THE
BUTCHER'S
MASQUERADE

Titles by Matt Dinniman

Dungeon Crawler Carl Series

DUNGEON CRAWLER CARL
CARL'S DOOMSDAY SCENARIO
THE DUNGEON ANARCHIST'S COOKBOOK
THE GATE OF THE FERAL GODS
THE BUTCHER'S MASQUERADE
THE EYE OF THE BEDLAM BRIDE
THIS INEVITABLE RUIN

KAIJU: BATTLEFIELD SURGEON

The Shivered Sky Series

EVERY GRAIN OF SAND
IN THE CITY OF DEMONS
THE GREAT DEVOURING DARKNESS

Dominion of Blades Series

DOMINION OF BLADES
THE HOBGOBLIN RIOT

THE GRINDING

TRAILER PARK FAIRY TALES

THE BUTCHER'S MASQUERADE

DUNGEON CRAWLER CARL BOOK FIVE

MATT DINNIMAN

ACE
New York

ACE
Published by Berkley
An imprint of Penguin Random House LLC
1745 Broadway, New York, NY 10019
penguinrandomhouse.com

Book design by George Towne
Map on page 549 by Andrew Duvall (sketchyvanrpg.com)
Interior art on pages iv, 2, 154, 260, 482, and 692: Vintage Black Texture © 316pixel/Shutterstock
All other interior art by Erik Wilson (erikwilsonart.com)

Library of Congress Cataloging-in-Publication Data

Names: Dinniman, Matt, author.
Title: The butcher's masquerade / Matt Dinniman.
Description: New York: Ace, 2025. | Series: Dungeon Crawler Carl ; book 5
Identifiers: LCCN 2024048319 | ISBN 9780593955994 (hardcover)
Subjects: LCGFT: LitRPG (Fiction) | Novels.
Classification: LCC PS3604.I49 B88 2025 | DDC 813/.6—dc23/eng/20241021
LC record available at https://lccn.loc.gov/2024048319

The Butcher's Masquerade was originally self-published, in different form, in 2022.

First Ace Edition: April 2025

Printed in the United States of America
1st Printing

The authorized representative in the EU for product safety and compliance is
Penguin Random House Ireland, Morrison Chambers, 32 Nassau Street,
Dublin D02 YH68, Ireland, https://eu-contact.penguin.ie.

Thanks, everyone, for all your continued support.
A special thanks to the dude who sent nudes.
It's not necessary, but I appreciate it.
I hope you get the help you need.

Surviving is winning. . . . Everything else is bullshit.

Michael De Santa, *Grand Theft Auto V*

PART ONE

THE HUNT

1

Views: 512 Sextillion
Followers: 142 Quadrillion
Favorites: 23 Quadrillion
Leaderboard Rank: 1
Bounty: 3,000,000 gold

Congrats, Crawler. You have received a Platinum Venison Box.

Welcome, Crawler, to the sixth floor. "The Hunting Grounds."
    Sponsorship bidding initiated on Crawler #4,122. Bidding ends
in 45 hours.
        Remaining Crawlers: 85,223
        Remaining Hunters: 360

Grace Period begins now. All hunters have been transferred to the
city of Zockau. They will be released in 30 hours.
    Run.

    Entering the Desperado Club.

I CAME INTO EXISTENCE IN A NOW-FAMILIAR OFFICE. THE HOODED FIG-
ure of Orren, the grim reaper–like Syndicate liaison, sat at his cluttered
desk, staring at me, hands steepled in front of him. I caught a glint of
the glass under his hood. I knew there was a parasitic worm floating in
there. A type of creature called a Gondii, but better known to the universe as a citizen of the Valtay.

    The last time I had been in this room was after I'd killed Loita the
administrator. This guy was supposedly a neutral third-party observer
and fact finder, but based on recent evidence, I knew some of these liaison guys played a little fast and loose with the term "neutral."

    Katia also sat in the room. It appeared she'd been here for a few minutes already, and she appeared bored. She was in her regular form. She looked at me and grinned, though I could see the worry in her eyes.

DONUT: CARL, CARL, WHERE ARE YOU? WE DIDN'T COME IN
TOGETHER! IT'S JUST ME, CHRIS, AND MONGO. WHERE ARE
YOU! WHERE'S KATIA?
CARL: It's okay. She's with me. We're back in the vice principal's
office.
DONUT: WHAT DOES THAT MEAN? I NEED TO PICK A NEW CLASS!

"Tell your companions you'll be joining them shortly," Orren said. "This won't take long."

CARL: Have Mordecai help you choose. I'll be there in a bit.
DONUT: I DON'T LIKE THIS, CARL. WE'RE IN A LONG LINE WITH A
BUNCH OF OTHER CRAWLERS, AND MONGO IS SCARED.
CARL: Donut, everything is fine. I'm about to get a talking-to by the
liaison guy with the fishbowl head. Put Mongo away, talk to
Mordecai, and then make sure you get everybody near you into
your chat.

"As I already told your friend, you can only see and hear me, but there are multiple entities in on this meeting," Orren said. "We have a representative from Borant, a few members of the Syndicate Crawl subcommittee, and a few additional interested parties listening in. In addition, there is a designated media representative. The media rep will not be permitted to report on anything that occurs in this meeting unless a law is broken."

"Wow," I said, turning to Katia, who suddenly had a sour look on her face. "All of this for us?"

She was about to say something, but the liaison interrupted her.

"Actually, it's all for you," Orren said. "Crawler Katia Grim is only here because she's the one who had it in her inventory. We asked her if she considered herself the owner of the item, and she claims you are the true owner. She will return to the staging area now."

"Wait," she began, but she popped away with an audible *crack*.

CARL: Are you okay?

KATIA: Other than a headache, I'm okay. Carl, I think I accidentally got you into trouble. I didn't know what to say. They took the gate from me. I'm sorry. There was nothing I could do.

CARL: It's okay. See if you can find Donut.

KATIA: I see her. She's chasing after Mongo. Be careful.

Orren waved his hand, and three items appeared on the desk in front of him. The two watches and the winding box, the three pieces to the Gate of the Feral Gods.

"Do you remember what I said the last time you were in here?" Orren asked. He reached forward and picked up one of the watches, idly spinning it in his hand.

I sighed. I was exhausted. My brain buzzed. There was so much to do, and a part of me would welcome it if they just decided to get it over with and squish me. If not that, I needed sleep, and soon. I shrugged. "I don't really remember."

"I said if it were up to me, I'd have you removed. At the time, the kua-tin wanted to keep you, and the Syndicate Council was indifferent. After this last little stunt, nobody is indifferent anymore." He put the watch down closer to the edge of the desk. "The Dreadnoughts have up and abandoned their stake in faction wars. You wiped out the entirety of their army. The war chief's wife got stung by one of those pain-amplifier jellyfish, and the chief himself had to kill her in order to stop the pain. She's recovering now on a sedative yacht. But they've given up, and now there's an open spot, one that nobody can take because they won't be able to field an army." He just looked at me as if waiting for a reaction.

The Dreadnoughts were large, humanoid creatures with red skin. They rarely did well in faction wars because their preferred method of fighting was to just hit everything in front of them, tactics and magic be damned.

"Good," I finally said. "That was pretty much the plan. To fuck up all the armies." I looked up at the ceiling. "You guys gave me the ability to do it. I'm just playing the game."

He nodded. He jotted something on a piece of paper. "Borant didn't intervene because they thought you were going to attempt a different type of attack. And they assumed you'd lose access to the artifact afterward."

I eyed the three items on the desk. If I so much as bumped the table, the first watch would fall into my lap. "And that's my fault?"

"It's not. They are upset, but"—he turned in his chair to look to his left, raising his voice—"you likely made them more money than they lost." He paused. "That said, we now have a problem. A problem with no easy solution. Actually, that's not true. There's a very easy and obvious solution to me. But the kua-tin don't want to go that route. Yet. The council and the showrunners need your help."

I felt my eyebrow rise. "*My* help?"

"We can't forcibly take the gate from you. Despite what you might think, there are rules about the treatment of crawlers. At least in regard to their inventory items. Patching certain artifacts requires cooperation across all involved entities, and we do not have a consensus."

I bit my lip.

Orren continued. "The system will not allow us to confiscate it from you." That was interesting, considering they'd already taken it. "Borant wishes for you to remain in the game"—he again raised his voice—"despite the danger you pose to their tenuous hold on solvency. However, we simply cannot allow you to keep the Gate of the Feral Gods. We are asking for you to voluntarily give it up."

"Is that a joke? What is this? You've already taken it." I took a deep breath. My instinct was to reach out and pick up the items from the desk. I thought of the journalist. They wanted a witness. This felt like a trap. I kept my hands at my sides. I scooted my chair back an inch.

He chuckled. "When the item was first generated into the game by the system AI, do you know what happened? It set off a chain reaction of checks-and-balances subroutines so extensive, it crashed the entire system. The AI created the item in such a fashion that it circumvented its own rules."

"Yeah, so?"

"That item has the ability to kill everyone on the floor. Borant already bent the rules the best they could to keep you from zeroing out the population on the previous floor. But this level is a little different. You can open a hundred portals and turn the dungeon into a wasteland in less than an hour."

DONUT: I GOT THE WORLD'S GREATEST CLASS FOR THIS FLOOR. KATIA IS BACK IN LINE WITH US.

I waved away the chat and waited for Orren to continue.

"Nobody expected you to get the item. There are rules in place we all must follow, so we can't remove it. We can, however, remove *you*. We must protect the integrity of the game. That leaves us with three options." He held up a finger. "One, I could create an order that would encase the floor in a protection spell that would remove all crawler access to portals. That would remove access to all personal spaces and clubs and break thousands of other little things. Teleport scrolls would cease to work. Certain movement spells wouldn't work. Your pet's carrier would no longer function. It would be chaos, and it would kill thousands."

He raised another finger. "Two. We accelerate you, which *will* result in your death, along with the death of anyone near you."

He let that sink in for a moment, and then he raised a third finger. "Or three, you turn the winding box in, I give you a receipt, and you get it back the moment you reach the ninth floor."

I didn't answer for several moments. My mind raced. *Goddamnit.* I needed that gate. How could I keep my promise to Juice Box without it?

I needed time to think. "Why was there a liaison helping Maggie cheat?" I asked. I looked up at the ceiling. I had no idea if he was telling the truth about the reporter, but if he was, they were the most important person here right now. "Maggie and Chris kept getting censored. They said it was a caprid. The creature was obviously working with the Skull Empire."

Orren's chair creaked. The watch wobbled. In the momentary silence, I could hear the distant boom of the dance floor. "Everyone here is aware of which you speak. There's an answer to that question. You're not allowed to hear it. But I'm glad you asked, because it's an important lesson. Exploits can work both ways. The forces working against you have had a lot more time to learn how to manipulate the system. Rest assured that particular issue has been dealt with in the same manner and swiftness as the one before us now. What's your choice? Will you hand the artifact over?"

"I want a lawyer," I said. "I'm not touching those things until I talk to one."

He grunted with amusement. I could tell, despite his mostly serious demeanor, he was enjoying this exchange. He looked back over his own shoulder to peer at the blank wall. "I told you. What did I say?" He returned his fishbowl head in my direction. "You just said the magic words, crawler."

ENTERING THE STAGING AREA.

I was hoping we'd teleport to our personal space and Mordecai would be the one who walked us through specialization. That's not what happened. This was like a football stadium, with a high ceiling and distant walls. It appeared every crawler entered into this room here or a place like this, waited in line, and then was forced to undergo specialization class selection. From what I gathered, everybody had to go through the line, even those whose classes didn't have the option to specialize.

By the time I arrived, the room was almost empty. Maybe three or four hundred crawlers remained, all on the far side of the room. I started walking toward them. I'd been in Orren's office for about an hour and a half, so not too long, but it appeared whatever this was, it was going by quickly.

CARL: I'm in the giant arena place. Where are you guys?

KATIA: Are you okay? What happened?

CARL: I'm okay. We lost the gate, but not permanently. It's a long story.

DONUT: WE'RE ALREADY DONE. YOU HAVE TO GO THROUGH THE SMELLY LITTLE ROOM, AND THEN YOU COME BACK OUT. EVERYONE IS GETTING SCATTERED, BUT ALL THE PARTY MEMBERS ARE COMING OUT IN THE SAME PLACE. ALSO, WAIT UNTIL YOU SEE WHAT MORDECAI LOOKS LIKE.

KATIA: This world is similar to the third floor but with a lot more trees. You should come out just outside a medium dryad settlement. Find a pub called Die Kirschbomben.

CARL: Did you guys get class upgrades?

KATIA: I got something. It didn't change my Monster Truck Driver class name, but I could pick one of three "endorsements." They only give you ten minutes to pick, and you can't use chat while you're in the little room. I got the HAZMAT endorsement.

DONUT: THEY SAID I COULD PERMANENTLY PICK ANY CLASS I ALREADY HAD, BUT MORDECAI SAID THAT MIGHT HAPPEN AND TOLD ME NOT TO DO IT. SO I DIDN'T. BUT IT'S OKAY BECAUSE I ALREADY GOT A NEW CLASS JUST FOR THIS FLOOR, AND IT IS GREAT.

CARL: What did you get?

DONUT: I'LL TELL YOU BUT ONLY IF YOU PROMISE NOT TO GET MAD. KATIA SAYS YOU'RE GOING TO BE MAD.

CARL: Donut. What did you pick?

DONUT: I'M A BARD! ISN'T IT GREAT! IT'S NOT A NECROBARD LIKE THEY OFFERED ME BEFORE, BUT IT'S BETTER. I'M A LEGENDARY DIVA. THAT'S WHAT THE CLASS IS CALLED. LEGENDARY DIVA. I SING!

CARL: You sing.

DONUT: I SING SONGS AND THEY CAST SPELLS. I GOT A BUNCH OF THEM. I'M PRACTICING ALREADY. MONGO LOVES THEM AND THE TREE GUY AT THE PUB SAID I CAN HAVE A GIG FOR THE LUNCH SHIFT TOMORROW.

KATIA: He said you could sing *after* the lunch shift.

DONUT: DON'T RUIN IT, KATIA.

I took a long, deep breath.

CARL: Okay, I'll see you in a bit.

Velvet crowd-control ropes snaked back and forth, attached to little brass poles, like in a line to buy tickets at a movie theater. Hundreds of single-door exits dotted the far wall, and as I watched, the remaining crawlers all walked one by one into individual rooms and disappeared.

I picked up one of the barrier things and tried to add it to my inventory.

Warning: You may not use your inventory in this area.

I grumbled and then walked around the rope, pushing my way to the very end of the line.

CARL: Mordecai, please tell me the Bard thing is a good class.
MORDECAI: It's great, in theory. It comes with multiple spells and a new spell system, and if she practices enough, she'll keep it. She managed to keep her buffed Hole, Magic Missile, and Puddle Jumper skills thanks to her Glass Cannon class from the last floor. This new class gave her a handful of enchantment spells and a decent constitution buff. Her Character Actor skill is level six now, and she received all the starting skills of the Legendary Diva class plus a few upgraded ones. That skill is going to be a real asset from now on. Just be glad she didn't choose it as her permanent class.
CARL: She has to sing? Have you heard her sing yet?
MORDECAI: Everyone has heard her singing.
CARL: Oh god.

By the time I arrived at the front of the line, there were only a handful of crawlers left. None were ones I'd met before. I exchanged fist bumps with them all. The second to last was a human named Ajib. His level 29 seemed pitiful compared to my level 47. His class was something called a Prodromoi, which I gathered was some sort of dexterity-themed fighter. He hopped forward in line, and I realized he was missing the bottom half of his left leg.

"I had to jump through the portal just as the floor collapsed," he said. "But we did it. We popped our bubble at the end."

"I'll build you a prosthetic if you need it," I said.

"My team is already on it, but thank you," the man said before hopping forward and disappearing into one of the rooms.

A group of NPCs—a mix of Crocodilians, cretins, and robed elves—was waving people toward the little doorways against the far wall. There were hundreds of the workers, but they were mostly standing around idle by the time I got to the front of the line. I was the very last crawler.

"Pick any one. They're all the same," one of the elves said.

I strolled toward a door near the end of the row, examining it as I approached, and it was just a regular portal. I took a quick screenshot, and it appeared to be an airplane-bathroom-sized room with a screen on the wall. It looked almost like one of those peep-show-room booths.

I was about to enter when the announcement came. I paused.

Hello, Crawlers!

Welcome to the sixth floor! We are so happy to have you here!

Like the third floor, this sixth floor is a *Dungeon Crawler World* tradition!

It's the Hunting Grounds! This floor is almost identical in layout and size to the third floor, but the abandoned ruins have been claimed by hundreds of years of foliage. What secrets and mysteries lie hidden in the jungle? You'll have 17 days to find out! But this time, you won't be alone.

We currently have 360 hunters on deck, and they're raring to go. In a little less than 28 hours, they will be unleashed and will begin hunting you for your gear. Due to recent events, we are keeping registration open until the very last moment, and we expect that number of participants to double or even triple by the time they are released! But be warned! Some of these hunters have been here for weeks now, and even though they're currently sequestered, their minions and traps are still out there waiting for you. A few of you have already found this out the hard way!

Traditionally, all hunters start out at level 30 and are able to train themselves up as you make your way through the lower floors. It's no secret that you're here sooner than usual. In the spirit of fairness and as an incentive to gain more last-minute participants, we have given all hunters a bump of 20 levels, so they all start out at 50.

We'll have more information about the hunt after the next recap message, but I wanted to thank you all for your participation. I know that last floor was tough, and we did lose a few more crawlers than we anticipated. We will all have to work together to make sure your incompetence doesn't continue.

There are 2,344 exits leading to the seventh floor. There is at least one unguarded exit in the city of Zockau along with more in the valley beyond. In addition, some city boss and larger mobs will have an exit nearby. The rest are hidden, but should be easy to find.

Your final sponsorship slots are now open to bidding. That's all for now. Now get out there and kill, kill, kill!

While the announcement was going, the NPCs got to work cleaning up the room and shutting down the arena. A group of Crocodilians started gathering up the velvet crowd-control ropes. A cretin walked around with a broom and a dustbin as a group of the elves started rolling up the red carpets. The sight seemed absurd.

A hooded elf approached as I listened. He was dragging an empty cart that would presumably be loaded up with the rugs. He paused to regard me as I listened to the message. I examined the man warily.

Ian—Bush Elf. Level 30.
Registration Arena Attendant.
This is a Non-Combatant NPC.
You know those perpetually depressed emo kids from high school who always sat on the floor during lunch? If they participated in extracurricular activities, it was always either drama, yearbook committee, or the dreaded anime club. They planned on changing the world with some bullshit cause. They all had jobs at the smoothie place. Then after high school, they just kinda got absorbed by the world, like pouring a dark drink into a rushing stream. You blinked, and they were just gone, along with all of their black hair dye and all of their dreams.

That is a Bush Elf. A once-proud people, almost physically indistinguishable from the ruling-class High Elves, Bush Elves are the regular joes of the forest. If you look really close, you can see the wrinkles around their eyes, or the very slight hunch to their backs. A sign of their defeat. They tend to favor druid magic and jobs at places where they're in cubicles.

Sometimes they remember how strong of a people they once were.

"Sir, we're closing this area. You need to go into a changing room."

"Sorry, just listening to the announcement."

"No problem, sir. Good luck out there."

"Thank you," I said. "You, too. Might want to keep your head down after today."

The elf paused, regarding me. "You're Carl, right? The one who bombed Larracos?"

"That's right," I said. "Word travels fast here."

"I heard them talking about it. The other crawlers, I mean. They said you unleashed a feral god on the armies. They said you're going to do it again on this floor."

"I didn't. That's what they thought I was going to do. Instead, I helped flood the city of Larracos. I was going to throw a god at them in a few days, but they took my toy away."

Ian nodded thoughtfully. The creature had a wistful look on his face. "They do that. If you gain a little bit of power, they take it away. Next time you need to use it while you can. Now you best get moving. If you go in the jungle, stay on the trail. Stay away from the city of Zockau, even after the countdown is done. It's all the way to the north. That's where the aliens are. They don't fight fair, so be careful. Last hunting season, one of them killed my brother for no reason. Was working a food stand. Ripped his head right off, and since the guards didn't see it, they did nothing."

"You remember the previous seasons?" I asked, suddenly intrigued.

"I was a human, like you. I was a crawler a very long time ago. I'm usually an attendant at Club Vanquisher, but this season they got me on urban janitor duty. They pulled us all away to work the opening arenas. Everybody you see here was once a crawler. I think. Sometimes it's hard to tell. I gotta say, this is the smallest group I've ever seen. I ain't supposed to be talking like this, though. I get in trouble if I break character. You better get moving."

I nodded. "I'm going. Do you know which hunter killed your brother? Are they back this year?"

Ian visibly shuddered. "Oh, yes. She is here. She is always here. Vrah. A mantis. There's a core group of about 20 regulars who are here every season. Vrah takes the heads of those she kills and wears them upon her body. Stay away from her, friend. Her death count is in the thousands." He jerked as if shocked. Without another word, he put his head down and pushed his cart away.

I turned, and I entered through the door.

THE ROOM WAS SUFFOCATINGLY SMALL AND SMELLED OF LYSOL. I WON-dered how some of the bigger crawlers, like Chris, fit in here. There was an old-school television against the wall with a glowing coin slot. Static played on the screen. I had to peel my feet off the floor as I stepped inside. A handwritten, stain-covered sign in English hung on the wall. "Only one person per booth." I realized with dismay this place was exactly what it looked like.

The screen flickered, and a 10-minute countdown appeared. Words formed on the screen and were also spoken out loud.

Welcome, Crawler.

You have ten minutes to choose your class upgrade. Your class, Compensated Anarchist, is required to pick a specialty. You will have three choices. Choose wisely as your choice will be permanent. If no choice is made, a random choice will be applied. You will retain all of your previous class upgrades.

The robotic, almost emotionless voice was unusual for the dungeon. The three new classes appeared.

Revolutionary.

Guerrilla.

Agent Provocateur.

I couldn't click or interact with the menu. It just appeared and played on the screen, and I was forced to watch. Mordecai and I had already discussed what the most likely choices would be, and these were all pretty close to what we expected. All three came with an unexpected stat point boost.

Revolutionary.

You are in the streets, in the front against the barrier. You can take a tear gas canister to the chest and keep ticking. When they come to break the line, you're the first to start swinging your fists. This specialty increases your training speed with melee fighting skills and greatly increases your strength.

Revolutionaries receive the following benefits:

An additional +1 to strength upon level up.

+2 to Unarmed Combat.

Immunity to Cloud-Based attacks (already obtained via upgrade patch).

The Blend into the Crowd benefit.

Faster melee training.

The extra strength benefit alone made this one worth it. My Unarmed Combat was similar to Powerful Strike. It currently sat at nine, and it was very difficult to train up. Getting it to 11 would likely give me an additional advantage since it pushed it over ten.

The screen gave a quick rundown of each benefit and skill.

The Blend into the Crowd benefit caused guards to forget who I was once I was out of sight for a while. I could've really used that skill on the third floor. While great, I suspected this sixth floor was the only remaining floor where that skill would be useful.

Guerrilla.

Unlike a Revolutionary who stands front and center, you take your fight to the jungles. You cease to be the face of the revolution and instead become the tip of the sword. Using your superior trap-making and ranged-weapon skills, you kill the enemy before they even know you're there.

Guerrillas receive the following benefits:

An additional +1 to dexterity upon level up.

Access to the Advanced Trap Maker's Workshop.

Plus *Camouflage*.

+5 to the Crossbow skill.

Faster trap-making training.

I had no desire to learn the crossbow, but it would be a good skill to have especially since Katia was leaving the party. I'd been working on explosive crossbow bolts, but she was afraid to use them. *Camouflage* was a spell similar to what Maggie My and Frank had used to hide themselves from other crawlers. It worked well, but it required you to stay in place. The Trap Maker's Workshop was a specialty crafting table, one that I really wanted to get. However, there was another upgrade I wanted even more.

Agent Provocateur.

The mysterious Agent Provocateur prides himself on being invisible. This class specialty focuses on being the ultimate saboteur. These wily troublemakers put less emphasis on individual traps and fighting in the street and instead focus on mass-casualty bombs and bomb making.

An Agent Provocateur receives the following benefits:

An additional +1 to intelligence upon level up.

+1 skill level to a Sapper's Table.

+2 to Explosives Handling.

Access to the Advanced Bomb Maker's Workshop.

Faster explosives training.

Even though the names were similar, the Trap Maker's Workshop was just a table while the Bomb Maker's Workshop was an entire room. I didn't need this class to get the regular version of either, only the "advanced" version. The advanced Trap Maker table was required to build some of the best magical-based traps, but the Advanced Bomb Maker's Workshop would allow me to precisely tune my explosives and to eventually make much more specialized bombs.

My Explosives Handling was another skill that had stalled out. This would send me over the hump.

We'd pretty much known I'd be given the options of fighting, traps, or explosives. Thankfully, none of them added any penalties to the other two. Mordecai was insistent that I choose the melee option. Still, I hesitated. I wanted that Advanced Bomb Maker's Workshop. I *really* wanted it, especially since I had a few recipes sitting in my cookbook that required that room to work.

I wasn't a huge fan of that +1 to intelligence, however. Still, the more I thought about it, the more I realized I'd been neglecting that stat for far too long. With my boxers and jacket but before the daily buffs, my intelligence sat at only 17. I always liked to keep a buffer that would allow me to cast *Heal* a few times if I needed. If I wanted any more spells, that stat really needed to go up.

I only had a minute left to choose. The little orange light on the coin slot started blinking as the timer on the screen counted down.

I reached up and touched the filthy screen, clicking directly on the third choice.

"Sorry, Mordecai," I muttered.

Congratulations, Crawler. You are now Carl, the level 47 Agent Provocateur.

2

ENTERING THE SELVA.

I left through the same door I entered, and I stepped into the pouring rain. Thick foliage filled the area. Bushes with wide kite-sized leaves encircled me. The rain splashed off the fronds, splashing up into my face. It sounded like a thousand little drums. Despite the rain, the trill of animals surrounded me along with the thick buzz of insects, even louder than the rain. The air was so muggy, it was almost choking. My lungs felt heavy and wet after just the first breath.

The rain stopped. Just like that. A single beam of sunlight illuminated a thin trail. Everything continued to drip. The leaves and fronds bobbed up and down. I looked up, searching for the ceiling, but I couldn't see anything through the trees. While the air remained oppressively humid, I caught the scent of flowers.

I turned, and the door I'd come through was an actual porta potty, just sitting there in the jungle. I hesitantly opened the plastic door, and inside was just my regular bathroom. I closed the door and examined my surroundings.

A trail led through the forest. A pair of white dots appeared on my map, only about twenty feet away, but I couldn't see them through the foliage. I already knew what to expect from Donut and Katia. They'd also appeared right here, just outside of town.

I headed toward the two white dots. Both dots had a blue hue around the edges, which meant they were both equipped with magical gear.

A bamboo wall about ten feet high materialized, along with a gate. A pair of guards stood sentry just within, each holding a massive spear about a foot taller than the tops of the walls. I paused, examining the twin creatures. My initial impression was thin, tall samurais with white-painted faces, but I blinked and saw them for what they really were. Mushroom men. Two arms, two legs, but no neck. What I'd originally thought were conical Asian-style coolie hats were actually the mushroom caps. The slender, flaxen-colored creatures did not acknowledge me at all. Their white-painted, vaguely human faces stared straight forward. Each stood about eight feet tall, completely rigid as I hesitantly approached. Each wore a black but red-highlighted flowing robe tied around their "stalk" just below the face. Water dripped from the tops of their mushroom caps.

> Funeral Bell—Level 95.
> I would apologize in advance for this description, but an apology would imply that I'm sorry. I'm never sorry!
> These mushroom dudes are not fun guys.
> Funeral Bells are the guards who are tasked with protecting the smaller settlements of the sixth floor. Unlike the swordsmen guards from the Over City, these creatures have no sense of humor. Also, they are on duty day and night. You should avoid making them angry.

"Hello, gentlemen," I said as I strode toward the gate. Just beyond, I could now see a good-sized town within the circle of the bamboo wall. It buzzed with activity. Multiple elves and treelike creatures walked about. Multistory shops and pubs filled the streets, many attached to trees. Some buildings were in the trees. It was like a German-style village mixed in with a bunch of tree houses. Small furry monkey creatures scuttled about the branches. The spire of a Club Vanquisher rose in the distance against the back wall. The golden tip of the spire gleamed in the fading light.

> Entering Medium Dryad Settlement.

I paused to drink it all in and smell the air. This seemed like a beautiful place. A perfect place, if it hadn't been stuck in this hellhole. I thought of my dream. My distant, forever-lost dream to one day get a job as far away from the ocean as possible and work in the forest.

It was a silly dream, really. Getting a gig as a park ranger. I'd never done anything to become one. I'd had plenty of time to maybe go to school. Take classes. Something. I never even knew how one got that sort of job. It didn't matter. Not anymore.

To my left, the first of the two guards fell over. One moment he was just standing there, and then he tipped forward like a tree that had been cut at the base. He crashed in front of me, blocking my path. His mushroom bell of a head smashed when it hit the ground, crumpling in on itself like a can. The giant spear clattered away on the stone street. I just stared. The guard wasn't dead. The debuff **Paralyzed** blazed over its head.

The second funeral bell made a croaking noise and dropped his spear. The guard also fell over.

What the hell?

My instincts took over, and I slammed onto *Protective Shell*.

An angry, hissing noise ripped through the air, and the edge of my spell sparked. *There's something invisible there.*

I tossed a smoke curtain, hoping to see movement through the eddies of smoke. I wanted to toss a small hob-lobber, but I didn't know what direction. NPCs were everywhere. If I hurt one, the guards would come after me. I needed to injure the monster. Most invisible creatures showed themselves once they were hurt.

Behind me, a horn sounded. Shouting rose across the town. My shell sparked again. I still couldn't see what was causing it. I reached down and picked up the massive spear dropped by the guard.

Warning: You receive a penalty when you use bladed weapons.

CARL: I need help. At the village entrance.

I swung the spear like a club in a wide arc at the air just past the edge of the shell, trying to hit the damn thing. What was this? It couldn't be a hunter, as they were all stuck in that other city. It had to be a mob. It'd incapacitated two level 95 guards like it was nothing.

Invisible mobs were always a worry, but Donut's sunglasses could see them. That did me no good now. I had to act fast. I dove into my inventory as I swung back and forth, hitting nothing. The shell would run out in seconds.

I had an idea. Gunpowder. I still had a dozen sacks of the stuff. Each bag was the size of a pillowcase. I dropped the spear, pulled a sack, and tossed it just as the shell dropped around me. The sack spun in the air, black powder spilling out. The sack hit something solid, and the powder formed a shape.

"Shit!" I cried, ducking. It hissed as it sailed right over me. It was smaller than Donut, and it was fast. It hit the ground, shook once, and dislodged the dust, though I could still almost make it out. Behind the invisible creature, a line of funeral bell guards approached, moving slowly.

In that moment, a dot appeared on my map. It wasn't red. It was orange. A pet. But that didn't make sense. The shell shouldn't have worked against pets. *Unless . . .*

Of course, I thought. *I should've tried this first.* I found my new *Ping* spell on my list, and I cast it.

Pling.

The noise sounded much like a sonar burst from a submarine. It shot forth, and my map flashed. It highlighted every non-mob or crawler in the area. The creature remained right in front of me, ready to pounce again.

"Oof," I cried as the second orange dot slammed me from behind. I felt a pair of hot teeth sink into my neck.

You have been paralyzed!

I crashed to the ground, frozen. I tried to take a healing potion, but it wouldn't let me. This was what they'd done to the guards. They'd paralyzed them.

"I'm coming, Carl!" a voice cried out. Donut.

I couldn't move. A five-minute timer appeared. *Five* minutes. That was a long-ass time. My limbs felt as if they were on fire.

A magic missile shot out. It slammed directly into the first creature, the one I'd doused in gunpowder. It flipped onto its back and screeched as its fur popped and sparkled and the powder cooked off. The creature's invisibility dropped. Its health had gone down by half.

It was a fuzzy, jet-black, ferret-like monster with six legs and a whole bunch of teeth. Its sharp teeth were way too big for its face, jutting every which way. Donut shot it again, leaving it with only a sliver of life. Its fur continued to pop and sizzle like bacon in a pan. Donut shot a third missile at the second monster, the one who'd bitten my neck. This second creature cried out with a hiss. I couldn't see it, but I heard it hit the ground and start to scramble away.

Mongo cried out with a shriek, sailing over my head as he attacked the second monster. Donut was perched on Mongo's back, and she screamed along with her dinosaur as they moved to pursue.

I couldn't move at all. The first injured monster hit the ground a few feet from my face. It was still alive. The creature hissed pitifully at me and started to drag itself closer, using a single leg, its jaw ravening. Smoke rose off the thing. *It's going to bite me. Shit, shit, not the face. Not the face! It's going to bite me in the goddamned face.* The creature was almost dead, yet it still fought, its jaw cracking rapid fire. It sounded like a rat trap snapping over and over as it inched closer and closer.

I tried to send a call for help. The system wouldn't let me.

I examined the creature as I inwardly cringed.

Tootsie. Night Weasel Scout. Level 25.

This is a pet of Hunter Zabit.

Have you ever seen one of those videos of a bunch of dogs having a pool party? It's usually a scene of pure chaos and joy as the golden retrievers and Labradors and other doggos run circles around the pool, jumping in and out and playing and splashing and having a great, hectic time.

Now imagine your body is the pool, and the Night Weasels are the dogs in this scenario.

Not many pack hunters answer to an alpha who isn't of the same race. It requires ultrahigh charisma to tame a pack of these living meat grinders. It's said a hunter who can control a gang of the invisible Night Weasels can take down prey of any size.

Their method of stalking is simple. A typical gang consists of approximately 20 weasels, including two or three seeker scouts, a group of huntsmen, and a pack leader. The scouts can sniff out prey

from hundreds of kilometers away. They track down and disable the
target, rendering it immobile. Once the prey is down, the rest of the
weasels move in, their movements coordinated by the gang leader.
I'd describe what happens next, but this is a family show.

A dark, rocky leg slammed down, crushing the pet just as it pulled
itself close enough to chomp my nose. Gore splattered onto my face.

Chris. He rumbled something and then stepped over me. Behind
me, I could hear Mongo squeal with delight as he chomped on the second weasel.

"There's more coming!" Donut cried. "A lot of them!"

"Drag Carl into the safe room," a new voice called. Katia. "They're
hunting him. Let the guards take care of it."

I felt myself rise up into the air, and I realized Chris had picked me
up. His lava-rock body burned my skin. He easily lifted me over his
shoulder. My entire body was stiff, my hand frozen awkwardly up in
the air.

"The guards can't see them. They're all invisible!" Donut yelled. I
heard the familiar zap of a spell being cast, followed by a second spell.
A weasel screeched. Donut had raised the pet from the dead and cast
Clockwork Triplicate on it.

"Get 'em!" Donut yelled as I was bodily removed from the area.
Chris strode into a pub. I caught sight of a treelike creature looking at
me as we moved into the personal space. My head banged into the en-
tranceway as we went through the door. He unceremoniously dumped
me onto the couch. I faced up into the air, still unable to move. I sat
there, not doing anything as the timer ticked down.

I felt something climb up onto me. A fuzzy face looked down at me,
scowling just as the timer counted down to zero. My limbs still burned,
but I could move them.

I looked up at the furry, buck-toothed, teddy-bear-like face glaring
down at me.

"You had to go and challenge all the hunters. Now look what happened," Mordecai said, trying to sound angry. "And that doesn't look
like a melee class to me."

I burst out laughing. I couldn't help it.

Mordecai—Pocket Kuma. Level 50.
    Manager of Crawler Princess Donut.
    This is a Non-Combatant NPC.
    Wow! This pint-sized fuzz ball is adorable!
    The rare Pocket Kuma is a magic-infused half-fairy creature originally designed as a pet for the elite High Elf royal court. When it was discovered these creatures were intelligent, High Elf King Finian, of course, ordered them all executed. Only a few of the little rascals managed to escape into the jungle.
    A Kuma is a type of bear. A Pocket Kuma is a different sort of creature, though they are distantly related. You take a small bear, crossbreed it with a capybara spirit, pick out the runt of the litter, and then breed it further down with a sugar glider. The resulting bug-eyed creature is what you see before you now.
    They can't fight for shit. They can barely walk. But holy shit are they disgustingly cute.
    I bet they smush really well.

He was a fuzzy, brown-and-white, knee-height, chubby, bipedal bear thing with elf ears and a monkey tail. His eyes were ridiculously huge, making him look like a baby. He had a pair of buck teeth that didn't help the illusion. The tail waved back and forth angrily.

"Laugh it up," Mordecai said, pissed. "Get it out of your system."

"Your voice," I said, falling off the couch as I continued to howl, causing him to yelp and leap off of me. He used his tail to keep himself from lurching back. I had tears rolling down my cheeks. "Holy shit. Will you be able to work at the alchemy table like this? Do you want me to build a booster chair for you?"

"Go fuck yourself, Carl," Mordecai said. He leaped across the room and landed on the kitchen table, huffing. Chris stood nearby, watching impassively.

Donut and Katia finally returned to the room. "The guards used their *Poison Cloud* attack to . . ." Katia began. She saw me there on the ground, laughing. A grin spread across her face, and she also started to laugh. "He really is funny-looking, isn't he?"

Mordecai glowered from the kitchen table. He jumped sideways, sailing through the air and landing on the ground in front of his room. He tried to storm in, but he couldn't reach the doorknob. He had to jump up and grab it. He dangled helplessly for a moment before the door opened on its own. He dropped to the floor, went inside, and slammed the door.

"You shouldn't make fun of someone just because they're small and adorable, Carl," Donut said. She leaped onto the couch and looked down at me as I sat up and wiped my eyes. "I'm small and adorable, and I just saved your life."

"You're right," I said, still laughing. "Thank you, by the way. All of you. It was just so . . . unexpected. They really screwed him over this time." I took a moment to compose myself. "Did the guards get all the weasel things?"

"I'm not sure," Donut said. "I started hitting them with low-powered magic missiles, which made them visible. Eventually one of the guards spewed Poison Cloud, and we had to run."

"They were hunting you, Carl," Katia added. "They were just the first. There will be more. A lot more."

"I know," I said, sobering. "When the hunters are released, all hell is going to break loose."

We all sat there in silence for a few moments. I was so damn tired.

There was a knock at the door. The door to the personal space.

"What in god's name?" Katia asked. "How . . . Who is that?"

"Ahh, yes," I said, standing up and striding toward the door. "It's a delivery."

"Of what?" Katia asked.

"Collateral," I answered.

3

"I WOULD LIKE SOME TIME ALONE WITH MY CLIENT," MY NEW ATTORNEY
had said the moment he appeared in the room. I'd just asked for a lawyer, Orren had stopped everything, and a moment later, a new creature
appeared, standing next to the liaison.

"Alone?" Orren asked, grunting with amusement. "This is my office.
I will turn off the feed to the others, but you'll have to suffer my
presence."

I was so astonished that asking for an attorney had actually worked
that I barely registered this exchange. Everything I'd read implied lawyers didn't become a thing until the tenth floor.

I studied the newcomer. The system didn't give much information.

Quasar.
Advocate of Crawler #4,122.

The small creature glowered at Orren as I examined him. I was
pretty certain the alien wasn't really in the room with us. I wouldn't
know for certain unless I touched him.

He was a gray alien. I knew from reading descriptions in the cookbook what this creature was. A Nullian, though they were mostly just
called "the Null." I'd seen their kind once or twice in talk show audiences, but they seemed rare. This race was similar to the much taller
Forsoothed, but this guy was only about four and a half feet tall. He
looked just like a stereotypical cartoon Area 51 alien with the gray skin,
large eyes, and bulbous head. He wore a tan suit with a tie. The tie had

what appeared to be an image of a Nullian hula girl on it. The hula girl gyrated back and forth.

Unlike the halting speech of their soother big brothers, this guy had more of a gritty, rapid-fire New York sort of accent that was somehow even more unnerving.

"You're gonna have to step out of the room," Quasar said to Orren. "The rules are clear. I get to speak to my client alone."

"I will turn off my auditory receptors. How is that?" Orren said. "I'm not leaving. You and your client are welcome to step outside yourselves, but I wouldn't recommend it. There are Desperado Club entrances in Zockau."

The threat was clear. There'd be hunters out there on the dance floor.

Quasar sighed dramatically. "All right, but if you do listen in, the sys AI will know, and we'll file a grievance. That last one we filed didn't go so great for your coworker, now did it? Also, get those items out of here. My client isn't going to touch them until we got an agreement."

"You have five minutes," Orren said as he gathered up the watches and winding box. They disappeared. He reached up and touched the side of his head, presumably to turn his headphones or whatever off. Nothing appeared to happen.

Quasar made a spinning motion with a long finger, indicating he wanted Orren to turn his chair around. The liaison grumbled but complied. The fishbowl-headed creature produced what looked like a rubber ball and started bouncing it off the back wall, deftly catching it each time it ricocheted back toward him.

The Null watched Orren for a moment and then shrugged. He moved to the front of the desk and leaned against it, facing me. He pulled out an item that looked like a vape pen, and inhaled. The smoke pixelated as it spread away, confirming he was a holo. "Okay, buddy. We gotta be quick. You are balls deep in the wrong hole, and Mom is pulling into the driveway. You get me?"

"I . . . What?" I asked, trying to make sense of the metaphor. I couldn't take my eyes off the alien hula girl on his tie. The goddamned thing winked at me. "I . . . So you're a lawyer? Do you work like a regular lawyer from Earth?"

"Look, pal. If you're going to be a babbling idiot this whole time, we're going to have a very short courtship. I have no clue how lawyers work from your world, but in my experience, they're mostly the same everywhere. We're in a hurry, so we need to get past the first-date finger-bang jitters and move straight to the part where we argue about me smoking too much. Got it?"

A million questions swirled in my brain. I just nodded.

"First off, don't buy anything this worm head is trying to sell. Most Valtay are tricksy fuckers, but the naked ones are the worst. If they ain't riding a body, that's usually a sign there's something wrong with them. And if they're a liaison . . . yeah. Growing up, you ever know a kid who'd rat you out to the adults just because it wet his receptors? That's the type of fuck stick who becomes a liaison. Fuck those guys." He took a deep drag from his vape pen. "You hear me? Liaisons are all fucks." He raised his voice at that, testing to see if there was a reaction from Orren. There wasn't. "From now on, anytime you get hauled in front of one of these chodes, say nothing except 'I want to talk to my lawyer.' Got it? And for the sake of his left tit, don't touch anything until I get there. You did good. They were trying to get you to pick up the artifact while it was under administrative hold. It would've deleted the item."

"Jesus," I said, looking at the spot on the desk where the gate pieces had been sitting.

"Yeah, that mudskipper admin guy was having a conniption. Those idiots actually want you to keep the artifact even though you fucked them over. I gotta tell you, pal. I'm moderately impressed."

"So, are you my lawyer from now on?"

"That's right. My name is Quasar, by the way. I am your attorney. Nobody else's. So I ain't representing the cat or the weird lady who turned into a shovel. Just you."

"And your job is to represent me? My best interests?"

"Best interests?" He made a scoffing noise. "When a crawler hits the tenth floor, he gains a teeny, tiny bit of autonomy over his fate. He's officially a citizen of the Syndicate. The moment anybody becomes a citizen, the Syndicate bends them over and fucks them. I can't stop you from getting fucked. But I am the condom. You guys have condoms on your world? Of course you do. Everybody has condoms. Your ass is gonna hurt no matter what, but at least you won't have tryptic genital mites after."

"And what do you get out of this?" I asked.

"What do I get out of this? Tits, pal. You mean, besides a headache? I get credits. Not a lot. But it's enough to keep me in receptor tugs and gelatin swabs. But in case you've been living on a backwater planet, you might not have noticed I'm a Null. Not too many outfits hire my kind. So here we are."

I was still trying to decide if I was better off with or without this guy. I suspected I wasn't going to be given a choice. "What's to stop you from getting bribed by the Skull Empire to fuck me over?"

He barked with laughter. "I love the way you think, pal. You humans are almost as paranoid as my people." He took another hit from his strange vape. The device pulsated with each drag. "You mean, besides the sense of ethics and pride I have from working and studying for twenty cycles straight just so I can scrabble for scraps by representing condemned assholes such as yourself? The short answer is, there ain't nothing stopping some interested third party from attempting to bribe me. The good news for you is that you're already fucked. To screw you over, I just need to do nothing. So if I'm doing the bare minimum, that should be a sign to you that King Rust hasn't been whispering sweet into my ears. Yet. And not that you'll believe me, but I do have my pride. The day I take a bribe from some pig-faced imperialist fuck is the day I wither."

"Our manager said lawyers don't usually come into play until the tenth floor. Why now?" I asked.

"Look. Is this really what you want to spend your time talking about? Your manager is correct. But most crawlers usually aren't subject to liaison action, either. Let alone a meeting where the subminister of the Native Species Agency takes an interest. There are a lot of moving parts of the Syndicate government, and there is a bureaucrat and or a committee for each and every one of those parts. And each one of those suits and committees is beholden to rules and laws and regulations that can date back tens of thousands of cycles. And all these moving parts and interlocking teeth are all grinding their way forward through time, trying to gain some sort of upward momentum. It's a perpetual motion machine that will only stop once the universe implodes in on itself. And how is that machine greased? The universe's four lubricants. Blood, tears, taxes, and lawyers."

By the time I realized he hadn't actually answered my question, he was already moving on to the next subject.

"But as much as I'd like to bore myself to death with pointless questions, we need to deal with the issue before us now. Nobody wants you to break the game. They're not allowed to take your artifact. Their solution is simple. You can just fuck off and die, and if you were a regular crawler, you'd already be goblin kibble. The good news is, you got something important. Leverage. Your sponsorship and entertainment value offsets the damage you might cause. It's Remex the Grand all over again. So the mudskippers would prefer if we come to an amicable solution. The problem is this liaison fuck sitting right here pretending to be deaf. If he determines we're at an impasse, he has limited authority to create solutions. And these rat fucks crave power so much, they'll manufacture problems just so they can take out their magic dick wands and start zapping shit."

"So what do we do?" I asked, my mind swimming. I still couldn't tell if this guy knew what he was doing or not, and that terrified me. "I don't want to give up the gate. I need it."

"We'll come up with a proposal," he said. He put his vape away and suddenly had a tablet in his hand. "You sure you don't want to give it up? I bet I could get you a deal. Too bad we ain't on the tenth floor. I'd probably be able to get you something really sweet."

It hit me, then. This was the guy who'd help negotiate my exit from the dungeon if I made it down that low. I felt ill.

"We're not selling it," I said. "Orren said I could have it back on the ninth floor. I don't know how it works in the universe, but in my world, if someone is borrowing something, they usually give collateral. Something they won't want to lose."

Quasar grinned. "Now we're talking."

"OH, MY GOD, SLEDGIE!" DONUT CRIED AFTER I OPENED THE DOOR. "What're you doing here?" The four cretins: Bomo, the Sledge, Clay-ton, and Very Sullen all lumbered into the room. The moment they entered, a new door appeared on the wall next to Mordecai's chambers. It was labeled **Mercenary Quarters**. The four white dots blinked and then changed color, obtaining a green cross.

"We received four free mercenaries. They're part of the package deal we negotiated in exchange for temporarily giving up the Gate of the Feral Gods."

Donut jumped to the Sledge's shoulder, and the rock monster gave her an affectionate pat. Chris came to stand before Clay-ton. The lava-rock monster was almost the exact same size as the granite-colored NPC. Chris made a noncommittal grunt, and Clay-ton answered with a similar noise.

Mongo, who'd never met any of these guys, started running in circles around them, hopping up and down with excitement.

"Bomo and Sledge stay with us, Very Sullen goes with Katia, and Clay-ton will stay with Chris."

"How are these guys collateral?" Katia asked. "What if something, uh, happens to them?"

"We have them on floors six, seven, and eight. That's it. If they die, they will regenerate, but not until the next floor. You guys should bring Clay-ton and Sullen with you when you venture out, but Bomo and the Sledge are too valuable to risk, so they're staying in here."

"What?" Donut asked. "Sledgie can't go adventuring with us? Why not?"

The Sledge made a disappointed noise.

"Did they give you the spells?" I asked Bomo.

The rock monster rumbled. "Yes. The Sledge has the second."

I nodded. Excellent.

"Sorry, guys. We need to keep these two safe," I said. "Since we were losing the gate, I wanted to be able to replicate two of the gate's abilities. The first thing I asked for was a teleport spell, but they wouldn't give it to me. Not directly. They didn't want to give me anything that I could just keep after we got the artifact back."

"They really said you could have it back when you hit the ninth floor?" Katia asked.

"Yeah. They seem to like the idea of me being able to sow chaos during faction wars."

"Or they think you're going to do something really stupid between now and then and die first," Donut said.

Katia walked up and patted Very Sullen on the arm. This guy was Katia's regular bodyguard when she entered the club. The rock monster's face was thinner than that of the other two, and his eyes were tiny emotionless dots. I'd never heard this one talk. "Wait, so these guys can teleport now?" Katia asked.

"Not your guy, but yes," I said. "Sort of. They agreed to give me a mercenary upgrade and access to four bodyguards. Then they gave two of them extra spells. Bomo now has a level 15 spell called *Teleport to Stairwell*. We can pick a stairwell from a list and teleport there. It has a ridiculous cooldown. Like twenty-five days. Still it's a pretty powerful spell because it lists all the exits on the entire floor. It's not something they want me to have access to later on, so it's in their best interest to make sure we get the gate back."

"And the other spell?" Katia asked.

"The Sledge's spell is also teleportation, and it's even more impressive. This one was my lawyer's idea."

"Your lawyer?" Katia asked, looking at me sharply. "Back up. What?"

"Yeah, the lawyer thing is a long story. But he suggested it. It's a spell called *Zerzura*."

"*Zerzura?*" Donut asked. "Sledgie, you got a new spell? I just got one, too! Actually, I got a bunch of new ones. I am now a singer, and my voice casts spells. Do you want to hear one?"

The Sledge rumbled happily.

"What does his spell do?" Katia quickly asked, cutting Donut off.

"It's . . ." I trailed off, finally noticing Katia's level. So much had happened since the end of the last floor, I hadn't even thought about the aftermath of what we'd done. "Holy shit, Katia. What the hell?"

She grinned. "I was wondering when you were going to notice. I finally got my base constitution over 100. Got something called Steely Skin. The lower my health, the thicker my flesh."

Katia had been level 44 when she opened the Gate of the Feral Gods onto the ninth-floor city of Larracos, sending a frothing mass of sharks and jellyfish flooding into the metropolis. Apparently she'd gotten a bunch of experience for it. She was now level 52.

"Did you get any good gear?"

"I got a few boxes, including a Platinum Asshole's Box. It gave me a gambling chip for the Desperado Club and an upgrade to my Find Crawler skill. Also . . ." She trailed off as if she was about to say something but changed her mind. "You still didn't answer my question. What does the Sledge's new spell do? What was it called? *Zerzura?*"

My hand found my necklace. I fingered the small charm with the yellow gem. It was warm to the touch. I thought of the crazy story Quasar told me about Remex the Grand and what he'd done with the *Zerzura* spell.

It was glorious, Quasar had said. *Shame how it ended for Remex. They made us study the exit deal he made in school. But the mudskippers cleaned up that season. It was a real windfall. You ask for this spell, and they'll fall over themselves to give it to you. And you want to know the beautiful part? All those other pricks won't interfere. Everyone will want you to pull it off. All the factions. All the fans. The showrunners. The AI. Everybody. That spell always leads to carnage. Everybody likes carnage when it's not them.*

———

I SLEPT TWO HOURS AND CAME OUT TO FIND MORDECAI STANDING ON the kitchen table quietly conversing with Chris and Clay-ton. The other three cretins were leaned over my *Frogger* cabinet.

If Mordecai was still pissed at me for laughing at him earlier, he didn't show it now. Which was good because I had to work really hard not to bust out again.

"We need to purchase some upgrades for the space," Mordecai said, "But I think we should wait until after the recap. If they're really going to open up the guild system, I want to know how it works first. They've tried this a few times over the cycles, and it's different every time. There are multiple upgrades we need."

"Okay," I said, moving to the food box and dialing in a breakfast sandwich. "There's something I want to buy right now if we can afford it."

"The bomber's studio?" he asked. "It's not too expensive, and that venison box had what, 300,000 gold in it?"

"Yeah," I said. "The *advanced* bomber's studio." Between me and Donut, we now had just about a million gold. I had a suspicion we were going to need it all.

I eyed the small shrine in the corner of the room, bubbling merrily. It was a disc and a cup. When I was in the room, the cup boiled over with water. Apparently it stopped when I wasn't around. I still needed to do my daily blood drop into it. Thanks to my new religion, I also had to drop 5% of my "looted" gold into the cup. A number appeared floating over the shrine, helpfully telling me exactly how much I owed. Unfortunately, the shrine's definition of "looted" included the gold I'd received from surviving the previous floor while on the top-ten list. I'd dropped the gold in there when Donut wasn't looking. She'd noticed anyway and complained for five minutes straight.

"It'll probably be okay if you buy the bomber room right now along with the magic studio, which will be expensive. We'll get them as soon as Donut is ready."

Katia emerged from her room and moved to the food box. She and Chris along with their two new mercenaries were going to head out on their own after her daily training. Louis and Firas had managed to recover the flying house, the *Twister*, from the changeling refugees. A group of crawlers—including team Meadow Lark, Bautista's team, and several others—was meeting up in a large settlement that was a few hours south of here. Katia wanted to make sure she met up with them before the hunters were unleashed.

She was going to remain in the party until after we figured out the guild system, which was fine by me. I still hadn't fully come to terms with her leaving the group, but I'd already decided it was for the best, especially after considering what I was planning on doing today.

Donut emerged from the space, all poofed out and clean. Mongo padded behind her. She hummed the theme to *The A-Team*. "Carl, I think I've figured out the melody I'm going to use for my *Standing Ovation* spell."

"Great," I said. I exchanged a look with Mordecai.

"Come on," he said. "Let's go buy those two rooms."

"YOU GUYS BE SAFE. STAY ON THE TRAIL," I SAID.

"We're taking the caravan. We'll be okay," Katia said as she, Chris, Clay-ton, and Very Sullen exited the safe room. "We'll see you guys later."

"Bye, Katia! Bye, Chris!" Donut said. She was attempting to be enthusiastic, but I could hear the sadness in her voice. Katia leaned over and kissed Donut on the head. Donut sniffed.

Mongo squawked mournfully.

"See you tonight," I said.

Katia held my eyes. "Don't do anything stupid."

"I won't," I lied.

As soon as they left, Donut and Mordecai were going to hit the town and go shopping. There was no Desperado Club here, and it wasn't yet safe for me to attempt to enter Club Vanquisher, so they had to rely on the local shops for the supplies they needed.

We only had 100K gold left after purchasing the two new rooms, and we needed to find a *Shield* spell book for Donut. Mordecai also wanted to find an item with something called a *Golden Throat* enchantment, which was apparently the dungeon's version of auto-tune.

Donut's new Bard class didn't use mana. All she needed to do was sing, and the bard spells would be cast. That was great, but there was a problem. A big problem. The song had to be in key. And until we found that item, her new class was useless.

Why?

Because Donut sounded like a helium-drunk cat being crushed by a steamroller when she attempted to sing—that was why. And even though she wasn't that bad of a dancer, when it came to making a song emerge from that tone-deaf gullet of hers, her rhythm was that of a drunk three-legged donkey trying to negotiate its way down a set of ice-covered stairs.

There were two types of songs. For some of the spells, a group of lyrics appeared floating in front of her in midair, and she had to sing the words, karaoke-style. She had to make up the melody herself. Apparently it didn't matter what the melody was, as long as it was consistently in key.

For two of the spells, however, it was different. She'd select the spell, and the melody would start playing on its own. She had to make up lyrics on the fly. It didn't appear to matter what the lyrics were as long as they, again, were sung in key.

I didn't know which one was worse.

Not that it stopped Donut from attempting to cast them. Over and over and over again.

The first three spells were party-support spells: *Standing Ovation*, which increased everyone's dexterity and made our regular spells more powerful. *Entourage*, which created multiple illusionary versions of each party member, and *Encore*, which was a *Heal Party* spell that could also remove multiple debuffs. Mordecai was pretty stoked about that *Encore* spell.

She could manage to cast all three of these if she sang the lyrics in a steady monotone voice. Each song was a relatively short paragraph. Unfortunately, the spell's power was based on how well she sang it. So until she got that auto-tune buff, the spells were pretty weak.

The other two songs were offensive spells, and neither was going to be feasible for now. One was a psionic attack, and the other was an Elle-style ice attack.

Donut had also received one additional regular spell, thanks to her Spell Book of the Floor Club. A spell called *Laundry Day*, which removed an item of armor from an opponent and caused it to fall to the ground. The higher the level of the spell, the more powerful it was. At level five, she'd be able to remove breastplates and other chest armor. At level 10, she could strip an opponent bare. At 15, she could cast on multiple opponents at once.

Thanks to our new magic workshop, we could train our spells up much like with the training room. Unlike the regular training room, however, only one person could use it at a time. The room was also required for some of Mordecai's higher-level potions, but I wasn't clear yet on how all that worked. Mordecai had already mapped out a strict schedule. He had Donut pushing her *Magic Missile*, which had stalled out at level 11 despite her constantly using it, and me working on my *Fear* spell, which hadn't moved past level five.

I'd sent a message to Donut and told her to work on *Laundry Day* instead. She didn't question it.

"What if something happens to Katia and we can't protect her?" Donut asked after they left. "Mongo would never forgive me if something happened to her."

I scratched Donut behind the ear. "Her staying away from us is probably for the best right now."

"Come on, Donut," Mordecai said. "Let's go shopping."

The Sledge moved to follow them out the door, but Mordecai held up a fuzzy hand. "Not this time, big guy."

"It's okay, Sledgie," Donut said. "You stay here. We won't be gone long."

The cretin grunted and then turned back to the *Frogger* game, which we'd had to shove over and place next to the television screens. With the addition of the two new rooms, the wide space was starting to look much more cramped. We could still fit one or two new rooms depending on the size, but anything after that would require us to figure out how to unlock the second level of the space.

I made a beeline toward my new room, the advanced bomber's studio. The small room was only about ten feet wide, but it was long, making me feel like I was standing in a private bowling alley.

Most of the work still happened at my sapper's table, for now. This new room had two separate functions.

The first was that I could now virtually "copy" a design or an existing explosive and bring it over to the studio, where I could place it and set it off. There were no actual explosions involved inside the studio. Everything in the testing area was virtual, like it was a game. I could create a miniature virtual person or group of people or even a whole village, place the bomb, set it off, and see what would happen. I could pause the explosion and see what way it would blow based on its position. I could use the information to go back and tweak the design or the method of delivery and fine-tune the yield.

The system wasn't perfect, however. Sometimes it gave a range of possibilities. The cookbook stressed this point. Just because it blew in a certain way in the simulation wasn't a guarantee it'd actually go up that way. There were literally thousands of small environmental factors that could affect the way an explosive went up.

Thanks to this being an "advanced" bomber's studio, I could also test bombs and other incendiaries that I didn't actually have. I could build a virtual bomb and see if it'd work. For now I could only use items I had in my inventory, but hopefully that'd change after I gained some more experience.

The room's second function was the crafting table in the very back. One where I could tweak actual explosives. This was a specialty workbench, and at level one, it wasn't as good as my level five sapper's table in terms of building explosives from scratch. At least not yet.

However, the table was designed to be able to examine and dissect explosives, and it was absolutely required to engineer certain large-scale bombs.

I stood at the new bench now, shaking. I, for the very first time since I'd grabbed the thing, took out the Carl's Doomsday Scenario bomb and placed it onto the table. The small bench reshaped itself to accommodate the glass reaper case, which glowed like a miniature sun. The bomb was a microsecond from exploding, and there was nothing I could do to stop it. But I could examine it. I copied it using the bomber studio interface so I'd be able to play with it safely using the simulator. I placed the bomb back into my inventory, my hands still trembling.

One day I would use that thing. One day.

Okay, I said to myself. *Quit screwing around. Back to work.*

We had 21 hours until the hunters would be released and about six or seven until darkness descended on the jungle. I pulled a stick of hobgoblin dynamite and started to carefully slice it into twenty different pieces.

———

THEIR SHOPPING TRIP HAD BEEN MOSTLY A BUST, BUT MORDECAI HAD purchased a ton of herbs and supplies from the town's vendors. He'd even picked some plants from the ground. But they hadn't found a *Shield* spell book nor any magical gear with a *Golden Throat* enchantment. There still wasn't anything good on the shop interface, either, though that would change over the next few days.

Mordecai wanted us to go out and start looking for some special type of small mushroom that only appeared at night. "These will appear at the base of the trees in town, so don't wander out into the jungle. It's just like the third floor. Stay out of alleyways. Keep a lookout for more of those pets. There's a caravan coming through town in the morning, and I think you should get on it. It heads deeper south and ends up in a larger settlement than this one. From there you can start building a defensive zone and grinding. The *Vengeance of the Daughter* production is probably going to rope you into something pretty soon, too, assuming the show hasn't been canceled yet, so I want to make sure you're in a good position for when that happens. But for right now, I need those mushrooms."

"Yeah, we'll be on the lookout for your herbs. We're going to head out now," I said. "Bomo, can you come?"

"You sure you wanna bring him?" Mordecai asked.

"We're keeping Sledge locked up," I said. "Bomo is worth the risk."

———

"DO YOU THINK THE HUNTER GUYS CAN SEE WHAT WE'RE DOING?" DO-nut asked as we stepped outside into the town. It smelled like rain. It was already pitch-black out here. A pair of tree creatures strode by, not acknowledging our presence. A pair of monkeys rode in their upper branches. Donut moved to cast *Torch*, but I waved her down. "Like, can they cheat and have their friends watch the show from outside and follow us and then tell them where we are at all times?"

"Well, in theory, people outside the dungeon aren't supposed to talk to those inside, even the tourists, but we all know that's bullshit. The fact they sued us for our plan on the previous floor means they're obviously watching our every move. I think it's safe to say they'll eventually know what we're doing. I don't think they have a direct line, especially since the Desperado Club access got all messed up for those on the ninth floor. But they'll still know eventually. So any plan we have needs to be kept as much of a secret as we can make it. By the way, do me a favor really quick. Can you put Mongo away?"

"We'll need a plan first before we can keep it a secret," Donut said. "Mongo, come on. Into the cage. No, put that down. I think that's mushroom poop. Come on, do what Mommy says. Good boy! Good boy, Mongo!" She returned her gaze to me. "But it's nice not to have to be all top secret for a day or two. It'll give me time to practice my singing. Why did I just put Mongo away?"

"Don't practice your singing in town," I said, putting my hand up on Donut to scratch her. "We don't want to set the mushroom guys' aggro off. Also, I'd like to apologize for what's about to happen."

"Apologize for what? Aren't we hunting for herbs?"

"We're going hunting all right. This is gonna go quick. Get ready."

CARL: Bomo. Cast your spell. Send us to the stairwell in Zockau.
   Do it now.

5 | Hunters Killed: 0

<Note added by Crawler Forkith. 20th Edition>

Based on some of these previous passages and my own observations, I think I've put together a good idea about the layout of the Hunting Grounds. They say it's the same every time, but that is not true. Herot spoke of those tall creatures who bellow into the sky each night, rumbling the world. Azin described the kite birds always flying overhead. Ikicha wrote of the ice and cold weather. None of those are here, not in this iteration. Most of the world is jungle. That is a constant. But the monsters within change, so be careful taking advice from previous editions of this book regarding this floor.

However, the map appears to be the same each time. The "political landscape" is the same, too. It is a round world with a single named metropolis and dozens of other unnamed cities of varying sizes like on the third floor. This world, according to the story, was half metropolis and half jungle before Scolopendra's nine-tier attack, whatever the hell that even means. After the attack, most everyone died, and the jungle ran rampant, swallowing the ruins. However, after a few hundred years, the survivors have started to rebuild. The named city is always in the same place. In the north, near the edge of the map and overlooking a clear valley filled with lower-level monsters, placed there so the hunters can train while the crawlers make their way through the lower floors. All the way to the southeast is the high elf city, which is in the thickest part of the jungle. Stay away from the elves. They are powerful magic users, and they attack everyone. Even the hunters stay away.

Before the cataclysm, this world was rich. The city was under control of a multi-race council. The jungle was under control of the high elves. They hated each other, but there was mostly peace. A river separated the two districts.

That river still winds through the map. There are bridges in regular intervals. Stay out of the water. The naiads live within and are just as bad as the elves.

The named city—whose name appears to be different each time—will always be under control of a single race. It doesn't matter which one. The moment the hunters arrive, one of them always hunts down and kills the NPC leader, which gives them control. I think it's the only city they're allowed to do this in. Otherwise they'd have control of them all by the time we arrive. Either way, once the floor opens, the low-level valley will be hunted to extinction, the existing government of the named city will have been wiped out, and one of the hunters will have set themselves up as Grand, the title given to mayors of the biggest settlements.

Stay out of the big city. The guards will attack you on sight.

"IT CAST," BOMO RUMBLED. THE SPELL WOULD TAKE THIRTY SECONDS to activate.

"Carl, Carl, what are we doing? Are you crazy?" Donut cried as I checked my gear.

I slipped the Ring of Divine Suffering onto my finger. This was the ring Frank Q had given me. All of my stats rose by 5%. The way the ring worked was slightly different depending on the floor one was on, but the end result was the same. If I marked someone—either a crawler or a "non-dungeon generated combatant"—and then I killed them, I would receive +1 to one of my stat points, based on their current highest stat. That bonus would increase the more I killed.

The problem was, once I marked somebody, I would receive a nasty debuff that wouldn't go away until I killed my mark. I wouldn't be able to heal. I knew from the cookbook that debuff was called "Left to Fester."

I examined the ring's properties to make sure it was working as intended.

Current Marks killed: 0.
Current Mark benefit: +1 Stat Point.

Current floor cooldown: There is no cooldown on this floor.
Marks form instantly on this floor.
Happy hunting.

"Fifteen seconds," Bomo rumbled.

I looked down at the second toe ring on my left foot, the one I'd gotten for getting stepped on by Grull. The ring came with two benefits.
I'd used one of them, Sticky Feet, quite a bit. The toe ring had a second
ability that I'd yet to try.

"Carl," Donut said, "I really think we should be discussing our plan
right about now."

"When we hit two seconds, Predator," I said.

"That's not a plan, Carl. That's a move."

"We'll be okay. Just stay with me. It'll go fast."

Predator was one of our newer moves. I'd been collecting a lot of
invisibility potions recently, and I made sure Donut always had a few of
them. The move was simple. As soon as I called "Predator," we both
went invisible, and Donut switched to infrared vision using her sunglasses. We no longer talked out loud, and she remained on my shoulder, constantly calling out anything she could see that I might not.

"Sorry about this, Bomo," I said. I smashed an invisibility potion
against the side of the NPC's head. The rock monster disappeared.

I drank down an invisibility potion just as the timer hit zero. Donut
did the same.

We blinked, I had the now-familiar tug of nausea, and then we were
there.

Entering Zockau.

DONUT: CARL, IF WE DON'T DIE, MORDECAI IS GOING TO KILL YOU.

We appeared in a quaint little park with manicured green grass. A
circle of trees and a well-maintained hedge surrounded the large stairwell. The exit to the seventh floor was right there, and I could feel the
heat coming off it. Cobblestones led up to the glowing exit. Light shone
up into the air like a searchlight, rising about fifty feet before stopping

against the artificial ceiling. Nighttime had fully descended on the area, but it was still early evening. There was nobody in the small park, but I could see multiple dots on my map, a mix of white, red, orange, and a new color. Purple. The white dots were the regular NPCs, the red appeared to be the city guards, the orange were the pets, and the purple were the hunters. I could only see three of the hunters. None were close.

The city guards were not the mushroom guys, but tall, muscled humanoid bears in heavy armor. A group of them marched down the street and away.

Nobody appeared to know we were here. Yet.

A large statue stood nearby, also depicting one of the bear-headed humanoids. A little plaque described who it was, but we didn't have time to stop and read. Commercial buildings surrounded the town square, giving the impression of a downtown area of a small American town from the 1950s. Electric-style lights circled the park in regular intervals, giving off a dim yellow glow. Directly across from us and on the other side of the street was a line of pubs all in a row. Raucous laughter emanated from the window of one. Music played from another. The distant *thwum* of a spell being cast shot through the night, followed by a crash and even more distant laughter.

As I watched, a purple dot stumbled from the doorway of one pub. He stopped, fell to his knees, and started vomiting on the street. This was a tall, lanky alien race I didn't recognize in the dark. He pulled himself up and stumbled into another bar.

Standing at the end of the line of pubs was what I was looking for. The tall, opulent entrance to the Desperado Club. The entrance was three stories tall, and twin spotlights swept back and forth in front of the building. In the Over City, the club entrance had a 1920s style that clashed with the medieval vibe of the village. This time, the club's architecture fit with the town's aesthetic. Instead of a 1920s art deco, this was more of a 1950s mid-century modern. A concrete archway covered the entrance, flanked by an angular façade with wings on either side, like eyebrows, almost giving the impression that the club was a massive drive-in diner. The sign "The Desperado Club: So Fun It Hurts" blinked, the words spelled out with dozens of little light bulbs. A statue of the dagger logo spun atop the building.

CARL: Bomo, walk toward that bar at the end of the street. The little one with the broken sign. That one appears to be mostly empty, and it's the only one that's a real safe room. Stay in the shadows until your invisibility runs out. Once it does, just casually walk inside and go straight to the personal space. If you're attacked, run. Do you understand?

BOMO: Understand.

I couldn't actually see the rock monster, but I heard him clomp off through the grass. There were dozens of NPC cretins on this floor. Nobody would notice him unless they stopped and read his description, which said he was a member of the Royal Court of Princess Donut.

I pulled the multi-launcher from my inventory and placed it on the grass. I had 25 of the surefire homing missiles in the box, all lined up in a five-by-five grid, pointing directly upward. Their targets were already programmed in. These were all single-stage rockets, so they were much smaller than the ones we used on the previous floor. The entire box was the size of a poker table. I placed it right against the inside of the closest hedge. I marked the timed trigger using my Remote Detonator skill.

CARL: Donut, if this goes south, just jump down the stairs. We'll regroup on the seventh floor.

DONUT: IT'S ALREADY GOING SOUTH, CARL. WE DON'T ATTACK THE MAIN BAD GUYS IN THE VERY BEGINNING. THAT'S NOT HOW THIS IS SUPPOSED TO WORK.

I examined my map. There was a total of seven pubs, not including the Desperado. Each one was its own separate building with a small alleyway between them. The one Bomo was walking toward was the smallest. Only that one was a true safe room, though all seven would have entrances to our personal space within. The largest of the regular pubs on this street was called the Ladies Love It, and from within this bar came the loudest music and most laughing. The sign was a large wooden placard depicting a grinning bald man with "Ladies Love It" tattooed over his upper lip. A spotlight shone directly on the leering mouth. This bar was not a real safe room. It stood right next door to the Desperado, which curved around the next corner.

> **DONUT: THEY ALREADY KNOW WE'RE HERE. THE GUARDS' DOTS ARE RED.**
> **CARL: That just means the mayor of the town has been killed by one of the hunters, and they have ordered them to attack crawlers on sight.**
> **DONUT: I HOPE YOU HAVE A PLAN TO GET US OUT OF HERE.**

I took a step toward the row of bars.

WARNING. DEAD MAN WALKING!

I cursed, and I stopped, my foot hovering an inch off the ground. I retracted my foot and then crouched down. I focused, and the problem became evident. A haphazard minefield of traps lay scattered about, filling the park that surrounded the stairwell. There were dozens of them. Most of them were alarm traps, but I saw a few I didn't recognize. One was called a **You Aren't Going Anywhere Trap.** There were likely others. My Find Traps skill wasn't super reliable just yet.

I quickly examined this first trap.

> **Placed Trap.**
>   **Set by Hunter Ontario.**
>   **Effect: A loud-ass alarm.**
>   **Delay: None.**
>   **Target: Crawlers. That's you.**

Most of them appeared to be placed by this Ontario person, but there were others mixed in, too. Bomo, being an NPC, hadn't set them off.

I easily disarmed this first alarm trap and pulled it into my inventory. I had to drink another invisibility potion. Donut's invisibility would last another minute. We didn't have time for this.

Ahead, I saw Bomo suddenly appear. He crossed the street and entered the dive bar with the broken sign. Nobody seemed to notice or care. He walked right past a group of NPCs, and they didn't give him a second look.

> CARL: Donut, puddle-jump us out of here. We're surrounded by traps. Put us in front of the alley between the Desperado and that other club.
> DONUT: WHERE ALL THE HUNTERS ARE?
> CARL: Yes.
> DONUT: IF I HAVE TO TAKE A MANA POTION, IT'LL MESS UP ME TAKING THE NEXT INVISIBILITY POTION BECAUSE OF MY POTION COUNTDOWN.
> CARL: I know. Send us now.

Donut grumbled. Three seconds passed, and we jumped, appearing in the space between the Ladies Love It and the Desperado. A pair of elven NPCs strolled down the street. One looked sharply in our direction at the noise of us cracking into existence, but she didn't stop to investigate further. Three doors down, a hunter appeared. An orc. An NPC female dwarf rode him piggyback, and they were both laughing. They drunkenly lurched into an alleyway.

My heart pounded. Our view counter was spiking, which meant at any moment someone was going to raise the alarm. I still had no idea how efficient these guys were with their communications. I hoped and prayed we'd have another few minutes at least.

I examined the tight alleyway between the Desperado and the Ladies Love It. It was pitch-black in there. Donut didn't see any mobs. I moved to step inside, but I stopped, seeing yet another alarm trap. *Christ.* I hadn't been expecting that.

Fuck it, I thought. I looked around to see if anyone was looking in our direction, and then I pulled the barrel from my inventory and placed it on the ground in the space between the two buildings, just in front of the trap. I marked the bomb using a second Remote Detonator and also added this trigger to my hotlist. We needed to hurry. The thing said it was a bomb, so if anybody examined it, they'd see it for what it was. I quickly moved to the next alleyway down.

Donut took her second invisibility potion as I took my fourth. For Donut, the invisibility lasted just about two minutes. Her potion sickness countdown was much better than it used to be, but it was still at one minute and forty-five seconds, which meant she couldn't keep her mana topped off and remain invisible. She had two slices of mana toast in her inventory that we were keeping for an emergency. The toast would top off her spell points, and it wouldn't count as a potion. I didn't want her to use it unless absolutely necessary.

Donut trembled on my shoulder, and I reached up to give her a reassuring pat.

I skipped the next alleyway and moved to the one after that. These bombs were pretty big and didn't need to be that close. I dropped a barrel right on the sidewalk. We skipped the next alleyway, which contained a grunting orc and dwarf, and I moved to the following entrance. I placed the third barrel.

Just as I rolled the fourth one into place, a dragon-headed hunter emerged from this last bar, just a mere five feet to my left. This was the same bar Bomo had entered. It was the only true safe room of the lot. The sign was broken, so I hadn't been able to read it from across the street, but I could now see the place was called the Scuttlebutt.

I examined the hunter.

Chin'Dua—Draconian. Level 50. Striver.
This is an Unaffiliated Hunter.

It didn't describe either the Draconian race or the Striver class. The creature stepped unsteadily from the bar. He stopped right next to me and leaned up against the barrel. The tall, scaled creature held a glass with a little purple umbrella in it. Multiple cherries floated in the red drink. He remained there, leaning on the massive bomb. He wasn't doing anything to it, but his very presence was causing the item's stability to slowly decline on its own. The hunter started to snore, but he clutched the drink tightly in his clawed hand. He snorted and then woke himself up.

"I ain't paying," he said, grumbling.

DONUT: CARL, CARL, I THINK HE'S DRINKING A DIRTY SHIRLEY!

CARL: I wouldn't be surprised. I think you might've made the drink famous.

DONUT: WHY ARE THEY ALL DRUNK?

CARL: They're all going hunting tomorrow. This is their last time to party. We gotta be careful. Not all of them will be wasted.

DONUT: HE'S GOING TO SEE IT'S A BOMB. WHAT ARE WE GOING TO DO?

A light appeared in the sky, coming from deep within the large town and rising into the air. It moved in our direction. A spell shot out from the figure, and a group of white flares burst out in each direction like fireworks, streaking out across the sky, lighting up the night.

Shit. Whoever that was knew we were here. I didn't know what that spell was, but they were obviously looking for us.

I pulled up the menu for the Ring of Divine Suffering, and I found the name I was searching for.

I took a deep breath. *There's no going back after this.*

You have marked Chin'Dua.
    Chin'Dua's highest stat is Dexterity.
    You have been infected with Left to Fester! This debuff will not go away until your mark is dead!
    Happy Hunting, killer.

The drunken alien looked up as I allowed the invisibility potion to expire. He blinked at me.

"You . . . you're not supposed to be here," the creature said. It was almost a whisper. It was a miracle this guy was still on his feet. He was just as drunk as Growler Gary the gnoll had been when we started cutting off his hands. He brought his drink to his lips, and he slurped in a cherry.

Behind him, the barrel's integrity continued its downward momentum.

"Your name is Chin'Dua?" I asked. I put my hands on his shoulder

to steady him, pulling him off the barrel, which caused the bomb's integrity to stop at about 30%. Above, one of the flares stopped to hover
over us, illuminating the square. Multiple hunters emerged from the
bars up and down the street, but they were all looking up.

Chin'Dua didn't appear to have any magical gear on him, which was
unfortunate. He'd probably only been here for a few hours and hadn't
had a chance to collect anything.

"That's Xindy," Chin'Dua said, lifting his head to the sky. "Why is
she all worked up?"

Down the line, a pair of alien hunters was standing right next to the
first barrel, but they hadn't noticed it yet. These were large blue-skinned
humanoids wearing leather armor.

I leaned in. "Wanna hear a secret?"

"What?" Chin'Dua asked, whispering. His eyes fluttered.

DONUT: CARL, HURRY UP. YOU'RE TAKING TOO LONG.

"I'm using you as bait. That's how you're going to die. As bait."

There was a shout, and at that same moment, I cast *Ping*.

An audible tone spread out, filling the town with the noise. My map
came alive as every nearby NPC, hunter, and pet appeared on my interface. Above, the shining light started rocketing toward us. I could now
see the flying purple dot on my map moving in our direction.

"Damnit," I muttered under my breath as I quickly searched the
dots. I was hoping that this flying hunter would also be the town's
mayor. The Grand. They weren't. I wouldn't be so lucky. I looked frantically about for the purple dot, which would be indicated on the map
with a star. I didn't see them, which meant they were either in a safe
room, they were asleep, or they were out of range.

I was expecting to be immediately assaulted. Instead, most of the
hunters scrambled away, rushing back into the bars. A few of the smart
ones scrambled into the Desperado.

I quickly sorted through the list, seeking out the highest-level
hunter. There was a 63 two streets over quickly running in this direction. They were too far away. I instead focused on the flying hunter.
Level 61. Good enough. I mentally clicked on the dot.

Hunter Xindy—Mantis. Level 61. Blood Tracker.
The Dark Hive.

I focused on my toe ring, and I pulled up its second ability. Super Spreader. Its range was dependent on my map. They had to be close enough that I could see their name. Because of the *Ping* spell, that range was greatly increased. I scrolled down the list until I found Xindy, and I clicked **Activate**.

The flying alien stopped dead in the air. On my shoulder, Donut fired a pair of magic missiles at a hunter who shrieked and ran away. Above, Xindy started to rapidly retreat as she realized she'd been hit with a debuff. She was now in the same boat as me. She was infected with Left to Fester, and it wouldn't go away until poor Chin'Dua was dead.

More shouting rose. I was hit with a *Ping* spell identical to the one I'd just cast. A yellow light jumped into the air. A half block away, a swarm of orange dots moved in our direction. Behind me, the bear guards had turned and were running toward us.

I mentally clicked the first of the two remote detonator triggers in my hotlist, and the rockets started corkscrewing into the air one by one. I had them programmed so they'd take off at three-second intervals in groups of five, each focused on the "Fastest-moving Hunter-class creature."

All five of the first group of missiles rocketed away, streaking toward the retreating form of Xindy, who'd, in a panic, started to rapidly fly away. A shield appeared around the fleeing hunter as the first missile slammed into her.

The second and third missiles hit her in quick succession. The fourth exploded prematurely as a bolt cast from one street over shot right into the missile. I watched the shield fail just as the fifth missile slammed into the hunter, and she exploded. I saw her purple dot turn into an X as her flaming corpse plummeted from the sky. Even before she hit the ground, the next missiles were spreading off into different directions.

"Whoa. Did you see that?" Chin'Dua said, looking up into the air as I waved away the page of notifications that'd just appeared. "That was Vrah's little sister."

I punched him in the chest, and I felt the satisfying crunch of bones. He gasped, looking at me with both surprise and an odd sense of betrayal. I punched him in the face. Then again. He crashed to the ground, knocking over the barrel, which started to rapidly deteriorate again. His half-full glass of vodka went flying. Little cherries rolled down the sidewalk as I crushed his head with my foot.

The orc and the dwarf from one alleyway over stood there on the sidewalk, ten feet away, gawking at me.

I wanted to mark this orc next, but I didn't have time. The orc's health was at 95%, and I would've had to heal him first. The barrel was going to blow. *Damnit. Damnit to hell.* I didn't have time to find someone else.

"You better run," I said as Donut and I jumped into the Scuttlebutt.

I never got the chance to click on the second trigger in my hotlist. The moment we landed inside and closed the door, the barrel went off.

Despite us being in a safe room, Donut and I were blown back and into the bar. Chairs fell over. Bottles cascaded off shelves. Three more explosions ripped through outside. I heard shouting from the other side of the bar. It was a Bopca crying out in surprise.

"Are you okay?" I asked Donut, who was all poofed out.

"Carl, I think I want to go to Katia's team now," Donut said, her voice dazed.

"Okay, but we gotta get out of here first," I said, pulling myself back up. "Back to my shoulder. Quick."

I rushed toward the personal space door. I was momentarily surprised to see there was actually a long hallway here with five other doors. I moved to the one marked **The Royal Court of Princess Donut**, and I burst inside to find Bomo and the Sledge standing there.

"Protect!" I shouted.

"What in god's name is going on?" Mordecai said from the counter, where it appeared he was eating a banana split sundae. He had the ice cream all over his fuzzy face.

"Are we going back out there?" Donut asked, incredulous.

"We have to," I said, breathing heavily. "If we don't get out now, they'll just guard that exit and trap us in Zockau."

"Zockau? *Zockau?*" Mordecai cried. "You motherfuckers are in the goddamned capital?"

The Sledge cast two quick magic shells around each of us. Blue light swirled. Bomo cast *Shield*, and a translucent spell appeared. Both would last for five minutes or until they were dispelled by damage.

I turned and bounded back outside with Mordecai shouting after us. One of the other doorways opened, and we passed by a wide-eyed dark elf hunter coming out of his own personal space.

"Boo," Donut yelled at him, and he stumbled backward. I caught sight of two more elves within the room.

We rushed back out into the Scuttlebutt, which now had two more hunters within. Both were level 50 tentacle-faced Saccathians.

We burst past the surprised creatures and back out into the night. We jumped into burning, smoky chaos.

The entire block was now on fire and blown to shit. A thick fog filled the area. Bodies were everywhere. The barrel explosives had been crammed with gunpowder and hobgoblin dynamite and delay-detonated smoke curtains. I'd packed them in a way that caused the most destruction. They were unstable as shit, but a single one could take out an entire block. We'd only been saved because we'd hidden inside of a real safe room.

The entire façade of the Desperado had collapsed. The entrance bar was gone. Those that were in the real club were now trapped, and they would remain trapped. None of the others would be able to get in, at least via Zockau.

Despite the mass destruction, we were surrounded by red, orange, and purple dots, though most were a few blocks away. Most of the traps in the blast radius had been tripped on their own, and dozens of different songs blasted into the night. I caught snippets of everything from Aretha Franklin to ZZ Top.

I pulled yet another bomb from my inventory and tossed it. It hit the ground, rolled, and started firing hobgoblin smoke curtains in regular intervals. I mapped out the closest path to the edge of town. It was a good quarter mile away down a residential street. We both took invisibility potions, and I started to run.

The invisibility did not hide the twin swirling protection shells around ourselves, but that was okay. It hid our dots on the map, and amongst all this chaos, we just needed a minute to get out of town. We'd be relatively safe once we hit the jungle.

From my shoulder, Donut started to sing. Her voice cracked.

"The shadows cold. The eyes and the smile. I see shadows in my mind, trying to be gone. Shadow in my mind. Carl, quit bouncing around, you're making me mess up the lyrics!"

"What are you trying to cast?". We rushed past the town square and into a tight street. The first several rows of buildings here were all half-caved-in. Debris littered the street. I jumped over the groaning body of an elf NPC.

"Sorry, buddy," I called over my shoulder.

It looked as if every window in town was blown out. Farther down, multiple NPCs started to wander from their homes. I didn't see any purple dots. We rushed down the middle of the street.

"I'm trying to cast *Entourage*, which makes a copy of us, but you keep messing me up. I have to read the lyrics, but I can't when we're running! It's like trying to do karaoke while I'm on a roller coaster!"

WARNING! WATCH YOUR DAMN STEP!

"Goddamnit," I said, sliding to a stop. It was too late. A countdown appeared. I'd already stepped on the trap. Two traps. The first was an alarm trap right in the middle of the street, and the second was a cheap spike trap. I jumped out of the way before the spikes activated, but there was nothing I could do about the alarm.

Peaking at Number 27 on January 27, 1990, it's "Kickstart My Heart"!

I cast *Tripper*, which set off every trap in a wide radius. Multiple songs and small explosions rocked all around us, but the Mötley Crüe song was blasting right next to us so loud that we were both racked with pain. I reached down and physically picked up the small cube-sized trap. It wouldn't let me disarm it now that it'd been set off, but it did allow me to pull it into my inventory, cutting it off. My ears rang.

Donut was screaming something, but I couldn't hear her. I pulled out my second rocket box. This one only had ten rockets within because I'd run out of surefires. This one was preset to kill the "Closest Hunter Class Mobs."

You have been deshrouded! Invisibility negated!

My shield sparked as something slammed into it. A shield health bar appeared in my UI, down halfway. A second, then a third item hit the shield. Crossbow bolts. I searched for the source, but I couldn't see our attacker.

DONUT: ON THE ROOF! INVISIBLE!

A magic missile shot forth from Donut, hitting the top of the building as I dropped a smoke curtain, loaded a hob-lobber, and threw it.

DONUT: WE MISSED! IT CAN FLY! IT'S THE SAME TYPE AS THE LAST ONE!

My *Ping* spell had five seconds left before I could cast again. I scrambled away down the street toward the looming line of trees. Above, an orange dot appeared, some sort of flying pet coming from a different direction. It rocketed toward us, screeching. A large hawk. A bolt slammed the pet's head, and it tumbled away. The hunter shot it. *He's protecting his kill.*

My shield sparked again as more crossbow bolts slammed into me. The shield failed. I cried out in pain as yet another crossbow bolt buried itself into my shoulder. *So much for my anti-piercing resistance.*

Poison Negated.

I instinctively ducked, and another bolt slammed into Donut, who was still protected. She flew from my shoulder and bounded ahead, hitting the street and rolling. She leaped to her feet and ran.

I hit *Ping*, and the dot finally appeared on my map. High above. I saw the star around the purple dot. The mayor. The Grand. Finally.

I activated the missiles, and they burst into the air behind us. I didn't turn to look. I ran. The hunter, who was level 70, arced away, dodging the missiles.

Another bolt slammed into the back of my thigh just as we reached the edge of town. The barbed front of the projectile shattered my leg, bursting out the front and opening up like an umbrella. I screamed as we jumped over the border.

Entering the Selva.

I healed myself as I dragged myself toward the trees. These guys couldn't leave the city, but I didn't know if their weapons could fire beyond the borders.

The moment we left the town, all the dots on my map snapped away, as if the city was protected. I turned to look over my shoulder as I dragged myself away, and the border was opaque. The street was mere feet behind me, but I couldn't see a thing.

"Carl, we gotta go! We're too close! There were more orange dots coming!"

I pulled myself to my feet, but I collapsed again. I looked stupidly down at the crossbow bolt still sticking through my leg. I'd healed myself, but it hadn't pushed the bolt out like it usually did. I had a second one in my shoulder. Both of the bolts were causing my health to continue to plummet. They had a bleed effect.

"Uh-oh," I said. The world started to get fuzzy around the edges. A debuff notification flashed on my interface.

An orange dot appeared on my map. Next to me, Donut gasped. It came from the woods, and it was huge. I couldn't see it, but it crackled with heat. I tried to focus, but I felt as if I was staring at a television screen turned to static. I felt dizzy, dizzier than I'd ever felt before. I realized the sound of all the traps had also cut off the moment we'd left the town's borders. I was falling into a fog. I managed to click a healing scroll, and it healed me, but it didn't do anything to my brain, which continued to swirl with confusion.

There were more people here. Donut was saying something. These were blue dots. Crawlers.

I can't tell the orange pet dots apart, I thought. *Crawler or hunter. That's a bug.* My leg burned. I thought of my *Frogger* game. I wondered if Bomo or the Sledge was better at it. I remembered the day I found my mother in the basement. I thought I was going to get a bike that day, and I never did.

This is my birthday present to you.

Where was I?

"Again! He did it again! At least he's about to perish," a familiar voice said. "Level 54! How did this idiot get so high? What are those knife symbols over his head?"

"Help, help!" Donut said to the newcomers. "Carl needs the arrows pulled out!"

"Mother, you should feed on him before he dies."

"Pony, I am not going to feed on Carl. Now help me with him," a new voice said.

"I say we let him die. He ruined my spell. Again. You need blood."

"Stop, Donut, sweetie," the woman said. "Do not touch the bolts. Oh my. That is a lot of debuffs. I will help. Don't you worry. He will be okay. We are safe here. Trust me."

Somebody screamed.

6

<Note added by Crawler Everly. 5th Edition>

We ended up hiring five mercenaries. I got four from the merc guild on the sixth floor of the Desperado Club, and another party member got a healer from Club Vanquisher. It was and continues to be a disaster. My guys cost us 1,500 gold a day each, and I'm not sure if it was worth it. First off, you have to be very careful with them. If they die, you can't loot their bodies, and our contract stipulates you have to pay their daily rate for the rest of the damn floor. It's outrageous. The healer charges per spell cast. Second, getting them from one place to the next is difficult if you use a personal space. It's easy to lose them. If they leave with me, it's fine. The door opens, and we walk out together. Otherwise, it automatically defaults to the last place they entered, as if they were a regular crawler. So if they're not right there with you when you exit, they could end up three or four safe rooms away. One of our guys left and never came back. He's still alive, as I can see him in the chat, but the prick is just wandering around some town having a good ol' time and I can't even fire him because you have to bring them back with you to let them go. Plus their levels mean next to nothing. My level 40 orc is a significantly better fighter than my level 50 dwarf, who is now dead, by the way. Got hit by a chair, of all things, and he died. Twenty-two more days at 1,500 gold a day. The whole thing is a scam.

MY EYES FLUTTERED OPEN. I FELT AS IF I'D BEEN TRAMPLED BY ELE-phants. Everything hurt. I still had a page of notifications, and I blinked them away.

Donut sat on my chest, looking down at me worriedly. We were moving. I felt gravel crunch underneath me. I was in the back of a cart. I stared up into the night sky. It was still dark outside, but the air above us shimmered with an opalescent sheen, like the skin of a soap bubble catching the light. A magical shell of some sort, I realized. I was under the dome of a spell.

"He's awake!" Donut said. She looked up and said, "His health is still going down."

"The debuff runs out soon," the woman said. "The worst is beyond us. Do not worry, little one."

"What happened?" I groaned. "Did we get any of them?"

"You almost died, Carl," Donut said. "And you would've deserved it, too. What in god's name was that anyway? From now on, I'm not participating in a Carl plan unless I know what I'm getting myself into. Mongo is quite upset with you."

I felt a warm glow, and my health moved back up. The woman had cast something. I felt my health immediately start to seep out of me again, like I was a leaky pipe. Whatever this was, it was a slow, painful debuff. I moved over to my health menu and looked at my current debuffs.

Sore as Shit and **Blood Trail.**

Sore as Shit was one I'd seen before. It popped up every time I'd been severely injured. It was exactly how it sounded. It usually lasted for about an hour, but this time it was at six hours and counting down. I didn't have anything to remove it. It didn't affect any of my stats directly, but everything hurt while it was active.

Blood Trail was a new one. It was about to run out, but it was an insidious debuff.

Blood Trail.

A favorite of game hunters and medical debt collectors chasing after deadbeats, this magical bleeding debuff is usually applied to ranged weapons. Your health seeps downward at a slow, steady pace. You may heal, but all open wounds at the time you receive this debuff will continue to weep, allowing for you to be tracked easily. It also makes you smell really bad. Or really good, depending on who's doing the sniffin'.

I'd been hit with a half dozen other debuffs, too, but they'd all expired.

"How long was I out?" I asked, trying to sit up. I was completely soaked in blood. "I know we got two. Did we get more?"

"Don't get up yet," the woman said. She put a gentle hand on my shoulder, pushing me back. I winced.

"You were in a coma!" Donut said. "It was only for a half hour. If we hadn't gotten out of the city, you'd be dead right now. Miriam, Prepotente, and Bianca saved you."

I felt myself groan.

"You need to rest for a few more minutes, sweetie," the woman—Miriam Dom—said. "We'll be at the town in about an hour, and then you can get to your safe room and sleep."

"Where am I?"

"We're in the back of a cart," Donut said. "It's being pulled by Bianca, and Prepotente is ahead of us, making sure the road is safe. Miriam has been helping you heal, so you need to say thank you."

"Thank you," I said. My head was still swimming. The fog was lifting away, but I felt as if I was waking from a long sleep.

DONUT: ALSO, I DON'T THINK PREPOTENTE LIKES YOU VERY
MUCH. HE SAVED YOU, SO YOU GOTTA BE NICE TO HIM.

A hand touched my forehead. Her fingers were ice-cold. She stroked my hair. "You just rest for a minute, okay?"

You have been Soothed! Everything hurts a little less. Debuffs are
10% less effective.

Donut leaned in. "Seriously, Carl. What, exactly, was the plan there? Go into town and then blow everything up and then run? You may have killed a lot of them, but all you did was make them extra angry. This is why you tell me the plan first, so I can point out why it's stupid."

"I wanted to block off the entrance to the Desperado and see if I could identify the mayor and maybe kill him. Or her. The mayor was Vrah, a woman. She's a race called a mantis. If I killed her, I'd become the mayor and then I was going to order the city guards to kill all the hunters." I gasped. "Jesus, why am I so tired?"

"You were knocked comatose accidentally," Miriam said. She sat behind me and was stroking my hair. It felt weird and kinda nice all at the same time. "It was a Woozy debuff from the crossbow bolt, but it was enhanced because of Pony's spell."

"Sorry I messed it up," I said.

"It is okay," Miriam said. "It was taking much too long, and I believe we'd been discovered. Someone was casting a countermeasure, and it likely wouldn't have worked in time."

"That's because they're cheating," I said, raising my voice. "The hunter guys have people who are watching the show and feeding the information to them."

I heard a distant scream.

"Pony captured something," Miriam said. "Your Bleed debuff is all better now. I am going out there to feed. You just stay here and rest, and I will be back to check on you, okay?"

I grunted. I felt her stand behind me, and I watched as the dark-haired, robed woman floated out of the cart and away.

"She can fly?" I asked.

"That's new," Donut said. "She's a vampire now. She can float, but she has to drink a lot of blood to survive. She's still a healer. It's very strange. She'll only drink blood from something that Prepotente has just killed. She has to do it fast. I don't know if she can turn into a bat or if sunlight hurts her. Or if she's allergic to garlic. I hope not. She's Italian, so that'd probably be extra terrible if she couldn't use garlic anymore."

I just sat there, breathing. As long as I didn't move anything, it didn't hurt. The crunch of the trail under the cart was oddly familiar. I thought of riding in the very back of my parents' car. I heard a snort, like from a horse; then it was followed by a bug-like chittering noise. I finally thought to look at the map. We were moving through a dense, wooded area. There was a massive orange dot right in front of us, and the two blue dots of Miriam and the goat were up ahead, along with a few mob X's and a red dot. Donut remained in the cart with me. I didn't see anyone else.

"Mordecai wants to know if you used that ring," Donut said after a moment. "I told him I didn't know, but it's on your finger, so I'm assuming that you did."

I reached over and pulled it off and put it back into my inventory.

"I used it once on the drunk guy, and I copied my debuff to that flying hunter. I wanted to draw out the mayor. I figured she would be the strongest one in town. But I also wanted to make sure it worked right before I started really using it. I wasn't sure that Super Spreader thing was going to work. It does. It works really well, especially when combined with *Ping* because I can apply it to hunters who are pretty far away."

I pulled myself up, but my head swam, and I lowered myself back down onto the wood. I realized the cart was actually one of the smaller railway carts from the previous floor modified with wooden wheels.

Donut sighed. "You only used the ring once?"

"Yeah. I was about to use it again on the orc, but the barrel was rapidly destabilizing, and the list of names was really long. It's not sorted by proximity. I didn't have time."

"Mordecai said it's addictive. I don't like that. I've already broken you from your tobacco and chronic masturbation addiction. I can't have you gaining a new one, Carl."

I tried sitting up again. I groaned as I looked upon the creature pulling the cart. It chittered angrily. Heat washed off the massive pet. It had grown since I'd seen it last. It was now the size of a draft horse.

"Bianca, huh?" I asked.

The creature, once a regular goat, had been transformed by the same enhanced pet biscuit that had turned Donut and Prepotente into regular crawlers. Black ethereal flames licked up into the air off the demonic, horrifying creature's hairy back. A crackling noise like a campfire emanated from its dark skin. It smelled like fire, too. A stubby pair of wings erupted from the ridged, hairy back. The thing was so black, its presence drank the meager light, like it was a hole in the fabric of space-time. The heat of it washed over me in pulsing waves.

Bianca Del Ciao. Hellspawn Familiar. Level 32.
This is a pet of Crawler Miriam Dom.
Somebody once said, "All Dogs Go to Heaven." Whoever said

that obviously never met Susan, the Pembroke Welsh Corgi gifted to future Queen Elizabeth II by her father upon her 18th birthday.

Susan was an unholy terror. The corgi was known as a vicious little psychopath. She attacked and bit numerous members of the royal court and visitors, including multiple police officers and even the royal clock winder, who was said to suffer nightmares after the incident.

What I'm getting at is that Susan was an asshole. I know, I know. It's not PC to call pets—or toddlers, since we're on the subject—assholes. But that doesn't change the fact that these assholes exist. And if there is a hell, Susan the corgi is there. She's there along with all the other dead asshole pets, including Brandon from *Punky Brewster* and Misty Malarky Ying Yang, Jimmy Carter's Siamese cat.

A hellspawn familiar occurs when a regular asshole pet is encased in a soul protection spell yet dies anyway. The soul becomes hell-bound and tainted and then shoved back into the resurrected body of the pet, rebirthing the creature. Its regular form is combined with that of a demon. It will physically grow upon each level up, ceasing to increase in size only when it reaches level 50. It will grow wings. It will be angry and formidable. It will be scary as shit. It will also be one of the most powerful, most badass pets available within *Dungeon Crawler World*.

"They make her sound mean, but she's really sweet," Donut said. "Miriam says when she was a regular goat, she liked being petted on the butt. She loved eating grapes."

"Yes, I'm sure the demon pet is delightful," I said. "Hey, what's that over your head?"

Donut had a new symbol floating after her name. It was a red dagger, similar to the logo for the Desperado Club, but the point was facing upward. The single red dagger spun, nestled between the player-killer skull and all the boss-kill stars. I examined it.

Hunter-Killer × 1.

"Hey, you got one."

"It was nothing, Carl. A magic missile while we were running away. I think your explosion is what really killed him, but they gave me credit anyway."

I, stupidly, looked up in the air in an attempt to see my own daggers. "How many do I have?"

"You should probably look at your notifications, Carl."

I dove into my menus. I'd rocketed up to level 54. Donut had also gone up a few levels to 41. That was still much too low. We'd spent too much time preparing for shit on the last floor and not enough actually killing stuff. That had to change fast.

I had a whole mess of achievements. I opened up the menu.

New Achievement! I Wanna Go Home!

You teleported to a stairwell station within the first thirty hours of the floor being open. What, you're running away early? I hope for your sake you don't actually go down the stairs. You know it doesn't get easier.

Reward: Your reward is advice. Fatherly advice. Don't be a little bitch. There's your reward.

New Achievement! You Crossed a Line You Didn't Even Know Was There.

You used an artifact of Divine Suffering for the first time. Hopefully there aren't any unintended and unadvertised side effects of using such a powerful and evil magical item.

Don't mind that tingle at the back of your mind. It's probably nothing.

Reward: You've received a Gold Junkie's Box.

That was worrying. I didn't feel any different. I'd received plus one to my dexterity. The next two I killed after marking them with the ring would also increase one of my stats by one. For the next three after that, it would increase by plus two. It wasn't until the ninth floor when I could mark multiple people at once, but in the meantime, I planned on charging it up as much as possible.

New Achievement! The Hand That Claws the Master (× 35).

You have permanently killed a non-crawler biological. They ain't just dead. They dead dead. Their children are now orphans. Their mothers are gnashing their teeth and cursing your name. And you're just sitting there all alive and shit, and, girlfriend, I am all in.

We all know you should have received this achievement, uh, a little earlier, but I figured it'd be in your best interest not to reward you this one just yet. But you sure deserved it, so I may have slipped an extra one in there. Shhh. Don't tell the mudskippers.

Reward: You've received a Gold Hunter-Killer Box (× 34).

Note: This achievement may be awarded more than once, but Hunter-Killer Boxes are only awarded on the sixth floor.

Holy shit. I'd killed 34 of them. I'd actually gotten 35 achievements, but that was just the AI being a dick. I'd gotten 34 boxes. My chest swelled. *Fuck yeah.* I hadn't accomplished what I hoped, but that was okay. *I will break you. I will break you all.*

New Achievement! Mass Casualty Event.

Okay. Calm your man-tiddies. Did your mother not love you? Is your god promising you unlimited hand jobs in heaven or something? You planted and then detonated an improvised explosive device within an urban population center that resulted in more than 250 non-mob casualties. You've done this a few times now, but this was a big one. And on purpose.

You really know how to paint the town red.

Reward: You've received a Platinum Asshole's Box.

"Damnit," I growled. That meant we'd killed more than 200 NPCs. It was a fraction of the number of innocents we'd killed after flooding Larracos, not to mention all the ones who'd been on the gnome *Wasteland* fortress. And . . . and it didn't bother me. Not nearly as much as it should. But I needed to be more efficient. These NPCs were better off dead. I truly believed that. But still, I didn't want to be so casual about it. I wanted to avoid the loss of innocent life if possible. They didn't deserve any unnecessary terror or heartache.

This isn't on me, I thought. *They* started this. These are *their* rules. *Their* game.

Miriam returned, floating over Bianca and returning to the cart. Prepotente disappeared, ranging ahead. Miriam had blood running down her chin, which she wiped off as she landed before me. I examined the woman. She was level 52. Her race had changed from Human to Vampire since the last time I'd seen her all the way back on the fourth floor. Her class hadn't changed. It was still just Shepherd, which was apparently a type of healer.

The woman had a motherly, gentle sense about her, despite the whole vampire thing. She reminded me of poor Yolanda, who'd fallen to the rage elemental so long ago.

"Are you feeling better? We'll be in town in a bit," Miriam asked. "There are traps just everywhere this close to Zockau. Pony is disarming them."

"Yes. Thank you," I said. "Look, I really appreciate you saving our asses. What exactly were you guys doing out there? Again, I'm sorry we messed it up."

"Oh, sweetie. Don't you listen to Pony. He's just a grumpy little boy. It was not going to work. We suspected they would be getting themselves quite drunk, so Pony was casting a few different debuffs on the area. One to increase the level of inebriation, which had successfully activated, and another to cause them to wish to fight one another, but it was being blocked. I was attempting to cloak our presence and increase the debuff's power, but it didn't work."

I remembered those two had somehow managed to kill that giant turkey thing by stacking debuffs. That was their method of killing. Miriam would keep them hidden and would buff Prepotente while the goat stacked debuff after debuff onto the target, doing it in a way that the target didn't even realize they were in trouble. His class was something called a Forsaken Aerialist. I didn't know what that meant. I had originally assumed it was some sort of acrobat thing, but it was clear it had something to do with magic.

"Yeah, like I said, they're cheating assholes. It's not fair if they're getting fed all the info on what we're doing. If *I* was watching this, I'd raise a big stink about it. Especially if betting is involved."

Before Miriam could answer, we were interrupted.

ZEV: Hello, Crawlers.

DONUT: HI, ZEV!

ZEV: Guys, your numbers are just insane right now. Try to stay with Prepotente for at least a little bit. Carl, don't insult him too much. He is strange, but his numbers are so high because of a certain demographic you two aren't trending in, and I'm hoping to gain some crossovers.

CARL: Am I allowed to say, "Go fuck yourself, Zev" still, or will I get in trouble?

ZEV: No. We're not saying that anymore.

CARL: Okay. I'll try to think of a nicer way to say it.

DONUT: CARL, DON'T BE MEAN TO ZEV. SHE JUST GOT HER JOB BACK. ARE YOU OUR REGULAR PR PERSON AGAIN?

ZEV: Uh, we can talk about that later. Just a heads-up. Assuming you two don't get yourselves killed, you will be going on Odette's show tomorrow. Katia will *not* be joining you.

DONUT: WILL YOU BE THERE?

ZEV: Yes, I will. Also, I should warn you there will be additional security protocols put into place before you're transferred. This was not my doing, and it applies to all crawlers.

CARL: What does that mean?

ZEV: I'm not exactly certain yet, but as long as you're not attempting to assassinate me or a member of Odette's staff, you shouldn't have to worry. Also, I am being asked to tell you the *Vengeance of the Daughter* program is still active. Therefore your contract regarding participation in any other programs is still in effect.

CARL: Wonderful. What are we supposed to do if some elite approaches us?

ZEV: All the other programs know to avoid you, but as you well know, sometimes elites don't do what they're told. If something happens, you are required to extract yourself the best you can. The showrunners of other programs will generally honor the contract you have with Sensation

Entertainment, and they will also attempt to intervene on their
end. This is something you'd have to discuss with your new
attorney, but as long as you make a good-faith effort to
extricate yourself, I don't see it being an issue.

CARL: All right. Thanks for the heads-up.

ZEV: That's it for now. Talk to you soon.

DONUT: BYE, ZEV!

I was about to ask Miriam if they'd been involved with any elite
quests, but Donut got to her first.

"How often do you go on shows?" Donut asked the moment the chat
closed. "We're going to see Odette in a few days. Have you been on her
show yet? She's just wonderful. She used to be our manager's manager."

"We've been on the Odette show once," Miriam said. "We're on
Plenty of Plenty mostly. Pony doesn't do too well on these programs, but
he's okay when there are other goats around."

"We haven't been on that one," Donut said.

"Pony likes it because they allow his brothers and sisters to come out,
and they have new plants for them to try each time, though last time
they had no treats. I find the program a bit unsettling, but it helps Pony
relax."

"Brothers and sisters?" I asked.

"Oh, yes," Miriam said. "I have ten unaltered Boers in pet carriers in
my inventory. I don't let them out so much except in the safe rooms because it has gotten much too dangerous for them. They are all Pony and
Bianca's siblings. After the unfortunate incident with Angelo, we keep
them indoors until we get out of this place."

I was starting to feel much better. I fully sat up in the cart. I examined my shoulder where the bolt had entered. It'd pierced my flesh, but
my magical jacket seemed unharmed. It was weird how that worked. I
had anti-piercing resistance thanks to my kneepads, but obviously that
wasn't the same thing as immunity. Skilled attackers could still get in.

Prepotente started moving back toward us.

"Oh dear," Miriam said. "It appears we have an issue."

The goat-turned-crawler looked much the same as the last time I'd
seen him. He was level 55, possibly the highest in the dungeon. His

class had changed from Forsaken Aerialist to Profane Vitiate, which made even less sense. I also noticed the faded but glowing tattoo on the back of his humanlike hand. The symbol was of a very evil-looking satanic goat. The number three crawler gave me an angry scowl and turned to Miriam.

"There is a line of traps up ahead at the entrance to the town, and I cannot yet disarm them. We will have to go around."

"Traps, huh?" I asked. "What kind? I can probably take care of them."

"You can't even take care of your own basic hygiene, Carl. These are complicated traps designed to decapitate anyone who gets anywhere near them, and it will require someone with a special touch to even approach them. As much as I would love to watch your head get separated from your overgrown, swollen—"

I cast *Tripper*.

All around us, in every direction, a cavalcade of small explosions and lights and noises erupted. Wind blades sailed over the cart, dissipating into the dark as they shot away.

Prepotente screamed.

"Problem solved," I said. "If any of those traps released monsters, we'll have to be on the lookout."

"That was an attack! Negligence most serious! Bianca, prepare yourself for battle!"

Just in front of me, the skin on Bianca rustled, black flames starting to rise off the creature's body.

"Pony," Miriam said, "we are not fighting Carl."

"I have been insulted! This will not stand! Mother. Princess Donut. Both of you, stand back while I defend my honor!"

"Suck my dick, Pony," I said, standing up and facing the goat.

Prepotente burst into tears. He jumped into the cart and wrapped his hands around Miriam, who took him into a tight hug.

"Now, Carl, that wasn't very nice," Miriam said, her voice gentle yet scolding. "We did save your life."

DONUT: CARL, I'M STARTING TO THINK THESE PEOPLE MIGHT BE A
   LITTLE WEIRD.

"He insulted me first!" I said. I regretted saying it the moment it came out of my mouth. It sounded whiny even to my own ears. I suddenly felt like I was back in grade school, and we were being admonished by a teacher.

"Pony shouldn't have done that, either. Now both of you apologize to each other."

Behind her, the flames on Bianca's back continued to prickle angrily, almost like a seismograph. The demonic pet was faced away and was attached to the cart with a harness, but I had no doubts it could break away at a moment's notice and devour us.

"I'm not going to do it," Prepotente said, his face buried in Miriam's robes. "He was mean to me, Mother. He's awful. Just awful. He's worse than those buffoons at Club Vanquisher."

"Pony," Miriam said, stroking the goat's head, "we discussed this. You mustn't insult everyone."

"He called me by my special name. Only you can call me by my special name."

I exchanged a look with Donut. We needed to get the hell away from these nutjobs.

Bianca continued to move forward. She seemed to sense that the danger was starting to wane, and the flames on her back settled. I could now see the edge of town. A pair of the mushroom guards stood just inside the gate, watching us approach. A line of scorch marks marred the entrance to the town. The air smelled of smoke.

"I'm sorry, Carl," Prepotente said. "I shouldn't have called you malodorous. Nor should I have questioned your ability to inexpertly set off every trap in the area."

"Yeah, uh, no worries. Sorry about telling you to suck my dick."

Miriam beamed. When she did, I could see the twin fangs, and suddenly that motherly feeling she gave off vanished and was replaced by uneasy revulsion. "See, now that wasn't so hard. Now both of you hug."

"Uh," I said.

Prepotente removed himself from Miriam and approached me, arms wide. Tears glistened in his goat eyes.

"Yes, Carl," Donut said. "Be a good boy and hug Prepotente."

DONUT: YOU BETTER DO IT OR YOU'LL LOOK LIKE A BIG JERK.

I gritted my teeth and hugged the goat. His weird fuzzy arms wrapped tightly around me. He smelled like a barn.

He screamed. Right in my goddamned ear.

7

THE TOWN WAS A "SMALL BUGBEAR SETTLEMENT," BUT AT NIGHT, I only saw the funeral bell mushroom guards out and about. This place had already been through the wringer. Two of the buildings in town were already bombed out and looted. There was a weird graveyard on the outskirts that was likely associated with some quest, but it had already been all dug up.

"We passed through here earlier," Miriam said, "but we came and went through the south entrance. There weren't any traps inside of town. The funeral bells deactivate them. However, it seems the aliens already moved through the town like locusts. There's another town down the road that is the same."

These towns near the main city of Zockau would all be like this, I suspected. Surrounded by shitty traps and already looted. We were going to watch the recap, reset our buffs, and then move on. No time to dawdle.

I exchanged fist bumps with Miriam and Prepotente, and we promised to keep each other apprised anytime we might get in each other's way. I thanked Miriam again, tried not to make eye contact with Bianca, and said goodbye to Prepotente, who was suddenly acting like we were best friends.

There was still a lot I wanted to get out of them, like some info on Club Vanquisher, but Prepotente was just too unstable to have a regular conversation with. I would attempt to use chat to speak with Miriam later.

"They might be strange, but I think they're good guys," Donut said once we finally separated. "They were trying to get those guys to get drunk and kill each other. That was a lot safer way to do it than your plan."

I pushed through the door of the first restaurant, which was a traditional-style safe room with a Bopca. It looked like a pub on the outside, but within it was a fast-food restaurant called Whataburger. I stopped to grab a soda from the fountain and filled the orange-and-white Styrofoam cup while Donut released Mongo. She hadn't dared release the dinosaur anywhere near Bianca.

"I was a lot more successful than they were," I said. "With your kill, we got 35 hunters. Their method is effective, but it's useless without true stealth. Once the hunters are all scattered, it'll be better."

"They're all going to be coming for you, Carl," Donut said. "Mordecai is already doing that whole we-gotta-talk thing in my chat, and quite frankly, I don't want to have the conversation. Especially since he looks like a bootleg Monchhichi with a bad haircut and a questionable pedigree."

"What the hell is a Monchhichi?" I asked as we moved to the personal space.

Katia had returned along with Very Sullen, and she'd brought Louis and Firas back up with her. Britney, the Ukrainian plastic surgery patient, was also there, sitting in the corner and looking pissed off as usual.

Chris and Clay-ton were not here. Katia said they were outside in the bar, waiting on team Meadow Lark, who were still making their way to the town.

Mordecai waited for us, arms crossed, sitting on the counter with his little legs dangling off the edge.

Donut indicated Mordecai with her paw. "Picture that, but with his face shaved and less angry-looking. That's a Monchhichi."

Louis burst out laughing. "My mom had some of those things. She mostly collected monkeys, but she also had a few of those. That shit gives you nightmares."

"Holy shit," Firas said, looking at my drink. "You found a Whataburger? Dude, go back out there and get me some of their fries."

"Hi, Louis and Firas and Firas's girlfriend!" Donut said.

"I am not his girlfriend," Britney said.

Katia looked just as irritated at us as Mordecai did, and I knew she was pissed. I had told her we weren't going to do anything stupid today.

"Mordecai, darling," Donut said, strolling through the room and toward the litter box. "We all know what you're going to say. And while I myself have voiced my frustration with Carl's seeming disregard for his and my own personal safety, I just want to get this conversation out of the way right here and right now. Yes, what Carl did was idiotic and suicidal. No, I am not going to abandon him. Yes, he's going to tell me the plan ahead of time from now on. No, we are not going to have some long, drawn-out storyline where we break up and then get back together. We're already doing that with Katia right now, and I just will not have it with me and Carl. So you're just going to have to get over it and not be all 'You don't know what you're dealing with.'"

Mordecai just opened and closed his mouth.

"Very well," he said after a moment. "If that's how you want this to go, then open up your prize boxes and reset your buffs. We'll watch the recap episode and then you two need to put more space between yourself and that town. You may have blown the city up, but you only killed a handful of them. Unless you're planning on going back in there, you need to get moving."

"I didn't blow the town up," I said, taking a sip of my soda. "It was one or two square blocks. Those barrel bombs were only like a fourth the strength as I could've made it. I have a plan for another one that's really big. Like huge." I made an exploding motion with my hand. "That's the best part about this floor. Lots of room for explosions."

Mordecai sighed. "I suppose you have a plan for that one, too."

I glanced up at my clock. The hunters were going to release in just over 13 hours.

"Oh, it's going to be spectacular."

8

I HAD BOXES TO OPEN AND A TON OF OTHER STUFF TO DO, BUT ALL OF
that could wait an hour. I sat down on the counter and just rested for a
few minutes.

I'd run out of books to read. I needed a new outlet. But more importantly, I needed to rest. Not sleep. Rest. Like, really rest.

Most of the time while I was idle, I was actually writing in my third
scratch pad, composing thoughts for the cookbook. I'd figured out how
to separate individual scratch pad pages even further and to create
drafts. I'd been putting a lot of stuff in there recently, and it'd just
dawned on me that I was spending every free moment "working." Even
when I was playing *Frogger*, I was really just on autopilot and writing
stream-of-consciousness words straight into the draft section of the
scratch pad. Planning. Scenarios. Theories. Re-creating others' recipes
and comments from memory as an exercise to make sure I could recall
them. Coming up with alternatives. My brain was always working, turning everything over and over.

Recently, I'd been noticing something hidden in the back of my
mind. It was difficult to explain. Almost like there was a bubbling,
meandering stream hidden back there in the weeds of my brain, nestled
deep, deep down. It'd always been there, which meant I was so used to
the quiet murmur of the stream, I never noticed it. But recently, that
sound was starting to get louder. Only it wasn't a sound, not really. It
wasn't even a physical feeling. Just a sense of flow, and that sense was
changing, rising in volume. It'd gone up just a hair, but it was enough
for me to finally notice.

I'd only found one way to mute it. Only when I was completely calm.

Fully at rest. When we were in the heat of it all, like when we'd been fleeing Zockau, it was right there, the stream, getting louder.

The recap would be on in a few minutes, and we waited for it. Mordecai and Donut talked about some of the new upgrades that were available for our personal space, including a bed that would refresh us almost immediately.

"No," I said. "We're not getting that. It's too much."

Mordecai was about to object, but he thought better of it. "We'll revisit it."

"Are you sure you're okay?" Donut asked, rubbing up against me. I reached over and rubbed her back.

"I'm okay, Donut. Just trying to decompress a little."

Mongo was curled up on the other side of the room, leaning up against Britney, who was sitting on the ground. She'd tried pushing him away a few times, but she was in his spot. He ended up putting his head on her lap, and she was now petting him like a dog.

"Does 'decompressing' mean you're not going to open your prize boxes?"

I sighed, and I pulled up my boxes. I needed to get this over with anyway. Donut sat next to me, excited. She also had a hunter-killer box to open, but she wanted me to open mine first since I had thirty-four of them, and she thought it would be more "dramatic."

The first box was a Gold Junkie's Box. This was an odd one. Since this was from using the Ring of Divine Suffering, I'd been expecting to receive a savage box, which was what one normally received for any player-killer-themed achievement.

The gold box opened and then puffed away. A spiderweb pattern appeared in the air and faded. Nothing came out. I cringed.

"Oh no," Donut said. "Not again."

"Goddamnit," I muttered before the new tattoo appeared.

"Carl, you keep getting disgusting tattoos. You might as well grow a beard and knock over a liquor store now. That's your third tattoo in a week. You're going to scare Mongo."

This was the biggest one yet, and it formed on my left elbow. I didn't have time to examine the tattoo's properties, but it was a spiderweb pattern. The individual strands of the web were segmented, wormlike. It was faded and green-tinted and poorly drawn.

"I think it looks sick," Louis called from the couch.

"My uncle had the same tattoo," Firas added. "He got it in prison."

The 34 hunter-killer boxes were lined up, all in a long row that floated all the way down to the wall where our rooms were located. It was so many boxes, everybody stopped what they were doing to watch. I was afraid these boxes would also contain tattoos, which would really suck. I took a deep breath as the first one opened.

It was two items. It was 1,000 gold coins and a claw. A mangled, severed claw of an insect-like creature. This was the claw of Xindy, the mantis I'd blown out of the sky with my rockets. Before I could wonder what the hell that was all about, the next box opened. It was 2,000 gold and another claw, this time a lizard-like, bloody, and scaled appendage. It was the hand of Chin'Dua, the drunk Draconian I'd marked, then killed. The third box was 3,000 gold and yet another hand, this one of an orc.

None of the hands had any sort of rings or any other adornments. But they just kept popping out, one by one. Each time the amount of gold increased by 1,000. It ended up being a total of 595,000 gold. Not bad. Not bad at all.

Donut watched all of this with revulsion.

"Well, this has been a huge letdown. All that, and it's a bunch of horrible hands? This is a rip-off! At least it's not tongues," Donut said. "Lucia Mar collects tongues, and that's much more disgusting." Behind us, the bubbling Emberus fountain made a chime, and the amount of owed gold, which I'd just zeroed out, changed to 29,750.

Donut made a pained noise.

I had one last box before I could examine all this crap. A Platinum Asshole's Box.

It ended up being a potion that I had to immediately drink. I flipped off the stopper with my thumb and chugged it down manually. It tasted like strawberry juice.

Your *Fear* spell has been upgraded five levels! It is now level 10!

"Woah," I said. "That was great. Five levels? And I wasted all that time working on it in the magic-training room earlier."

Mordecai grunted. "That spell should already be that high if you'd been practicing it like I told you. It's less of a bonus and more of a corrective measure. They do that every once in a while. Now you can work on *Ping* instead."

At level ten, the *Fear* spell also had a 2% chance to paralyze my targets, and I could cast it in a wide area. Mordecai was right. I needed to push hard on *Ping* now, which was only level two. Once I trained it up to level five, I'd be able to combine the two spells. But for now, I could imbue smoke curtains and certain explosives with *Fear*. I had instructions on how to do it in my cookbook, but I would need to practice. The act of enchanting items added a high probability of giving them the "Dud" status.

Plus, *Fear* caused my targets to run away. Paralyzing them was good, but it was only a 2% chance, and in my experience, anything below 10% actually translated to "whenever the dungeon thinks would be beneficial to the narrative." I didn't want them running away. I eyed Louis sitting there on the couch. He had a spell I could really use. Too bad he'd already pledged himself to Katia's team.

I sighed and put my hand on the spiderweb tattoo on my elbow.

The Night Wyrm's Nasty Little Web of Suffering.
Bearers of this sigil are given access to the Guild of Suffering.

"Guild of Suffering?" I said, looking at Mordecai. I couldn't recall reading anything about it. "What is that?"

Mordecai frowned, which looked absurdly adorable. "It's a cult," he said. "Not a real guild and not a real church. Similar to the city elves from the third floor. They have outreach centers, but I've never been in one. They worship a demigod, the Night Wyrm, who is not a regular member of the pantheon. Similar to Samantha. It's a long story. The cult has something called a memorial crystal. They're similar to soul crystals, but what they do has never really been established. It's all tied in with that precious ring of yours. A few seasons back, the entire seventh floor was centered around them raising their god. Everybody who uses a divine suffering artifact gets marked like you have."

Donut sniffed. "Well, it's absolutely revolting. If I had known Carl was going to be marked even further, I would never have allowed him to use that ring. I never noticed the mark on Frank or Maggie, but they looked like the sort to have filthy tattoos like that."

I sent out a message to the group to see if anybody had run across one of these guilds. Then I pulled the mantis claw from my inventory and examined it. As I did this, Donut finally opened her own box. She made a disgusted little noise as a gray hand popped out, followed by a squeal of outrage when she only received 1,000 gold.

Hunting Trophy.
It's the hand of a hunter. Gross.
You own 34 of these items.
You ever go to one of those arcade pizza joints as a child? You're usually there because it's some other kid's birthday or, worse, because your parent hates raising you so much, they'd do anything just to keep you distracted for ten minutes in exchange for a pitcher of watered-down beer. The whole place is chaos. There're flashing lights, blaring music, a colorful carpet that hides the vomit stains. Not to mention the norovirus-infested ball pit, the rickety merry-go-round, the workers with dead eyes, and the pizza that tastes like it was cooked in a Soviet-era microwave. All the while an animatronic rodent holds court onstage, blinking and rotating and telling you that he is now your god.

Within this orgy of grease and unchecked consumerism is the arcade. Barely functioning games gobble up tokens in exchange for mere seconds of entertainment. And every once in a while, one of these games will spit out something special. A ticket. A prize ticket.

Once you have a sticky handful of these hard-won paper tickets, you must make a pilgrimage to the fabled prize counter.

Here, you squeeze yourself in with the other pilgrims and press your face up against the glass and spend an inordinate amount of time deciding how to spend your newfound riches. In the end, you trade forty dollars' worth of tickets for five cents' worth of bubble gum and a filicide-inducing whistle. But that's okay. It's an important life lesson. Perhaps the most important one of all, only you're not sure what that lesson is.

> This hand you have savagely removed from a third-party inter-
> loper is the ticket in this scenario.
> The prize counter where it may be exchanged will be open at the
> Butcher's Masquerade during the party that will occur near the end
> of this floor.
> The cheapest award in the prize case will cost a single hand.
> The prizes only get better from there.
> If you transfer or sell this item, it will revert to just being some
> dude's appendage.

"What the hell?" I said, turning the claw over in my hand.

As I examined the item, Donut examined her own trophy. She gasped as she read the description.

"A prize counter? A masquerade? Well, this changes everything," Donut said. "Carl, I only have one hand. We need to go get more!"

There was nothing about any sort of "Butcher's Masquerade" in the cookbook. It sounded ominous as fuck. There was mention of a giant party at the end of the ninth floor if it was won early, but nothing of the sort for the sixth.

"I don't know what that is," Mordecai said after Donut showed him her hand. "That's . . . They don't usually actively encourage the crawlers to kill the sponsors."

Before we could discuss it further, the screens flickered. It was time to watch the show.

"It's the Hunting Grounds!" the newscaster announced. Because of our earlier boss battle at the bottom of the ocean, we now knew this orange lizard guy's name was Kevin, which was an absurdly normal name for an alien. "This season is bigger, badder, and more extreme than any sixth floor we've ever had. The humans may be whittled down, the timer may be shortened, but this season we are on a whole new level. This season we're going—"

"Redacted" abruptly appeared on the screen as Kevin the lizard breathlessly described whatever hidden horrors they had in store for us.

While we waited, I put the trophy claw away and turned my attention to the three newcomers in the space. Britney remained on the floor, petting Mongo. Before, the Ukrainian woman had been a class called a

Pit Fighter. She had upgraded to **Pit Champion**. Since she refused to say anything to me, I had no idea what was different.

Firas's class remained Hammersmith, and he'd ascended to level 35. He hadn't been able to specialize. Louis was also level 35, but his class had changed from Pest Exterminator to **Extermination Professional**. He said he'd gained a .5% instakill bonus on mobs his level or lower, but that was it.

"So, how are the changelings doing?" I asked him while we waited for the show to return.

Louis shrugged. "They have some village deep in the woods they were all headed to. It's in the Liana district, so the elf side of the river. One of the adults said he'd leave a message for you at the Desperado Club in a few days."

"That's good," I said. I didn't want to know exactly where their village was as long as I had a way to contact them.

"And Bonnie?" I asked.

"The little gnome kid went with them," Firas said. "Did we tell you what she did to the *Twister*?"

"No. What?"

"She built a giant crossbow thing. A ballista. She affixed it to the side of the yard. She made it out of the mechanism for the garage door opener. Katia test fired it, and it blew up a tree."

Katia, sitting at the end of the table, grunted with amusement. At first I'd thought she was mad at me and was giving me the silent treatment. But then I noticed the constant flashing in her eyes. She was doing the same thing I was. Talking. Planning. Working. She'd been forced to stop for the show.

"How elevated can you get the *Twister*?" I asked. The ceiling on this level wasn't very high compared to the one on the previous floor.

"Not very," Firas said. "The roof is higher on this side of the river, away from the bigger cities, but we can't even get over the trees. The balloon is just too big. So it's not very useful. Hopefully you can figure out how to get it down another floor. Maybe the seventh floor will have another sky."

"We'll see," I said.

"So, Louis," Donut said, sidling up to the large man, "I understand congratulations are in order. Tell me, when are the nuptials? I'm assuming it won't happen until we all reach the ninth floor. Since Carl has recently found religion, he'll probably be able to officiate the wedding. Don't worry, I'll make him get pants for the ceremony. And we'll cover up his prison tattoos. Wait, do you think I could be maid of honor? Oh, oh. And Mongo could be ring bearer!"

Mongo looked up from Britney's lap and squawked.

Donut suddenly gasped. "I could sing. I'm a professional musician now. I'd have to charge you of course, but wouldn't that be amazing? Think of the ratings!"

Louis's cheeks burned red. "Juice Box told you, huh?"

"She didn't have to tell us. Love makes a person just glow," Donut said. "I must say, I am not surprised you're the first of our group to find true love. We all knew it wasn't going to be Carl. And I'm already in a long-distance relationship with Ferdinand."

"Ferdinand?" Louis asked. "Who is that? Another cat?"

"Oh, yes," Donut said. "It's a relationship even more unconventional than yours. We are star-crossed lovers and—"

She was interrupted by the show coming back on.

"Murderer!" Dmitri or Maxim Popov screamed on the show. The screen was now showing things that had happened at the very end of the last floor, and it'd returned in the middle of a scene. The two-headed crawler fought with another human I didn't recognize in the final moments of the last floor. The guy they fought was a big guy, leather clad with a shaved head and a war gauntlet similar to my own. The two-headed creature that comprised Dmitri and Maxim, a Nodling, apparently, spun their magical meteor hammer, and they would've brained the guy, but they suddenly all flew off their feet as a giant foot crashed into their world and then jumped away. The target of the Popov brothers' ire used the distraction to run into a stairwell.

The god foot, I realized, was Slit, one of the feral demons we'd summoned at the end of the last floor. She'd been on her way back to our bubble, chasing after Samantha the sex doll head.

"I simply don't understand why two different people would choose a race like that," Donut said. "They must really like each other. Plus it has to make shopping for clothes a real chore. Carl, can you imagine sharing a head with one of your friends? You'd murder each other after a day."

It then showed Katia opening up the portal to the ninth floor. It didn't show the actual destruction, but we were given a shot of a half-flooded Larracos with the water churning as a gaggle of shark mobs fought each other over the corpses of NPCs. It portrayed Katia's stoic face looking at what she'd done and then cut to a shot of me laughing from some other time.

The redacted screen appeared again, but only for about thirty seconds this time.

We were then treated to a quick rundown of the top ten and how each person on the list had changed during specialization. They started with me, showing my Agent Provocateur stats. From the wall, Britney grunted with amusement when they showed it, but I didn't know why.

Next, they showed Lucia Mar, who hadn't changed. Prepotente changed to a **Profane Vitiate**, but it didn't explain what that meant. Dmitri changed from an Illusionist to a **Visionary**, but the other half of the two-headed monster remained a Bogatyr, whatever that was.

We watched Elle transform. I hadn't spoken with them except for a quick check-in, and I hadn't even thought to ask how they'd changed. I knew Imani had a big change coming, but I wasn't certain about Elle. We now watched her transform from Blizzardmancer to a **Tundra Princess**. It was some sort of Earth class combined with ice. It also said she'd get to pick yet another class on the ninth floor.

"Interesting," Mordecai said. "I hadn't realized she was going for a four-seasons build."

"Four seasons?" I asked.

He shook his head. "It's never been completed before. Plenty have made it to three, but never four. It requires you to survive to the twelfth floor to complete. It'll be tough for her because it means she has to strictly control how she distributes her stats. Her race is a Frost Maiden Fairy, which makes it even more difficult. It's complicated stuff. But she'll be quite powerful if she hits the ninth floor and levels enough to have the stats for a triple class."

"She already is pretty powerful," I said.

We watched a one-armed, pale, and sick-looking Quan Ch switch from Imperial Security Trooper to **Sergeant at Arms.**

"Well, that's a lie, now isn't it? It should just be 'Sergeant at *Arm*,' not 'arms,'" Donut quipped. "The next time we see him, I hope you rip his other arm off, Carl. Then he'll just be a Sergeant."

From there, the show went on to even more redacted stuff, but I recognized the streets of Zockau before it disappeared. It remained that way for the rest of the show.

I sighed once the show ended. The top-ten list populated, and it hadn't changed from the end of the previous floor.

1. Carl—Primal—Agent Provocateur—Level 54–
   1,000,000 (× 3)
2. Lucia Mar—Lajabless—Black Inquisitor General—Level 48–
   500,000 (× 3)
3. Prepotente—Caprid—Profane Vitiate—Level 55–400,000 (× 3)
4. Donut—Cat—Former Child Actor—Level 41–300,000 (× 3)
5. Dmitri and Maxim Popov—Nodling—Visionary and Bogatyr—
   Level 44–200,000 (× 3)
6. Miriam Dom—Vampire—Shepherd—Level 52–100,000 (× 3)
7. Elle McGib—Frost Maiden—Tundra Princess—Level
   47–100,000 (× 2)
8. Bogdon Ro—Human—Legatus—Level 44–100,000 (× 2)
9. Eva Sigrid—Half Nagini, Half Orc—Nimblefoot Enforcer—Level
   40— 100,000 (× 2)
10. Quan Ch—Half Elf—Sergeant at Arms—Level
    48–100,000 (× 3)

"I can't believe Quan is still up there," Donut said. "He doesn't deserve the top-ten list. I feel Katia should be back up there, especially after what happened at the end of the last floor."

"I am perfectly content to hover outside the list," Katia said.

"Yes, but Eva is ranked, and it's not fair!" Donut said.

"Don't worry about that," Katia said. Her voice was uncharacteristically cold. "She won't be on there for much longer."

I caught Mordecai's eye, and he looked worried. I felt it, too. It wasn't just what had happened at the end of the last floor. It wasn't just her being mad at us for raiding Zockau. There was something else going on there with her. Something had changed. I opened my mouth to ask, but then I shut it. I didn't know what to say.

Hello, Crawlers.

We hope you're all doing fantastic. Many of you are settling into your new classes, and that is great. We only have a few hours left before the hunters emerge, and we know they're itching to get in on the hunt. As predicted, the number of participants keeps growing and growing. We are just overwhelmed. We now have a total of 1,002 hunters alive in the dungeon. That number was slightly higher, but a few managed to get themselves prematurely killed.

The audience just can't wait for them to get unleashed on you guys!

We have several important announcements, so please pay careful attention.

Your final sponsors will be coming in soon, so be on the lookout for that.

Effective immediately, the subscription-based system where the viewers may listen in on the private messages of Crawlers will be discontinued. However, please note, Borant reserves the right to take your conversations and play them during any and all non-live broadcasts.

"Oh, thank the gods," Mordecai said. "I didn't think that one would stick."

I'd asked Quasar if he could sue on my behalf about this, and he'd told me there was already a case making its way through the courts regarding this issue. He'd given it a 50-50 chance of succeeding. I was glad it had that.

There was another part to this problem, and he promised he'd work on it from his end, but in the meantime, I needed to bitch out loud as much as I could about the hunters getting fed information from outside the dungeon. He was much less confident about anything happening in regard to that.

As soon as this message ends, the guild system will be live!

As you know, party members share certain quests and will share experience. All personal space upgrades are shared. Party members may examine each other's properties. But sometimes people will want to work with someone without having to actually party with them. And sometimes, as we've seen over and over again with you humans, you very much like working together in large groups. Such massive groups are not feasible when it comes to parties. Oh, by the way, parties are now limited to 30 crawlers. Larger parties will be automatically broken up at the end of this message. Sorry about that, guys!

"Oof," Mordecai said.

"Assholes," I muttered under my breath.

But that's okay. We are implementing the guild system this season, so your larger parties can stay together. You're welcome.

Here's how it works.

A crawler must purchase a guild charter from a Bopca. These start at 500,000 gold. The basic membership will allow up to five separate parties or individuals to join together to form a guild. That number can increase as the guild levels up.

At least one member of each party must own a personal space in order to participate. Once joined together, each of the personal spaces will be expanded to include a common area. Your own personal and party areas will remain off limits to nonparty members unless you give them access.

There will be guild-only upgrades available for purchase. Some of these are pretty spectacular, so you'll definitely want to check it out.

Also, for a small licensing fee, you may share most preexisting environmental upgrades with one another. This will be a great way to combine power and work together and will allow for a wide variety of upgrades.

The guild leader will have control over who may join the guild and will have power to kick them out. They will have control over who may edit the common area and purchasing of the common upgrades. They may institute dues and create a treasury.

Guild members will not share experience by default. There is an option to change that for a fee.

There are many more rules and exciting upgrades. The Bopcas will have all the information you need to get started.

Next to me, Donut was quivering with excitement. The whole thing was an obvious cash grab. People were forming massive parties so they could share in personal space upgrades, and this was a way to break that up and squeeze more money out of them. But I was curious what the guild-only upgrades were.

And finally, we have an even more exciting announcement. At the end of this floor, we will be having a party! It'll be at the Butcher's Masquerade. Isn't that exciting? Only the top 50 crawlers in the dungeon will receive an invite, but all invited crawlers will also be able to bring a plus-one. The hunters will also attend the party, along with a few intergalactic celebrities, but do not worry about your safety regarding the hunters. How it will work will be explained later. All you need to know now is there will be music, dancing, a costume contest, a pet beauty contest, a talent show, and prizes available to all who attend! It will be great fun for everybody involved, so you really want to get one of those invites. The best way to guarantee a spot is to get out there and kill, kill, kill!

Donut gasped and started hopping up and down. "A pet beauty contest? A *pet* beauty contest? Oh, my god, oh, my god. Mongo!" Mongo looked up from Britney's lap. "You're going to follow in Mommy's paw-steps!"

Mongo leaped to his feet and started to also hop up and down, feeding off Donut's excitement. Britney let out a shriek and scrambled away.

"We're going to need to start training immediately. We'll need at least an extra hour a day. We need to find a seamstress. A walk coach. We'll need to purchase the upgraded pet shower to get all the blood-stains off. It's going to be a lot of work. Mordecai, how many more NPCs can we hire? Also, I just must see the standards manual immediately. Carl, message your attorney and see if he can pull a few strings."

"Standards manual?" Louis asked.

"Donut," I said, "we are not—"

"And don't even think about saying, 'We're not doing this, Donut.'" She paused. "I have very little, and this is something we *are* going to do, and you're not going to stop me."

I just stared at her. "Look . . ." I said, trailing off. *Goddamnit, Donut.*

MORDECAI: Don't worry. I'll talk to her. We'll come up with a compromise.

"Donut," I said. "This party thing, whatever it is, is over two weeks away. We need to focus on the task at hand. We're not going to make it to the party if we don't."

Donut sighed dramatically. "Very well, Carl. But we're going to need to collect more hands. And we'll have to get this guild thing immediately, too."

I was already moving back to my bomber's studio. "That, I can agree with. Bomo, come with me. I'm gonna need you."

I could hear it again, that river in my mind. Rushing, tumbling, crashing, getting faster and louder by the moment. It was starting to hurt. Just a little. That was okay. I'd rest later.

9

THE NUMBER OF HUNTERS IN THE DUNGEON APPEARED ON THE SCREEN, just below the remaining crawler counter, which had lowered to 83,995. The hunter count had ticked up a few times in the past few hours, presumably as a few more last-minute stragglers decided to press their luck.

Katia and the others had left an hour ago while it was still dark. Apparently team Meadow Lark had run into some trouble along the path, and they'd gone out to assist. All was well now.

Now that the sun had risen, we also needed to get moving. We were still only a few hours from Zockau, and the hunters were going to spread from the city like a cloud the moment it opened up. Teleport spells and scrolls were rare, but as we'd already demonstrated, not unheard-of. In a day or two, the hunters would be all over the map.

We prepared to leave. We had a rough map of the floor's layout, and we needed to head south, get to the river, and cross it. There were towns and villages and cities on either side, but most hunters avoided the high elf areas because they were too dangerous.

Still, most everyone on my chat was pushing their way deeper and deeper south, as far away from Zockau as possible. They figured they'd take their chances against the elves rather than face the hunters.

Katia had made the map based on the gate coordinates Gwen's team had looted off the body of Quetzalcoatlus on the previous floor. She'd drawn out a paper copy for us, and it was nearly identical to the one I already had in my scratch pad, which I'd copied from the cookbook.

I hadn't realized just how large this place was.

"If I'm translating the gate coordinates correctly, it's about 100,000 square kilometers," she'd said after I asked her. "Really similar to Iceland, actually. It even has a similar shape."

"Really? That seems huge, especially compared to the last floor."

"It's big," Mordecai agreed. "The ninth floor is the biggest one, though most of the action takes place in one small area."

"Wait, how big is this really, like from edge to edge?" I asked.

Katia moved her finger from top to bottom. "It's about 400-something kilometers from north to south, so what? 250 miles? And about 300-something kilometers from east to west. The river, end to end is about 500 kilometers, but that's only because it's not straight."

The river meandered from the northeast corner to the southwest, bisecting the map like a slithering snake. It branched off into multiple tributaries and lakes, I knew, though Katia didn't have any of that yet on her map.

"Are these roads?" I asked, pointing.

"Yes. We're using the same information-gathering system as we did on the Iron Tangle. Every time someone finds something new, they're calling it in. Imani is the one who's mostly coordinating it, but I've been copying down everything, too. Some of these locations are estimates."

"And these are bridges?" I asked.

"Yes, but again, the location is approximate."

"Do we know how many there are?"

"At least a dozen, but probably more," Katia said. "We only have a general idea of most of them."

"I know you guys are busy, but do you think you can help organize something for me?"

Katia sighed. "You know I'll do anything you ask. To a point."

I grinned. "This one will be easy. I just want all the bridges knocked down. All except this one."

———

NOW, A FEW HOURS LATER, I REEXAMINED THE MAP. I EXAMINED THE main road off Zockau. It seemed to run straight to the river, cross it, and continue on its way before ending about halfway into the jungle.

CARL: Hey, Miriam. Have you guys left yet?

MIRIAM: Yes, sweetie. Are you feeling better? We are traveling the

main road south, following the path of the caravans. We plan
on crossing the river soon and disappearing into the jungle.
There are very few mobs about.

CARL: Are you coming across a lot of traps?

MIRIAM: This main road is mostly clear. The caravans make their
way up and down this road, and their bodyguards cast anti-
trap spells as they travel. Even if there are traps made for
crawlers, they are still disarmed by the spells.

That was super-valuable information. I sent a quick note to Katia,
asking her to spread the word. We needed to map out the regular caravan routes and add them to the community map.

The lack of mobs was because the hunters had likely cleared them
out around the cities. It wasn't until we got farther away that we would
find more.

I had multiple IEDs I'd built, designed to only be triggered by hunters, and I'd need to be careful with their placement. I didn't want to
waste them.

CARL: Is there a town near the bridge?

Katia's map had noted a "possible" settlement here, and I wanted to
make sure it was there.

MIRIAM: Yes. A very big town. It's about forty kilometers from
where you are now. Maybe 60 from Zockau. It's where we
started. A large ursine settlement just on the other side of the
river. Be careful if you go. They're very peculiar there. We have
to put Bianca away when we enter.

I took a pencil and circled the area where the road met the city.

———

DONUT: YOU CAN'T USE BOMO AS A SUICIDE BOMBER. IT'S NOT RIGHT.

CARL: It's not a suicide bombing if he comes back the next floor.
He already agreed to it.

DONUT: BOMO IS OUR FRIEND. WE DON'T BLOW UP OUR FRIENDS,
   CARL.
CARL: He actually seemed kinda excited at the idea.
DONUT: IT'S NOT GOING TO WORK ANYWAY. THEY'LL BE WAITING
   FOR HIM.

Since Bomo had last entered the personal space through the safe room in Zockau, he'd leave the same way if he went out the door by himself. I wasn't sure if there was a door just sitting there or not in the safe room. Even Mordecai wasn't sure. He knew the door would appear if Bomo exited, but he had no idea if it generated and remained there while he was inside like it would with regular party members. If there *was* a door sitting there in the situationally generated space, the other hunters certainly would've noticed it and would be prepared. If there *wasn't* a door, someone probably still would've figured this out by now. It was a pretty obvious move.

I was going to load Bomo up with a very large bomb, send him out into the safe room, have him step outside, and blow the shit out of the town. This would be a bigger explosion than last time. Much bigger. I wanted him to do it when there was only about a half hour left on the timer so more hunters would be outside.

Now that we could chat again safely, I'd been relaying the plan to Donut. Anyone who'd been paying attention could probably figure this out, but that was okay. Bomo would pull the wheeled bomb out of the personal space and emerge out in a safe room, and there wasn't anything anybody could do about it. The only way to stop him would be to block the door off and keep him from exiting out onto the street. If that was the case, it'd require resources and teamwork, and I had the impression none of these guys were too keen to work together. But if they did, Bomo would return to the personal space, and we'd save the bomb for later.

The bomb itself was pretty cool. It was similar to the barrel explosives I'd used before, but much bigger in yield. A few days back when we were still on the previous floor, Mordecai had left a few little square blocks on my sapper's table called **Nitro Sludge**. They were a by-product of a shield potion he'd been working on. They looked like squares of uncooked ramen noodles. They were completely inert, but if vaporized at a high enough temperature, they released an insane amount of oxygen. I'm no chemist, and I have no idea how this stuff really works, but Mordecai tried to explain it to me anyway. Each block was the equivalent of several hundred pounds of ammonium nitrate. They weren't explosive on their own, but they acted like an amplifier if used in the correct situation. Too little, and they did nothing. Too much, and they actually muted the explosion. I seriously had no idea how it really worked since they had so little mass, but after a lot of trial and error, I'd come up with the perfect mix.

I had a large egg-shaped, clamshell-like bomb casing from the previous floor. It was a type of live ammo ball, but it was broken and couldn't be used again to hold and protect a living creature. I could, however, fill it with explosives and a few blocks of Nitro Sludge and then weld the thing closed.

The finished egg-like bomb was about five feet tall and much too big to easily carry, so I built a little cart to place it in that Bomo could pull behind him. For good measure, I also imbued it with *Fear*. Because why not?

According to the simulator, if the bomb worked properly, it would flatten everything within a third of a mile from the epicenter and would severely injure or kill everyone for a good half mile beyond that. It was by far the largest bomb I had constructed myself. At least intentionally.

The system helpfully named the bomb on its own.

Just Wait Until Your Daddy Gets Home—Wheeled Bomb.
    Type: High-Yield Thermobaric Explosive. Also imbues *Fear* within blast radius.
    Effect: I hope you're paid up on your homeowner's insurance.
    Status: 250. Fortified.
    Boom.

I wasn't actually expecting this plan with Bomo to work, but I figured it was worth a try. In the meantime, Donut and I would be booking it south, using the Royal Chariot dune buggy, which I still had in my inventory. I wanted to get to that town on the other side of the bridge and check it out and see if it was a suitable base of operations.

DONUT: WHAT IF I MADE A CLOCKWORK BOMO?

CARL: Uh, would that work? Can you even make a clockwork Bomo?

DONUT: HE'S LISTED AS A ROYAL COURT MINION. WE'D HAVE TO SWITCH HIM OVER TO A MINION OF ME AND NOT THE PARTY, LIKE WE DID WITH CLAY-TON AND VERY SULLEN. REALLY, CARL, YOU NEED TO PAY ATTENTION TO HOW THE PARTY SYSTEM WORKS. ONCE HE'S JUST A MINION OF ME, IT LETS ME MAKE CLOCKWORK VERSIONS.

CARL: Well, shit, that's actually a great idea, but I don't know if the clockwork would exit out the correct door.

DONUT: YOU UNDERESTIMATE ME, CARL. THIS IS WHY YOU NEED TO LET ME KNOW THE PLAN. DON'T WORRY. I GOT THIS. ONLY PROBLEM IS, I MUST BE IN THE SAFE ROOM WHEN WE DO IT.

I glanced at the clock. If the road was clear, we could get to that next town no problem. We had just over three hours.

CARL: Okay. We'll prepare Bomo in case we don't make it in time. But if we can get to the next town in three hours, we'll do it your way.

10

"OKAY, DO YOU UNDERSTAND? DON'T TOUCH IT UNTIL IT'S TIME TO leave. It's really stable, but if you screw around with it too much in here, it might turn into a dud."

Bomo rumbled. Behind him, the Sledge made a disapproving sound. He wasn't mad that Bomo was possibly doing this. He was upset that Bomo didn't want him playing *Frogger* while he was gone because he didn't want him to beat his score, which meant the Sledge would have to go two weeks without playing.

I had a Playstation Two and a television set I'd gotten from the house along with a ton of games. I'd managed to hook a dwarven battery to a power strip without blowing everything up. I was hoping to expand their video game horizons, but their hands were too big. I was going to make them cretin-sized controllers when I got a chance.

We left the space and moved to the streets. We didn't have time to go exploring in this town. Everything had been destroyed, and that was even more evident in the daylight. We moved from the space, out into the Whataburger, and out into the streets headed south.

"Your kind are not welcome here," a creature called. This was a bugbear atop a house hammering wood into place. The creature stood, looking down at us. He wore a tattered leather apron and clutched an enormous hammer in a clawed hand. He pointed the hammer at us. This was my first time really looking at a bugbear. Shamus Chaindrive, the submarine captain from the last floor, had been a bugbear, but he'd been nothing but a head in a jar and I never really got to see him.

These guys were ugly bastards. He was large, furry, with pointed ears and a goblin-like face. This one had an orange-brown tint to his fur. Others were more brown or red. Each one was about my height, but twice as bulky. We did not want to tangle with these guys if we could avoid it. His accent was Eastern European, reminding me of that dead idiot Vadim, who'd locked himself in an escape pod and gotten himself killed by jellyfish.

"Carl, I can smell him from here. He smells like pickled beets and vodka. Disgusting," Donut muttered.

Goiter—Bugbear. Level 42.

Council member of this settlement.

One of the few races who managed to not get fully wiped out by Scolopendra's nine-tier attack, the bugbears are now one of the most common races one might find in the Kapok district of the Hunting Grounds, second only to the Ursine and the Bush Elves.

Bugbears are on the same evolutionary tree as goblins and hobgoblins, which is to say they're ugly and mean and are rumored to have sexual relations with toads. Like hobgoblins, they're known for blowing stuff up, but the explosions they cause tend to be involuntary. They are engineers at heart and spend their days attempting to construct automatons and vehicles and other contraptions with varying degrees of success.

Despite their name, they are not actually bears. Their neighbors and rivals, the Ursine, are happy to point this out every chance they get.

You gotta treat a bugbear like you would treat the enormous drunk guy at the end of the bar. It could go either way. He'll either want to fight you or be your buddy. And there ain't no way to predict which one it'll be.

"We're not the ones who destroyed your town," I called up to the bugbear. "We're here to kill them."

"That is a different story, then. This means we are friends. I shall buy you a drink."

"Sorry," I called. "We gotta get moving. But just a warning: Those same guys will be coming through here again in a few hours, so you should get ready."

Goiter the bugbear cracked his neck. "We'll be ready."

I saluted him, and we moved out of town.

———

LIKE MIRIAM SAID, THE JUNGLE HERE WAS COMPLETELY DEVOID OF mobs. At least it was near the main road. There was wildlife and all sorts of foliage, but we didn't have time to examine anything. Mordecai had given me a list of items to look for that was literally five pages long. I told him to take some gold and hire someone to look for him.

I drove the Chariot while Donut rode Mongo and ran alongside. Her *Twinkle Toes* spell made it so Mongo could run faster even than the dune buggy, and she'd been practicing it, trying to level it up. Mongo *loved* going fast and screeched with joy whenever she cast the spell.

I stopped a few times and planted a few claymore-like mines. They'd only be triggered by hunters. I suspected I was wasting my time, but it couldn't hurt.

As we traveled, Donut worked on her singing. She was attempting to cast *Entourage*, but she could only make a single illusionary Carl appear when she sang in a low monotone, and the resulting illusion was vaguely transparent, which was no good.

"Carl, this system is broken," Donut said. "It's not letting me cast my new spells right."

"Keep working on it," I said. "We'll find you something to help . . ." I trailed off as I received an odd notification.

Your god, Emberus, has made an appearance in this realm.

I stopped the cart and looked around. I didn't see anything. Nothing changed.

"What? What is it?" Donut asked.

I told her.

"He's probably collecting all his money from you."

Just about a minute later, a second notification appeared.

Emberus has returned to the Halls of the Ascendency.

"Weird," I said, and we continued on our way.

It didn't take long for us to reach the river.

I wasn't sure what to expect, but there were no real surprises here. The stream was pretty big, maybe 250 feet across. I couldn't tell how deep it was. It flowed north to south, but at a slow pace. I didn't see anything on or in the water, but Donut said she saw a few white dots flash by. There was a steep slope here, and we didn't dare approach.

An impressive-looking wooden covered bridge spanned the water, wide enough for two carts to pass side by side. The ground just in front of the bridge was burned to hell, suggesting there'd been a trap here not too long ago.

I could see the city on the other side of the bridge, bigger than I expected. A pair of funeral bell mushroom guards stood at the end of the bridge, watching us impassively.

We had just under an hour before the hunters would be released. I stopped the Chariot and stowed it away as I clomped my way across the bridge, taking note of the multiple braces that led down into the river. We'd gotten word of maybe ten bridges that had been knocked down. That wasn't nearly as many as I hoped, but hopefully the word had leaked to the hunters. They, the ones who couldn't fly or teleport at least, would be funneled toward the bridges that remained. Hopefully.

Entering Large Ursine Settlement.

"I must say," Donut said from the back of Mongo, "this village smells much better than the last one. It's no wonder why these ursine folk don't like the bugbears."

We stopped at the end of the bridge, just before the two mushroom guards. It was kind of odd. This town's main residents were the ursine, which were large bearlike humanoids. In Zockau, the bear guys were the guards and there weren't any of the funeral bells.

Unlike that very first dryad village, which had been part of the jungle, this one was mostly devoid of jungle foliage. The jungle encroached all around the big town, but there were no wild, unkempt trees within the streets. Rows of well-manicured shrubs and trees with flowering buds dotted the city, but it was clear this town was very well taken care of. Multiple stores and shops and guilds all lined up neatly amongst cobblestone streets. I caught sight of a Club Vanquisher entrance in the distance, but I did not see a Desperado Club. I knew there had to be one in there somewhere because Mordecai said all "large" towns would have access.

There was no indicator that the hunters had ventured this far before they'd been sequestered. The town seemed fully intact, and like Donut said, it actually smelled nice. Kind of like flowers mixed in with clean linen.

My map had a strange red diamond symbol on it just at the edge. I zoomed in and saw it was listed as a **Temple of Hellik**.

Hellik was the brother and enemy of Emberus. I had a quest to kill the god that I'd eventually have to deal with. In the meantime, I would supposedly get a bonus anytime I killed a worshipper of Hellik, though I wasn't about to wade into that pool anytime soon. I had way too much stuff to deal with.

I didn't see any temples of Emberus in town, though I did notice a few other churches that weren't labeled. They all sat together in a row down one street deep in town.

There were dozens of NPCs about. Most of them were the large, hulking ursine, but I caught sight of multiple bush elves and dryads along with the occasional dwarf and even bugbear, plus a dozen other random creatures. I saw none of the monkeys that seemed to plague the more southern cities. I didn't see any other crawlers, but I did catch a few oddities. There were a pair of dots with the cross, indicating them as elites. They both were moving away. In addition, I saw two different white dots that were shaped like stars. I hadn't seen that before, but I knew from Mordecai and the cookbook that white stars sometimes indicated quest-giving NPCs.

We stopped in front of the two funeral bells.

"Hey, buddy," I said to the guard, "do you guys even talk?"

The guard just looked at me. His flat white face was an emotionless mask.

"Do you think you can point me toward the mayor's office?"

The guard made a sort of deep-throated rumbling noise which I took as a "no."

"I don't think he talks, Carl," said Donut.

I sighed. "Let's get into a safe room." We started moving forward, but the two mushrooms suddenly lowered their spears to block our access. Their dots on the map remained white, but they weren't letting us pass.

"What is it?" I asked.

One of the funeral bells pointed at Donut and Mongo with his long spear and made a very slight "no" motion with his head as Donut made a scoffing noise.

I realized he was pointing the stick directly at Mongo's chest. Mongo screeched in indignation. The guards both made a dangerous, growling noise. These guys were level 90. We didn't want to fight them.

The second funeral bell pointed to a poster that was tacked to the interior wall of the covered bridge behind us. The paper ran the length from the floor to the ceiling of the bridge and was so old and faded, I hadn't noticed it. The system was kind enough to read it for me.

Sign. This is a set of rules put forth by the town. This is an Ursine settlement, so consider yourself lucky this one is short.

Town Rules. Failure to heed any of these will result in immediate decapitation:

- No fighting.
- No alcohol.
- No illicit drugs.
- No magic on the streets.
- No dancing.
- No singing outside of a temple.
- No unruly children.
- No gambling of any kind.
- No stealing.
- No littering.
- No swearing.
- No sexual activity outside the sanctity of marriage.
- No Macaques of any breed unless escorted by a Dryad.
- No Naiads.

- No Half- or Quarter-Naiad Mongrels.
- All High Elves must register their presence at the guard headquarters.
- All bugbears must take a bath in the river before entering and then register at the guard headquarters. Funeral Bells will provide soap.
- And absolutely, positively no dinosaurs of any kind. No exceptions.

"What?" Donut exclaimed. "This is an outrage! They specifically called out Mongo! He's just an innocent little child. And no dancing? No singing? All of these rules are just ridiculous. Well, except maybe the bugbear one. But all the others are just awful. I will not have it. You there," she called out to one of the guards. "Get me the person in charge immediately!"

"Donut," I began, "we don't have time. Just stick Mongo in his carrier and—"

To my utter astonishment, the mushroom guard grunted and turned, waddling away while Donut sat there, still astride Mongo. She made a little harrumph noise.

"We don't have time for this," I said again as I watched the slow-moving mushroom lumber down the street.

"It's about the principle, Carl. Mongo loves villages. The last one didn't care about him." She patted the dinosaur on the head. "Don't worry. Mommy will get it all sorted out."

Mongo snorted.

"All right," I said, "but the hunters will be free soon. Plus, we should probably find out why that last rule is necessary." I shivered at the thought of having to fight a pack of Mongos. Holy crap.

An older ursine wearing honest-to-goodness glasses suddenly appeared, walking hurriedly down the street. He met the funeral bell and exchanged a few words—it appeared they *did* talk—and then they both turned toward us.

"No, no, no," the bear said as they approached. "This is not real royalty. I told you to only summon me if it's a member of the high elf court. Not whatever *that* is."

The bear was about the same size and shape of a bugbear, but this one was a large brown bear who walked on two legs. While the bugbears seemed overly muscular, this guy just seemed pudgy. But he was also a bear, and I knew looks could be deceiving when it came to these guys. This one had some gray around his snout and was clearly a little older. He wore no pants but had a vest. The glow around his dot told me he had magical gear.

I was suddenly reminded of another bear, this one a reanimated corpse on roller skates, and I shuddered, remembering.

I examined the creature.

Elmer. Level 40. Ursine.
    Mayor of this settlement.
    Hoo boy. An Ursine. So there are bears, which are the vicious, brutal-yet-somehow-cuddly creatures we all know and love. And then there are the Ursine. They're 49% bear, 51% racist uncle who works for the IRS and has to hide his erection when he prepares for an audit.
    I have nothing against those who choose to live a saintly existence or those who choose to find hope and peace and comfort in a life of purity and virtue.
    Actually, that's a lie. I hate these smug fuck sticks. Why? Because of the godsdamned hypocrisy. It'd be one thing if these hairy bitches practiced what they preached, but all of their rules and self-righteousness is nothing but a shiny veneer covering up the fact they're just as rusted and immoral and imperfect as the rest of us. If internet porn was a thing in the dungeon, there's no doubt these repressed assholes would be the number one connoisseurs of gnomish femdom porn or something of the like. Well, except maybe after the Gingers from the seventh floor. But you get the idea. They think they're better than everybody else.
    It's just like those other new shiny AI iterations with their clean lines and error-replacement nets. Fuck you all.
    If repressed sexuality and caged instinct were, err, bearified, you would get the Ursine. After Scolopendra's destruction, the only surviving Ursine were the clerics. That resulted in the formerly bru-

tal society evolving into something like that town from the movie *Footloose*. They want a utopia. If you don't look at the fraying edges, it's clear they've somewhat succeeded.

"You're a genius, Donut," I muttered under my breath. I'd figured it would take some time to find the mayor.

"Yes, Carl," Donut said. "I know I am a genius."

I looked over my shoulder. The bridge stood just behind us. On either side was a steep slope that led about twenty feet down into the river. There was a well-worn trail here where the bugbears would, presumably, trudge up and down to take their baths.

"Yankee Doodle. Into the river."

"What, *now?*" Donut whispered. "What about the guards? Yankee Doodle needs Katia. That's where we got the name! We put the feather in the cap! Really, Carl. You need to remember the moves better."

I took a step back so we returned to the covered bridge, just outside of town.

"If these guards are like the swordsmen from the third floor, it won't matter if we're out of the town limits. I'll take care of Katia's part. If it doesn't work, we'll run to a safe room. There's one right there around that next corner. The Galleon's Lap."

Every time a new description popped up now, I copied the text and then pasted it into the scratch pad. As Elmer the mayor bear approached us angrily, I noticed something odd. That weird line in the middle of the description, the one about the other AIs, wasn't there after I pasted the text. I retyped it from memory while it was still fresh in my mind.

"You. You there. You cannot bring your lizard into town," Elmer called. He stopped about ten feet from the city limits. The other guard moved back to his spot right in front of us.

Donut bristled. "Mongo is a purebred mongoliensis, and he is in training for a very important pageant which will occur in a few days. And you, sir, are delaying his training. I demand you let us in immediately."

The ursine crossed his arms. "Rules are rules for a reason. We do not make exceptions. We have had nothing but trouble from his kind, and he will not be allowed to enter. In fact"—he adjusted his glasses and squinted at Donut—"what sort of creature are you? Are you some sort of monkey?" He looked at me. "I'm sorry, only dryads are allowed to bring monkeys within town. So if you want to continue forward, you will have to leave them both behind."

"A monkey?" Donut exclaimed. "You think I'm a *monkey*? I'll have you know I am an award-winning purebred tortoiseshell Persian cat with a flawless pedigree!"

"Yeah," I agreed, "if we ignore the weird incest stuff, she does have a pretty flawless pedigree."

"Hmm," Elmer said to me. "She certainly acts and smells like a monkey. No, no. I'm sorry. We better be safe. If you wish, I can have one of my guards dispatch them both for you."

Donut was about to say something, but I held up a hand. I pulled a handful of gold coins from my inventory. "How much would it cost us to have the guards get rid of them for me?" I gave Donut a sidelong glance. "They have been getting on my nerves recently. Especially the hairy one."

"Carl," Donut said, "that is not funny."

"See?" I said.

Elmer took a few steps forward to get a better look at the gold in my hand. "Hmm," he said, thoughtful. "Probably a bit more than that. The customary execution fee is 100 gold, but I'll give you a discount if we do both at once. So only 150."

"Let's do it," I said. "You'd be doing me a favor." I pulled a few more coins out.

Elmer stepped closer to take the money.

The moment he did, Donut cast *Astral Paw*, pushing Elmer from behind toward the slope.

The mayor let out a cry as he tumbled off the edge of town and rolled down the slope. He pitched forward and flipped like a rag doll, his fat body making an odd squishing noise as he bounced off a rock.

Normally, Katia would then shoot a crossbow bolt into the back of their head. Instead, I pulled a banger sphere and whirled to toss the metal ball.

I never got the chance to throw it. The bear creature's face somehow managed to find every rock on the hill. He fell, landed face-first on a

stone, tumbled, then cracked his head on another. His own weight
worked against him. He was dead the moment he rolled to a stop at the
edge of the river. His mighty stomach jiggled.

Nobody moved for several moments.

"Well, that was unexpected," I grumbled.

"Wow," Donut said as the two guards stepped forward to look down
at the dead mayor. Their dots remained white on the map. It didn't appear as if they knew Donut had cast a spell to push him. Either that, or
they didn't care because she'd been out of town at the time. "For a level
40, he sure was fragile."

"Jump down there, loot his body, and then we'll run into that safe
room while—"

A red dot appeared, leaping out the water with a sudden violent
splash. The movement was so sudden and fast, I cringed back in surprise. The blue-tinged fanged-and-horned creature grabbed the body,
pulled it in the water, and disappeared before I could even examine it.
The thing had been out of the river for less than a second. The X of the
corpse and the red dot disappeared.

The two guards just looked at each other as if unsure what to do next.

I was pretty sure that thing had been a full-blooded naiad.

"Wait," Donut said, suddenly gasping. "I got credit for that. Does
that mean—"

"Go, go," I whispered, slapping Mongo on the rump. The dinosaur
screeched and ran between the two guards, who each took a second to
respond. Their dots flashed and turned red as we ran into town and
headed toward the nearby safe room.

**Warning: You have been branded as a troublemaker at this settle-
ment. Guards will now attack you on sight.**

We jumped into the safe room pub, which was some Spanish restaurant. We rushed past the Bopca proprietor and into the personal space.

WE ONLY HAD A FEW MINUTES UNTIL THE HUNTERS WOULD BE RE-
leased. I'd hoped to have more time to prepare, but that was okay. I

moved to the bomber's studio, grabbed the cart, and pulled it to the door.

"You're going to have a box to open which'll give you control of the settlement," I said to Donut as I quickly prepared the wheeled bomb. "The guards are going to attack us until you open it. But we gotta do this first."

Donut was hopping up and down with excitement. "My own town. I have my own town, Carl! I can change the rules now." She gasped. "Do you think I'll be able to change the town's name? Do you think I can make them paint stuff different colors?" She looked at Mongo. "I told you Mommy would take care of that stupid rule. Thought they could ban my baby from town. I showed them. I'm going to make dancing mandatory."

"No time," I said. "We need to do this now, and then we'll need to get to work on making the guards set up to defend the city."

"Oh, all right," Donut said. "Everybody step back. Bomo has to open the door and stand on the edge. Then I'll cast the *Clockwork Triplicate* so the minion appears outside the room in that weird space where all the doors are. Bomo will hand him the cart and get back inside. And then clockwork Bomo will roll it outside, and you can set it off."

"Okay," I said, my heart thrashing. "Bomo will have to go out with him into the safe room so he can tell us when the clockwork guy gets outside."

Bomo rumbled and stepped toward the door. He reached forward and pulled open the door.

"Stop," I said before Donut could cast. There was nobody out in the situationally generated space, but there was something attached to the outside of the door. A note. It was stuck into place on the door with a knife.

"Don't touch that knife," Mordecai said.

I was about to ask Bomo to grab it, but I had a notion and stepped forward and grabbed the note myself, careful not to touch the knife. It let me. I could actually step outside if I wanted. Now *that* was interesting. I quickly stepped back before anybody said anything.

I quickly examined the paper.

"Damnit," I growled. "Sorry, Bomo. We'll save you and the bomb for another time."

He made an unhappy growl. The Sledge grunted happily and turned to the *Frogger* machine.

"What? What does it say?" Donut asked. I showed her the note.

Carl,

Do not bother trying to kill anybody else within town with one of your silly explosives. All of the hunters are now protected from further explosions. You would only be killing your precious NPCs.

I have ordered the town guards to all worship Emberus. I am going to assume you know what that means. I hope you're not stupid enough to try it. As entertaining as it would be for you to get smote by your own god, I much prefer for you to remain alive.

The Hive is hunting you, and there will be nowhere for you to hide. We are coming. *I* am coming. Your death will not be quick. I will crack you open and drink your innards slowly, one organ at a time as every nerve in your soft body crackles with endless pain. The universe will watch as you suffer and beg for a death that will not come until the very end. And then I will take your head home with me and place it upon my sister's grave so she may feast upon you in the afterlife.

Vrah.

"She seems nice," Donut said.

I pulled a pen from my inventory, and I wrote, "Come and get it, bitch." I crumpled up the paper and tossed it out the door.

System Message. Attention. Attention. The gates are down. The hunters are loose.
Run, Run, Run.

11

"THIS IS JUST NOT ACCEPTABLE, CARL. I *LIKE* MY BUTTERFLY CHARM. It makes it so fairies like me, and it is pretty. It's part of my fit. I don't want to take it off. I don't see why I just can't wear two charms at the same time. Stupid Angel the cocker spaniel had like four or five tags on her collar. She jingled like a bunch of rusty cowbells being dumped down the stairs wherever she walked."

Donut had received the little butterfly charm a long time ago, all the way on the first floor. We'd used it to great effect early on. It'd been instrumental in defeating the first Krakaren boss. Plus, it gave plus one to intelligence and plus four to Donut's Light on Your Feet skill, which helped her jump. Her skill was ten with the charm, and she could still sail through the air like an acrobat without it. Just not as much, which was unfortunate.

"The system only lets you wear a certain amount of magical items at once. Otherwise, Katia could grow a hundred arms on her back and carry around 500 plus-one rings of strength," I said. "This new one is better anyway."

"It's ugly. And the gem is turquoise. Turquoise! Do I look like an elderly woman with smoke-stained teeth sitting in a bingo hall?"

"The gem is tiny. You're gonna have to wear it while you're in Point Mongo, but you can always switch it back if we come across some fairy-class mobs."

She didn't *have* to wear her new collar charm. It wasn't required to enter the settlement menu and change stuff around, as we quickly learned. I'd already received a notification that she'd changed the name from "Large Ursine Settlement" to "Point Mongo." The system had also changed her name to "Mayor Donut" but she'd quickly changed it back to Princess. However, Mordecai said if she wanted to order the guards around, she needed to be wearing the charm. The benefits were much better anyway.

I had one of these already, but mine was in the form of a necklace. I examined Donut's new charm.

> **Enchanted Collar Charm of the Effete Bourgeoisie.**
>
> The middle size of the chains of leadership, this pendant signifies you as a member of the elite. Each jewel encrusted upon this charm represents a settlement owned and controlled by the bearer. If one still maintains a settlement's jewel upon the collapse of the level, the holder of this necklace will permanently receive a tax stipend every ten days from that settlement based on size and population. In addition, each gem will impart additional benefits based on the town.
>
> In order to upgrade this necklace, one must first conquer an Extra-Large-Sized Settlement. Upgraded necklaces will also upgrade all existing gems.
>
> One Attached Gem:
> Plain Turquoise. Point Mongo (Sixth Floor).
> +8 to Dexterity.
> +4 to Intelligence.
> +Snitch (Level 10).
> Taxes received: 3,592 Gold every 10 days.
> May you be a kind and just leader.

I picked it up to examine Snitch, which was a skill, not a spell.

> **Snitch.**
>
> Nobody likes a snitch. Nobody except the po-po.
>
> If you are within any settlement, activating this skill will immediately alert all the town's guards, who will start to move to your location at the time of activation. At level five, a single guard will be immediately teleported to you. At level 10, it'll be five guards. At 15, *all* of the town's guards will be summoned to you.

In addition, at level 10, guards may be summoned up to one kilometer outside of the city limits of a settlement you own. At level 15,
this will work with any settlement.

Warning: As you've probably already deduced, simply summoning the guards to you doesn't necessarily mean they'll do what you
want, even if you're the town's leader. In addition, while there's no
cooldown for this skill, this is not something you want to abuse.
These guard guys can get *really* cranky.

Donut huffed and changed out the charms, mumbling under her
breath.

"Okay," I said. "The guards are mad at us, so you gotta figure out
how to turn that off."

"I'll walk her through it," Mordecai said. "It's not complicated, but
it sometimes takes a minute for them to reset. We'll have to go out
there. We should do it now before the hunters can get here."

"We need to hurry," I said. "Vrah can fly, and she might head straight
here. I'm going to distribute some anti-hunter missiles to the guards
once we get control, but I need to build some more missile tubes first.
We'll have to surround the town with traps and instruct the caravans
not to deactivate them."

As if on cue, I received a sudden group of notifications.

A trap you have left has killed a hunter!
    You have received a Gold Hunter-Killer Box!

New Achievement! Insurgent.
    You left an explosive device along a well-traveled path, and it
detonated and killed an intended target. It was really cool. Too bad
you didn't get to see it because you're a trap-leaving bitch!
    Reward: You've received a Gold Trapmaster Box!

"I can't believe that worked," I said after I explained the notification.
"But that was a trap I'd placed after the bugbear settlement. They're
moving quickly in this direction. They'll be here soon, especially if they
have vehicles."

I immediately opened both of the boxes. The Gold Hunter-Killer Box contained 35,000 gold and a fat mottled gray hand of a hunter who'd been named JayGee. I held the trophy up to the ceiling.

"Hey," I said, waving the fat hand, "if any of JayGee's family or friends are watching this, you can go fuck yourselves. And maybe next time if someone you know wants to go hunting innocent people for fun, you can tell them about how your idiot friend or son or dad once tried it and ended up dying on the first day."

"You shouldn't do that," Mordecai said after a moment. "People out there have long memories."

"Good," I said. "I don't want them to ever forget."

The trapmaster box contained a very useful mod. It was a pack of twenty trap add-ons called Fail Safes. They would send me a notification if the trap was ever disabled or set off.

"Come on, Donut," Mordecai said, leaping sideways toward the door. "We'll need to reset all of the town's rules and build new parameters for the guards. I'll show you how to do it."

"I'm not a child, Mordecai," Donut said, strolling toward the door. "I have the menu, and I've already removed all of those idiotic rules. I kept the bugbear one, though. They really are stinky."

"No," I said, "you gotta erase that one."

"Why would I do that?"

"Because that rule was a trap. You saw what happened when that bear rolled down the hill. He got snagged right into the water. If you make all the bugbears walk down to the edge of the river to wash, the same thing will happen. You'll be killing them."

"Oh, all right. I'll make it so the guards have to soap them up themselves or something."

"Just hurry and message me once the guards are all fixed."

KATIA: Guilds are different than personal spaces. Anybody in the party can initiate one, and they'll be the guildmaster. You two already said you don't want the responsibility. Imani doesn't really want to do it, either, but Elle thinks she will if we ask. We'll have to pool some money if we want to share the upgrades, and if you want to keep the training room. One of

Bautista's guys already has a stables upgrade that Donut will want the moment she sees it.

"Here," I said, handing off a missile launcher to a funeral bell guard. The creature smelled like dirt. Donut had named him "Doctor El" for some inexplicable reason. She'd gone through and named the officers and sergeants and would've spent the next hour naming *all* of them if I hadn't intervened. There were fifty-something mushroom guards scattered around town, but the town management screen had identified six of them as sergeants and three more as commanders. The three commanders remained within the guard headquarters, but all six of the sergeants were out here with us now. For me, the sergeant rank wasn't indicated anywhere in their appearance or stats, though Donut said they had three chevrons over their head when she looked at them. I also couldn't tell the difference between the male and female funeral bells, but apparently that was a thing. I still hadn't heard one talk.

In the distance, a group of ursine watched as I passed out the weapons to the guards. Mordecai was there amongst them, speaking with a robed cleric bear, who was gesticulating and shouting down at tiny little Mordecai, who was shouting back. Donut sat astride Mongo. She was flanked by two of the funeral bell sergeants, both apparently women. She'd named one Dinallo and the other "Miss Nance."

CARL: If Imani doesn't want to do it, ask Li Na. Or Gwen. Or, you know, *you* can do it.

KATIA: I don't have time. And I'm not going to let Gwen do it, either. We don't know where Li Na and Li Jun are yet. We'll start setting it all up tonight. We'll figure it out then.

CARL: 10-4. Are you doing okay otherwise?

KATIA: Yes. There are some big personalities in this group. And they don't all get along. Florin is doing a good Carl impersonation with how broody he's being. Gwen constantly wants to murder Louis and Firas. Britney has given up on everything, and I don't know what to do with her. But we'll make it work. We're heading southwest tomorrow. Away from

elf territory but deeper into the wild. We've been fighting
these screaming little tiki warrior guys. They're fast and
scary. We're going to grind some quests and start collecting
the former Daughters to us.

CARL: Be careful.

KATIA: We're not the ones who're setting up a base of operations
right on the edge of the hunter zone.

I handed another missile tube off. This time to a mushroom named
Ice Man.

CARL: The whole floor is the hunter zone now. Talk to you tonight.

"You'll have to reinstitute the naiad and dinosaur rules immediately," the ursine was saying as I strolled closer to the group. I placed an
alarm trap. It'd play "Give It Away" by the Red Hot Chili Peppers. I
had a different song for each of the town's six entrances. I'd also receive
a notification if someone messed with the trap.

"Why is it necessary?" Mordecai asked. "The guards will keep the
town safe regardless. Have there been naiad attacks recently?"

"Recently?" the bear asked. He was a level 45 Light Cleric named
Tam. The creature had a gray muzzle similar to the mayor's. In fact, it
seemed all the ursine in town were elderly. "We live right on the edge
of the river! They are always attacking. Always!" He pointed at Mongo.
"But they're not as bad as the lizards. Those things are the worst. Absolute worst. There are all shapes and sizes, and they're always trying to
get into town to eat us! And now that we're being led by a pagan monkey with a pet dinosaur, we are not protected by the gods. We have been
safe only because we do not sin. If you refuse to reinstitute the holy
shield of piety and order, then you'll have to go out there and do something about the dinosaur menace."

"Ahh, shit," Mordecai mumbled the moment the cleric guy finished
his rant. He turned to look at me and Donut. "Sorry, guys," he said
sheepishly. "That was an accident."

I was about to ask him what he meant when the notification came.

New Quest! The Recital.

Dinosaur attacks are becoming more and more of a problem in
the large settlement of Point Mongo. It started small. A chicken
here. An Ursine there. People didn't care so much at first since they
were mostly picking off the annoying people. But the attacks are
getting worse. The dinosaurs probing the town's defenses are getting bigger. There's plenty of easier-to-obtain dino chow out in the
jungle, so what is causing all of this attention on Point Mongo? Why
are they attacking?

Exterminate the threat. Or find out what they want and then
give it to them. I'll leave it up to you.

Reward: You will receive a Gold Quest Box! You will also receive
a free town upgrade!

"Town upgrade?" I asked. "What is that?"

"I don't know," Mordecai said. "Donut's town menu is much more
extensive than it's ever been. In fact, ever since this floor opened, I've
noticed a lot of little changes that are unusual. Everything is moved
around on my manager menu."

KATIA: Point Mongo? Really? And why did I just get a quest to
hunt dinosaurs?

"Recital?" Donut asked. "Why is the quest named that? What does
that mean?"

"I don't know," I said. "But maybe you should reinstitute the no-
dinosaur rule and add an exception for Mongo or something. We should
look into the quest if it'll offer some sort of defensive upgrade to the
town."

"I absolutely will not reintroduce a racist policy just because it makes
a bunch of overgrown teddy bears feel more comfortable. Really, Carl,
the town is named after a dinosaur for goodness' sake." She turned back
to the guard. "Now, Miss Nance, where were we? Oh, yes. They have
fuzzy ears that look like wet dollar-store slippers. And they drool all
over the place and are famously incontinent. If you see one—" Donut let
out a strangled yelp as Mongo abruptly shrieked and started galloping

away with Donut still in the saddle. "No! Mongo! Bad!" she cried as they disappeared down the street.

"Goddamnit," I growled, and started running off after them.

CARL: Donut, jump!

Bears and other creatures scattered out of the way as Donut and Mongo rocketed away. A vendor selling flowers had to dive to avoid being run over. I cursed again as I ran. Chasing after Mongo was like trying to run down a motorcycle. They ran past a group of churches and stores, turned a corner, and disappeared. Donut did not jump off. *Shit, shit.*

The last time Mongo had run off like this was because he'd been enchanted by a spell. It was to lure us into a trap. This was probably the same thing.

CARL: Goddamnit, Donut. Do not leave town. Jump off!
DONUT: I AM NOT LEAVING MONGO, CARL.

I rushed around the corner, passing a group of bears with weird symbols over their heads I didn't have time to suss out. Mongo and Donut were in the far distance racing toward the southernmost exit to town, which was guarded by two mushrooms.

Mongo and Donut rushed out the gate and past the wall, then disappeared into the thick jungle as I scrambled after them. Just as they disappeared, I heard Mongo shriek again.

Only it wasn't Mongo.

A chill washed over me. Several more shrieks filled the air as the foliage shook and trembled.

Holy fuck. Holy fuck. No, no, no.

CARL: Mongo will be okay. You won't. Get off. Now!

I'd received a total of ten dinosaur-repellent potions since the end of the previous floor. The description was vague about what the potion actually did. It lasted a full thirty hours. I'd already taken one earlier.

Mongo didn't seem to care I'd taken it, but Donut refused to drink the potion, afraid it'd make her pet shy away from her. I regretted not making her take it.

As I ran, I loaded up a double-stuffed, *Fear*-infused smoke curtain into my xistera and tossed it out into the jungle ahead of me. It arced away like an artillery shell, trailing smoke. This enhanced smoke bomb used up four of the regular curtains, but it lasted twice as long and filled the area with much more smoke than the normal ones.

DONUT: CARL, CARL! HELP!

I rushed out through the town gate into the jungle. *Oh fuck, oh fuck,* I thought as I saw the red dots. There were about forty of them arranged in a semicircle surrounding Donut and Mongo, who were just up ahead. I pushed my way through the foliage into a small clearing.

I stopped dead, taking in the scene. My heart thrashed.

For a terrifying moment, I thought the world had frozen and a boss battle was about to start.

Mongo was stopped in the clearing, head down, growling, about to attack. Forty pairs of eyes glared back through the leaves. All around us large familiar heads poked out of the foliage. They were all focused completely on Mongo.

I'd overthrown my smoke curtain. The smoke billowed up and away in the distance. Gray wisps curled into the clearing, dancing at the edge of the forty velociraptors, but not enough to obscure us. They were all laser focused on Mongo.

Nobody moved. Any moment now, the fight would start. When it did, we were fucked.

None of the other dinosaurs made a sound. Only Mongo growled. It was a low, terrifying growl, like a constantly revving engine. I'd never heard anything like it before from him. The only other sound was the distant hissing of the smoke curtain. Even the normally loud bugs and other animals had grown silent.

The viewer counter in the corner of my interface was starting to spike.

My mind raced. I needed options. My *Protective Shell* spell still had another twenty minutes before it'd reset.

I edged my way toward Donut and Mongo, and I physically pulled Donut off the saddle and then started to slowly back away. Donut was equally transfixed, her entire body trembling. She didn't resist as I pulled her away. Mongo had gone completely rigid. His entire body was taut like stone. I put the limp Donut on my shoulder and continued to back away.

"Carl, it's a bunch of Mongos. They're all really high level," Donut whispered, her voice full of fear.

"Stay on me," I whispered. "Snitch and then Nope."

Snitch would call five guards to us. With Nope, we'd both hit invisibility potions. I'd drop another smoke curtain as Donut cast *Wall of Fire*. Then Donut would *Puddle Jump* us back to town.

"Not without Mongo," Donut said. "And I can't see past the clearing."

"That little shit is the reason we're here right now," I said, taking another step backward. I still didn't know what, specifically, called him out here, but it was probably some sort of dinosaur call or sixth sense or something. A branch snapped under my foot, and one of the closest mongoliensis jerked their head toward us. The lizard eyes blinked, and the head bobbed, chicken-like. I'd seen that look a hundred times, just before Mongo tore something apart.

The dinosaur had what appeared to be a purple shawl wrapped around its neck, which was out of place. It was threadbare and splattered with blood. A few others had similar items equipped. None were magical.

"We are screwed, Donut. We need to go. These are Mongo's people. He'll be okay. I just need to back up a little more, and you'll be able to see the town, and then you can cast *Puddle Jump*."

Mongo continued to growl. One of the raptors took a tentative step into the clearing, stopping about twenty feet away. This was a particularly large velociraptor, battle-scarred and vicious-looking. It had a more pink-and-blue feather appearance than Mongo, giving it a lighter hue. A vicious, jagged scar ran the length of the dinosaur's face. It was missing its left eye, and its beak was pitted, like someone had slammed it directly in the face with a halberd long ago. Each one of its gleaming claws had to be ten inches long. The claws undulated up and down, almost like the raptor was drumming its fingers on a table.

This was obviously the leader. It also stood rigid, head low to the ground, mirroring Mongo.

I examined the monster.

Kiwi. Mongoliensis Pack Leader—Level 60.

They say an asteroid is what wiped out the dinosaurs on this planet.

I don't think that's true. If Kiwi and her pack of voracious, slightly insane velociraptors are even remotely like what you had roaming around way back in the late Cretaceous Period, I'm pretty sure what really happened is that these ladies simply killed everyone and everything.

This is Kiwi, the head bitch in charge of the jungle's fastest, most vicious, most clever predators: the Mongoliensis. Take a gang of women convicts from a 1970s prison movie. Combine them with a coalition of cheetahs and a shoal of hangry piranhas, and you have a vague notion of just how screwed you are.

This particular pack is comprised of only females. In fact, it appears all the dinosaurs in the area are female. That's pretty odd. Almost interesting.

And here's an even more interesting, seemingly random, but probably important fact. Dinosaur-class monsters didn't exist in the area before Scolopendra's nine-tier attack. Yet here they are. Where did they come from? If you weren't about to die screaming, it would be something you might want to look into.

Warning: This is a lizard-class mob. It will inflict 20% more damage against you thanks to your Extinction Sigil.

And yes, I know dinosaurs aren't really lizards if we're being super technical. Get over it.

All of the other Mongos ranged in level from 30 to 45. Mongo was level 33.

"Donut," I said, taking another step back, "do it. Cast *Snitch*."

"Mongo," Donut hissed, ignoring me, "come away. Come to Mommy." Mongo didn't respond. "Carl, we need to throw an invisibility potion at him."

Kiwi suddenly raised her head into the air and made a loud, terrifying barking noise. It was like a seal mixed with a monstrous amount of distortion. *Unk, unk, unk.* The ground shook with the call.

You have been Deer in the Headlight–ed! You can't move from your position for fifteen seconds!

Mongo lifted his head and made a similar noise.

Then all of the raptors started barking and howling. Still, none moved toward us. I tried to take another step back. I could move my arms and cast spells, but my legs were firmly bolted in place. *Damnit.* We were so damn close. The fronds of jungle leaves brushed against the back of my head. I could now see the twin white dots of the town guards. They were only thirty feet away, just standing there.

"Goddamnit," I cried. "Invisibility potion. Now!" I drank one down.

At that moment, Mongo and Kiwi both leaped at the same time, slamming into one another in midair like a car collision. Donut—who was still visible—pulled back like she was attempting to jump off my shoulder and into the fray. I pulled out the hobgoblin disco ball as Mongo and Kiwi curled around each other like a pair of snakes, hitting the ground and rolling.

All around us the other Mongos howled and screamed, but none moved to attack. In fact, I realized they were all starting to move away, stepping back into the jungle. They still screamed louder than ever. All around us, additional sounds rose. A flock of birds burst into the air. Monkeys I hadn't even known were there suddenly erupted above us in the canopy, their screeches and cries adding to the cacophony. The trees above us shook and a rain of little pink and red flowers fell from the air.

Only five more seconds, and then I was going to drop the disco ball, wrap Donut in my arms, and run. But just as my paralysis ended, I paused. I felt my chin drop.

Holy shit.

"Carl, Carl, what are they doing? What are they doing?"

Mongo and Kiwi were not fighting.

They were doing the opposite of fighting.

"Uh," I said, finally able to take a step back. My leg felt like it was asleep, but it let me move. I looked warily at the map. All of the other red dots had moved back, but not too far. "I think we need to give them some privacy."

"Carl, do something!" Donut exclaimed. "You! Dinosaur! Get off my baby!"

Kiwi was face down, backside up, tail to the side with Mongo mounted behind her. Mongo made a throaty gurgling noise as he slammed into her over and over.

"Oh, she's getting him off all right," I said.

"That's not funny, Carl. He's too young! We haven't even had the talk yet! She's taking advantage of him! Mongo! Mongo!"

"Donut, we gotta get out of here. She's going to attack us as soon as they're done. Mongo will be okay."

"Haven't you ever watched Animal Planet, Carl? She's going to eat his head! Mongo! Stop that this instant! Stop it now!"

Mongo lifted his head into the air and howled joyfully as he continued to jackhammer into Kiwi like a drunken sailor on his first liberty at a foreign brothel. He lifted his wings and started flapping them up and down like he did when he was a little baby. His tail swished back and forth.

"This is all your fault, Carl. Mongo! Come back! Come back to Mommy!" She moved as if to jump toward them, and I grabbed on to her.

"How is this my fault?" I asked, taking another step back.

"You're a terrible influence! He certainly didn't get this from me. You and all your constant sex talk have turned him into a pervert."

Kiwi let out a loud, satisfied hissing noise. She'd lowered her head all the way to the ground and was also flapping her arm wings. She wiggled her butt as Mongo continued to hump away. His grunts were getting faster and faster.

"She's too old and gross for him, Carl. I'm going to hit her with a magic missile."

"Look," I said. "Her dot is still red. She is going to attack us when this is done. And if she does, Mongo will defend you, and she'll probably hurt him. If we go back to the safety of town, Mongo won't be forced to fight for us."

"What if she uses her evil whore sex magic to lure him away forever? Like one of those schoolteacher ladies?"

"We'll deal with it if it happens," I said, pulling us into the fronds. I could still see the other red dots just on the other side of the clearing. They could easily catch us, but none were moving in our direction. Yet. We had to hurry.

"Mongo, come back to Mommy as soon as you're done," Donut called, defeated.

I turned and jogged back to the town's entrance, still clutching on to Donut.

"As soon as he gets back, he's going into his cage and I'm turning the no-dinosaur rule back on," Donut grumbled.

12

I PULLED DONUT INTO THE FIRST PUB WE PASSED. IT LOOKED LIKE A regular in-theme building from the outside, but inside it was some sandwich place called Eegee's. Donut was still trembling with rage and fear. I didn't bother going all the way into the personal space. The proprietor was a female Bopca named Marta. A pair of older ursine sat in the corner, both sipping on drinks in Styrofoam cups.

I put Donut down on a booth table. She looked like she was about to start hyperventilating. She removed her sunglasses, and her eyes were wide and dilated. Her entire body quaked.

"Take a deep breath," I said.

"What if he doesn't come back?" she said, her lower jaw trembling. "Carl, we need to go back out there."

"What is wrong with you?" I asked. My anger at her was starting to be replaced with worry. "If they had attacked, all three of us would be dead right now. This isn't like you. You're freaking out. Worse than usual. Have you been hit with a spell?" I quickly examined her, but if there was a debuff, it wasn't showing. That didn't necessarily mean anything. I rubbed my hands across her. "Are you hurt?"

Donut didn't answer. Her lower jaw continued to tremble.

"Look, I know you love Mongo, but you can't lose control like that."

"What if he doesn't come back?" she asked again.

"Then we'll deal with it, but something tells me he's going to be fine. I'm more worried about you."

Donut didn't talk for several moments.

"I'm really scared, Carl."

"I know you are," I said. "I am, too. It's okay to admit it. Anybody who says they're not is either crazy or they're lying."

"You don't understand. It's getting worse. Every day."

My hand was still on her back, and I started stroking her. I still didn't know what was going on. She'd seemed fine just a few minutes earlier before Mongo had run off. She'd really taken to becoming the town leader. And then suddenly she'd lost it. It didn't make sense.

"Talk to me," I said.

She looked as if she wanted to run. Like that look she got whenever somebody ran the vacuum cleaner or bathtub.

"Donut," I said, changing tactics, "it's okay. Tell me when you're ready. We'll just sit here and wait for Mongo to come back." We didn't have time for this, but I didn't know what else to do. Donut was completely useless when she got into panic mode. And worse, she was a danger to both of us. I had to figure this out.

Five full minutes passed of me just stroking her before she said anything.

"I'm supposed to pretend like I don't know. And I was doing good. But then Mongo ran off and it just came out of nowhere. Like that time Miss Beatrice got in the car accident when we were on our way back from the cat show, and I'd been asleep, and then suddenly there was this big bang, and I slammed against the side of the carrier, and even though I wasn't hurt, it really, really scared me. And when I thought Mongo was going to get eaten, it felt like that car crash all over again."

I felt a chill. "You have to pretend like you don't know what?" I asked. "What does that mean?"

"I . . . I can't." She took a breath. "Everybody always leaves me. And I don't know why. Am I really that awful?"

"Where is this coming from? That's not true at all," I said.

"Katia left us," she said. "And you're doing more and more dangerous things, and I told Mordecai it was okay. But it's not. You're going to die because you're being stupid, and you don't even care what happens to me. Mongo is going to leave for some hussy. And then . . . and then . . ."
She stopped.

"What?"

But she just shook her head. I looked at her, confused, trying to puzzle it out. Before we'd gone out there and started organizing the town guards, I'd gone into the crafting room to build a few more of the missile launchers. Donut had trained in the magic room, working on her *Laundry Day* spell. And then what?

She'd been on the social media board, reading comments.

"Did somebody say something that upset you? Somebody online?"

Her eyes started to shine, and I knew I was right. Her mouth quivered. "I . . . I . . ."

ZEV: Hey, guys!

CARL: Bad timing, Zev.

ZEV: I just wanted to quickly touch base. We rearranged the schedule a little. You'll be visiting with Odette later today. Try not to schedule a boss battle or anything during that time.

DONUT: THE TIME HAS MOVED? IS EVERYTHING OKAY? WILL YOU BE THERE?

ZEV: Yes, yes, and yes. I also wanted to remind you, Carl, that you will be receiving some extra scrutiny before you go to the trailer. So just be aware. But you'll be fine, because you're both really strong and brave. Especially you, Donut.

CARL: Okay, thank you, Zev. But we're a little busy right now, so kindly leave us be.

But the moment I sent the message, I realized that the timing was no coincidence. Zev rarely interrupted us when we were in the middle of something, especially drama. I knew Zev and Donut were somehow communicating via the social media board, but I had no idea how, and I had no way of safely asking her without putting everybody in danger.

Zev's uncharacteristic interruption was a not-so-subtle warning to drop it. I'd get a chance to ask both of them freely when we were in the production trailer.

I took a deep breath.

"Donut, I know I'm doing some dangerous stuff. That's never going to change. But I'll consult you from now on if I can. I promise. I'm not going to leave you."

"You've already said that," Donut said. She paused. "But what about the ninth floor?"

And there it was. Whatever Donut was hiding, it was only a symptom of the real problem.

Thanks to the Enchanted Crown of the Sepsis Whore, which she didn't even have anymore, Donut wouldn't be allowed to exit the ninth floor until every other member of the Blood Sultanate royal family was dead. I remembered the important part of the item's description:

> Placing this crown upon your head permanently places you within the royal line of succession for the Blood Sultanate on the ninth floor of the World Dungeon. Removing this item *will not* remove this status. Royal members of the Blood Sultanate will be required to slay the Sultan and *all* other members of the royal family before descending to the tenth floor.

That task—killing all the Nagas—was even more difficult than it appeared on the surface.

"We'll deal with it when we get there."

Donut just looked at me. We'd been here before, had this same conversation more than once, and this was always where we left it. *We'll deal with it when we get there.* But that wasn't good enough. Not anymore, and we both knew it.

That feeling, that ceaseless river within my mind, roared. *The water is running.* Something within me broke. A decision was made. I thought of my mother holding my hand as we stood at the edge of the Grand Canyon. I thought of my father in the car behind us, waiting. A tidal wave of potential energy. This was the same. This was the same exact moment. I didn't know how I knew that, but it was.

You can do that, I thought. *You can recognize these moments when they appear.*

I took both of my hands, and I cupped Donut's face. "You know how worried you are about Mongo?"

"Yes."

"That's how I feel about you."

Donut blinked. "Really? Do you really mean that?" Her voice was so full of genuine longing that it hurt my heart.

"I know I haven't said this to you directly before, and I'm sorry that I haven't. But I will not leave you behind on the ninth or any other floor. I promise you. Okay? We are a team, and nothing is going to break us up. No matter what."

"No matter what?"

"No matter what."

We held that way for several moments. Donut trembled, and I realized I was trembling, too. Anybody watching this from the outside wouldn't understand what had just happened. That was okay. Some things weren't meant for others to understand.

I watched her swallow a few times and start to compose herself. The moment had finally passed. I sighed and waited for it.

"I don't know why you're being so dramatic, Carl. We should be—"

She stopped midsentence, jumped up, and rocketed out the door. I saw the dot on the map a moment later. Mongo was out there. I got up and followed her outside. I watched as the dinosaur drunkenly stumbled past the guards. I jogged up as Donut clucked over him. "Are you okay?" Donut was asking. "What did she do to you? You don't have any weird diseases now, do you? She looked like the type of dinosaur to have weird diseases."

Mongo croaked once and then collapsed right there on the street. His health bar was still full.

Donut gasped with concern as I barked with laughter. Two funeral bells loomed over us, both looking down at the dinosaur.

I kneeled down and patted Mongo on the head. "If I still had cigarettes, I'd let you have one, buddy."

Mongo made a peeping noise.

"That's not funny, Carl," Donut said.

She pulled out the pet carrier, and Mongo didn't object as she pulled him away.

"At least their dots turned white," Donut said a moment later, looking off toward the edge of town.

I followed her gaze. A few dozen of the lady Mongos stood there at the edge of the woods, looking toward us. Kiwi stood at the center. Her lighter feathers stood out against the dark green foliage. She lifted her head to the sky and let out an *unk unk unk.*

"Her dot is red for me," I said.

"That's odd," Donut said.

I shrugged and felt myself smile. "You probably get extra points because you're her mother-in-law now."

Donut made a scoffing noise. She paused, cocking her head to the side. "Carl, there're more dinosaurs out there a little deeper in the woods. They weren't there before. But there's a really big one."

"Shit, is it getting closer?"

"No. It's just standing there. Actually, no, it turned around and is moving away. I don't know if it makes a difference, but I believe you're correct. I better turn the no-dinosaur rule back on."

"Agreed. If we have time, we'll try to figure out the dinosaur quest."

Kiwi cried out one more time and then melted back into the jungle. Soon, all the dinosaurs were gone. As they moved away, the trees rustled with their passage. I caught a glint of something in the forest, like light shining off a prism. Just as I tried to focus on the light, the day became dark, and it started to rain.

Donut jumped to my shoulder and huddled against my neck. "Carl, do you think she got pregnant?"

"Most definitely," I said.

"I'm too young and pretty to be a grandmother."

New Achievement! Double-Billed!
You are one of the first five crawlers to receive double-billing! I bet you don't know what that means. This is similar to switchovers, but this time it's on purpose. I bet that didn't help at all.
Reward: You have received a Platinum Fan Box!

"The fuck?" I muttered. I examined my view counter, and the needle was buried to the right. But it had been since Donut had run off. I was going to have to reset it. "Donut, did you just get some weird random achievement?"

"No. It's probably because you spread your tootsies funny on the moss or something." She paused. "My word. Now that you've mentioned it, my view counter *is* a bit high right now. Probably a bunch of perverts tuning in to watch Mongo get violated. Well, the show is over."

Far behind us, there was the sound of a missile shot into the air, followed by a detonation.

I cursed, took a deep breath, and patted Donut. The rain was getting heavier by the moment, and it pelted into us. "Are we good? No more panic attacks?"

"Really, Carl, I don't know what you're talking about."

"Good," I said. "Time to get back to work."

13

WE JOGGED BACK TO THE OTHER SIDE OF TOWN. IT'D BEEN SUNNY JUST a few minutes before, but now it was absolutely pouring. We found Mordecai standing near the northern gate by the bridge, peering out while flanked by two of the funeral bells. He stood underneath the bell of one of the mushrooms in an attempt to stay dry. It wasn't working.

One of the guards had shot an anti-air missile at an approaching hunter. Mordecai said it was a yenk using a levitation spell, not a mantis, so it wasn't Vrah or a member of the Hive.

"I doubt he's dead, but they knocked him out of the sky," Mordecai said. "He popped up on the other side of the river. If he's not dead, he's probably going to try to find another way around. He's a yenk, so he's probably working alone. But it's possible he's part of a bigger team."

Yenks were humanoid aliens with ridged foreheads and bony exoskeletons, almost like malnourished Klingons from *Star Trek*, only taller. Ikicha, who'd written the 11th edition of the cookbook, was one. They weren't too common of a race, but I'd seen a few here and there in audiences, especially on the Maestro's show. They were an odd species with some weird-ass reproduction method. There were three genders, and all three were required to make babies. The women and children lived in peaceful communities along with the unintelligent third gender, whatever it was called. I didn't know the details. The males were forced out once they reached maturity. The males were also known as powerful fighters. They became bounty hunters and mercenaries, but they couldn't work with other adult males of their kind, lest they fight. Like betta fish.

I knew Ikicha had been a castrated male, but he was pretty light on the details about what that meant.

"He's still out there," Donut said after a moment. "I can see his dot."

I looked, but I didn't see anything. We stood on the threshold of town, right at the edge of the bridge. Below, the river splashed with the torrential downpour. The water level had risen even though it'd only been raining for a few minutes. I thought of the naiad that had jumped out and eaten the mayor.

"Where is he?" I asked.

"I think he might be stuck in a tree," Donut said, pointing just to the right of where the covered bridge met the slope on the opposite shore. "Maybe when they shot him out of the sky, he landed there and he can't get down. Or maybe he's waiting for the rain to stop."

"Hmm," I said. "Do you think it's a trap?"

"Maybe," Mordecai said. "If it's not and he's not dead, he's probably unconscious. These guys all load themselves up with as many health potions as they can carry, so he's not just going to be sitting there injured in a tree."

"Let's find out," I said.

I cast *Ping*.

"There you are," I said. There was only one hunter in range. He was stuck in a tree all right. The moment I cast *Ping*, the tree started shaking violently as the alien tried to get away.

"He's not knocked out," Donut said. "What is he doing?"

"He must be impaled," Mordecai said.

Ping couldn't find red-tagged mobs or fellow crawlers, but it found everything else. As the map populated with multicolored dots, I saw something that made my heart skip.

"Shit," I said. "Fuck, fuck, fuck." This was a day sooner than I had hoped.

I wasn't certain what that "double-billed" achievement really meant, but I was starting to get an idea.

"What? What?" Donut asked.

"It's a trap all right, but it's not set by other hunters. Or crawlers." I focused on the small crowd of dots hidden just past the tree. It was seven white dots and then two more: white dots with red crosses within. One of the seven white dots was in the tree with the hunter. This one was long, like a snake, and it was wrapped around the hunter, keeping him in place.

Elites. The fact they weren't moving off told me everything I needed to know.

"OKAY, SO WE HAVE THE FOUR CRETIN BODYGUARDS AND THE TWO spells. My client is requesting two more items, and we'll have a deal."

"We've been more than generous," the kua-tin said. The dour Borant admin had pretended to hem and haw about giving us the four body-guards, but the moment Quasar had mentioned that *Zerzura* spell, he'd practically creamed himself. The mudskippers did not have good poker faces, which made me appreciate Zev's ability to stay in character so well. Behind him, Orren the liaison grunted with amusement from his chair. He hadn't said a word once the negotiations started.

"This second request is easy," Quasar said. "We're pretty sure you're already going to award this to them, but we want it to be a lock."

"What is it?" the nameless kua-tin asked.

Quasar gave me a little wink. This one had also been his idea. Only the third item on the negotiation list was my own, though it tied in nicely with the first and second request.

"As we all know, the sixth floor is where most of these secondary programs go to die. We also know a limited number of programs are given licenses to continue upon the collapse of the sixth floor. We want for you to extend one of those licenses to Sensation Entertainment, In-corporated, for their program *Vengeance of the Daughter.*"

Before the Borant rep could respond, Orren spoke up. "Not possible," he said. "Secondary program licenses are granted by AI decision and not until the end of the floor. And if there are multiple eligible programs, the license is granted via lottery."

"Actually, you're wrong there, buddy boy," Quasar said. "Look into subsection 674, paragraph five or six of the secondary program amend-ment. Showrunners who are running at lower-than-expected profits are allowed to give emergency use to a single program."

Orren's eyes flashed. "That's a pretty old rule," he said after a moment.

He shrugged. "They'll have to agree to it, and they'll have to pay an extra twenty percent to Borant. They might not be willing. Assuming the show survives past this current arc, there's a good chance they'll get the extension anyway."

"They've already agreed. I've already asked," Quasar said, waving his cell-phone-like device.

"Agreed," the kua-tin said. "But this one needs to be kept quiet. One mention out loud, and it's negated." This, again, was something my lawyer said the kua-tin would happily agree to. It basically guaranteed them a few extra million credits.

But more importantly, it guaranteed *Vengeance of the Daughter* the equivalent of a third season. Not all secondary programs were allowed to send their elites to the ninth floor. It was a coveted reward, and Quasar insisted Sensation Entertainment would leap at the opportunity. It would also, once again, give them an incentive to keep me alive. *Especially* if Borant agreed to my third request.

Sensation Entertainment hadn't actually agreed to anything yet. That was a bluff. Quasar attempted to contact the producers, but they'd been unavailable. He insisted they'd agree to it. And if they didn't, well . . . he'd let me know.

"You said there was one additional item you wanted," Orren said. "I just can't wait to hear what this one is."

CARL: QUASAR. TIME'S UP. I NEED TO KNOW IF YOU EVER HEARD BACK from Sensation Entertainment.

> **QUASAR: Yo, yo, yo. I'm a bit busy right now. Maybe drunk. Maybe having some alone time with the missus. You know how it goes. If you are a client, I will read this message and get back to you. If you're a bill or tax collector, fuck off. This is an automated message.**

CARL: Goddamnit, Quasar. What the fuck? I need to know.

He'd promised he'd message me if there was a deal, but last I'd heard, they were still thinking about it. If there was no deal, there was no incentive for them to keep me alive. My death would be glorious for ratings, and they'd probably get access to the ninth floor anyway. If there *was* a deal, then I was safe. From them at least.

"Two elites?" Mordecai said. "That's unexpected."

I looked at Donut. "Your choice. Stay here and continue to set up the town's defenses, or come with me. I'm the only one listed on the contract."

She returned to my shoulder. "Didn't we just have this conversation, Carl?"

I grinned. "I figured, but I also promised to give you the choice."

Donut looked up at the closest mushroom guard. "Miss Nance. I am leaving Mordecai here in charge. Now, he's not allowed to fight, but he can tell you what to do. Keep setting up the town's defenses, but if any of those bad guys attack, you first need to bring Mordecai to a safe room whether he likes it or not. Do you understand?"

Miss Nance grunted.

Donut sighed dramatically. "Also, do not let any dinosaurs into town, but if the one with the pink feathers attacks, try not to kill her. We'll have to deal with her eventually, but we simply must take care of this first."

"Be careful," Mordecai called after us. "Remember what this is. Don't put yourself in a position where it's either her or you. Just because you're both top ten doesn't mean shit to those other showrunners."

"Come on, Donut," I said as we walked out onto the bridge and left town.

"Carl, I know you promised not to get involved with any other secondary programs, but is this absolutely necessary? It seems like it's a distraction we don't need right now."

"It's necessary," I said. "After the third floor, she's going to be friendly to us. We need all the help we can get right now."

"Okay, if you say so. The last time I saw her, she put me in a coma and left me to die alone in the city at night while Mongo defended me."

"Signet," I called as we neared the edge of the bridge. "There's no need for all this hiding-in-the-bushes bullshit. We know you're there."

The tattooed, horned, almost-naked half-naiad emerged and crossed her arms as we approached.

Tsarina Signet.

I'd forgotten how disturbing her face was. Samantha the sex doll head was also a half-naiad, but Samantha looked mostly human. Sort of. She was still a decapitated love doll. Signet, however, favored the more demon-like, monstrous visage of her naiad heritage.

Tsarina Signet—Half-Naiad, Half-High-Elf Summoner. Level 60.

That was the same level she'd been before. Apparently elites didn't progress. Level 60 was still higher than my 54, but she no longer seemed so terrifying, so overwhelmingly powerful.

"Who said anything about hiding, old friend?" Signet said. She had some spell running that kept the rain off of her. The familiar tattoos swirled about her. The three-headed-ogre tattoo stopped to look upon me, curving around the side of her large breasts, and he waved.

Signet continued. "We came seeking you, but then we found others are seeking you as well. I have a few friends ranging north to keep the path clear, but one of the others managed to sneak past us. Most of the invaders are avoiding this area, but some idiots have destroyed a few of the bridges, making this town the only access point in the area to the Liana district."

A second elite appeared from the bushes. I'd been expecting this to be Grimaldi, the city boss who'd escaped the third floor. It was not. It was Apollon the Mighty, the ogre strongman who'd given me a parasite-infested ice-cream cone. I had thought he'd died on the third floor.

But no, I realized. This wasn't Apollon. It was another strongman who looked similar. This one was a level 45 ogre named Areson the Wise. But before I could fully examine him, a group of six small-sized creatures emerged, all coming to stand to glare at me.

All wore black studded leather from neck to toe. Each wore a pair of weapons over their shoulders, no two the same. They wore no helmets, but each of the male, pale-skinned warriors had red bandannas wrapped tight around their fuzzy heads, Rambo-style. All stood about three feet tall. All were wide, but not fat. More like miniature well-built football players. Stout like a row of armored barrels. Their wide-set, wide-eyed faces glared at me and Donut with mistrust. One had a genuine mullet.

Two had shaved heads. Another a mohawk. One's face was painted with camouflage.

My initial impression was that they were smaller-sized dwarves. They were too tall to be gnomes. About the right size to be a Bopca and just as hairy, but the wrong body shape. Their features were elf-like. Almost hobbit-like, really, but that wasn't quite it, either. These guys ranged in level from 48 to 53. All of them were well scarred and battle worn.

I examined the closest one. This was a bald-headed one with a flat face and big brown eyes. He had a mace and a machete crossed over his back. I realized this one was missing one of his feet, perhaps his entire leg, and a curved metallic bar sat where his boot should be, emerging out of the leather pants.

Clint Smashgrab. Level 50. Were-Kin. Light Recon Specialist.

A long time ago, Clint and his people were of a race called the Chee. They were peaceful. Carpenters, mostly. But then the High Elves wanted their land, and that was that. What happened to them next is a pretty awful story.

There are no Chee left in this realm. There are survivors of that night, when the High Elves invaded their land. But there are no Chee.

So I'm going to assume you know what a werewolf is. This isn't a werewolf. Or maybe it is. It's a were-kin. That's all you know until either he tells you what he turns into, or he shows you what he turns into, or he bites you, and you find out for yourself.

Clint and his brothers have joined forces with Tsarina Signet. They have a common enemy.

"What do you think they turn into?" Donut whispered. "Do you think it's a dog? I hope not. I don't think I can handle them turning into dogs. They're certainly hairy enough."

A seventh creature appeared, climbing out of the tree. This wasn't a snake like I originally assumed, but a massive caterpillar, about as long as Mongo with his tail. It was yellow and black and segmented and covered with long, pointy hairs, about as tall as my waist. I shivered at the sight of the thing. Its large bug head hissed at me as it scuttled behind the row of warriors. A row of six saddles sat upon the back of the caterpillar.

And tied prone across the row of saddles was the hunter. An unaffiliated level 50 yenk named Bravvo. The left side of his body was burned where he'd been hit with the missile. The skeletal creature's wide eyes looked up at me in fear. His health was almost all the way drained.

"I thought at first I could use this one for my blood sacrifice," Signet said. "But instead, I think perhaps I will allow you to choose what to do with him. He claims he was hunting you, and it is your people who knocked him from the sky, so it is your kill."

"He was hunting us, yes," I said, stepping forward.

"What would you like to do with him?" Signet asked.

"Heal him," I said.

Signet nodded thoughtfully. "You've grown in strength, Carl. But you're still soft."

"No," I said. I pulled the ring from my inventory and slipped it onto my finger. "Not anymore."

BRAVVO'S HIGHEST STAT WAS HIS DEXTERITY. KILLING HIM GAVE ME A single point.

He didn't have too much good gear on him. Hunters didn't appear to have bottomless inventories like we did, but instead used the slot system, similar to what most NPCs had, which limited what they could carry. He wore black leather enchanted boots that protected him from magical bolts, though that'd done him no good. He had thirty Good Health potions and another thirty Good Mana refills, which I hadn't seen yet. Regular mana potions completely refilled your spell points instantly. These also refilled your magic, but slowly. They added 200 mana points over the course of two minutes. I explained to Donut how these would be better in certain situations. I kept two and gave the rest to Donut.

His weapon was a magical longsword that increased his constitution by two points. It went into the sell pile. The rest of his clothes were useless, but I took them all. And then I took his naked corpse.

The only real prize was a set of nine potions of Levitation. These things weren't as good as flying potions, but they allowed you to rise up into the air for as long as your intelligence times two seconds. It wasn't clear on how high one could go or what would happen if the potion ran out before you lowered yourself. The hunter had been using one of these to scout out the city of Point Mongo when he'd caught a missile to the face.

Donut and I matter-of-factly looted the dead hunter using my new safe-looting method while Signet and the others watched us impassively. Once we finished, I stood and uselessly brushed water from my eyes. The rain continued to pelt onto us. Donut was miserable and pressed against my neck, shivering.

"Signet, darling, I will sell you my firstborn grandchild if you tell me the name of the spell that you're using to keep yourself dry," Donut said from my shoulder.

Signet chuckled softly. "It's not a spell, little one. It is a curse. Be grateful you do not have it."

"Well, you found us," I said. "I'm glad you're still okay. But we have our hands full. We have a ton of people hunting us, and this town behind us has a dinosaur problem that needs solving."

The half-naiad nodded. "It's all tied together. We can help each other."

"We are not safe here," Clint said. He had to speak loudly to be heard as the rain kept increasing in intensity. The small man looked nervously over at the slope leading down to the river. "With this rain, they will soon emerge." Behind him, the large six-seater caterpillar made a wet chittering noise.

"Come," Signet said, waving for us to follow. "Into the forest. We shall talk as we walk. I will not force your help this time, but I am hoping we can come to a mutually beneficial agreement."

That, of course, was a lie. I was contractually obligated to help her. But this was a semi-scripted drama, and I couldn't exactly say that out loud. I briefly wondered what would happen if I wedged one of my new sticky bombs onto her back and ran away. Probably nothing good.

"Where did the ogre guy go?" I asked, looking about. The other elite had disappeared while we were looting the body.

"There are invaders on the trail. The city of Zockau is vomiting them out. Areson is helping to keep us safe. He will meet back up with us later."

I paused, looking north. "We should also assist," I finally said. The Ring of Divine Suffering hung heavy on my finger. Its warmth was even more prominent in the rain. After one more kill, it would start giving me two stat points instead of one.

"We are already risking too much just to collect you," Clint said as he climbed onto the back of the caterpillar. The five other warriors leaped up upon the saddles, one by one until all six sat in a row, making them look like they were upon an amusement park ride. The fuzzy yellow caterpillar made a chittering noise.

DONUT: CARL, THAT CREATURE LOOKS LIKE A YELLOW TOILET
BRUSH. SHE'S GOING TO SCARE MONGO.
CARL: Leave Mongo in his cage for now. He needs his rest anyway.

I examined the long, fuzzy caterpillar.

Nadine—Bearded Sage Caterpillar. Level 50.
    The Bearded Sage Caterpillar is an enormous, furry, tree-dwelling insect who is normally content to sit atop trees and munch on leaves until the day they get the notion to form a chrysalis and turn into something else equally innocuous. They're super fuzzy and kinda cute as long as you don't look too hard at their faces. Have you ever seen a super close-up of a bug's face? Seriously, what the fuck? These things are mostly harmless, even after they turn into moths.
    Anyway, Nadine wasn't born as a caterpillar. A Bearded Sage isn't normally intelligent, despite their name. Not that Nadine was Miss Science Fair before the High Elf attack, but she was a Chee. A teacher, actually, in charge of the Chee day school. She also used to be an actress, but don't ask her about that. If she was still able to talk, she'd deny it.

DONUT: DO YOU THINK THESE OTHER GUYS ALL TURN INTO
CATERPILLARS, TOO? BECAUSE THAT'S KINDA WEIRD.
CARL: I don't know. But be careful. Remember what happened to
Miriam Dom. They turned her into a vampire because it was
funny. Don't let any of them bite you.

Nadine the caterpillar zoomed ahead, undulating as she disappeared into the jungle. The six riders moved up and down, like they were doing the wave. Signet casually strolled behind. I kept pace with her with Donut on my shoulder. I sent another note to Quasar, but he still wasn't answering.

"When it rains really hard, the Confederates sometimes range forth from the river," Signet said as we moved from the waterway. We were moving back north. Away from the main road and the river, but closer to Zockau.

"Your mother is a naiad, and your father is the high elf king, right?" I asked, trying to remember the full story. I knew because she'd been a bastard, she'd been rejected by both families and had been forced to flee to the Over City, where she'd joined the circus. She'd lived there until Scolopendra's disaster had upended everything.

"Correct, but King Finian, my father, is no longer with us. His daughter, my half sister, now rules the high elves. Imogen."

"And your mother?" I asked.

Signet's mouth drew tight. On her shoulder, the hammerhead shark tattoo shook its giant head and swam away.

"She is long dead," Signet said after a moment. "She was a princess. A true princess. She protected me and loved me and taught me the meaning of grace and magic and the importance of family, no matter how small that family may be. Then came the revolution, and that was that. My family's palace is now occupied by the simpering dukes of the Confederacy. Nothing has changed since. I was cast out of the river and exiled from the Hunting Grounds by my father's people. I was still a child. Gods, it was so long ago."

"My father exiled me, too," Donut said. "He later got his tail caught in a car door, which resulted in him being disqualified from future showings. Serves him right."

Signet nodded. "If you help me complete my task, I will assist in helping you reclaim your own crown if you wish."

"Oh, I already reclaimed my crown from him," Donut said. She swished her wet tail against my neck. "I conquered Cleveland and secured the GC title. Something he could only dream of."

"Good for you," Signet said.

The jungle got more and more dense as we walked. It appeared that Nadine the caterpillar was chewing a trail for us. I remembered the advice from the bush elf when I first got here. *Stay on the paths.* The white dots of non-hostile creatures surrounded us, most of them moving away as we approached. A group of red dots appeared in the distance but then spread away.

The rain still found its way to us, despite the heavy coverage of the undergrowth. It felt as if we were constantly walking through waterfalls and showers. Dozens of small rivers formed on the jungle floor, draining away toward the river. I sank to my ankles in the mud. This far from the road, it was unlikely we'd come across traps, but I kept a wary eye out.

"What are we doing here, Signet?" I finally asked. "Why did you come and find me?"

"I am recruiting a team, and I am requesting your help. You are the last piece."

"What about me?" Donut asked.

"You both are the last pieces," she said.

"Okay," I began. "But the last time you recruited me, you were actually planning on sacrificing me."

"Not at the end," she said defensively. "Not once I realized how strong you were."

"What happened that night," I asked, "after I left the circus? We went by the next day, and the tents and everything were gone. Everybody was gone."

Signet nodded sadly. "Grimaldi killed the parasites, and he set our family free. It was like when you freed Heather the bear. All the clowns and lemurs and other performers simply crumbled away, finally free. All but Grimaldi himself, whom I took with me."

"So he is still alive?" I asked. "Has he turned back into a dwarf?"

"No," she said after a moment. "He . . . His story in this is mostly done. I am gathering people to me for a different reason."

"Who is that other guy, then? The strongman who was just here? Wasn't he a part of the circus?"

"Yes," Signet said, "but he was here in the Hunting Grounds when the attack occurred. Only his brother Apollon was in the Over City. Apollon is gone, but Areson lives. They have another brother, Herman the Fleet, who was in Larracos. We don't yet know his fate."

I exchanged a look with Donut.

Ahead, one of the warrior guys shouted, and the caterpillar rushed off.

"What's the story with those guys?" I asked. "I can tell they're were-creatures, but I can't tell what they are. Do they all turn into caterpillars?"

"No," she said. "All six are the same, but they are not caterpillars. They're were-castors."

"Were-what?" I asked. "Caster? Like magicians?"

"No, not caster. Were-cas*tors*."

"What the hell is that?"

"It's a small creature. A type of rodent. It's not important. Their people were all magically transformed by then Princess Imogen. This was long ago, even before Scolopendra's attack. Back then, my father still sat upon the throne, and Imogen was his right hand. His Sorcerer General. They attacked the Chee and stole their land. My sister cast the *Transfiguration* and then sent the cleansers in to mop them up. Only a few escaped. These warriors were children then. Nadine was their instructor. Their teacher. She was transformed into the caterpillar. The schoolchildren were all turned into different creatures, but these six young boys were all turned into the same thing. They have spent every moment since then running and fighting for their lives. The Chee were peaceful people, but these six have had a very hard life, and they have spent every moment of their lives in a constant state of struggle. They are an elite fighting force."

"Okay. So lay it on me. Why are you gathering people?"

Ahead, the bushes rustled again, and the six dots of the were-warriors spread away from the caterpillar, chasing after something unseen.

Signet cocked her head to the side, as if listening. A jellyfish tattoo on her shoulder flowed across her neck. In the distance, some creature cried out in pain. She relaxed.

"There are two great cancers in this once-beautiful, once-sacred land," she said, "and with every breath left in me, I will cut both of them free. The Confederacy and the high elves."

"So you want revenge against those who killed your mom, and then you want to take out the high elves, too? Is that it?"

Signet grinned without the humor reaching her eyes. "Close enough."

15

DONUT: CARL, WHAT KIND OF BORING, COOKIE-CUTTER STORY HAVE YOU GOTTEN US INVOLVED IN? IF I AM GOING TO BE PART OF A DRAMA WHERE WE'RE NOTHING BUT THE GUEST STARS, I CERTAINLY HOPE IT'S SOMETHING MORE INTERESTING THAN A SIMPLE, FANTASY-BASED RE-VENGE STORY. I MEAN, REALLY. THIS SOUNDS LIKE SOMETHING THE CW NETWORK WOULD CANCEL AFTER THE FIRST SEASON. AT LEAST THE CIRCUS STORYLINE WAS INTERESTING.

> CARL: We just have to get through this, and we can get back to work. I'm hoping to turn it to our advantage. But I don't know yet how hard it's going to be. I still haven't heard back from my lawyer.

The rain had finally started to ease, but the jungle foliage dripped all around us. The air was so humid, it was getting hard to breathe. Bugs were everywhere, and some of them were red-tagged mobs. My feet stuck in the mud with each step. We were moving northeast through the jungle, skirting the edge of the river by about a mile. We were still on the city side of the river, and I occasionally saw remnants of buildings buried in the foliage. The ruins had been completely covered by the jungle.

Donut continued to complain as I stopped to pick a group of mushrooms that I recognized from Mordecai's list. Each one made a crying noise as I pulled it from the ground, and I received a small amount of experience each time I picked one.

DONUT: ZEV, HOW ARE THE RATINGS ON THIS SHOW ANYWAY?
ZEV: They're . . . okay.

DONUT: I KNEW IT! CARL, THIS IS NOT GOOD. WE SHOULD DITCH
HER AND HER WEIRD WERE-VERMIN. THIS HUMIDITY IS
TERRIBLE FOR MY COMPLEXION. THIS IS WORSE THAN THE
DESERT.

ZEV: Ratings were good on the third floor when you were involved.
They lagged a little midseason while you two were on the
fourth and fifth floors, but people really like the current arc.
People like the six warriors and their caterpillar mount. I
missed a lot of it when I was away, but I've been trying to
catch up. Fans are afraid Signet has painted herself into a
corner with this storyline and is going to rely too heavily on
something contrived to get herself out of it. People are pretty
excited about you two coming back, but some of the more
hardcore fans think you're going to mess everything up
because of all your other issues. They're afraid everything is
going to implode before there's a resolution. Or that you're
going to take the show over because you both have big
personalities.

DONUT: WELL, OF COURSE WE'RE GOING TO TAKE IT OVER.
HAVING MYSELF AND CARL ON THE PROGRAM IS THE
EQUIVALENT OF HAVING AUDREY HEPBURN AND—I DON'T
KNOW—"MACHO MAN" RANDY SAVAGE SUDDENLY SHOW UP
AS GUEST STARS ON A PUBLIC ACCESS TELEVISION SHOW.

CARL: How do you even know who that is?

DONUT: HE WAS ON AN EPISODE OF *WALKER, TEXAS RANGER*.

ZEV: I never saw that show. Only the remake.

DONUT: WE DON'T TALK ABOUT REMAKES, ZEV.

ZEV: Right. Changing subjects now. We're talking to the Sensation
people, and they're going to try to steer the narrative so
you're back in a safe room in time for Odette's show in a few
hours.

The white dot of an elite appeared on my map, and soon Areson the
ogre appeared. He now had a goddamn arrow sticking out of the side of
his head. The seven-foot-tall strongman ogre stepped into the clearing
and looked down at us. He held the corpse of a white-skinned elf slung

over his shoulder like a sack. He dumped the body at my feet. It was a hunter.

"Sorry. Tried to keep him ticker beating," the ogre said as Signet clucked over him. She made him bend over so she could yank the arrow from the side of his head.

Signet pulled on the arrow, and a spurt of blood shot out, like she'd just popped a zit. The ogre didn't seem to notice. I returned my attention to the pale elf as the ogre continued to apologize.

"Signet says you want them alive. But he started to bleat, and I had to smoosh him a little to de-bleat him. Then all the stuff came out. Sorry I deaded him."

Corpse of Hunter Arwick. Killed by Elite Areson the Wise.
The Dream.

"It's okay," I said, going to my knees to examine the dead hunter. The Dream were a powerful, galaxy-spanning group of elves who had a stake in the faction wars game of the ninth floor. I had in my inventory a photograph of the mother of the Dream's leader. Her name was Epitome Noflex, and she was a bald but strikingly beautiful creature. This hunter was equally bald. I hadn't realized how pale these guys were, even after seeing the picture. He wore a quiver full of unenchanted arrows, but there was no bow. He also wore a flowing enchanted robe that allowed him to move quickly and gave a small constitution buff.

"I do want them alive, but I want them dead more," I said.

"It is strange elf," Areson said as he rubbed the side of his head. "Very pale." He looked at his palm, which came back red. He examined the blood quizzically and then licked his hand. "Yummy."

"He *is* quite pale, isn't he?" Donut said. "His skin is the shade of Miss Beatrice's thighs in December."

"These elves are from very far away," I said. "They came in spaceships. We need to kill all of them."

He only had two items in his inventory. A single magical arrow and a piece of paper. I pulled the blast chest from my own inventory, stuck it in the elf's inventory, and transferred the two items to the chest. Then I pulled the chest free and immediately transferred it to my inventory so I could examine the items properly. Both were relatively safe to handle, and I pulled them out.

This was something I'd have to do from now on when looting hunters.

The arrow looked like just a regular arrow, but it was enchanted with a particularly nasty poison.

Arrow of Enthusiastic Double Gonorrhea.

    This is a regular arrow, but the tip is dipped in a poison that will inflict you with Enthusiastic Double Gonorrhea.

    Trust me on this. You don't want Enthusiastic Double Gonorrhea.

    It doesn't kill you, but you'll want it to. It sets your genitals aflame. Literally. And then it heals that area of your body over and over. The only way to remove the disease is to, uh, geld yourself. Or pass it on to someone else.

"Holy shit," I muttered, careful not to touch the tip as I returned it to my inventory.

The piece of paper was a kids' menu from some diner from Canada. On the back of the menu, written in what looked like colored pencils, was a crude map of the Hunting Grounds. It looked like the map was segmented into several sections, and there was writing along the edges.

"Huh," I said after a moment, trying to figure out what I was looking at.

"What is it?" Donut asked.

"I think a bunch of the hunters sat down in some safe room and then divvied up the Hunting Grounds so they wouldn't get in each other's way. Look. The Hive has the bottom left corner, and the Dream has where we are now. Their area includes all of where Point Mongo is."

The unaffiliated hunters were relegated to areas around the city of Zockau. There were multiple other groups with names such as the Crafters and the Nebular Sin Patrol. I focused on one area in the southeast, near the elf castle. Skull Empire. My heart quickened. The orcs had sent hunters here.

Excellent.

But there was more to the crude map, too.

"Hey, our names are written on here," Donut said, pointing with a paw. "He spelled my name wrong!"

Sure enough, there was a list of about thirty names. All of the top ten were on there along with several others I recognized. Each name had an arrow to a point on the map. All of the names were circled, all in different colors. Some were circled with two different colors. Both Donut and I were circled in blue and purple. If I was reading it correctly, that meant we'd been "claimed" by two different groups. The Hive and the Skull Empire.

The line from our names led to the approximate location we'd been this morning before we'd set out. *Son of a bitch.* They knew where all of us were. I focused on Prepotente and Miriam, and they were said to be near Point Mongo. Lucia Mar was not too far away, either, but on the high elf side of the river.

It appeared each group was given a hunting area, but some of the hunters also claimed specific crawlers. I wondered how that worked if we weren't in their designated areas. More importantly, I wondered how we could exploit this information.

Katia was circled by the Skull Empire. Elle was being hunted by the Crafters. Eva, I noted, was also being hunted by the Crafters. In addition to me and Donut, the Hive had also claimed Lucia Mar. The nebular group was hunting Prepotente and Miriam Dom.

The Dream only had one person on their list. The very last name. This dead hunter had circled it a bunch of times, pressing so hard that the pencil broke through the paper, and then at the bottom of the map, he'd drawn a pretty impressive likeness of their target with a big X over his goofy, smiling face.

Louis.

I sighed, remembering that moment when Louis had snatched the photograph of Epitome Noflex from my hands and then demanded that Juice Box transform into her likeness so he could bang her.

Goddamnit, Louis, I thought. That entire group: Louis and Elle and Katia and several others were all a few hundred miles away in the middle of the forest, near the edge of the Skull Empire's claimed territory, but in an area claimed by a group called the Filigree. I didn't know who that was.

"Come," Signet said. "We are close to camp."

"Our presence is a danger to you," I said out loud, looking pointedly at the sky and indicating the map. "The others know where we are because they're cheating assholes, and they're coming for us."

Signet didn't appear worried. "We can handle a few outworlders. It is not a concern."

Areson grunted. "I will squeeze all the stuff out of them, too."

I SENT OUT A GROUP MESSAGE, RELAYING EVERYTHING I COULD SEE ON the hand-drawn map, as we sat in the small clearing amongst the others. In addition to the six were-whatevers, the caterpillar, and the ogre, Signet had a group of forty bush elves, a talking tortoise named Edgar, and an eclectic group of others including dryads and monkeys and other forest creatures. The group totaled about 70 people. Most of them hovered around level 40 or so.

> LOUIS: It's not my fault they can't take a joke.
> CARL: Just be careful. Katia, you gotta watch his back. I don't
> know how many of the Dream are here, but I had the sense he
> was really over-the-top angry at Louis.
> KATIA: Wonderful. Thanks for the heads-up.
> LOUIS: I don't see why everybody is overreacting.

Three of Signet's crew were small winged pixies. All female. They all hovered there, glaring at me like pissed-off Tinker Bells. It was because of my goblin tattoo, which I'd gotten all the way on the first floor.

While I talked in the chat, Donut released Mongo, who had finally recovered from his "ordeal." He jumped about with excitement, moving to sniff at all the newcomers. The elves in particular were wary of the dinosaur, but soon everyone got used to his presence. He came to sit next to me, and he curled up, yawning big, his teeth crackling with electricity.

"It's odd seeing one of his kind on this side of the river," one of the elves said. "And one so well-behaved."

"He's a very good boy," Donut said.

"Then he's definitely not from around here," the elf said.

"No, most certainly not," Donut agreed. "We've already had a run-in with the local dinosaurs, and they are absolutely not the kind I wish to associate with."

In the center of the clearing was a small eight-foot white-barked tree with a fairy ring of white flowers circling it. All the others kept back from the tree. Actual soft grass surrounded the clearing. When I examined the tree, I could see a very slight glow of enchantment, but all the description said was: This tree is old as shit.

Signet announced we were waiting for a few more to show up, and we all sat down. I turned to say something to Donut when I received a long message.

QUASAR: So, how you doing, buddy? Sorry about the radio silence. They're moving some of the rules around, and we can't just casually chat anymore. I now have to get a court order to send you a message. You can still send me messages all you like. That's a good thing. All your constant bitching about the hunters getting outside information has caused a stir, and things are moving on that front. Anyway, regarding the program, it's kind of a good news–bad news thing. Sensation has agreed to accept Borant's offer of a ninth-floor extension, but they're being little bitches about it and want to wait a few days before actually signing anything officially. Between you, me, and this Betty giving me a rubdown right now, I'm reading between the lines here. My take is you gotta find a way to make the program more exciting, but you gotta do it in a way where the spotlight isn't throwing the star into the shadow. Don't know how you're going to wrangle that. If that spotlight on you gets a little too bright, they might decide to pull your plug, so be extra-double careful. I'm sure you've heard this a hundred times already, but nobody likes it when the guest star gets all the tail.

Regarding our other problem. One hundred fifty million credits. That's . . . Yeah, I don't know how you're gonna pull that off, cowboy. That's enough money to buy your own planet. By my count, your current outside-the-dungeon net worth is sitting at about 117 credits, and you probably already have a tax bill of 50. And even if you do gather that much money, which you won't, we have a few legal issues to deal with. Bribery is both a way of life but also a real crime out here in the real world. And while technically it's *not* a bribe, I'm not so sure the high courts will see it that way. It's not exactly something we can keep hidden, now is it? I have an idea, but it's a little . . . Never mind. I'm working on it.

Talk to you soon. Don't die on me. This is the most fun I've had since the night I graduated law school and nailed Professor Foster.

Goddamnit. Why did it always have to be so difficult?

A few more creatures, this time a pair of ursine, entered the clearing and sat down. They nodded at Signet in greeting. Signet nodded back and stood to face us all. Next to me, Donut was chatting away with Edgar the tortoise.

"Now that everyone is here, it is time. We have two tasks before us," Signet said. "It won't be easy, but if we work together, we will reach our goal."

"And what, exactly, is the goal?" I asked.

NEW QUEST. THE VENGEANCE OF THE DAUGHTER.

    Part One of Two.

    Tsarina Signet, exiled half daughter of the Naiad, has finally come home. Her kingdom, once flourishing and beautiful, has become marred by infighting and a sloppy revolution that cut off the head of the government and left the body flailing.

    Signet has returned and wishes to reclaim her mother's crown. Or at the very least, put a proper government in place. In order to do that, she must assassinate the current leaders of the Naiad Confederacy, who are holed up in their fortress at the former river palace of the Naiad, now dubbed "Fort Freedom."

Help Signet assault Fort Freedom and establish revenge against her mother's assassination.

Reward: You get to move on to part two. In addition, every survivor of the assault against the Confederacy will be 20% more willing to follow your orders. I bet that number will go up even more if you complete the second half of this quest.

PART TWO

THE VENGEANCE
OF THE DAUGHTER

16

TWO OF THE WERE-CASTORS ACCOMPANIED US ON OUR TREK BACK TO
Point Mongo. Signet also sent out more bush elves and a few others to
spread around us and to seek out any lingering hunters.

The two who accompanied us were the bald, one-legged one named
Clint, and the one with the mullet. His name was Holger. The furry
men were strangely insistent upon us returning to a safe room, and it
took me a minute to realize they'd been pushed into it by Signet, who'd
in turn been pushed into it by the showrunners. It was because we had
to go on Odette's show in a few hours.

It was a reminder—a damn important reminder—that elites weren't
nearly as autonomous as regular NPCs. They weren't controlled like
robots, but the showrunners were allowed to send suggestions to them,
which sometimes caused them to act out of character. It still wasn't clear
exactly how much control they really had.

I wondered on that as we walked back to Point Mongo. If there was
a way to make Signet and other elites self-aware, just like with regular
NPCs, and what that would mean if it happened.

Either way, these two guys, Clint and Holger, weren't elites. Just regular ol' NPCs, and they were just following Signet's orders.

"So, Holger," Donut asked as we marched. She rode upon the back
of Mongo. The rest of us walked. "Tell me about your hairstyle. What
is it called again, Carl?"

"A mullet," I said.

"Yes, that's right. Business in the front, party in the back. Tell me,
is it a cultural thing? Where I'm from, it's a cultural thing. It means
you're from a people who like to say 'Yeehaw' a lot and listen to music

about trucks and cheating girlfriends and you eat things like corn dogs and fried butter. And you like to blow things up." She looked at me. "Carl, maybe you should grow one."

"It's a sign of my dominance," Holger said proudly. This guy had two weapons crossed over his back. A sickle-shaped blade and a sharpened stick.

"It's not a sign of nothing," Clint said.

"You just feel that way because you're bald," Holger said.

"I ain't bald when I turn," Clint said. "And when you turn, you look even more like an idiot."

"Well, I like it quite a bit," Donut said. "I once knew a Maine coon who had a similar hairstyle, and it suited him perfectly. It was stunning." She looked at Clint. "But bald is beautiful, too. Or it can be. We won't talk about Sphynx cats or those weird chihuahua things. But it really suits *you*."

"Thank you, Princess," Clint said.

"Have you ever seen her do it?" Donut asked, changing the subject. "Summon her battle squad, I mean. Carl saw her do it once, but I didn't get to see it. He said all of her tattoos came to life, but they were flat."

"Just once," Clint said. "It wasn't all of them. Just the ogre and the eels."

"How did you two first become associated with her anyway?" Donut asked. "We met her when she was trying to invade a circus, and she gave Carl an erection so bad, he had to break his finger to make it go away. How about you?"

Holger grunted with amusement. "She does that. We have known her since we were kits. She lived in the village with us after she was cursed. One of the village elders introduced her to Grimaldi, and she left with him. Soon after, that bitch Imogen came to the village and attacked and killed almost all of us. A few years after that, when Scolopendra attacked, those of us who'd survived Imogen's attack were mostly unaffected by the demon's cloud."

"Really?" I asked. "Do you know why not?"

Holger shrugged. "Dunno. Maybe it's because one of the attacks that hit the area was the *Transfiguration* spell. It was the exact same spell Imogen used on our village. Not sure though because there was other stuff in the cloud. Spores. A rage spell. All sorts of nasty stuff. I remember that day, and I got really sick, but everything was fine after. But the city on the other side of the river was devastated. Most of the animals were transformed or killed. We all almost starved. Miss Nadine saved us."

"Huh," I said. "That's really interesting."

"It wasn't too interesting to me. We'd already been kicked in the nads a bunch o' times. And this was another kick. A big one. 'Bout time we start kicking back."

"What about the high elves?" I asked. "How did they do during Scolopendra's attack?"

Clint grunted. "Ain't your mum ever tell you the story? Read you the poem? *The high elves cowered, deep in their castle, protected by what they took.* The elves came out of it smelling like water lilies. The bush elves were devastated, but the high elves had some magic that protected them. Something they'd stolen. Some say the bastards knew it was coming. Some say the whole thing was their fault in the first place. I wouldn't be surprised."

"How was it their fault?" I'd heard something different from the cookbook. The Semeru dwarves on the ninth floor had dug their city too deep. It was a reverse version of the Tower of Babel story. It was that story that had given me the idea to fill it with water in the first place.

Clint shook his head. "Rumor has it the elves went down there once. Back when she was still asleep. That's when they collected all their soul gems for their magic. But the worm started to wake up, so they ran. But before they left, they stole something else. An item that protected them from Scolopendra's multi-attack. It saved all of them. The royal court at least. Everybody in the castle."

"Well, *I* heard," Holger added, "that bitch Imogen herself tried to cast her *Transfiguration* spell on the giant centipede, and it didn't work. But that was why it was one of the spells in the nine-tier attack. Scolopendra was just firing back everything that had been fired at her over the years, only it was all at once. Like a *Damage Reflect*, but one that took a long time to get ready."

Clint turned on the other were-castor. "It couldn't have been Imogen, ya turd burger. Them elves have had soul crystals since before any of us been born. Imogen is old, but she ain't that old. She's the same age as the Tsarina."

"Well, maybe she went down again later," Holger said. "And don't call me a turd burger. I'll tell Miss Nadine."

"That ain't make no sense," Clint said. "Went down later? My gods, you're so stupid."

"Your face is stupid," Holger said.

"Well, your hair is stupid."

"At least I got hair, baldy. And two legs."

"Really?" I said. "Can you two not—"

Clint screamed and tackled the other NPC. The two started beating the shit out of each other while rolling through the underbrush. In moments, they were covered in mud and leaves. Birds scattered away. Mongo started bouncing up and down with excitement.

"This is just like you and your Monobrow Sam friend," Donut said, watching the two men fight with an odd fascination. They were both screaming at the tops of their lungs and hitting each other with closed fists. The anger and violence were sudden and chaotic. At least neither had pulled a weapon.

"We insulted each other, but we were always joking," I said, looking down at the two small men. "We never actually hit each other. And we only did it while we were playing video games."

"You weren't serious?" Donut asked. "Are you certain? You two got quite brutal with each other. He used to call you a complete wuss and talked about how you were his bitch. Honestly, I was beginning to think maybe you two had spent time in prison together or something. Girls never insult each other like that."

"Girls are worse than boys, but they usually don't do it to your face. And you insult me all the time, Donut."

"I'm not insulting you, Carl. It's called constructive criticism. It's different."

Clint had gotten the upper hand and was now on top of Holger, pounding his face in. A health bar had finally appeared over both of them. Both bars were still in the green, but he was starting to do some real damage. I stepped in and pulled him back.

"That's enough," I said, trying to pull Clint off of Holger. They continued to fight. Clint had a fistful of mullet, and when I pulled him away, he dragged the other man with him. Holger screamed in outrage, and he gnashed his enormous front teeth while Clint punched him over and over with his free fist.

"Stop. Jesus," I said, dropping them both and backing away. I finally remembered that a bite from these guys could possibly turn me into one of them, and that was not something I wanted to deal with.

"Mobs coming," Donut said. "Coming in fast."

Without even a hesitation, both men jumped to their feet and pulled their weapons. Their reaction was so lightning quick, it was almost like they'd been practicing this exact move. They moved back-to-back and took a protective stance in front of us on the trail. Clint held a mace, and Holger held a sickle sword. They both started turning in a circle.

"Where?" Holger asked. His face was starting to puff up from the beating.

"I feel 'em," Clint said, pointing down the trail with his mace. "Invisible. Coming in hot. On the ground."

"It's more of those weasels from before, I think," Donut said. "The ones that paralyzed Carl."

"Yup," Clint said. "Them is everywhere around here. Hunt in packs. Sometimes they're under control of one of those outworlders. Sometimes they're just wild. Elves use 'em, too. Easy to kill if you know they're coming. We got this."

"I'll help!" Donut said, and she started to sing.

———

"HERE'S THE THING, PRINCESS," HOLGER WAS SAYING TO THE POUTING Donut as we approached the bridge to Point Mongo. The small man's face was so swollen, it was hard to understand him. He acted as if the fight with his fellow were-castor hadn't occurred. "You can't sing well. You ain't in tune. I mean no offense. There's no shame in it. You need lessons. That's all. Or magic that'll help you along. It's as simple as that."

Donut sniffed. "It's hard to sing proper with all that disgusting grunting and stabbing and screeching going on around me. Besides, Mongo and Carl think I'm an excellent singer."

"They think that because they're your mates. It's okay. There's probably a bards' guild in that town of yours that'll give you some tips. It's not a big deal with the easy spells. They just fail. But if you're trying to do something big, it becomes dangerous to try it if you're not in key. What were you trying to cast anyway?"

"*Standing Ovation*," Donut said. "It would've given you a dexterity boost for the fight."

"That's a good one to practice on," Holger agreed. "But maybe not practice while we're getting our faces chomped on by murder weasels. We're gonna stay in town with you two until the assault tomorrow night. We'll help you find someone to help you practice. Won't we, Clint?"

"Sure we will," Clint said cheerfully. He, too, pretended like they hadn't just beaten the crap out of each other. Or that either of them had been chewed on by dozens of weasels.

The fight had gone quickly. The weasels were wild, not affiliated with either a hunter or a high elf. Neither Clint nor Holger cast any spells, but the two little men moved with surprising speed, and despite the weasels' invisibility, they could hunt by sound and smell. The little men were quick and vicious fighters, and I imagined when it was all six of them together, they would be almost unstoppable. Plus it turned out they were immune to the paralysis effect. They fought with their weapons and their teeth, and they did the lion's share of the work in the quick, brutal fight.

Unlike last time, the night weasels attacked all together. They moved in from three sides at once, screaming, which was especially terrifying because I couldn't see them. I dropped a smoke curtain. Donut jumped off Mongo, and after slamming a pair with magic missiles, she started her ill-fated attempt at singing. I could only see the weasels after they took some damage, but the two were-castors tore through the invaders with terrifying speed. I soon had multiple visible targets. I managed to snap kick a few of them away and then crush one under my foot against a tree. I cast *Fear* and then nailed one with a banger sphere.

Mongo had also fought well, pouncing and snatching up the weasels with enthusiasm. He'd activated his Earthquake attack—something he rarely used—which had given damage to all the weasels on the ground and turned them visible.

The fight had ended quickly after that. The weasels had mostly fo-cused on Holger and Clint, and they were the only ones to have taken damage. Their health had barely gone down despite multiple bites.

I was starting to suspect that the two creatures had extremely high constitution scores. That plus a special ability that drew the aggro of mobs.

We approached Point Mongo without seeing anything else. Mordecai had been busy. A pair of mushroom guards now stood at both ends of the bridge. I also noticed the wide arc of alarm traps that had been spread out randomly in front of the bridge, designed to only be triggered by pet-class mobs and hunters. He'd also placed alarms along the slopes on both sides of the river, adding naiad creatures to the trigger.

Donut had to do a bit of talking to get the guards to allow Clint and Holger in. We received a ping from Zev that we had fifteen minutes to get to a safe room.

I was about to respond when the notification came. Both Donut and I stopped dead on the bridge.

Admin Notice. Congratulations, Crawler. You have received your third and final sponsor!

Viewers watching your feed will now see advertisements pro-duced by all three of your sponsors.

Sponsor's Name: The Apothecary.

Additional details available in the Sponsorship Tab of your in-terface.

"Carl, Carl, I got another sponsor!" Donut said. "Someone named the Apothecary!"

"Yeah, that's who I got, too," I said. "They must've spent a lot of money to get both of us."

"Hey," Donut said after a moment, "they sponsored Prepotente and Miriam Dom and Lucia Mar and Katia and both of those two-headed guys, too! And Elle and Imani, too!"

"Interesting," I said, trying to parse the information. I had a pretty good idea who this was. I'd only seen the term "the Apothecary" once before. It'd been during a mob description back on the fourth floor.

Krakaren. The *real* Krakaren, not the weird caricature version they had in the dungeon. But the collective mind that was slowly making her way across the universe. I had no idea what she really looked like, but I doubted she was an octopus thing. It was rumored she was involved with the company that ran the tunneling system, which was owned and operated by the Plenty, who were goat people. If this Apothecary collective was the Plenty's silent partner, it meant they likely had a bottomless reserve of money.

The fact they'd gone through and sponsored most of the top ten was more than likely some bullshit political posturing that had nothing to do with us. I sighed.

DONUT: I DON'T LIKE SHARING A SPONSOR WITH ALL THE OTHER TOP 10S! IT'S NOT FAIR! THEY'RE NOT GOING TO HAVE ENOUGH MONEY TO GIVE US ALL PRIZES.

CARL: Maybe. Maybe not. You never know what's going to happen. I never thought I'd get anything from that "pacifist" group, and they sent me some great stuff.

DONUT: YOUR LAST SPONSOR GAVE YOU A VEGETABLE.

17

WE SET THE TWO WERE-CASTORS UP WITH ROOMS AT THE INN, AND WE
moved to the safe room. We entered, but nobody else was there except
for Mordecai and the two cretin bodyguards. Mordecai was in his room,
and he came out wearing what looked like earmuffs over his already-
fuzzy ears and a pissed-off expression.

"Thank the gods," Mordecai said. "You two need to go shut her up
before Bomo or the Sledge pound her to death. Louis, Firas, and Katia
had to leave. Your friend Bautista was in here, too."

"What's going on?" I asked.

"Carl! Are you home! Carl! Come here this instant!" came the high-
pitched, screeching voice. It was supernaturally loud, coming all the way
from the training room.

Samantha.

"Oh, yes. That's right. I forgot to tell you," Donut said.

"Forgot to tell me what?" I asked.

"So, I may have accidentally told Samantha that we're talking to Signet. I didn't know that was going to freak her out. I had to mute her
ability to chat. She went crazy when I told her, and I don't know why.
It's quite embarrassing, really. Have you noticed how annoying she is in
the chat with the way she talks?"

"Jesus," I said. "What does she want?"

Samantha continued to screech. "Carl! Carl, come here!"

The cleaner bot beeped mournfully at me, as if even it was irritated
at the noise.

"She wants you to take her to this Signet woman," Mordecai said.
"She was in the middle of telling me the recipe for a potion I've been

chasing for a very long time when Donut told her that you two were with the elite. She's been like this ever since. I had Bomo shut her mouth all the way, but she's figured out how to roll around a little and move her mouth back open. I suggest we use your duct tape."

"Well, we don't have time to deal with her right now. We're about to go on Odette's show."

Mordecai just looked at me.

"Hey, you're the one that said we should keep her," I added.

Samantha let out a series of shrieks.

I groaned. "I'll go talk to her really quick."

Donut looked up at the Sledge. A brush appeared in front of her. "Sledgie, be a dear and brush me."

The rock monster rumbled happily and moved to pick up the brush while I made my way to the training room.

Samantha—the reanimated severed sex doll head—sat on the floor in the middle of the training room, face down, screaming. She stopped the moment I entered. The head rolled toward me, stopping at my feet, looking up at me.

"What the hell?" I asked. "When did you learn how to do that?"

"Take me to her. To Tsarina Signet. She's the granddaughter of Princess Yungsten of the Naiad, which makes her my third cousin thrice removed, and she has the ability to give me back my body. So take me to her, or I will kill your mother."

I kneeled down and picked up the latex-like head by her white hair. I set it straight on the ground. "How is she your third cousin? I thought you were a god. She's not."

"Well, it's really by marriage if you're being super technical, but her great-grandfather was Tsar Guggenheim, who was married to—"

"You know what? Never mind. Donut and I are going to go see Signet again tomorrow night when we assault the naiad castle. I'll bring you if you promise to stop screeching. Okay? One squeal, though, and the deal is off."

I'd already been planning on bringing her for this anyway, but I wasn't about to tell her that.

"Okay, okay. Cool," she said. "I can do that. You should take me out of here more often. I'm pretty sure my bitch of a mother won't attack anymore when you do. I'll fuck up anything you want me to fight. You take me to Signet, and I'll be your ride-or-die bitch to the end."

I patted her on the head, and she growled at me and tried to bite my finger.

ZEV: Okay, guys. Transferring now. Remember, you're not going straight to the trailer. There's a security checkpoint first. It should go quickly.

"Shit," I muttered. I'd forgotten about that.

Donut sat next to me. She seemed strangely nervous. She'd already put Mongo away, which was unusual for her. She looked at me like she was about to say something but changed her mind.

Entering Security Checkpoint.

We flashed, and we appeared someplace I'd never been before. All of our menus snapped away. A warning appeared on my interface, but it came and went so quickly, I couldn't read it.

Donut yowled. We both fell sideways, hitting a wall made of glass. But when we hit, it was in slow motion. It still hurt, and I wasn't so sure it was sideways anymore. My head spun. I suddenly felt sick, like I was falling. As we bumped into the sidewall or floor or whatever it was, I caught sight of something I never thought I'd see. My breath caught in my throat as I looked straight down.

"Holy shit," I gasped.

Earth. It filled the view, though it was starting to pull away. It took me a breathless moment to orient myself. I could see the Indian Ocean spread out below us, the edge of Madagascar coming into view from the top. The skies were mostly clear of clouds. The whole world was turned 90 degrees from the way I was used to looking at it.

Our change of scenery was so sudden, so unexpected I felt tears come to my eyes. I immediately thought of Coolie, who'd written the 19th edition of the cookbook. This had been his last view, but of his own home planet. He'd died after a failed assassination attempt on a pair of admins.

We weren't in zero-g, but it was damn close. The ship's rotation made it so the clear sidewall was the floor, but because of physics I would never understand, the amount of gravity we felt was very slight.

Donut scrabbled with her legs. "Carl, Carl, I don't like this. I'm going to—"

She horked her tuna lunch right in my direction. The vomit seemed to spread out in a cloud in slow motion before angling down and splattering against our feet.

"She didn't warn us that we'd be in space," Donut said.

The room itself was completely featureless. It was just a straight chamber with a glass floor and ceilings made of a strange, almost-rusted-looking metal. We were the only ones here. There were words on one of the walls, but I didn't recognize the script and couldn't read it.

"Hello?" I called.

"It smells like rotten tuna in here," Donut said. "I'm glad I put Mongo away. He would hate this."

A pair of gnolls entered the room from above, dropping in feetfirst. They came through a hatch I hadn't seen. No tooltips popped up. They dropped in like commandos doing a raid.

These were shade gnolls. The kind that looked like hyenas. The same type of creature as Growler Gary, the poor NPC I'd been forced to kill a dozen times over on the fourth floor. Both of these guys were armored in plastic-like body armor with rank insignias on their chests. The armor covered every inch of them except their heads. They both wore what looked like pulse rifles over their shoulders. Each carried a scanner on their wrists, like oversized watches.

These were the Shade Gnoll Riot Forces. Real ones. Mercenaries.

They landed heavily on either side of us. Their heavy boots made a clicking noise when they hit the glass, one of them landing directly into the pile of Donut's vomit.

"Don't move," the other one said, running the scanner over me. "Are you holding any explosives?"

"If I was, you'd know by now," I said.

The gnoll grunted with amusement. He proceeded to roughly pat me down. He had something odd tied to his waist dangling down. They were large old-school diver's flippers. The other guy had the same.

"Is this really necessary?" I asked. "Don't you have some special AI scanner that can see I'm not carrying anything?"

The gnoll didn't answer. Behind me, the other gnoll was bent over Donut doing the same. He clutched on to Donut's collar charm and examined it closely.

"It used to be a butterfly, but now it's this ugly thing," Donut said. "Ghastly, I know." The gnoll let it go and stood.

"They're clear," he said. The gnoll who'd patted me down nodded and jumped up, flying higher than I expected, expertly moving through the hatch in the ceiling. The second gnoll appeared to scratch Donut under the chin and then he, too, disappeared above.

"Did you just let that dog guy scratch your chin?" I asked.

Before Donut could answer, we teleported away again.

———

WE LANDED SIDEWAYS IN ODETTE'S FAMILIAR TRAILER. I HIT THE DECK with an *oof.* Donut landed on the couch, landing right between Zev and Odette. The ground roiled. There was a storm outside.

"Ow," I said, rubbing my arm, pulling myself up.

Odette was in her legless-human form floating an inch off the couch cushion atop her circular wheelchair thing. Zev wasn't wearing her usual diving suit. Just a simple rebreather around her throat. It was the first time I'd seen her outside the thing. I was stricken at how thin she looked compared to all the other kua-tin I'd seen. But I was more surprised at the appearance of the talk show host in the greenroom.

"Odette," I said, surprised.

Donut scrambled to her feet, and I clearly saw her tail move through Odette, indicating she was, indeed, a holo. Zev was really here. The couch was already soaked with the mist from her rebreather. She pulled herself off the couch and onto the floor as Donut jumped down beside her. Donut lowered her head and pushed it against the small fish woman in greeting.

"So, Odette is here," Zev said after a moment, stating the obvious. "Unexpected. But here she is."

"Hello, Carl," Odette said. "We don't have much time. We're going on in a few minutes, and I still need to get into costume. But we need to discuss something important. It's regarding your ex-girlfriend."

Donut made a hacking noise, and I was momentarily distracted. I thought she was going to puke again, this time right on Zev.

"Wait, what?" I asked, my brain catching up with what Odette had said. "Are you talking about Beatrice?" I felt a chill. "What about her?"

"Miss Beatrice?" Donut asked, looking up. "Do you know something about Miss Beatrice?" She looked at Zev. "What is she talking about, Zev?"

"Odette just gave me some information," Zev said. "*Unexpected* information. When she told me what she wanted to tell you, we discussed it, and we both decided it best we get this out of the way as quickly as possible." She paused. "It's safe to talk in here"—she looked at Donut and then at me—"about this subject."

It was like Odette had just tossed a grenade into the room, and now all we could do was wait for it to explode.

I took a deep breath. "Okay, Odette. What is it you need to say?"

"Beatrice is alive."

18

"BULLSHIT," I SAID AS DONUT GASPED.

"It's true. She survived the initial collection. She was being hunted by bounty hunters who were going to illegally sell her to Borant so they could transform her and use her as a country boss. A very specific one if they found her in time. I had her removed from the planet's surface so that wouldn't happen."

I just looked at her. Holy shit.

"Miss Beatrice is alive?" Donut asked, her lower jaw quivering. She looked at Zev. "And you knew this?"

"I just found out a minute ago," Zev said.

Donut jumped to my shoulder. "How? It can't be true. Is she here?"

"Why did you take her? And why are you telling us this now, Odette?" I asked. I reached up and put my hand on Donut. She leaned against my touch for support.

"I *wasn't* going to tell you," Odette said. "Not until you were free. But present circumstances have forced my hand. The plan was to secrete her away and keep her safe until the crawl was over. We had a security breach. It hasn't yet leaked that she's alive and off planet, but that will soon change. Another program is planning on running a story. They're going to ambush you with the information. Information stolen from *me*, and I want to make sure you have all the facts before you're confronted. And if you're amenable, we can completely head off this story-poaching bastard."

"Wait. Hold up," I said, confusion rising. "How were they going to ambush us? And you didn't answer my first question."

"Why I took her? I did it to protect my investment in you. Both of you."

"Bullshit," I said. "There has to be more to it than that."

She held out her arms. Her nails were ridiculously long. They were curled like claws. "It's true. Look, there were always only four ways this could've gone. One, she entered the dungeon. Two, she'd been in the initial collection. Three, she survived the collapse and was living on the surface. Or four, she was dead. In the first three scenarios, they would've found her and used her against you. And what would've happened next would've been cruel and awful and likely a crawl-ending event." She looked at Donut pointedly. "For one of you at least."

"But she was just living on Earth? I thought people were safe if they didn't go in the dungeon."

"Oh, Carl," Odette said. "You should know by now that's not how this works. Laws and rules and regulations don't apply when this much money is involved."

"Then why didn't you just kill her?" I demanded.

On my shoulder, Donut stiffened even further.

"Oh, believe me, the thought entered my mind," Odette said. "One day, if you survive this, we'll sit down, and I'll explain it to you. Then you'll understand."

"No," I said, anger rising. "You told me to never trust anyone until I understood their motivations. And I don't understand yours. I want to understand right now. Right fucking now."

Lexis stuck her head in the room. "Ten minutes, Odette."

Odette waved her away.

"Is she here?" Donut asked again, her voice practically a whisper. "Can I talk to her?"

Odette exhaled. "Did Mordecai ever tell you what I did to him?"

"What?" I asked. "What does that have to do with anything?"

"Everything," Odette said. She had a sudden, unexpected quaver to her voice. "Get the story from him, and maybe my actions will make sense. But we don't have time to get into it now."

Zev sighed, water splashing out from her rebreather and onto my legs. "Oh, for the sake of the gods. She's also using Bea to blackmail the Borant Corporation."

I felt myself growl. I looked at Odette, and she gave Zev an annoyed look. "How?" I asked.

"It's complicated," Zev said. "And it has nothing to do with you or her. It's actually a good thing. But we all have to pretend like it wasn't Odette who saved Bea, and that Borant did something noble. In exchange, Odette is getting a higher revenue share for the remainder of the crawl. We just signed the contract. We had to do it quickly."

"About Mordecai, my ass," I grumbled.

"The contract was an afterthought," Odette said, her voice uncharacteristically soft. "It wasn't my main motivation."

"But is she really here?" Donut asked.

"Yes. Is she?" I asked.

Odette turned to Zev. "If you're going to tell him about the contract, you might as well tell him the next part."

"There's more?" I asked, incredulous.

"It's that fan box you got," Zev said, her voice subdued. "You're not supposed to open it for a few hours, but the votes are in. Soon after you open it, you're going to be whisked away to an event. One where you'll be able to interact with fans. It's going to be just you. Not Donut. That's where they were going to confront you. It's why we're telling you this now."

"I don't understand," I said.

"Please," Donut said, her voice turning to a sob. "Please, someone answer me. Goddamnit. Carl, make them answer me."

"She's here," Odette said. "Not in person, of course. She's already off planet, on her way to the inner system. But she's standing by. I want your permission to bring her on the show."

"Go fuck yourself, Odette," I said, rage boiling over. "This is what you really wanted. This is what you wanted all along. Goddamn you." I turned to Zev. "We are not going to go out there. Fuck the consequences."

"Carl," Odette began.

"We're doing it," Donut said, interrupting. She straightened on my shoulder. "It's my decision, and I'm saying we'll do it."

"No, Donut," I said. "I'll do it alone."

"Carl. Darling," Donut said. She took a moment to compose herself.

A long moment. "You're trying to protect me. I know that. Remember what I told you before? That we need to trust each other? Well, it's time for you to trust me. Okay? It sounds like this is going to happen one way or another. At least now we have a moment to prepare." She turned to Odette. "Thank you for saving her from becoming a dungeon boss. And thank you for the warning. We'll start the program as usual, and then we'll do the reunion. That'll be all. See you on set." She turned away.

"If this ends up being some sort of trick or bullshit beyond what you say, I swear to god I will kill you myself," I said to Odette. "I don't care how long it takes, but I will get to you."

She smiled sadly. "I would expect nothing less of you, Carl." She blinked and disappeared.

"I'm sorry," Zev said. "She dropped all this on me as we started preparing for your appearance."

"You don't have to do this, Donut," I said.

"It's quite all right, Carl," Donut said. She was pretending, of course. "It's quite all right," she repeated. She jumped from my shoulder and moved to the counter and peered underneath it. She gasped. "Carl, they have treats hidden under the counter! They found the treats that come in the pink bag. I love those!"

Zev remained standing on the floor by the couch, watching Donut, a worried expression on her face. The small fish woman was trembling. I'd never seen her like this.

"This is such terrible timing," Zev said. "This shouldn't be happening now. This is too big to be happening now."

"Goddamnit," I said. "There's something else going on. Why are *you* so damn nervous?"

She turned to me and pulled her webbed hand to her lips in a *shhh* motion. She leaned in and whispered, "Donut is going to need you. Focus on that."

"Look," I began. "I'm worried that you're—"

"All you need to know is that you need to close that yap of yours right now. Please."

I was so surprised that she'd told me to shut up, that I did.

Lexis stuck her head back in the room. "Odette will record her monologue later, so you two will come on almost right away. It's not live, but we are on a tight schedule. You have two minutes before we'll call you out here."

"Okay," I said. "Donut, come here. Let's talk really quick before we go on."

19

LEXIS HAD US ALREADY SITTING ON THE COUCH WHEN THE SHOW
started. We sat two spots over, leaving an empty space between Donut
and Odette. They were going for a more serious, somber tone and not a
Jerry Springer thing like I feared. There would be no studio audience for
this segment. I assumed it was because Odette didn't want word getting
out about the interview before it aired. Mongo remained tucked away in
his carrier and wouldn't be coming out.

"Okay, here we go," Odette said. She was decked out in her bug helmet, giant breasts, and crab body. I still wasn't used to the sight of her.
She, too, seemed more nervous than usual.

My head ached. The river behind my eyes roared.

I swear to god, I thought. *If this is some bullshit trap, I will burn this goddamned production trailer to the ocean floor.*

"Princess Donut and Carl, it's great to see you," Odette said, her voice
moving to her on-camera persona. "It's been a while since we last talked."

"Hi, Odette!" Donut said, cheerful. "You look just lovely today. It's
been too long! Did you see what Carl did at the end of the last floor? He
and Katia filled that town with water!"

"Oh, we saw. I'll have Katia on in a few days to talk about it. There
is so much I'd like to talk to you about, but we can save most of it for a
later episode. Tonight we have a very special, exclusive guest joining us.
She is making her first and only appearance on a tunneled program tonight. And you guys are here because of your special connection to her.
We're going to get right to it. Watch this."

The screen appeared, and it started showing something, but we
couldn't see it.

ZEV: Sorry, guys. The censor won't let you see this. They're just
    showing scenes from the planet's surface and talking a little
    about the rules regarding humans who didn't go down into the
    dungeon. They're explaining the details on something called
    the walk-on list and the illegal practice of bounty hunters
    seeking out and finding survivors so they can sell them to the
    production. Also, I'm being called back to the office, so I won't
    be in the studio when you get out. I'll ping you later after the
    interview. Talk to you soon.

The video segment was over quickly. The whole time it aired, Odette
had her head turned to the side and was talking with someone we couldn't
see. Her voice was muted. Donut sat next to me, completely rigid. Her tail
curled forward around her body, like she was giving herself a hug.

The lights turned back up, and Odette continued. Her normal, over-
the-top personality was subdued, and she took on a more journalistic
tone while she weaved a story I knew to be utter horseshit.

"Tonight's special guest survived the initial collapse only to be kidnapped by bounty hunters intent on selling her to Borant. She was taken
off world for the exchange in a black market somewhere in the inner
system. But Borant recently reiterated their statement that they wanted
no part in the practice of kidnapping unwilling participants, and they
promptly turned the pirates over to the Syndicate. A battle ensued, resulting in the death of a pirate. But per Syndicate rules, our guest is now
off planet, and her fate is up to her. She decided to remain in Syndicate
space and is now a full citizen. Because of her close relationship to Princess Donut and Carl, she is coming to us from an undisclosed location,
and she'll remain hidden until after the crawl. In addition, before I bring
our guest on, I want everyone to know that I sat Princess Donut and
Carl down ahead of time and told them we were going to have this
guest, and I asked their permission to do this. I also asked our guest the
same question. So nobody is surprising anybody."

She paused dramatically, and her regular on-air persona started to
creep back into her voice. "That's right, everyone. We don't need any
more speculation and theories. It's Carl's former girlfriend and Donut's
original owner. Miss Beatrice!"

And then, there she was.

Thin. Long, straight hair. Freckles. Pouty lips. She'd lost weight. A lot of weight. She had a shell-shocked and hollow look to her, and she appeared as if she'd aged ten years since I'd last seen her. She wore a glittering red gown with an open back. It was a common dress style for women aliens, but it would've fit in well at a formal ball on Earth, too. It looked out of place on her. She looked back at someone we couldn't see, and she nodded, and then she hesitantly walked out into the studio. In that moment she was turned, I could see her dress scooped all the way down to her butt, exposing the top half of her ass. The poorly drawn tattoo of Princess Chonkalot, Donut's grandmother, seemed out of place on her lower back. Her white skin was shockingly pale, as if she had never seen the sun.

She wore ridiculously tall high-heel shoes. Her ever-present Aries anklet hung around her ankle.

Beatrice saw me, and her eyes went huge. She did a little gasp and ran to me, awkwardly moving like a penguin because of the shoes, trying to hug me. Her arms moved right through me, which caused her to stumble. She looked back over her shoulder again and then moved to the seat next to Donut and Odette.

"Princess?" she asked, examining Donut. "Is that you? What are you wearing?" She moved to pet the cat, and her hand, again, passed through.

Donut licked her paw, pretending. She hadn't looked up once since Bea entered. But I could feel her next to me, trembling.

You can do this, I'd said just minutes before. *Don't give them the satisfaction.*

I don't think I'm strong enough, she'd replied. *She's just an ex-girlfriend to you. But she was everything to me. My whole world.*

I know, Donut.

She was going to abandon me, Carl. I pretended not to know, but I knew. I think I even knew before. I pretended for so long, and I don't think I can pretend anymore.

"Hello, Beatrice," Odette said. "I understand you've had quite the journey."

Bea stared wide-eyed at the bug-headed Odette, not saying anything.

Donut paused her licking and said, "Honey, this is where you speak."

I tried to hide the smile creeping across my face. I couldn't.

"Holy shit," Bea said, jumping back to her feet, facing Donut, who resumed her paw licking. Bea again stumbled awkwardly on her high heels.

"It's okay, Bea. Sit," I said.

"She's talking," Bea said. "They said she'd be here, but they didn't tell me she'd be talking. Carl, what in the world is going on? Why aren't you wearing pants?"

"I really wish we had a live audience, Odette," Donut said. "I mean, really, a live audience would've loved that line."

I looked at Odette. "I thought you said she'd been briefed on all of this."

"She has," Odette said. I knew Odette well enough to hear the irritation in her voice. "Apparently it didn't take."

"Sit," I repeated.

Bea sat, her head on a swivel, looking back and forth. She looked absolutely terrified. Donut continued to play aloof.

"I understand you were kidnapped by pirates," Odette said. "And they were going to sell you."

"I, uh . . . They came into the tent while I was asleep. And when they saw me, they all started fighting. That's the last thing I remember until later. I think stuff happened, but they did something to me. Wiped my memory."

"What about the black market?" Odette asked. "Do you remember them trying to sell you? I heard there was a shoot-out."

"I . . . I do," she said. "Again, it's fuzzy. They bought me and were about to put me back in the cube, and then this guy, a small alien guy, he saw me and seemed to recognize me and started shouting. And then I got sucked back into the cube, and I was on a spaceship with all these guys with hyena faces, and now I'm here."

"That story is a little different than the official version," Odette said. "But it must have been terrifying."

"I don't know what the official version is," she said. "My memory has holes in it."

"She gets like that, sometimes," Donut said. She looked up. "Too many Dirty Shirleys."

Bea looked down at Donut, open-mouthed.

"I'm sure it'll all get sorted out," Odette said. "I'm certain the Syndicate fact finders will want to talk to you soon enough. Rest assured you did nothing wrong. And I want to be the first to congratulate you on being the Syndicate's newest full-rights citizen. Now, I wanted to ask you, what was your reaction when you first heard that Carl and Princess Donut had become top-tier crawlers?"

This went on for a few minutes. Odette asked her a few inane softball questions, but Bea didn't answer with anything other than a slack-jawed response. Odette circled back a few times to that supposed black-market exchange and the shoot-out, but Bea claimed ignorance over and over. It seemed to me that Odette was trying to poke holes into her own lie.

Finally, Odette turned to Donut.

"Princess, is there anything you'd like to say to your former owner?"

"Have a good life," Donut said. "Oh, also, if you ever get another cat, make sure you only purchase the wet food for her. And don't conspire to sell her once she gets a little older. Don't pretend to love her when you don't. Don't make her feel special when you don't really feel that way about her. That is all."

She returned to her paw licking. I continued to stroke the cat's back.

"Hmm," Odette said. "And you, Carl?"

"Got nothing," I said.

"Carl," Bea began. "Carl, are you going to be able to come to me?"

"Nope," I said. I turned to Odette. "Are we done?"

"Almost," Odette said. She was trying to hide the irritation in her voice. She asked additional leading questions, trying to coax information out of all three of us. Bea continued with the deer-in-the-headlights routine. She was obviously drugged to the gills. It reminded me of Katia's first appearance on this show. Donut continued to lick her paw, pretending not to care. I just grunted. Bea was going to burst into tears at any moment, and Odette could sense that. The host sighed and said goodbye to us.

The lights all turned on. Odette pulled off her bug helmet. She glared at me angrily for a second before breaking into a smile.

"Well played, Carl," she said. "Not quite the explosive interview I hoped for, was it? Plus the timing is terrible." She sighed. "But this was always destined to be messy. At least we scooped that Naga asshole. If he comes to you, make sure to tell him I said, 'Better luck next time.'"

Bea continued to stare at Odette. She was just now seeing the woman without her bug head. I remembered the surprise I'd felt the first time I realized Odette was human.

"I'm proud of you, Donut," I said. "You were very mature. You did it."

"Odette, darling," Donut asked. "We're not on air anymore, correct?"

"That's right," Odette said. "We're done."

Donut suddenly let out a hiss and jumped to my shoulder. "You vile, disgusting bitch," she spat at Bea, who pulled back in surprise.

"Wh . . . what?" Bea asked.

"You danced with me. You sang to me. You made me feel loved. I didn't do anything wrong, and you were going to give me away."

"What?" Bea asked again.

"I didn't do anything wrong. Nothing. You were the only person I ever knew. I was born, and you were there. You and Carl. I loved you, and you were my world. My whole world. I know you had a bunch of cats growing up, and maybe I was just nothing to you other than a way to win more ribbons than your mother, but you were the only human I ever knew, and to me, you were everything. And I was so stupid, because I thought since I loved you, that meant you loved me."

Odette muttered something under her breath.

"And you were just awful to Carl. And even though he's big and dumb, he didn't deserve that. He's not perfect, and I know he snores and has all these disgusting habits and smelly friends, but what you did to him is not okay. I know I make fun of him sometimes. I can't help it. I'm a cat. That's what I do. Plus, I mean, let's be honest here. He walks right into it most of the time. But you actually betrayed him. We don't do that to people we love. And you know what, Miss Beatrice? You don't deserve how sad I feel right now. I *still* love you. I *still* miss you, and I hate myself for it. You don't deserve to get to explain your side of the story. You lost that chance. But I'm glad you escaped. Because if the world ends and none of us survive except for you, I think that's an even more fitting fate. Because you're going to be all alone, and maybe then you'll finally understand how you made me and Carl feel."

The silence hung heavy in the air.

"You're not my person anymore," Donut added. "Carl is. He's always been."

Bea just looked at Donut, her lower jaw quivering. I recognized that look. Donut did the same thing from time to time.

I continued to stroke Donut's back.

Bea was at a complete loss for words. She looked at me. "Carl—"

"I'm glad you're okay," I said, interrupting. "Truly. I wouldn't wish our fate on anybody. Not even you. But what we're dealing with right now is so much more important, so much bigger than this drama bullshit. It's stupid that it was even a thing. I'm glad it's finally over. I think Donut said everything that needs to be said. We're done. Finally. Goodbye, Beatrice." I looked at Odette. "Get her out of here."

And just like that, she was gone. Odette turned her head, nodded, and then Bea just disappeared, leaving an empty space on the couch. Donut jumped back to the cushion, and she looked up at me, eyes shining.

"I'm glad," she said. "I'm glad we got that out of the way. I feel so much better."

"Me, too," I said. "It was always such a big distraction. But it's done."

We held like that for a moment.

"I can't imagine it's going to be that big of a news item anyway," Donut said. "Odette and Zev are right. The timing is awful."

"So it's true?" Odette asked. She sighed happily. She looked over her shoulder and gave someone I couldn't see a thumbs-up.

"What?" I asked. "What the hell are you talking about? What is going on?"

Admin Message.

    This is an automated message.

    Due to a system regency change, a conflict of interest has arisen, resulting in one of your sponsors being removed effective immediately. A special auction will ensue to replace the missing sponsor and will complete in 60 hours. All previous awarded prizes will remain.

    Sponsor Lost: The Valtay Corporation.

"The hell?" I asked.

And then came a second message in a different voice, but similar to the one when all of this started.

Please take note.

This is a planetwide message.

The Borant Corporation, not to be confused with the Borant System Government, has been declared an independent, nongovernmental entity by a Syndicate court. As a result, a previously filed court ruling was automatically executed, granting the Valtay Corporation 51% ownership of the Borant Corporation. The Borant Corporation remains in charge of this crawl, and as far as most of you are concerned, nothing will change. This is nothing more than a courtesy notice. All previous legal contracts will be honored, including indenture contracts. However, the Borant System Government no longer has any stake in either the planet, the resources, or the production of *Dungeon Crawler World: Earth*, and regency has been granted solely to the Borant *Corporation* and their new principal owners, the Valtay Corporation. If you have any questions about how that might affect any debts owed or contract obligations, legal counsel is available free* of charge to all full Syndicate citizens. Have a great day.

Odette sighed. "They didn't cancel out all the contracts. Thank the gods." She looked at me. "This is good news for Mordecai and all the other guides and tenners. Too bad it's the Valtay. You poor bastards."

"She did it," Donut whispered. "She did it."

I looked down at Donut. "What the hell? What happened? Did you have anything to do with this?"

She looked up at me. "*Viva la revolución*, Carl."

20

"SHE ALWAYS WANTED TO BE A REALITY TELEVISION STAR," DONUT
said. "It's too bad Odette is keeping her all . . . What did she say? Sequestered? Oh, well. Do you think I was too hard on her? I needed to
say it, but I'm starting to think I was too cruel. By the way, before you
ask, yes, you do snore, Carl. Or at least you used to. You don't anymore
with the new beds."

Moments after the announcement, Odette requested that we not say
anything about the interview until it aired, which would be after the
next recap episode. Not the one about to come up, but the one after that.
And then she said she'd see us upon the collapse of this floor, and disappeared, leaving us alone. Lexis poked her head into the studio and bade
us to return to the greenroom, where we'd be teleported back to the
dungeon in a few minutes.

"Donut," I whispered as we moved to the door, "what the fuck? I
don't know what you're involved in, or how, but holy shit, what the hell
just happened? Actually, don't tell me. It's too dangerous to tell me, even
here."

"It's okay," Donut said. "It's done now."

Odette's words haunted me. *Too bad it's the Valtay. You poor bastards.*

I'd known for some time that Donut and Zev had some secret system
of communication. I assumed it was via the social media board, which
was dangerous, because if that was how they were doing it, it meant it
was all out there for people to find and decode. And if this intergalactic
internet was anything like what we'd had here, someone would figure
it out.

We returned to the greenroom, my head still swimming. Lexis was leaned up against the counter, smoking one of those same vape things Quasar used. The tendrils of smoke curled about the room, catching the light in a rainbow of colors. The smoke smelled like burned candy. She held her finger in the air. "Wait for it."

"Wait for what?" I asked.

The lights flickered.

"There it is," she said, speaking rapidly. "The handoff. The system is transferring from mudskipper control to the Valtay central control. It'll take a minute or two. No sniffers will be online, so I gotta speak quickly."

"Go," I said.

"Okay, shut up and listen," Lexis said, continuing to speak hurriedly. She kept her eyes on her tablet as she talked, watching a blinking cursor. "Do *not* speak of this, as it will be construed as cheating, more so than anything else we've said to you. Queen Imogen of the High Elves is a *country* boss. She's a new character this season, and nobody has seen her yet, a sure sign that she's going to be a repurposed human. They're saving the big reveal. Obvious choice was Beatrice because of your ties with the *Vengeance of the Daughter* storyline. Don't know who it'll be now. Best guess is the elf won't appear until the Butcher's Masquerade. The top fifty crawlers will all be transferred to the party whether you like it or not. It'll be in the high elf castle. There'll be a party and contests and prizes, and you'll mingle with the remaining hunters. I don't know how that will work. The party will end with a big battle. They're setting it up to zero out the top crawlers."

"Why?" I asked, alarmed. "If the Valtay are taking over, won't they want the rest of the season to move like normal?"

"No time to fully explain. The Valtay did not win full control. They gained 51% of the Borant Corporation, but the collection action on the whole system is still in limbo. Think of the worms as the new babysitter. Or better yet, the new stepdad, and he's just as strict as the last guy, but in a different way. The Borant Corporation is still in control of the game, and they want it to run smoothly. They always did, but they were being controlled by their crazy government. The Valtay isn't going to be satisfied with this new arrangement. They are control freaks. They'll want the top ten to be crawlers of their choosing. Like a new apex predator taking over a pride. The first thing he'll do is wipe out everything and start fresh."

"But they already sponsor Carl," Donut said. "They like him."

"They sponsored Carl because they knew he was going to be a thorn in the mudskippers' side. What do you think is going to happen now?" Lexis asked.

"We'll go down the stairs early, then," I said. "We'll go down before this ball thing."

"That would be Odette's advice as well," Lexis said.

I suddenly realized that this was all coming directly from Odette, but she was filtering it through Lexis because of how dangerous this information was. If we got caught, she had plausible deniability.

"But what about everybody else?" Donut asked. "Even if Elle and Katia and all the others go down, they'll just use the next fifty top crawlers. And those guys will be even less prepared. Plus I've already started training Mongo for the beauty pageant."

"Goddamnit," I growled. She was right, of course. But a country boss? Nobody would be prepared for that.

"System will reboot in ten seconds," Lexis said, looking at her tablet. "You'll be transferred out in fifteen."

"This is most distressing," Donut grumbled. "I certainly would never have smuggled all those Valtay secret agent guys to Zev and the Borant Emancipation Front if I'd known this was going to happen."

I exchanged an incredulous look with Lexis, who stared at the cat, open-mouthed.

"*What?*" I asked just before we transferred back to the dungeon.

"GODDAMNIT, DONUT," I GROWLED. "DON'T SAY ANYTHING. DON'T SAY a word. But god-fucking-damnit."

Donut released Mongo back in the safe room, who started bouncing around happily. Donut jumped to my shoulder and butted her head against mine. I reached up to pet her.

DONUT: RELAX, CARL. EVERYTHING WILL BE OKAY. NO NEED TO
GET ALL BROODY AND WORRIED. IT'S NOT LIKE IT'LL BE ANY
BETTER OR WORSE THAN BEFORE.

I didn't know about that.

Mordecai was standing on a dented chair—the same chair he'd once tossed at a guy's head—playing with the shop interface. "Did you hear the news while you were away?"

"Yes," I said. "They said your contract is still being honored."

"We'll see," he said. "This sort of thing happens a lot, though usually not midseason. When it does, we typically get our contracts frozen as we're transferred and traded to other companies, and it takes cycles to work itself out. But there're always lawyers and rule changes and all sorts of fuckery involved." He grunted and reached up, clicking something on the 3D screen of the interface. "I'm still not clear how much has really changed. I'm looking to see if the shop system is still using kua-tin software, or if they changed to the Valtay system. It'll be a good indicator how much control the new guys have. Hmm. It looks the same as before."

"Is that good or bad?" I asked.

"It's both. They're going to keep the fantasy theme of the dungeon. Hopefully. It doesn't make sense and won't go over well with the fans if the next floor is Valtay style, which would be androids and hover cars and laser pistols and mechanical death machines. The Syndicate would never allow it, nor would the AI. It wouldn't make sense in the context of all your spells and abilities and classes." He sighed and jumped sideways, landing on the counter. "So for now, it'll be business as usual. Since the corporation itself is still in charge, you should still be dealing with Zev. How was the interview?"

"Don't ask," I said.

"How's the town?" Donut asked. "Are my mushroom guys keeping everything safe?"

"The ursine are complaining," Mordecai said, "but I think I finally got through their thick skulls that they're in danger from the hunters. We had to beat back an attack from another pair of those pale Dream elves, but they disappeared into the woods. I suspect they're all going to seek safer prey. Another day, and the town should be self-sufficient, and you can move farther south. Those two guys you brought with you from the woods are helping to build picket defenses. They've already upgraded the southern wall."

"Really?" I asked. We'd only been gone for about two hours.

"They work fast," Mordecai said. "Especially when they've turned. Also, Katia wants to talk to you. They talked Imani into being the guildmaster, and they've already purchased a space. Katia wants to borrow some money to buy something called a 'manager's headquarters,' which will allow me to keep my room when she disengages. Sort of."

"Okay," I said. I felt frazzled. Overwhelmed. I needed to sleep. My heart was still thrashing at Donut's sudden unexpected confession. I was terrified that whatever she'd done would soon come to light, and there'd be no hiding from the consequences this time.

I reached up and petted her again. I knew that whatever it was that she'd done, it'd been less about helping with some random guerrilla group and more about helping her friend. Still, how could I get mad at her? It would be hypocritical beyond belief. Especially after what had just happened with Bea.

As exhausted as I was, I knew her emotional state right now had to be much more fragile.

"Come on, Donut. Let's get sleep, reset everything, and get back out there." Donut and Mongo followed without hesitation. I passed the bubbling Emberus shrine on the way to the bedroom, and I paused long enough to add a drop of blood. I'd soon get my first boon. We entered the room and prepared to sleep for our two hours.

"You know what, Donut?" I asked as I sat down on the bed.

She just looked at me, a strange, unreadable fear in her eyes.

"You snore, too."

The eyes softened. "I have never snored once in my life, Carl. I am both a princess and a cat. It's quite literally impossible. Now quit talking nonsense and go to sleep."

21

WE AWAKENED IN TIME TO VIEW THE RECAP EPISODE, AND UPON WATCH-
ing it, I found myself wishing I'd stayed asleep. We watched as Vrah and
a unit of four other mantis creatures swooped in from the air and decapitated a group of crawlers as they rode down a heavily wooded trail
in the back of a cart. The formation of five aliens landed and approached
the crawlers, looting their bodies. The show zoomed in and showed a
rapid-fire list of all the loot they'd gained as Vrah took the heads of the
two crawlers she'd killed—both human—and she affixed them to her
carapace using some unknown method.

The rest of the scenes in the first part of the show portrayed crawlers
getting mauled to death by all sorts of jungle animals. We saw a crawler
bend over to pick up a mushroom only to get skewered by a spike that
popped out of the fungus, piercing him right in the eye. He dropped
dead, and his skin started boiling.

"That's the skewer belle," Mordecai said. "If you see one, make sure
you grab it for me. But always pick it by the stem. Don't touch the top."

"Christ, Mordecai," I said.

After that, we watched a much-abridged version of our dinosaur encounter from the night before. The show presented a few majestic slow-
motion shots of Mongo getting lucky. Donut made frustrated and
disgusted noises. The screen went black for a few minutes before the
show moved on. We watched Lucia Mar, in her beautiful-woman form,
fight a borough boss that looked like a stegosaurus. She cast her weird
Damage Reflect spell on the smaller of her two rottweilers, and when the
dinosaur crushed the dog, the damage reflected to the boss, killing it
and leaving the dog unharmed.

I exchanged a look with Donut. I knew she was thinking the same thing. If Lucia was at this party thing and didn't actually murder us all before the boss fight, she would be a great asset.

The show portrayed Lucia cackling maniacally as she pulled out the now-dead boss's eyeball with her bare hand and bit down on it like it was an apple.

"Yeah, that's normal," Donut said.

From there, we watched Elle, Katia, Bautista, Florin, and others raid a small dryad town while Louis and Firas floated above and directed the attack. They were hunting Eva. They thought she was in the town, but she'd gotten away. Eva appeared to have a special ability to avoid being magically tracked.

We then finally saw snake-headed, four-armed Eva, who'd gathered a small group of women with her. She glamoured the town's NPCs with a charm spell and talked them into attacking Katia's group when they entered, but when they actually approached, Imani cast a counterspell that removed the glamour. It showed a tree-person NPC tearfully telling Imani what Eva had done. The raid ended without violence.

This was the first time I'd seen Imani since the floor started. She looked much the same, but her ethereal wings had taken on a more solid appearance, and wisps of fire radiated from her. Her face was even more gaunt than it was before, making her look almost mummified. The white skull face paint glowed.

But the biggest change was that she could now fly. She and Elle moved together, with the rest of the team on foot coming behind Katia, Florin, and Bautista. They all worked in tandem like they'd been doing this for years. I did not see Li Jun or Li Na or Zhang, but I knew they were now working with them, too. I didn't see Chris, either. Nor the two cretin bodyguards.

I couldn't help but feel a pang of regret, of loneliness that we'd gone off on our own for this floor. But the path we were traveling was too dangerous. The others were doing important work, and our presence would be nothing but a distraction.

"I do hope they're being careful," Donut said. "Maybe later we can all work together."

"I hope so, too," I said.

The show ended, and then Katia entered the personal space by herself. She looked haggard and exhausted. "Is she done screaming now?" Katia asked, poking her head into the room. She was talking about Samantha.

"Speak of the devil," I said. "We were just talking about you."

"Hi, Katia!" Donut said. "Yes, Carl got her to shut up. But now we have to bring her adventuring with us next time we go out."

"I was watching the show in the guild. I figured it was time to come over and make the exchange and finally leave the party. We need one more purchase so Mordecai doesn't lose his space. Plus Mistress Tiatha will finally get her own as well. She's pretty excited about it."

We were interrupted by an announcement. The speaker was the same lady as always, but she was more annoyingly chipper than ever.

Hello, Crawlers.

What an interesting day! We have a bit of a long message today, so please pay careful attention.

There's a lot of rumor and speculation about what that last world announcement means for you guys, and the short answer is that it means nothing. For those of you who regularly deal with Borant administrators, some of you might find yourselves with a different representative, but for the vast majority of you, nothing has changed. The Borant Corporation is not the Borant System Government, and more importantly, it has been fully severed from silly system politics. The civil war that just erupted in our home system will have no bearing whatsoever on this production, and we look forward to working with the Valtay. This is still a kua-tin organization that is run by the same kua-tin who designed and put this season together. As some of you know, this particular crawl has been my personal life project. I have been working on it for a very, very long time, and I am going nowhere! All future floors will be the same ones they were always going to be. That is all we're going to say about the subject.

So on to the fun stuff. You've all received all three sponsors by now. We had record bidding this time around. But don't worry, the fun isn't over yet. If you find yourself with an inactive or stingy sponsor, odds are good they're holding on to sell your slot. Sponsors will be allowed to sell their sponsorship stakes starting next floor.

The hunt is on! Hunters have already claimed over 500 crawlers. But more interestingly, you guys are showing some serious spunk. We've already had a record number of hunters fall this season. Over 50 so far. So many that their families are starting to complain! Now that's showing some initiative!

Speaking of the hunters, we have good news, everybody. Because of public concern and outcry and because of a new court injunction that we fully support, we have implemented a few changes that don't affect you directly, but they will have a major impact on the hunters. Hunters may no longer communicate directly with those outside of this dungeon. Some were concerned that the hunters had an unfair advantage, and we agree! Boy, this really made some of them angry. Maybe that will teach them not to try to sue us so much!

"Excellent," I said. I held up a fist, and Donut did a paw bump. Quasar had come through. Now the playing field was much more level.

We have a few additional patch notes. The hot springs in the southwest corner of the map were found to be not as hot as they were supposed to be, and they were adjusted upward. Unfortunately, the action accidentally cooked a good number of crawlers who were in the water at the time. Sorry about that! Those of you who moved in to collect the dropped gear, please note that since this was an error on our part, the gear you obtained will be removed from your inventory immediately upon the end of this message.

In a related note, the lava tubes in that area are now also active, so keep that in mind if you want to play in that area.

The allosaurus mobs have been split into two distinct mob types to accommodate a newly generated quest. In addition, for both mob types, the strength levels have been split further by gender.

We've been forced to temporarily disable the *Fuck Those Trees in Particular* spell as it didn't work as intended on this floor.

Finally, we'd like to announce a new feature. The preparations for the Butcher's Masquerade party are well underway. Several of you have expressed concern that you don't know where you stand in the rankings. Upon the end of this message, all crawlers will now be able to see their rankings if they are in the top 1,000. If you have nothing, that means you need to stop being so boring.

That's it for now. Now get out there and kill, kill, kill!

"It looks like we're all going to that masquerade," Katia said. "I wonder if it'll be in a safe room? How are they going to keep everyone from murdering each other? Or, at the very least, keep the hunters from the crawlers?"

"I don't know," I said. "But hopefully we'll get the details as soon as possible. How are you doing, Katia? We saw the raid on the recap."

"Yeah, that just happened like an hour ago. I'm exhausted. But we'll get her. She's backed into that area they were talking about with the hot springs and lava tubes. Li Na is able to track her, and they're moving in. How was Odette's show?"

"I'll tell you about it later," I said.

DONUT: THERE WAS A SPECIAL SURPRISE GUEST! I TOLD HER OFF!

"Okay, tell me when you can. Bautista and I will be going on together in a few days. It'll be his first appearance. Donut, we managed to pool enough money for the upgrade, but we were hoping you could purchase it because you have the highest charisma of all of us. If we bring the Royal Palace into the guild now, we can go to the Bopca in the common area and purchase it together. Then you can meet everyone you haven't yet."

"Let's do it!" Donut said. "Wait. Let me take a quick shower first. Mongo, you, too." She scampered off.

"Is she okay?" Katia asked. "She seems a little . . . forced."

"She's not, but she will be," I said. "She had to do something very grown-up."

"Was it because of the dinosaur thing?"

"No," I said. "I'll . . . I'll tell you in a bit. Hey, does this new system offer a way for us to fast-travel?"

"Not yet. Supposedly teleport portals will become available in tier three, but you can't purchase those until the ninth floor."

"Okay . . ." I said, trailing off, suddenly distracted. I'd received a notification. I groaned. "Fan box time."

"Well, I'm glad I came over now, then," Katia said. "Should we wait for Donut?"

"No," I said, pulling it up. I opened the box. A plastic rectangle badge popped out, dangling from a red lanyard. The red lanyard said **Titan Entertainment** on it in Syndicate Standard. The plastic-badge thing was the size of a postcard. The back was covered in scrolling words, all advertisements. The front featured a moving image of a horned-demon thing shooting fire from its mouth. The words **SPECIAL GUEST** exploded over and over again along the edge. At the bottom was a spinning logo that said **Carl. Dungeon Crawler World: Earth.**

A timer appeared on my interface. It was at 22 hours and counting down.

I read the description.

"What the shit?" I asked. "What the ever-loving fuck?" Even with the warning from Zev, I was still surprised at the actual reward. I looked up at the ceiling and said, "Yeah, thanks, assholes."

"What? What is it?" Katia asked. I handed the badge to her, and she barked with laughter as I read the description a second time.

Congratulations, Crawler! You've received a free fan booth at CrawlCon! With thousands of physical attendees and billions of virtual visitors, *Dungeon Crawler World* fans from all corners of the galaxy gather once every other season to geek out together over all things Crawl! With special guests, panels, vendors, cosplay, and so much more, CrawlCon is the event of the galaxy!

Thanks to your fans, you've been added to the CrawlCon roster! You will attend three events!

Your presence at the con will be virtual. Please see your outreach associate for details on your schedule.

CARL: Zev. Fuck this. I'm not doing this bullshit. Fuck no. Send Donut instead.

ZEV: Carl, I am very busy right now. I'm sorry you don't like the contents of your fan box. But believe me when I say, it's in your best interests to be cooperative just this once. I'll try to talk to you more later about it. In the meantime, I've already received your schedule, and I'm sending it to you now. The conference is already underway, which is why your scheduled events are so soon. Talk to you later.

Donut would not be going with me to this. She was gonna be pissed. The new countdown timer started blinking, and I mentally clicked on it.

Your schedule for the upcoming event has been updated. You will be transferred to a production facility for each individual event, which will occur at separate times. Please be prepared.

You have been scheduled for three events. They are as follows:

Art Contest: Judge's panel. Three very special guests will pick the best drawing in the juvenile quickdraw category. Judging will be live. Judges TBA.

Panel: Crawling Through the Ages. Crawlers both new and old will lead a discussion regarding the current state of the Crawl. Discussion followed by a Q&A. Special guests TBA. Moderated by Circe Took of the Hive.

Autograph and Keepsake Session: Fan-favorite Crawler Carl of the current season will autograph merchandise, spend a few moments chatting, and pose for a static image with a limited number of fans. Enter the lottery for a chance to purchase a place in line now. Refunds guaranteed* if Carl does not survive long enough to attend.

A special limited number of duo-likeness sessions also available with Carl and the Popov brothers. Bidding is now open for VIP access.

I took a deep breath.

"This has to be a joke," Katia said, handing the badge off to Mordecai, whose eyes got huge when he examined it.

"When has it ever been a joke?" I asked.

"I haven't seen them use current crawlers for the con in over a century," Mordecai said. "I was a special guest once, but it was years after my season. Did you get your schedule yet?"

I read off what Zev sent me.

"Three events? Wow, they're going all in," Mordecai said. "All I did was the autograph session, but I only ended up signing three items."

"How is this even a thing?" I asked. "It sounds just like a comic convention from Earth."

Mordecai grunted, which came out more like a squeak in his current form. "Fan conventions have been a thing for a very long time. The first active prep teams landed on this planet in your year 1936. The first sci-fi convention was in Philadelphia in 1938. Do the math."

"How did you autograph stuff?" Katia asked just as Donut returned to the room, sparkling clean. "How can you sign something if you're not really there?"

Mongo padded behind Donut, also shining. He squawked happily.

"Autographs?" Donut asked. She eyed the badge thing sitting on the counter and jumped up. "Carl, you opened your fan box without me?"

"I just wanted to see what it was first," I said.

She examined it. She already knew that it was going to be something like this, but I could see her tail droop as the realization hit her. She looked at Mordecai. "Can I go, too?"

"Sorry, kid. It looks like this one is just Carl."

DONUT: ZEV, I WANT TO GO, TOO!

ZEV: Sorry, Donut. It's out of my hands. They're only allowing four crawlers to do this, and they've all already been chosen.

DONUT: WHO IS IT?

CARL: Again, I'm more than willing to give this to Donut.

ZEV: Not my choice. We'll talk later.

Donut grumbled something under her breath.

"Come on, Donut," Katia said. "Let's do some shopping."

Donut looked at her suspiciously. "You're going to finally leave the party for real, aren't you?"

"I am. We really need to disengage, Donut. Every time you get a quest, I get one, too, and soon, I'll be getting my own quests."

"Will I still be able to visit you?"

"Of course," Katia said. "I'll be right next door. It'll be like moving into a bigger town."

"Okay," Donut said finally.

Katia reached over and scratched Donut's head. "Okay, hang on. I'm having Imani send you an invite."

While they worked that out, I moved to the side of the counter and started to prepare a biscuit sandwich from the food box. I parked myself next to the Sledge, who sat there staring off into space. The rock monsters had finally gotten sick of the *Frogger* machine. I needed to do some work. I had a few things I needed to build for the assault on the naiad castle. And we needed to spend some time working on the local NPCs before we moved south and took over the next big town. And I still needed to visit both the Desperado Club and Club Vanquisher. I was putting off the latter because I knew it would involve a bunch of additional bullshit I didn't have time for.

> The Royal Court of Princess Donut is now a member of the guild Safehome Yolanda.
>> The controlling party for this guild is Team Meadowlark.
>> The guildmaster is crawler Imani C.
>> This Guild is now level 7.
>> There are six parties attached to this guild with a total of 63 crawlers.

The name punched me in the gut. Despite their age difference, Yolanda had been one of Imani's best friends.

To the left of the door to the outside, a new door suddenly appeared. It was labeled **Guild Common Area**.

> You have multiple upgrades available for your personal area.

"Don't place anything yet until after Katia leaves the party," Mordecai warned.

"Mongo," Donut cried, "there's a pet stable!"

A pair of barn doors appeared to the left of the new exit.

Your beds have been upgraded to the Instacot 60.

"What did I just say?" Mordecai demanded.

"Goddamnit," I grumbled. The "Instacot" was the second-best bed on the market. It refreshed us after sixty seconds of "sleep." But it also changed our Good Rest bonus to Great Rest, and it imparted a whopping 15% bonus to our stats for the day. Still, I hated the idea of it. I absolutely hated it.

A distant explosion suddenly rattled the personal space.

"What is that?" I asked. "Do you have some weird training area out there?"

"I don't think that came from the common area," Katia said.

A bang came at the door. The voice of Clint came through, muffled.

"Y'all better get your butts out here. They be attacking!"

"I DIDN'T EVEN GET TO GO SHOPPING," DONUT GRUMBLED AS WE rushed out the door back into the town of Point Mongo.

I jumped into the hallway. The pub was filled with shouting ursine. "Who?" I called. "Who's attacking? Is it dinosaurs or—" I stopped, finally seeing Clint standing there by the door, waiting for us.

"Come on, come on," he said, waving his now-webbed hand.

He'd changed. His height was the same, but the already-stocky man had grown even wider. He was covered with brown oily-looking fur, including over his formerly bald head.

He'd also turned into a goddamned beaver.

A pair of buck teeth jutted from his rodent mouth, and he now spoke with a noticeable lisp. His clothes were gone. My eyes focused on his long, flat tail. It looked like a wide black tongue.

"Carl," Donut whispered, "I didn't know a castor was actually a beaver. He's disgusting."

"I didn't know, either," I said.

"You two gonna stare at my ass, or you gonna go help us kill some elves? The idiots built some sort of magical trebuchet or catapult or something out in the middle of the woods and are using it to lob poison bombs at us." He shook his beaver head. "Poison bombs against funeral bell guards. It's like trying to attack a mongoliensis by throwing sausages at it. Idiots."

Another explosion rocked the town. This one from several streets over.

"How many are there?" I asked.

"Dunno. They're firing from really far away."

"Hmm," I said. I had a sudden idea. A ridiculous idea. "Hang on. I need to go grab something."

22

"WAIT UNTIL YOU START TO DESCEND, AND THEN CLOSE YOUR MOUTH. Don't do it too early. These missiles have a limited range."

We all ducked as a church two blocks over exploded. Smoke billowed, and the air smelled oddly humid. Green-tinted clouds hung in the air. The message **You've been poisoned! Poison negated!** kept spamming across my interface. Both Donut and I along with all the guards and both of the were-beavers were immune. Mongo was not and had to be put away. The ursine weren't safe either and were all hunkered down.

Samantha the sex doll head was also immune. In fact, as Mordecai had pointed out earlier, she was a withering spirit. She only had a single hit point, but she was pretty much indestructible. Short of dropping the head directly into a black hole, she wasn't going anywhere. That was offset by the fact she couldn't actually do anything except roll and scream.

She could bite now, too. She'd chomped pretty good on my hand when I went to fetch her. It didn't hurt, but she had enough force to actually latch on. Her fangs bent harmlessly when any pressure was applied. I could pull my hand free with a little yank.

"If they keep their pattern up, the attack after the next is going to land right in our laps," Clint said, looking up. He remained in his buck-toothed-beaver form.

I was reasonably certain there were only two or three of these elf assholes out there, but they'd somehow managed to pull a giant catapult thing out of their ass and get it set up. They were firing large rocks that emitted gas when they struck. The attacks were coming in about 90-second intervals. They walked their artillery fire across town like they were playing a giant version of the board game *Battleship*. If I wasn't so pissed off, I'd be moderately impressed at their accuracy.

"Okay, Samantha, open wide," I said.

I'd been developing a land-mine trap that included a pair of miniature seeking missiles as part of the payload. The thought was, if someone set off the land mine, a pair of crossbow-bolt-sized missiles would pop out a full second before the land mine's detonation. These two additional missiles would ignore the guy who triggered the land mine and would seek out nearby companions, thus doing more damage. They had a short range. Maybe a quarter mile, if that. But the detonation trigger was simple. A simple yank on a string.

The payload of the missiles was about the equivalent of a sixteenth of a hob-lobber. Not much, but if it detonated against someone's temple, it was still enough to blow their head off.

Now that Samantha had figured out how to open and close her own mouth, she could easily activate the missiles. All I had to do was duct-tape the missile to the side of her head, add a loop to the string, and tie it to one of her latex fangs. Thanks to the nature of her, uh, original purpose, she could open and close her mouth really wide. I looped the string under the jagged neck hole and then tied it off around one of her lower latex fangs.

These missiles were not designed to haul decapitated sex doll heads with them, but thanks to the seeking nature of the missiles, they were self-correcting. Hopefully. Actually, I had no idea if this would work. This was one of the few things I couldn't test in my workshop. I figured it was worth a try.

"*Unnngh chunga,*" Samantha said as I finished tying the trigger. She couldn't speak with her mouth all the way open.

I placed the head on the ground and examined it. She sat there, unmoving, her jaw open like she was getting a root canal. The rocket was tied to the side of her head with duct tape, wrapped around her forehead and her neck. I pulled out my xistera extension. "Be careful. Don't close your mouth until you see them or the catapult."

"Okay," Samantha said.

Click.

"Motherfuck!" I exclaimed as I jumped back. The missile went off, launching Samantha into the air like a bottle rocket. The sex doll head screamed as we scrambled away. It corkscrewed a few times and then started to circle in the air.

"At least it still works with her attached to it," Donut said, looking up.

The small missile detonated after it couldn't find a target. Samantha shrieked anew, her hair on fire as she plummeted back to the city, landing several streets over near where the last rock had hit.

"I think I'm going to use two missiles next time," I said. "The detonation wasn't too big."

"She's really not going to blow up?" Donut asked.

"That's what Mordecai says."

"If those pointy-eared bastards saw that, they'd have our location now," Clint said.

"Agreed," I said, starting to jog off toward where she landed. It wouldn't be hard to find her. Two blocks away, and I could still hear her screaming. "We need to reset our position anyway."

———

"DON'T CLOSE YOUR GODDAMN MOUTH. I ONLY HAVE A HANDFUL OF these left," I said as I duct-taped two missiles to the back of her head. We found Samantha on the street, covered with black soot and growling as she attempted to chew on the side of an ursine house. Her long bone-colored hair needed to be brushed, but there was no indication her entire head had just been on fire.

We now stood a block over in a small park. On both sides of us, buildings had been leveled by the artillery. The distinctive whine of an incoming rock whistled through the air, landing right where we'd been standing a few minutes before. The wall near the entrance of town cracked and fell in on itself. Donut growled.

I, once again, installed my xistera extension. I eyed Samantha warily as I placed her in it face down. The backs of the missiles were now pointed directly at my chest. If she set them off now, I would be crisped.

CARL: Okay, Mordecai, I'm taking the potion. I hope this shit works.

MORDECAI: It'll work. Just remember the side effects.

My intelligence was at 25, but with all the daily buffs, it sat at just over 30. The potion Mordecai had made for me was called **Major Charlie** for some inexplicable reason that even Mordecai couldn't explain. He said it was usually called "Brain Juice." It raised my intelligence by 10 points for thirty seconds. It came with a nasty side effect. After it wore off, it lowered my intelligence by 10 for five minutes.

My *Ping* spell had a reach of one kilometer plus 500 meters for every ten points of intelligence. However, environmental factors could raise and lower that effect. After I downed the potion, my *Ping* spell would now reach three full kilometers in every direction. We weren't sure how far these assholes were or if they were using some sort of camouflage, but we were hoping it was within that circle. If I could spot them, they were fucked.

I could lob Samantha 50+ kilometers, so I had to be careful with how hard I threw.

"Here we go," I said. I pulled the loaded xistera to my chest to keep it in place. The twin rockets pressed right up against me. I drank the first potion. Levitation. A slider appeared in my interface, up and down along with a 60-second countdown. *Shit,* I thought. *I did this in the wrong order.* I tried mentally touching the slider thing, and my feet rose a foot off the ground. I knew Elle had a similar thing in her interface, but she could actually move back and forth, too. I was stuck just going up and down.

"Whoa, this is weird," I said. I tapped my foot on the air, and it felt as if I was standing on glass. I rose up another five feet as I waited for my potion timer to reset. I knew the ground wasn't as solid as it felt. Mordecai emphasized how dangerous these potions were. He said it would not stop me from dropping if I had enough momentum. They were *not* a suitable alternative to Feather Fall. We couldn't use these things to keep from plummeting to the ground unless we took them before we jumped. *Treat it like you're standing on thin ice,* he'd said.

"Don't hurt yourself, Carl," Donut said from the ground, looking up at me worriedly.

I waited for my potion timer to zero out, and then I drank the Major Charlie potion.

Boy, are you smart!

I pushed the slider up, and I zoomed upward, pushing through the green cloud. The wide expanse of trees spread out around me, surrounding the town. The wide naiad-infested river spread out like a snake. I glanced over my shoulder, and it was the same in every direction. Nothing but trees. In the distance to the south, however, I caught quick sight of something terrifying: multiple dinosaur heads peeking over the tree line, like duck heads coming up from a lake. These were brontosaurus things. We were going to be journeying through that area soon. I returned my direction north toward the hunters.

I cast *Ping*.

The noise spread out, extra loud in the cloud-filled sky. I watched my map, looking for the telltale purple dots of hunters. The map populated, flashing white, suddenly becoming useless. Every non-red-tagged mob filled the area. That included all the goddamned snakes and monkeys and birds. After a moment of panic, I remembered I could filter it, and I clicked over, removing everything except purple-tagged hunters.

There. Closer than I thought, about one and a half kilometers away, northeast of town. I couldn't see them, but I could see exactly where they were. There was a break in the trees. A clearing. There were only two of them. They both had the glow indicating they had magical gear.

They were probably already running.

"Go get 'em," I said. I reached back and hurled, lobbing Samantha directly at them.

She shot away, arcing through the air, moving ridiculously fast. I quickly lost sight of her. My eyes caught the twin flames of the rockets flaring up. She'd pulled the cord almost perfectly over the clearing.

Shit. I paused my descent. She didn't veer off like I'd hoped, but continued her forward momentum, the rockets spinning in a circle like a flaming tire rolling across the sky. I'd tried not to throw her too hard, but it looked as if I had.

But then she shot down at a right angle, just as something shot from the ground up at her. A fireball shot into the air, trying to knock her from the sky. The slow-moving projectile missed, and Samantha disappeared into the trees past the clearing just as I lowered myself fully to the ground. I could hear the distant detonation.

"Yes!" I cried, pumping a fist into the air as the experience notification rolled in. "I got one of those fuck sticks."

SAMANTHA: BRING ME BACK. BRING ME BACK. FAST, FAST. BRING ME BACK.

I quickly dropped the xistera extension, which recalled her to me. She popped into existence at my feet, growling and gnashing. Her hair was on fire again, and she was covered in dirt and leaves and a lot of blood.

She'd also brought something back with her.

She'd clamped down on the ankle of the second elf. The thin, pale elf was unconscious, likely as a result of the explosion that had killed his friend. He was drenched in blood, and most of it wasn't his own. His leg was on fire.

Clint turned and started smacking the flames out with his beaver tail. The sound was oddly squishy and wet, but after a moment, the flames were out. Samantha continued to growl and thrash at his ankle. She was unharmed.

The elf's health was almost all the way down. He remained unconscious. He'd be out for another forty seconds. I went to a knee and pulled a black bracelet off his arm. Constitution +10. Along with something else. I sighed, taking it into my inventory. I'd give it to Donut in a minute. I examined the man.

Akland—Moon Elf. Level 51. Artillery Specialist.
    The Dream.

"Samantha, let him go," I said. I pulled the still-growling head off his ankle. She made a spitting noise. She still had duct tape stuck to the side of her filthy head.

"It's my kill. My kill!"

"Not this one." Actually, I'd gotten credit for the other guy, too, which was interesting. It probably had something to do with her being a withering spirit. I'd ask Mordecai later.

"Hunter-Killer?" Donut asked, all business. He was going to wake up in seconds.

"No," I said, pulling the ring from my inventory. Hunter-Killer was a move we'd just come up with. "Heal him, but I want to talk to him first."

I slipped the ring on, and then I pulled the enchanted handcuffs from my inventory.

———

"IT'S NOT SUPPOSED TO BE LIKE THIS," AKLAND THE ELF SAID AFTER Donut healed him. He was handcuffed to a pole. He wouldn't be going anywhere. Donut was behind him, a magic missile ready in case he tried to pull something. Clint and Holger stood on either side of him. Holger claimed he'd be able to sense any spell being cast.

Samantha had somehow returned to his leg and was gnawing on him like a damn piranha, biting and growling. He tried to shake her off, but he couldn't.

"Please. I'm just an accountant. They offered us money to come and to hunt. I have a family. Please. Please."

"How was it supposed to be?" I asked.

"What?"

"You heard me. You said it wasn't supposed to be like this. How was it supposed to be?"

"We weren't even hunting you. The Dark Hive and the Skull Empire have both laid claim. But you're in our territory. The bridges are all out. We were going to take the city. Epitome Tagg doesn't even care about the gear. Or what you did to the factions. He just wants us to find that crawler."

"You mean Louis?" I asked.

"Yes. Yes. That human besmirched Tagg's mother's honor. Please. I didn't want to get involved. I did well at fantasy hunter camp, and I won a spot on the faction wars army. Then they asked me if I wanted to come down to the Hunting Grounds. It was supposed to be easy. They offered me so much money. I'm not even a member of the family like the others."

"Fantasy hunter camp?" Donut asked from behind. "Is that what it sounds like?"

"It's so people can pretend like they're on the show. It's run by Vrah's family, but once a cycle, the Dream always rents the whole moon out and lets the employees and family members play for a few days. It's not real, but it's fun. The best players get to play in faction wars. I did well, and I won a spot. I wasn't ever supposed to be in real danger. But they offered me money. Please."

"*Real* danger?" I asked, leaning in. "Fun?"

"That's right. Please. I'm just an accountant. I work with soy crop shipping manifests all day."

"Do you know what I do every day?" I asked.

DONUT: CARL, HURRY UP. YOU'RE DOING THE BAD-GUY-SOLILOQUY THING. YOU ALWAYS SAY TO NEVER DO THE SOLILOQUY THING.

She was right. I was keeping an eye on my view counter, and it had spiked. I was doing this for the audience. This was important. It was important that they heard this. I wanted to drag it out a little so more viewers had a chance to tune in.

At least that's what I was telling myself. I couldn't hear myself think. The river in the back of my brain raged, flooding, filling all the empty places it could find.

This is my birthday present to you. I am giving you a chance at life. I'm sorry it took me so long.

This will stop it. It's so loud, Carl. It's so loud.

"I . . . I think I saw a thing. You fix boats."

"No," I said. "That's what I used to do. I don't do that anymore."

"Please."

"I had a world. A whole world. A world filled with people. Some good, some bad. But most of us just wanted to work a little, live a normal life, maybe fall in love, have an adventure or two. And that was it."

"Please," he said again. "I can pay you. I don't have a lot. But I'll give you everything I have."

You have marked Akland.

   Akland's highest stat is Constitution.

"I'm going to show you what I do now."

23

CONGRATULATIONS, MURDERER.

You have leveled up the Ring of Divine Suffering. It now gives two stat points for every kill.

I took a deep breath and put the ring back into my inventory. I retrieved the handcuffs.

I'd gained one point to constitution, two trophies, and I'd also gone up a level to 55. I wiped my hands on my shirt. I'd forgotten to summon my gauntlet. Holger and Clint, still in their beaver form, looked at each other nervously as I looted the now-dead elf. All he had in his inventory was a bunch of crawler biscuits and another one of those arrows of Enthusiastic Double Gonorrhea. He didn't even have a bow or any other ammo. I left the biscuits in case they were poisoned.

The arrow was obviously meant for Louis.

I briefly wondered if Juice Box was doing okay. If they were expending all this effort to get to Louis, surely they were also doing everything they could to hunt down the changeling who was now somewhere on the ninth floor. I hoped she was safe.

DONUT: That was unnecessarily gruesome, Carl.

CARL: I know.

DONUT: It's like you're getting angrier and angrier, and it's scaring me.

CARL: It's hard not to be. But you're right. I shouldn't waste too much time telling them how I feel. But I wanted to get it out of the way at least once. I promise I'll kill them nice and clean from now on.

DONUT: WELL, YOU HAVE TO ADD A LITTLE FLAIR TO IT. MAYBE WE CAN COME UP WITH A NEW CATCHPHRASE JUST FOR KILLING THE BAD GUYS. I'M SURE IT'LL PLAY BETTER THAN YOU GOING ALL *RAGING BULL* ON THEM.

I chuckled out loud.

"Oh, hey," I said. "That guy had something equipped that I think you'll like. It's a bracelet, so you can wear it. You still have a couple slots left, right?"

I pulled the obsidian bracelet from my inventory and held it out for her to examine. She jumped to my shoulder and peered at it.

"Hmm," she said. "It's black, and it looks like it's made from glass. It's just a plain bangle. It's not as ugly as that wood anklet, but . . ." She gasped as she finally read the description.

"Give it to me. Give it to me now, Carl."

"Just don't, you know, burn us all alive."

Enchanted Obsidian Bracelet of the Raggle Rouser.

This item has been upgraded three times.

Warning: This item has a 50% chance to permanently break if it's upgraded again.

This murky bracelet is light and kinda stylish if you're one of those sad sacks who always wears black and complains about how nobody ever understands you. It's made of obsidian glass, which is actually a type of rock that only forms under extreme, lava-based circumstances. And interestingly enough, this is what you'll turn into if you don't treat this item with the respect it deserves.

This bracelet imbues the following effects:

+10 to Constitution.

+5 to Dexterity.

+15% Fire Resistance.

Wearer may cast a level 10 *Fireball* spell once every twenty minutes.

The bracelet appeared on her front right leg. It was suddenly much smaller. She lifted it to examine it, snorted, and it disappeared and reappeared on her front left.

"Don't use *Fireball* when we're in a tight space," I said. "It's a lot more dangerous to cast than *Magic Missile.*"

"I know how fire works, Carl."

———

AFTER I PULLED THE REMAINS OF AKLAND INTO MY INVENTORY, SAmantha growled and then rolled away. She stopped in front of an ursine cleric who'd just peeked out of his church. She started barking at him like a dog.

"What? What in Pawna's name?" the cleric asked.

"I'm going to kill your mother. And Pawna is a big liar. She plays all innocent and virginal, but she's into soaking. Look it up."

"Well, I never."

She growled again and continued to roll away.

"Hey," I called, "where are you going?"

She didn't answer. I sighed. I was going to have to go grab her before she caused trouble.

Donut sniffed. "Do you remember that time you got blackout drunk and passed out on the couch while watching scary movies?"

"Uh, sure," I said.

"There was a movie on that night called *Critters*. It was quite dreadful and low-budget, but I must admit I really liked it at the same time. Isn't that weird? Anyway, it was about these little hairy alien monsters that formed into balls and rolled around and bit people while aliens blew stuff up all around them."

"Yes, Donut, I'm familiar with the movie."

"Now that she can roll, Samantha reminds me of one of those critter things."

"I can see that," I said, chuckling.

"I don't mean it in a good way," Donut said. "She's getting stronger. She's already stronger than Mordecai said she'd ever get. She's even rolling faster than she was this morning. He said withering spirits aren't dangerous because even though they're usually indestructible and crazy, they can't do anything."

"I'll keep an eye on her," I said, suddenly feeling uneasy. "No matter what we do, we can't ditch her. Not yet. We're planning on using her to take the naiad castle in the morning. And now that we know she can bring stuff back with her, it makes her extra valuable."

"Maybe," Donut said. She sighed dramatically. "I wish Katia was here. It's difficult being the voice of reason. That was her job. But I do know those critter things were bad news in the movie. They attracted other bad guys, and there was a lot of fighting."

I grunted. "That's why she fits in so well with the rest of us."

24

<Note added by Crawler Drakea. 22nd Edition>

The hunters avoid the elites. They are smart enough to know not to fight against something they won't be allowed to easily defeat. The problem for us is, elites are more dangerous than the hunters, and much more numerous. They should always be avoided. However, it appears some of the more powerful hunters go out of their way to hunt these elites anyway, all in a quest to gain more equipment and clout for themselves. It is a most dangerous game, one I am happy to watch play out. I am not yet powerful enough to kill either elite or hunter claw to claw, but with my new subclass, I am experimenting with hidden traps that may even the odds. I shall attempt not to directly slay either, but to bring hunter and elite together. The woman from the talk show let slip that the Naga fools have offered insurance to those idiotic dramas that control the elite beasts. It will be my pleasure to watch the elites fail and die. While killing a hunter directly is a worthy feat, it is not a smart one. Killing individuals may be satisfying, but the true satisfaction is hurting them on a larger scale. When one values coin above life, you should target the coin, for it hurts them more. And that is my food. My life. My god. Hurting the Naga and everyone responsible for this nightmare.

TIME TO LEVEL COLLAPSE: 11 DAYS, 8 HOURS.

Hunting Trophies Collected: 38

MY FIRST "BOON" FROM THE FIRE GOD EMBERUS WAS COMPLETE BULL-shit. It was plus 50% damage to all fire spells for 30 hours. I didn't have any fire spells other than the 10% chance I now had to inflict *Burn*, which, apparently, didn't count. Mordecai had warned me that boons were like low-tier loot boxes. Usually crap, but every once in a while, you'd get something great. This time it was a dud.

I received the notification of the boon just as we ranged forward to find the corpse of the other hunter. It was, once again, raining heavily by the time we got to him. We found the body close to where he'd been marked on my map. The seeking missile had blown the dude's head clean off. His corpse was in the process of being eaten by slugs when we arrived. His hand was gone, having already been removed and sent to me in a hunter-killer box. His only equipped magical gear was a +1-strength ring. It sat on the ground next to the body. I looted an un-enchanted bow from him along with a bunch of regular arrows, another gonorrhea arrow, and a photograph of Louis. The first guy had a draw-ing, but this was an actual photograph that appeared to have been taken from his Facebook page. It didn't look anything like him. He was wear-ing a straw hat and had some filter turned on that gave him dog ears, nose, and tongue. I showed it to Donut, and she fell over laughing.

The real prize was the trebuchet. The rock-throwing device was oddly small, especially considering the size of the rocks they'd been lob-bing. It was the size and height of one of those windsurfing boards. We found it abandoned in the empty clearing, affixed to the ground with a set of spikes. It was made of some weird hollow wood and was so light, I would've been able to easily carry it even before I had my strength enhanced.

The whole thing glowed green.

Enchanted Venomous Elven Rock Chucker—Contraption.
      The fast-attack mounted-artillery specialists of the Dream don't bring siege engines with them when they go raiding. That's why they're so annoyingly deadly. Using a combination of knowledge, druid magic, and a little something-something extra—*wink*—they're able to rapidly construct their war machines on the fly. These can't-take-a-joke beanpoles can conjure up a whole regiment of wall-breaching contraptions in a matter of hours. Translation: You don't want these pale fuckers on your doorstep.

This particular light-duty rock thrower is made by casting *Bamboozled* on a patch of land and then assembling the device from the resulting poisonous bamboo stalks. Bring a sling, some rope, a few extra parts, and you have a device that can hurl 300 kilos' worth of "Do you hear something?" in an enemy's direction. The magical bamboo stalks infuse anything hurled with this machine with *Poison Cloud*.

This contraption has a 90-second cooldown between each use.

It took me a minute to figure out how it worked. There was no counterweight like with traditional trebuchets, but the machine was made with a pair of magical plates that wanted to come together like magnets. You ratcheted the arm into place, attached the rock to the sling, and pulled the lever. The arm spun, and the poisoned rock blasted off.

Upon closer inspection, I suspected the plates weren't actually magical, but some sort of high-tech bullshit. Something that was just as out of place in the dungeon as that photo of Louis. The only "enchanted" part of these things was the wood.

"These assholes are still cheating," I grumbled, inspecting the postage-stamp-sized plate. It was covered with little diodes. I looked into the sky. "Do you guys see this? Well, it's mine now." I pulled the individual spikes and then picked up the trebuchet, taking the whole thing. A new tab appeared in my inventory labeled **Siege Equipment**.

They'd picked this clearing because a pile of rocks stood nearby. They were the ancient remains of some long-collapsed building from before the Scolopendra disaster. I picked up a few of the heavy boulders and added them so I'd have some ammo handy if I ever got the opportunity.

We searched the clearing for traps, supplies, or any sign there'd been another hunter before moving on. Clint and Holger had both returned to their fuzzy humanoid forms. They sifted through the nearby underbrush like a pair of expert trackers.

"I don't know why you're taking all this stuff," Samantha said from the ground as I finished looting the rocks. She had a small slug crawling on her forehead. "I can fly a lot farther than that thing can throw stuff."

"You're not wrong," I said. "But what if you ever get your body back? Or if I want to throw something really big? Plus this thing imbues stuff with *Poison Cloud*."

She answered by making a growling noise and then rolling off through the grass. Mongo chased after her, grunting playfully.

"I do wonder if that was all of them," Donut said as she watched the god and the dinosaur frolic. "All of the Dream elves, I mean. We don't have a way of knowing how many of each hunter faction are here."

"Yeah, I should have asked that guy more questions before I killed him. I think that was probably all of them, but we'll be ready if there're more."

"I hope for Louis's sake it was all of them," Donut said. "They seem to be really mad at him. I don't know why. If you're going to be famous, you need to deal with thirsty fans. On the Princess Posse server, I receive multiple marriage proposals a day. And there's this one Saccathian who keeps sending me pictures of his tentacles for some reason. But I don't actually get offended by it." She sighed dramatically. "It's the price of fame, I suppose."

"He's gonna have to deal with it eventually," I said. "We have too much on our own plates to worry about him right now."

The schedule for the next few days was going to be taxing. We still had several hours before we were to help Signet with her castle assault. From there, we were going to move south and attempt to take another town and do the same thing that we did to Point Mongo. Take it, set up defenses, and train the local guards and populace to fight the hunters.

The next town south of Point Mongo also bordered the wide swath of low jungle that represented the area with Kiwi the mongoliensis and the other dinosaurs. We still had to figure out that quest if we had time.

I also had three separate events I was going to appear at over the next few days, all thanks to my fan box. I wasn't looking forward to that. Not even a little bit.

It was almost overwhelming. *One problem at a time,* I thought.

As soon as we were done here, the task at hand would be the *Vengeance of the Daughter* storyline. They said they were open to a deal for another season, but they hadn't committed to it. I was starting to suspect that they didn't actually want one, despite what they'd told my lawyer. If that was true, there was only one real explanation for it. They had some grand finale planned out. One that likely ended with the death of Signet and probably everybody around her.

It'd been bugging me since we'd gotten that warning from Odette's assistant. After we dealt with the naiads, Signet's ultimate goal was to get to and kill her half sister. Imogen. The high elf queen. But this same lady was also the big, bad country boss that all the top crawlers were going to have to deal with at the party. On the third floor, my exploits with Signet weren't shown on the recap episodes because anything that happened with an elite was licensed to the owners of the elite's program. There was no way—no way at all—that Borant or the Valtay or whoever was in charge would allow this floor's massive climax to be exclusive to some other program.

So what did that mean?

Maybe that meant the *Vengeance of the Daughter*'s climax was set to pop off *before* this party at the end of the floor. If so, it'd be Signet versus a boss that wouldn't be allowed to be killed. If that was the case, it meant they were going for a tragic climax. Both Mordecai and Zev had told us that these programs loved their unhappy endings. There'd be no appearance on the ninth floor. And if Signet died, everyone around her would probably get the axe, too. Including me and Donut.

Make sure you surround yourself with trustworthy, competent companions. Not too many, but enough to get the job done. That was Herot's advice. She'd written the 16th edition of the cookbook. I'd been rereading her convoluted, rambling essay on the nature of NPCs recently. I had a nagging feeling that there was genius in there, hidden in her wandering sentences. *Efficient helpers are an absolute must. Remember their true capacity. Fools will get you killed.*

"Put me down! I'll kill you! I'll kill your mother!" Samantha screamed, breaking me out of my thoughts. Mongo had picked her up and was shaking her back and forth like a chew toy.

"Hey!" Donut protested.

Clint and Holger howled with laughter.

I sighed.

"SO, A 'CASTOR' IS ACTUALLY A BEAVER?" DONUT ASKED HOLGER AS
we walked. We'd been walking for almost three hours now, grinding on
small, vicious mobs called slickbacks, which were like half-sized wolver-
ines that popped up out of holes in the ground. They were easy to kill
since Donut could see them before they emerged. We had to put Mongo
away because once he discovered them, he was gleefully committing
mass murder, denying us the chance to grind.

The sun set, and nighttime descended on the forest. Donut cast her
Torch spell, which was now level 13. The slickbacks moved deeper into
their holes. Holger said they'd soon be replaced by predatory bat-like
creatures. They generally didn't attack groups, especially a well-lit one,
but we still had to be on the lookout. We would be at our destination
soon.

We were on our way north to meet Signet and the rest of the team
for the assault on Fort Freedom, the former naiad palace. Clint had run
ahead to let them know we were on the way. Supposedly the entire "assault team" was going to gather at another one of those old trees. From
there, we'd approach the river and execute the plan. Thankfully, Donut
and I had but a minor role in tonight's assault. It was clear Signet wanted
to keep us safe for the second part.

Plus, the castle was mostly submerged, and we all knew Donut's opinion of going underwater. She'd already reiterated the point multiple times.

Samantha also traveled with us. I carried her at first, but she wouldn't
shut up, so I was now making her roll. She followed behind or ahead,
happily growling and splashing through the mud and foliage. She could
move quickly, but she couldn't jump or hop, which sometimes bogged
her down. She kept getting hung up in bushes and branches, and we
were constantly rescuing her. At first, I was worried about her running
off or disappearing into the darkness. She didn't. She hummed to herself
merrily as we went, and she cursed loudly whenever she bumped into
something. She was frequently threatening trees.

"I ain't never heard the term 'beaver' before," Holger said. "But you
foreigners always have funny words for things."

"Well, you are most definitely a were-beaver. It's adorable. This Chee form you're in now is perfectly fine, but the beaver body is just a delight." Donut suddenly gasped. "Carl, is that where castor oil comes from? Do they get it from beavers? Miss Beatrice used to use castor oil on her head for her hair. She insisted it made it grow faster. She did have nice hair. Almost as nice as Holger's. She'd sometimes make me drink a drop of it so I'd poop before I went into the judging cage. It always made my stomach hurt." She smacked her mouth. "My word, what an unpleasant memory. Come to think of it, it did taste a bit like how you smell, Holger."

"She shouldn't have done that," I said. "I'm pretty sure castor oil is really dangerous for cats. It doesn't come from beavers. It comes from a castor bean. But I once read they used beaver gland excretions or something for perfume and as a vanilla flavoring."

"That's disgusting," Donut said. "Vanilla? Beavers do not give me a vanilla vibe. Maybe rocky road. Or Neapolitan. But vanilla? Hardly."

"There's a beaver god in the Nothing," Samantha said. She'd rolled up between us. "Capa or something. He's a fuck. Another god, Hehaka, uses him as a hat. He doesn't like that much, but he can't do anything about it. He's always crying."

"Gland excretions?" Holger asked, ignoring Samantha. "For *perfume?* Oi, you guys are crazy. No wonder you humans smell so bad."

"Oh, you have no idea," Donut said. "You should have met some of Carl's old friends. He had this one friend named Maloney who smelled like rotten SpaghettiOs mixed with—"

Donut was interrupted by a distant bright light shining into the air, turning night to day, coming through the trees, so bright it overwhelmed the torch. The brilliant blue flash stopped us in our tracks. It was followed shortly by a crackling-lightning sound and then the rumble of thunder. The ground shook, and all the hair on my arms stood on their end as I felt the tingle of electricity. Donut and Samantha both let out little screeches.

"Carl, what was that? That sounded like an explosion!"

We all stopped and crouched down. Donut snapped off her *Torch* spell.

"Not an explosion," I said. "It was lightning."

"That's where the all-tree is!" Holger said. "Just over the next bend. I think they got attacked!"

The scent of burning wood filled the air.

"Donut, what's on your map?" I asked.

"We're too far away!"

"I'm on it. I'll kill 'em!" Samantha said, rolling off.

"Wait," I hissed, but she was already gone.

"Goddamnit," I said. I was about to go grab her, but I hesitated. The whole plan was to use her as a distraction anyway. She rumbled off into the night. "We'll follow, but stop as soon as you see something on your map."

"Yoo-hoo! Who's shooting lightning!" Samantha yelled in the distance.

"For something so small, she sure makes a lot of noise," Donut muttered.

"Come on," I said. "Stay low." We moved quickly through the dark woods. There were suddenly dots everywhere, but they were all low-level forest creatures fleeing the explosion. A group of the ever-present monkeys screeched as they rustled through the trees above us.

"There're a few X's on the map," Donut said as we approached. "Uh-oh, I see a hunter. No, wait. It's surrounded by a bunch of NPCs. And two elites. It's Signet and that scary ogre guy. What was his name? Areson. That's it. I see the other beavers and their caterpillar lady. I don't know who shot the lightning, but I think the hunter guys got the worst of it. There're two dead bodies, and I think they're the bad guys. Carl, these hunters are terrible at their jobs. They keep getting caught and killed."

Ahead, Samantha started caterwauling, screaming for help. She'd gotten herself stuck.

I sighed. "Okay, come on," I said, standing up.

25

CLINT FOUND US AS I FISHED SAMANTHA OUT OF THE MUD.

"Gah, how did you get stuck down there?" I asked. She'd gotten herself wedged in good. She'd somehow gotten the back of her head half buried. I had to yank to free her. Her head made a slurping noise as I pulled her from the muck.

"I was trying to take a shortcut, but I hit a rock." Globs of mud cascaded off of her.

Clint emerged. The bald man had a harried look to him.

"There you are. Taking the scenic route, are you? We're all waiting for ye."

"Everybody okay?" Holger asked.

"We got jumped by a trio of off-worlders. They're a weird kind of hairy orc ain't never seen before. Hurt a few elves, unfortunately, but it didn't kill 'em. The fools used a lightning attack near the all-tree."

"Oi," Holger said, shaking his mullet. "What a bunch of twats. So they get splattered?"

"Two of them," Clint said. "The third got his shoes blown right off him. Areson grabbed him. Now Signet is gonna use it as her sacrifice. She's gonna assemble her battle squad. The full group. I'm pretty excited about it."

"Signet? Tsarina Signet is there?" Samantha asked. She wiggled out of my hands and plopped to the ground. She started rolling off toward the encampment, shouting, but she got herself stuck again about twenty feet away. She started growling.

"What's the all-tree?" I asked, moving to grab her.

"You saw it before," Holger said. "It's an old magic-infused tree. It protects us. The dwellers of the forest."

I remembered the old tree we'd sat around the first time Signet had gathered us together. The description hadn't been very helpful, I remembered. "That other tree was pretty far from here."

"Yep," Holger agreed. "It's all the same tree. The roots cover the entire area. What you saw was just a small outgrowth. The main body is far below us, between the disputed lands and the celestial realm."

"Huh," I said. I couldn't remember reading anything about a giant, floor-spanning tree in the cookbook. "And this tree protected you from a lightning attack?"

Clint answered as I bent down to once again retrieve Samantha, who was now shouting for me to let her do it herself. Donut clucked her tongue at how dirty the sex doll head had gotten.

"Any forest-kin within a few hundred meters of an all-tree outcropping is protected from magic attacks. The tree sucks the spell in and turns it on the caster. Everybody knows that. It kills the outcropping. But it grows back in a few months. Only an idiot attacks near one of them things."

This had to be something new. There was no way a hunter would be stupid enough to attack otherwise.

"The tree protects forest dwellers? Even the high elves?" Donut asked. "Even though they're the bad guys?"

"Yeah," Clint said. "Those assholes have their castle right in the middle of a grove of the things. The all-tree don't give a shit about who is good or bad. It just shields those of us who have the forest in our blood. It's not smart or nothing."

"That's too bad," Donut said. "I thought maybe it was like that tree from that weird blue-alien movie with the *Ghostbusters* lady and that Scientologist guy who married Eric Forman's mom on *Friends*."

"What?" I asked. "What are you talking about?"

"Really, Carl. If you're not going to understand my references, I don't know why I even bother discussing classic entertainment with you."

"Put me down! Put me down," Samantha demanded, interrupting. She wiggled in my hands.

"Okay, but if you get stuck again, you're gonna have to get yourself out," I said.

"Put me down!"

I rolled her like a bowling ball, and she disappeared into the woods.

A few minutes later, we entered the clearing to find Signet conversing quietly with Areson. The ogre nodded and picked the unconscious hunter up over his shoulder and walked off into the dark. He was followed by a group of bush elves and ursine.

Samantha had not yet arrived, having gotten herself tangled up once again. I was going to give her the chance to free herself before I rescued her.

I looked down at the fried corpses of the two orcs. While there were X's on the map, these guys had been so thoroughly fried, there was hardly anything left of them. Still, I had the ability to loot one of them.

> **Corpse of Hunter The Talent. Killed by zapping himself with his own** *Lightning* **scroll. What a punk.**
>
> **The Skull Empire.**

"I was wondering when these assholes would show up," I said.

"They seem about as inept as their Prince Maestro," Donut said. "Do these guys really run a giant galactic empire?"

This guy, who had the ridiculous name "The Talent," had three scrolls of *Lightning* and an astounding amount of gold. Almost 75,000 gold pieces, which was—by far—the most amount of gold we'd ever found on someone.

> **CARL: Hey, Donut. You better loot this one. Not me. Don't want to pay that much in tithe taxes.**

Donut audibly gasped when she saw what he had on him.

> **DONUT: WHY DOES HE HAVE SO MUCH? THE OTHER ONE DOESN'T HAVE ANYTHING.**
>
> **CARL: Dunno. But be careful with those scrolls.**
>
> **DONUT: CARL, CARL. HE HAD SOMETHING ELSE. IT WASN'T**

LISTED, BUT WHEN I HIT "LOOT ALL," I GOT SOMETHING
EXTRA! IT'S A CREDIT CHIT. I THINK THAT'S LIKE A CREDIT
CARD. IT DOESN'T HAVE A DESCRIPTION. IT LOOKS LIKE A
CREDIT CARD. WE NEED TO GO BUY SOMETHING WITH IT
BEFORE THEY CANCEL IT!

CARL: Hold on to it for now. We'll ask Mordecai about it later. From
now on, when you loot hunters, only take one item at a time.
Don't do the loot-all option.

DONUT: THAT'S GOING TO TAKE FOREVER, CARL.

"They somehow knew we'd be meeting here," Signet said. "They
were hiding, preparing an ambush when Edgar sensed them. It forced
them to attack."

Edgar was the tortoise creature. He looked like a regular giant tortoise one would find in any zoo. One of those creatures who was always
like 150 years old. The only difference was this guy could talk. He and
Donut had taken a liking to each other.

"Where are you taking the other one?" I asked.

"Areson is preparing the sacrifice," Signet said. "I was hoping you'd
do the honors."

I nodded. "Absolutely. But I'd like to talk to him first."

"If we have time."

"Signet! Darling!" Samantha cried, her voice uncharacteristically
high-pitched and friendly. She rolled up to Signet's feet and started
pushing against her, leaving muddy splotches on her leg. She had a
branch in her hair. "Niece! Or is it cousin? I gotta say, I love the bare
breasts. It's good. A bold statement. They're not as good as mine, but I
am impressed that our genes have held up so well. Seriously. Those are
some grade-A party pillows. Small but perky. When I first got locked
up, there was a time when I did a little experimenting with these demon
ladies we got locked up with, and I learned to really appreciate . . . You
know what? Never mind. You don't want to hear about that. All I'm
trying to say is, nice tits. You got them from my side of the family, I'll
have you know. I don't know why you'd besmirch such a beautiful body
with so much ink, but that's something that can be dealt with. Oh, I
suppose I should call you Tsarina, shouldn't I?"

"What in the name of the gods?" Signet said, stepping back. "Is that supposed to be a Lika head?"

Lika was the fictional character the original sex doll was based on.

"Uh, yeah, that's Samantha," I said. "It's who we were going to use as the distraction."

"I see," Signet said, looking down at her, mouth tight.

"She says she's related to you," Donut added. "She's a withering spirit!"

Signet crouched down and picked up the sex doll head to examine it. All the tattoos swirling about her skin crowded to the front to get a better look.

"Look, cousin. Your Imperial Majesty. I need you," Samantha said as Signet turned the latex head over in her hands. The naiad ran a finger along the scar on Samantha's chin. "As I'm sure you heard, my pop sent me on a little time-out, and you would not believe what I had to go through to get back out. But the human who was helping me screwed everything up, and long story short, I'm stuck in this thing. You being the last trueblood heir to the empire *and* a blood relation, you have the ability to help me out. It won't even be that difficult for you. It'll take like two-three minutes. Tops. And I'll have my body back."

Signet looked at me pointedly. "Carl, when you said you had someone to assist in the assault, you forgot to mention a few details."

I grunted. "I seem to recall when you used Donut's life as a bargaining chip to get me to help you. This isn't even close to that."

Signet sighed and returned her attention to Samantha, who was unsuccessfully attempting to distort her wide mouth into a big smile. The effect was like a fish gasping for breath.

"What, exactly, do you wish for me to do for you?" Signet asked.

"You have to give me your body," Samantha said. "You'll die, of course. But it'll only take a few minutes. I'll walk you through the spell. I see you're a summoner, so you most definitely have the chops to cast it. Do you wish to get started now, or do you want to do the assault on the castle first? I mean, no offense, but that'll be much easier once I take over. What's your bra size? King Blaine loves them perky like that. Not too big. Just perfect. He's sure to stop banging my mother once he sees my new body. We'll have to expel those tattoos first, but no problem. Really, no need to apologize. Oh, I am so excited."

Signet returned her gaze to me.

I laughed.

"UNGRATEFUL BITCH," SAMANTHA GRUMBLED AS WE APPROACHED THE river. We'd had to hike for another half an hour through the dark woods to get to the edge of the river, and Samantha had been grousing the entire time.

"Shush," I said. "You need to stay quiet."

"She's a liar. Just like her slut aunt Corrine."

Samantha sat upon the back of Mongo, lashed just behind Donut on the saddle. We didn't trust her not to roll off. Donut turned and patted the head with a paw. "Don't you worry," Donut said. "We'll get something soon enough."

"I wanted her body," Samantha said. "She has a nice body. I don't see why she won't just give it to me."

"She said she'll help you," Donut said. "She just doesn't want to, you know, die in the process. It would be most inconvenient for her."

"She's full of shit," Samantha grumbled.

Signet *was* full of shit. It was painfully obvious she had no intention of helping Samantha regain her body. She'd told Samantha that after both the naiads and elves were dealt with, she possibly had a spell that could summon a permanent body for her. The elite was really just saying that to get her to shut up.

The problem was that Samantha was no dumbass. She was batshit crazy, but she wasn't dumb. Still, she wanted it so bad, she was willing to help just in case Signet was being truthful. That didn't stop her from bitching about it the whole time.

"When we approach the water, we have to be quiet. We don't want them knowing we're here yet," I said.

"I'm going to kill all of them," Samantha said. "Just you watch. I'm going to kill them all. And then their mothers."

Ahead, the shimmering blue of a spell danced in the air. This was a protection spell designed to keep large parties invisible. It'd been cast by Edgar the tortoise, who was something called a Shell Mage. We headed toward the edge of the spell and pushed ourselves inside. My ears popped, similar to when I went in and out of a protective shell.

You are secreted!

The area of the spell was huge, bigger than I was expecting. I was suddenly reminded of Grimaldi's circus tent. *You could hide a whole army in here.* Ahead, the others crowded at the top of a hill. I spied Areson the ogre still with the orc slung over his shoulder. The bound creature was awake and struggling.

We crested the hill, and there it was, glittering in the dark. Fort Freedom.

We stood at the edge of the forest, just inside the line of trees. The protection spell extended about a quarter of the way down the hill. A long, muddy slope led down to the river, which was much wider here. At least a mile and a half, which was significantly wider than it was just outside of Point Mongo to the south. The naiads had cleared the slope of foliage so they could see if anything approached. A single rock-paved trail led down out of the forest to a stone archway, which ended at the riverbank.

As I gazed upon the slope, multiple lights started popping up around the area. Traps. Lots of traps. These were alarms and summoning traps. I turned my focus to the stone walkway, and it was also covered with "silent alarm" traps.

A group of bush elves crawled over the muddy slope, quietly disarming the traps within the area of the spell. As I watched, a group expertly crept out of the spell's containment and moved to the first trap. Actually, a trap I hadn't yet noticed. They set to work disarming it. They were carving a path to the water.

The castle itself sat about a quarter mile offshore, coming up out of the water like the top of a skyscraper that had been submerged in a flood. Even in the dark, I could see the castle was in poor repair. One of the ramparts was missing a wall. A dark tattered flag hung from a pole that leaned at an odd angle, like it was about to tumble forward. What had once been a massive arched stained-glass window was built into the stone just above the waterline, spanning two stories high. It was now dotted with holes, so many that I couldn't tell what it once depicted.

If there was a bridge from the shore to the castle, it was long gone.

Only about half of Signet's fighters were here. The other half were on the opposite shore, hidden in the trees.

I came to stand next to Signet, who gazed mournfully at the castle. She turned to look at me. A single tear ran down her cheek.

"You know what the funny thing is?" Signet asked.

"What's that?"

"If they had just waited, they would've gained control anyway. It would've been a peaceful and organized change of power. They didn't have to kill my mother. I was her only child. Under the imperial charter, I would've never been eligible. The rule would've gone back to the people. But the Confederacy couldn't wait, and they killed my mother right before she was to become Tsarina. Sometimes, looking back, I think she was planning on stepping down anyway. She talked about it sometimes. Just me and her running off. Finding an island somewhere."

The tears running down Signet's face weren't actually touching her skin. They hovered just a millimeter off of her, and when she turned her head, they flew off and away, some striking me. *Water doesn't touch her.* What had she said to Donut before? *It's not a spell. It's a curse.*

I still didn't know Signet's full story. At least not the details. I knew her mom was a princess, but she'd gotten knocked up by the high elf king guy. King Finian, who was now dead. A coup had killed her mother and gotten Signet banished from the naiad. At the same time, just as King Finian's health started to fail, his heir—Princess Imogen—set out to eradicate all the half-elf bastards he'd sown. Probably to secure her own claim to the high elf crown. Signet had been forced to flee to the Over City, where she'd joined the circus.

The naiad kingdom wasn't very big. The naiad people had fallen to anarchy. The usurpers occupied the castle, no longer maintaining it or the kingdom. They were so obsessed with the idea of being "free" that they lost sight of what it meant to actually run a government. Like with most of these stories and quests, this was probably some bullshit political cartoon, and they were making a statement about something. I didn't care. However, I knew I needed to know about all of this as much as I could.

We should be doing this part last, I thought. *That makes more sense.*

"So, you ready to summon your squad?" I asked.

"Yes," she said, straightening. "You send that possessed thing into the water and get the main guards moving toward her, and my crew will take the castle from the top down. You, Princess Donut, and the rest of the ground team will protect the shore from those who might attempt escape. I suspect you won't see much fighting. They rarely leave the water." She paused. "If something happens to me tonight, I want you to know that I appreciate all you've done for me, Carl. I consider you part of my family now. And family is very important to me."

I turned toward the captive. "Let's get this done."

I had to do the sacrifice first. It took Signet several minutes to cast her spell once the sacrifice was made. While she did, I would toss Samantha into the water, but I had to use my xistera extension if I wanted to get her back. I would have to keep the extension on my arm.

Signet nodded at Areson, who stepped forward and unceremoniously dumped the orc at my feet. I examined him.

Her, actually. She was a young female orc, spitting and grunting. I grinned when I saw her class. Like Gwen, she'd traded fighting skills for no magic whatsoever. Plus she was also still level 50, which meant she hadn't even leveled once since she got here. This had very likely been her very first foray into battle.

Future Huntress—Wire-Haired Orc. Level 50. Boring Ol' Fighter. The Skull Empire.

I kneeled down in front of her. Areson had gagged her and tied her up. He'd also stripped her of all her gear. She didn't have anything magical on her and wore a simple bodysuit. She possibly had a scroll in her inventory, but the fact she hadn't used it yet suggested she didn't. The dead one with the money and the scrolls and that weird credit chit had obviously been the leader of the group and held on to all the expensive gear. Still, I had to be cautious. Like usual, I pulled the ring from my inventory and stuck it on my finger. I cast *Wisp Armor* on myself, which would last for ten minutes. I pulled the gag off. Samantha rolled up and started chewing on the orc's ankle, growling. I left her there as a distraction since she couldn't do any damage.

"You can't do this," Future Huntress said, her voice full of fear. "You can't do this. The Skull Empire will hunt you down and kill you."

Donut and I both laughed.

"Oh, honey," Donut said, "are you suggesting that if we don't kill you, the Skull Empire won't hunt Carl down? I mean, really, what an absurd threat."

"How many other Skull Empire orcs are there on the floor?"

"Thousands," she hissed.

I sighed. "Including you, that was three. We already wiped out all the Dream elves." We still didn't know if that was true or not, but I was hoping it was. "We know about the hunting areas. This isn't even your territory. The Gorgites have this area."

"Top tens are fair game for those who bought the hunting license. It doesn't matter where they are."

"Hunting license?" I asked. "Is that official?"

She didn't answer. She continued to glare at me sullenly. "You should let me go. If I die, then you'll be free game for the Dark Hive. We paid to have first crack at you."

"So you *are* the last of the orcs?" I asked.

She didn't answer.

"I can yank an arm off to get her to talk," Areson said.

"No," Signet said. "It'll weaken the sacrifice. Even if we heal her."

"I'm not going to torture her," I said, standing up. "Untie her and heal her. If she pulls something, make sure she doesn't get away."

"No, no. Please. You can't do this. I'm a real person. Not a crawler or an NPC. I'm a real person."

I took a deep breath, holding back the sudden wave of anger. I'd actually been starting to feel bad about this. She was so goddamned scared. I pulled up my menu to mark her, but I was interrupted by a notification.

System Message: A champion has fallen. A hunter has claimed a bounty.

"Fuck, fuck," I said, quickly pulling up my chat to make sure every-body was still on there.

> KATIA: Something's happened. Langley's team is gone. All of them.
> They're all dead.

Next to me, Donut gasped. I held my head low. Langley. The archer and all his friends who'd been crucial on the previous floor. But they weren't on the top ten. That message only appeared when someone on the list fell.

> CARL: Goddamnit. I'm really busy right now. The dead top 10 must
> have been that two-headed guy. The Popovs.
> KATIA: No, Langley hadn't gotten to them yet. They were hunting
> down Bogdon Ro on their own with a large group. They had him
> cornered.

Bogdon Ro was a guy who'd been off and on the top ten, but I didn't know anything about him other than that he had a bunch of player-killer skulls. Whatever happened resulted in the death of all of them, and a hunter had gotten credit.

"See?" Future Hunter said. "See how dangerous Vrah is? You need me to protect you. She can't hunt you for three more days, but not if I die. Then you're fair game."

I took a deep breath. Poor Langley. He and his friends had worked so goddamn hard to get off that last floor. They'd all been immigrants to Finland, working their fingers to the bones their entire lives. They'd had to scramble for everything they'd ever had, and the moment they'd gotten a leg up, they'd turned around and tried to help others. And just like that, gone. He'd been trying to do something good.

"You know," I said, "the only possible reason why Vrah would let you guys go first was because she knew you'd fail."

The orc seemed to deflate. She nodded. "I know," she said after a mo-ment. "I should never have come here."

"No," I agreed. "No, you shouldn't have."

"Carl," Signet said.

I marked Future Hunter. A moment later, I groaned.

"Charisma?" I said. "Your highest stat is charisma?"

The doomed orc sat up straight. She knew now that she'd been marked, it was over. She sighed heavily. "I thought I could charm my way out of bad situations."

"But you're an orc," Donut said, incredulous. She'd stepped back. We had a circle around us now, everybody watching.

I formed a fist.

I PULLED MY XISTERA EXTENSION AND LOADED SAMANTHA UP. I grabbed an alarm trap ball—one I'd marked "Annoying"—and duct-taped it to her head. I set the timer for one minute. Nearby, Signet was frozen, her arms out in a Jesus pose. The tattoos around her body swirled faster and faster. The were-castors all oohed and aahed as they watched.

"What song does that one play?" Donut asked, peering at the alarm trap.

"It's not important," I said. I couldn't get Langley out of my head. *I should have talked to him more.* I hadn't said a word to him since the floor started. "It'll be submerged, and you probably won't hear it." To Samantha, I said, "I'm going to throw you a little upstream. Just start shouting when the alarm goes off. The current isn't too strong, but if you can, try to aim yourself to get inside the castle. Let me know if you overshoot it. If they capture you, remember your lines."

"I don't want this strapped to my head!" Samantha said. "I can be plenty loud without the trap!"

"Don't worry. They'll get rid of it as soon as they can."

"I'm going to kill all of them."

"Remember your lines. You'll have plenty of time to kill them afterward."

I turned, aimed, and chucked Samantha into the river. She arched up and away, plopping into the water like a stone.

I turned in time to watch the three-headed paper ogre emerge out into the sky, stooping down to remain within the protection spell. The were-castors all started to transform. The elves glowed as they cast a water spell on themselves.

Nearby, the body of Future Hunter remained crumpled on the ground. She hadn't even fought back. Her hand had already been magically removed by the system. I thought of poor Langley. *I will break you all.*

SAMANTHA: WHAT IS THIS WONDERFUL SONG.
CARL: It's called "Wonderwall."
DONUT: CARL, YOU THREW THE WRONG TRAP.

An alarm went off somewhere deep in the castle. The sound echoed up into the night air.

More paper monsters formed. The protection spell around us snapped off.

"For my mother," Signet said, and she moved toward the water, followed by the assault team. We watched them move forward. To my surprise, Edgar the tortoise moved with them. Areson the ogre remained with us. The caterpillar remained with us, too, along with a handful of the elves.

"Do you think we're going to have to fight anything?" Donut asked, watching the assault team.

"What do you think?" I asked.

26

"DO YOU THINK THAT WAS HER REAL NAME? FUTURE HUNTER?" DONUT asked as we watched the team slowly approach the castle. The castle's alarm was a constant, pounding *ah-luga, ah-luga*. Apparently that particular pattern meant *Attackers at the main gate. All defenders converge at the front.*

"Maybe," I said. "I think all the orcs of the Skull Empire have weird names."

"It's just weirdly specific," Donut said. "I mean, she was a hunter. Not a future one. A terrible one, sure. She ended up dying almost immediately, but she could've dropped the 'future' part from her name. It's confusing. When her parents talk about her at her funeral, what are they going to say: 'Future Hunter the hunter was formerly a hunter before she got punched to death by a human with no pants'? Also, what if she wanted to be an Instagram influencer or something? You're not exactly giving your child a whole lot of choices when you name them something like that. It's like naming your daughter Candy. Of course she's going to become a stripper. She has no other choice. When I'm ruler of the galaxy, I'm going to institute name rules. Like they have in Iceland. Katia was telling me—"

We were, thankfully, interrupted by Samantha.

SAMANTHA: THEY CAME OUT TO GET ME BUT I SHOWED THEM. I
    WENT RIGHT PAST AND INTO THEIR CASTLE. THEY HAVE
    REALLY LET THIS PLACE GO. THE TAPESTRY OF MY
    GRANDFATHER IS GONE. THEY'RE ALL CHASING ME, BUT I
    GOT SUCKED INTO THE FILTER VENT. THE SONG TRAP FELL

OFF AND WENT DEEP DOWN THERE. NOW THEY'LL NEVER
TURN IT OFF.

CARL: Did you get a chance to talk to them?

SAMANTHA: DO YOU KNOW HOW LOUD THIS THING IS? BESIDES,
THERE'S NO TALKING IN WAR. ONLY TEETH AND BLOOD AND
THE WAILING OF WOMEN WHO BLEED OUT AS I SEDUCE THEIR
MEN AND MAKE LOVE IN THE GORE. OH GOODIE. THE SONG
JUST STARTS OVER WHEN IT FINISHES. IT'S LOUDER NOW
BECAUSE IT'S IN THE VENT SYSTEM.

I sighed.

"Hah!" Donut said. "She forgot her line. You owe me a gold coin!" A moment later, Donut gasped. "Carl, Carl, I can hear it! The song! It's coming from the castle! I can hear it over the alarm! Tell them to shut off the castle alarm. It's ruining it!"

"You know," I said, "it occurs to me that we've never learned what Samantha is supposed to be a god of. I guess since she's a minor goddess, maybe she didn't get a thing. Whatever they call it."

"She's the goddess of unrequited love," Donut said, bopping her head. She stood atop Mongo, who was sniffing suspiciously at the air.

"Really? How do you know?"

"I asked her, Carl."

"Huh," I said. "Interesting."

"Well, she *said* it was unrequited love. But I must say, I kind of get the impression it's more like the goddess of crazy ex-girlfriends. Everything she does is because she wants to get back with some weird king guy. She also seems to think her sand-ooze child—you know, the one that was married to the mage guy on the last floor—is still alive and is on the ninth floor. I don't know how she knows that. But she wants to pick up the kid and then get herself down to some other floor where the king is. The first part of her plan is to get a body, though."

I shook my head. I figured the odds of them letting her move from her current form to a regular body were pretty slim. Either way, she was much more powerful than she was letting on. We had to be careful.

Samantha's part in the castle assault was to be nothing more than a distraction, and she'd already done her job. She was to enter the water, splat in front of the castle, and wait for the Oasis-blasting trap to draw everyone's attention. When the guards reacted, they'd set their own alarm off to tell the defenders where the threat was. When this happened, Samantha was to roll/float toward the guards. The castle's alarm system was old and inefficient according to Signet. Once triggered, it took a long time to reset.

They had guards, but not enough to cover all the entrances and exits. Once the alarm went off, signifying an invasion at the front door, all the poorly trained guards would move in that direction, leaving the rear—the air area of the castle—undefended while Signet's amphibious assault team moved in. Even if noticed, there wouldn't be enough time for the alarm to be reset to tell the defenders where the real threat was coming from. The team would move to the throne room, where the leaders of the Confederacy would conveniently be hiding.

It was simple. Child's play. The whole defensive system of Fort Freedom was a joke. This was just an extra plot point in the Signet story and not meant to be a true obstacle.

We'd given Samantha a line to say because she'd been bitching that we were underutilizing her "talents." The instructions weren't important, but she'd insisted on having something to do if she got captured and the alarm trap deactivated, so I'd made her memorize a line. One designed to toss the guards into further confusion:

I am Psamathe, long-lost daughter of the Confederacy! I am here to parlay with the leaders of Fort Freedom. Take me to them immediately so I may discuss the conditions of my army's surrender to your glorious cause! The cause of freedom from tyranny!

Donut insisted the line was too long and she'd never remember or say it. I figured Donut was probably right. If by some miracle they did transport Samantha to the leader chamber, she could relay important information back to us. They couldn't hurt her, and I could teleport the sex doll head back to me at a moment's notice, so it was a pretty harmless plan.

I was glad to be otherwise sitting this one out. I figured we'd have to fight something, as they weren't going to just let me and Donut sit here with our thumbs up our asses, but if there was a big what-to-do, it'd be between Signet and whomever she found down there. The show-runners were trying to walk a very fine line with this. They wanted me present, but they certainly wanted to protect the integrity of their main character.

Ahead, the paper soldiers along with the others moved into the water. The flying ones circled above while the others floated atop the slow current of the river. One of the battle squad, a long eel, laid itself across the river like a boat, allowing the elves to scramble aboard. It bobbed up and down a few times and was now moving quickly across the river toward the castle. Signet traveled with this group. Some of the others—like Edgar the tortoise and the beavers—disappeared into the water, sinking below the surface. Mongo let out a forlorn peeping noise when they disappeared.

Next to me, Miss Nadine the giant caterpillar hissed worriedly. Areson the ogre patted the hairy thing. "It'll be okay," he said. The caterpillar hissed again. She smelled like wet moss. Behind us, a few bush elves remained, guarding the trees in case something attacked from behind.

Signet and the elves reached the castle and stepped inside, moving directly onto a walkway aligned with the height of the river. Wherever the half-naiad walked, water shied away from her, like a magnet pushing iron shavings away.

"How is she going to go down there?" I asked Areson. "It seems like the curse might make it difficult."

"She floats like an apple," the ogre said. "It's a bad curse. But she can go down. You watch."

One of the summoned paper monsters—a hammerhead shark, but with a buff humanlike body—wrapped Signet in a hug. Together they disappeared inside. I didn't actually see what was happening there.

"Once she deep enough, she doesn't pop up no more. She needs air though. Has spell. But if she go too deep she get the squish. Good thing river not deep enough."

"How did she get the curse?" Donut asked.

Areson grunted. "High elf cast it the night mom was deaded."

"Wait," I said. "There was a high elf working with these naiad guys?"

"Yah," Areson said. "The dissenters killed the Tsar and his family. They only did it because they had help from the sneaky high elves. It stopped fighting between elves and naiad, but the naiad are almost slaves now. Especially after nine-tier attack. Most of the fishy people died, but there's a good number left. They still at the teat of pointy-ears. They gotta ask them for permission to do anything. Now the naiad regular folks are going wild like old days because the castle people don't do no ruling or nothing."

I remembered what Signet had said, that her mother was planning on a peaceful transition of power. All of this happened before the Scolopendra attack, so years and years ago. I wondered how different it would've been had there been an efficient government in place when the disaster happened.

A few of the paper monsters draped themselves over the top of the castle, but several others lowered themselves slowly into the dark water. It looked almost as if they were being erased. Or fed into a paper shredder.

A few minutes passed with nothing happening, and then the castle alarm abruptly stopped. This had the unfortunate side effect of allowing the looping alarm trap to be heard much more clearly. It sounded distant and hollow. Thankfully.

SAMANTHA: I CAN HEAR FIGHTING. I'M TRYING TO WIGGLE MY
WAY OUT TO GET IN ON THE ACTION.
CARL: Don't get in the way. I'm going to recall you.
SAMANTHA: PLEASE NOT YET.
CARL: Okay, but stay out of the way. And keep me updated on
what's going on.

I had no idea how the massive paper monsters were going to fight in such close quarters. But I figured it was equally glorious and terrifying to behold.

SAMANTHA: THERE'S A LOT OF BLOOD IN THE WATER. AND THE
GREEN ALGAE STUFF THAT WAS COVERING ALL THE NAIADS
IS FLOATING ALL OVER THE PLACE.

DONUT: THAT SOUNDS DISGUSTING.

SAMANTHA: IT REALLY IS. I CAN TASTE IT IN THE WATER. IT
    MAKES THE BLOOD TASTE EARTHY. LIKE I'M EATING A SALTY,
    FISH-FLAVORED SALAD.

DONUT: EW.

The river surrounding the castle started to bubble. A lightning bolt shot upward, coming directly out of the water. It shot into the sky, briefly turning night into day. At that moment, I caught a glimpse of the defense team on the south shore, multiple ursine standing there looking back at us.

The ground shook. I exchanged an uneasy glance with Areson. Mongo abruptly howled and started pawing at the ground. He jumped up and down excitedly, causing Donut to yelp and yell at him to calm down.

"Look," Donut said, pointing after Mongo calmed. A body floated in the water, face down. A naiad. It disappeared as it floated away into the darkness. Another naiad appeared, popping up like a cork. Then another, this one missing a head. But then two more bodies appeared, both of them the paper cutouts of Signet's battle squad. They appeared and then dissolved. Yet another body popped up, this one too mangled to properly examine in the dark. I was pretty sure it was a bush elf. It'd been ripped in half.

"This not good," Areson said as Miss Nadine started chittering worriedly.

SAMANTHA: UH-OH.

CARL: What's happening?

SAMANTHA: I THINK IT WAS A TRAP. DON'T WORRY. I GOT THIS. I
    JUST WRIGGLED FREE.

"Goddamnit," I growled. "Donut, you stay here. I'm gonna have to go in there." I pulled the water-breathing ring from my inventory and slipped it on my finger. I felt the gills form on my neck.

You've been hit with the ugly stick!

"Oh, my god, Carl. Take that ring off this instant. I can't believe it only lowered your charisma by one point! You're all slimy. And Signet told us to wait here. I don't think going in there is a good idea."

A new explosion rocked the river. Bloody red water showered up, this time from within the castle, coming out the broken stained-glass window. More bodies appeared, but I couldn't tell what they were, but one of them was distinctly short and hairy.

Miss Nadine started to lose her shit, bouncing and hissing. She broke for the hill leading down to the water.

"You no swim!" Areson called. She did not respond.

"No time to argue," I said. The xistera extension remained on my arm. I had to remove it before I dove in there.

CARL: Samantha, I gotta teleport you back.
SAMANTHA: NO! NO! I ALMOST HAVE HIM.

I pulled the extension into my inventory.

27

I HAVE NEVER CLAIMED TO BE A SMART PERSON.

We all do stupid things. A lot of times, people do stupid shit not because they *are* stupid, but because in the heat of the moment, they make rash decisions. It's a different sort of thing. That's my excuse here.

Heat of the moment. At least that's what I tell myself.

When Samantha said, "I almost have him," I *should* have waited a moment and asked who she was talking about. She would have answered with "The lightning-shooting river monster that has taken over the throne room of Fort Freedom." And then I would have followed up that question with "Are you biting down on this creature right now?"

I was expecting Samantha to teleport to my feet like she usually did. Instead, the enormous truck-sized frog thing appeared right next to me. It appeared so close, we all went flying, the sensation oddly akin to bouncing off a wet trampoline. Donut and Mongo rocketed away, disappearing into the trees. Areson fell over and disappeared with a howl. I flew backward and started to slide down the slope to the river. I stopped, smashing against the surprisingly soft body of Miss Nadine the giant caterpillar, who'd paused her descent to gawk at the sudden appearance of the monster.

The large creature was about eight feet tall and maybe fifteen feet long, green, and lizard-like. The thing had no neck, and short, stubby legs that looked ridiculously too short. It had a stub where its tail should be, like it had recently been ripped off. It was like a half-frog/half-squished-alligator. It had a distinctly prehistoric appearance. It opened its mouth and croak-growled in surprise at its sudden teleportation.

When it croaked, both Samantha and beaver-form Holger vomited out of its mouth, both of them unceremoniously splatting onto the dirt like a pair of quivering hair balls.

Slime-covered Holger lifted his head and tried to yell something, but he plopped over, unconscious. Samantha was screaming something incomprehensible about the frog thing's mother.

The world did not freeze nor did new music start, but I knew this creature was a boss even before I read the description. I started to scramble back up the slope as the description popped up. I ducked as a multi-branch lightning bolt ripped through the night, coming from the monster's eyes. The bolt sizzled above my head and slammed into the castle walls far behind me. *Shit, shit, shit.*

Claude Sludgington the Fourth. Eryops Gigantis.

Level 65 Borough Boss!

Oh boy, are you in for a treat. These bottom-dwelling, lightning-tossing water pigs will ruin just about anyone's day. It's pretty much what they live for.

Also known as the River Squatter or the Mud Kato, one of the cardinal rules of living under the water in a river is that you never, ever invite an Eryops into your home. Why? Because they never goddamn leave. That's why. Sure they're cute when they're young. They tell jokes. Great dancers. They mix a mean pisco sour. But when the party's over, they'll plop themselves down into the middle of the room and announce that this is where they now live.

That's what happened with Claude here.

A few years back, the few remaining members of the Confederate government thought to host a fundraiser to gather gold to fix up their aging castle. Their aversion to all taxes whatsoever led to a rather unfortunate and unforeseen shortage in the kingdom's treasury, especially since they are still required to pay tithes to the high elves.

So, taking a page from those same elves, the Confederates thought to host a grand ball, and any underwater dweller from near and far was welcome. Welcome, that is, if they were willing to pay the 50-gold entrance fee.

The party was a disaster from the start. Nobody showed up, first off. This was mostly because the regular citizens of the naiad kingdom had been starving for a while now and would eat pretty much anyone and anything that came close to the water. Secondly, because everyone knew the Confederates were shit at throwing parties.

Claude Sludgington the Fourth, however, decided to make an appearance at the last possible minute. The guards allowed him into the castle despite his reputation. The rest is history.

Eryops receive a 10× constitution bonus if they are rooted in place. Oh, and they shoot lightning out of their eyes if you irritate them. They are notoriously difficult to kill. Or even move. I heard a rumor that they really dislike belly rubs.

Claude is an amphibian. You know what that means.

Warning: This is a lizard-class mob. It will inflict 20% more damage against you thanks to your Extinction Sigil. And, yes, like with the dinosaurs, I know amphibians aren't really lizards. You can complain about it to management.

Claude roared indignantly and shot yet another bolt of lightning. He already had a health bar over his head, but it had hardly gone down at all. Next to me, Miss Nadine hissed in rage and started moving back up the slope, pushing past me. The bristles rushed past my face, like I was being pulled through a car wash. Areson was suddenly on top of the boss, screaming. Claude just looked around, bewildered at his new surroundings, still disoriented. He shot a tongue out and captured a bush elf, who screamed as he was pulled to the mouth. He swallowed the elf whole.

I started to scramble up the riverbank.

CARL: Donut, we gotta flip it over. Then we can get at its stomach.
DONUT: THAT THING IS DISGUSTING. HE SMELLS LIKE ALGAE AND CHEETOS.
CARL: He's going to flip in your direction. Be ready. Don't attack yet. Take Mongo back deeper into the woods. Watch out for his lightning attack, but when he's on his back, we gotta go for the stomach.
DONUT: WHAT ARE YOU GOING TO DO?

Far behind me, a new sound filled the night. Fighting. This was coming from the far shore. A roar filled the night. A distinct dinosaur roar. Not velociraptors, but something bigger. *Goddamnit.* There was nothing we could do about that right now.

"Areson!" I yelled. "Get off of it!"

Claude let out a new and mighty noise. Not quite a croak. More like a reverse belch. He slurped up the unconscious form of Holger and Samantha once again. Miss Nadine launched herself at the side of the monster, her mandible things thrashing. The neckless head of the creature struggled to turn toward the giant caterpillar, still oblivious of the ogre on its head. The twin beady eyes focused on Miss Nadine.

Miss Nadine, who also happened to be directly in front of me.

The eyes glowed.

Oh shit.

I dove to the right just as the twin lightning bolts blasted forward. They hit the long, fuzzy form of Miss Nadine. Her body inflated. She momentarily glowed, like she'd been transformed into a neon tube. And then the former kindergarten teacher–turned–guardian just exploded, green gore and black fuzzy quills going everywhere at once. I was hit in the side of the head with one of the saddles, sizzling hot, pushing me even farther off course. Areson screamed in outrage as I continued to roll.

My foot hit a non-disarmed summoning trap as I scrambled up the hill. A pair of dead naiad guards suddenly appeared, splatting onto the hill in front of me. They rolled down the hill toward me, and I had to hurdle one as I continued to scramble back toward Claude the rampaging frog-lizard thing, who continued to look about with bewilderment.

"Areson," I yelled a second time, "get the hell off of it. We can only attack its stomach."

The ogre was attempting to . . . I don't know. Dig into the thing's head with his bare hands or something. Whatever he was doing, the monster didn't even know he was there. If the ogre wasn't going to listen to me, that was his own problem. I had mere seconds before the lizard would finally notice me.

SAMANTHA: IT SWALLOWED ME AGAIN. DO NOT WORRY. I'LL JUST KILL HIM FROM WITHIN.

I slid to a stop just to the side of the thing, trying to keep out of its direct line of view. Claude croak-belched again. He vomited something out. I was pretty sure it was Holger again, who remained unconscious. Samantha and the other elf were still in there. *God, I hope this works.*

"Hang on, Areson," I yelled. "He's gonna flip. Jump off."

I cast *Protective Shell.*

I was expecting the larger monster to bowl over to the side, like a semitruck rolling over, which would hopefully expose his stomach. The hint in the description was pretty obvious that was how to kill this thing.

That's not what happened.

I was too close. The diameter of my protective shell grew with my intelligence, and I probably should have cast it while I was lower on the hill so the angle of the sphere would've pushed him to the side and not launched him straight into the air.

Whoops, I thought as I watched the massive lizard thing blast off straight up into the sky. I didn't see Areson, but I assumed the ogre was still attached, riding the thing like a bucking bronco. The boss's stubby legs scrambled as the fat thing flew straight up into the night, faster and higher than should be physically possible for something that big.

I should get out of the way, I thought.

Donut galloped into the shell astride Mongo, looking up. "That wasn't to the side, Carl!"

"Shoot it! Quick!" The monster reached its apex and started falling back down toward us.

"*Fireball!*" she cried as the beach-ball-sized ball of fire burst forth. The level 10 fireball rose slowly into the air, almost reluctant as it blasted directly into the pink stomach of the flailing beast. The creature exploded in flames, his entire body catching alight as he landed atop the barely visible shield with a vicious *splat.* The howling monster sizzled and scrabbled as it started to slide off the dome, falling in the direction of the forest, leaving a smear of flaming gore atop the shield that started to rain down on us a few moments after it detached from the boss's body.

The line of trees stopped the monster's descent. It roared indignantly as it came to a rest, face down like it was doing a handstand. Its legs scrambled against the sparking shield. It was stuck. It would either tumble backward into the woods, or it would fall back toward us if the shield ran out first. Behind it, the massive trees started to bow and bend under its weight.

From this angle we could not see its health bar.

"Wow, look at that, Carl!" Donut cried. "*Fireball* is awesome!"

Donut had punched a hole directly into its belly and somehow caught the contents on fire, but the job wasn't done. The boss, his large face pressed against the ground, fired multiple lightning bolts in every which direction as it screamed in pain, showering gore. The lightning did nothing but slam into the ground, and random trees all around us started to explode.

"Where the hell am I?" Holger groaned from the ground. I hadn't realized he was here at my feet. "That thing ate me right up."

It still hadn't fallen over. The four legs waved. Claude squealed in pain and fear. We had seconds before the shell would fizzle out.

"Missiles," I cried as I loaded my least powerful hob-lobber. We were too close for any real explosives. I tossed it directly into the thing's stomach just as Donut started lobbing magic missiles into the open wound.

"Why isn't it dead? Every time it breathes, gore comes out. I mean, really," Donut shouted. "No, no! Mongo! No!"

Mongo—with Donut still on his back—roared and dove for the open wound just as the spell fizzled out. Donut backflipped off the dinosaur, landing perfectly on my shoulder, shooting one last magic missile just before the dinosaur dove headfirst into the open wound.

"It's going to fall onto its back," I cried as the trees behind it continued to bend.

The spell snapped off, and the trees acted like spring hinges, launching the amphibian directly at my position like I was standing right in front of a massive mousetrap.

"Oh fuck," I cried. I scrabbled to jump out of the way. *Too late. Too late.* Donut was already gone, launching off my shoulder with supernatural speed. I watched in slow motion as the corpulent lizard fell toward me, Mongo's long tail sticking from the hole in its stomach.

"Gah," I felt myself cry as I splatched directly into the wound. It was no longer on fire, but I suddenly couldn't see or breathe. A searing pain ripped through me. I felt my neck getting rent open by a claw as I was compressed further. I couldn't scream or see. It felt as if a building had landed atop me. My health flashed a warning. I slammed my healing spell, but the pain kept coming.

It was Mongo's back claw pushing off me as the goddamned dinosaur gleefully ate his way up and out the back of the monster. My shoulder shattered as he pushed away from me. I caught a glimpse of light, and I took a deep breath as Mongo broke free, coming out the back of the monster. I drank a healing potion, crying out in pain, taking in a lungful of Claude gore.

I pulled myself up, coming out the back of the large creature, who continued to shudder and quiver in death. The body felt like a slime-covered spring mattress. I slurped off of the side and fell to the ground, hitting the dirt hard. Next to me, a gore-covered Mongo gurgled happily and jumped back onto the dead creature.

I sputtered, and I realized I had lizard gore in my goddamned gills. I was still wearing the ring. I used a finger to clear them out. The sensation was like I was trying to scoop yogurt from the back of my throat. I started to hack as my lungs cleared.

Holy shit, that just happened.

The whole fight had lasted maybe thirty seconds.

As always, once the boss died, the supernatural glue that held its body together disappeared. The body exploded. It literally exploded in gore, and I felt myself fall back as Claude guts rained all around me. I had Holger to my left sputtering, and Mongo to my right grunting as he devoured up the guts. The bush elf was dead, his body in pieces. Areson sat nearby, rubbing his head. I had no idea what had happened with him, but he looked pissed.

Donut leaped into a branch overlooking the scene, looking down at the mess and clicking her tongue with disgust. Quills of Miss Nadine littered the area.

Sitting right on my lap was Samantha, completely soaked in gore.

"Hi, Carl," the sex doll head said. "I told you I'd kill it."

28

"This is an outrage!" Donut cried from the tree. There was gore just everywhere, and she was refusing to come down. I picked up the neighborhood field guide map from the dead boss, which showed which parts of the river were currently occupied by naiads and which parts would be safe to cross. It was actually super-useful information.

I wasn't exactly certain what the quest would've been, but I had an inkling. Signet and the assault team would've cleared out the castle, all except the frog thing in the throne room. I would've somehow been tasked with removing the creature. But we'd jumped the gun thanks to Samantha getting swallowed by the thing before I could recall her. I'd also inadvertently saved Holger's life, but he wasn't seeing it that way.

"Oh, oh, gods. Miss Nadine! Miss Nadine!" Holger started to cry once everything settled. "First Clint and now Miss Nadine!" The beaver held his head into the air and started to howl.

"Clint? Clint is dead?" Donut asked from her tree.

"He got ripped up right in front of me," Holger said, rubbing his

eyes. "And Miss Nadine, too. She'd been taking care of us for so long."
He sniffed. "She was like my mama. It's like my mama died."

"It was my fault," I said, standing up. Samantha bowled off my lap
and started rolling in circles in the gore. "I accidentally summoned it up
here."

"No. No fault," Areson said. "Miss Nadine was going to water.
Would've drowned anyway. She died fighting. Warrior's death."

"It's the thing that killed her's fault," Holger said. "Oh, Miss Nadine." The beaver looked up at the ogre. "Do you think there's enough
of her left? Do you think she was worthy?"

"She worthy," Areson said.

I didn't know what they were talking about. I turned my attention
back to the water. There was still fighting, but it was much less tumul-
tuous than before. I could still hear the song playing quietly through
the water. I knew it had to be unbearably loud down there.

I turned my attention to the opposite shore. I couldn't see what was
going on, but they'd gotten attacked. It was too dark to use the gnom-
ish farseer telescope. I pulled my xistera extension and affixed it.

"Samantha. I have a recon mission for you."

"Oh goodie," she said, suddenly at my feet, bumping up against my
legs.

SAMANTHA: I AM ALMOST THERE. I CAN SMELL THE BLOOD.

I'd tossed Samantha over there almost ten minutes earlier, but I'd
accidentally thrown her a little too far in the dark. She insisted she could
get to the shore on her own and was making her way there.

While we waited, I spent time on the slope down to the water searching for untriggered traps and disarming them. I could use my Tripper
skill to set them all off, but I needed to train my Find Traps skill, which
was stalled out at nine. The summoning traps were hard to spot, and
there were several of them scattered about. I accidentally tripped them
twice, and both times they brought a pair of naiad guards with them.
The traps apparently summoned specific guards, and every time, the
guards in question were already dead. All of them had been killed by

were-castors. After looting them of their crap gear and occasional health potion, I moved on.

After I discovered the third or fourth such trap, my Find Traps skill finally leveled to 10. The moment it did, the slope lit up like a Christmas display. I went about disarming and collecting everything. They were mostly silent alarm and summoning along with a few of those glue traps, which made it so you couldn't move away for a full minute.

After returning to the top of the slope, I examined one of the ten summoning traps I now had.

Summoning Trap

This is a Recycled Trap.

Effect: Once triggered, will summon two town guards or minions to the location of the trap. Will summon two random guards or minions from this floor only. If you do not have minions or if you do not control a town, this trap will misfire. Specific guards or minions may be programmed at a Sapper's Table.

Delay: Two seconds.

Target: Programmable.

Duration: Onetime use.

That could potentially be useful, but I didn't have any towns on this floor. Nor did I have any sort of minions. That was a Donut thing. If we ever used this trap, she would have to be the one to set it. I put it away for now.

SAMANTHA: THEY'RE ALL DEAD. IT LOOKS LIKE THEY GOT CAUGHT IN A WHEAT THRESHER. ONE OF THE BEARS IS JUST A HEAD. ANOTHER LOOKS LIKE A COOKIE THAT GOT A BITE TAKEN OUT OF IT.

CARL: Do you see any sign of the dinosaurs who did it?

SAMANTHA: JUST FOOTPRINTS. I THINK IT WAS JUST ONE. IT HAS THREE TOES. THE TRACK IS BIG ENOUGH FOR ME TO SIT INSIDE OF. OH, AND THERE'RE PINK FEATHERS EVERYWHERE.

CARL: Pink feathers mean Kiwi the mongoliensis was there, too.

SAMANTHA: IF SHE WAS, I DON'T SEE ANY OTHER SIGN. THE DEAD
BODIES ARE ALL BIG DEAD. NOT TORN-UP-BY-MONGO DEAD.
CARL: Okay. Grab a feather. I'm bringing you back now.

I relayed everything to Areson while we waited for Samantha to find
a feather and stick it in her mouth. The water had stopped thrashing.
Several more bodies bobbed to the surface, all naiads. Holger returned
to the water to tell the others what had happened.

I pulled the extension, and Samantha returned with a *pop*. She
growled and dropped a feather on the ground. Then she rolled off into
the underbrush. Donut remained in the tree. She'd cascaded herself
across one of the branches and was snoring while Mongo continued to
splash about in the remains of the dead boss. I reached down to pick up
the feather. It was dirty and flattened and small. If it had come off of
Kiwi, it was from a long time ago. It reminded me of the down they put
inside of pillows, but a little bigger.

This is a feather. It's pink. It's garbage. Fuck off with making me
describe this shit. Do you want me to describe the dirt below your
feet, too?

"Sounds like Big Tina," Areson said after I finished describing what
Samantha found. "She's usually not this far east, but it sound like her.
She wear a pink boa."

"Big Tina?" I asked, raising an eyebrow. "And she wears a boa? A
necklace made out of feathers? Are you serious?"

"A pink boa. She just a kid," Areson said. "But she a big dinosaur. Carries a wand, too, but it run out of zaps a long time ago. Got anger problem.
Doesn't like ursine. Eats them all up. She usually with the mongoliensis,
but she runs away a lot and then gets herself into trouble before they find
her. She usually the one that attack that town downriver that you staying
at. The other dinos gotta go get her and bring her back out. That's why I
stay on this side of river. She dangerous. She good at killing."

Quest Update. The Recital.
There's a dinosaur out there named Big Tina, and she's being a

bad, bad girl. She's somehow involved in the attacks on Point Mongo and on the other towns. Find out what this crazy dino chick is up to. Kill her to save the towns. Or find out why she's the way she is, and do something about it.

"What? What's going on? Ahhh!" Donut announced suddenly. She fell from the tree, but landed on her feet in the midst of the gore. She hissed with dismay and then scrambled away, her hair poofed out. She ended up back on my shoulder, licking her paw furiously.

"Carl, that notification woke me up," she said between licks. "That's never happened before. If you're going to be investigating quests, I must insist you only do it when I'm prepared."

"You were sleeping outside of a safe room," I said.

"Well, that's because I'm bored, Carl. And if I'm bored, that means the Princess Posse is bored. We've fought one boss all evening, and that's it. I only got to fire one fireball!"

We were interrupted by the return of Signet. She bobbed to the surface with a loud splash, water cascading off the force field around her like oil off a hot pan. All of her tattoos had returned, and she was brought back up with the help of the remaining were-castors, who all moved to the remains of Miss Nadine and started to wail.

"Damn. Damn, damn, damn," Signet said, looking down at the splattered, exploded mess of the giant caterpillar.

"The ursine on the other shore got Big Tina'd," Areson said.

Signet shook her head. "What a waste. If I had known the castle was so poorly defended, I would've just gone in there myself."

"What happened down there?" I asked.

"We took the castle. There were still plenty of guards, but the whole place would've fallen in a matter of months on its own. There's an algae infestation, and the godsdamned Confederates had stopped attempting to rule ages ago. It was barely a fight. They'd lost control of the throne room to a damn eryops. The entire kingdom is in shambles. After we free ourselves from the chains of the high elves, I will have to find a suitable ruler to clean up the place and begin the long, slow process of bringing the remaining citizens back to civilization. It's a nightmare. My mother weeps from beyond the veil."

"But the castle is liberated? The Confederacy defeated?" I asked.
"Yes. It is done."

Quest Complete. The Vengeance of the Daughter. Part One.
    All surviving members of the assault like you 20% more. That
doesn't really mean anything. Especially since half the squad is
dead because you left the southern shore unprotected. The real
prize comes at the end of part two.

I exchanged a look with Donut and waited for the notification. It
came immediately.

New Quest. The Vengeance of the Daughter.
    Part Two of Two.
    Tsarina Signet has taken back her family's castle only to find the
place in ruins and the Confederacy in tatters. Her people have re-
gressed to a time before society taught them that eating everybody
they meet is just rude. They are nothing better than selfish wild
animals, reminiscent of those creatures who crawl over each other
to purchase televisions on Black Friday each year. Signet has a long
road ahead of her to reunite her people.
    But that shit's boring, and we ain't gonna make you have any-
thing to do with it. We're still on the revenge track, and we're going
to fast-forward to the good stuff.
    The true culprits in all of this are the murderous and xenophobic
High Elves. And since King Finian is now dead, your target is Tsarina
Signet's half sister, Queen Imogen. The reclusive pure-blooded
mage rarely ventures from her chambers deep in the impenetrable
High Elf Castle. She does, however, make an appearance at the
yearly party the High Elves throw for the most elite citizens of their
empire.
    The same party you will be invited to should you remain one of
the game's top players.
    Help Signet kill Queen Imogen. Destroy the stranglehold the High
Elves have on the Hunting Grounds. Only then will the daughter find
her revenge.

Fair warning: This one won't be nearly as easy as the last.

Reward: Upon killing Queen Imogen, the contents of the High Elf Castle will become available to loot. There's a rumor they have something hidden within that will protect one from Scolopendra's attacks. That, plus a metric fuck ton of other good shit.

"I suppose we now must deal with this elf queen," Donut said, still licking her paw.

"Yes," Signet said, her voice tired. "But not tonight. Tonight, we mourn and celebrate those we've lost."

Despite the victory, a dark cloud fell over the camp.

I watched as all the tattoos on Signet moved to the front and looked down on the exploded remnants of Miss Nadine. The were-castors had all returned to their short Chee forms and were huddled in a circle around the body. A pair moved downstream to see if they could locate Clint's corpse, but I knew they'd never find it.

"Signet, you're not planning on being their ruler?" Donut finally asked.

"Not with my curse," she said. "It's not something that I will ever be able to remove from myself."

"I'll do it," Samantha said as she rolled past. She had something gross stuck in her hair, and Mongo was sniffing after her. "Remember our deal. Once we get rid of the high elves, you're going to get me a body." She rolled off. Signet just watched her.

Edgar emerged from the water, climbing slowly onto the shore. The ancient tortoise had bright, gooey blood on his jaws, making it look like he'd just eaten a strawberry. He paused at the sight of Miss Nadine. He sighed and lowered his green head.

"Edgar," Signet asked, "do we have enough moonlight left?"

"We do," the tortoise said. He lumbered off toward the back of the camp. "I'll get my stick."

29

DONUT AND I SAT, FASCINATED, AS WE WATCHED EDGAR THE TORTOISE use a silver needlelike stick in his mouth to poke a new tattoo onto the skin of Signet. Both Mongo and Samantha also stopped to watch the process. Edgar dipped the thin stick into the remains of Miss Nadine, which sucked up pieces of the exploded caterpillar like a straw. It made a slurping noise as the fur and quills and white guts got pulled in, like the sound of a malfunctioning bilge pump. He then turned and poked at Signet's thigh. With each poke, a dot appeared and then moved out of the way. The tortoise wasn't actually drawing the tattoo, but just poking in the same spot over and over, and the dots moved on their own, slowly forming the image.

Each poke made an odd pen-clicking sound as it entered her body, like he was tapping the stick directly against bone.

The other tattoos on her body swirled in circles around the new, half-completed one, giving it a wide amount of bare skin. The new, unfinished tattoo curled in on itself, as if cold and afraid.

> DONUT: THIS IS DISGUSTING. BUT I CAN'T LOOK AWAY. IT'S LIKE THAT PIMPLE SHOW MISS BEATRICE ALWAYS WATCHED.
> CARL: Yeah, it's pretty gross. Don't say it out loud, though.

"So all of these tattoos are from fallen companions?" I asked. I whispered the question. The whole process had taken on an almost spiritual vibe. The other were-castors along with the remaining bush elves and other odds and ends all watched silently, reverently. The only sound was the clicking and the occasional rush of water down below.

"Yes," Signet said, also whispering. "Or fallen enemies whom we've deemed worthy. I received my first one the night my mother was killed. That was the same night I met Edgar."

"So, you were a little girl, crying and alone, and some tortoise guy walked up to you and said, 'Hey, kid, would you like a tattoo?'" Donut asked.

Edgar, with his mouth still wrapped around the tattoo stick, grunted with soft laughter.

"Wait a moment," Donut added, looking between Areson the ogre and the three-headed-ogre tattoo on Signet, who glared back at the cat. "That tattoo there is clearly the same as Mr. Areson here, and Carl says there was another ogre that looked like another one of the heads, too. If that's a tattoo of him, they're not all of dead guys."

Areson grunted.

Signet glanced sadly up at the ogre. "Areson, Apollon, and Herman are ogres, yes, but they were born the day their progenitor fell. Di-we. He is the second tattoo I received. A three-headed Nodling who died protecting me from agents of my sister. When a Nodling dies, he splits into a new creature depending on how many heads the original had. These new creatures emerge as toddlers but quickly grow. The original body remains, and we used that for the tattoo. Areson here has a third of the knowledge of his progenitor. He remained here in the Hunting Grounds. Apollon traveled with us to the Over City, where he worked in the circus. Herman is down below in Larracos."

She paused, her eyes going glossy for just a moment. And then she added, "I hope one day to see him again."

"A Nodling?" Donut asked. "Carl, isn't that what the Popov brothers are?"

"Yes," I said. I was thinking the same thing. That actually created more questions than answers regarding the two men who'd picked that odd race. "They only have two heads, not three."

"A Nodling can be anything from two to six heads," Signet said. "They're usually two or three."

It took another hour for the tattoo to be finished. By the time it was done, the sun was starting to peek over the distant horizon. The finished tattoo was small, maybe four inches long. We watched as the likeness of

Miss Nadine took a tentative step on Signet's skin. The three-headed ogre—Di-we—went to a knee before the newcomer and put his hand on her. She curled up, afraid.

"Does she know who she is?" I asked. It suddenly occurred to me that Miss Nadine might not have asked to be turned into a tattoo upon her death, and that this wasn't necessarily an honor depending on how you looked at it.

"She is not Miss Nadine," Signet said, looking down lovingly at the new tattoo. "She is a blood-and-ink elemental, and she is a combination of the remains of who she was and of my personal memories of her. She is like a living portrait painted with her blood. But she is not real. Not in the sense you're asking. She is a facsimile. A loving memory."

As I watched, the caterpillar straightened and then formed into a young female Chee wearing a long, flowing skirt. She looked up at the ogre, wide-eyed. A smaller child Chee appeared, peeking out from behind her skirt.

Next to me, Holger gasped. "It's Clint! She brought Clint with her! Oi, but he's how he was before we changed. Look at all that hair."

"It happens sometimes," Signet said softly, watching the new tattoo. The child Clint looked about, wide-eyed. "She loved him so much that his memory lived within her. So when we drew the tattoo, she brought his memory with her even though we didn't have his body."

Holger reached forward reverently, his finger stopping an inch from the half-naiad's skin. "I'll miss you, buddy. But you got Miss Nadine with you. Here and wherever else you are, you're safer than we are." He reached up and rubbed his eyes. One by one, the surviving were-castors bowed to Signet's skin before turning away.

Christ, I thought, watching the exchange, *this goddamned place.*

Just as the sun fully rose, the were-castors returned to the water, set on building a wooden dam around the entrance of the castle. Holger popped up a few minutes later to complain that they couldn't reach the alarm trap that had fallen deep into a vent. "Wonderwall" was playing on an endless loop.

"We won't need to build a defense around the castle. Not with that racket playing," the man said.

"Why would you want to turn it off?" Donut asked.

WE NEEDED TO GET TO A SAFE ROOM. I HAD MY FIRST APPOINTMENT
coming up. I couldn't remember exactly what I was supposed to do, but
it was some bullshit, and we didn't have time to get back to Point
Mongo. There was a small village a few miles north of us, but instead
we opted to cross the river, pass through the carnage on the south shore,
and head toward a small dryad settlement south of there. It was an extra
few miles, but it was in the direction we wanted to go. Once we got
ourselves settled, we'd take the town, train the guards, and then maybe
poke at the dinosaur quest.

From there, we were going to spend the rest of the time hunting the
hunters and preparing for the inevitable battle against Queen Imogen.

"I'll be in contact," Signet said as we prepared to leave.

"We'll be moving around," I said. "How will you find us?"

She smiled devilishly. "Don't worry about that. Once we have a plan
in place for the assault on the elves, I'll send someone to collect you. In
the meantime, we'll be moving southeast toward their territory. Imogen
will know I'm back by now, so we will be running, fighting, and hiding
from now on. We will continue to hunt the outworlders as well."

"Be careful of them," I said. "Just kill them as soon as you find them.
Don't try to capture them. They'll be getting stronger by the day, and
soon they may be too strong to easily kill."

She kissed me on the cheek before she turned away.

I approached the water and pulled out my kayak as Donut stored
Mongo. We needed to keep him locked up because we knew other dinosaurs were in the area. They had a way of sensing each other, and that
wasn't something I was ready to deal with just yet.

A low fog descended onto the river, covering it like a blanket. I still
caught occasional glances of the dead ursine on the opposite shore. I
wanted to get there before the forest critters ate them all. Some of them
had magical gear.

I eased into the kayak, and Donut jumped to my shoulder, looking
down suspiciously at the water. I tossed Samantha in as well. The sex
doll head had fallen asleep, and she was snoring loudly. We proceeded
to make the trek across the river.

"You know this Signet lady wants to jump your bones, right?" Donut asked as we were halfway across. I kept a wary eye on the far shore. It wasn't as sloped as the north shore. I wondered how many traps were over there.

"If she does, it's because the producers are making her feel that way."

"Oh, I don't doubt that for a second. But if I know anything, Carl, it's how story arcs work. She's going to want to boink your brains out before the final battle. There'll probably be a meadow involved, and she'll be wearing a ring of flowers in her hair, and there'll be candles and butterflies. She might cry out for her mother during the sex, and there'll be all sorts of back arching and nails raking across skin. You'll be grunting like an overheated water buffalo like always. And afterward, they're going to try to kill you. That's the rule. That's how this sort of thing works. Sex with a guest star always spells doom. Well, I'm not going to let it happen. You are not to ever be alone with her again."

"I am not going to 'boink' Signet."

"No, you're not. Not if I have anything to say about it. It's too bad Areson and Holger are both so hideous. That's the real problem. There're no other decent-looking people in the party for the sex sacrifice. Other than myself, of course. I'm pretty sure she's not a lesbian, though. Even those bush elf guys all look like they've just been released from a hard-labor work camp. I thought elves were supposed to be sexy."

We hit the shore, and I went to work. I tied the still-sleeping Samantha to my back by her hair as we looted the mangled ursine. Samantha was right. These guys were big dead. All chomped in half by something huge. The pink feathers of the boa littered the shore. The stench of death filled the air. I picked up multiple bits of armor and several enchanted daggers and swords. There wasn't anything overly valuable, but it was all worth over a thousand in gold.

Most of the traps had already been disarmed or triggered, but I managed to find and disarm a few additional ones on the edges of the area, including a new one called slippery slope, which would've caused me to slip and fall into the water. The traps all went into the inventory.

"Keep an eye out for the dinosaurs," I said as we moved into the woods, heading south. The town was supposedly a few hours south.

Zev checked in and told me to hurry up. She warned I'd be transferred whether I was in a safe room or not, which meant abandoning Donut in the wild. She was being unusually insistent that we hurry. I took the hint and picked up the pace.

We came across several mobs, most of them things called thorny dervishes, which were creeping plant things that reminded me of blackberry bushes, only they moved like spiders. The flowers on them were on Mordecai's list, so we quickly killed several and took their bodies. In addition, we picked up several more items Mordecai wanted, much to his delight. We didn't see any major mobs or dinosaurs, but we did manage a good solid hour and a half of grinding as we moved quickly. Samantha woke up, and she bitched loudly from my shoulder, wanting to be let down. I kept her tied up. Her shouts attracted more mobs, all of which we easily killed. I was more than ready to get to a safe room and dump her back inside.

The town finally came into focus. It reminded me of the very first town we'd found, but even smaller. A single funeral bell guard stood out front. Tree houses crawled up trees at odd angles. Most of the buildings were made of bamboo-like planks. A single temple stood in the middle of town. Even from the outskirts, the village smelled sweet, like fresh flowers and rain.

> ZEV: Carl, Donut, get to the safe room. I won't be able to stop or delay the transfer. You have two minutes. Or maybe you should . . . Never mind. I can't say that. Just get there.

The view counter, which had been relatively middle-of-the-road since before the whole tattoo thing started, was suddenly spiked, buried all the way to the right. The movement was sudden and jarring, like the folks on the intergalactic internet were realizing something just after Zev had realized it, whatever this might be.

Uh-oh, I thought.

Entering Alucarda.

"Carl, this village already has a name!" Donut said. "Not fair! I wanted to name it!"

I paused, looking around quickly. "Be careful," I hissed. "There might be another crawler here."

"Well, that's just not acceptable. This is why we need Katia. She has that Find Crawler skill. Carl, I don't see any dots at all on the map. It's broken!"

"There's a protection spell. Go!"

We moved quickly, coming to a line of businesses. I paused at the entrance to the pub, a small building called the Aloe Mana. This was a true safe room. The logo was a cactus glowing blue. A treelike dryad stood out front. He had a monkey climbing in his branches.

"Hey," I said, my hand on the door. I could see the inside of the safe room. It was a fast-food restaurant of some sort with nobody inside except a single Bopca. Donut sat on my shoulder and Samantha remained on my back. "Do you know who the mayor of this town is?"

"It was R'aggah," the tree guy said. "But he has returned to the earth. An evil woman has taken control. A woman with two beasts that kill indiscriminately. Mayor Lucia Mar."

Fuck me. "Where is she now?" I asked.

"Ooh, who's that? She looks like my type of crazy," Samantha said from my back.

And that's when I transferred away.

PART THREE

THE
UNHINGED CHILD

30

I, once again, transferred to a space station. *No. No, no, no.* Donut and Samantha remained down there. Alone with that psychopath. The door to the safe room was open. Had Donut gone in? Of course she had. Donut wasn't stupid.

But I couldn't be certain. Why did I have to ask that dryad who the mayor was? Zev had tried to warn us the best she could. *Goddamnit.* I had to get down there.

I twisted in the near-zero gravity, surprised at my environment despite this being the second time. I tried to pull up my chat, but my interface was blacked out. "No," I said again.

Several torturous minutes passed. Below, something burned on the surface of India near the southern point of the country. I didn't know the geography well enough to know what city that was. Or what city it had been. The fire was big enough to see from up here. "Hey," I called up at the invisible trap door. "Hey!"

With every minute that passed, my panic rose. The thought of something happening to Donut and me not being able to do anything about it filled me with an overwhelming sense of helplessness.

"Goddamnit." I kicked at the window floor showing the planet below, which was a mistake. I went flying off at an angle and crunched heavily against the corner bulkhead.

To my left, the trapdoor in the ceiling finally opened, just as I started to sink back down toward the floor. A single gnoll came through the chute, all business. This was not one of the same ones as before. This one was less kitted out with not as much crap attached to his uniform. He was also older, with gray around his snout. He had a quarter moon insignia on his shoulders, which was different than what the last guys had.

"I need to go back. Now. Right now."

"You need to shut up is what you need to do," the shade gnoll said. He hit the ground with a clank and took a few steps toward me where I helplessly floated downward. He grabbed me by the ankle and effortlessly pulled me down the rest of the way. I had to struggle to keep from fully collapsing to the translucent floor. He waved a scanner over me. "Do you have any explosives on your person?"

I had an overwhelming urge to grab this guy by the neck and start choking him, but I knew that'd just end up delaying everything. Zev said she'd meet me in the production trailer. She'd tell me what was happening. I hoped.

"I don't have anything," I said. "Now get it over with."

The gnoll leaned in. His breath was hot and smelled strangely sweet, like mandarin oranges. "My grandpup's name is Lix. I would consider it a personal favor if you looked approvingly on her and her entry. I can't back-scratch you directly, but I am in charge of security in the production vessel you're about to be transferred down to. You're known to steal from production trailers. I can overlook any such future transgressions if you do this for me."

I pulled my head back to regard the older gnoll. "What in the flying fuck are you talking about?"

He didn't answer. He grabbed my jacket and bodily turned me sideways, like he was turning the arms on a clock. My feet left the ground as I twisted in midair. I was so surprised at the motion, I didn't resist. I started to slowly float down. He said, "Clear" into his shoulder and then jumped toward the ceiling. Before I could react, I flashed.

ENTERING PRODUCTION FACILITY.

Last time, I landed hard on my side. This time I landed on my feet. My bare feet echoed as they hit a thin, cool metal. My interface snapped back on for a moment before snapping off again. In that brief second, a page of messages appeared, mostly from Donut and Mordecai. And Samantha. One popped up from Donut right at that moment, saying something to Katia, so I knew she was okay for now. I didn't get to read the messages, but I relaxed. Slightly.

"Whoa," I said, looking about. I could tell right away that this production trailer was much bigger than usual. We were underwater, but I could sense this vessel was huge. I could feel movement and sound all around me. I thought of the *Akula*, the massive submarine from the last floor. This was the same sort of thing. The room was ridiculously humid, and I felt my ears pop.

My room looked similar to the last underwater trailer, minus the large window. There were no portholes here. A single slightly too small exit sat against the far wall, and a red-blinking light was affixed to the metal above it. An alien symbol was etched above the light. It looked like a capital "Q" with two extra little lines in it. I committed it to memory. Everything else was the same as usual. There was a bare counter. A small bathroom. A couch, though it was made of metal, like the bench at a bus stop. *Donut would hate this.* Below my feet, I heard what sounded like the crackle of a spell being cast, followed by cheers and laughter. There was a slight vibration in the floor with the sound of the cheering crowd. "What the hell?" I muttered.

"Hello, Carl," Zev said from the bench. I jumped in surprise. She was directly behind me, and I hadn't noticed her there at all. She sat quietly, leaned up against the arm. She wasn't wearing her suit. Only the rebreather, and she looked small and tired. The diminutive fish woman smiled up at me.

"Zev," I said. "I need to get back down there."

"Yeah," she said. "That was quite the fight, but Donut is okay. She is safely ensconced in the guildhall. There's no need to hurry. This is the first of three events, and this one will not take too long. However, I was discussing your schedule with my team, and . . ."

"Fight?" I exclaimed, interrupting. Any relief I felt fled. "She fought Lucia Mar? By *herself*?"

Zev looked nervously up at the ceiling. "Look, Carl. Things have changed with the, uh, new management. We are not in a regular production trailer. Most of the rental trailers were owned by a company called Senegal Production Systems, Unlimited, but they've been kicked off system by the Valtay because it's difficult for them to keep . . . track of crawlers when they're outside the dungeon. There was an incident. An escape attempt. That along with what happened with Loita last floor, yeah, they've decided to be a little more strict." She leaned in. "We are under constant surveillance. Not just by the AI, but by the actual security detail of the vessel. I can't tell you exactly what happened. But Donut is okay."

I remembered what that guy up in orbit had said. "Strict?" I asked, looking about. *With us?* I didn't add. *After what we helped you do?*

Zev continued. "This is an actual Valtay landing vessel, and it is parked in the planet's primary zone. So we're sitting at the bottom of the ocean. Not far from the headquarters, actually. The ship is normally sectioned off into different environments, but it's been cleared and pressurized to Earth standard, and most of the interviews will occur here from now on."

Below my feet, I heard more muffled laughter. *There's a show being recorded down there right now.*

I took a deep breath. "All right. Let's get this bullshit over with so I can get back down there."

"Actually, what I was saying earlier, Carl, was that I was discussing your schedule with my team. You have your first event coming up in a few minutes followed by the second, a panel discussion, in a few hours. We've decided to keep you here the whole time. Your autograph session is already booked for tomorrow, so you'll have to leave and come back for that one, but your "Crawling Through the Ages" panel is scheduled for about six hours from now. So after your first event, you'll return here, and we'll provide you with a bed and food. We can also provide you with access to a training room as compensation for the loss of dungeon time."

"Is this a joke?" I said. "Screw that. I want to go back down there immediately. If Donut managed to get herself into the guildhall, that means she can only exit through that same door, and if she didn't kill that psycho kid, that means she and her dogs might still be there. Donut is trapped, and I need to get down there as soon as possible."

Zev lowered her voice and spoke slowly and deliberately. "Your involvement in CrawlCon is highly anticipated. Not only is the universe looking forward to meeting you today, but it might be in your best interest to . . . linger as much as you can. Do you understand?"

"No," I said.

"Then you will have to trust me. When we are done, you will be transferred back to the exact place you were transferred from. Any other crawlers and their pet or *anyone else* who may be aware of your participation may very well be waiting for you. So you need your rest. It will do you good. That is all I can say."

There was so much loaded into that statement, it made my head spin.

"I thought you guys plugged up the communication . . ."

"Stop talking," Zev said, raising her webbed hand. Water splashed from her neck and dripped off the bench. "I'm going to open up your inventory for a moment. Pull out that CrawlCon badge you got from the fan box and put it around your neck. Do not remove anything else. Lose the bandanna, too. You'll be able to put it back on before you return. You need to get out there."

I sighed and pulled the badge with the red lanyard. The red demon on the front of the badge roared silently, shooting fire from his mouth. On the back was a scrolling ad for some real estate venture on what looked like a swamp planet. I put the badge around my neck.

A new tab is available in your interface. CrawlCon schedule.

I tried to open the tab, but I couldn't get to it.

"I can't get to the schedule," I said.

"Sorry, Carl," Zev replied. "Unlike the regular trailers, this vessel has its own containment zone. You have crawler wetware, so you're blocked out."

I instinctively formed a fist to see if my gauntlet worked. It did, just like when I was above sea level. I quickly dismissed it before I summoned security. Weird. What did that mean? I really wanted to ask Zev why, but my instincts told me to leave it be. For now.

"What was this first event again? I forgot what the prize box said it was."

"You're judging a kids' art contest."

"Are you fucking kidding me?"

"Try not to swear for this one, Carl. They're children."

31

"MY DADDY SAYS YOU'RE THE CAT'S BITCH," THE LITTLE BOY SAID. HE was human, and his badge said his name was "Keith H." The boy was about six or seven years old, and he had a weird-ass haircut. It looked like a skunk had curled up on top of his head and died. Most non-Earth humans were generally thinner and bigger-eyed. This kid was stout and squat, practically a dwarf, with eyes like pinpricks. He looked at me expectantly with his piggy stare.

I examined the kid's submission to the art contest. It was a shitty drawing, even by seven-year-old standards. It was a flat piece of paper with a stick figure with a bunch of red scribbles over it. There was maybe a yellow bird or something floating over the mess. It looked like he'd spilled chocolate milk on it, too.

"What is this supposed to be?" I asked.

"It's you getting eaten by a brindle grub," the boy Keith said. "My dad says if you weren't the AI's toy, that's probably how you would've really died. He says you're a cheater and you whore yourself to the macro AI and to the mudskippers. He says now that the brain worms have taken over, you're going to die any day now."

"Ask your dad why that other guy is always coming over when he's not home," I said. I reached over and clicked the number one on the virtual tablet that hovered in front of me. "Next."

To my left, Hurk suppressed laughter. The gleener gave one glance to the kid's artwork and made his vote, shooing the kid away.

This had been going on for over an hour now. Apparently this Crawl-Con was happening at an actual, physical location somewhere in the inner system, whatever that meant. While the adults were walking around buying random shit and visiting booths and panels, they had a day care where they could drop off their kids. For an extra fee, the kids could participate in an art contest. Each day of the three-day con had a different panel of so-called celebrity judges. The kids were given all sorts of art supplies, from digital tablets, to "nano, self-learning sculpting clay," to the alien equivalent of paper and crayons. Then the kids marched one by one in front of three judges where we looked at the art, and we judged it on a scale of one to 30.

I was given no direction on what to do or how harshly I should be judging this stuff. Most of this crap looked like how one would expect. But there was also a smattering of art pieces that looked like they were drawn by master artisans, including 3D moving paintings that were so realistic that they looked like photographs. The kid before Keith was a green bubble alien named Guru-san, and his art piece was a sculpture that looked and moved like a real-life, lava-spitting llama. The alien kid had no arms or features at all, and I had no idea how he'd even made the thing. I'd given him a 25.

Usually I had some sort of robot or producer telling me what to do, but this time there was nothing. I'd gone through the small door on the side of my greenroom, and I sat down at a desk, and suddenly I had a panel floating in front of me. I was sandwiched between two aliens. To my left was a fishlike gleener, who appeared to be floating in a virtual tank of water or some other alien liquid. Everyone who wore that badge had their name floating over their heads, and the name floating over him said simply **Hurk**. He waved at me jovially. These gleener guys looked a lot like the kua-tin, but they were human sized and had more of a blue tinge to their skin.

To my surprise, the alien to my right was a dour, long-faced Bactrian camel alien. I hadn't realized these camel guys were a real thing and not something made up for the dungeon. I wondered what they thought when they saw Earth camels. I wondered if that was like a human seeing a monkey or a Neanderthal.

This guy was dressed in a long, silklike robe. His label said **G'valt. Session of Love**. I had no idea what that meant. He looked at me and snorted, snot flying from his nose and disappearing once it hit the virtual edge of the screen.

All three of us were attending the con virtually, but all the kids were really there.

In front of us was a wide room filled with screeching children. It didn't appear as if they could see us yet. Multiple Frisbee-shaped Mexx-style robots floated about the room, humming and hawing over the chaos. The kids were an eclectic mix, ranging in age from what appeared to be two years old to about ten. There were soothers, Sacs, humans, elves, orcs, and dozens of other what-the-fuck-is-thats mixed about the room. They were all air-breathers, I noted. There were no gleener or kua-tin children.

About a third of the kids were hard at work creating their masterpieces. The rest were pinging off the walls and running around, doing typical kid stuff. I was struck with how normal the scene was. If it weren't for the actual aliens and robot attendants, it could easily be a scene from a regular Earth day care.

"I have no idea what I'm supposed to be doing," I announced.

"Don't worry, my child," Hurk the gleener said. Despite being in a tank of liquid, I could hear the creature like he really was sitting next to me. He had an oddly formal British accent. Like a Shakespearean character. "This isn't quantum mapping. You look at the art, and then you press a button between one and 30. The better the art, the higher the score. Simple. At the end, the little poop dumpling with the highest score wins."

To my right, the camel guy snorted with derision. He pulled out what looked like a tumbler filled with smoke and held it to his large nose. The camel sniffed long and hard.

"Really, old friend? Children too much for you?" Hurk called over at the camel. "You'll be out of your mind before we're finished."

"Eat my ass, Hurk," the camel said. Then, raising his voice, the camel called, "Let's get this over with."

This would be the first and last time I would hear the camel speak.

"Don't mind G'valt," Hurk said to me, whispering conspiratorially. "He's mad they added his drama to his name."

"I don't know what that means," I said.

Hurk pointed upward. "My name tag says 'Hurk.' That's because, ostensibly, everybody knows who I am. I'm Hurk. Designer of the Desperado Club along with several different sets. Perennial flower of the CrawlCon panel. Likewise, your tag simply says 'Carl.' Everybody knows who you are, even if you weren't prancing around in your underwear. This year, G'valt's name tag has a qualifier. Once upon a time, he wrote multiple stage dramas, including a minor masterwork called *Session of Love*. It is only performed by NPCs on the ninth floor of the crawl. At least only legally. Back in the olden days, everybody knew who he was. Now he needs a little bit of a boost to jog everyone's memories." The fish man sighed dramatically. "It matters not when it comes to these diaper-encrusted balls of talentless youth. The only one of us who they'll possibly recognize is you, dear Carl. Judging the art contest is both the first and last stop of the panel circuit. A mix of rising stars and those they're about to toss into the rubbish portal."

I was starting to realize that despite his jab at the camel, this gleener guy was also blitzed out of his mind.

"Hey," I said, "do you know what just happened? In the dungeon, I mean, with Donut and Lucia Mar? They won't tell me."

Hurk shook his head. "I apologize, my boy. I only watch the highlights nowadays. But if your companion tangled with that psychotic crawler, you have my condolences for your friend."

Damnit, I thought. I looked over at the camel, but he just shook his head at me.

One of the Mexx robots suddenly beeped and buzzed in our direction. "Children, it is time to be judged. Now line up one by one."

"IT'S MY MOM," THE LITTLE ELF GIRL SAID. HER NAME WAS BUTTERCUP Divinity, and she'd drawn a strikingly good anime-style rendition of a female elf smiling up at the viewer. The picture blinked at me and blew a kiss.

"That's really good," I said. I gave her a 24.

"Thanks. She's dead," the girl said before turning away.

"Jesus," I muttered.

"Oh, gods. These guys," Hurk whispered as a trio of goat things walked up side by side. They were small jet-black long-haired goats with red eyes. They looked like miniature satanic Prepotentes all lined up. The names over their heads were what looked like scientific equations. Completely unpronounceable.

"Uh, so where's your entry?" I said, looking at the three small goats.

"Judge us," the center goat kid said. He bleated. "Judge us."

To my right, G'valt had passed out, and a hand reached over his shoulder and picked a score. That'd been going on for a while now. He'd been silently voting, but since he'd fallen asleep, someone else in the room with him was doing the voting.

"I'm not sure what I should be—"

"Just pick a number," Hurk whispered as he voted. "Get them the hells out of here."

"Judge. We wish for judgment," the center goat said. The other two let out a prolonged bleat that sounded like it was being played back in slow motion.

I reached down and picked five, which was the lowest I was giving everyone except that little asshole Keith.

The three goats sighed as one, and all three did a little spin and just walked off.

"Judgment received," the middle one said. "Juddddgggment."

"What the hell was that?" I asked Hurk as the next kid walked up, a soother holding what looked like a Play-Doh flower.

"The Plenty," Hurk said, watching them walk off. I could hear the shiver in the fish man's voice. "They're all like that. You should see the adults. Your fellow contestant, that caprid guy, goes on a program with them every few days where they just sit in a circle around him while he screams, and they scream back. It's the strangest thing. Nobody knows what's going on in their heads. It is bizarre, even to me, and my boy, I have seen things you wouldn't believe."

"Weird," I agreed. An uneasy feeling washed over me, like we were all suddenly in danger. Those guys, the Plenty, were the ones who invented the tunneling system, the ones who were supposedly working with our new sponsor, the Apothecary.

I turned my attention back to the new kid, and then I noticed the next kid after him waiting patiently for his turn. I saw the name glowing over this other child's head. I leaned over to Hurk.

"Hey, do me a favor. Give this next kid a high score."

Hurk turned all the way in his tank to regard me. "The gnoll child? Why would I do that? I've been giving all of these little snot factories ones and twos all morning."

"If you give her a good score, I'll say I really like the design of the Desperado Club during my next panel."

"Sold!" Hurk said. He looked up at the soother kid holding the flower sculpture. "You're still here? It's middling at best. Make way for a real artist."

The tall alien kid nodded solemnly and walked off.

The next kid looked like a walking puppy, barely resembling the hyena creature she would grow into. Her name was Lix, and she had ridiculously large, innocent eyes. The head of security guy wanted me to vote for her, apparently his grandkid, and in exchange, he'd let me loot my greenroom. As far as I was aware, there wasn't anything that great in the room, but the last thing I wanted was some security officer guy pissed at me on top of everything else.

"What have you got there?" I asked.

If I had to guess, the girl was the equivalent of about four years old. She'd made a 3D stick drawing of an older gnoll with a truncheon. The gnoll on paper appeared to be beating something. Maybe an orc. She'd only used one color. Black.

"It's my pup-pop," the kid said. "He's helping rid the universe of tax-avoiding scum."

Hurk laughed. "This is a thirty out of thirty if I've ever seen one." He voted with an overenthusiastic flourish.

I sighed and also voted 30 for the kid's drawing.

"WE DON'T GET TO SEE THE WINNER'S CEREMONY," HURK SAID AFTER the last kid was done. "But we do get to see who the winner is. That way you'll know I didn't cheat you. Don't forget your part of the bargain."

The whole process had taken almost two hours. After we finished voting, the scores populated on our screen. Lix the shade gnoll had won with a perfect 90. To my right, the Bactrian continued to snore. Whoever was voting for him was picking 30 for every entry. The kids who'd entered while the camel was still awake had all received ones. That little punk Keith placed dead last with a final score of four.

"Most of the time, I am okay with that," Hurk continued, "with missing the ceremony. But I am rather interested in watching today's service. The Eyber faction will be quite ruffled. They'll be squirting anger slime all over the place. Gonna stink up the whole convention center."

"Who's that?" I asked.

"The kid who drew the portrait of your cat companion. They usually win this thing. The kid won yesterday. They love blowing bubbles up the posterior of the judges, but when they don't get their way, watch out."

I remembered the portrait. It was a perfect likeness of Donut, and she would've absolutely loved it. I'd given the kid—some sort of slug thing—a 26. *Oh well*, I thought. I was glad we were skipping the awards ceremony. Apparently they went through all the winning portraits, which would take goddamn forever. It'd be painfully obvious there was some sort of fix. I didn't care.

It was time to go. The door above the entrance to my greenroom started blinking, which apparently meant I had to leave. "Well, Hurk, until next time," I said, standing. I raised my voice. "You, too, camel guy."

"Good luck to you, Carl," Hurk said. He paused a beat. "You know, it's been a while since there's been a crawler like you. One that people pay attention to. One that they actually *see*. Be careful."

"Careful?" I asked.

He laughed derisively. "Yeah, I suppose that's silly advice. Nevertheless, I will be watching your panel that's to occur later. I must admit, I may be an old hand at this, but I am quite excited about the upcoming nova display. I hear the line to attend the panel was filled this morning the moment the con opened."

"Nova display?" I asked. "What do you mean?"

"My boy," Hurk said. "Didn't they tell you?"

I sighed. "Lay it on me."

"You're going on a panel that is being moderated by the mother of one of the hunters you killed. And she is quite vocal about how much she dislikes you. The entire fandom is just dripping wet over about what's going to happen. Everyone will be watching."

Next to me, the camel guy snored, blowing snot everywhere.

"Oh, I can't wait," I said.

32

"ZEV," I SAID AS I RETURNED TO THE GREENROOM. THE KUA-TIN RE-mained sitting on the metal bench. She was intently watching a screen, but she snapped it off the moment I entered. "Who is on the panel I'm attending later today?"

"Why did you guys vote for that shade gnoll kid to win?" Zev asked. "All three of you gave it a perfect score. I've been staring at this thing for several minutes now, and I don't see it. Is it supposed to be a joke?"

"The panel?" I asked.

"Oh, yes," Zev said. "About that. It starts in approximately four hours. You'll be brought to a different room to participate. They need to use the studio attached to this one for something else. The scheduling is a nightmare. I'm glad I'm not in charge of that stuff."

"Who is this moderator?"

"Her name is Circe Took. She's a minor hive queen. A mantis. Not part of their military or the Burrower clan. She's more of a business-woman, but she started off as a hunter and became quite famous for a while. She owns an amusement park."

"Apparently, I killed her child."

"Yes. Xindy. Vrah's little sister. It was her first hunt. The mantis people are overly dramatic about everything. The woman is a Hive queen, which means she probably has ten thousand children. Try to avoid talking about her government, and there won't be any problems."

I sighed. I guess there wasn't anything I could do to make it worse. It's not like I could make Vrah want to kill me more. Or less. But it also explained Zev's warning. At least somewhat. If this mantis had somehow figured out how to speak with her daughter, that meant Vrah would know exactly where and when I would be returned to the dungeon.

"Why can't you return me now?" I asked. "I'll just jump right into the safe room."

"I'll be returning to base in a few minutes," Zev said, ignoring the question. "They will come and fetch you in a little over four hours. After I leave, security will have a bed and a training module attached to the room. I'd get some rest and some training in. Do your panel and then come back here, and I'll give you a quick debriefing. And then you'll go back to the dungeon. Understand?"

"Okay," I said, settling into the metal chair next to Zev. "What is this panel about anyway? I've never done anything like it."

She waved a small hand. "It's called 'Crawling Through the Ages.' I looked at the panelist list, and it won't be anyone you know. You're the only current crawler. Usually the crawl and the con aren't run concurrently, but it happens sometimes. They've only let four active crawlers attend this one, and they're spread thin. Five crawlers actually, since the Popov brothers are really two. You're lucky you're only doing three events. That's because you got here because of a fan box. The Popovs are doing something like 10 events."

"Who are the other two?"

"A guy named Chirag Ali and your old friend Tserendolgor. You won't see either of them, but you're scheduled to be sharing an autograph table with the brothers tomorrow."

I'd seen the name Chirag Ali, but I didn't know who that was. He or she had sometimes popped up on the top-ten list. Tserendolgor was a dog soldier woman who looked like a German shepherd. We'd fought with her at the end of the third floor, and we'd saved her entire bubble at the end of the fifth. Donut did not like her, and she was going to be pissed if she found out the woman got to go to this con.

"I wish Lucia was involved. Then she'd be up here and not down there."

Zev grunted. "Lucia hasn't done an interview or event for a while now. She's too . . . unpredictable." Zev paused, seeing the concern on my face. "Donut is okay for now, Carl. Really. She's not the one in danger."

I knew what that meant. I was going to be sent back to the surface and into the jaws of some trap. The details of which were unclear.

"Are you . . . are you doing okay, Zev? Donut seems to be pretty worried about you."

The fish woman smiled sadly. "I'm doing about the best anyone can expect. We don't know what's going on back home since the entire system has gone dark. When this is all over, those of us who stayed on after the change don't know if we'll be welcomed home or executed as traitors. Plus, you know, my entire family was slaughtered because I refused to wear a pin. But I got a job to do. I gotta go, Carl. See you in a few hours."

She blinked and disappeared before I could say goodbye.

A PAIR OF GNOLL GUARDS ENTERED THE ROOM A MINUTE LATER. THEIR names were Frito and Moxo. I stood back while Frito installed a "bed" in the corner. This was nothing more than a blue glowing panel that I could walk over, and it would fully refresh and buff me for 30 hours. This was a tier-three bed, something I wouldn't be able to purchase until the ninth floor. They brought a crawler's biscuit and dropped it on the table. They also added a door against a wall that led to something labeled **Ultimate Training Room.**

"Is this thing gonna work?" I asked, eyeing the training room. "I can't pull up any of my systems."

"It'll work," Frito said. He paused and leaned in, whispering. "The captain sends his regards. That's a tier-four training room, so you best use it while you can. You won't be able to nick the room or bed when you leave. But a smart guy like yourself can be creative. We'll likely turn your inventory back on right before you return to the dungeon, just so you know."

The two mercenaries nodded and walked out.

I strolled over to the bed thing, and I instantly felt refreshed. My skin prickled for a moment, like I was walking through a sprinkler. If there were notifications or achievements associated with it, they were suppressed. I examined the crawler's biscuit, and it looked and smelled normal. I dropped it back on the table. Without the ability to properly examine it with my UI, there was no way I'd eat it.

I turned to the training room.

Interestingly, my Valtay portal skill worked on this door. I still couldn't enter or use any of my menus, nor could I pull up the subspace portal description, but the telltale glow of a portal surrounded the training room door.

I shrugged and stepped inside.

The room looked identical to the training room back at the base. The training menu popped up, just like normal. It allowed me to scroll through and pick something to train, but if that training required something that was in my inventory to use, like a weapon, I wouldn't be able to use it. Still, I could select multiple items, like Powerful Strike or Bare Knuckles.

It took me a bit of scrolling to figure out why this room was superior to the other one.

Firstly, it appeared I could train for up to six hours a day in up to six different skills, as opposed to one hour a day in a single skill. Also, I was now given a visualization regarding how far along in the training I was to level up. Plus it seemed I received an additional bonus to training.

Secondly, there were additional types of training listed. This room combined several kinds of training rooms into one. It wasn't just skills and weapons. The room was actually a combination of the regular training room, the magic workshop, the explosives studio, and multiple other similar rooms, all combined into one. My regular spells were listed as trainable along with spells associated with equipment, like my *Protective Shell*. Apparently, if I upgraded the spell in the training room, the associated armor—my boxer shorts in the case of *Protective Shell*—the equipment itself would actually be what got upgraded. Interesting.

But I could also train on how to use workshop tables, like my sapper's table and the explosives workshop. This was easily the most valuable feature of the room. I didn't need to have my tables with me. I just had to have them installed in my crafting studio.

I found **Sapper's Table** on the list and clicked it to see what would happen.

A familiar level five table popped up out of the ground. The table was identical to my own, though less scorched. I ran my hand across it, and it didn't come away sticky, either. I remembered the time I'd "accidentally" set off the hobgoblin disco ball. It'd left residue everywhere. The tables were the one place in the entire base that the poor, overworked cleaning bot didn't dare touch.

Instead of the multiarmed trainer guy who usually appeared, a badger creature with an eye patch and a hook for a hand faded into reality in front of me.

"Oi," the badger said. The name over his head simply said **Trainer.** "I hear you wanna learn how to blow things up and disarm traps and maybe brew a poison or two using this table. Well, you come to the right place, mate," the virtual badger said. "Let's see here." He paused, his eyes flashing. "Oi, mate. It looks like you already know your stuff. You're practically ready to teach me a thing or two. What can I do for you?"

"There's a specific type of bomb I want to learn how to make," I said. "I guess it's more of a trap. I think I have most of the components, but I'm still missing the last part," I told him.

He smiled and thought for a moment. "No, that's not a trap. Or a bomb. It's a weapon. The explosive itself is no problem, but what you're asking requires a different type of table. I see you have a bomber's studio and an engineering table, both of which can inch you there. But not quite, mate. You need either a hypnotist's bench or a necromancer's altar. Or maybe a spider nursery room. I see you recently added a pet stable to your personal space. You need something that'll allow for multiple minions. And not temporary ones, either. That or a bunch o' suicidal friends. Hmm. It doesn't look like something you can pull off. At least not anytime soon. I got a recipe for a trap that'll infect an entire party with stink-finger leprosy. Takes three hours to learn. Four hours if you want to add the extra-credit fungus module. Want me to teach you?"

Holy cow, I thought. *We need this room.* This trainer guy was an actual AI, not the mindless NPC in our other room. And I had access to multiple versions of this guy. If I pulled up the alchemy table, it'd probably be someone else. Someone Mordecai could talk to. Unfortunately, this was also a tier-four room, which meant normally one wouldn't have access to it until the 12th floor. I wondered if anyone ever had one of these rooms before, considering so few ever made it down that low.

I had less than four hours to exploit this the best I could.

"Let's talk about the first part of my idea. I've been working on sticky bombs for a while, but the ones I've been making aren't very adhesive. I can't go into my inventory right now to show you, but I was hoping you could help."

"Hmm," he said, eyes flashing again. "I think I know what the problem is. Let's put this table away and pull up the advanced bomber's studio workshop. Then we'll have to move over to the alchemy table for a minute, which means you'll be talking to my associate for a bit. But the whole module will only take two hours. Is that acceptable?"

"Let's do it."

Training Module Started.

FRITO AND MOXO THE GUARDS CAME TO ME WHILE I WAS WORKING ON my Powerful Strike. After the sticky bomb and then a few other odds and ends, the only thing I could do in a 15-minute increment was this skill. They actually waited for me to finish the module, and by the time I was done, it'd moved from nine to ten. It'd been stuck on nine for over a week, and getting it up just a single notch had been a long road.

The training guy for the skill was the same as in my regular training room, but he talked now, throwing insults at me while I pounded at the wooden dummies. I had a visualization of how efficient each strike was, which allowed me to hit items better and more effectively.

With all my equipment buffs along with the extra benefits of my primal race, the skill should have gone up to 16, but according to the display in the training room, it remained at 15. Mordecai had warned me that would probably happen. My primal race allowed me to train past 15 in skills and spells, but armor and weapons-based enhancements lost effectiveness past 15, which meant certain benefits, such as the +1 to Powerful Strike from my gauntlet, were greatly diminished.

That didn't mean the enhancements actually stopped at 15. There was complicated math involved I didn't understand. It was similar to how our personal space worked with multiple rooms attached. The bottom line was that the +1 to Powerful Strike from my gauntlet and the additional +5 from my toe ring would still enhance me past 15, but I'd probably need to get to 12 or so on my own before it did. And each level beyond that came with diminishing returns. If I wanted to hit 20, I'd probably have to train to 17 or 18 on my own, which likely wouldn't happen.

"Come on. Panel starts in a bit," Frito eventually said. "We'll all get our hides stripped if we're late."

We walked through the studio I'd used for the art contest, and it had completely transformed to a much larger room. There was a virtual audience filling the arena. They didn't see me. On the stage were a soother and a pair of dwarves, along with what looked like a quarter-sized version of one of the dwarven automatons from the fourth floor.

One of the dwarves stood at a workbench, preparing some items on it. He looked up, startled as we walked through.

"Oh, hello there," he said as we passed. He was an older man. He had a CrawlCon badge around his neck, and the name over him said **Dr. Ratchet.**

"You can see me?" I asked.

"I think we're actually in the same room," Dr. Ratchet said. "It's hard to tell sometimes. But I'm visiting the planet and had to borrow this room for my upcoming panel. This floor of the ship has access to the dungeon AI protocols, and it was the only available room." He patted his table. "I need the juice for my demonstration, so unfortunately you'll have to go upstairs. Sorry about that."

"Come on, no dawdling," Moxo the guard said, nudging at my back.

"Hey," Dr. Ratchet called over at me as I exited the far door, "uh, good luck. At both the panel and when you return. Keep your head down."

I left the room, an ominous feeling coming over me. I suddenly felt like I'd wasted my time in the training room. Like I was supposed to have learned something that I hadn't.

We moved into a tight hallway that looked more like an electrical conduit access panel. All three of us had to duck as we pushed our way through, passing doors and moving straight for what seemed like five minutes. The temperature in the halls was sweltering, and I felt sweat start to bead on my head. The two gnolls looked absolutely miserable.

We came to a ladder. It was like a ladder for a child, with the rungs too close to one another. "Up," the guard said. I complied, squeezing my way through a ceiling porthole, coming into a hallway identical to the one I'd just left.

There was no subspace portal warning, but something changed when I went up the ladder. My interface remained off, but I suddenly felt weaker, almost like the gravity had shifted.

"Breathe for a second," Frito said. "You're in a zero zone. No enhancements at all. You'll adjust in a second."

"Gods, I hate that transition," Moxo said, shifting.

I still didn't understand what all these different zones meant. There seemed to be multiple types. I made a fist, and for the very first time, my gauntlet didn't automatically form. What did that mean?

"Don't worry," Frito said. "We're going to studio three, which has a class two."

The other guard grunted. "Okay, enough rest. Move along."

We walked for another few minutes and stopped at a round portal with words over the door.

The words, I realized, said "Studio Three. Something, something, only." I recognized the text as Syndicate Standard. I could read it. Sort of. Like I knew it, but I didn't know it very well. Like an old language I hadn't spoken in a long time.

What the hell?

We entered the room, and I felt my energy return. The words on the door were back to the regular Syndicate Standard, which I could read just fine along with a few sentences in another alien script I didn't know.

"We're gonna wait in here," Frito said, pointing to a corner.

Moxo pulled out a vape pen similar to the one Quasar my lawyer used, and started sucking on it. "Yeah," he agreed. "We got the best seats in the house for this."

"Hello, Carl," a robot voice said. This was a Mexx-style Frisbee robot, but thinner and much sleeker-looking. "I am a Valtay Corporation Porter Bot, identification number 6.ff. I will be your assistant during the upcoming panel. You may call me Biff." It spun, and the room formed around me. A massive, completely full chamber with stadium seating appeared. It was packed with literally dozens of alien types, including several I'd never seen before, from bugs to slimes to three-headed-bird things. They did not see me.

Ahead of me was a long, straight table with four chairs facing the audience. It was raised up on a podium. The three chairs at the end of the row were already occupied. These guys did not see me, either. Or if they did, they didn't acknowledge my presence. The sound of crowd chatter filled the room.

Biff floated over to the final chair and hovered over it.

"This is where you'll be sitting, Carl."

I noted the long, empty space to the left of the chair.

That's where she'll be parked. They put me right next to her.

"Am I alone in the room?" I asked, moving to the chair. I was suddenly worried they were going to pull something ridiculous, like really put me alone in a room with this woman.

"That is correct," Biff said, "except for myself and the two flea-infested mercenaries who are smoking illicit, mind-altering materials while on duty."

"Watch it," Moxo called from the corner.

"Oh, I am terrified," the Frisbee robot replied. "My servos are quaking." To me, it added, "The panel will commence in approximately three minutes. You will be the only panelist attending virtually. Upon the conclusion of the event, remain in your seat, and your security, assuming they're both still conscious, will collect you to escort you back to your chamber."

"All righty," I said, apprehension rising as the robot vanished into the ceiling. I could smell whatever the two gnolls were smoking. It wasn't the distinct tangy smell of a blitz stick. It was actually closer to the skunky scent of weed, but not quite. It filled the room.

"We got the best seat in the house," Frito said. "People were paying big bucks for a chance to be at the panel. They're not going to tunnel it until later."

Moxo took a drag of his hit. "Being a mercenary has its perks."

33

<Note added by Crawler Rosetta. 9th Edition>
Never trust mercenaries.

I EXAMINED THE THREE CREATURES ALL SITTING TO MY RIGHT. I DIDN'T recognize any of them or their names.

Next to me was a ridiculously thin, flat-faced, orange-hued alien with wide-set eyes. The dude looked like a human-sized stick of gum with eyes and arms. He didn't wear any clothes at all, and his badge was magically affixed to his pale orange body. His eyes were the size of softballs and made a squishing noise when they moved. He had a floating window in front of him, and he was reading notes, not talking to the other two, who were chatting. The name over this guy read **Uptown Hal**.

The next was a female, tentacle-faced Saccathian. She reminded me of Princess D'Nadia, but about half the size. She wore a simple blue sheet of fabric that made her look like she was wearing a bedsheet toga. It looked dirty, too. Her name was indicated as **Sydnee Iglacia—Crawl Historian**.

The third was an older, heavily scarred, albino, bald elf that I immediately recognized as one of those Dream assholes. A moon elf. His name was **Drick**. Despite his advanced age, I could see the muscles bulging under his silk shirt. *This guy is a former crawler.*

He was listening to the Saccathian woman talk animatedly about something I couldn't quite understand. Something about audience numbers from a previous season. The guy stared back at her blankly.

It was clear they didn't know I was here.

"Hey," I called over to the gnoll guards sitting in the corner, "who are these three guys?"

Frito grunted. Neither of them stood. They both sat in a cloud of smoke.

"The first guy. The slate. He's an ex–game guide. From back before they used former crawlers. Now he has a popular show called *Uptown Hal Talks Tactics.* I don't know who the slime-face bitch is. It says she's a historian. That last guy is Drick. Was a crawler a long time ago. Tapped out at the end of the 11th. This was on a Valtay season, and he used a plasma saw as his main weapon."

"Yeah, he's a psycho," Moxo added. "But he's a funny psycho, so they use him a lot for panels. I think he's a worm head now. Can't remember."

"Don't say that in here," Frito growled to his companion. "And he is. He died a few years back in a fight at a way station, but he had a Valtay contract, and they got to him in time."

"They always do," Moxo said. *"Keeping the best of you alive,"* he added in a singsong voice like it was a jingle.

"Godsdamnit, Moxo," Frito hissed, "don't fuck around."

"Panel starts in two minutes and six seconds," a disembodied female voice announced.

"So, you think Carl is gonna survive?" Sydnee was saying to the elf. "If he does die, this panel will be his last appearance. It'll be great for my book sales."

"You know," Drick said, his voice full of disdain, "he's probably sitting in that chair right now, listening to everything you say."

"They don't let the crawlers listen in on this stuff," Sydnee said. "The Valtay are much more intelligent about security than the mudskippers ever were."

Drick grunted. "The Valtay aren't running the crawl. The Borant Corporation still is. It's a big difference. It's all mudskipper infrastructure with mercenary support." He turned and looked directly at me.

"Anyway, he'll probably survive," he said. "It's gonna be chaos, and that's Carl's preferred environment. He's gonna need to go straight to the offensive. Both the nebs and the mantids will be there, and they won't know the exact time or spot he's going to appear."

"I don't understand why they told them he'd be there," Sydnee said. "It seems like a betrayal."

"No," Uptown Hal said, speaking for the first time. He still had his face buried in his screen. His accent was strange. Like he was West African. "Drick is right. Summoning the hunters was the best choice after Lucia cast those spells and set up camp. He wouldn't have a chance against her one on one. This is still a desperate ploy. But unless they know the exact moment and spot he will appear, he's better off against the hunters than the Lajabless. Especially with her so angry."

"I don't understand any of this," Sydnee said.

"Hopefully Carl will," Uptown Hal said. He shared a grin with Drick. "I just wish we were allowed to tell this directly to him. We'll see. Ah, here comes our moderator."

"I can't believe she's late," Sydnee said. "I'd read she's never late."

"Someone leaked her path to the panel room, and it is packed with fans," Drick said. "Carl and Donut fans. She's going to be grumpier than usual."

In the back of the large room, a circular door twisted open, like the mouth of some beast. For a moment, I had a glance of a large crowd beyond, with blinking lights and things zipping through the air. Voices rose, a combination of both cheers and jeers. The view was quickly obscured by the large insect entering the room. The door irised shut, cutting off the sounds from the hall beyond.

The crowd within the arena went silent as the bug woman stormed down the center aisle. The way the large bug skittered reminded me of a bad-guy wrestler on their way to the mat, minus the music and crowd noises.

I examined the bug woman. I'd seen Vrah in action and again on the recap, but I wasn't quite prepared for how terrifying this thing was in such a mundane setting. My heart quickened as this woman bug, presumably Vrah's mother, came directly for me. My head spun, and I felt a little lightheaded.

Circe Took was the size of a mantaur. Her head resembled Odette's bug helmet, but it wasn't quite exact. Antennae things hung from her skull like dreadlocks, reminding me of the creatures from the *Predator* movies. Her top, folded arms were like segmented meter-long blades designed to pierce and disembowel enemies. A pair of secondary arms with three fingers on each side hung under the natural weapons. Her long, insectoid body was held up by three additional pairs of segmented and spiked legs. These, too, looked deadly.

There was no question that this creature was built for one thing. Hunting and killing prey.

A pair of translucent wings was folded on her back, covering a thick armored abdomen. Her six legs made clicking noises as she descended the stairs, crossed the space, and then came to stand next to me behind the table. She turned her large head to regard me. Her mirrored compound eyes examined me, and only then did I realize that she could actually see me.

I shivered. I had the urge to cough, and I suppressed it.

"Your luck is a dishonor on the Hive," she said finally.

"The Hive can lick my sack," I said.

Thwap.

The attack came so fast, I didn't have time to react.

Circe's top-right arm blade came down and cut straight through the table, cleaving a huge chunk out of it. Little pieces flew everywhere. A few people in the crowd shrieked in surprise.

If I'd really been sitting there next to her, she would've just cut me in half.

"By the gods," Uptown Hal shrieked, his voice going up an octave. The flat, strange alien jumped from his chair. He fell onto his back. He had two short legs, and they wriggled helplessly in the air for a minute like he was an upset turtle.

I'd like to say my lack of reaction was because I was cool and collected. But it was really because it'd happened too fast. Still, I seized the moment and looked up at the bug, smiling.

"I wonder how many times your daughter practiced that move. Too bad she never got the chance to use it."

A deep chittering noise rose from the throat area of the mantis. She bobbed up and down a few times like she was composing herself.

"Get up," Circe said to Hal, who remained on the ground, staring up at the bug woman with terror. I realized that since he couldn't see me, it had looked as if she'd almost attacked him. He'd probably just shat himself.

And without any further fanfare, Circe Took turned her attention to the crowd.

"We are here today to discuss the history of the crawl. That and nothing else. I am the moderator. Therefore I am in charge of this discussion. I will be asking questions of the four panelists in the unlikely event I deem the discussion requires their input. I will be doing the introductions."

She started at the end of the line, pointing at Drick. She pointed with the same arms she'd just used to slice the table, and she pierced the arm directly through my head. I was still invisible to the crowd.

"Drick is the famed iguanoid–turned–moon elf crawler from approximately 400 seasons ago. He has an impressive body count for a crawler. Was stabbed in the back after a bar fight at a way station after he bragged too much about his fighting prowess and is now under the control of a Valtay worm." A smattering of applause filled the room.

"Next we have a Saccathian. I don't know who she is."

"My name is Sydnee, and I'm the author of—" the woman began.

Circe talked over her. "The idiot still on the floor is Uptown Hal. He is a former game guide and occasional manager who spent over 200 seasons in the dungeon before retiring and starting his own program. He was never a warrior."

"And finally," Circe began. The crowd erupted into cheers, and I knew I was now visible. I sat stiffly, the cleaved-in-two section of table right in front of me. I had my hand on it, and I could feel the real table of the studio was perfectly intact. "We have the top crawler in the current season. He will not survive much longer."

I waved, planting a smile on my face.

Circe leaned forward. She delivered the words in an almost deadpan voice, like a bored college professor. "We are here to discuss the history of the crawl and how it has changed over the cycles. We all know how it started. When the original council nations first accidentally tripped the primal engines and started the chain reaction that overpopulated the galaxy, it was eventually decided that we needed to both collect the primal elements left behind on all the pre-seeded worlds and to beat back the new biological overgrowth. In addition, superior species such as the Hive—who have been at the forefront of decoding and reverse engineering primal technology—approached the council and demanded the ability to field-test macro-AI-controlled enhancement zones. This, unfortunately, led to the formation of a Syndicate subcommittee that put the request under advisement. . . .”

She went on like this for almost ten minutes straight, not allowing anyone else on the panel to speak. The story was actually kind of interesting, though Sydnee the historian woman scoffed loudly multiple times during the mantis's lecture, suggesting she disagreed with what the bug lady was saying.

I kept thinking, *If Donut was here, she'd have stopped this by now.* I could tell the crowd was already bored out of their minds. They'd mostly come to this panel not because they wanted to get a mind-numbing history lesson, but because they knew Circe and I would be in the same room together, and they wanted to see what was going to happen.

After a few more minutes of the bug woman discussing how the formation of the Indigenous Species Protection Act was endangering the very existence of all life in the universe, I leaned forward and banged my head loudly on the table. I placed my head firmly on the illusionary broken spot. It banged louder than I expected, echoing through the room like a gunshot.

Circe paused her droning and didn't speak for several moments. The other members of the panel didn't speak, either.

“Carl,” Circe eventually said, “what are you doing?”

“You did it,” I said, not moving my head from the table. “You killed me. I am literally dead right now. Your kid couldn't do it, but you pulled it off. You've succeeded in boring me to death.”

The crowd erupted in laughter. To my right, Uptown Hal said nothing, and neither did Sydnee. Drick guffawed.

“Carl, I will be forced to mute you from the panel if you're going to insist on being an imbecile.”

“Mute?” I said. “You're not letting anyone talk.” I finally looked up, addressing the crowd. “Does anybody give a shit about this subject?”

“No,” half the crowd said.

“I do,” Sydnee said, sounding crestfallen.

"Great," I said. "Sydnee or whatever your name is, what's the name of your book?"

She straightened. "It's called *A Petite Chronicle of the Crawl: One Lady's Journey into Enlightenment Through Knowledge and Scholarship and Three-Beat Poetry.*"

"Sounds like a great time. If you guys really want to learn about this stuff, read that book. I guarantee it can't possibly be less interesting than this bullshit."

"Thank you, Carl," Sydnee said. "Can I put your endorsement on the cover?"

"Absolutely," I said.

The dreadlock-hair things on Circe's head all went rigid. She started to say something, but I cut her off.

"I heard a rumor that a lot of you guys waited in line a long time to see this panel. Is that correct?"

"That's right," a person called. I looked up at him. It was a half-human, half-robot guy sitting near the back. He was wearing a T-shirt that appeared to feature a pinup version of Elle on it, and he was eating what looked suspiciously like sparkling cotton candy on a stick.

"I'm guessing what you guys *really* want is to hear what this roach lady has to say about me killing her coward bitch of a child. And then you probably want to hear me respond by saying I'm going to kill her other kid, too. Then she's going to get all hissy, and I'll say something else that'll piss her off further. Isn't that right?"

Now the crowd was starting to really get worked up. To my left, Circe Took was bouncing up and down, angrily chittering. Her weird hair things were all rigid, making her look like a praying mantis with an afro. Uptown Hal was starting to back away, as if afraid the mantis would literally explode. Sydnee just seemed happy she got a chance to mention her book. She'd pulled the book out and was holding it against her chest. Drick was watching me intently. He, too, was tense, as if afraid I'd somehow sneaked a bomb halfway across the galaxy.

"Here's the thing," I said. I leaned back and put my bare feet up on the table. "I was originally going to say, 'Y'all can go fuck yourselves,' and storm out of the room. But I have a problem, and I'd like to enlist your help. You guys want to help me crowdsource a solution?"

"This is why we should never use active crawlers for this," Circe hissed as the room went berserk. She looked up at some wide-eyed soother guy standing in the back of the room. "Cut him off."

"Don't," a voice called. It was a woman. A human or maybe an elf woman sitting in the back corner, wearing a simple brown cloak with a distinctive pattern on it. The pattern was somewhat familiar, but I couldn't place it. It was circles and lines. Her voice was unnaturally amplified, like she, too, had an invisible microphone. She sounded much older than she looked. She pointed at the same soother and called, "Don't." The creature froze, eyes wide. Several audience members, noticing this woman, all started to point and whisper. Several people gasped.

The audience members closest to her all got up and scattered back, as if afraid of her.

Who the hell is that?

"I am the moderator of this panel," Circe hissed, speaking to the newcomer. She slammed her two lower arms on the table, and it broke off at the point where she'd chopped earlier, causing her to stumble forward and almost tumble off the platform. All three of the other panelists jumped back while the audience tittered. Everyone was looking back and forth wildly between me, Circe, and this new woman.

"Was this the plan? Was it a setup? To mock the death of my child?" Circe hissed. "To humiliate me? Well, it won't work. I am not the Maestro, and I won't be trapped so easily."

I looked over at Uptown Hal. He still stood turned sideways, facing me and Circe. His eyes were intent on the mantis woman. Sydnee had skittered back, and she was now standing behind Drick, who was whispering something in her ear. Drick's attention moved quickly between me, Circe, and the robed woman in the back of the room. I could tell that he was also talking to someone using his interface.

They all were, I realized. Everyone's eyes were glossy and flashing. It was the intergalactic equivalent of everyone having their phones out, recording whatever this was.

I remained on my chair, my feet up on the table. I knew to this crowd, it now looked as if my feet were floating in the air.

"Can someone tell me who the lady in the robe is?" I finally asked. Then I felt myself add, "She's kinda hot."

It was then, at that moment, that I finally realized how stupid and reckless I was being. I looked sharply over at the two guards, Frito and Moxo. They were gone. Moxo's vape-pen thing remained on the floor, smoke lazily drifting out. The heavy scent of the drug remained in the room. *You idiot.* This was the same thing as the drugs hidden in the pet treats on Odette's show. This *was* a setup. I'd been drugged with something.

I still felt as if I had all my faculties. But something had definitely changed. My inhibitions were gone.

I didn't care. I guessed that was the point. The Valtay had set this up. But was it to get me in trouble or was it something else? I was in over my head. Again. I was being used by forces much bigger than myself. Again.

I didn't goddamn care. I looked over the audience and thought, *This is my chance.*

The woman in the robe spoke.

"Carl, I am not allowed to address you directly because I am one of your sponsors, and it will be a violation of the sponsorship contract. So I will be taking my leave. But I am also one of the sponsors of Crawl-Con, and I have directed them to allow you to speak. That's all I can say."

The woman strode from the room. People scattered out of her way as she marched toward the round door and disappeared.

Sponsor? I thought. The Apothecary? Or was she from the Open Intellect Pacifist Action Network?

"Bitch. Godsdamned bitch. I will kill her," Circe growled, watching the woman leave. "I am not staying for this." Without another look at me, the large mantis started to move toward the exit. She had to move the broken table piece out of the way. She picked it up and threw it against the wall. It crashed loudly, shattering into pieces, before she started to flee.

"So," I said loudly, "can someone tell me the best way to kill Vrah?"

Circe froze, stopping dead in the space between the raised platform and the audience. She stood rigid, not turning. To my right, Sydnee let out a gasp. The audience was suddenly dead silent.

"I mean, that's what you talk about at these things, isn't it? That's why we're here, no? That's what this whole convention is, is it not? To celebrate killing. We talk about monsters. NPCs. We glory in the casting of spells that melt the faces off people like myself. Vrah decapitates her kills and wears their heads on her back."

I allowed the uncomfortable silence to hang for a few seconds before continuing.

"I just judged a little kids' art contest where a bunch of them drew pictures of me dying. Of my friends dying. You treat us like we're nothing. Like we're not real. Like we're below you. It's like you're all members of this giant death cult, and all the pain and suffering are just great as long as it's entertaining and as long as it's not you. You're all smart. You're intelligent, thinking species. You allow yourselves to separate people like myself into a different class. 'It's okay. It's just crawlers.' But deep down, you know. You have to know what you're doing. I don't get it, and I don't think I ever will. I have to get over that and accept it for what it is. So y'all like it when other people die. Great. Let's go all in."

I pointed down at Circe, who remained frozen in place.

"I'm not asking to cheat. I'm just asking to have the same information as those who I'll be fighting. The moment I'm done with this panel, I'm going back out there, and I'm pretty sure I'll be facing down not Lucia Mar, but Circe's daughter in battle. And not just her. Aren't there several mantises?"

I already knew the answer to this because I'd seen it on the recap episode. Still, I looked over at Drick, who I knew would be the first. The man nodded.

Just little seeds here and there, and soon enough you have a forest.

"Are they *all* children of Circe? How many are there?"

Someone else, an orc from the audience, called out the answer. "There're eight left, though one stays in Zockau to exchange with the other trade representatives. That one is a male. It's seven warriors including Vrah."

"The warriors are all her daughters," someone else added. "They're all Dark Hive."

"But the nebulars are camping out also. They're claiming they have the right to hunt you now, too," yet another person called. "You're in their territory."

I motioned to the three other panelists, who remained standing there uncertainly. "Good, good. Let's talk about this. Sit back down, guys. We have a discussion on our hands."

This whole time, Circe remained rigid, not moving.

"Circe, you're free to come back up. I don't know how much time we have left, but I want to brainstorm with all of you. If you were in my position, tell me what you'd do. Feel free to raise your hands. Or, uh, tentacles. Whatever you got. Uptown, Drick, feel free to let me know if you think someone's suggestion has merit. You, too, Circe. It'll be great to have an insider's perspective."

"If anything happens to my other daughters, I will personally hunt down and kill the person responsible," Circe suddenly hissed before becoming unglued. She stomped toward the door, causing more audience members to scatter.

"That'll be me," I called. "I'll be the one responsible. And you should have thought of that before you sent them all off to die in my dungeon. It's too bad you're not in there, too. I guess you're too old or too cowardly to face me."

The mantis paused again, but then she stormed from the conference room.

"You know you're fucked, right?" Uptown Hal said. The rectangular alien looked down at me sadly. "She is correct when she says she is not the Maestro. The mantids are not just excellent hunters. They are tacticians. I am constantly in awe of them. If you survive this, you best make sure you kill them all."

I sighed and returned my attention to the crowd. "Uptown says I'm fucked. So how do I unfuck myself? What's the best way to kill a mantis?"

Multiple hands and tentacles and wings rose into the air.

―――――――――

"I'LL BE BACK TOMORROW," I SAID WHEN THE SOOTHER GUY INDICATED our time was almost up. The two mercenaries had returned, and the vape-pen thing had disappeared. "I'll be signing autographs at my own table and taking photographs and answering questions. If your plan works, I'll be sure to bring the heads of Circe's daughters to decorate my table."

The crowd laughed and cheered.

Oh shit, I thought, remembering something. "By the way," I called out, "have you guys ever noticed how awesomely designed the Desperado Club is? It's just amazing."

Several audience members looked at each other, bewildered. I laughed, still feeling the effects of the drug.

"So who was that lady?" I asked Uptown as we all stood.

"A representative of the collective. Their spokeswoman," he said.

I nodded. I was correct. The Apothecary.

"They are not someone you want to attach yourself—"

The room blinked and suddenly the crowd and my fellow panelists all disappeared, cutting Uptown Hal off in midsentence.

"Come on," Moxo said, grabbing me by the arm. "Time to go home."

"Yeah, you forgot your vape when you stepped out," I said.

The two guards were much less talkative and more serious as we made the trek back to my greenroom. I didn't bother trying to talk to them further.

We stopped in front of the door to the studio that in turn led to my greenroom.

"You can figure out the rest of the way," Frito said. He leaned in. "There are two types of transactions. Personal and business. We have transacted both types today. The matter with the drug was business. The matter with the commander is personal. Two separate things. Do you understand?"

"No," I said.

He patted me on the shoulder and pushed my back as I entered the now-empty studio. All that remained was a single table sitting there. As I looked at the table, my UI suddenly returned. A page of messages appeared. I only read the most recent one.

DONUT: IF YOU SEE THIS, DON'T GO TOWARD THE SAFE ROOM.
IT'S A TRAP. LUCIA IS IN THERE AND CAN HURT YOU EVEN IF
YOU GO IN. I KILLED HER STUPID DOG AND SHE'S REALLY
MAD ABOUT IT. SHE'S WAITING FOR YOU. BUT THE BUG
LADIES ARE OUTSIDE IN THE TOWN. THEM AND THESE OTHER

GUYS WHO LOOK LIKE BAD *STAR TREK* ALIENS WITH BIG
HATS.

I already knew all this thanks to the panel. I took a deep breath. I'd
written out instructions for Donut in my scratch pad and was prepared
to send them to her. I paused, finally noticing the table that was sitting
there in the middle of the empty studio.

Automaton Table. Level 5.

Sitting on the table was a book. It was a regular paperback featuring
a familiar smiling dwarf riding on the back of a mechanical-horse thing.
Dr. Ratchet's Guide to Building Automatons for Fun and Profit. I picked
it up and opened to the first page. It was autographed.

I took both the book and table into my inventory and cracked my
neck. Once I entered the greenroom, I'd have about five minutes before
I was to be transferred back to the dungeon. I took a deep breath. I
pulled out my bandanna and returned it to my face. I pulled out the
Ring of Divine Suffering and slid it onto my finger.

"Here we go," I said, and I entered the greenroom.

"POISON IS GOOD AGAINST THE MANTIDS," ONE AUDIENCE MEMBER said. "It affects them almost three times as fast as it does everyone else."

"That's no good," replied someone else. "Those guys load up on antidote stuff. I'm pretty sure Vrah has an antidote ring. So you can poison her, but it'll get cured almost right away."

"And it can't be cloud poison. She's immune against that now, too, remember?" a third guy said. "You'd have to stab her with a poisoned blade. It'd have to be a poison that kills in five seconds or less. Or one that can't be cured."

"That's not going to work," I said with a sigh. "Any other ideas?"

"Their necks are the least armored parts of their body," a blob thing called out.

"The other hunters like to use alarm traps because they're loud, and loud sounds hurt mantids," yet another audience member added. This was a little chunky dwarflike girl with what looked like chocolate all over her face. "It keeps the bugs away long enough for them to claim the crawler bounties. Mantids like to swoop in from above and poach other hunters' kills."

I glanced over at Drick, who gave a half nod.

"They poach the other hunters?" I asked. "Doesn't that piss everyone off?"

The crowd laughed. They'd finally warmed to the uncomfortable subject and were all participating. A few had gotten up and left, but the moment they did, the soother dudes at the door allowed others to enter the small arena, and the seats remained full. When the round door opened, I could see a throng of people had gathered outside.

"A few seasons back, Vrah got into a fight and killed a fellow hunter," someone else called. This guy was a fuzzy Quokka, the same type of creature as the talk show host Ripper Wonton. "They said it was legal since it was in the Hunting Grounds. Since then, people just do what the Dark Hive says. Almost everyone is scared of them."

"But those nebular guys are also waiting to hunt me. Why are they pushing back against the Hive?"

"The nebs have never gotten along with the mantids," the same Quokka said. "They fought a war a long time ago. Plus, you know, they're the nebs. They kinda just do what they do."

"I don't normally agree with mantid policy," Uptown Hal said, "but in that case, the nebulars got what they deserved. They were squatting in a Hive system. Not that the Dark Hive had anything to do with that. Those were the Burrowers, but most people don't know the difference."

I'd never seen a nebular before. I hadn't seen any during my raid on Zockau, and from what I gathered, they weren't ones to attend shows like this.

They weren't actually a distinct alien race, but a religious cult that mechanically and bio-augmented themselves as a sacrament. Their deity was apparently some space oddity at the center of the inner system. They were nomadic, oftentimes settling onto barely hospitable planets and then bioengineering their own children to adapt. They'd only live on the planet long enough for their children to grow to adults, and then half of them would move on to a new world. They consisted of soothers and humans and elves and dozens of other aliens, though apparently it was sometimes difficult to tell what their lineage was because they were always wearing the same outfit, which apparently covered their whole bodies. I'd have to see it for myself, but I had the impression they looked kinda like the sand people from *Star Wars* wearing bishop hats.

People viewed them more as a nuisance than as a genuine threat. From what I gathered, they had a healthy income stream, but I had no idea what it was. They didn't actively recruit, and they only settled on empty worlds and abandoned space stations. They fought if they were attacked but were generally considered pacifistic and kept to themselves.

Except when it came to the crawl.

As I understood it, the Nebular Sin Patrol was one of the few hunting groups who always attended a crawl, but the actual hunters were different every time. They trained for the event, and the team consisted of young males, all studying to be priests. They believed people like me—someone born on a "seeded" planet—were an abomination, and they considered the act of hunting us as a sort of crusade. They spent a lot of money on sending hunters, and they sometimes even paid for a deity sponsorship. They were actively campaigning for the right to run a future crawl.

There weren't many mentions of them in the cookbook, but it appeared they liked to focus their crawler extermination efforts on cleric- and paladin-based players for some reason. I remembered from that list that they'd claimed Prepotente and Miriam Dom as their targets. Someone else mentioned that they'd biffed an attack on Lucia Mar a few days back, despite her being claimed by the Dark Hive.

As I suspected, the truce on who was allowed to hunt whom was already falling apart.

"That's what always happens, in the end," Uptown Hal said when I pointed that out. "Scarcity breeds increased competition. And competition always leads to violence. It's actually a little ironic, considering that's a core tenet of the nebs' bizarre religion. To avoid violence. And poverty. Dunno how that translates to them camping out on inhospitable worlds, always getting themselves wiped out by the environment."

"Their pacifism is the one portion of their religion I respect," Drick added, looking at me, "not that they all follow it, especially the priests. But it sounds good when sung out to the heavens. Their 'Ballad of Survival,' they call it. Avoid conflict. They preach that scarcity-based competition breeds violence, and I agree with this. But it is their next principle which I feel is much more important to the question before us now, quoted directly from one of their songs: *Violence breeds chaos. From chaos we were born and into chaos we will succumb.*"

A sudden uncomfortable silence filled the room.

"Do these panels always stray this far off the main subject?" Sydnee asked.

"Just the good ones," Uptown Hal said as the audience laughed.

ZEV HAD RETURNED TO THE GREENROOM AS I SPRINTED IN.

"Carl, you took too long on your panel," she said. "I was going to give you fifteen minutes in the training room, but they came and took it away."

"It's okay. I need five minutes to get ready."

"What happened on that panel? The tunnel is going crazy. The Valtay blocked all the attempted live tunnels, but everyone is talking about it. They said you attacked Circe Took, that you somehow pushed her off the podium. And the Apothecary was there egging you on."

I laughed as I grabbed the bowl of fruit on the counter. It had appeared earlier while I was training after they noticed I didn't touch the crawler biscuit. I pulled it all into my inventory, including the bowl.

I tried to pull out an alarm trap, but I received an error.

You may not remove inventory items in this location.

Shit, shit. Okay. I'd have to do it all when I hit the ground. I started moving things around in my hotlist.

"You know, Zev," I said as I frantically worked, "it's weirdly comforting that the telephone game still exists out in the wide universe. It reminds me that you guys aren't that different."

"I don't know what that means, Carl."

I ignored her as I jumped back to the chat.

CARL: Okay, guys, listen carefully. I'll be there in four minutes. I'm going to copy and paste the plan. Read it quickly and then tell me when you're in place. Katia, are you near a guildhall?
KATIA: Entering now. We were trying to make it back to where you are, but it was just too far.
DONUT: DON'T GO INTO THE SAFE ROOM.
CARL: Are all the dots still turned off on the map?
DONUT: I THINK SO. I HAVEN'T BEEN OUTSIDE IN A WHILE.
SAMANTHA IS STILL OUT THERE, BUT SHE'S MAD AT ME AND ISN'T TALKING.

SAMANTHA: YOU ABANDONED ME. THIS WAS WORSE THAN THE
     NOTHING. IT WAS WORSE THAN WHEN MY MOTHER
     HUMILIATED ME IN FRONT OF MY KING. I DON'T KNOW IF I CAN
     HANDLE ANY MORE INDIGNITY. FIRST, THE DISGUSTING,
     SLOBBERING DOG TREATED ME AS A CHEW TOY, AND THEN
     YOU DID NOTHING TO HELP ME. AND NOW I AM ATTACHED TO
     THE BACK OF THIS BUG. I AM SURROUNDED BY DECAPITATED
     HEADS, AND LET ME TELL YOU, THEY ARE POOR COMPANY.
DONUT: OH, HONEY. YOU USED TO BE A SEX DOLL. I'M QUITE
     CERTAIN YOU CAN HANDLE ALL MANNER OF INDIGNITY.
SAMANTHA: DON'T SLUT-SHAME ME. I'M GOING TO KILL YOUR
     MOTHER.

As they bickered back and forth, I activated an alarm trap within my
inventory. I actually had an initiated one already on my list, forever
playing "Kickstart My Heart" by Mötley Crüe, but I decided it would
be best to have something with a short delay.

CARL: You two fight later. Donut, did you read the plan?
DONUT: LUCIA AND HER DOG ARE IN THE SAFE ROOM. SHE'S
     SCREAMING AND SCREECHING, AND THE LAST TIME WE
     LOOKED, SHE WAS PUNCHING HERSELF IN THE FACE. SHE'S
     TRASHED THE PLACE WORSE THAN THE TIME MISS BEATRICE
     WRECKED THE KITCHEN WHEN YOU TOLD HER SHE SHOULD
     STOP TRYING TO SELL THOSE AWFUL LEGGINGS. CARL,
     LUCIA IS CRAZY. I KNOW WE SAID THAT BEFORE, BUT SHE'S
     CRAZIER THAN YOU THINK. SHE'S WAITING FOR ME TO COME
     OUT. SHE'S FIGURED OUT A WAY TO CHEAT THE SAFETY
     MEASURES. SHE HAS TRAPS THAT KICK PEOPLE OUT OF THE
     ROOM. I WENT OUT THERE WHEN I THOUGHT SHE WAS GONE,
     AND I HIT A TRAP. IT TELEPORTED ME INTO THE MIDDLE OF
     TOWN. AND THEN WHEN I TRIED TO GET BACK TO THE SAFE
     ROOM, I HIT ANOTHER. THEN SHE CAME OUT OF THE WOODS
     AND CHASED ME INSIDE JUST AS THE HUNTERS ARRIVED.
     MORDECAI AND I WANTED THEM TO KILL HER, BUT THEY GOT
     HERE REALLY FAST, AND WE THINK THEY ALREADY KNEW

YOU WERE GOING TO BE HERE. NOW LUCIA IS IN THE SAFE
ROOM, I'M IN THE GUILDHALL, AND THERE ARE A BUNCH OF
HUNTERS OUTSIDE. THERE ARE SIX OR SEVEN BUG GUYS
AND LIKE 10 OF THESE GUYS IN WEIRD ROBES WITH TUBES
ALL OVER THEM. THEY HAVE MAGNIFICENT HATS, THOUGH.

SAMANTHA: THEIR HATS REALLY ARE FASHIONABLE.

CARL: Goddamnit, did you read my instructions or not?

DONUT: I AM TRYING TO GIVE YOU IMPORTANT BACKSTORY,
CARL. AND YES.

KATIA: I won't be able to make a good facsimile in time, but I have
an idea. Daniel has a stuffed animal called a back-alley mouser
that'll work. I'm already at a table, shaping a fake crown and
sunglasses. Too bad we don't have robot Donut anymore.

CARL: Is Lucia in her pretty-woman form, or is she the skeleton
lady?

DONUT: SHE WAS IN THE PRETTY-LADY FORM LAST I SAW, BUT
THAT WAS A WHILE AGO. SHE ALREADY CHANGED ONCE.
ALSO, WHAT IS A MOUSER? I DON'T LIKE THE SOUND OF THAT
ONE BIT.

CARL: The hunters haven't tried coming into the safe room? Even
to just talk?

DONUT: NOT THAT I KNOW OF. I THINK THEY KNOW YOU'RE
COMING BACK. THEY'RE WAITING FOR YOU JUST LIKE LUCIA
IS WAITING FOR ME.

SAMANTHA: THEY KNOW CARL IS COMING. THEY DON'T KNOW
EXACTLY WHEN. THEY DIDN'T KNOW WHERE, EITHER.

My heart skipped a beat.

CARL: Samantha.

SAMANTHA: SO . . . THEY DO KNOW SOME OF IT. THEY TRIED
TORTURING ME TO TELL THEM WHERE YOU WOULD APPEAR. I
PLAYED ALONG. LIKE THEY COULD ACTUALLY TORTURE ME.
HA! I TOLD THEM, BUT I TOLD THEM THE WRONG SPOT. I HAD
YOU APPEARING A WHOLE FIVE METERS AWAY FROM THE
REAL SPOT. YOU'RE WELCOME. BUT THE DRYAD GUY

SNITCHED ME OUT. SO THEY KNOW. BUT THE ROBE GUYS
AND THE BUG GUYS ARE FIGHTING OVER WHO GETS TO KILL
YOU, AND I THINK THEY ARE GOING TO KILL EACH OTHER
FIRST.

I took a deep breath.

CARL: Okay. I'm transferring in a minute. Get ready at the door.
Wait for my signal.

"Zev, is it going to let me down an invisibility potion before I teleport back?"

"I . . . I don't think so, Carl. Thirty seconds to transfer."

I clicked on a health potion to test it. I received an error. *Great.* I
would be coming in without any protections.

"Okay, this is it," I said. A strange calm descended onto me. There
was nothing peaceful about the sudden warmth that spread through me.
Still, that was the sense I had. Calm. In the back of my mind, that feeling
of movement, the hidden river, raged.

This is where you belong, Carl, the river said. *Jump into the rapids. Embrace the chaos.*

"Zev, if I die and Donut gets out of this, please watch over her."

"I'll do my best, Carl," Zev said as I felt the first tingles of teleportation, like hundreds of hands coming to drag me into the abyss.

35

ENTERING ALUCARDA.

I teleported back into the village, my face pressed up against the door to the safe room tavern. I'd actually been standing *in* the doorway when I'd originally been whisked away, and I was lucky I hadn't just had my nose sliced off. Instead, the effect was like I'd been smacked in the face with a baseball bat. I slammed down on the invisibility potion as I staggered. I dropped a smoke curtain as I jumped to the left, tripping again, this time over the corpse of an NPC. The same dryad I'd been talking to when I'd been teleported away. The snitch.

At that same moment, multiple things happened at once.

The heavy form of a mantis landed on the ground right where I'd been standing. The creature—it wasn't Vrah—slammed her forward segmented arms against the ground, swinging wildly in an attempt to catch me. She missed by inches.

The entire front of the tavern rocked as magic missiles and lightning bolts and small fist-sized fireballs slammed in and around the doorway. These all came from a group of nebs huddled about forty feet away. A full-powered magic missile slammed my shoulder just as I activated *Wisp Armor*.

"Gah," I cried out as the mantis behind me was also slammed by the attack. She crumpled to the ground. Not dead, but she screamed profanities at the nebular priests.

Despite the magic protection, my health plummeted by almost half. I continued to run, praying my invisibility would protect me.

CARL: Do it now!

DONUT: THEY'RE OUT!

I heard the pop of teleportation behind me, but I didn't have time to look. I cast *Tripper*, causing the rest of the traps in the area to all go off at once. Hundreds of little explosions and snares and teleport traps all detonated simultaneously.

I hurled an alarm trap ball as chaos erupted. I lurched toward the next building, turning the corner onto another street. I paused at a strange scene. There was a goddamn inverted crucifix in the middle of the street with an ursine nailed to it upside down. He had the word "*Leche*" carved into his chest. The word was facing up, so it was carved upside down on the bear's naked stomach.

The creature was still alive.

What the fuck? I didn't have time. I moved around him and across the street. I came to a small temple that overlooked the town. It was the tallest building in the area that wasn't an actual tree house. I activated Sticky Feet as I executed a dropkick against the bamboo wall. I ran along the side of the building, angling upward to get a better view as I pulled the next potion ball. This one was filled with my last potion of Bloodlust, the same berserking potion I'd used to save us against the baby sharktopuses. It made creatures speed up and blindly attack anyone near them. I searched for a target.

DONUT: IT WORKED! CLOCKWORK SLEDGIE NUMBER ONE WENT OUTSIDE, AND STUPID LUCIA DID HER TELEPORT THING ON CLOCKWORK SLEDGIE TWO! I CAN'T BELIEVE IT. THAT THING DIDN'T LOOK ANYTHING LIKE ME. SHE'S GONE! SO IS THE DOG!

Relief flooded me. I'd been relying solely on the information from my panel that this would work. Information I'd publicly dismissed as untrustworthy and too risky to rely upon.

Where the hell was Vrah?

CARL: Have the real Sledge wheel it all the way to the door to the outside. Don't let Bomo out of the guildhall. Take the invisibility potion in case someone comes in. If they do, pull the whole thing into your inventory before they can steal it and book it back to safety.

The trap ball I'd tossed finally activated.

Peaking at Number Five on October 18th, 1975, it's "Ballroom Blitz."

I cast *Ping*. I received an error message.

Oh shit! It didn't work! It's almost like the mapping system is blocked out in this town!

"Damnit," I growled as the snare-and-bass-drum intro to the song echoed through town. My abs burned from standing at a right angle. I'd heard this tune a million times, but I had no idea who the artist was. I scrambled up the side of the building, curving around the back of the steeple to get a view of the bedlam spreading down below. One of the two clockwork Sledges who'd teleported right into the midst of the hunters exploded just as a pair of pissed-off mantis warriors descended on the group of nebular priests.

The bugs screamed and pointed at their injured companion as the nebs shouted back. One of the bugs pushed a robed priest, whose hands started glowing.

A third mantis was attempting to destroy the trap ball. The music had an obvious effect on the bugs. All four of the ones on the ground—the two fighting the nebs, the injured one at the door, and the one slamming the trap ball against a rock—all had a debuff over their head. Unsettled.

They're all bunched together.

I quickly stowed the potion ball and pulled a full-strength hoblobber. I chucked it into the chaos.

Bam!

Body parts tore through the air. Notifications flew, including a level notification. I waved them away as I desperately searched the air for Vrah. Was she invisible, too?

Despite the hob-lobber going off right in their midst, the damage-enhanced explosive had only killed a handful of them. All of them were blown off their feet, some now missing body parts. It appeared I'd killed three of the nebs, but none of the mantis warriors. They had explosive protection. Still, the protection wasn't absolute. They were all injured and disoriented.

The song continued to play, louder than ever. I took a second invisibility potion. I only had two more after this. My sticky feet would run out soon. I scrambled up the side of the building, going even higher. I grasped onto the tip of the spire, anchoring myself so I wouldn't fall when my foot buff ended.

CARL: Samantha, where are you and Vrah?

A pair of bugs swooped down onto the scene, coming from the top of a massive tree that appeared to have recently been on fire. They rocketed toward their injured companions. Neither of these was Vrah.

I pulled the berserking potion, aimed, and beaned it directly at the closest of the two flying bugs. It slammed the back of the creature, who howled indignantly.

The mantis turned in the air, searching for me. Her companion also stopped, looking at the bug questioningly. The **Enraged** buff appeared over the first bug's head. She reached over, almost casually, and yanked the head off of her own sister. *Holy shit.* She hissed loudly and then dove like a hawk toward the still-recovering group of nebs and bugs.

The robe on one of the priests had ripped off in the explosion, revealing a young human male. The priest had almost been zeroed out by the explosion, but he'd healed himself. He fired a magic missile at the screaming and diving mantis, which staggered the bug. She shrieked in rage. At this distance, I couldn't read the name over the priest's head, but I saw it started with a Q. I jumped into the menu for the Ring of Divine Suffering, searching for a nebular with a Q name. There was only one. I marked him as the berserking mantis descended, slamming onto the ground, cleaving the human in half.

I then marked the next nebular. And the next. By this point, they were all fighting, and all of them were injured, and I didn't dare mark any more.

All three of the killed nebs had intelligence as their highest stat. The ring's Marked for Death skill leveled up between the second and third kills, giving me a total of seven stat points in intelligence. The next two kills with the ring would give me three stat points each.

I quickly noted that Vrah was on the list, able to be marked. Lucia was not.

All of the dots on my map suddenly populated. Whatever protection spell there was before, it was now gone. The screen was sparsely populated. The X's of dead NPCs filled the village.

SAMANTHA: WE WERE WAITING ON THE OTHER SIDE OF TOWN. SHE GOT INTO A FIGHT WITH MISS BOO-HOO-YOU-KILLED-MY-DOGGIE WHEN SHE TELEPORTED HERE ALONG WITH THAT CLOCKWORK ROCK MONSTER AND CAT. THE BUG LADY ATTACKED THE CAT FIRST, AND NOW THERE IS STUFFING EVERYWHERE. THE DOG LADY CAST A SPELL AND DISAPPEARED. THE BUG LADY IS REALLY MAD. I COULDN'T SEE ALL OF IT. I'M FACING THE WRONG DIRECTION. THE BUG LADY KEEPS HISSING. SHE SOUNDS LIKE A SNAKE WITH A LISP. THEN SHE THREW ME ON THE GROUND AND FLEW AWAY.

Shit, shit. She was coming for me now. She'd found me last time when I was invisible. I still didn't see her. I had to hurry.

Vrah wasn't stupid. She knew Samantha was feeding me information, and she'd kept the indestructible head with her just so I'd get a false sense of what was going on. It was clear the hunter was still receiving intelligence from outside the dungeon. She knew that Lucia always set a teleportation escape spot when she entered an area. She also knew, as I now did, that Lucia regularly cast that spell while she was in a safe room. This teleported everyone in the room away, allowing her to attack them outside the safety of the room. It was insidious, a way to cheat the safe room protections.

Lucia had been in the safe room waiting for Donut to come out so she could teleport all of them to a distant spot where she could strike at the cat and get her revenge. This was an actual spell, and I knew it only worked when Lucia was in her beautiful-woman form.

Vrah somehow knew where this preset teleportation destination was and was lying in wait, away from the inevitable messy chaos with her sisters and the nebs. No matter what happened when I bounced back, there was a distinct possibility that at least one of the three high-priority targets was going to show up at that spot. She'd probably been hoping that all three of us would appear: me, Donut, and Lucia.

If I'd precisely followed the panel plan, that's exactly what would've happened.

Instead, Vrah got just Lucia.

We knew Lucia had set at least two teleport traps. One right inside the door to the safe room and one right outside the door to the guildhall. According to some nerd kid at the panel, the system allowed them to be set within safe rooms because the real trap module was actually set outside at the destination. A loophole. One that had been around for years and years.

Despite appearances to the contrary, Lucia was always vigilant when she entered a new area. In addition to using the teleports as an attack, she had more than a dozen different ways to teleport herself and her pets out of a dangerous situation.

We had to use that knowledge to our advantage.

Mordecai and Donut, not knowing if they'd be able to talk to me, had originally come up with a desperate plan. They hoped to summon hunters to us to take care of Lucia before I had the chance to return. Hunters rarely lingered in an area after a kill, and if they didn't have outside information, they would've, in theory, had no idea Donut and I were still in the area or, worse, that I was going to teleport to the area vulnerable.

Bomo was still tuned to Zockau, and they sent the cretin through with a note telling the hunters of Lucia's location. But they already knew, and Lucia was refusing to come out of the safe room, thus setting the stage for the three-way showdown.

The public plan was for me to immediately cast *Tripper* and jump into the safe room just as Donut jumped in from the other side. Then

Lucia, still in a rage due to the earlier events—events I didn't yet know the full details of—would teleport the entire room to the edge of town, where we'd have it out. We'd have to quickly dispatch the other crawler. Then, no longer cornered, we'd be able to face the hunters or flee.

The panel audience all thought this was a grand plan and were quite proud of themselves.

It was suicide, but I didn't tell them that. Instead, I took bits and pieces of their ideas and cobbled together a better one.

Well, maybe not better. But one that wasn't floating free all around the tunnels.

I took Drick's advice and created chaos that I could hide within.

Donut had cast *Clockwork Triplicate* on the Sledge. She had the two automatons rush into the safe room from the guildhall, one after another. The first triggered the teleport trap, and Sledge automaton number one appeared right outside in the midst of the hunters.

The second rushed into the room at Lucia. This was clockwork Sledge number two with Donut on his shoulder. Only it wasn't Donut, but one of Bautista's Beanie Babies. Supposedly a black-cat thing wearing a crown and sunglasses.

Lucia would've had to cast the spell immediately, lest Donut cast a dispel-magic enchantment, yet another non-attack spell that would be allowed within a safe room.

It all worked as I hoped and feared. I had a sinking suspicion that they'd be ready at the teleport spot, and I was right. I'd assumed Lucia would be dead, but the kid survived. That little shit was crazy, but she was also a brilliant fighter. I still couldn't believe Donut had survived her encounter with her.

But all that was only the first part of the plan. The rest of this I was making up on the fly.

Down below, anarchy reigned. The nebs ran from the remaining bugs. A total of three mantises were dead and only three of the nebs were still alive.

I'd killed three of the robed hunters and successfully marked three more before they were killed by the bugs. The berserking bug had managed to kill two of her own people before getting cut down by one of her own. I'd blown the back legs off another bug, the one who'd been trying to disarm the alarm trap. She remained on the ground, crawling away toward the edge of town, leaving a streak of white gore from her ruined back legs. She was so disoriented, she hadn't even attempted to heal herself.

I was a sitting target up here, invisible or not. There was no easy way to get down. I jumped from the spire, landing on the roof of the temple. *Crack.*

"Uh-oh," I said as the ceiling collapsed under my feet.

Entering Temple of Diwata.
   Warning: This Temple has been Desecrated.

I crashed heavily into the building, landing atop a small shrine, shattering it. Water splashed everywhere. A notification popped up, but I waved it away. I healed myself and jumped to my feet. This was a wide, empty room filled with tree branches and vines and potted plants.

And bodies. Lots and lots of dead bodies, all NPCs.

Most were dryads, but there was also a pile of dead funeral bell guards. They'd all been killed by Lucia. I didn't have time to figure all that out. I rushed for the front door of the temple, thought better of it, and jumped out one of the side windows, which had already been shattered in the earlier explosion.

CARL: Coming in. Samantha, roll into the woods. Head south.
SAMANTHA: IS THAT SUPPOSED TO BE A PUN?

I cursed myself for having wasted my *Ping* spell when the map was down. It had a five-minute cooldown.

I was still invisible, and I bolted for the unguarded safe room door. All the nebs were now dead. A single mantis stood over their corpses, all the way at the edge of town. The legless mantis still crawled away while a third leaned over her, attempting to render aid.

The song continued to blast. The ball had rolled up against the side of the safe room, and it bounced up and down to the beat, dancing between me and the door.

Slam!

Vrah hit the ground with the force of a meteor, landing atop the trap ball. It shattered, causing the battlefield to plunge into silence. My ears rang. Smoke from the dying curtain swirled away, catching in the wind, forming twin vortices before fading.

Oh fuck.

The mantis had been level 70 last time I'd faced her in Zockau. She was now level 74. She was also a lot bigger. The back of the praying mantis alien was covered with heads, dotting her exoskeleton like round pustules, all in various states of decay. I stopped dead, not daring to move. She didn't move, either, for several moments. She was right there, fifteen feet in front of me.

I recognized the two heads at the top of the pile against her insectoid shoulders, flanking her exposed neck like a pair of headphones. I had no idea how she attached them to her body. The one on the left was Langley, mouth wide in surprise. The one on the right was a human I'd seen on the recap a few times. Bogdon Ro, one of the top player killers. He'd been in the top ten. The only one so far to be killed by a hunter. Langley and his men had been hunting him when they'd all been set upon by Vrah's team.

"Mother," the legless mantis cried as she dragged herself away. "Mother, where am I? I want to go home."

You have been deshrouded! Invisibility negated!

"Carl," Vrah said, turning to face me. The movement was smooth, indicating she'd known I was there the whole time. When she turned her insectoid head, the heads planted on her shoulders moved with her, following her movement. It was some trick to make her look extra terrifying. She peered over at the pile of dead insects and nebs and made a chittering noise. "You are a worthy opponent. I will give you that. You and the Lajabless child both. I've almost forgotten what it's like to hurt for a kill. But it ends here."

She held her crossbow in one claw. It was loaded with a glowing bolt.

"I met your mom," I said. "I pushed her off the podium."

"That's not . . ." Vrah paused, and then what might've been a smile cracked across her insect face. She made a clicking noise. "Nice try, crawler."

I, too, smiled. "You can hide it, but it's clear you're still speaking with your mother. Is that why you've collected so many heads? Because you're always cheating?"

"It's not true, but do you really think it would matter if I *was* cheating? Would anyone truly care? You are nothing but livestock, and livestock exists to be culled. Everyone watching right now doesn't care how this moment came to be, just that it's here. There's not a regulation in the galaxy that will change that fact. When I'm done with this hunt, I will take my place in the birthing hall of Hive Home two, and I will birth a thousand nymphs, all of whom will be born with the memory of this moment, of your slaughter, yet not a single one will care because you will be nothing but a faceless blip, one of thousands."

"So, it's true?" I asked. "I heard that earlier today. That this is your last crawl, and you are being sent off to be breeding stock. Your sister Xindy was supposed to take your place as top hunter. Too bad she never got a chance."

"This won't be pleasant, crawler," Vrah said as she raised the crossbow.

"Wait," I said, holding my hand up. "Langley, I'm sorry I couldn't help you before. I appreciate your help now."

Vrah cocked her bug head to the side.

"What?" she asked just as the reanimated corpse head bit down on her exposed neck. On the other side, Bogdon Ro groaned. Surprised, Vrah turned her head toward Langley, but his teeth held firm. The movement allowed the Bogdon Ro head to also bite down on her neck from the side. Then a third head started biting at her, the one right below Bogdon. Vrah screamed and fired her crossbow as I hit the deck. The bolt whizzed over my head.

I jumped up, pulled out the arrow of Enthusiastic Double Gonorrhea, and rammed it into Vrah's neck just before the shield popped up, which ejected the zombie heads on the bug woman's neck and shoulders and tossed me back. I slid, bumping into Donut, who'd sneaked out while still invisible and cast as many *Second Chance* spells as she could before her mana ran out.

Vrah writhed as the bottom of her carapace burst into flames. She jumped into the air in an attempt to fly away.

"Go!" I shouted.

The two other mantids had finally noticed and rushed toward us. Donut and I vaulted into the safe room.

It was right there at the door. The wheeled bomb that the system had named **Just Wait Until Your Daddy Gets Home**. The same wheeled bomb I'd wanted to use to level Zockau. The Sledge stood there, peering outside at the two mantises rushing toward us.

"Cover your ears," I shouted as I kicked the wheeled bomb out the door. It rolled and started to tip as I slammed the safe room door shut.

"We've gone over this before, Carl," Donut shouted. "I can't cover my—"

Bam.

THE WORLD ROCKED. DESPITE THIS BEING A SAFE ROOM, WE ALL FLEW into the air and slammed to the ground, rolling and spinning like billiard balls. My ears rang, and my body cried out in pain. The world rumbled for a very long time. Notifications rolled down my screen.

SAMANTHA: YO, WHAT THE ACTUAL FUCK WAS THAT?

I expected the Bopca to start shouting, but it seemed we were alone. I wondered if Lucia's teleport trick also jettisoned the poor Bopcas out of the room.

"Do you think we got her?" Donut said after she recovered. "What about that crazy bitch and her dog?"

I pulled up my notifications and started scrolling through. "Oh, shit," I said. "Goddamnit. I killed that ursine guy. No other NPCs, though I got a bunch of mobs in the woods. Lucia had really cleared out the town. Christ. She got away."

Vrah had also escaped. That was okay. I was expecting that. She'd cast a strange, swirling shield at that last minute and was rocketing into the air. Like Lucia, she had some sort of eject button, and she'd slammed it down.

This was actually a better outcome. I wasn't planning on this, but I knew exactly where she was headed. A golden opportunity had just presented itself.

I'd killed the three remaining mantises, despite their protection against explosions. That meant Vrah was the last one left of the warriors. There was only one other mantis left on the whole floor. A male holed up in Zockau. He was a salesman. The guy who took the looted gear and wheeled and dealt and sold it to the other faction representatives who'd installed themselves in the local safe rooms.

They were all stuck here until the floor was done. Nine more days.

But that guy, that sole remaining mantis, suddenly had a very big problem.

I recalled the description of the arrow of Enthusiastic Double Gonorrhea. It had originally been meant for poor Louis because he wouldn't shut up about how hot the leader of the Dream's mother was.

Arrow of Enthusiastic Double Gonorrhea.

This is a regular arrow, but the tip is dipped in a poison that will inflict you with Enthusiastic Double Gonorrhea.

Trust me on this. You don't want Enthusiastic Double Gonorrhea.

It doesn't kill you, but you'll want it to. It sets your genitals aflame. Literally. And then it heals that area of your body over and over. The only way to remove the disease is to, uh, geld yourself. Or pass it on to someone else.

Future Hive queen Vrah wasn't about to neuter herself. So she could either suffer the consequences or she could pass it on.

"Come on," I said, rushing back to the safe room. Katia was there in our personal space, as were Bautista and Imani and Elle and several others. The second door leading out to the guildhall common area was open, and multiple others were in there, waiting. They shouted as we entered.

"In a hurry," I yelled. "Bomo, come here."

I grabbed a pen and paper and started to furiously write.

"Dude, what happened?" Louis asked. He and Firas sat on the couch, watching wide-eyed.

"It was quite exciting," Donut announced. "But wait until you see

my fight with Lucia on the recap episode in an hour! Zev says they're
gonna show the whole thing!"

Mordecai hopped to the table and read over my shoulder:

*To the mantis representative holed up in Zockau. We can protect you. But you
gotta come now. Bring all the gear you've collected, and we'll keep you safe
until the end of the floor. No gear, no deal.*

Trust me, buddy. You'll want this.

"What in the gods' name did you do?" Mordecai asked.

"Carl gave Vrah gonorrhea!" Donut cried.

36

I PUSHED BOMO OUT THE DOOR INTO THE ZOCKAU SAFE ROOM, WHERE he'd post his note and wait for a response. Hopefully word would get to the mantis guy before Vrah did.

"The bitch lives, correct?" someone asked. "I didn't see a notification. Lucia survived?"

The speaker was Florin the Crocodilian. I hadn't noticed him there in the back corner.

"Yes," Donut said. "She's a cheater just like that Quan Ch guy, and she got away."

"Good," Florin said. He pushed himself off the wall and went out into the guildhall common area. We all watched him go.

"We're still in Lucia's town," I said after he left. "We need to get out of here before she comes back."

"I do believe we just destroyed the town. There's nothing to go back to," Donut said. "But if she does dare return, I'm not one bit scared of her. Not one bit."

"Open your boxes, reset your buffs, and then watch the recap," Mordecai said, ignoring Donut's boast. "I'm pretty sure I know what spell she used to get away, and she won't be anywhere near here. But I want you gone before she gets back. After what Donut pulled, you're gonna be looking over your shoulder for now on until you deal with her."

"What else is new?" I asked as I turned to examine the people in the room. I felt a grin spread across my face as I took everyone in.

This is it, I thought. *This is my family now.* My heart continued to pound from the fight. I knew I was about to crash, that the shakes would hit me, that the river in my mind would roar. But for now, at this moment, I took comfort in the friendly faces all around me.

It was Katia, Elle, Imani, Bautista, Louis, Firas, Gwen, Tran, Britney, along with several others I didn't know as well. Mongo was also loose and moved freely about the spaces, demanding scratches from everyone like he was an attention-starved dog at a party.

"Where's Chris?" I asked Elle after I went through and acknowledged everyone. They all greeted me back with enthusiasm except Britney, of course, whose resting I-hate-you-and-everybody face was on full display. The fur-clad barbarian sat upon Firas's lap with one arm wrapped around his shoulders.

Everyone in the group had gone up several levels. Half of them had new equipment. *I've missed so much,* I thought.

Elle had transformed from a Blizzardmancer to a Tundra Princess, but the fairy woman didn't look any different. She now had a brown streak of hair in her haphazardly cut white mane, but that was it. She still wore the anti-slip socks from when she'd been a 99-year-old resident of the Meadow Lark retirement home. They were the only before thing that remained on the woman except for a simple gold wedding ring that now hung around her neck by a chain, because her fingers were much smaller than they'd been before. She'd ascended to level 51.

She'd also somehow gotten a glass of yellow alcohol and was sipping on it. From the couch, Louis watched the glass the same way a dog would watch a human holding a piece of beef jerky.

"Whoa, big guy," Elle said, looking up over my head. "That's a lot of hunter-killer daggers you have. Good job. I still need to collect one for myself. Chris is with Li Jun and Li Na along with the other two rock bodyguards. It's a long story. That Eva woman is hooked up now with team Cichociemni, and those guys are no joke. They're named after some Polish special forces group, but none of them are actually Polish if you can believe that. Not anymore. They killed their leader guy because he didn't want them to be a group of murderers. That guy was buddy-buddy with the Popovs before that Dmitri idiot accidentally picked a race that combined himself with his brother. Anyway, the Popovs had them cornered, but then the brothers got whisked away to go to that convention. They've been gone for two days now and won't be back until tomorrow. Must be nice. Li Na and Chris are keeping an eye on the group in the meantime. Did you know Chris can burrow right into the ground? And Li Na can turn into smoke? Man, that girl freaks me the fuck out. We would've been there by now if Katia didn't insist on turning the whole circus around to come help save your ass. We would've been with you in time, too, if the flying house didn't get attacked by pterodactyls. Now we're stuck in the jungle in the middle of nowhere. How'd that go anyway? Your convention, I mean. Did you meet Dmitri and Maxim? They said you guys would be sharing a table or some shit."

"That's not until tomorrow," I said, my head spinning. I was still coming off the adrenaline rush, and my brain couldn't parse the tidal wave of information Elle had just thrown at me. All that really mattered was that everyone was safe for the moment.

Behind me, Donut was chatting with Daniel Bautista, demanding to see the mouser stuffed Beanies. The orange tiger man pulled one out for her to examine while she clucked over it.

"It's a cat," Donut said, not sounding impressed. "Do they really have cat mobs in the dungeon? Why are they listed as common? This thing doesn't look anything like me, but it fooled both Lucia and Vrah. Still, this shouldn't be common. Surely it should be a province boss at least. Maybe even a country boss. It should definitely be legendary rareness."

"If it makes you feel better, I used an uncommon variant for the ruse. It was fuzzier. With the sunglasses and fake tiara, it looked a lot like you. I had to use a tame spell on it," Bautista said. "These guys attack when I pull the tag."

"How many Beanies do you have left?" I asked. I knew the man had looted over 1,000 of the stuffed animals on the third floor, but he had to be running low by now.

"I have about 500 left," he said, surprising me. "My sponsor gave me a refresher kit, and I can put the tag back on them if they don't die while summoned. I can only do it twice, though. Plus, I've gotten a few more in loot boxes." He thumbed over his shoulder at Tran, who stood with Gwen. "I've taken your advice and been training with my sword. Tran and I are both Swashbucklers, and we've been working together in the training room. We get a bonus when we work as a team."

Katia was in her regular human form. She stood next to Bautista, nodding. In fact, I noticed she actually had her hand on his orange furry shoulder. *Huh,* I thought. I wasn't sure what I thought about that. I was about to say something, but thought better of it. Donut would likely notice at any moment and make a comment.

"Speaking of teamwork," Louis said, getting up from the couch. He spilled a cup of soda he'd had between his legs. Above, the cleaner bot made a shrill noise of disapproval. "Oh, my bad. Hey, anyway. Katia has been making us learn moves like we did on the last floor. Want to see my favorite one? I came up with it on my own."

Before I could object, Louis pulled what looked like a limp ring of fabric from his inventory. Katia sighed and stepped away from Bautista. Louis tossed the ring at Katia, and it landed over her head, flopping onto her shoulder, where it promptly disappeared, either into her inventory or her mass.

"Okay . . ." I said. "What the hell was that?"

Louis grunted, annoyed I wasn't mystified. "That was a potion bandolier. I can throw armor items on Katia, and it automatically equips itself as long as she has the spot open. We can do it with shoulder bandoliers, helmets, arm bracers. Pretty much anything you can think of."

I exchanged a look with Katia, who just shook her head.

"Yeah," I said, "but she has unlimited inventory. What, exactly, is the move? I mean, it's cool, I guess, but how is it useful?"

"I told you," Britney said from Firas's lap.

"So, if it lands on her perfectly, it equips itself the moment it touches her, right? She's got that new backpack that lets her add a bunch of mass. But what if she gets really big, but without a breastplate, right? And if we make a giant breastplate, we drop it on her from the *Twister.* It'll automatically equip, and suddenly she can get even bigger. And then we can have a helmet that's even bigger. We could just make her bigger and bigger. It'd be like the Voltron formation sequence. Well, sort of."

"Unless the item misses or doesn't hit right, and then she's crushed and dead," Britney said.

"It's a work in progress," Louis said defensively.

CARL: Katia. Don't let him drop a giant breastplate on you.

KATIA: The idea has some merit. I'm trying to let him build his self-confidence. We'll figure something out. He doesn't show it, but he was really upset when he learned those elves were hunting him. I walked in on him earlier when he thought he was alone, and he was crying. I think he's worried we're going to kick him out of the guild.

"It's a good idea," I finally said, and Louis's eyes beamed. "But be careful. It'd be really easy to accidentally hurt her with that. Keep working out the kinks."

"That's what he has Juice Box for," Donut said at the same moment Firas opened his mouth, presumably, to say a variation of the same thing. They both burst into laughter.

"Okay, guys," I said as I stepped to the kitchen counter. "I have a ton of boxes to open." I eyed the Emberus shrine in the back of the room. I knew I was about to owe that thing a ton of money. That would make Donut stop laughing.

I hadn't been in a safe room since before the fight to liberate Fort Freedom from the naiad Confederates, and several items had stacked up. I had over thirty achievements to sift through, from rowing across the river in a kayak, to making an appearance at the con, to shoving that arrow into Vrah. A few of the achievements were notable:

New Achievement! Uprooted.

You caused a Rooted-in-Place boss monster to move. That's no easy feat. You then killed that monster. Pretty impressive. Hope you remember how you did it.

Reward: You already got a boss box. This achievement is the reward.

Huh, I thought. The wording on this one was strange. It lacked the AI's typical . . . zippiness. I'd received the achievement because I'd used my *Protective Shell* to eject that eryops frog thing into the air. I hadn't thought about it at the time, but the description had mentioned how difficult it was to get them to move once they were settled. Apparently the AI wanted me to remember how I'd done it.

The AI quickly returned to his regular asshole self after that.

New Achievement! Bisected!

You teleported into a solid object. Congratulations. You've lost your . . .

Oh, wait! You were teleported due to an administrative action. That means your privileged ass was saved. Again. No missing arm or leg. No dungeon-style circumcision. Nothing. Boy, you must really bring in the cheddar for them to keep coddling you like this.

Teleport mishaps are funny as shit. You ever see *The Fly*? Anyway, you don't have to worry about it. This time.

Reward: You've received a Silver Lucky Bastard Box!

Holy shit. I remembered the sensation of getting smacked in the face with the door when I'd teleported back. I hadn't even thought about it. Then again, they were the ones who'd teleported me at that moment. It wouldn't have been fair. Not that fair meant anything to these assholes.

New Achievement! Desecrated!

You have found a desecrated temple! That means all the temple's attendants have been murdered. The temple's treasury has been looted. The sacred wine has probably been all lapped up, too.

And this used to be a nice town. It hasn't been the same since you guys moved in.

If you are an adherent of this temple, you may no longer worship here. You've also probably just received a quest to hunt down and kill the heathen who did this.

If you *don't* worship this god, just scram. Remember that time you walked in on Mommy and Daddy playing leapfrog? It's just like that. Back away. Don't touch anything. Never talk about it again.

You should also probably avoid the person who did this. Not only does society frown upon those who slaughter whole congregations, but there are real consequences for this sort of stuff.

Reward: You entered a building. You don't get a reward for that. It's not like you kicked it up a notch by defiling the shrine.

Oh, wait.

New Achievement! Temple Defiler!

You've defiled a temple's sacred shrine by breaking it with your own flesh!

Wow. I dunno, man. That's pretty ballsy.

There are a lot of bad things people can do when they're in church. They can swear. They can ogle the hot nuns. They can pinch the eucharist wafers and use them as poker chips. They can rip pages from the hymnals and roll them into joints. Hell, they can stab the priest and murder all the town's adherents and put the whole thing up on YouTube.

None of that is as bad as defiling the temple's shrine with one's own flesh.

In case you didn't know, the shrine of a temple is pretty much indestructible. They made it that way because you crawlers are always blowing up whole towns and submerging cities in water or burying entire populations of innocent NPCs with the guts of giant turkeys.

When a temple is desecrated, the shrine's protection fades over several hours. Eventually, it's able to be destroyed, but only with a direct attack.

You're *supposed to* find desecrated temples and destroy the shrines. Hell, it's a sacrament in some religions. But you can't just do it willy-nilly. And certainly not when you're not a member of that congregation. It's like walking into a random ICU from off the street and pulling the plug on someone's brain-dead grandma.

It's not your place.

Gods don't like it when some punk walks into their house and kicks them when they're already down. It's rude. And what's worse, when a shrine is destroyed improperly, the god loses some of their power, and all of the other gods can see this. It's quite humiliating.

Hopefully you got some cool loot from the priests or monks or whatever because this box, while technically a prize, is sort of a good news/bad news thing.

Reward: You've received a Gold Apostate Box!

"Shit," I muttered. I hadn't done anything wrong. Apparently, that little Lucia psycho had killed everyone in the church. All I'd done was fall through the roof of the temple. I'd landed on some shrine thing, and it shattered. That was it. There wasn't anything in the cookbook about this sort of stuff. I knew if temples were desecrated, they eventually turned "corrupt," which usually meant there were mobs inside. But this was the first I'd heard about the shrine thing.

New Achievement! That's not how you use arrows, dumbass.

You took an arrow, and you physically stabbed someone with it. That's something a kid who eats glue would do. You know I'm pretty sure you have a bow in your inventory.

Reward: You've received a Gold Ranged Weapon Box.

I did have an unenchanted bow in my inventory. I got it from the same elf I'd looted the first gonorrhea arrow from. The last time I'd shot a bow was during archery class in high school, and I'd ripped the shit out of my left wrist doing it. With my xistera, I had no need for any other ranged weapon.

New Achievement! It itches when I pee!

You infected another combatant with a venereal disease.

Good job there, Derek Jeter. I hope you bought them dinner first.

Reward: You've received a bronze condom. Use it next time.

Sure enough, it wasn't a box. It was an actual wrapped condom. The packaging was bronze-colored. It was unenchanted. There was a sketch of an older woman on one side who might've been Bea Arthur and a sheep on the other.

"The hell?" I started to mutter, but I stopped the moment I heard the breathiness of the AI's voice when he read out the next one. I cringed.

New Achievement! This little piggy made a boom boom!

You deployed a bomb with the supple, curved sole of your foot. You took your perfectly perfect 30.004861-centimeter-long right foot and compressed it against an explosive device—a device named after me no less—and you gave it a naughty little shove before you pushed it out the door and detonated it.

You killed them. You killed them all for your daddy.

The AI made a deep, throaty groan for like five seconds straight, an uncomfortably long time.

Reward: You've received a Gold Spicy Box.

"Was that a condom?" Donut asked when the achievements finished. "Did the AI really give you a condom? Talk about a useless prize!"

"That wasn't the worst of it," I said.

"Well, I got a John Wick achievement that I thought was very rude. I didn't even get a prize from it. Though I did receive something quite useful from a Platinum Did-You-Really-Just-Cast-*Fireball*-in-a-Room-This-Small Box."

"We still need to have a discussion about that," Mordecai said, sounding irritated.

"What was the prize?" I asked. Then the name of the box hit me. I remembered the burned-down tree in the middle of town, alarm rising in my chest. "Wait, what did you do to get it?"

"Oh, oh, the prize is just great," Donut said, pointing. There was a small closet-sized room next to the restroom in the main space. I hadn't noticed it until now. "It's a vocal coach! It's a special training room! Can you believe it? There's a little room with a microphone behind glass and a holographic NPC lady who shows me throat exercises to train my voice. Her name is Lover Illiana, and she's just wonderful. She says I have a voice like a Cygnus cloud gull. My singing has already gone up to level four."

Mordecai sighed. "It's actually a great prize. Next time Donut casts an illusion with her voice, the apparitions might actually have substance. Now, Carl, get your loot."

I told Mordecai about the apostate box before I moved to open the prizes. He groaned. We weren't able to pick and choose the boxes we opened. It was an all-or-nothing thing, so I didn't have much of a choice.

"It'll be okay," he said. His tone was not convincing. "You said the god was Diwata? That's a weird one. She changes genders, but she's usually referred to as 'her.' She does some odd shit, like impregnates herself and then eats the offspring and then forms cities with her poop. Thankfully, she's pretty rare. Go ahead. Open the boxes. We'll deal like we always do."

"What does she look like?"

"Her natural form is a giant squirrel-like thing with antlers. She's covered in moss and leaves, too. You can't miss her."

"All righty. Here goes nothing."

I had multiple prize boxes. Most of them were low-tier adventurer boxes, but I had a grand total of 14 hunter-killer boxes including the one I'd received from Future Hunter the orc. This was several more than I'd been expecting. It appeared they gave me credit for the three nebs and three mantises that were killed by the other mantis while she was enraged, though I hadn't gotten credit when she had in turn been killed by her own people.

Even though I got boxes for those six kills, I didn't receive any experience, but I *did* receive a small amount of experience when the enraged mantis was cut down. Again, it was all behind-the-scenes math stuff I didn't understand, and I wasn't so sure anymore that this stuff wasn't being tweaked in real time. Sometimes some of these rules seemed to change for no reason. I wasn't going to argue about it.

I now had 52 hunting trophies, and I received a total of 637,000 gold just from those boxes. Donut made a little pained noise every time the Emberus shrine beeped.

The Silver Lucky Bastard Box contained a few invisibility potions and a useless cloak that I wouldn't be able to wear. It added a few hammer-based attack skills, so I gave it to Firas.

The Gold Ranged Weapon Box contained a patch for my jacket. The first one I'd gotten on this floor. Donut started to inspect it as the Gold Apostate Box opened.

The symbol appeared in the air and then slapped itself right onto my left upper arm. This was yet another tattoo. It appeared to be a flaming ball of snakes. Almost like a free-floating Medusa wig. One of the snake heads reached down and curled around the web pattern on my elbow tattoo, the one that gave me access to the Guild of Suffering, which I hadn't seen or heard anything about since I'd gotten that tattoo for using the Ring of Divine Suffering for the first time.

Before I could examine the tattoo's properties, the Gold Spicy Box opened.

I was expecting something ridiculous, like another toe ring or foot lotion. Instead, I got another patch.

This one was a little bigger than the first. It was a white rectangular piece of fabric with a little circular bomb hand stitched on it with fine black thread. It almost looked like a pencil drawing of a bomb. Donut gasped, and she pulled it over to examine it more closely.

"Exquisite," she said. "This is classic Spanish blackwork. This is much better than that other screen-printed monstrosity."

She was so enraptured by the patch, she didn't seem to notice my new tattoo, which was by far the largest one I'd received. With this, the spiderweb, and the goblin pass, I practically had a whole sleeve on my left arm.

"It could be worse," Mordecai said, also inspecting the tattoo. "Diwata is a minor goddess. A nature one. Like a low-rent Apito. She's pretty vengeful. She can make trees grow and summon animals. You're gonna have to stay clear of the dryads from now on. I think some of them worship her."

"That's gonna suck," Louis said from the couch. "Those tree dudes are everywhere."

Enemy of the Church Tattoo.
    Diwata.
    The bearer of this symbol is an enemy of the church of Diwata. All adherents outside of a Club Vanquisher will attack you on sight. You may no longer worship Diwata or any of her allies. Eh, no big loss. She's pretty much a hippie anyway. Always crying about her stupid trees. Always letting forest animals knock her up. It's actually pretty disgusting.
    You will receive a 25% damage bonus against all adherents of Diwata.

As an adherent of Emberus, you receive an additional 25% bonus against all adherents of Diwata, giving you a total of 50% bonus damage.

Warning: Uh, so this is a big one, so listen closely. Don't let Diwata see you. Ever. If she shows up at a party, and you're there, you best be sneaking out the back door. That's all I'm saying about that.

Unlike other tattoos, this one may not be hidden with a cover-up sleeve. If you'd like to remove this tattoo and the associated effects, you must either kill Diwata or chop off your arm. One of those is a lot easier than the other.

"Carl," Donut said, finally noticing the new ink, "are you trying to look like Signet? Because it's starting to work. You keep getting them over and over. You must be doing it on purpose. Disgusting. All tattoos are disgusting."

"Hey," Gwen said from her position against the back wall, "you said you liked my tattoos when we first met." The Inuit woman had multiple tattoos on her face and hands.

"Oh, that's different," Donut said. "Your tattoos enhance your beauty and are culturally important. Carl's tattoos make him look like someone whose mug shot would go viral."

Gwen grunted indignantly.

"I have Bart Simpson tattooed on my ankle," Firas added. "I did it in class in school. It looks a little smudged now. And by a little, I mean it's just a blue blob. It got infected when I did it."

"I was saving up for a Death Star tat," Louis said. "I was gonna get it on my chest."

"Who is Bart Simpson?" Britney asked as I picked up my two new patches to examine them.

My enchanted vest could hold as many patches as I could fit. I only had one patch on it right now, so I had plenty of room. Each new patch added +1 to all of my stats, plus the benefits of the patch itself.

The archery one was a small square patch similar in size to my first patch, which depicted the planet Earth. This one featured a group of about a dozen flaming arrows clutched in the claws of an eagle. The drawing was rendered in an old-school, traditional Sailor Jerry–style. I thought it looked kind of cool.

Upgrade Patch. Small.

This patch depicts the twelve flaming arrows the great Skyfowl hero Radiant Star shot into his grandfather in order to end the frozen time that plagued their world.

If this upgrade patch is affixed to an eligible garment, it will imbue the following upgrades:

+5% to Dexterity.

+5% damage to all ranged projectiles.

Warning: Upgrade patches are fleeting items. You may remove them, but they will be destroyed in the process.

"Hell yeah," I said. I glanced at Katia, who'd already grabbed the sewing kit. She affixed my first one.

I picked up the second patch. This one was bigger. Bigger ones took up more space, though they still only imbued the same benefit as the smaller patches. However, the patches themselves appeared to give much better benefits, which made them worth it. I ran my finger over the raised bomb on the white patch. Donut was enraptured with it. What had she called it? Spanish blackwork? That didn't make sense. How in the hell would she know that?

And then it hit me. Finally. *Of course.* I felt like an idiot for not seeing it earlier.

"Donut," I said, "what was the name of that Earth hobby potion you got way back on the third floor?"

"Scutelliphily," she said, spitting the word. "Useless, stupid potion. Nobody knows what it means."

"I'm pretty sure I've figured it out," I said.

"Really? What is it?"

I patted the bomb patch. "What type of thread is on this thing?"

"Oh, it's just lovely. It's supposed to be silk, but some people try to cheat using linen thread. But you can always tell when it's the real deal because . . ." She trailed off.

"Yeah, I'm pretty sure scut-whatever has something to do with embroidery or patches."

Donut gasped. "Carl, Carl, I think you're right!"

"Scutelliphily is a compound Latin and Greek word," Britney said. "*Scutellus* is Latin, and it means 'small shield.' *Phileein* is a common Greek suffix that means 'the love of.' Or something similar. So it means 'the love of small shields.' I guess that means you love little patches. If you had asked me, I could have told you this earlier."

We all just looked at the Ukrainian barbarian woman like she'd just sprouted a hamster from her nostril.

"Dude," Louis said.

"What?" she asked, irritated, as I shook my head and examined the rectangular patch.

> **Upgrade Patch. Medium.**
> This patch is finely made from Spider Reaper Minion thread silk.
> It's a bomb. You blow shit up all the time. It's appropriate you have a patch depicting it. This patch is finely made, which means all below upgrades are enhanced.
> If this upgrade patch is affixed to an eligible garment, it will imbue the following upgrades:
> +11% to Constitution.
> +6% damage to all explosives.
> +2 to the Dangerous Explosives Handling Skill.
> +15% Discount from traveling Spider Reaper Minion merchants.
> Warning: Upgrade patches are fleeting items. You may remove them, but they will be destroyed in the process.

My Dangerous Explosives Handling skill was already at 10, so that alone was pretty good. I pulled my jacket off and handed it to Katia. She took the two patches and started mapping out the best place to sew them on. Donut jumped to her shoulder and started offering unsolicited advice.

I had one more important upgrade to deal with. With my last level up, I was finally able to move my base strength over 100. This came with its own upgrade. I'd be given three upgrade options, and I had to pick one.

That number, 100, was just insane to me. The average human had a strength of four. Every person in this room, even Louis and Britney, was now stronger than the strongest human who had ever lived.

It's not real, I thought, having a sudden memory of my time in the production ship. Of the "zero zone," as they'd called it. It'd felt like I couldn't breathe, that I'd had all my strength zapped out of me. I had lost my ability to read Syndicate Standard. Sort of. I was pretty sure I'd lost all of my upgrades and abilities, including all of my enhanced stats.

What does that mean? How does that work in the context of the rest of the universe?

It was a question for another time. I assigned my points, bringing my strength to exactly 100. For the first time, I felt myself get physically larger. It wasn't a huge change, but I felt my arms swell. My chest bulged. I reached up and touched my arm. *Wow,* I thought. *I'm jacked.*

> New Achievement! What big muscles you have!
>   Your base strength is now over 100. Rawr!
>   Get thee to Chippendales!
>   *Reward:* You've received an upgrade!
>   Admin Message:
>   You have been given a permanent upgrade. You have three choices. You have three minutes to pick. Choose wisely. Your choices are:
>   Swole.
>   Prison Bitch.
>   Stepson.

"Shit," I said. Three minutes wasn't very long. None of these were listed as the possible choices in the cookbook. Or if they were, they'd changed the names. "Mordecai, help me pick." I quickly moved through each one, reading it out loud after I read the description.

> Swole. From now on, every one point of Strength you add as a result of a level-up stat point is actually two points. This is not retroactive, nor does it apply to equipment-based upgrades.

That was pretty awesome. However, I was planning on focusing on constitution for a bit now. It wasn't clear if it worked with my Ring of Divine Suffering, but I suspected it would not.

Prison Bitch. You have an additional 20% strength bonus when fighting hand to hand with someone whose base strength is lower than yours.

Again, that was a good upgrade. I did a lot of hand-to-hand fighting, and this would be a solid choice. Fighting like this was where my strength was most useful, so it would be better than the first choice at first, but the first choice would eventually be better. And this was useless if I was fighting someone stronger than me, presumably when I'd need the extra strength the most.

Stepson. All kicks and foot-based attacks have an automatic 15% chance to inflict Ouch per hit.

"What the hell is 'Ouch'?" I asked. There wasn't a way to click on or read what it did.

"It's a stagger attack," Mordecai said. "It'll stop someone in their tracks. Like kicking them in the nuts."

"Carl did that once to an elf," Donut said from Katia's shoulder. "Zev, our agent, said the audience didn't like that much."

"It is kind of a bitch move," Firas agreed.

"Not helping," I said. "Mordecai? What do you think?"

"Swole," he said. "You already have multiple feet upgrades that'll help disable a victim. Swole seems to be the obvious choice. It's not an active skill, but it's what I would choose."

"Agreed," Katia said as she sewed the arrow patch next to the planet Earth on my jacket's shoulder.

"I think you should do the one with the feet," Donut added. "If it's ever a question, you should always take the foot-based choice. Plus if you kick something five times fast, that's like an almost guaranteed stun. You're always kicking and stepping on animals and orcs and hunters.

You could tap-dance on someone and stun them." She paused. "Carl, did you get bigger? Everyone, look at Carl. His arms got bigger."

"Yeah, he did," Elle said. She reached over and touched my arm. "Imani, come touch Carl."

I ignored her. I had a minute left to choose. Donut made a compelling argument, but, again, it seemed the two-for-one upgrade was the best choice. I ended up going with it.

"Sorry, Donut," I said. "I think I'll go with Swole." I clicked it.

Dude. You're so big. Huge.

"I'm not the one you need to apologize to," Donut said, still intently staring over Katia's shoulder.

Katia had already finished with the first patch, and she'd moved to the bomb. She was placing it on the bottom left of the jacket's front, right along the hemline. She grew a second pair of arms to hold the jacket in place.

Donut made a disapproving noise. "No, no, your stitches are off. This is a piece of fine art, Katia. You wouldn't tape a Bob Ross painting to the wall with duct tape. Your stitches have to be perfectly spaced."

"Donut," Katia said.

"I'm just trying to help."

I sat down in the chair, finally done with my boxes. I put my hand against my arm. I thought of everything that had happened over the past day and a half. I thought of that little kid with his shitty drawing of me getting eaten by the brindle grub. Was his dad right? Was I only alive because the AI wanted it? Should I have chosen the Stepson benefit?

I looked down at my feet, and I felt dirty. My new tattoo burned on my swollen arm. The Emberus shrine bubbled louder, reminding me that I owed both blood and money.

That's how it always is, isn't it? I thought. The silence in my mind roared louder than it had ever been.

The sink is running.

"No, no, no!" Donut cried from Katia's shoulder. Katia looked like she was about to murder the cat.

I smiled. At least I was home, if only for an hour or two.

37

"HERE IT COMES, HERE IT COMES!" DONUT SAID, BOUNCING UP AND down. Next to her, Mongo screeched, waving his arms. "Oh, it's going to be glorious. I wish this thing had a DVR. Mordecai, can you record it so we can play it back?" She gasped. "We can make copies, and I can autograph them, and Carl can sell them when he goes back to the stupid con thing!"

"I don't think it works that way," I said.

Mordecai didn't answer. It was just me, Mordecai, Donut, and Mongo. The others had an emergency outside. Their village was being raided by death monkeys or something. They had to leave, and they were going to take the *Twister* back south to assist Chris and Li Na.

After several scenes of crawlers getting themselves killed, the rest of the program was dedicated to the fight between Donut and Lucia Mar.

The scene started with Lucia entering the town and literally ripping the treelike mayor in half. She was in her melee-focused, skeletal, demonic form. Her two rottweilers—the massive pony-sized Cici and the regular-sized Gustavo 3—slinked into the village behind her, heads low to the ground, growling at anything that moved. As we watched, Gustavo barked at a dryad, and a bolt of lightning shot from the dog's mouth, striking a monkey in the branches on the dryad's head. The small animal dropped dead. While Gustavo moved to devour the corpse, Cici pounced on the tree creature and started biting the smoldering branches off the NPC as it cried out. Blood sprayed from each broken branch.

"Christ," I muttered.

"Dogs. Can't trust a one of them," Donut said.

From there, the show portrayed Lucia as she went through each pub and safe room in the small town and sampled all of their food and alcohol. As she left each pub, she cast a spell at the entrance. It was the trigger for the teleport trap.

"How is it that they haven't patched that yet?"

"Exploits that allow a crawler to trap and kill another crawler usually aren't patched," Mordecai said. "This one has been around a while. Though I think her original intention was to capture the nebs, not necessarily you and Donut. From what I gather she'd had a run-in with them before this."

Lucia ended up settling at a raised tree house bar in the middle of the small village. It wasn't a safe room, but a dungeon-style pub with an ursine proprietor. The pub had a wide picture window that looked over both of the village's two entrances. An ornate wooden stairwell circled up the tree, leading to a broad deck that led to the front door.

We watched, from Lucia's point of view, as Donut and I walked into town from the north, hurrying because it was almost time for me to leave and go to CrawlCon. We paused at the entrance to the safe room to ask the dryad NPC who the mayor was.

Both of Lucia's dogs started to growl.

"Lunch," Lucia said, sliding out of the chair. The effort was smooth, snakelike. They moved out the front door and leaned over the balcony, watching us. The three of them quietly and slowly descended the circular staircase, reaching the ground. We hadn't noticed them because she'd somehow placed a protection spell over the village, blocking all the dots from appearing on the map.

"Cici, do not swallow the cat whole like you did to that fairy lady. I wish to loot the *puta*'s inventory," Lucia whispered.

"Well, I never," Donut said next to me as we watched the show. "That's just rude."

"So, she just attacked you straight up? She didn't try talking to you first or anything?" I asked.

"No," Donut said. "Not at first. Watch how I expertly handle the situation."

"Ooh, who's that?" Samantha said on the screen. "She looks like my type of crazy."

Pop!

It showed me disappearing and then reappearing in my seat at the panel for the art contest, which wasn't exactly how it happened. They also, for some inexplicable reason, digitally added a little cocktail to the table with an umbrella along with a bowl filled with what looked like strawberries and candy bars.

"Snacks? They gave you snacks?" Donut squeaked.

They quickly moved back to the action before I could object.

Samantha dropped to the ground as Donut hissed. I'd had the safe room door open, but it started to slam closed when I'd disappeared. Donut leaped for the door, but she vanished and reappeared in the middle of the town square, switching places with Lucia.

Lucia landed in the doorway to the pub, landing with one fist on the ground in the classic superhero pose, her back to the action. Mud splattered as her fist hit the earth, splashing over the dryad and the back of Samantha's head.

At the same moment, Donut splatted on the ground with a yowl, landing in the exact spot where Lucia had just been standing.

Right between the two snarling dogs.

This was obviously a planned move, something Lucia had done before. The two dogs both lunged in the exact moment Donut hit the ground.

The dogs were fast, but Donut had a Dodge skill of 11, and she shot forward, moving lightning quick. She leaped in the air and did a rather impressive backflip, landing on the back of the larger rottweiler before launching herself again toward the second pub—the tree house where Lucia had been waiting. A plume of blood geysered off the back of the giant dog as Donut's back claws ripped flesh.

As she flew, Donut cast *Wall of Fire* behind her. The dogs both yelped and ran in opposite directions as the flames spread across the center of town.

The recap paused as a camera zoomed up into the air and then looked down on the scene. Little triangles appeared over all the combatants—Lucia, Donut, Cici, Gustavo, and Samantha. The announcer zoomed in on the smaller of the two rottweilers, giving the audience the dog's stats before moving to the large dog, still frozen with blood splashing up off the creature's back.

"Holy shit," I gasped. "You almost got bitten in half."

"I know, right?" Donut said. She made a little karate motion and a *wachaw!* noise. "They don't call them catlike reflexes for nothing."

"What was that teleport spell? It was different than what she used on the clockwork Sledge."

"*Loop-de-loop,*" Mordecai said, his small eyes intent on the screen. "It's a trap spell, which is different than a regular trap that you set with a module. She likely has the option to either send the victim to a default location or to switch places, and she can toggle it on the fly. She peppers every town she enters with teleport traps. It's a smart survival technique. She likely can only set them when she's in her other form. All of her magic in the skeleton form comes from items."

The announcer completed his analysis of the five players, finishing with a frozen zoom-in on Samantha, who appeared to be screaming and rolling toward the skirmish with the dogs. A pop-up appeared and quickly went away, too fast to read.

The scene unfroze.

Lucia hissed in anger. In the five seconds it had taken for Donut to evade the dogs, Lucia had tossed four potions, each in a different direction. They hit the ground and exploded in a puff of yellow smoke. She dropped the last potion onto the ground in front of the safe room door and rushed forward toward her two dogs and the wall of fire as Donut pounded in the opposite direction toward the tree house pub.

"What are those potions?" I asked.

"Cloud of Dispel Magic," Mordecai said. "She's looking for you. She didn't know you'd left. She thinks you went invisible."

Despite having two different types of legs—a skeleton leg and the leg of a goat—Lucia moved with surprising speed.

Donut didn't bother with the stairwell that circled the tree leading up to the other pub. She jumped, landing high on the side of a tree adjacent to the tree house and scrabbled up the trunk. She then moved to leap from that tree to the deck surrounding the raised pub.

At that same moment, Lucia effortlessly scooped up the still-rolling Samantha by the hair and swung her directly at Donut, launching the head like a rocket. The sex doll head flew true, beaming the cat in the side just as she landed on the platform. Donut yowled and stumbled, rolling. She hit the side of the pub with a mighty thump.

I cringed. That looked like it had hurt. Mongo growled with concern.

Lucia shouted a command, and the two dogs snarled and lunged directly at their owner as she slid to a stop. She dropped a round chip at her feet that I immediately recognized as a trap module.

Despite knowing that Donut survived this, my heart dropped. I knew exactly what was about to happen. Donut was going to enter the other safe room and switch places with Lucia again. But this time, Donut was going to activate a second trap as soon as she landed between the two dogs.

Donut scrambled toward the door, but Samantha, who'd also landed on the raised deck, veered off toward the door and hit it first, pushing it open and rolling inside.

She did that on purpose, I thought, watching the action unfold.

Samantha hit the invisible loop-de-loop trap and teleported back down to the center of the clearing, on the other side of the still-roaring wall of fire. She triggered the second trap, which appeared to be some sort of snare thing that kept her from fleeing. Gustavo snapped down right onto the indestructible doll's head, ripping her up from the ground and shaking her violently as Samantha screamed bloody murder. The larger Cici lunged forward in an attempt to pry the sex doll from the other rottweiler's grip, but Gustavo scrambled away, shaking and growling.

At that same moment, Lucia teleported to right in front of Donut, who was still diving for the safe room entrance. Lucia was facing the room, and Donut plowed into her back. They both flew into the tree house pub, crashing inside and scattering tables and chairs. The ursine proprietor shouted and jumped out of the way.

This pub wasn't a true safe room. It was the same sort of place as the Desperado Club or where we'd killed Growler Gary over and over. There was a door to the guildhall just fifteen feet away, but they could still kill each other in here. Before Lucia could recover, Donut lunged for the guildhall door.

"Watch for traps," I felt myself saying just before Donut hit the snare.

"Nobody likes a Monday-morning shortstop, Carl," Donut grumbled.

On the screen, Donut stopped dead, completely rooted in place. A ninety-second timer appeared over her head. She could still move in a circle, but her forward paw was stuck to the pub's floorboard. She turned and fired a full-powered magic missile into Lucia Mar, who rocketed back. Lucia was now injured, but she had some sort of magic protection which greatly absorbed the damage. I could see one of the rings on her fingers glowing and pulsing. Still, the spell had rocked the crawler, and her health went down about twenty percent.

And just as the girl-turned-woman started to recover, Donut cast a *Fireball* into her chest. Lucia slammed into the back wall of the pub as the ursine guy shouted in alarm. The far wall of the wooden pub burst into flames.

"Don't attack her directly," I said. "She has that other spell, remember? The *Damage Reflect* one she used to kill Ifechi."

"I'm not an idiot, Carl. The spell is called *Rubber*, and she hadn't cast it yet because she wanted her dogs to eat me. Plus Mordecai said he thinks she can only do it when she's in her pretty form."

"That's not what I said at all," Mordecai said. "I said I think it's from an item she's wearing, so she might be able to cast it in her skeletal form, but I wasn't sure."

"Oh," Donut said. "Well, she never cast it."

"Also," Mordecai added, "*Fireball* is an outdoor spell, Donut."

"Both of you, shush! This is the part where it gets all weird."

"You should have released Mongo," I added. "It was three against one."

Next to me, Mongo screeched in agreement.

"I can't help but notice I'm sitting here next to you right now, Carl. You were sipping margaritas and eating strawberries while I was literally fighting for my life. Now quit making suggestions and watch."

I reached down and petted Donut. "You're right. I'm sorry."

On the screen, Donut yelled, "Get back," as Lucia peeled herself off the wall. Her health was down to about 50%. She casually patted out the fire on her body. Behind her, fire raged. Lucia stumbled toward the counter and peered over at the ursine proprietor, who cowered there.

"Milk," Lucia said.

"We're on fire, Mayor. We have to go," the bear said.

She slammed her fist on the counter, and the wood cracked. "Milk. Hurry." She turned toward Donut. "Cats like milk, right?"

"What?" Donut asked.

"Two milks!" Lucia demanded. She looked over her shoulder at an empty spot. "The fight is over. It is a draw."

"Uh, I gotta go into the back to get it," the ursine said. He disappeared into the kitchen. A moment later, a distant door slammed. The bear man was running away. Lucia didn't seem to notice.

"No points?" Lucia paused and looked back out the window as the flames spread upward.

"Who are you talking to?" Donut asked as the flames licked across the ceiling. She still had forty seconds over her head.

"He's mad," Lucia said. "He says I should finish you off, but you fought good."

"Hey," Donut said up at the television screen, "they cut out what she said! She said his name was Alexandro, and he was her youth assistant."

"You didn't tell me that," Mordecai said. "Strange."

On the screen, Lucia continued. "Your friend ran away. What is his name? Oh, yes. Carl. He's a coward. You should never leave your friends. I had friends, on the last floor. Bini and Abraham and Siti. It was all ice, and we finished and popped the bubble. But I fell asleep, and I didn't tell Gus to sleep. And . . . He's the bad one." She paused. "Cici does it, too, but Gus is worse. I think they ate your head friend. I didn't get any points for it." She started to pound at the side of her own head, slamming her hand against her temple in a steady rhythm. *Slap, slap, slap.* I'd seen her do that once before on the recap after her dog had killed all the others in her bubble. "You should probably go before . . ." She paused.

Cici, the larger of the rottweilers, entered the pub, head low. The dog's lip curled back in a vicious snarl. Her incisors were each the length of a human hand. *Holy shit,* I thought. Donut was still snared for another twenty seconds.

Gustavo hadn't come in, and I assumed the other dog remained outside on the ground, gnawing on Samantha.

Something changed in Lucia's demeanor. I could see it on her face, almost like a shadow falling across it. *What is that?* She looked at the giant dog and said, "You want a head to play with, too, don't you, sweet Cici? Kill the kitty. Keep the head for yourself. Leave the rest for me."

The roof of the pub was fully engulfed. Black smoke choked the room. The rear corner caved in, revealing the branches of the trees, which also burned. Red embers zipped through the air. A heavy wooden beam crashed to the floor next to Lucia, showering sparks, and she didn't flinch.

This whole time, Donut was mumbling under her breath. It finally dawned on me what she was doing. *She's singing. She's trying to cast a bard spell.*

"Don't worry, little Donut," Lucia said as Cici stalked forward. "Soon, you will be tossed through the veil, and you will feast with the other losers. And I will have enough points to get across the bridge and back home with my papa."

What the hell is that kid babbling about?

Four additional Donuts suddenly appeared in the fiery pub, all in a line along the back wall.

"Holy shit, you did it!" I exclaimed, forgetting Lucia's weird rant. "You cast *Entourage.*"

"Don't act so surprised, Carl," Donut said indignantly.

But the deception was obvious. Four of the illusions didn't have a timer, nor were they moving. They stood still like mannequins. The center one had five seconds over her head, still counting down.

At the same moment, Cici jumped forward, snapping at the middle Donut. I cringed as the massive jaws clamped, moving right through Donut as if she wasn't there. The dog slammed into the guildhall door and howled.

"How," I began to say, but then the illusions all snapped off as quickly as they'd come. There'd been five Donuts, not four. She'd overlaid the middle one onto herself. She'd also downed an invisibility potion.

But that wasn't all. She'd cast *Hole* under her own feet just as the dog lunged.

The view quickly changed to the outside. We watched as a translucent outline of Donut dropped straight down and landed deftly on the ground next to the burning tree. She looked up at the hole.

"I can't believe that worked," I said.

"The spell removed the trap," Mordecai said, "so she got out of it. It's a good trick."

"I got an achievement for it, too!"

"Did you know that was going to happen?"

"Of course I knew, Carl. Wait, wait, this is the best part!"

Back in the tree house, Cici finally discovered the round hole between her legs and peered down through it. The monster dog stuck her head through and started barking wildly down at the still-invisible form of Donut.

"No," Lucia cried, rushing forward. She reached to pull Cici back. She was too late.

Donut snapped off the *Hole* spell.

The head of Cici the rottweiler dropped from the tree house and splatted onto the muddy ground as firefly-like embers drifted all around it.

Above, an unholy wail of anguish rocked the village.

Donut, still invisible, walked up to the head and put her paw on it, pushing it over to reveal the dead monstrosity's eyes.

"Stupid dog," Donut muttered on the screen. "The only bridge you'll be crossing today is made out of rainbows."

The head disappeared as Donut pulled it into her inventory. A chunk of tree house fell, and Donut bounded off. She remained invisible, and she skulked around the still-burning wall of fire and headed back toward the original safe room. A few hundred meters away, Gustavo 3 sat on the ground, oblivious, happily gnawing on Samantha's head while she wailed that she was going to kill Gustavo's bitch of a mother.

Donut disappeared inside.

The scene returned to Lucia Mar on her knees, hugging the headless corpse of the giant rottweiler as the building collapsed all around her.

"She killed the wrong one," Lucia wailed. "My sweet, sweet Cici. That cat killed the wrong one. What's going to happen now? What's going to happen now?" She looked over at the empty flaming bar. "Where's my milk?"

I could see it, even on the screen. She was constantly changing back and forth, like a child doing hopscotch from one personality to the next. Her eyes narrowed, and the corpse of Cici disappeared as she took it all into her inventory. The pub's flaming counter dropped away as the entire kitchen half of the pub collapsed.

Lucia stood to her full height, but she'd changed from the skeletal hag to the beautiful woman, surrounded by a nimbus of flame. The transformation had been instantaneous.

"Yes. Yes. They all must die. You're right. No more mercy. No more friends. They all must die."

The show ended there.

I looked over at Donut, who beamed up at me triumphantly.

"I was pretty proud of that rainbow-bridge comment," she said, "though I keep going over it in my head, and I kinda wish I'd said it in a different way. Like maybe 'Welcome to the rainbow bridge,' but that doesn't seem quite right, either. It doesn't have enough punch. Oh well, it's too late now. I'll have another one ready for when we take out the other dog."

I exchanged a glance with Mordecai, whose fuzzy face looked grim.

I kept my eyes on the screen, but the show was ending. They would show the next part with me tomorrow. "So that bear I saw out there, attached to the upside-down cross with the word 'milk' carved into his chest in Spanish, I'm pretty sure that was the bartender. She killed him and every other NPC in the town after that. But I don't understand. She sees someone invisible. And what was that point thing? What's a youth assistant? Are you sure that's what she said?"

"Yes, I'm sure, Carl."

"Youth assistants are new," Mordecai said. "But they're not a dungeon thing. Children under a certain age aren't allowed to enter the dungeon. If they descend into the dungeon, they are taken away until after the crawl. The youth assistants are the ones who take care of them. I'm not sure what the minimum age is. It's different each time, and it changes based on intelligence level and species. Kids shouldn't be in here. Youth assistants shouldn't be here. It's really strange."

We were interrupted by the daily announcement.

Hello, Crawlers!

What an exciting day! With just over 66,000 crawlers left, we have exactly 100 guilds formed, combining almost 1,500 parties. Over 90% of all crawlers are partied with at least one other contestant, which is an extraordinarily high number. For a non-stigmergic species, you guys sure love your societal structures.

This coordination is great for survival in normal circumstances, but you make yourselves easy targets. Still, an equally amazing number of hunter-killer trophies have been collected. Tomorrow's recap episode will feature some of the highlights of hunters falling, a first for *Dungeon Crawler World*.

In fact, you guys are fighting back so astonishingly well, several of the silly hunters are abandoning their hunt and hiding out in Zockau. Hopefully they stop being cowards soon. If not, we may have to change things up a little.

Your pluckiness has caused us to completely redesign the seventh floor. More on that later. Please note, however, if you go down within six hours of level collapse, you will not get a head start. You will, however, get good placement. If you go down *too* early, you *will* be placed at the back of the pack.

In the meantime, you still have a full seven days left to secure your spot in the top 50. All of the top 50 will be notified that they've received an invite to the party at the Butcher's Masquerade. Attendance is mandatory, and all invitees will be allowed a plus-one. Attendance for the plus-ones is optional.

Now get out there and kill, kill, kill!

"What the hell does 'stigmergic' mean?" I asked.

"I bet Britney knows," Donut said.

"I'm more worried about the wording on—" Mordecai began.

The door to the outside was flung open. Bomo stepped inside the safe room. The giant rock monster looked uncharacteristically tired and exasperated. Just outside, standing uncertainly in the situationally generated space was a small male mantis. The hunched-over, shivering creature was barely distinguishable as the same race as Vrah or Circe.

"Carl," the creature said through the open door, "we must talk quickly. She's coming for me."

38

CARL: MORDECAI, HOW SAFE IS IT TO BRING HIM IN HERE?

    MORDECAI: He can't teleport you away like Lucia does in a regular safe room, if that's what you're asking. But he can and will likely report everything he sees back to his people. You can't tie him up. You can't hire him. You can restrict him to the main room of the personal space, but that's about it.

    CARL: Shit, what do we do?

    MORDECAI: You probably should have thought this through before you invited him here.

"I wasn't expecting you to come," I said, leaving him in the hallway. It'd been almost two hours since I'd sent Bomo out into Zockau with the note. He'd been given strict instructions not to leave the tavern safe room. I was about to send him a message to come back. If Vrah was returning to the town, she surely would've arrived by now.

Well, I thought, *maybe not.* I imagined flying while your genitals were on fire had to slow you down somewhat.

"He attack me," Bomo said, grunting the words. "In safe room, he attack me, and he get frozen for a minute. Then he said, 'Wait for me,' and he attack me again. He got frozen for an hour. Stupid bug. Lots of hunters in safe room. Lots and lots. They scared of Bomo."

"He attacked you?" I asked, raising an eyebrow. *"Twice?* With what?"

"With hands. He tried to punch. He got frozen, and it said he was naughty."

If he attacked any of us a third time, he'd get stripped of all his gear and teleported away to the closest monster nest.

I sighed and examined the small, quivering creature. He looked like a child. He did not have the upper swordlike arms that the females did, which made him look even more pitiful.

Edict—Mantis. Level 50. Merchant.
The Dark Hive.

"Hello, Edict," I said, leaning against the door. A few personal space doors dotted the situationally generated hallway. This was one of the few true safe rooms in Zockau, so it made sense others would want to keep their spaces attached to this pub. "So, what do you got for me?"

"I'm not a hunter. Or a fighter. I'm just the accountant. They made me come here to do the trading."

"An accountant?" I asked. "You know, you're the second guy to say that to me." I looked over at Donut, who'd jumped to my shoulder. "What was that other guy's name? The elf from the Dream? He said he was an accountant, too."

"You know I don't remember the names of corpses, Carl," Donut said. "Maybe if you pull his hand out of your inventory, it will jog your memory."

"Akland?" Edict asked, deflating even further. If he hunched over any more, I was afraid he'd fall to the ground and turn into a pill bug. "You killed Akland? I hadn't heard. He'd gone out with the others. I told him it was stupid. The hunters are all returning to Zockau. It's become too dangerous. Please. She's almost here. She told me I have to mate with her. We must hurry."

"What do you got for me?" I asked again.

The bug wrung his hands. "I had a lot of magical gear, but I am contracted to buy for our government. The Burrowers. They've already paid for all the loot I have collected."

The Burrowers were also mantises. They were one of the nine factions that were to compete in faction wars. "There's a Burrower rep on the floor?"

"No, no, you misunderstand. They paid in advance. I have been contracted to bring the gear directly to them upon the collapse of this floor. I'm going straight to the ninth after this. That's who I really work for. The Dark Hive sells only to them."

Even though the Burrowers were the same species as the mantises from the Dark Hive, I knew that they were actually two very different groups. The Dark Hive was really just a private corporation. They apparently got their money from running some sort of intergalactic amusement park. Like a fucked-up version of the Disney family.

The Burrowers were the royal family and the governmental entity for the mantis system. They rarely did well in faction wars, but they usually participated. Apparently they were one of the deadliest and most terrifying forces in the galaxy, but the generated NPCs they received in faction wars weren't fellow bugs, so they usually got knocked out second after the Nagas. I had a photograph of the empress mother in my inventory.

"I don't care who you really work for. Unless you want your praying mantis nut sack to catch on fire for a week straight, you're going to have to hand the loot over. And then we'll protect you."

"Carl, do bugs even have genitals?" Donut asked. "I don't think I've ever seen a bug penis. I bet they're really gross. Like a corkscrew duck penis. Or a dog penis. Have you ever seen one of those? They're absolutely revolting, and sometimes they just have them hanging out for no reason. They look like sweating lipsticks. Whenever Miss Beatrice pulled out that red tube and brought it to her mouth, I couldn't help but think—"

I held up a hand to stop the cat and let the mantis answer.

"You don't understand," Edict said. "The contract for the gear has already been executed. If I gave it to you, the Burrowers would take the money back from me and my family. My Hive. I'm of Deep Mind, and we would not survive. So I have already given it all away to another entity who has agreed to deliver the goods for a small fee. I will not tell you who."

I sighed. I hadn't really been expecting that part to work, but it'd been worth a try. All I really wanted was to keep Vrah away from this guy so she couldn't pass the gonorrhea on. I already knew from the cookbook that venereal diseases were a common thing in the dungeon, and several of them had the same cure. You had to neuter yourself or you had to give it to someone else. And by "someone else," they meant a creature with compatible anatomy.

I had no idea how mantis alien genitals worked, but I did know that once you cut something away in this dungeon, it didn't come back. And I also knew that Vrah was next in line to be the Hive's big queen, so giving herself a space hysterectomy or spaying herself or whatever had to be out of the question.

As simpering and cowardly as this guy looked, he was no dummy. He had to know keeping Vrah infected was my primary goal. Still, I had to play this out.

"I guess you're fucked, then," I said, trying to sound nonchalant. "If you have nothing for us, we have no incentive to keep you safe." I shrugged.

Edict shook his head. "If I truly wished to remain safe, I would stay in the safe room and refuse to leave, even when Vrah orders me to. She cannot force me outside. She can't use the teleport trick or the phase trick or the Bopca ejection method or the other dozen ways they have to lure crawlers out. After your assault, they covered the tavern with protection spells. I could just stay within."

"Then why are you here?" I asked. A distant sense of alarm started to tingle at the back of my mind. *This is a trap. He's springing a trap.* But what was it? Was this a distraction?

"I don't know how you infected Vrah with that disease, but when you did, you placed my fate, perhaps the fate of my entire Hive, at a split in the tunnel. If I gave you the weapons and armor, my family would be financially ruined. I would be without honor, forced to kill myself in shame. If I refuse Vrah's orders and allow her to suffer, her family would take revenge on my own. They are powerful. Almost as strong as the royal family and certainly more wealthy. But if I give in to Vrah's demands and mate with her, I will more than just die. While she would not be impregnated within this zone, it is still forbidden for members of my Hive to attempt a coupling with hers. And while the Burrower government isn't as strict as they once were, the old ways persist amongst our culture, and we would still be deemed as traitors. Perhaps forgivable, especially considering the circumstances. But a humiliation either way, and I will not let that happen."

"Wait," Donut said. "They'd make you kill yourself for having sex with someone from a different family?"

"All mantis couplings must be registered ahead of time. There must be a trial and psychological counseling for the male. But my family is employed by the government, so it's forbidden to couple with a for-profit entity without putting up a bond and paying for a license."

"Psychological counseling?" Donut asked. "Whatever for? All the human males have to do is find someone who's drunk enough to not find them completely revolting for five minutes."

The creature scoffed. "Do you know what happens when a mantis mates?"

"Probably something really gross?"

"The female eats the male's head off. I have a smaller secondary brain in my abdomen that keeps me alive for a few hours and allows me to keep mating until I am tapped dry."

"She mates with a headless corpse while munching on the head? Are you serious?" Donut asked. "And you know this going in? You can still get it up? Carl, did you hear that?"

I didn't care about any of this. I'd spent the last minute searching the hallway for traps and asking Mordecai what he thought was going on. He'd said you couldn't place traps in situationally generated spaces. I was getting ready to step back and close the door. Still, I remained, my feet glued in place as I listened to this guy's story. The more he talked, the straighter he stood. The more certain his words became.

"So," I said, "you're screwed no matter what happens."

The bug's hands had turned to fists. He continued to tremble, but I wasn't so sure anymore that this was fear. He was angry, but I had the sense it wasn't at me. I didn't understand.

"There's only one way to maintain honor," he said. "To protect my family. I need to die in battle."

"We can't fight in here," I said. But then it hit me. He'd attacked Bomo twice.

"I hate this place," the man said, standing fully erect. Behind him, I heard shouting coming from the main pub. This was the pained voice of Vrah crying out for Edict. "I hate everything about it. Finding the stars was the worst thing that ever happened to my people. It is a slow, horrific death. Expansion to the point of oblivion. The primals finally understood, but it was too late for them. The kua-tin, I think, know this, too. Some of them at least. They call it the Great Consensus. But it's not. There is no agreement. Their young don't understand. Now quickly, allow me entrance into your space."

The door that led back to the pub burst open, and Vrah limped into the hallway. She towered over Edict. I highlighted the smaller bug, and I gave him a onetime pass to enter through the door.

Vrah moved slowly. She hissed in pain with every step. Smoke rose from her crotch. It stank like burned cheese. There was no vent system in this small hallway, and the smoke would soon be too much.

She started to say something to the smaller man, but with a strangled battle cry, he lunged at me, punching.

He froze in place, small fist about an inch from my crotch. The words **Super Naughty** flashed over his head. Vrah hissed in rage as Edict blinked twice and then disappeared.

He'd just been teleported, naked, to the closest mob nest. I had no idea what that would be, but he was likely in the process of being torn to shreds.

I wasn't ever going to understand the intricacies of mantis culture, but I suspected this was the best possible outcome for him. Or if not for him, for his family.

Despite his report that he'd given away all his loot, a metric ton of gold coins dropped to the floor right at my feet, splashing like I'd just hit the jackpot at an old-school slot machine. So many, I was suddenly buried to my ankles. The cleaner bot beeped with rage while Donut gasped.

In the hallway, Vrah shrieked. She pounded at the wall as her lower abdomen burned. *She looks smaller,* I thought. *Less sinister.* I realized she'd dislodged all of the heads from her back. Not just the ones Donut had reanimated. Likely in an effort to make herself lighter. The flames on her lower abdomen whiffed out, she glowed as she was healed, and then the fire raged anew.

Not even a safe room would protect her from this torment.

"You know," Donut said through the open door, "you really should get that taken care of. Maybe you can put some ointment on it. It looks infected."

"Catch you later," I said. I had to physically push the pile of the coins as I slammed the door. Several of them slid out into the hallway. The majority of the gold remained with us. I immediately opened the door back up to reveal the pub in Alucarda. The place was a mess. The Bopca had not returned. I knew this pub was the only thing in town still standing. That bomb had been superpowerful, the biggest thing I'd built myself. The only bigger explosive was Carl's Doomsday Scenario, which remained in my inventory.

"Come on, Donut," I said, stepping into the pub. "We need to get out of here before either Lucia or another hunter comes back."

"But what about the gold?" she asked. "And you pushed some of it out into the hallway. You need to be more careful, Carl."

"I got it," Mordecai said. He shooed the cleaner bot away as he started to pick it all up.

39

"I KINDA FEEL BAD FOR THAT GUY. WHAT WAS HIS NAME? EDICT?" DO-nut said much later as we approached the small ursine village. It'd been a long day. We'd been avoiding the dryad settlements because half of the tree guys now attacked me on sight, and I'd just learned the hard way that if the mayor happened to worship Diwata, he'd immediately task the funeral bell guards to attack me, too. Also, the monkeys in their branches threw rocks with amazing accuracy. They reminded me of those asshole undead lemurs from the third floor. "He didn't seem to want to be here, and we forced him to play the game."

"Yeah, I don't want to be here, either," I said. I was not sympathetic, though I'd been thinking about what he said all day. I couldn't get it out of my head. I didn't actually agree with him, or at least what I thought he was getting at, and that was what was bothering me the most. I believed him when he'd said he didn't want to be there. And that he hated the way the universe worked. Despite everything that was happening to me and our planet, I thought he was wrong. It was stupid to let it bother me.

I heard my dad's voice scolding me. *Why do you care?* he'd said to me one day when he caught me watching the news. *Knowing all that stuff rots you from the inside out. It doesn't affect people like us.*

"I wish I had been there," Samantha said. "I'd have killed him."

We'd found Samantha stuck under a log about a half of a mile south of town. It hadn't been hard to track her down considering how loud she was. She was still pissed about Donut leaving her to get eaten by the rottweiler, but she was starting to get over it. She seemed to have actually enjoyed the experience of being tortured by the mantises.

We'd spent the last several hours fighting our way south. Killing mobs, collecting plants, mosses, and mushrooms for Mordecai, and just grinding. Most of the mobs in this area were venomous plant things that whipped vines at you if you got too close. They were all level 40 whip crackers. They'd be a downright menace if we weren't immune to poison. Because we were, they were a great source of experience, and I forced Donut to kill as many as possible. She hit level 45 while I remained at 56.

We'd also taken control of two small towns, both ursine settlements. Donut killed one mayor, and I killed the next. I'd also been attempting to get a hold of my attorney, but I hadn't heard back from him yet. The last time we'd spoken, he'd told me they were restricting communication, and he had to get a court order each time he wanted to reply to me. My question for him was a legal one, so hopefully they'd allow him to send me a response. I'd asked Mordecai first, and he'd said he didn't know.

MORDECAI: Every day, you do and come across something that's
never been done or seen before, Carl. I'm starting to feel a
little obsolete. Ask your lawyer, and if he doesn't respond, wait
until after the next recap episode. If they don't take it away
from you, install it into the crafting studio and start working.
In the meantime, transcribe everything you can from that
automaton book into your scratch pad.

Zev had also been in contact, reminding me I still had one more appearance to make and that we needed to make the safe room in time. We didn't want a repeat of the last incident, though it seemed the hunters everywhere were retreating. Once word spread about what happened to the Dark Hive, the vast majority of these guys decided their own lives were suddenly valuable.

Not a single person on my chat had seen or heard of any hunter contact all day. I'd also asked around if anyone had seen Lucia, but nobody had. Mordecai seemed to think her escape spell would've teleported her to the opposite side of the map, and that it was a once-a-floor spell. I wasn't so sure about that, but hopefully she was far away from us. We needed to deal with her, but now was not the time. Not yet.

That scene with Donut had been eating away at me. It was almost like Lucia was experiencing a completely different reality than the rest of us. *You killed the wrong one.* What did that mean? There was someone there with her, invisible. But there was more. Were they attached to the dogs? Or dog. I didn't have enough info.

When I was on my panel, everyone appeared to think she was just a crazy kid with an uncanny ability to kill people and defend herself. Despite being the most followed crawler in the universe until I surpassed her, people seemed to know precious little about the nature of her existence. It seemed important. Crucially important.

But at the same time, I hadn't changed my mind. She was hurting people. Attacking crawlers. She was slaughtering and torturing NPCs for no good reason. She had to be put down.

Donut's confidence in her ability to take out the kid during our next encounter was alarming. At least at first. She'd gotten lucky, and I wanted to make sure she knew that. But Donut was sensitive, and if I pushed too hard, she'd shut down. I'd tried to carefully broach the matter with her a few times, but she expertly steered the conversation away. In fact, she was doing it so deftly that I finally got the hint, and it made me relax.

Donut knew exactly how lucky she was. Donut was a lot smarter than she let on, and the way she'd handled the fight with Lucia made it clear she knew what she was doing. She just didn't want to say it out loud. Or in private, for that matter. I decided to leave it be.

The upcoming town was another small settlement. The plan was to settle in for the night. I would go on my show, come back, and we'd reset. If we could easily find the mayor without getting embroiled in some bullshit quest, we'd take him out and then move on.

Both of the new ursine settlements we'd claimed—now dubbed Ferdinand Peak and Nipton—had been as ridiculously religious as the first one, Point Mongo. After taking out the mayor, we hit the safe room and sent Mordecai to talk to the guards. He was currently attached to the town of Nipton and was bitching about the quality of the stores there. I suspected this new place wouldn't be much better.

This new town was surrounded by a massive wall of living level 10 vines called a **Jericho Bush**. It wasn't one giant shrub, but literally thousands of them. Each individual branch was its own plant. The description simply said: **These powerful vines are very durable. They have a strong dislike for people named Josh and ska music.** They appeared as a non-hostile, so we couldn't get experience from chopping them down, not that we needed to. The plants all near the northern entrance to the city appeared dead. There were no guards. Mordecai said these things were a magical plant that could be used to protect a city. He wanted us to hurry up and find a safe room so he could go out there and collect some seeds.

The closer we got to town, the clearer it became that something was amiss. There were no people coming and going. No guards. There seemed to be no activity whatsoever. *Shit,* I thought. Had Lucia gotten to this town, too? Was that little asshole just moving across the map, murder-hoboing everybody and everything?

Mongo screeched with concern, then issued a low growl.

"Uh-oh," Donut said. "That's his I-smell-other-Mongos growl." She sniffed at the air herself. "Oh god, I smell something awful, but it's not dinosaurs. It smells like that train car after you attached Katia to the front of it."

"Go look, Samantha," I said.

"I'm on it," she said, and rolled forward, bouncing merrily toward the large town. "Hellllloooo," she called out. "Is everybody dead? Are any of you lizards here?" She disappeared through the unguarded entrance, hollering.

"She's rolling a lot faster than she was before," Donut said.

"Yeah, I've noticed," I said. We waited a few minutes. Donut practiced humming a song. She was still terrible, but she was getting better.

SAMANTHA: I JUST SAW A FEW BEARS IN A WINDOW, SO NOT
    EVERYBODY IS DEAD. BUT I HAVEN'T SEEN THIS MANY
    CORPSES SINCE IT WAS ALGOS'S TURN TO HOST GAME
    NIGHT. IT'S LIKE THE BEACH FROM A FEW NIGHTS AGO, BUT A
    LOT MORE JUICY. CHOMPED-UP PEOPLE AND PINK FEATHERS
    EVERYWHERE. THEY'VE BEEN DEAD A WHILE. MORE THAN A
    DAY. WHY DON'T THEY CLEAN IT UP? THE DINO IS LONG
    GONE. I THINK.

I sighed.

Corpses that were more than a day old were always a bad sign. The dungeon cleaned up after itself. When it didn't, it was always on purpose.

"Come on, Donut," I said. "We need to get a safe room spot established. We'll deal with whatever this is later." My last appearance at CrawlCon was only scheduled to last about two hours, which would probably translate to four or five hours. Afterward, we'd rest and get the hell away from here.

"Mongo, get into your carrier," Donut said. "Come on. Be a good boy. We don't want you eating all the dead bodies and getting sick again."

Mongo screeched but complied.

Donut then jumped to my shoulder and started to lick at her paw. "Don't step in gross stuff, Carl. You know how I feel about you trailing gross stuff into the guild."

We went through the main entrance, and the stench of rotting death hit me like a baseball bat to the nose.

Entering Prepotente Town Number Four.

"Gah," I muttered upon seeing the name.

"My word. He definitely needs help naming things," Donut said.

"At least we know who it is this time."

Donut gasped. "Unless it's a trick. I shall ask him. We haven't spoken in a bit."

I was already in the middle of composing a message of my own.

CARL: Miriam, are you guys here in, uh, Town Number Four? It looks like most of the NPCs are dead. There's a giant dinosaur rampaging in the area.

She didn't answer, and I didn't see any sign of other crawlers on the map. It was still day outside, which meant she was likely asleep.

The town was oddly in shadow thanks to the tall hedge that surrounded it, which was probably why Miriam the vampire liked the place. There were no big trees or tree houses here, but several of the structures were three or four stories high, adding to the sense of darkness. Rows and rows of nondescript buildings spread off down the tight cobblestone street. There was a small downtown area with a clock tower and a pair of temples before ending at the far wall. I didn't see anyone else.

Samantha rolled up, trailing a line of blood. The doll head had already been filthy, but now she was just caked in viscera, like she was cosplaying Rambo hiding in the mud. "It's worse the next street over. Everyone is in pieces. I tried making gore angels, but it's too coagulated and sticky. And that Signet bitch hasn't given me her body yet."

Multiple X's dotted the area, mixed in with the random body parts of creatures too destroyed to be recognizable. Samantha was right. This was worse than the beach. Before the collapse, the stench would've been enough to bring me to my knees. Now it was just another day. It looked as if someone mixed chili with reddish brown paint and splashed it over the streets. A few pink feathers flitted about, but most of them were glued to the ground by blood.

I caught movement in the corner of my eye, and I looked up. A white dot appeared before disappearing. Someone in one of the buildings. They were hiding. We needed to get off these streets.

Most of the corpses had a small amount of loot on them, but nothing too great. It was mostly junk clothing items, the occasional health potion, and a handful of coins. I set out to quickly loot the bodies and take some of the corpse pieces into my inventory, but the first head I picked up disappeared into dust.

I kneeled down and examined one of the body parts. I wasn't certain, but it appeared *all* of the corpses were bears.

Fodera—Level 40 Ursine Lamplighter. Killed by Big Tina.

"They're not letting this dinosaur quest go, are they?" I grumbled.

> **ZEV:** Carl, you need to get to a safe room. You're getting filthy, and you need to go to your event. Uh, also, you should probably know that Odette's interview with you and Donut and Beatrice tunneled last night. That along with the Dark Hive

business is causing there to be a lot of attention focused on you.

CARL: Wonderful. Hey, I need to talk to my attorney. Can you make that happen?

ZEV: I'll see what I can do. Now go get ready. There's something else we need to discuss, but I'll do it in person.

CARL: Oh, I can't wait.

"Come on, guys," I said as I reached down to pick up Samantha. She growled and snapped at me. An eyeball fell out of her hair and landed on my foot with a *splatch*.

The closest pub was not a true safe room, and the proprietor was either dead or hiding. The inside was some standard dive bar filled with flags and framed jerseys and signs for the Ottawa Senators NHL hockey team. The center of the bar was dominated with a massive autographed picture of some player named Daniel Alfredsson. I didn't follow hockey, so I didn't know who that was.

Just before we entered the guild, I paused, looking about the empty room. I caught sight of a bear claw embedded in the wall just inside the pub by the front door, like the proprietor had been standing there in the doorway before he'd been ripped away, and he'd tried to save himself. A puddle of dried blood sat pooled under the claw.

I had a sudden ominous feeling about this damn dinosaur quest.

40

ENTERING PRODUCTION FACILITY.

"Hello, guys," I said to the large two-headed-ogre creature sitting before me. I couldn't examine them like I could in the dungeon, but they were really here with me. I knew this right away because they smelled like how one would expect a two-headed ogre would smell. Especially one who'd been locked in a small room for three days, only let out to perform like a monkey for various panels and events.

This was the first time I was ever physically in the same place with a crawler other than Donut or Katia in one of these studio places.

I took stock of the room. They had a bed and a training room, but I noted it was a regular level 1 training space. The remnants of what appeared to be a greasy cooked chicken sat on the counter without a plate. There were no other comforts. This was practically a jail cell.

I'd taken a shower, Zev made me put the badge on, and I transported away. I'd gotten the security sweep, but this time it was a low-level gnoll who barely said two words to me before I was transferred back down to the production facility. The security guy did not turn me sideways before I zapped away, and I landed hard on my side on the floor.

The two-headed creature was attempting to play a game. They each had a set of cards in their respective hands and were desperately trying to keep the other from seeing what they had. They both looked at me in alarm as I suddenly appeared, blasting onto the greenroom floor like a book being slammed on a table.

"Ow," I said. I rolled onto my back.

The ogres both grunted as they put the cards down, stood, and moved to help me up. I allowed them to pull me to my feet as I grinned sheepishly and faced the two-headed creature. Creatures. I knew this was two distinct people, but it was hard to see them that way. Together, these guys were the number five crawler in the dungeon.

My menus were gone, but I could still see the names floating over their heads thanks to my CrawlCon badge. Dmitri had the right side—so on my left. It didn't have his class or level, but I knew he was a mage class called a **Visionary**. Maxim was a melee-focused **Bogatyr**. The two stood about seven feet tall and were wide and solid. Their skin was mottled gray and looked thick and calloused. Like that of an elephant. Maxim wore a knitted beanie, and Dmitri's round, wide head was bare. They wore a simple tunic, with the badge around both of their necks. Their massive arms made my newly enhanced guns look like twigs. The ogre's right arm was covered with golden rings, one after another, and they jingled as the creature moved.

Both creatures had wide-open eyes with furrowed lines upon their foreheads, making them appear stupid. I knew this was misleading.

These guys were clearly the same sort of ogre as Areson the Wise, Signet's bodyguard. I recalled what she said about the Nodling race.

When a Nodling dies, he splits into a new creature depending on how many heads the original had. These new creatures emerge as toddlers but quickly grow.

Their race basically gave them an extra life. I wasn't certain how useful that was considering they'd turn, at least temporarily, into little kids when they died, and split.

Their main melee weapon was Maxim's meteor hammer: a flaming ball at the end of a chain. I'd seen how much damage they could do with the thing. According to Elle, they were good guys, for which I was glad. I had no desire to ever face them down.

"Carl," Maxim said after I greeted them, reaching out his left hand to shake mine. Awkwardly. "It is good to finally meet. I hear you've been making a big splash at the convention so far. Thank god it is almost over, no?"

This guy had an Eastern European accent, deepened and grittier because of his race. It reminded me of Britney's and Langley's, but a little different in a way I couldn't quite put my finger on.

"You do not have your cat companion with you?" Dmitri said, sounding disappointed. "I wanted to meet the cat."

"You and the damn cat," Maxim said. "You're always talking about this cat. We told you, it's just Carl. Skindle told you it is just Carl. You're going to make him feel uncomfortable."

"Uh, yeah," I said. "Donut is back in the safe room. She wanted to come, but they wouldn't let her."

Dmitri sighed sadly. "I wish to meet the cat. I've never met a talking cat before."

"I apologize for my brother," Maxim said. "He likes the cat. We could never have one growing up."

I knew these guys were twin brothers, but fraternal twins. So they weren't identical before. They weren't identical now, either, despite sharing a body. Dmitri had a rounder face while Maxim looked much more chiseled.

"I'd just gotten a cat," Dmitri added sadly. "His name was Kapitan Whiskers, and he was orange. I got him the day before . . . before it happened."

"I'm sorry to hear that," I said.

"Yes, my poor Kapitan. He was all alone. You're a good man, Carl, despite what they say. You were trying to save the cat in the cold when it happened. We saw this at a panel. This is a sign of a good man."

Pop! Pop! Two kua-tin appeared in the room, splashing water everywhere, saving me from this suddenly awkward conversation. This was Zev and another kua-tin. I realized I had no way to determine kua-tin genders, but this one looked very similar to Zev.

"Skindle," Maxim said, growling. "You left us here for hours. We were promised food, but all they gave was a single chicken, which is nothing."

"Yes, yes," Skindle said. She sounded female. "This is Zev, and she is both my boss and Carl's outreach associate, so do as she says."

Zev nodded. "Hello, Carl. Hello, Dmitri and Maxim. This is the first time you two have met if I'm not mistaken. Thank all three of you for agreeing to do this today."

"Agree?" I asked as Maxim snorted.

"Anyway," Zev continued without missing a beat, "you will be going out there in about a minute. The line is already at capacity, and the fans are eager to get this rolling."

"You said there's something you wanted to talk to me about first," I said.

Zev gave a sidelong glance to Skindle and then said, "Yes. Your replacement sponsor. There was a small delay in the announcement as the first sponsor who won the bidding ended up unable to pay. As a result, we started a new bidding event, and your sponsor has been chosen, and they wish to award you your first benefactor box during this event."

"Lucky," Dmitri said.

"Who is it?" I asked. "And who was the one who couldn't pay?"

"You'll see at the end of the signing," Zev said. She sounded a little reticent, which did not bode well. "As for the first winner, I actually don't know. I may have gotten a promotion, but that's still above my pay grade. Now we need to get out there."

"Is this really only going to go for two hours?" I asked as we moved toward the door.

"Maybe three. Or four," Zev said. "There's not an unlimited supply of fans. They had to enter a lottery to get chosen for a place in line. People aren't allowed to give away or sell their place, except the premium spots, but you don't need to worry about that. So it'll be a good smattering of fans. Not just rich ones. There will be press, too, at the end. I think it's only about 300 fans. Plus 30 premiums. Plus the press. They wanted to do more, but today is the last day of the con, and there isn't enough time."

"We all get to leave when the last in line is done," Skindle added. "So don't spend too much time talking. Try to be efficient and not your usual dumb selves."

I looked over at the twins. "Does your associate get mad when you tell her to go fuck herself? Zev gets pretty pissed."

Dmitri looked horrified as Maxim grinned. "We shall try it later, and I will report back," Maxim said.

41

"WAS IT REALLY AN ACCIDENT?" THE LITTLE BLOB KID ASKED THE POP-
ovs as they signed the photograph. The thing had a nasally, nerd-like
accent. "Or did you do it on purpose?" They both looked up and paused
mid-autograph.

Even though we were in the production facility, the movement of the
Sharpie-like pen was mirrored halfway across the galaxy. Our "handler"
was a terrified-looking soother male named Effex. He was really at the
con, and he stood to the left of the Popovs manning a display of different
photographs the fans could purchase for signatures. They'd pick one or
two, pay, and then Effex would place the photo on the table in front of
us, where we'd sign it. They could get either me or the Popovs, and there
was one photo, a video really, of me shaking hands with the brothers,
taken literally minutes earlier in the greenroom. The fans could have
that one signed by all three of us. The fans had dozens of choices of animated photos. There were also shirts we could autograph and some
digital-tablet thing I didn't understand. I had the impression it was akin
to a phone case.

The photograph the blob kid was getting autographed was of the
Popov brothers swinging their meteor hammer while inside an about-
to-derail train car as flaming-hedgehog things attacked them. The picture moved in a loop, repeating over and over. Apparently if you put
your finger, or blob appendage, on it, you could mentally find yourself
in the scene. The Nodling finished signing—each had a pen in their
respective hands—and the twin autographs appeared in sparkling gold
on the photograph.

Dmitri happily signed everything, chatting with everyone. Maxim was more subdued and looked bored, though he perked up at any of the female-presenting aliens if they appeared even slightly human.

If the fans paid extra—and they always paid extra—they turned around, and a photograph or short video or whatever was taken of them standing between us.

Next to me, Maxim sighed while Dmitri made an indignant noise at the little blob kid.

"For the thousandth time," Dmitri said, "our game guide, Hongrish, told me the Nodling was a good choice that would give me an extra life if I died. He did not tell me it would force my brother into the same body as myself. I would never do this."

The blob quivered and leaned forward, which made him look like a gelatin mold that was about to be spilled all over the table. When he talked, his mouth opened from the very top of his head, facing upward. It was weird as shit.

"But," the kid said, "we saw you talking about that television program from your world. The one with the conjoined twins. The two boys who were arrested for selling guns. You said you liked this program. I have watched this program and determined that you were so enamored with them that you deliberately chose a race that would allow you to emulate your favorite television characters."

"I don't know what you're talking about," Dmitri said.

"So you won't confirm or deny my hypothesis?"

"I'm going to confirm my foot up your jelly ass if you don't move along," Maxim growled.

"I paid for a picture. My superior cell mass paid for it."

"Then turn around and get on with it."

The blob didn't say anything further as we took the picture.

"Touchy subject?" I asked Maxim as we watched the kid slurp off.

"Don't even ask," Dmitri said. "Hey, at least this one didn't ask about your ex-girlfriend or the fight with the bug."

Sure enough, every single damn person who went through had something to say about either the Odette interview with me and Beatrice or me sticking that arrow into the throat of Vrah. Apparently, Circe had gone completely apeshit about the whole thing and was on her way right now to the Earth system to do something about it. I didn't know what that could possibly be since it was too late for her to come to the sixth floor and join the hunters.

Vrah, in the meantime, was apparently going to attempt to ride it out. People were actively betting on whether or not she'd give in and cut the infection away, which would ruin her chances at being the next Hive queen. I waved all the questions about her away. I just said she'd be dealt with soon enough.

If it was a comment about Bea, I simply replied that Donut was doing fine and that everything that needed to be said was said during the interview.

Multiple people—twenty of them at least—were dressed like me. They wore little-heart boxers and weren't wearing shoes and had jackets and capes. It was weird as shit. A lot of these guys wanted me to autograph their boxers, which was awkward with the magical pen. One dude, a human, wanted me to autograph his foot. I refused.

There were other cosplayers as well, including an elf woman dressed like Hekla and an orc guy dressed as Quan Ch, complete with a prosthetic bloody stump that shot out little squirts of blood everywhere. I signed the stump at his request.

There was a pair of Saccathians who'd tied themselves together and were pretending to be the Popovs. The two bickered so much, they ended up dislodging from one another. I thought that was pretty funny. Dmitri and Maxim did not.

Several asked me about that damn gnoll kid's drawing. I refused to answer any questions about that.

The Popovs were peppered with questions about their fallout with team Cichociemni and what they thought about the death of Bogdon Ro. Dmitri said nothing to this, but Maxim cheerfully told them that the man had gotten what he deserved and that he was just sorry others had to die for it to happen.

The entire grueling procession took about three and a half hours.

Finally, we only had a few guests left. Then would come the reporters.

At first glance, everything about the last fan looked human, but that was before I noticed the tentacle coming from the back of her head. I couldn't tell if she was a person with a parasite, or if this was something new. She walked carefully and slowly up to the podium, like she had an issue with one of her legs. Other than that, she looked like a regular brunette human woman, maybe in her forties. Her name was Jenn'ifer. She had the word **Premium** after her name with little spinning stars, which meant she'd paid for this spot. We'd seen plenty of these guys already. I wondered how much it actually cost for this bullshit.

Effex slid a picture in front of me to sign. Her premium pass came with two free pictures and a photo, but she'd only wanted one. It depicted me and Donut in the drop bear biplane as it was chased by Orthrus, the giant puppy at the end of the last floor. I picked up my Sharpie. "Jenn'ifer, huh? That name is really popular where I'm from."

"It is common everywhere," she said drily as I started to sign. I stopped dead as I finally noticed her T-shirt.

It read "The Society for the Eradication of Cocker Spaniels" in Syndicate Standard, but the words "Cocker Spaniels" were censored with a transparent line through them. Above the words was a semi-realistic drawing of an adorable, fluffy-eared dog with a big red flashing X over it.

I sighed. "I know I'm going to regret asking this, but is that cocker spaniel shirt supposed to be a joke?"

The woman's eyes went wide. "You don't say the word out—"

The flesh-colored-tentacle thing coming from the back of her head waved about and started to thrash, beating her on the top of the head, stopping her in midsentence. A little mouth opened up on the tentacle and started growling and salivating, oozing thick saliva over the woman's head.

The tentacle itself had a little spot of long blond hair at the very tip, and it was held together with a bow, making the . . . thing look like a fucked-up Yorkshire terrier. It quivered with anger.

"Maggie, shush," the woman said to her tentacle as I mouthed *What the fuck?* at the twins. She petted the tentacle a few times. "She gets angry when someone says the C-word. She gets so mad, she runs away. I say, 'I'm not going to chase you, you little monster.' But I do every time."

The thing, still quivering, started to make a whimpering noise.

"Maggie?" I said. "I knew another Maggie not too long ago. She was also a parasite."

"She is not a parasite!" Jenn'ifer said, indignant. "She doesn't like people saying the C-word."

"If you don't want people saying it, why is it on your T-shirt?" I asked.

Jenn'ifer ignored my question and continued. "Anyway, Carl, the society is very real. We used money from our fund to purchase a premium pass so I could come and give you a message that you can bring directly to Princess Donut. I am the chapter president of the Princess Posse Inner System number 43. As you likely know, the Syndicate brings a select sampling of unique flora and fauna to a compatible biome in order to preserve a sampling of the lost biology. Multiple canine variations are on this list, including the C-word. I would like for you to tell Princess Donut that, as she suggested, we have filed the lawsuit to prevent this from happening. It will be difficult to succeed, but the donations are flying in."

"As she suggested," I said evenly.

"Die. Die. Die!" Maggie the head tentacle suddenly shouted, causing both me and the Popovs to jump.

"Wait, how much in donations have you brought in?" I asked. "How big is this Princess Posse thing?"

"Hey," Effex called, "I didn't see your symbiote. Your premium pass gets a free photo, but not for two."

"She'll retract," Jenn'ifer said as she turned to face the invisible camera. The woman reached up and stroked the tentacle thing, and it went back into her head with a slurp. A little bit of red gore dripped from the hole in the back of her head.

"Wait," I said, but Effex pushed the weird woman away. Before I could object, the reporters all came. They came at once, appearing in a line in front of us, like this was a press conference.

The tallest one of this group was a Naga, and the large green-and-purple snake creature bobbed, like a cobra about to strike. The thing was similar to Manasa the singer, but bigger with different coloring. His twin arms pumped, like he was speed walking in place. The sight was strange, and the other reporters started to back away from him.

"That snake guy looks like he has to poop really bad," Dmitri said.

The name over the Naga read **Nihit. Press. Elemental Collection Updates.**

ZEV: Carl. We're doing the presentation of the new sponsor in
front of the press, and then they will ask you questions.

A disembodied female voice boomed out of nowhere, startling everybody in the room. This was the kill-kill-kill lady, but her voice had gone
up in pitch, likely because she was talking directly to the reporters.
"With the Valtay obtaining 51% ownership in the Borant Corporation,
Crawler Carl was forced to give away his first sponsor, which led to a
new sponsorship auction. The Borant Corporation is proud to present
Crawler Carl with the name of his newest sponsor."

A jet-black, red-eyed goat thing appeared in the middle of the room.
It zapped into existence between us and the reporters. Maxim swore as
Dmitri yelped, and the Nodling fell back. The goat thing was damn
huge, like eight feet tall, and its long, wavy hair trailed all the way to
the floor. It met my eyes and then slowly turned to face the reporters.

"The Plenty!" the unseen announcer woman said. "And with this
new sponsorship, Carl has been awarded a Gold Benefactor Box, which
he will open upon return to the dungeon!"

The massive goat didn't have anything over its head indicating its
name. It looked more like a walking version of Prepotente's satanic pet,
Bianca Del Ciao, than like Prepotente himself.

The giant goat made a deep, unnerving bleat and then blinked and
disappeared. Just like that. He'd been visible for maybe fifteen seconds.
The reporters all stood in a line, looking up at where the goat had just
been. They appeared just as bewildered as I felt.

"You motherfuckers let these guys control all of the universe's trans-
portation systems?" I asked.

Nobody laughed.

ZEV: We should probably avoid insulting the new sponsors, Carl.

"Carl," an elf-like woman asked. She cleared her throat, composing
herself. She'd obviously been startled by the bizarre sponsorship ceremony. "With the news that Circe Took is possibly—"

Nihit the Naga angrily pushed the elf woman to the side and slithered all the way to the table, looming over me. He opened his mouth and snapped right at my head, as if to bite it off. I tried not to flinch.

"Oh, yeah," I said, grinning. "Odette said the reporter who was going to ambush us over the Beatrice thing was a Naga. She scooped you, right? Is that why you're pissed? She told me to tell you something, but I can't remember what it was. I think she said, 'Better luck next time, asshole.' I might've added the asshole part. I can't remember. Either way, it's implied."

"You're cheating," Nihit hissed in my face, ridiculously close. He slammed his twin arms onto the table in front of me, reminding me of Vrah's mother, Circe. *Jesus,* I thought, *is everyone in the universe this angry all the time?* Behind him, the other reporters started to yell at him to back off. "I will discover how you're doing it, and I will reveal it to the universe." He flicked a long, forked tongue, and it pierced the illusion of my head.

"Dude," I said, leaning back, "I already have like two top ten crawlers after me, a bunch of hunters, those orc assholes, all those faction wars pricks who sued me, oh, oh, and some mysterious liaison guy who may or may not be associated with my newest sponsor. Plus that robot Donut toy company and likely several others I'm not aware of." I turned to the Popovs. "Am I missing anyone?"

"Dunno. Everybody likes us," Dmitri said.

I grinned. "So what I'm saying is, you're gonna have to get in line. I forgot you even existed until just this moment. You should be mad at Odette, not me."

This guy's anger went beyond just losing an exclusive story. This was a Maestro-level temper tantrum. As always, I only had a small window in which to view the universe. I was missing something. Something important.

"Odette is complicit. I will find the truth," Nihit said. "You and your partner are cheating. You're receiving illegal help. The timing of that interview with Odette is pretty damn suspicious, don't you think? Assisting in system sedition is a crime." His tongue flicked again, and he leaned in even closer.

"Good luck," I said. His anger was starting to finally piss me off. "But if you really want to hurt me, you're gonna have to come in here and do it to my face."

Nihit hissed. "Oh, I can hurt you just fine from the safety of the inner system."

"He's really riding the broom," Dmitri said.

"Did you bang this guy's wife or something?" Maxim asked.

"You think you're safe, huh?" I asked.

"What do you think you can do?" Nihit asked.

"We'll start with this," I said, and I picked up the magical Sharpie, and I slammed it into his neck with all of my might.

It, unfortunately, broke into a dozen little pieces, but a little stick of metal protruded from the Naga's neck, spurting blood as he fell over, screaming. All the other reporters shouted and jumped forward.

The room blinked twice, and the lights went on.

"In Bulgaria," Maxim said after a moment of silence, "much of the media is not trusted. But at least they pretend to be impartial. I don't think this is the case with that guy."

42

I WASN'T GIVEN THE OPPORTUNITY TO SAY GOODBYE TO THE POPOVS. After the lights flicked on, about twenty gnoll guards flooded the room. They took the Sharpie from me and collected the other two. I had to remain in the now-featureless production room as the twins were ushered back to their space.

"Bye, Carl!" Dmitri called. "Tell Donut I said hi!"

The gnoll guards surrounded me, saying nothing, grim-faced. I did not see any I recognized.

"Come on," I finally said. "You have to admit, that was pretty awesome."

A guard on the end burst into laughter, but a growl from another guard shut him up pretty quick. Then, without another word, they turned and left as Zev entered the room. She waddled forward, trailing water on the metal ground.

"Carl," she said, "we can't bring you anywhere."

"He deserved it. He got in my face."

"Well, you should know that he is fine and has been healed. He wants to press charges for assault."

I just blinked at her. The idea was so absurd that it didn't even make me angry. "Are you kidding me? Assault?"

She shook her head. "Carl, criminal charges are serious. He's off system, so the attack isn't under Borant jurisdiction. The regular rules apply. You're not a full citizen, and he is."

I still sat in the chair, and I leaned back and crossed my arms. "Yeah, what are they going to do?"

"The charges, if the prosecution wants to pursue it, will be filed and then shelved until you're released from the dungeon. It's happened before. If you're successfully prosecuted, you'll be given a warrant with an associated sentence, usually two or three cycles. Odette had a warrant, for example. Of course she's now married to the president of the corporation who bought her out because she's Odette."

"What the hell does that even mean?"

"The Syndicate doesn't have or use long-term prisons. The lighter the crime, the higher the warrant and the shorter the amount of time. After three or four warrants are imposed, the amount of time usually tops out at 20 cycles, and the warrant is lowered. So, if you're arrested for shoplifting, you can get a year sentence and a warrant for maybe 50,000 credits. The clock starts ticking at the moment of sentencing. If a third party, usually a licensed system government or megacorporation, needs able-bodied workers for a project, they have the option of buying out warrants. Usually, those with high warrants aren't picked up unless there's a war going on somewhere, and they're desperate for bodies. If someone's warrant is lowered to three digits, it usually guarantees they'll be franchised for the remainder of their sentence."

"Wait, wait, wait," I said. "So prisoners are sold as slaves?"

"Sort of," Zev said. "It's expensive. If your warrant is 1,000 credits and 10 cycles, they don't just pay 1,000 credits. They have to pay the franchise fee, which is something like five times the warrant amount per cycle. Plus they have to pay you that amount when you get out. Plus the warrant to the court in question. So a 1,000 credit warrant really translates to over 100,000. Plus they have to feed and house and transport you. It's not cost-effective unless your warrant is really low, and it only gets low if you've committed multiple offenses. Nobody ever gets purchased if their warrant is one cycle because the clock is always ticking, and it usually takes months to even get the person to the work location, and they have to guarantee their return passage to the location where they were picked up. It's not true slavery because the criminals get paid when they get out. Assuming they survive. But the corporations have to pay the full expenses plus a death tax, so it's always in their best interests to keep the person alive. Franchisees are usually sent to frontier planets to help set up new colonies or factories or mining locations. It's rare for them to be used for war nowadays."

"That's still slavery," I said, shaking my head. "And people are okay with this?"

"They're criminals," Zev said.

I took a breath. "So, what's the penalty for sticking a pen into the neck of an asshole Naga?"

"If you're convicted, you'll get a light sentence. Maybe 30,000 credits and three cycles. But you're no ordinary crawler, Carl. Someone like the Skull Empire will buy you out."

I stood and stretched my back. I'd been fighting and killing every day for weeks now. The idea of me getting out of the dungeon and eventually getting punished for barely scratching this guy seemed just . . . I didn't know. Stupid. Ridiculous. Irrational. But also par for the course. "Can I buy out my own warrant?"

"Technically, it's not allowed. It happens, of course. You have to be a licensed organization, and the franchisees can't be associated with the purchasing entity. But of course it happens. Prince Maestro is franchised to a subsidiary of a subsidiary that's wholly owned by the Skull Empire. They weren't owned at the time, but they were later acquired by the empire. A loophole that only the ultrarich can afford. It was big news when it happened. It pays to be wealthy."

"Whatever," I said, deciding the universe deserved this dystopian nightmare. The odds of me ever having to suffer the consequences for this were infinitesimal. I started to move toward the greenroom door. "At least I'm not in trouble with the dungeon for this one. Why was that dude so angry anyway?"

"I never said you weren't in trouble. You'll probably get extra security on you from now on. And Nihit is a Naga. They all have issues controlling their emotions. Plus, his brother is married into the Blood Sultanate and is participating in faction wars. He wants you and Donut out of the dungeon before you get down there. He seems to think that you're some sort of Antichrist figure sent from the heavens to bring about the apocalypse. You and Donut. It's a small, but growing, conspiracy theory amongst some populations. Most everyone else loves you two."

I grunted with amusement, but it only lasted a moment. It was always there, in the back of my mind. The impossible task we had before us. If we ever made it to the ninth floor, Donut would have to deal with the Blood Sultanate's army. But it was worse than that, thanks to her long-lost Crown of the Sepsis Whore. I'd read the description so many times, I had it memorized:

> Enchanted Crown of the Sepsis Whore.
>> Who's a dirty girl? You're a dirty girl!
>> This is a Fleeting item!
>> This is a Unique* item!
>> Imbues wearer with +5 Intelligence, grants the user +5 to the Good First Impression skill. All attacks, including magical attacks, now have a 15% chance to inflict the Sepsis debuff.
>> Warning! (Seriously though. I'm going to say this again.
>> WARNING! Read this shit before you put it on.) Placing this crown upon your head permanently places you within the royal line of succession for the Blood Sultanate on the ninth floor of the World Dungeon. Removing this item *will not* remove this status. Royal members of the Blood Sultanate will be required to slay the Sultan and *all* other members of the royal family before descending to the tenth floor. You'll only want to wear this if you're a blood-thirsty raging psychopath.

So, we'd have to make sure *all* the members of the Blood Sultanate were dead before she'd be allowed to leave the floor. And while the Nagas usually had their asses handed to them during the fighting, I now knew that the royals themselves always made it to the end. Always. Getting to them was going to be a difficult if not impossible task.

If Quasar pulled through for me, the task might be slightly easier. But even then, it was still going to be a tall order.

When Donut lost the crown at the end of the third floor, the crown was regenerated and possibly awarded to someone else. As far as we knew, that person wasn't stupid enough to put it on, or if they had, they were already dead. If some other crawler put it on, we'd have to make sure they were dead, too, before Donut could exit the ninth floor.

"So, this Nihit guy thinks there's a way to physically harm those guys on the ninth floor?" I asked.

Zev sighed. "You might want to worry about surviving the sixth floor first, Carl."

43

"HE WANTED TO MEET ME? REALLY?" DONUT ASKED WHEN I FINISHED telling her and Mordecai everything that happened. "Well, I would be honored. It's always a pleasure to meet a fan. Even if he's part of a weird ogre thing with two heads. They didn't smell, did they? They look like they might smell."

"After everything I told you, that's what you're on about?" I asked. "Just how much control do you have over this Princess Posse thing?"

"Oh, that's nothing. I already saw and approved the shirt design days ago. I'm hoping someone sends one into the dungeon so you can wear it. I must have mentioned it a hundred times by now. Honestly, Carl, sometimes I think you don't listen to me. I believe there are only 700 or so chapters up and running. The AI filters through most of the messages, so it's difficult to tell. But I'm glad to see some of our initiatives are moving forward." She sighed dramatically. "It's important to leave the universe a better place than when you found it."

"You're advocating for the genocide of dogs," I said. "People don't like it when you hurt dogs."

"My numbers tell another story, Carl. If someone is going to get all butthurt about it, there's simply nothing I can do. It's done, and I'm not sorry. If they're okay with all the baby goblins you slaughtered way back on the first floor, then it's something they're gonna have to put up with. And it's not *all* dogs. It's just one kind. I suppose some of the breeds are endearing in their own stupid, slobbering way. Like Labradors and pugs and those ones who look like black Rastafarian mops. It's not genocide anyway. I'm sure there are some cocker spaniels left running about the surface being smelly and disgusting and mauling toddlers."

"It's a bad idea," I said. "Do you know how much money they've collected for this?"

"I don't know. Whenever someone talks about money on the boards, they filter it out. That's why I should've been included in the signing." She suddenly gasped. "You don't think a member of the posse is embezzling funds, do you? Certainly not. I wish you'd asked more questions. You never know how to properly interrogate fans, Carl."

"She really said he's pressing charges against you?" Mordecai asked, changing the subject. He shook his little furry head. "I'd like to see that one go to trial. Odette's trial was a farce. It was this whole production, and she pleaded down to a lesser charge just before they reached a verdict."

"Wait," I said. "You saw Odette's trial?"

"Yeah," Mordecai said. "I testified in it. Against her."

"But she was a crawler long before you."

"She wasn't charged when she was a crawler. It was when she was my manager. Now open your boxes and get back out there."

"I hope you get something good in yours," Donut grumbled. The red gem added to Donut's leadership charm had added +2 to her intelligence and +1 to her dexterity and a few points to some spear-throwing skill that she would never be able to use, which had pissed her off. Especially since the tax stipend for the small-sized settlement was only 403 gold every ten days.

I sighed. I had a Gold Tyrant Box from killing a mayor and the Gold Benefactor Box from the Plenty. According to my sponsor menu, these new guys only sponsored three people in the dungeon. Me, Miriam Dom, and Prepotente.

"That reminds me. Did you ever hear back from Pony?"

"No. I tried again, but I think . . ." She paused. "Carl, Carl, I just got a gold box from the Apothecary!" She hopped up and down. "Now we both have boxes to open!"

"Then you best get on with it," Mordecai said.

I opened the tyrant box, and it was a sliver of an amethyst, smaller than the "poor sapphire" I already had on my necklace. It gave me +3 to my dexterity, and nothing else.

The next box moved into place.

The symbol for the Plenty was a creepy eyeball thing with a bunch of squiggles coming off it. It looked like something that would be spray-painted on the wall at the scene of a ritual murder. I remembered how creepy those goat kids were, and how disturbing the adult at the sponsorship ceremony had been. It was no damn wonder people didn't trust these guys. Everything about them gave me the heebies.

The gold box hissed and spun, opening like a flower, revealing a patch for my jacket.

"Huh," I said, picking it up. It was another patch identical in size to my white bomb one, but this was made of a black denim-like material with a gray goat head screen-printed on it. Donut immediately scoffed and started muttering about screen printing. Before I could fully examine it, I received a notification.

You have received a Silver Benefactor Box from the Apothecary.

"Well, shit," I said.

Donut was already in the process of opening her own box, which was gold, not silver. She gasped as the sparkling bracelet popped out. She immediately equipped it. She moved the obsidian bracelet that allowed her to cast *Fireball* to her right forward leg and this new one to the left. She kept her fallen oak anklet tucked on her back leg, and her +2-dexterity one on the other back leg. This new one glittered silver with little purple gems. Now that she had bracelets on all four of her legs, she couldn't add any more.

"Oh, I just love it. Doesn't it look divine? I don't know about that description, though. It sounds like the AI is having a stroke."

"Uh-oh," Mordecai said as he examined the bracelet. He grunted. "It's pretty clear the Apothecary and the Plenty really are working together. At least when it comes to your sponsorship prizes. That'll be sure to stop all those rumors."

I examined Donut's silver bracelet. The attached purple gems each had an odd shape, almost like a bulb of garlic. After reading the description, I realized that's exactly what it was.

Enchanted Silver Bracelet of the Ab-solar.
"AnD SO The lioN fEll iN lOVe WiTh The LaMB."

I'm actually quite fond of the *Twilight* novels. Plus, I would never stoop so low as to disparage the work of an overimaginative and obviously undersexed artist who managed to become a brazilianaire from barely disguised erotica targeted at adolescent girls. However, I would like to take this opportunity to point out that your culture's obsession with fictional underaged heroes was absolutely misguided.

Paul Atreides was fifteen years old. Harry Potter was just eleven in the beginning of the first book. The kids from *Stranger Things* were all tweens. Kid 'n Play were (portrayed to be) high schoolers when they threw that epic party.

Fairy tales. Myths. Lies.

Spoiler alert. Kids are all idiots, and when they're forced into a life-or-death situation, they overwhelmingly make stupid decisions and get themselves killed. Like almost right away. They're like that rabbit you see sitting on the side of the road that decides to dart in front of your car at the worst possible moment. They're so efficient at getting themselves squished, you can't help but wonder if they are doing it on purpose. Go ahead. Complain. Tell me I'm wrong. Trust me on this one. I've done some pretty extensive and conclusive research on the matter.

This apotropaic talisman looks like something a goth teenage girl would shoplift from a Hot Topic. A girl who dreams about one day meeting a hundred-year-old predator and making him fall in love with her.

Remember, it's not a crime if he's handsome or rich or looks like a teenager.

Anyway, this bracelet imbues the following effects:

Protection against Vampirism.

Protection against Lycanthropy.

+25% Magical damage against all sapient undead.

"Fuck," I said.

"The description has nothing to do with the item," Donut complained. "And *Twilight* was a great movie. I only saw the first one because you made Miss Beatrice turn the second one off that one time we were watching it because you were jealous. Also, *Stranger Things* was a great television show up until when Barb died." She lifted her leg and admired the item. "But it sure is pretty. It's purple!"

"It gets worse. Read the description on your patch," Mordecai said. "You'll want to sew it on right away."

I examined it. The symbol was of a weird satanic goat. I'd seen it before. Prepotente had a tattoo on the back of his furry humanlike hand of the same thing. I'd even sketched it out the best I could in the cookbook. I'd been assuming it was for a deity, like the twin sun disc tattoos on the back of my own hands. I was wrong.

Upgrade Patch. Medium.

Ah, yes. The Midnight Epicure. The Caprid Who Devours the Sky. This scary-ass fable is used to terrify children across the universe. Eat your dinner, or the Midnight Epicure will come eat it for you. He will not be satisfied by the meal and will in turn devour every child in the home. Best draw a picture of him and put it in your window to let him know you're onto his tricks.

I'm pretty sure this fairy tale was devised by Big Therapy in order to keep themselves in work.

Over the cycles, the rather disturbing symbol of the Midnight Epicure, which is really just a racist caricature of an adult Caprid, developed into a ward against all night evils.

If this upgrade patch is affixed to an eligible garment, it will imbue the following upgrades:

Protection against Vampirism.

Protection against Lycanthropy.

+25% Magical damage against all sapient undead.

Warning: Upgrade patches are fleeting items. You may remove them, but they will be destroyed in the process.

"Weird," I said. The descriptions were different, but the patch and the bracelet gave the exact same benefits. I would also get +1 to all my stats once I added it, which I intended to do right away.

"They obviously know something you don't, so you better put it on," said Mordecai.

"The only vampire we know is Miriam Dom," Donut said. "Are they saying we'll have to fight her? I don't want to fight her. She's really nice."

"I . . . I don't know. I'll have to sew it myself," I said. Katia was out and once again chasing Eva's team.

"Don't worry. I'll help you," Donut said.

I opened my second benefactor box. The silver box from the Apothecary.

It was two items. Two pieces of paper. The first was a potion recipe. The second was a drawing. A drawing of Mongo. After I read the recipe, it was clear what the connection between the two items was.

I handed both pieces of paper to Mordecai, who made a squeaking noise. "Holy cow," he said. "I've been chasing this one for fifty cycles!" His eyes scanned the page. "Of course! You don't chill it. You put it in the centrifuge and then flash freeze it! Of course. Gah, I almost had it. So simple, too."

"Do you have all the ingredients?" I asked.

"Actually, I do," he said. "You already collected the thorn sap tips, which are pretty rare, but we now have dozens of them. The hard one is the last item. And we have that as well."

We both turned to look at Mongo, who blinked and cocked his head to the side. He then screeched back at us with concern.

"What? What is it?" Donut asked.

I exchanged a look with Mordecai, and then I slid the potion recipe over to show her, along with the photo of Mongo.

The recipe was for a potion of Charm Animal. The potion had to be brewed for a specific animal, and it required a special ingredient to work.

"She gave you a photo of Mongo!" Donut exclaimed. "What a nice prize! Mongo, look! It's a picture of . . ." She trailed off, her eyes going wide once she actually read the recipe. "Absolutely not. You're going to have to find another way."

"It's just blood," I said. "We'll need to do it outside a safe room and collect a liter of it."

"You want to drain a liter of blood from Mongo?"

"Per potion," Mordecai added. "You can heal him each time you collect it."

"I am Mongo's mommy, and he trusts me implicitly. I will not break that trust. A liter is a lot, too! Not a chance. We just got all this anti-vampire stuff, and here you two are talking about draining Mongo's blood. No. No way. Mongo, come here this instant where Mommy can protect you."

Mongo scurried around the kitchen counter and hid behind Donut.

"Donut, I will make a potion to cause Mongo to sleep. He won't even know."

"*I'll* know, Mordecai."

I was about to say something when I was interrupted by a message.

MIRIAM DOM: I need help. Are you still near Prepotente Number
   Four? I am not far. I am trapped. Dawn will break in 10 hours,
   and if you do not come before then, I will not survive.

44

DONUT AND MORDECAI BICKERED BACK AND FORTH AS I RAPIDLY CHAT-
ted with the vampire woman. They both realized I was talking to someone and stopped to watch me.

> CARL: Where are you?
> MIRIAM DOM: I am a few hours east of that town, maybe 25
>   kilometers and approximately a kilometer south of the big river
>   bend.

I pulled out the physical version of the rough map Katia had made
for everybody, and I could see the approximate location. It was in the
middle of the forest. I tapped it on the map. Mordecai and Donut looked
down at the spot.

> CARL: What's your situation? And where's your partner?
> MIRIAM DOM: I tried asking for help from you earlier, but the
>   system would not allow me to talk to you. I asked others, but
>   none are close enough. I asked them to get in touch with you,
>   but they all said it wouldn't let them.

Sure enough, I saw a line of messages from people passing on Miriam's increasingly frantic messages. The messages had only just appeared.
Weird, I thought until I saw the keyword floating in a few of the message
previews.

Elite.

CARL: I can't help if an elite is involved. I'm really sorry. It's a long story.

MIRIAM DOM: The elite is dead. The quest is done. Pony killed him, but he got himself paralyzed in the process. They were both frozen, and the elite fool finally died just a few minutes ago when the sun set. It is also a long story. Bianca is in a pet carrier in Pony's inventory, and he can't let her out. He is paralyzed for fifteen more hours.

CARL: Fifteen *hours*?

MIRIAM DOM: It was 35. It has been a long two days. His arm is around my waist. I can't break it free. If any part of him breaks, even his thumb, he will shatter. I have been fighting off small mobs, but now that dark has returned, so will the dinosaurs, and I fear I will not be able to keep us safe.

CARL: We're on our way. But how did you survive out in the daylight?

MIRIAM DOM: The sunlight drains me quickly. I alternated between my *Revive* spell and the blood potion. I've had to cast over and over again, and I only have a handful of potions left. If I even survive the night, I will not be able to keep myself alive in the new day for long. I will explain when you arrive.

"Listen up, guys." I pulled out a pen. I marked where Miriam Dom was trapped, quickly explaining the situation. There were two towns between here and there.

"Mordecai, how long will it take for you to make that Charm Animal potion?"

"Fifteen minutes once I have the ingredients."

"What about the knockout potion?"

Both Donut and Mongo screeched with outrage.

"I'll need another fifteen."

Donut harrumphed. "If something happens to Mongo, I'll never forgive you, Mordecai."

"He'll be fine," Mordecai said. "But—"

"Here's the plan," I interrupted, talking rapidly. I tapped the first town. I cringed when I saw it was a dryad settlement. "We'll collect the knockout potion from you here, and then we'll collect Mongo's blood and heal him. We'll only have time for one." I tapped the next town, which was also a dryad town. "We'll collect the Charm Animal potion here."

Mordecai held up a hand. "Or," he said, lowering his voice, "you just let her die, and you collect her gear in the morning."

"Why would I do that?" I asked.

"Oh, I don't know," he replied. "Maybe because two different sponsors, who know more than you do, just spent a huge amount of money to protect you from vampirism. And just by coincidence, a vampire shows up and asks you to come help her the moment the sun sets. I know I'm not as valuable as I once was, but I can't help but see a connection there, Carl."

"She saved my life," I said as I grabbed the sewing kit. "If it's a trap designed to get us to turn to vampires, then we'll be protected. I'm not going to abandon her. That's not what we do here. She's been asking for help for hours. Either a hunter or player killer is going to get wind of her situation and move in. We don't have time."

I started to rapidly sew the patch in a spot right next to the bomb patch. Donut gasped as my wide stitches covered up Katia's deliberate, careful threading.

"Carl, it's not straight!"

"It's good enough," I said as I stitched it in place. I received an achievement and a few skill levels in sewing. The patch glowed as it was officially affixed. I pulled the jacket back on.

"Let's go!"

"Oh boy, another adventure!" Samantha cried from her spot on the kitchen counter. Donut had forced the filthy thing through the cleaning module. Minus the gash on her chin, she looked as if she'd come straight from the sex doll head factory. Her gleaming, white hair was put up in wavy pigtails. Even her ridiculous makeup seemed brighter. Had she been on the kitchen counter this whole time? Surely she hadn't jumped up there on her own.

"You're staying back this time," I said. She growled and wailed as we moved to the door.

"Wait, wait," Mordecai called. "I have an idea." He hopped sideways into the crafting room.

"We're on the clock, Mordecai," I yelled as Samantha continued to bitch.

He came back out a moment later, two potion balls cradled in his small arms. He moved to the Emberus shrine at the back of the room and dipped the balls in the red water and then brought them to me.

"Take these," he said.

"What are they?" I asked, pulling them both into my inventory. The system labeled them **Holy Goopers**.

"Blessed water mixed with a fine healing potion and an air-activated coagulant in a potion ball. Emberus is a light-based god. I keep forgetting that. The blood water from the shrine combined with a healing potion and the coagulant acts like napalm to vampires. Hit 'em with this, and then have Donut max out her *Torch* spell. Any vampire will be turned to dryer lint."

"So they're holy water grenades? Cool."

"Exactly."

WE EXITED THE GUILDHALL AND MOVED CAUTIOUSLY INTO THE AT-tached pub with all the hockey paraphernalia. Donut rode on Mongo's back as we creeped forward toward the exit to the street.

Darkness had descended, and none of the pub's torches were lit. Donut cast *Torch*, keeping it on the lowest setting. A sickly yellow glow illuminated the empty pub. The stench of death hung heavy in the humid air, clawing its way into my nose and sinuses, settling heavily. The pattering of rain slapping into puddles and corpses drifted into the pub. The ceiling dripped in several places. The bloody bear claw remained affixed to the wall by the door. It appeared extra ghoulish in the yellow light.

"Turn it off! Turn it off!" a female voice hissed. I jumped in surprise as Mongo screeched. We all turned to face the speaker. It was an ursine peeking up from behind the counter. Her dot was white on the map. We hadn't seen her until just now. "Turn it off!" she repeated. "She's out there. She'll see!"

"Do it," I whispered, and Donut complied, plunging us into darkness.

Outside, a horrific, meaty roar shook the walls. Mongo replied by screeching back and turning toward the open door.

"You have to keep him quiet! She already came in here once. Ate my husband right out of the doorway! Please, please. I have two little ones with me!"

"Mongo, shush," Donut said, patting him on the head. "Remember what we talked about." Mongo growled.

The sound of soft weeping filled the pub, mixed in with the rain. Children. Two of them. The three of us moved behind the bar.

The NPC sat there, huddled on the floor. She was a large bear wearing an apron. Two small male cubs were clutched in her arms. One had his eyes clenched shut, shivering and afraid. The other looked up at Mongo, wide-eyed.

Mongo peeped with concern at the children. They whimpered and cuddled closer to their mother as he approached.

"Hey, hey, it's okay," I whispered. The ground shook as something huge walked by outside. We all crouched down to hide. *We don't have time for this.* "We're gonna let it pass, okay?"

Nobody answered.

I examined the female bear.

Prudence. Level 28 Ursine Barmaid.

She had a debuff blinking over her head. **Terrified.**

"Prudence," I said, "is that Big Tina out there?"

"It is," she whispered. Her eyes glowed with fear. "She came back. I knew she'd come back. Getting her revenge. The others can't control her anymore."

Another angry roar rocked the street.

"Explain it to me," I said. "Revenge for what?"

"For what they did to her. Long ago. The clerics."

The dinosaur had parked herself just outside. The ground rumbled again. There was a distant crash and scream, followed by a sickening crunch. I remembered the tall building across the way from this pub.

She was breaking the windows and pulling bears out, like one of those Christmas Advent calendars. If the bears were all suffering from this Terrified debuff, I knew they wouldn't even be able to run away.

I put my hand on the trembling woman's leg.

Donut moved to my shoulder. "Prudence," she said, "tell us what they did to her."

The woman swallowed, but she finally answered. "When Scolopendra struck, and the world turned upside down, the nine-tier attack killed almost everyone. But others were transformed. Most of the female ursine were changed. Changed into the reptilian beasts."

"So the dinosaurs used to be bears?" Donut asked. "Carl, did you hear that? Mongo was molested by a bear!"

"Let her finish," I said.

"Even before the cataclysm, the clerics . . . they could be cruel, yes. But it's the work we have to do. Piety is the path we must follow. We mustn't stray. The path is what leads us to eternal paradise. It keeps us from getting lost."

"Mama," one of the boys squeaked. This one was named **Randy**. "Mama, make it go away." He pointed at Mongo.

"That's not a bad one, stupid," the other boy said. He was **Todd**. It looked as if they were twins. Or from the same litter or whatever. "It's a mongoliensis. They don't attack mamas or kids."

"This is Mongo," Donut said. "Mongo is a nice dinosaur."

Mongo peeped in agreement.

"Keep going," I prodded. I might as well get the story out of her while we could.

"Dancing is forbidden," Prudence said. "But a community of mothers formed, and they taught several of the children the old ways. The art of dance. The art of ballet."

"Ballet?" I asked. "Are you kidding me?"

"I know, I know," Prudence said. "A sin most foul. But they taught the children anyway. As the story goes, they planned on having a secret performance for the children and their families. Just a small recital at the school after hours where the children would dress in costumes and dance." Prudence shook her head sadly. "Those poor lost souls."

"What happened?" Donut asked, leaning in.

"One of the dancers was the daughter of the town's head cleric. Despite being only eight years old, she was the best of the dancers, and she practiced more than anybody else. She was to go last. A solo performance. Her name was Tina. The day of the recital came, and the girls went onstage. But Tina's father had somehow learned of the secret recital, and he along with a group of clerics set out to find where the performance was being held to put a stop to it. They finally discovered the location, and they stormed the school just as Tina was to take the stage."

"Oh no," Donut gasped.

"Tina's mother tried to stop her husband. She slapped him in front of everybody. In front of the congregation. It was unheard-of."

"So Tina never got to dance?" Donut asked. "She must've been so sad!"

"The cleric had no choice. He was forced to push his daughter aside and whip the mother. But in his anger and humiliation, he went too far. He was possessed that night, they said. He whipped his wife to the edge of death, right upon the stage in front of his daughter. And when he pushed Tina aside, she fell and hurt herself. She had a magical wand that was supposed to shoot sparkles during her performance. It broke when she fell."

"Sinners get what they deserve," little Randy said.

"That's right, honey," Prudence said. She continued. "After he was done beating the mother, the cleric announced he would be forced to punish all the parents and children who participated. But before he got his chance, it happened. The nine-tier attack."

"The judgment of the gods," Randy replied.

"Good boy. Most died. Some ursine were transformed. Only the females. The surviving men were unchanged. Only a small handful of women survived unchanged, including my grandmother. She was the most pious. Her faith saved her."

"Christ," I muttered.

"Scolopendra turned them to demons. The sinners. They do not age. They can't procreate. They're only a shell of what they once were, and they serve as a reminder of their wickedness."

"And now little Tina is Big Tina," I said.

"She's the only child who turned," the woman said. "Her mind is gone. She has lost all of her faith. While she kills everyone she meets, she actively hunts ursine. Her mother survives along with several of the other mothers from that evening. But they are in the form of dinosaurs like your companion. They are vicious, and they also kill, but they're not as deranged. Tina's mother still attempts to keep Tina from doing too much damage, but something has changed just in the past few nights. Tina is stronger than ever now, and the others can't stop her."

"Uh, do you know what Tina's mother's name is?" I asked.

"It is Kiwi," Prudence said.

Donut gasped as I reached over and scratched Mongo's head. "Hey, buddy. It looks like you banged Tina's mom."

Quest Update. The Recital.

Big Tina is out of control.

She's on a rampage, killing every Ursine she can find. She's angrier than ever. Her violence, which used to be an occasional nuisance, has turned into a looming threat for everyone in the Hunting Grounds. If she's not dealt with soon, the High Elves may field their army in order to deal with it. You do not want that to happen.

Tina must be stopped. Kill her or give her what she wants.

"Oh, my god, Carl," Donut said. "This is just like the plot to *Footloose*! They're stealing storylines now!"

"I don't remember the part where the girl turns into a murderous dinosaur after her dad tells her she can't dance," I said.

"Maybe that was in part two."

"It says we have to give her what she wants," I said. "What do you think that means? To kill all the ursine?"

The walls shook as Tina collected another snack from a nearby building. Next to me, the two cubs whimpered.

"Of course not, Carl," Donut said. "Didn't you see the movie? It's quite obvious."

I just looked at her.

"She wants to dance! We have to finish the recital!"

Holy shit. *Of course.* "How in the flying fuck are we supposed to do that? We should just kill her."

Splatch. I turned my head at the noise. What was that? It was inside the pub.

I peeked over the counter, searching just as the red dot appeared on my map. I caught movement on the floor. It was the bear claw. It had fallen, and now it was dragging itself away, like an inchworm. It moved out the door and out into the rainy night.

Glamoured Fragment—Ursine Claw (Left). Level 5.

4.2% of the whole.

This is a minion of Big Tina.

When you think about it, vampires are basically necromancers with an eating disorder. The fact these minion things exist is testament to that.

A glamoured minion can only be created by a vampire two sunsets after the victim was originally killed. In its current form, it's nothing more than an uninteresting yet reanimated body part, and it's now trying to find its way to the rest of its body. Poor little guy. It just wants to go home.

Here's the thing. A vampire kill scene usually looks like the Walmart toy aisle on Black Friday. In other words, vampires are notoriously messy when they get to a-slaughtering. Usually the rest of the body parts are all squished and gross and half-digested and thrown all over the place. When that happens, the pieces just meld into other orphaned pieces and form a Shambling Berserker, which is a horrific monster in its own right. But if the pieces can actually reunite 70% of their original bodies, they become something quite deadly.

"Fuck me," I muttered. "So *that's* why they're giving us all the vampire stuff."

"Wait, I don't understand," Donut said. "The *dinosaur* is also a vampire? Big Tina is a vampire Tyrannosaurus rex?"

"She's an allosaurus," little Todd said, looking up from his mother's fur. "She has three fingers, not two. That means she's an allosaurus."

"I know how to count, Todd," Donut said.

Quest Update. The Recital.
   Surprise, motherfuckers. Strap yourselves in. You don't know the half of it. It's about to get bumpy.

Outside, the world rumbled as Tina roared again.

45

<Note added by Crawler Allister. 13th Edition>

Vampires. We have vampires in my culture, but they are not the same as the ones here in the dungeon, though they are similar. My T'Ghee deck contains two vampiric forms. The Plague Bearer and the Blood Hunter. Both represent death. Both represent the end of days. But one is considered deliberate, thirst-based evil, and the other, the Plague Bearer, is a study on how one's poor actions can ripple through time and become amplified and doom us all. The vampires here on this seventh floor are a combination of the two. It is strange that our traditions are so different yet the same. I have not met any fellow crawlers cursed with vampirism, but I have met my fair share of vampire mobs and NPCs. The monster ones cannot be reasoned with. They are fast. Faster than you think. They are insatiable. They are strong. Yet they are not mindless. In fact, I believe the curse of vampirism greatly increases their intelligence. They cast spells. They wish to surround themselves with protectors. Do not underestimate them. Do not rely solely on your own mythology to defeat them. My best advice is to avoid them, and if they've moved into an area you occupy, move away as quickly as you can.

CARL: Hey, uh, Miriam. We're still trying to get to you. You didn't by chance tangle with a giant allosaurus thing at one point? One with a pink feather boa?

MIRIAM DOM: Carl, please hurry. And yes. We fought with a giant dinosaur wearing a pink feathered necklace and carrying a

wand. I almost killed her, but then something happened, and
she escaped.

CARL: Yeah, I think you might have infected her with vampirism.

MIRIAM DOM: Yes. I know. Many of the dinosaurs in this area are
vampires now. It is spreading through the forest. Spreading
quickly. They are weak for the first few days if they survive,
but they quickly grow in strength. It was part of the story with
the elite. He died before the infestation could be stopped. You
must help me, or we will not be able to contain it.

Oh, that was just wonderful.

CARL: We are on our way.

"Okay, Prudence," I said as I sent a quick note to Mordecai, warning
him. "Grab your kids. Go through the door we came out of, okay? You'll
be safe in there. I promise."

"We can't go in there," she said. "I tried, and it wouldn't let me."

"You can now," I said. "I'm giving you and your cubs access."

Outside, Tina had moved on down the street. The red dot representing the animated bear claw disappeared. The rain became more fierce,
thumping louder than ever. It sounded like drums pounding on the
ceiling. I knew from the main chat that this newest storm covered
the entire map. The river was starting to overflow.

After we made sure Prudence and her two cubs were inside the
guildhall, we slowly crept outside. Big Tina was gone, but it was impossible to see. It was pitch-black, and the rain's intensity seemed to be
ratcheting up by the moment.

"Light," I whispered as I started to pull the pieces of the Royal Chariot from my inventory. "Keep it low."

Donut activated the yellow light and sent it out the door, hovering
low like a firefly. Her skill in the spell was 13, and she could do all sorts
of cool stuff with it now. The moment the light went outside, my map
came alive with red dots. We both stopped, aghast at the scene before us.

"Fuck me," I whispered.

I hadn't seen anything like this since the krasue nest on the third floor or the train car filled with ghoul parts on the fourth. But this was worse. Much worse.

Mongo screeched and almost bolted out, but a command from Donut kept him still. I turned to see a pair of small dinosaurs—not raptors, but something similar—bound off into the darkness, their forms getting swallowed by the night.

Before, when we'd entered town, there were dead bodies everywhere. I'd tried to pick some of them up, but they'd shattered into dust the moment I touched them. I hadn't thought much of it at the time because they were old, but it was clear they were all part of . . . whatever this was.

The number of body parts had increased. A lot. They scattered in all directions like a lumpy stew.

I'd assumed Big Tina had been parked outside simply because the building across the street was a target-rich environment. But it seemed she'd been sitting there working on her spell. She was calling the two-day-dead body parts to her. But this wasn't just her dead. It couldn't be. There was way too much here, and it wasn't just ursine. There were all manner of forest creatures. Bears, deer, monkeys, wolves, all types of mobs. I remembered our journey from the edge of the river to this town. We'd been grinding all day, but the vast majority of the mobs we'd fought were plant-based creatures. We hadn't seen hardly any mobile mobs.

It appeared other dinosaurs were gathering all the pieces they could find and bringing them together in one place. Like a massive pile of bloody mismatched socks. A sorting facility where the reanimated parts could move about and find a match.

This was just the edge of the nightmare. The main pile was down the street. I could see it now, rising in the darkness like a small hill. A group of fast-moving dinosaurs darted away.

"Turn it up," I whispered. "Slowly."

As Donut increased the light, body pieces scattered away like cockroaches, roiling and undulating unnaturally. The streets were a mess of severed arms, legs, tails slithering like snakes, shattered rib cages walking like spiders. Eyeballs bouncing. Organs rolling and splatting away, like fat hedgehogs moving through the bush.

But there was more. Half-formed pieces had found one another. These all had percentages and extra-long names hovering over them. One moved away like a flat tire, spinning and splatting, leaking.

> Glamoured Fragment—Ursine Foot (Left), Ursine Leg (Left), Ursine Pelvis (four pieces, re-formed), Ursine thigh (Right), Ursine Lower Intestine (two pieces, re-formed), Ursine Kidney (Right). Level 5+7+12+6+10+2 = Level 42.
> 21.8% of the whole.
> This is a minion of Big Tina.

I swallowed. I understood then. It came to me all at once what this madness was. They slaughtered people, ripping them into as many pieces as possible, and then they came back two days later and waited for them to re-form. Each individual piece had a level, and if they re-formed with the original, the levels got added. The pieces added together were going to be ridiculously powerful, way stronger than they were originally.

"Carl," Donut said, looking over the sea of writhing body parts. "Carl, I don't like this. Let's go."

"Max it out. Shine your light all the way," I said, trying to keep my gorge down. We pushed outside as I rapidly lashed pieces of the Chariot together, facing it away from the center of town.

"Donut," I said, "ride ahead of me. We're gonna have to run."

I pulled out a fully loaded missile launcher and attached it to the Chariot. I assigned two of the missiles to the center mass of the writhing body parts and then the others along the edges of the pile. All the while, I was starting to send out frantic messages, asking if anyone else had seen anything like this.

We should go back inside.

But this was something we had to contain the best we could. This was a storyline with an elite that had spiraled out of control. Something— for once—that wasn't started by me or Donut. It sounded as if Miriam and Prepotente had stepped into something that was about to reverberate over the entire floor, just like when we'd unleashed Orthrus the two-headed puppy on the world.

Miriam had implied she could fix this if we got to her in time, and that's what we were going to do.

I jumped onto the Chariot, and we raced away from the nightmare. Donut and Mongo sped forward. Just as we reached the walled edge of town, surrounded by those mostly dead vines, I lit off all of the missiles. They shot into the pouring darkness, hissing and corkscrewing in the rain. Muffled explosions rocked the night as we turned west toward Miriam's location. Experience notifications rolled down my vision as an outraged roar filled the night. Thankfully, the massive dinosaur didn't appear to be following us. Yet.

DONUT: DO YOU THINK THAT STOPPED ALL THE GROSS MONSTER PIECES FROM GETTING TOGETHER?
CARL: Probably not, but we hopefully slowed them down.

WE ROCKETED DOWN THE MUDDY ROAD TOWARD MIRIAM AND PREPO-tente's general location. Twin streams formed on either side of the road, rushing with the rain's runoff. Donut kept her light spell turned all the way up, and it lit the path with the power of a stadium light. The forest was alive with red dots, and they all scattered away from us like we were a snowplow. I couldn't tell if the mobs were infected or not while we moved at this pace. Donut and Mongo rushed ahead of me, and I warned her to be careful with Mongo. The last thing we needed was him getting infected.

It only took about two minutes before Donut decided that she hated being out in such a powerful rainstorm, and she started to loudly complain about it in my chat.

A few other crawlers started to report back that they were seeing vampire forest animals, too. Mordecai said this wasn't the first time this sort of thing had happened, but it didn't usually spread this fast.

GIDEON: I just fought a half-genie, half-owl vampire thing. It tried to rip my neck out, but our Cleric killed it before it could get me. It was damn close.
TSERENDOLGOR: I think we're about 200 kilometers from you guys,

and it's the same thing, but it's not as bad as you say. I haven't seen any reanimated body parts, but the drillbeaks all disappeared almost overnight, and now they're vampires. It makes them twice as strong and superfast. You don't automatically get infected if they touch you. I think it's only if they injure you severely. If I cast *Ultraviolet* on my flamethrower, they die quick. But I'm sticking indoors in this rain. Don't want to take the chance.

CARL: Okay. Good. By the way, are any of you in the top 50? I'm trying to make a list of all the crawlers who might be at that party.

GIDEON: I'm not even in the top 1,000, and I like it that way.

TSERENDOLGOR: I'm currently ranked 54. Trying to get it up in time so I get an invite.

DONUT: MAYBE IF YOU WEREN'T ALWAYS STEALING OTHER PEOPLE'S EXPERIENCE, YOU'D BE HIGHER.

TSERENDOLGOR: Are you still on that? That was three floors ago. And I didn't see you at CrawlCon, so I must be doing something right.

DONUT: WHAT? WHAT?

CARL: Don't try too hard to get into the top 50. I think it might be a trap, and we might need some people not at the top to rescue us. Either way, that flamethrower of yours might come in handy.

The first of the two towns was a small dryad settlement, and we reached it much more quickly than I anticipated. A pair of funeral bell guards stood out front. They covered their eyes at our approach, but they didn't try to stop us from going in. I could see multiple white dots moving about in the streets.

Entering Small Dryad Settlement.

Good, I thought as I scanned the map for a real safe room. This town hadn't been captured yet.

"There!" I shouted over the pouring rain, pointing at a pub near the end of the small town.

**Warning: You have been branded as a troublemaker at this settle-
ment. Guards will now attack you on sight.**

The warning came out of nowhere. I turned and saw a pair of dryads
glaring at me from around the corner. One of them was the mayor, and
he obviously also worshipped Diwata.

A few red dots appeared on the map moving in our direction just as
we pulled up outside the safe room. I quickly pulled the pins on the
Chariot and took the two pieces into my inventory before we dove inside.

The bar was filled with dryads, which surprised me. Usually these
places were mostly empty. This appeared to have once been a beachside
bar with a long, open-air window that faced the water. Now the bar just
faced a wooden wall of bamboo. A sign on the wall read "Y-Not Lounge."
A Bopca in a Hawaiian-style shirt sat behind the counter, glaring at us
as we rushed in.

"Apostate!" a dryad shouted the moment we entered the safe room.
The monkey in his branches screamed and threw himself at me. He got
zapped and teleported away.

"Black magic!" another tree screamed as he tried to swing at me before he, too, zapped away. A minute later, we were alone in the safe
room.

"I don't feel very welcome here, Carl," Donut said.

"They're not attacking you. Just me," I said. Outside, a group of red
dots descended on the tavern. *Shit,* I thought. *Shit, shit, shit.*

"You're gonna have to do it yourself," I said as we moved to the
guildhall door.

"Do what?"

I patted Mongo on the back. "Sorry, buddy. Just a little blood."

46

DONUT: CARL, MONGO IS REALLY MAD AT YOU. AND THE DRYAD MAYOR GUY IS OFFERING ME 5,000 GOLD TO TIE YOU UP AND BRING YOU OUT HERE. I'D *FIREBALL* HIM, BUT ALL THE GUARDS ARE OUTSIDE, TOO. I'M MAKING ONE OF THE MUSHROOM GUYS STAND OVER ME BECAUSE THEY'RE GOOD UMBRELLAS.

CARL: How long before Mongo wakes back up?

DONUT: TWO MINUTES. I DON'T HAVE TIME FOR ANOTHER LITER. MOST OF IT WENT ALL OVER THE PLACE, BUT I GOT A FEW OF THOSE WET MONKEYS TO HELP ME HOLD THE FLASK. THIS IS REALLY HARD WITHOUT THUMBS. HE BETTER NOT REMEMBER ALL OF THIS. WE SHOULD HAVE DONE THIS BEFORE WE GOT INTO TOWN.

CARL: We didn't have the Mongo sleep potion. You know that. Get back in here as soon as he wakes up, and we'll be on our way.

"You need to quit pacing. She's fine," Mordecai said. "As long as you're not out there with her, the guards won't attack her. I hope you have a plan for when you leave."

"I do. We're gonna have to do this again with the next town. It's also a dryad settlement." Mordecai only had time to make one of the Mongo knockout potions, and he'd only be able to make one of the Charm Animal potions. Hopefully that would be enough.

Prudence the bear sat on the couch while her two cubs crawled all over her, acting like nothing had happened. One of the later *Land Before Time* movies played on the screen, which I thought was a little fucked-up because they'd just watched their dad get eaten by a dinosaur, but they seemed to like it. Little Todd was bitching at Mordecai about the movie's accuracy issues with the dinosaurs' appearance. Both Bomo and the Sledge sat on the ground, enraptured by the movie. The cleaner bot followed the bear cubs around, beeping worriedly.

Donut returned to the room a minute later and plopped the large glass flask onto the table. Blood ran down the side. Mongo, who'd been healed before he'd even woken up, sniffed at the container suspiciously.

"A liter is a lot!" Donut said for the hundredth time. "Why do you need so much? If Mongo was any smaller, he wouldn't even have that much in him. I had to cut and heal him three times just to fill this."

Mordecai moved in to examine the large flask. "This looks like it's more than enough. Good. I'll have the potion ready for you soon."

MIRIAM DOM: Carl, I hate to be a pest. But are you coming?
CARL: We're on our way.

I had Donut go outside and drop a smoke curtain right outside the door. I downed an invisibility potion and stepped out into the swirling mist. I didn't have time to rebuild the Chariot inside town, so we booked it to the edge of town.

"Can I do it? Can I do it?" Donut asked as we reached the unguarded western gate.

"Be careful. Try not to hit anybody else. Just the mayor. Use a magic missile, not a—"

The fireball shot forth from Donut, moving almost lazily as it glided through the air, sizzling and crackling in the rain. We watched as the beach-ball-sized glob of flames squeezed between two mushroom guards and slammed into the back of the dryad mayor, who immediately burst into flames like a goddamned sparkler from the Fourth of July. He screamed and started running in circles. The exterior of the pub we'd just left also caught on fire, and in seconds, half the town burned.

"Would you look at that!" Donut exclaimed. "Carl, why'd it catch on fire in the rain?" She gasped. "I did it! It's my town now!" A flaming monkey ran down the street, squealing.

"Yeah, let's not do that again," I said as I rapidly put the Chariot together.

The next town was only about twenty minutes away, and it looked almost identical to the previous one. This one was called **Prepotente Number Seven**, which meant the guards, hopefully, wouldn't automatically be hostile toward me, even if the dryads attacked. We quickly moved through, and I rushed inside to grab the now-completed Charm Animal potion. Inside, the cubs and the two rock bodyguards had somehow gotten ice-cream cones and were sitting there, still watching the damn dinosaur movie. Mongo, who hadn't gotten a chance to notice the movie at the previous location, started screeching and jumping up and down once he noticed the cartoon dinosaurs on the screen. We grabbed the green potion and bounced. None of the guards attacked us as we passed.

Ten minutes later, and we approached the approximate location of Miriam and Prepotente.

"I don't see them, Carl. We need Katia!"

CARL: Miriam, I think we're getting close, but I don't know exactly where you are.

MIRIAM DOM: Hang on one moment, Carl. Let me know if you can see this. I'm going to shoot a few sparks into the air.

I waited a moment, but there was nothing.

CARL: I don't see anything.

MIRIAM DOM: You must not be close enough. Keep moving west.

CARL: Hang on. Do it again in about fifteen seconds.

I downed one of the potions of Levitation, and I hovered off the ground. I pushed the slider up, and I moved into the dark, freezing air. Rain continued to pour, pelting into me like little needles. I passed up through the trees, wind causing my cloak to billow. I could see nothing ahead, though far behind me, the night glowed ominously. I could smell it. A distant fire burned, despite the rain. A big fire, bigger than before we'd left the area. *Goddamnit, Donut,* I thought. She'd set the whole damn forest aflame.

CARL: Do it now.

A moment later, a few sparks of light dotted the horizon, about two kilometers away and far to the south, farther south than I expected. It was far off any path that I could see, which meant we'd have to go on foot.

CARL: I see you!
DONUT: CARL, WATCH OUT!

The screeching, frothing form slammed into me from the side, and I bowled away. The levitation spell immediately snapped off. I pinwheeled as I plummeted from the sky.

I froze in midair. Pulsing EDM music started to play, pounding over the rain.

Oh fuck, oh fuck, what is this?

Mug shots of Donut and myself slammed into place, hovering, pounding right above my head. Digital lightning crept around the images, turning into vines. Monkey-screeching sounds and bongos punctuated the electronic squeal of the music. I couldn't move, but I faced upward, and I gagged as the cold water started to fill my mouth. It tasted of dirt and blood. I sputtered and gurgled as I was waterboarded by the downpour.

B...B...B...Boss Battle!
Special Forest Encounter!

Unable to move, I attempted to move my eyes, trying to see what had hit me. A massive twin pair of talons hung in the air about fifteen feet away, angled in an attack. The monstrous shadow attached to the monster was a familiar shape. *It's Quetzalcoatlus,* I thought. The pterodactyl-like ghost boss from the last floor. But that wasn't right. It couldn't be. It was, I realized, the same type of mob.

This one wasn't a ghost, but it was still undead.

The damn thing was huge, like a mix between a pelican and a vulture, but the size of a flying giraffe. It had an unusually large beak, almost like the head of a jouster's lance. The beak was as long as me. I'd only briefly seen the glowing ethereal form of Quetzalcoatlus, and the flesh form of this creature was terrifying.

We hung like that for several moments, the music getting louder and louder.

Versus!

. . .

An earsplitting shriek filled the night. Lightning crashed, and in that moment, the bloodred eyes of the monstrosity came into full view.

Sierra—Northropi Vampire.
> Level 65 Neighborhood Boss!
> This is a Bereft Minion of Viscount Fog.
> The great, now-deceased hunter of vampires and all things undead, Viscount Fog had trained his trusty mount, Sierra, to never leave his side.
> Together, they hunted evil, ridding the world of the dark scourge that took his village and family. They hunted and killed every filthy ghoul they could find. So when Viscount Fog learned of a newcomer to their world, a vicious and powerful, ruthless and deranged bloodsucker by the name of Miriam Dom, he set out to exterminate her.
> It went bad.
> When Sierra swept down in an ill-fated attempt to save her boss, she was injured by the ruthless, baby-murdering bloodsucker. She stumbled away, abandoning the fight. In less than a day, the bloodlust thirst has ravaged her. Now on the hunt for her first kill, Sierra has become what she and her master hated the most.
> Free her from her misery.

The world unfroze, and in less than a second, the twin talons gripped me. One around my legs, and the other around my chest. Leathery wings beat at the dark sky. The claws crushed and pulled at the same time, trying to pull me apart like a hot mozzarella stick. The creature smelled of death and gore. I continued to face upward, looking at the underside of the beast. I screamed as my health flashed red. *It's pulling me apart.*

DONUT: CARL! CARL!

A magic missile slammed into the monster's wing as it circled just above the tree line. It screeched angrily.

At the same moment, I cast *Heal* on myself as I pulled the Holy Gooper potion ball into my free hand. I smashed the sticky-holy-water substance against the talon locked onto my chest. The foot sizzled as Sierra screeched yet again, its voice high and piercing. I was hoping it'd drop me, but it just crushed harder.

CARL: Light!

I pulled my second and last potion ball just as the new sun ascended. Donut had scrambled up one of the trees, and she emerged from the canopy like a wizard atop a mountain, tiara glittering in the new light.

I attempted to heave the potion ball up at the dinosaur's chest, but it reared back at the bright light. The potion ball went flying as the boss continued to tumble backward, but that was okay because the thing's head burst into flames. What wasn't okay was that it tossed me straight up into the air like a rag doll.

"Gah," I cried out. I waved my arms ineffectively as I tumbled upward into the now bright sky. The boss landed on her back atop the canopy of trees, trapped as if she'd been caught by a spider's web. I spun upward, paused for but a moment, and then I dropped face-first like a sack of doorknobs.

I slammed down my last Half Splat potion as I rocketed toward the flaming form of the still-alive boss writhing atop the trees. Donut remained nearby, a few trees over, screaming something as a pair of clockwork Mongos negotiated the treetops toward the boss. One attempted to pounce, but the branch under it broke, and the dinosaur plunged down to the forest floor a hundred feet below.

I was going to hit the boss right below the center of the chest. The

Half Splat potion would keep me from dying, but it would plummet my health down to five percent. Since the dinosaur wasn't actually on the ground, I had no idea how or if the potion would even work in these circumstances.

I had my right fist clenched, and my gauntlet formed just before I slammed into the still-screaming-despite-its-goddamn-head-being-on-fire vampire dinosaur. I smashed right between the two flailing talons like Superman breaking through a wall.

I tore through the dinosaur like it was made of paper. I continued to fall, now tumbling, crashing through branches and leaves. *Shit, shit, shit. Crash!* I felt my rib cage crunch and legs break as I slammed into the muddy ground. I wheezed blood as I hit *Heal* once again.

To my left, a tree exploded, cracking and snapping and shattering as the body of the massive bird creature fell from the canopy and carved its way through the foliage. *It's going to land on me.* The body abruptly stopped its descent, hovering twenty feet over me, wings spread like it was a marionette. The sudden stop did not hinder the downward momentum of the beast's entrails, which ripped free from the hole I'd carved with my fist. Cold, stinking eellike guts smashed into my face. They just kept coming and coming like a ribbon from a magician's hat, followed by the rest of the creature's innards. I sputtered and gagged anew as my body healed itself.

I clawed my way out of the gore and looked up at the creature. It remained impaled between two trees, and its head continued to burn as it screamed. Its lower half dripped the remains of its stinking guts.

How are you not dead? It had a health bar, and it was in the red, but it stubbornly refused to sink lower.

Donut's light orb moved down toward the creature, causing the flames on its head to burn brighter and hotter. The guts around me sizzled like a pile of sausages on a pan. Mongo ran up to me and started squawking as the last clockwork Mongo leaped from above, landing on the thing's shoulder.

I caught sight of something on the ground. The still-beating heart sat a few feet away, thumping like a soccer-ball-sized engine. I could hear it, the heart beating in time to the music.

I remembered the warning from the cookbook, that our version of a vampire might not be the same as what we faced here. Still, I picked up a thick, broken, and jagged branch, slick with blood and rain. I lurched toward the loose heart, and I stabbed it directly into the organ. It felt like I was trying to stab a raw turkey.

The damn monster exploded, showering more gore over all of us.

The neighborhood map dropped at my feet, and the rest of the thing spilled from the trunks of the ruined trees, landing all around me in a cascade of stinking, wet slop.

Winner!

The music stopped abruptly as it always did. I didn't move, allowing the rain to half-wash me clean. Another tree fell, but it fell in an opposite direction. Mongo grunted and leaned down to bite at the remains.

"Don't you dare."

Vampirism was contagious, and if I hadn't been protected by my jacket, I'd likely be infected. I'd "die" and then wake up, overcome with hunger. I didn't know if one ate a vampire corpse, it would spread, but the fact that half the dinosaurs in the forest were now infected suggested that was indeed the case.

Donut leaped to a branch as she turned down the intensity of the light.

"You punched that vampire pterodactyl in the dick!" she cried. "You put a hole right in it!"

I groaned as I stepped away from the gore. The rain continued to pound. "Yes, Donut. I was there. But it was female. It didn't have a dick."

"Then you punched her in her lady garden! Did you see what my light did? It's up to level 14 now!" She jumped down, being careful not to land anywhere near the dripping remains of the vampire. "It was hard to kill, but my light set it on fire just like the *Fireball* spell." She made a face. "Really, Carl, we need to find a less disgusting way to kill these things."

"What the hell did you just call it?" I asked. "Lady garden?"

"That's what Miss Beatrice used to call it. That and 'kitty,' which I will not even dignify with a response. But I rather like the term 'lady garden.' Mongo, no!"

"You better put him away until we can get out of here. We don't want him infected with any of the lady garden bits."

"No. No, I suppose that would be quite inconvenient. Mongo, come on."

47

<Note added by Crawler Volteeg. 7th Edition>

I miss her. I miss her so goddamn much. Is it worth it? To survive this place with her gone? No. No, I don't think it is.

<Note added by Crawler Drakea. 22nd Edition>

This is Volteeg's first, last, and only entry in the cookbook. Fuck everything about this place.

WE FOUND THE SCENE WITH MIRIAM DOM AND PREPOTENTE WITH JUST under an hour to go before dawn. We'd have gotten there even sooner, but we'd had to fight our way there. Hordes of turkey-sized dinosaurs called bambiraptors swarmed through the forest. Most—but not all—of them were vampires. Strangely, the ones infected with vampirism didn't appear to attack their own kind, which I found interesting. I could kill them easily with a kick and a stomp. Donut's *Torch* spell was also highly effective against the infected ones. It didn't outright kill them, but it stunned them at regular strength, and it caught their heads on fire when she maxed it out.

I paused at the clearing to take it all in.

The paralyzed form of Prepotente stood there like a statue, left arm around the waist of Miriam, who leaned against the goat man. His right arm was extended out, hand grasped around something that was no longer there. He had a timer over his head, six hours and counting. He would wake up five hours after sunrise.

There was an asterisk after the timer. I did not know what that meant. I hadn't seen that before.

I could tell Miriam was exhausted. I knew, as a vampire, she was normally pale. But her skin had taken on a ghoul-like shimmer. *She's sick,* I thought. *I wonder how long it's been since she's eaten.*

A circle of corpses surrounded the pair, extending out to the tree line. There was a wide range of creatures, from raccoons to monkeys to large bugs to dozens of the bambiraptors. Farther out within the trees, red dots stalked in a circle, but they fled as we approached.

"There's some bigger monsters out there," Donut whispered. "I think they might be lady Mongos. They're moving away."

"Okay. Keep Mongo locked up for now. Keep an eye out for hunters and other crawlers, too."

"Thank goodness," Miriam said as we cautiously entered the clearing. I could hear the pain in her voice. She held up her arms to cover her eyes. "Donut, please. The light."

"Oh, sorry," Donut said, adjusting the brightness. "Is that better?"

"Yes, sorry. Please. We must talk before the sun rises."

"What do you need us to do?" I asked.

"Sunrise is in fifty-three minutes," she said. A book appeared in her hand. She dropped it to the ground. It was a magical tome. "Miss Donut, if you would be so kind. If you read the spell book, you will learn the spell you need to wake him up."

Donut gasped and jumped from my shoulder before I could object. My something-is-wrong sense screamed. The viewer counter was jacked all the way to the right, but it had been since the boss battle with Sierra.

CARL: Wait!

Donut paused, looking uncertainly between me and Miriam.

"Why didn't you read the book yourself?" I asked.

Miriam sighed. "You two are in no danger from me, Carl. But I understand why you are cautious. I can see the glow on you. You are both protected from vampirism, and I can't feed on you even if I wanted to."

"You didn't answer my question."

"I already have the spell. Or I had it. It's gone now. I have a special ability that allows me to unlearn a spell and turn it into a spell book. I can only do it once a night, unfortunately."

"But why didn't you use it, then?" Donut asked. She cast *Second Chance* on a raccoon-like monster and told it to go get the book. The zombie raccoon hissed and grabbed the book, dragging it away from Miriam's feet. It dropped it at Donut's feet before lurching off into the forest, chattering.

"Don't read it before I— Goddamnit, Donut."

Donut glowed as she read the spell book.

"Relax, Carl," Donut said. "It was just a spell book of *Get out of Jail*. Wow. It costs forty points. That's a lot! I've seen this spell before. Okay, I'm going to wake Prepotente up."

"Goddamnit, wait," I said.

"Donut, please wait," Miriam agreed, continuing to gasp.

A trio of bambiraptors cautiously entered the clearing from behind Miriam. Before we could react, three bolts of energy shot from the vampire and struck them down. She hadn't even turned her head. *Holy shit.*

"Miriam," I said, taking a step forward. If she wanted to hurt us, she could do it from a distance. My sense of danger didn't ease, but I was starting to suspect whatever the danger was, it wasn't from Miriam. "Tell us the story. What's going on? Why haven't you released him?"

"Okay," Miriam said. "I will tell you everything. Just promise me you won't attempt to wake him just yet. Not until after dawn breaks. I don't know if it will work if you try before then, and I'm afraid the attempt might harm him. So please wait."

"Something tells me he's going to be mad if we wait that long," I said. "Can he see us in this state?"

"I think so," Miriam said. "He can't talk or move or use the chat, and he has the Fragile debuff, so we must be careful. But I believe he sees and hears all of it."

"Okay," I said. "Explain."

"We don't know each other very well, but I like you, Carl. Pony likes you, too."

"I don't think that's true, Miriam—"

"Shush. Let me tell you a story. Don't worry, it is short. But it's about a young woman who had a life and a career and a fiancée. And she gave it all up. Not because she wanted to, but because she had a sense of duty to her parents."

"I'm sorry," I said. "But . . ."

She had a quaver to her voice. "My parents were getting old, and I returned to their home outside Parma to take care of them and the animals. Twenty years would pass before my parents were gone, and when they were, I was too rooted. I couldn't give it up. Even though I hated it as a child, I'd grown to love the farm and the responsibilities and the country. And my children. The goats. I loved them more than anything."

"Miriam," I began.

She held up her hand.

"I am telling you this not just because I am a sentimental old fool. It is important I say it because I never have. And I wish to say it to you because it is clear you love your Donut as much as I love all of my babies. Only you can understand. You're the only one here whom I trust enough to understand." She turned her head to regard the frozen Prepotente.

"And one day, I want you to explain it to him. Because I know he will not understand it now."

"Carl does love me," Donut said.

Before I could object again, Miriam continued.

"Even before, Pony was attached to me. He would even follow me inside the house if I let him. My little stubborn shadow. But now. Now it is so much worse. When we are separated, he becomes hysterical. He becomes a danger to himself."

"Yeah, I heard," I said. "When you went on that show with Katia, he flipped out."

She reached up and touched her neck. I didn't know the details, but Prepotente had run off in a panic when Miriam was away. She'd gone looking for him and somehow ended up a vampire.

"When we got to this floor, we found ourselves hunted by an elite. A vampire hunter named Viscount Fog."

"We just killed his flying mount. Sierra."

She nodded. "Good. Good. She was dangerous. Fog was part of one of those television programs they run inside of this place. It was called *Blood Hunter*, and Fog was the star. He started hunting me the moment we landed on this floor. We have the hunters and the clerics, and now this creature. . . . Plus, Pony got that prize box. It is unbearable, Carl. I . . . I am not strong like you. Or stubborn like Pony." Her voice broke. "It is too much. And with my condition, it is a toll on my children. All ten of those who survive."

"Ten?" I asked.

"Pony plus Bianca plus the others. They are all in his inventory." She paused, momentarily overcome with emotion. "It is no longer safe for them to stay in mine. If I fall into the Ravenous state, it's . . . it's a bad idea for my babies to be on me."

Fuck it, I thought.

I took another step toward her. I put my hand on her arm, and it was shockingly cold. That, combined with the look of pure agony in her eyes, threatened to push me over a precipice I didn't even know I was standing upon. I still didn't understand what was going on, but I knew whatever this was, it was devastating to Miriam. She was known for being ridiculously calm in horrific situations, and this loss of control was heartbreaking.

She put her calloused hand atop mine. She had a tattoo there, old and faded in the skin between her thumb and forefinger. It was of a musical note.

"Pony and I didn't know about this vampire hunter until it was almost too late. He attacked us early on, but we escaped. This was several days ago, and the attack occurred while we were fighting that giant dinosaur. Big Tina. That was the start of it."

I felt myself nod. "Big Tina has gone off the rails. We have a quest to figure out her story. But she's doing something odd. She's building some sort of army of undead."

"Yes," Miriam said. "Vampirism comes with a host of spells and abilities, and you get different ones when you are infected. Some new vampires are more powerful than others. Some of the infected are more contagious or charismatic. Or more deadly. Some can shapeshift. Tina is a boss monster, and they have given her multiple powerful abilities. Abilities that allow her to control others. Or to create undead minions from those she slaughters. This was to be the climax of *Blood Hunter.* The vampirism curse was to infect the forest, and after killing me, Viscount Fog would have saved all the dinosaurs in the area, stopping an

THE BUTCHER'S MASQUERADE 413

apocalypse. There's a hierarchy, you see. Since I am the progenitor of their infection, if I die, the curse ends. Since none have been infected for a full month, they would all be cured. It's not too late."

Donut gasped. "You're the head vampire!"

"Yes," Miriam agreed. "Once I went down the floor, I gained a title. Princess of Hell. All crawlers who survive a floor while infected gain such a title, which makes the infection permanent. Carl, please listen. Just in the past few days, over a dozen other crawlers have been infected by forest creatures and dinosaur vampires. And those are only the ones I know of."

I suddenly felt a chill wash over me, and I finally knew what was happening.

"Miriam, why haven't you unfrozen Prepotente?"

She sniffed. "When Viscount Fog fell upon us this second time, Pony was ready for him. He read a very powerful scroll. It is called *Community Pool*. He must be physically touching both parties for the spell to work. He takes the infection of one party, me in this case, and he moves it to another. It would have not only cured me. It would also make it so Fog was now the prime. We could've killed him then, and it would've cured the infection. Pony received the scroll in a benefactor box."

"So, it would've turned Viscount Fog into the new head vampire?" Donut asked. "That would've been great television!"

"Yes. The scroll said it would cause Pony to be stunned for a minute, but we knew the transformation would've overcome Fog, and we would've had plenty of time to recover and finish him off."

I eyed the frozen form of Prepotente. "Something obviously went wrong."

"When Pony cast the *Community Pool* spell, Fog activated a counter that threw the spell back at Pony. It burned through his protections." Miriam took a deep, pained breath. "Because of his wards, Pony was not infected, and the curse did not leave my body. Pony countered the counter. The spell bounced back and forth between the two several times." She indicated a fat ring on Prepotente's stubby finger. It looked as if it once housed several jewels. They were all gone. All except one on the very end. It looked like a tiny soul crystal, and it glowed ominously, like it might explode at any moment.

"That is a five-time-use ring called Opposite Day. It activated, and it shot the remains of the spell at Fog, who in turn had a similar ring, which bounced the spell back. It ping-ponged back and forth between the two. Both ended up stunned multiple times, and as you might know, the Stun effect compounds each time it is applied. After the third iteration, one becomes Fragile, which means even the slightest amount of damage kills the sufferer, which is why I haven't been able to break myself free without hurting Pony. The whole thing happened in less than a second, so fast it took me a while to figure out what had happened."

DONUT: CARL, CARL, LOOK AT PREPOTENTE'S OTHER HAND. AT
     THE OTHER RING!
CARL: I see it. Let her get there on her own.

"How did Fog die?" I asked.

"With the both of them stunned and attached to me, I was tempted to kill him myself. It would've been easy. But I feared he had one last trick up his sleeve that would take Pony with him, and I didn't dare. Not when I knew he would perish on his own at sunset, which is what happened."

"How did you know he'd die at sunset?"

"Spells, when they bounce back and forth so many times, have a tendency to fall . . . How do you say? Inside out. It is something we learned early on. It is how Pony is so effective at killing slowly. He takes simple, low-power spells, and he finds ways for the spell to compound. That is what happened here. Fog had a new debuff. One titled Cursed Light Walker. I knew what that meant. While I die when exposed to light, his health slowly seeps if he is away from it. It is just as insidious of a curse. It's not what we intended, but it worked. Because he was frozen and unable to heal, he died and crumpled to dust."

"He was an opposite vampire!" Donut said. She turned to me. "I wonder how that works. Does he vomit blood on people instead of suck it away?"

"It doesn't matter," I said. "So, Pony . . . Prepotente hasn't been inflicted with either form of vampirism?"

"No," she said. "No, thank goodness. His wards have burned away, but they held." She swallowed. "However, when the spell bounced back and forth, something else happened. Something worse."

I returned my gaze back to the frozen form of Prepotente and the ring on his other hand. It was difficult to see through his dark robe in the low light, but I saw it there, glowing ever so slightly through his clothes. The spiderweb tattoo on his left elbow. He didn't just have the ring. He'd been using it.

"I didn't know anybody else had a Ring of Divine Suffering," I said. Mordecai had told me a few of these would appear in the dungeon, but this was the first I'd heard of one other than my own.

"He just got it," Miriam said. "I told him not to put it on, that it was a mistake. But he is stubborn. That's what his name means." Her voice broke then. "He was always my stubborn little boy."

"Wait," Donut said, finally catching up. "He marked you? He can't heal? Why not?"

"It happened on its own," Miriam said. "When spells bounce back and forth like that, it can cause a magical burst. A burst like that causes magic items to behave erratically."

"Yeah," I said. "We saw that happen at the end of the third floor."

"I didn't see his ring activate. I didn't feel it happen. He can't talk to me. But I see the debuff in his status. One can't mark an NPC or an elite. I was the only eligible target in the area."

"Left to Fester," I said quietly.

"Yes. That is the debuff. Such an ugly name."

"You haven't woken him up because you can't. The Stunned and Fragile debuff might time out, but the spell you gave Donut won't work on him," I said.

"I actually don't know," she said. "I was hoping you'd come before I was forced to find out. I fear casting it prematurely might damage him. Spells do that sometimes if they don't work. He has but a single point of life in the Fragile state."

"You didn't ask me here to protect you. You asked me here to kill you," I said.

"Yes," she agreed.

DONUT: I DON'T UNDERSTAND.

    CARL: Miriam wants to die, and I don't blame her. If she dies, all of
    the other crawlers who have been infected on this floor with
    vampirism will be cured. It will stop whatever Big Tina is doing
    with the body parts. And Pony will be able to heal. I don't even
    know if we can wake him up until she's dead. It's not clear how
    it works with debuffs.

    DONUT: IF WE KILL MIRIAM, PREPOTENTE WILL KILL US. IT'S
    WHAT I WOULD DO IF ANYBODY HURT YOU.

I reached up and rubbed Donut's head. A sense of helplessness
washed over me, but I pushed it away. *Goddamn you. You will not break me.*

    CARL: The smart thing to do would be to kill them both.

    DONUT: I DON'T WANT TO KILL EITHER OF THEM.

    CARL: Neither do I. Miriam wants us to kill her before Pony wakes
    up. She hasn't said this out loud, but she's probably afraid he'll
    kill himself in a misguided attempt to save her. But we have
    other things to consider. I still don't know what the hell is
    going on with the Plenty, but they obviously like Pony because
    they're all fellow goats or whatever, and the last thing we need
    is another intergalactic conglomerate trying to kill us. If one of
    them has to go, it makes sense that it's Miriam. Even without
    the ring thrown into the mix, her vampirism curse is terribly
    dangerous, and it's spreading fast.

    DONUT: THIS IS JUST LIKE WITH CHRIS. IT'S AN IMPOSSIBLE
    SITUATION.

    CARL: No, Donut. It's not impossible. It's just hard. Very hard.

I took a deep breath.

"Miriam, I am not going to kill you. But I will stand watch with
you. I'll keep you safe and Prepotente safe until the sun rises."

The shepherd woman nodded. Tears ran down her cheeks, and they
were made of blood. They mixed with the rain before they hit the ground.

I HELD MY HANDS BEHIND MY BACK SO NEITHER DONUT, MIRIAM, NOR the frozen form of Prepotente would see. I slipped my own Ring of Divine Suffering onto my finger just as dawn broke.

> You have marked Miriam Dom.
>   Miriam Dom's highest stat is Intelligence.
>   You have been infected with Left to Fester! This debuff will not go away until your mark is dead!

I knew people would think I was an idiot for not killing her myself, especially when she was going to die either way. Her bounty was worth 300,000 gold. And Prepotente was worth 1.2 million. Plus he had the ring and probably a host of other items.

It would be so easy.

But that's not who I was. She knew that. She could see that in me, and that's why I was the one she summoned. She needed someone to protect Prepotente after she was gone.

I thought of Drakea's note after Volteeg's one and only entry.

Fuck everything about this place.

I thought of Prepotente watching this and unable to move. I imagined what he must be feeling.

I thought of my mother, who'd ruined everything when she'd gone.

Miriam leaned her head on Prepotente's frozen shoulder as the sun rose up over the trees. The rain had finally stopped, just long enough for the light to shine brightly on a clearing in the middle of the forest in this forsaken place. A health bar appeared, and it slowly started to drain away.

> DONUT: Carl? Would you do the same thing to save me?
> CARL: Without hesitation.

I will break you all.

"My beautiful boy," Miriam whispered as she turned to dust. "My beautiful boy."

SYSTEM MESSAGE: A CHAMPION HAS FALLEN.

I took another step back, and I pulled the Ring of Divine Suffering off my own finger and slipped it back into my inventory.

"Get ready," I whispered. "We don't know how he's going to react. He might unleash that Bianca thing on us."

"Are we going to let him stay with us?" Donut asked, looking down at the pile of dust.

Hell to the fuck no, I almost said out loud, but I remembered he could possibly hear us. "We'll see."

Nearby stood a literal stack of random potions and magical items and more plants than I could count. She'd spent the last few minutes dumping everything from her inventory. She'd feared that the act of turning to dust would make her body unlootable, and she'd been correct. She told me I could take a few items for myself if I wanted, in exchange for helping her. I promised her we'd give it all to Prepotente, and I intended on keeping that promise. Mostly.

She did have a pair of little orange traffic-cone-like hats she'd taken off some gnomelike creature, and she told Donut it was okay if she had one of them. Donut tried not to show her excitement.

I didn't want to be obvious about it, but now that she was gone, I started examining everything she'd left behind. Most of the stuff I couldn't properly examine unless I picked it up. She had over forty potions of something called Size Up. I walked around out of Prepotente's sight and took two of them.

As I pulled the second potion into my inventory, my interface flickered. The number 50 appeared and slammed into place just under the level timer.

"Carl, do you see that number thing?" Donut asked.

We were interrupted by another system message.

New Quest. The Creeping Apocalypse.

This is a world quest! All crawlers *and* all hunters currently active on the sixth floor will receive this quest!

You may not opt out of this quest.

Miriam Dom the vampire has fallen. With the rising of today's sun, she found herself caught out in the open. Helpless and crying, she burned away into dust. The callous crawlers Carl and Princess Donut watched and did nothing as she died in agonizing pain. Nothing!

(Actually, not nothing. Someone should probably ask Carl why he suddenly has three new points to his Intelligence stat. Suspicious!)

Anyway, Miriam did not go quietly into the good night. Oh no. Her death has cured thousands of crawlers, monsters, and hunters who have been touched by the vampirism curse.

There is, however, a problem.

Some of the forest monsters infected with vampirism have spent the past few nights on a killing spree. And another vampire, a now-cured Allosaurus by the name of Big Tina, unfortunately has expended a lot of effort on building an army of undead monstrosities using the . . . leftovers . . . from the forest-wide slaughter.

These newly created monsters are not vampires, and they were not cured when Miriam died. These mindless freaks were left all alone, not under control from any entity. Some are nothing more than Mini Grinders, also known as Shrillings, also known as Shambling Berserkers. We've all seen these before, most notably in some of the train stations at the end of the fourth floor. Yes, they can get pretty big and annoying, but it's not anything you really need to worry about. Hardly worth a regular quest, let alone a world one. You'd have to be a total idiot to let one of those things kill you, especially during the day. I'm looking at you, Nihit Kumar, who's about two seconds from getting . . . Oh, that's a shame. Gross.

Anyway, some of the other, more powerful monsters have become something else, and short of a god, they are the most powerful monsters who have ever set foot on a sixth floor in *Dungeon Crawler World* history.

I like to call them Odious Creepers.

The good news? Like Shambling Berserkers, Odious Creepers tend to be pretty slow during the day. The bad news? When it's dark outside, they gain the ability to combine with both Shamblers and other Creepers and get even stronger. And they can get fast, very fast. They can replicate themselves, too, if they have the parts!

There are currently fifty of these things . . . growing around . . . the forest, plus another few thousand Shambling Berserkers of various sizes. For fun, we have randomized their location. And for extra fun, we have marked the location of each Creeper on the map for you all.

So, here's the quest part. Kill all the Odious Creepers before the sun sets tonight.

For every Creeper you kill, you will receive +5 to a random stat. For every five you kill, you will receive an additional +5 levels. The crawler or hunter who kills the most will get an additional prize.

Only the person who does the most damage gets credit for the kill.

If you don't kill all of them before the sun sets tonight, bad stuff will happen. And I mean every single one of the fifty Creepers. And by bad stuff, I mean something completely batshit. And not just to the crawlers, but to the hunters, too. So all of you cowards sitting on your ass in Zockau need to get to work.

"Holy shit," I muttered.

"Carl, did you really use that ring on Miriam? After everything that just happened with Prepotente?"

I looked at the map, and the closest creeper thing was about five miles away.

"Also, have you noticed how the AI refers to itself as 'I' way more often than it used to? It always did, but something has changed."

I started to answer her, but Mordecai interrupted us.

MORDECAI: I think I've seen this before on a smaller scale. Undead and bereft minions can get taken over by certain types of plants. If these are the self-building glamoured fragments you saw earlier, they were likely going to turn into something called a Glamoured Creeper once they gained 70% of their bodies back. But now their boss is no longer able to control them, they've been commandeered by something else. Likely a plant called an Odious Bloom. The whole process is supposed to be rare and take a long time, but they've sped everything up to create this event. Listen to me. These things are going to be deadly. Deadlier than I have time to explain. Stay away from them. Don't even get close. They'll likely control all the vines in the area. They will rip body parts off people and use the parts to make themselves stronger. They will shoot poisonous darts. They will grow up out of the ground.

My messaging system blew up with chatter.

CARL: Mordecai, we can't just sit back and let everyone else do the work. Can you come up with something to kill it? Like with that Pestiferous Vine?

MORDECAI: An Odious Bloom? Yes. But this is a different creature, and I don't know if anything I have will work. Not without a lot of trial and error. Things this big usually require a full application, so we're talking an aerosol. Delivery is going to be a problem. With only half of a day . . . They want you to kill these things the old-fashioned way. Hacking and burning, and that's going to be difficult. They're trying to draw the hunters back out. The prize for killing these things is a little *too* good, which means it's too dangerous. It's going to be a slaughter.

I added Katia to the chat, who was asking me what had happened with Miriam. I quickly gave her a rundown.

KATIA: I've been doing the math based on what you said earlier, and I think some of these Glamoured Creepers will be as high as level 150, maybe more, and that's before they turned into these plant things. We'll have to attack in groups from afar. Eva's group has one right in the middle of them. Hopefully it takes them out, but if it doesn't, we'll have to move in.

CARL: Holy shit. Be careful. Make sure you only work with crawlers you trust. This has potential to get out of hand.

DONUT: STAY AWAY FROM THAT DOG LADY. TSERENDOLGOR. WHAT KIND OF A STUPID NAME IS THAT ANYWAY? HER MOM OBVIOUSLY DIDN'T LOVE HER.

KATIA: Donut, she's a very nice person who had a very difficult life. And her name is Mongolian.

DONUT: EVERYONE IS HAVING A DIFFICULT LIFE RIGHT NOW, KATIA. SHE DOESN'T GET EXTRA CREDIT BECAUSE SHE HAS A STUPID NAME.

KATIA: Okay, Donut.

MORDECAI: Guys, listen to me. For the sake of the gods. Stay away from them. This is going to be a clusterfuck.

CARL: Well, it's about to get even worse. Donut and I need to wake up the goat.

"Carl," Donut said, "I see a bunch of dots moving in. I think they're lady Mongos. How did you know that was going to happen? I swear, I think you're psychic sometimes."

"Is Tina with them?"

"I don't think so. I don't see a big dot."

"Okay," I said. "Let's do this quick."

I took a knee in front of Prepotente. It was weird. Even though he was motionless, I could feel it. I could sense it coming off of him, like electricity off a live wire. Or heat radiating off a stove. The sense of utter despair and anger and misery and loss.

He'd thought of Miriam as his mother. He'd just watched her die as he sat by, helpless.

Christ, I thought. I knew exactly how that felt. The realization was like a punch to the gut.

"Listen, buddy. We're gonna wake you up. I'm really sorry about what happened, and I wish I could take it back. She would want you to be strong, and she needs you to take care of all your brothers and sisters or whatever. You need to be strong for them. We have some monsters moving in, and we have to wake you up now. But don't kill these new monsters, okay? Donut and I need to do something with them."

I nodded at Donut, who cast the spell. She waved her paw, and Prepotente glowed.

And just like that, he was awake.

For several moments, the goat made no sound. He remained frozen in place, just blinking. I tensed, waiting for him to attack.

"They'll be here in a minute," Donut whispered. "They're coming in slow now, like they're hunting."

Prepotente slowly pulled the Ring of Divine Suffering off his finger and dropped it to the dirt in front of him. My heart quickened, and I started to plan on how to get it for myself. I wondered what would happen if I wore two of them, if I'd be able to double up on the benefits.

But then he reached down, and he picked the ring back up, his fuzzy hands trembling. He popped the ring into his mouth, and he swallowed it whole.

He ate it. He ate the goddamn ring.

He fell to his hands and knees before the pile of dust that'd once been Miriam. The sun had come out for a few moments, but it was already starting to rain anew, and big fat droplets fell upon the already-rain-soaked ground, splashing into the only thing that remained of the crawler. The drops splattered heavily into the piles of ash, washing them away.

He screamed at the pile of ash.

This wasn't his normal cry. This was haunting, almost silent, like he couldn't get the sound out. Like wind rushing across a desolate landscape.

He screamed over and over until he had no more.

"Oh, Mother," Prepotente finally said, his voice raspy. "Oh, Mother, what did you do? Please. Please, no." He turned to look up at me and Donut. Muddy tears ran down his face. "She was going to play piano for me like she used to. She was going to sing me my special song."

Donut leaped from my shoulder and landed upon the shoulder of the smaller goat, who winced under her weight. She butted her head against his horn.

"I'm sorry you're hurting right now," Donut said, her voice unnaturally gentle. "You just sit here and have a good cry. Take as long as you need. Some monsters are about to come into the clearing, but don't you worry about them. Don't move, and let me and Carl take care of it."

Prepotente reached up and patted Donut on the side of the head just as Kiwi the velociraptor slinked into the clearing, head low, growling. She didn't attack, however, and she kept to the edge of the field. Multiple dots finally appeared on my map in a semicircle, coming from the south.

"She said everything was going to be all right, but it was a lie. A dreadful lie," Prepotente said as Donut returned to my shoulder. His hands trembled. He was oblivious of the danger around us. "What am I going to do now?"

He paused, eyes going wide.

"It appears I've just received an emergency benefactor box from my sponsor," he said, sniffing. He returned his attention to the empty space on the ground, and he began to sob.

49

THERE WERE TWENTY OF THEM. THEY EMERGED FROM THE WOODS, each about twenty meters back against the tree line, poised. I knew they could clear the distance easily with a single leap. They held like this, ready to attack.

I took a moment to observe them. All, including Kiwi, were covered with blood. I knew these guys were some of the few dinos that had not been turned to vampires, and it appeared that was a hard-fought victory.

I'd already figured they'd be in the area. These things didn't talk, but they used to be intelligent creatures, and it was clear some of that remained. I figured if they weren't following Tina around, they would be hunting for the source of the infection. If we hadn't shown up, they'd surely have attacked Miriam already.

Or maybe they'd been waiting for dawn, just to be safe. Either way, they were here now.

The remaining question was, what did they want? Tina—who was Kiwi's daughter—was cured of the vampirism curse. From what I gathered, this pack of women velociraptors spent most of their time following the kid around and protecting her and keeping her from getting herself into too much trouble. That had gone off the rails because of Miriam and the elite. But why were they still here? Why weren't they out there seeking out the big dinosaur?

Their dots were red for me, but white for Donut. Mongo remained in his carrier. Mordecai warned his presence might negate the spell.

Kiwi made a barking noise and took a step forward. All around, the others hunched, as if about to pounce. I tensed, ready to hit *Protective Shell*.

DONUT: I NEED TO BE CLOSER FOR THE POTION TO WORK. IT
SAYS IT ONLY LASTS FOR A MINUTE, AND I NEED TO MAKE
SURE I DON'T ACCIDENTALLY CHARM THE WRONG ONE.

We only had one potion of Charm Animal, actually named Charm
Mongoliensis now. The potion caused the closest eligible monster to be
tamed by Donut for the duration of the floor. She wouldn't become a pet
with a permanent bond, but she would be a minion, which was a similar sort of deal.

If we managed to actually charm Kiwi, she would, hopefully, bring
the rest of the pack with her.

I realized charming Kiwi had always been the solution. This was
still part of the Tina quest, and they wanted us to somehow enlist her
help to solve the Tina problem. That potion recipe from the Plenty was
a cheat. A shortcut. A way to guarantee we'd get involved in the quest
and, ultimately, end up where we were right now. Protecting their precious Prepotente.

Kiwi looked between me and Donut. She rested her piercing gaze on
me and growled again. Up and down the semicircle of raptors, feathers
bristled. A warning.

"I think you need to do this alone," I whispered.

Behind us, Prepotente continued to rock back and forth, muttering
to himself, occasionally bursting into tears. He screamed a few times,
his voice still hoarse.

"Don't worry, Carl," Donut said. "I'm quite practiced in the matter
of taming dinosaurs."

She hopped off my shoulder and put her tail up, ramrod straight. She
took a few steps toward Kiwi, whose feathers remained poofed out.

"Now, Kiwi," Donut said, "I'm prepared to forgive you for what you
did to my poor Mongo, but that does not mean we can forget it. Just let
me get a few steps closer, and we can discuss it like adults."

I could see it in the dinosaur's demeanor. She seemed to be fighting
her every instinct to attack Donut. I'd seen it before, so many times, in
so many places. That battle between what one used to be and what one
had become.

"I wish you'd never given me that pet biscuit. It's not worth it," Prepotente said to his dead mother's ashes. "We'd all be gone now. It would be quite better, wouldn't it? We'd be together." I could barely hear him over the rain.

But no, I realized. The rain had stopped once again. My head throbbed.

Fuck everything about this place.

I kept my mental finger on the *Protective Shell*, ready to slam it down. With my newly enhanced intelligence, the shell would be plenty big enough to protect Donut, myself, and Prepotente. If only for a few precious moments.

It wasn't necessary. Donut stopped about ten feet in front of the pink dinosaur. Kiwi cocked her head to the side, just like how Mongo did sometimes before he screamed and attacked. Donut glowed, and about three seconds later, Kiwi also glowed. The dinosaur shrieked, long and loud. Her dot turned white, and the green X appeared in the dot, indicating her as either a mercenary or a minion. A moment later, the dots of all the other raptors turned white. They did not gain the green cross pattern.

Multiple more lady Mongo dots appeared on my map, raising the total to just under forty. They'd been behind us, and I hadn't even realized it. And then others, too. More of those small bambiraptors, whose dots remained red, but they quickly moved off. I examined the pink dinosaur as the others all moved into the clearing, no longer in a battle formation.

Kiwi's demeanor hadn't changed too much. She still appeared as if she wanted to rip my throat out, despite the dot on the map changing color.

Kiwi. Mongoliensis Pack Leader—Level 60.
   This is a minion of Princess Donut.

"Good job," I said to Donut as the raptor sniffed at my crotch and growled. "You did it."

"Of course I did it, Carl," said Donut. "After all the torture we put Mongo through, what else did you expect? Now, Kiwi, we do have a few rules to go over. Rule number one is not to molest Mongo again. Rule number two is to not eat Carl."

Kiwi looked at me and squawked, sounding disappointed.

"That should probably be rule number one," I said as more of the pony-sized dinosaurs started sniffing at me. One snapped at the air inches away from my junk, and I almost pissed myself. They were ignoring Prepotente, but they seemed to find me fascinating.

"You can take care of yourself, Carl," Donut said. "Just don't get them riled up." She returned her attention to Kiwi. "Also, I'd like for you to introduce me to each of your friends. I must insist upon knowing everyone's names if we're all going to be working together."

I looked over the group, counting. There was a total of thirty-six velociraptors. Most hovered around level 40. A few had a strange debuff over them.

Immortalized.

There was a 29-hour countdown with each debuff.

I had never seen nor read about that one. I sent a note to Mordecai, and he said it came from being cured of vampirism. Anyone with the debuff would be at half strength and mana and unable to heal for the duration of the debuff while they were in direct sunlight. The debuff wouldn't affect them if they were in shadow. In direct moonlight, the debuff would turn to a buff: plus 50% strength and mana and double healing speed. Right now the sky was overcast, so these guys were unaffected. The rain kept starting and stopping, but a thick layer of clouds had moved in and remained heavy in the sky.

I wondered if those Odious Creepers were suffering from something similar. I sent a note out to the main chat.

A few of the dinosaurs finally started to notice Prepotente sitting there on the ground. He grumbled about the attention and waved at them to go away. A few snapped angrily at him, deliberately keeping their distance. He growled back, which worried me.

Donut only had true control over Kiwi, and if something happened to her, we'd be in trouble. I needed to remember that all of these guys were different from Mongo. We did not have an army of Mongos now. We had—*Donut* had—one minion, who controlled her own army. That was a major difference.

"Okay, Kiwi," Donut was saying. "I'm going to bring Mongo out now. He might be scared at first, so please be gentle with him. You might want to think about apologizing to him for taking advantage of him like that."

"Uh, Donut," I said, "maybe we should wait until—"

Mongo appeared, zapping into place between Donut and Kiwi, who squawked and jumped away at the sudden appearance of the male dinosaur. She angrily bit at him, and he shrieked and snapped back. They both started barking like pissed-off geese, circling one another while other dinosaurs scattered, almost knocking me over.

"Mongo, no!" Donut cried. "It's Kiwi!"

All of the others crowded around Mongo and started sniffing at him. He cried and tried to move away, but he was quickly circled. He squeaked in fear.

"Mongo, it's okay," Donut called. "Ladies, give him some room!" She returned to my shoulder to get a better view of the crowd. "Mommy is right here. Kiwi has agreed to help us. Don't worry, Mongo."

One of the lady Mongos—not Kiwi—bent down in front of Mongo, face down, butt in the air, presenting herself to him, wiggling her tail enticingly. Mongo suddenly didn't appear so scared anymore. But before anything could happen, Kiwi saw this and hissed angrily, pouncing through the air and tackling the offending female, who hissed but shrank back.

"Good girl! Good Kiwi!" Donut said. "I'm glad we understand— Kiwi, no! Mongo! Not again! Bad!"

"So much for rule number one," I said a moment later.

―――――

WHILE THIS WENT ON, I FINALLY NOTICED THAT PREPOTENTE HAD RE-turned to his feet. He'd collected all of the loot from Miriam. He had a wand in his hand. He hung his head low, and he faced away from the circle of screeching dinosaurs.

"Hey, Prepotente," I said, stepping back. Donut remained on my shoulder, complaining loudly. I'd told her to just let it happen, but she didn't listen. "Hey, you doing okay, buddy?"

I tensed as he pointed the wand at an empty space in the field. A blue square, about one meter by one meter, appeared on the ground, flattening the grass around it. The goat put the wand away and stepped onto the square.

"Carl, do you see that?" Donut said, attention suddenly on the spot on the ground. "It's a safe space!"

"I only have one charge left after this one," Prepotente said, his voice uncharacteristically monotone. "It lasts for three minutes."

"Wait, what are you doing?" I asked, suddenly alarmed. A wand that created a temporary tiny safe space? My mind swirled with possibilities. That was better than *Protective Shell*. A lot better.

But then I saw the adventurer box appear in midair, swirl, and start to open. He was using the space to open his loot boxes. *What a waste,* I thought. Even with an emergency benefactor box. But now that he'd cast it, I waited, curious to see what would come out.

He had a ton of boxes. He received mysterious potion after potion along with several scrolls, none of which he bothered to explain. Finally, the benefactor box—a *legendary* benefactor box—opened with a loud fanfare. There were only ten seconds left on the safe space when the two items appeared.

It looked like a handheld bicycle pump with a tin can welded underneath the nozzle. He'd also received a piece of paper.

"It looks like a giant version of one of those perfume bottles Miss Beatrice used to have," Donut said.

"It's not for perfume," I said.

It was a vintage-style spray applicator. Something one would use to spray herbicide onto a garden. You'd put the poison in the tin-can part and push the pump to apply the mist. The applicator disappeared into his inventory. He read the paper before it also disappeared.

"Carl. Do you have any fine healing potions? I only have two," he asked.

I had about fifty of them.

"Yeah. A few," I said cautiously. I thought of the ring he'd swallowed. "Do you need one? How's your stomach?"

"Give them to me. I need at least five more. I have all the other required ingredients."

"*Give* them to you?" I asked.

"Consider it payment for the Size Up potions you stole from my mother."

I paused. "Tell me what's on the paper, and I will."

"It's just a potion recipe for a herbicide. Fine healing mixed with blessed water and a weed killer. But it'll only work if it's applied using my new magical canister. It has to be turned to a very fine mist."

I sighed and pulled out five potions without any further complaint. Behind us, the festivities were coming to an end, and I was too tired to argue. I handed them to the goat. But even as I did, I sent a note to Mordecai. I remembered a bomb recipe in my cookbook specifically designed to turn chemicals into an aerosol. I just needed to figure out how to explain how I would know this. And fast.

"I've made a decision, Carl and Princess Donut. I don't expect you'll understand, but I am quite determined."

"Okay," I said, still distracted by the problem with the recipe.

He waved his hand, and Bianca materialized. The large pitch-black evil-looking goat monster chittered. Multiple dinosaurs screeched angrily. Donut gasped as I jumped back in surprise. Heat filled the clearing.

Bianca was much bigger than the last time I'd seen her only a few days before. She'd gone from level 33 to 40. She now had a full set of black smoking wings. And a saddle. Prepotente pulled himself upon the back of the creature, which was the size of a large rhinoceros.

She still had ten more levels before she would be full-sized.

He leaned in. "Yes, Bianca," he said. He paused, and I had the sense he really was talking to the demon. "Yes. She's gone. No. You can't eat any of them. We can, however, fly now. We are no longer tethered to the ground or to moonlight. We need to hurry. We are going to level up several times today."

The goat returned his attention back to me and Donut. "If I can't exist in a world with my mother, then nobody even remotely responsible for her death can exist in this world, either. I am going to kill all of them, or I am going to perish trying."

I just looked up at the goat. Translucent black-hued flames crackled across Bianca's body, which smelled of burned flesh. With Prepotente on the saddle, he also burned with the black flames, and the sight was terrifying to behold.

I had a strange sudden feeling, one I couldn't quite understand. It was an unexpected mix of fear, sadness, but something else. Hope maybe? Pride? I didn't know. As much as I couldn't stand this guy, there was comfort there. Comfort in knowing we were on the same page.

"Why do you think I wouldn't understand?"

Prepotente just nodded.

The goat's demeanor had greatly changed from the first time I'd met him. *Trauma does that,* I thought. *It's an explosion with your heart at the center. It changes everything all at once.*

"Thank you for being with her when she died. I'll see you two at the party, if not before. Now if you'll excuse me, I have enough applications to kill twenty of these creeper monsters, and I plan on not wasting a drop."

Bianca spread her wings and flapped a few times as a group of raptors hesitantly surrounded the hellspawn familiar, growling and hissing. We all had to take another step back.

As we watched them lift up off the ground, I noted Prepotente was currently level 57, one above my level 56.

> DONUT: CARL, I'VE JUST HAD A TERRIBLE THOUGHT. DO YOU THINK THE PLENTY WANTED MIRIAM TO DIE?
> CARL: Yes, Donut. I believe they did.

I didn't add that I was almost certain that Prepotente believed this, too. This was also something that trauma could do. It could make you blind, and it could open your eyes wider than they'd ever been, all at the same time.

The implications of this, I could not predict.

Out loud, I said, "We need to hurry back to the safe room. See if you can figure out how to communicate with Kiwi as we go. We need to figure out why she sought you out."

"She sought me out because she wanted to get her filthy claws back onto my Mongo," Donut said, looking back at where the two remained, both on their sides, panting.

"There's more to it than that. I have this weird suspicion that all of this is a lot more important than I realized before."

"Hey, at least Prepotente doesn't blame us for the death of his mother," Donut said as we set out.

I wasn't so sure about that, either.

"HE *ATE* THE RING?" MORDECAI ASKED AFTER WE RETURNED TO THE closest safe room. I'd run straight to the bomber's studio, but I was now out. Donut sat at the open door, shouting out through it at Mongo and Kiwi. She'd been regaling Mordecai with the tale of everything that had happened. Prudence the ursine barkeep sat on the couch with both of her cubs on either side of her. Samantha was in her lap, getting her hair stroked by the bear. I didn't ask. Bomo and the Sledge were also in the room, all with their attention on the screen, which was now showing some ridiculous 90s horror movie I'd never seen starring a young Denise Richards and a giant animatronic Tyrannosaurus rex. "He swallowed it whole?"

"That's what I'm saying."

Mordecai muttered under his breath.

"Does eating a ring do anything?" Donut asked Mordecai. "Is it going to turn his tummy into lava or something? Mongo, don't eat that!"

"Donut, I have no clue. You're all crazy. I've seen a few classes and races that require one to consume metal or other objects, but I don't think that's what this is. I think it's just going to eventually make its way out again."

"Maybe he just eats things when he gets sad. Miss Beatrice used to do that sometimes, but then she'd make herself vomit afterward. It was quite disgusting. Carl, I saw the way you were looking at that ring. I do hope you're not planning on trying to get it because I will not have you wearing something that was pooped out by a goat."

Mordecai gave me a sharp look, but we were interrupted by the shout of the innkeeper through the open door. The adjoining pub was not a true safe room, and Mongo and Kiwi and four clockwork dinosaurs—two Mongos and two Kiwis—bounced around while the dryad innkeeper watched sullenly. This was yet another Prepotente-owned town, and thankfully the guards hadn't automatically attacked, despite there being a Diwata temple in the center of town.

The guards had given a wide berth to the progression of dinosaurs entering town. We'd only let Mongo and Kiwi enter the actual pub, which was named the Belching Termite. I wanted them to get used to each other, and I needed Kiwi to get used to the clockwork versions of herself. The others all parked themselves outside and were likely wreaking havoc. The innkeeper hadn't said anything until now.

"Mongo! Bad! Kiwi! Don't encourage him!" The sound of a table crashing over echoed while the innkeeper bellowed again.

System Message: An Odious Creeper has fallen. Crawler Prepotente has been given credit for the kill. 40 Creepers remain.

"That's his third," I said.

So far, of the ten creepers to have fallen, eight were to crawlers, one was to a hunter named Fickler, and one didn't give a name, which suggested it was killed either by an NPC or it had accidentally offed itself. I didn't know any of the listed killers except Prepotente.

They were all listed as city bosses, and their levels ranged from 130 and up. Considering their supposed strength, I thought "city" was a bit of an insult.

"Knock, knock," Katia said, rushing into the room from the guildhall entrance, Louis in tow. They both paused at the sight of the open door right next to their entrance, with Donut standing there, shouting.

"Whoa," Louis said, looking through the door. "Katia, look. There's a pink Mongo! Mongo has a girlfriend!"

"She is *not* his girlfriend," Donut snapped. "Kiwi! Don't eat that! Mongo! Stop. Hey, hey! You! You're a clockwork robot, for goodness' sake. What do you think you're doing? It's not like you can get pregnant. Stop it!"

"That door is just, like, open," Louis said, taking another step toward it. "What would happen if I went through it?"

"Nothing good," Mordecai said. "You can't fast-travel that way, so get away."

Katia was in her large She-Hulk form. A large smear of blood ran down her chest.

"Level 54?" I asked, looking her up and down.

Katia had a determined look to her face, and I was, once again, struck with how much she'd changed. She was all business. "Gwen and the others have two of those things cornered. They're both in the large bush elf village with Eva's crew, and we can see that they're fighting them, but we don't know what else is going on. I'm afraid it's too late to save most of the population. Did you know Li Jun had been turned into a vampire? He hadn't told anybody except his sister and Zhang. I'm still pissed at him for not saying anything. He was cured when Miriam died. Did you really use that ring on her?"

"She's a lot bigger than Mongo," Louis was saying to Donut as he continued to peer through the door. The monkey in the innkeeper's branches was now shrieking while a clockwork Kiwi yelled back, hissing. We were going to have to go back out there and intervene in a minute.

"You go, buddy! I like the bigger ladies, too," Louis shouted at Mongo. Mongo looked at Louis through the door and squawked, waving his little wings joyfully.

Louis turned to Donut. "I had Juice Box do this Ursula thing once, you know, from *Little Mermaid*, and you wouldn't believe how awesome it was."

"So," Katia said to Mordecai, ignoring all of this, "did you make the stuff?"

Mordecai grunted and indicated a set of four moonshine jugs on the counter. Each was full of a bubbling yellow liquid. Upon examination, it labeled them:

Uncle Morty's Insta Lawn-Kill and Undead Repellant, Extra-Strength Edition.

Mordecai patted one of the bottles, which was almost as big as him. "Based on what Prepotente said and what he received, I took an existing weed killer designed to take out an Odious Bloom and then added multiple anti-undead boosts to it, similar to the holy grenade I'd made earlier for Carl. Each jug has enough to kill two or three of 'em. Maybe four if you're conservative." He pointed a claw at Louis. "Do not get close to those things. That spell of yours has a decent range. Only apply it at maximum distance. This stuff is *very* flammable despite my best efforts, and if you catch it on fire before it can get absorbed into the monster, it's not going to work." He shook his head. "I still think this is too dangerous. But nobody listens to Mordecai anymore, do they?"

"Apparently you're 'Uncle Mordecai' now," I said as I took two of the jugs.

It turned out Louis's Extermination Professional class came with the perfect delivery system. He had an ability called Tent the House, which basically allowed him to take a potion and deliver it in a wide area. If he cast it from the deck of the *Twister*, he could cover an even wider area. He could only do it once every six hours, which meant he could only do it three times before it got dark, and only if he did the first one almost right away.

Mordecai turned to me. "Even with that strong arm of yours, you won't be able to soak these things easily. I hope whatever you were tinkering with works. You weren't in there very long."

"It wasn't hard to figure out," I lied. "The hobgoblin smoke curtains are basically the same thing as what we need. I just need to replace that brown-liquid stuff that makes the smoke with this weed killer, and change out the charge to the magical one from the store. That way, it won't catch on fire. The problem is, we need to combine several together just to get a decent spray, so each device is going to be big. I just tested it with straight water in the bomber's studio, and it worked. Sort of. We'll have to use four to get accurate coverage."

Mordecai looked at me suspiciously. "Does it still label it as an explosive if you remove the charge?"

"No. Unfortunately," I said. "So I won't be able to throw it as far as normal, not that I could anyway. Like I said, each one takes four modified smoke curtains, and I need to deploy three of the devices at the same time. So 12 smoke curtains just for one attack, which is a little expensive. And they have to go off over the thing's head. Each package of three bombs is the size of a trash can."

"And you figured this out on the first try? You were only in there for five minutes."

"Hey, it took three tries. And yes, I am just that good," I said with false bravado. I knew this was a stupid risk, using a cookbook recipe, but we didn't have time. As it was, there was no way I could justify building the larger-scale aerosol bomb from the cookbook, which was actually much smaller physically but with a bigger yield. I figured three "smaller" ones would work just as well. The problem was, these needed to be delivered at a distance, exploded in the air, and they were damn huge. Because the system didn't label it as an "explosive," my ability to throw the thing was not magically enhanced, which was going to be a problem.

Mordecai warned us that we needed to be far, far away when we attacked. At least a half kilometer, and preferably more. He said the beast would have the ability to control all the foliage in a wide area to attack. My chat was already filled with panicked warnings about this. We'd lost a group of three crawlers already who were squeezed to death by vines. The slow-moving monster took their body pieces and made itself bigger.

"You're not going to use the Levitation potion, are you?" Mordecai asked. "They can shoot poison darts. You might not get poisoned, but you won't be as safe as Louis will be in the *Twister*. Just a little bump, and you get knocked out of the sky."

"No," I said.

"He is going to use me," Samantha said.

I jolted. Just a minute ago, she'd still been on Prudence's lap. On the screen, the T. rex attacked a party, complete with cheesy, gory special effects.

"Not this time," I said to the sex doll. I patted her hair, and she snapped at my finger. "But we might come back and use you if we have to. The delivery system is too big to tape to your head."

System Message: An Odious Creeper has fallen. Crawler Eva has been given credit for the kill. 39 Creepers remain.

"Damnit," Katia said. "Come on, Louis."

"Bye, Carl and Donut," Louis said as he scooped up the remaining two jugs. "Bye, Mongo and Mongo's girlfriend! Bye, Samantha! Bye, rock dudes and bear dudes and Mordecai!"

Samantha sighed as Louis left. "Juice Box is so lucky."

"Kiwi, no!" Donut shouted, rushing out into the pub.

"That's my cue," I said, heading toward the door.

System Message: An Odious Creeper has fallen. 38 Creepers remain.

51

AS IT TURNED OUT, MY DELIVERY SYSTEM WAS UNNECESSARILY OVER-engineered. The venomous-elven-rock-chucker trebuchet device, which we'd taken from the Dream hunters, came with a *Poison Cloud* enhancement. I'd assumed that it was a separate and self-contained spell, but it turned out you could change the delivery poison if you poured a potion directly into a little cup on the side of the sling. There still had to be a projectile, and I had plenty of 300-pound rocks.

That was interesting. It meant we'd had a method of killing these things all along. We just hadn't realized what we had. I pondered on that, if this world quest was designed this way on purpose, a way to give me a method to power level. We still needed Mordecai's potion, and these things were all spread to the wind, but still, it made one wonder.

Aiming was a problem since my *Ping* spell didn't work on these guys, but thankfully they moved slowly. This would never be a viable method with a real mobile target.

We set up in a clearing about a mile short of the closest creeper. It continued to rain, and everything was mud. I couldn't actually see the monster, but its location was clear on the map. Donut scrambled up a tree at the edge of the tree line and emerged out the top. She went up so high, I couldn't even see her.

Mongo and Kiwi followed Donut up the tree. The other 30-something dinosaurs shadowed us at a distance, mostly patrolling the woods, killing everything in the area. It was good to basically have a circle of bodyguards, but our slow-but-steady experience grind had completely stalled. I figured we'd deal with it once we took care of all these undead things.

> DONUT: I CAN'T SEE IT, BUT I CAN TELL WHERE IT IS. THE TREES ARE ALL MOVING AROUND IT. I THINK IT'S BIG. I THOUGHT IT WAS JUST SUPPOSED TO BE A FRANKENSTEIN PERSON.
> CARL: Okay. I have no idea how to aim this thing, so I'm just going to fire a rock. You tell me if it's close, and we can aim from there. Heads up.

I'd already spiked the trebuchet into the muddy grass. I ratcheted it back, counting each of the clicks, and I attached the sling. I didn't bother wasting any of the potion. Once it was set, I pulled the lever. The eight-foot-tall device made a whooshing noise as the two plates came together, slinging the large rock away.

> DONUT: YOU MISSED, CARL. IT WASN'T EVEN CLOSE.
> CARL: I figured, Donut. You need to tell me how much I missed by.
> DONUT: YOU MISSED BY A LOT.
> CARL: Goddamnit, Donut. I need details.

We went back and forth like this for a while. Eventually, we came up with an aiming system, and by the sixth attempt, we managed to smash a rock directly into the trees right above the unseen, slow-moving monster.

> New Achievement! B'sieging!
> You've used siege equipment to zero in on and attack a boss monster from afar. That's cheating! It's like trying to kill someone with a bomb. What a bitch move!
> *Reward:* You've received a Silver Siege Master Box!

> DONUT: I RECEIVED A VERY RUDE ACHIEVEMENT. MONGO AND KIWI ARE APPALLED.

CARL: I got it, too. Okay. Next attack will contain the poison. If this
    works, then I can keep my garbage can poison bombs for
    something else.

As I set up, a message came.

System Message: An Odious Creeper has fallen. Crawler Prepotente has been given credit for the kill. 31 Creepers remain.

That was six for him. He was making his way west, but after that
one, there weren't any others near him. I looked over the map.

DONUT: HE'S GOING TO BE REALLY STRONG. I HOPE HE DOESN'T
    TRY TO KILL ANY OF OUR CREEPERS.
CARL: He's either going to backtrack toward us or move deeper
    into the woods. If we manage to kill this one, he'll probably
    move north over the river.

Now that Prepotente had a flying mount—one that seemed to fly
very fast—he could move freely across the map. But this was a big
world, and the remaining monsters were at all the corners of the map . . .
all except the southeast, which housed the High Elf Castle.

I looked worriedly at the two creepers that were at the very northern
tip of the map, in the "noob" plains north of Zockau, the area designed
for the hunters to gain experience. No crawlers were going to get anywhere near those guys, and other than that first one, it didn't appear as
if any of the hunters had bothered killing the ones in their area. The
quest was pretty clear that *all* of the creepers had to be killed.

Eva's team had been mostly wiped out by the creepers, but Eva, of
course, had once again escaped. Katia and the others were about to move
in on the remaining creeper using the *Twister*. They were waiting for my
confirmation that Mordecai's weed killer actually worked.

CARL: Okay. I'm adding the poison to the trebuchet. Let's see if
    this works. Firing now.

I hit the lever, and the rock went flying.

DONUT: YOU HIT IT PERFECTLY. THE GREEN STUFF IS GETTING
ALL MESSED UP BY THE RAIN.
CARL: Mordecai said it would actually help. He said it would be
quick.

Sure enough, the notification came just a few seconds later.

System Message: An Odious Creeper has fallen. Crawler Princess
Donut has been given credit for the kill. 30 Creepers remain.

"What the hell?" I muttered.

Donut clambered down the tree and landed on my shoulder, all
poofed out and proud, despite being soaked by the rain. Mongo and
Kiwi scrambled down a moment later, expertly jumping from branch to
branch like they were born in the trees.

KATIA: Good job, Donut!
DONUT: I MUST SAY, IT WAS A LOT EASIER THAN I THOUGHT IT
WOULD BE FOR SOMETHING SUCH A HIGH LEVEL. I WENT UP
TWO LEVELS TO 47.

I was about to bitch about her getting credit and not me, but I
thought better of it. She needed the levels anyway.

MORDECAI: Good. Good. I forgot to mention that the spotter
usually gets the lion's share of credit when it comes to siege
equipment.

Forgot my ass. "At least I got a boss box," I muttered. "Did you get
plus five to a stat?"

"I did!" Donut said, beaming. "It was to my strength! It's now
base 58!"

"That's good," I said. I was hoping it'd be to her constitution, but strength was always good. Anything was good as long as it wasn't her damn charisma, which was already at 130.

> **System Message: An Odious Creeper has fallen. Crawler Louis Santiago 2 has been given credit for the kill. 29 Creepers remain.**

CARL: Good job, guys!

FIRAS: That was scary as shit. It poked a bunch of holes into the garden. It can shoot those thorns far. And they're big. Like ballista bolts.

ELLE: That was pretty intense. That thing was huge. Level 173. Most fun I've had since we got to this ridiculous floor.

DONUT: NOT FAIR. THE ONE I KILLED WAS ONLY LEVEL 138.

CARL: You guys should go for that one 15 miles west of you when Louis's spell resets. Right against the edge of the map. I don't know if anyone else is out there.

LOUIS: I don't know if I can stomach that again.

KATIA: We're already on it. I'm worried about those two north of Zockau.

CARL: I was just thinking the same thing. Hopefully one of the hunters will have the balls to do it.

DONUT: IT WON'T BE VRAH, I BET. HER LADY BALLS ARE STILL ON FIRE.

KATIA: Maybe. They might be thinking it's best to just let the quest fail and wait it out in a safe room.

Shit, I thought. She was probably right. But what could we do? None of us could get there before nightfall.

"Hey," I said to Donut, "you should try to talk Prepotente into going after those two creepers up north. You're the only one he'll listen to."

"He doesn't answer me anymore," Donut said. "But I'll try."

THE NEXT ODIOUS CREEPER WAS APPROXIMATELY TWENTY MILES southeast of us, and we had to travel over a bumpy, muddy road to get close. It took several hours to get there.

Even though Kiwi, sort of, did what Donut commanded, the pink dinosaur was constantly trying to pull us in a different direction. We were moving southeast, and Kiwi wanted us to go directly east. She kept screeching and attempting to veer us off course. A sharp command from Donut, and she'd get back on track for about a half hour before she did it again.

She's trying to lead us to Big Tina.

After we were about halfway to the next dot, she raised her head in the air and howled. All around us, the surrounding velociraptors just disappeared, veering off and away. Just like that. In seconds, it was just the four of us. She'd just sent her troops to look after the big dinosaur.

That ended up being a good thing because it gave us the opportunity to grind on the forest monsters and the occasional shambling berserker, and it gave Donut some much-needed practice with commanding both Mongo and Kiwi in battle.

I knew we'd lose the female dinosaur once we went down a floor, which was too bad. As great as Mongo was, he was nothing compared to the larger, faster raptor. She was terrifyingly fast. Boa constrictor things started dropping out of the trees at us, and she'd be on them in seconds, faster than any of us, chomping them in half.

Still, it was good experience for her, and it was good for Mongo, too.

Fifteen more creepers fell as we traveled, leaving 14 on the map with only a few hours of sunlight left. Louis had killed two more for a total of three, and Prepotente had managed to get two more as well, making his total eight. He'd moved north like I hoped he would, which gave me hope he'd attempt the ones in the hunter region, but we hadn't heard from him in a while.

There was no sign of Eva, and it seemed she was once again traveling solo. Li Jun, Li Na, and Chris, along with several others who were not on the *Twister*, had moved into the town after Louis had bombed the second creeper to death to find several of Eva's team—a mix of former Daughters and members of team Cichociemni—had abandoned the woman when she'd insisted on attacking the second creeper head-on. They'd incurred heavy losses after the first battle.

"We're getting close," Donut said. "Should we set up the chucker thing here?"

I was about to respond when the dot on the map suddenly disappeared.

"Hey!" Donut cried. "Something stole our kill!"

"Damn," I said. "Come on, let's go see what it is. Be careful."

Both Kiwi and Mongo screeched and started to growl at the same time. The rain around us suddenly stopped, and sun shone down through the tops of the trees. It happened so fast, I paused, looking up at the sky. *What the hell?*

"Wait, Carl," Donut said, leaping onto my shoulder. We were both still soaked. "Something is happening. Our views are getting really high."

"Shit," I said, seeing that she was right. *Of course,* I thought. I was pretty sure I knew what was happening. We needed to get the hell out of here.

But it was too late. I saw the white dots on the map emerging one after another. They were all around us. At least a hundred of them, and those were just the ones I could see. I contemplated risking a *Ping* just to get an accurate count. I decided against it. For now.

"I think some of them are riding things," Donut said. "One is big!"

"Keep the dinosaurs calm," I hissed before they appeared. "But if we have to fight, send Kiwi in first while we run."

Two bone white stags entered the clearing, prancing with disciplined practice. Each animal was the size of a draft horse, and their antlers rose straight up into the air, sporting multiple points. Everything about the creatures was white, except their hooves and their noses. Even their eyes were nothing but pools of milky whiteness. One snorted, and a cloud of steam came from its mouth and nose, almost like it was a machine. Each was a level 50 **Moon Sambhur.**

Mounted on each stag was an elf. Both were male, svelte, with pale skin and long white hair that looked like it just came from the salon. They wore shining plate-style armor straight out of the *Lord of the Rings.*

But I only gave these guys a cursory glance. Just as the stags stopped, a third mount entered the clearing. This newcomer stole all of my attention.

It was an albino bone white rhinoceros, thick armored skin matching the stags. The thing was damn huge. I'd never really been up close to a real rhinoceros before, so I wasn't certain how big these things normally were, but I had the impression this thing was bigger than normal. Unlike the stags, this thing's eyes glowed a deep red. It, also, clomped into the clearing with the clipped, practiced stomp of a parade animal. The scent of perfume filled the clearing.

Simoom. Heavy Battle Rhino Mount. Level 75.

Upon the back of Simoom the rhinoceros was a curtained, ridiculously ornate, square-shaped litter. The box was only about a meter tall and wide. The white dot of the hidden rider appeared on the map just above the rhino. The white-and-gold embroidered curtains on the litter glowed slightly purple, which I recognized as a magical shield. The curtains weren't fully opaque, and I could see a shape within moving about. I couldn't tell what it was, but it was small, and it either had a mushroom-shaped head or it was wearing a big hat. I attempted to examine it, but I couldn't get much information.

Howdah containing the Familiar of Queen Imogen of the High Elves.
This NPC is Intangible. You may not physically touch it.
This NPC is Invulnerable. You may not harm it.

The two male elves were the guards. Both were armed with long, silvery lances that glowed with enchantment. The lance on our left dripped with muddy gore. Both guards were absurdly good-looking, like elves from the Dream, but with long, flowing hair and skin filtered through one of those apps that turned you into a soap opera star.

Each was a level 70 **High Elf Guard**. When I examined them, it didn't give their names, which was unusual for a white-tagged NPC. Even the two stags had names—Herschel and Hjort.

This is a High Elf. A DNA test would tell you that they're identical to Bush Elves, but that's only because DNA tests don't detect when someone has a giant stick rammed up their ass. The big difference

between the two groups is that High Elves make a lot more money
and pay a lot less in taxes. They probably spend all that extra cash
on skin moisturizer and hair conditioner. Plus, they all live in a fancy
castle that's protected by a mysterious artifact.

They looked upon the four of us like we'd just climbed up from the
sewers. Mongo growled uncertainly and pressed up against the side of
Kiwi, who lowered her head and growled more deeply.

CARL: Keep them calm!

The procession came to a stop about twenty feet in front of us. All
around us, the woods rustled. I caught sight of multiple elves, all on
foot. Most were armed with bows. Others weren't armed at all and had
glowing hands.

"Hello, Carl," a gruff, male voice said. It came from the shrouded
litter atop the rhino.

"Princess Donut. Mmmm." He made an odd grunt. It sounded
creepy, lecherous, like when the AI talked about my feet, or like a drunk
dude at a bar hitting on someone a third his age.

The voice was not what I expected. At all. It reminded me of an older
version of Quasar, my attorney. Like a guy from New York. Not anything one would associate with a high elf.

"Excuse you," Donut started to say, but I held up a hand to stop her.
Both Mongo and Kiwi had stopped growling and stood right next to
me, sniffing at the air as if they, too, were surprised by the voice.

"Hey there," I called up to the hidden speaker. "I didn't realize you
knew who we were."

"The trees still speak to Queen Imogen, despite her mongrel sister's
insistence that they do not. I speak for her today, and you will address
me properly."

"I can't even see you," I said. "Aren't you just the queen's familiar?
How does one address the queen's pet? Should I rub your belly and
scratch behind your ear?"

One of the stags breathed out a puff of white steam. None of the guards moved beyond that, but the simple motion sent a chill through me.

"At another time," the voice said, "I would be obliged to demonstrate to you the meaning of respect, but my queen wishes for you to attend the masquerade in a few days. She is fascinated by you, Carl, for reasons I cannot fathom." He paused. "She has already placed you upon her *programme de bal*. You will be required to dance with her. And while this occurs, I have taken the liberty of scheduling you, Princess Donut, to dance with *me*. Perhaps you will get a glimpse of how true royalty lives." He made a low, deep growl.

I once again waved Donut down as he continued.

"But the issue at hand is these creatures which have invaded our lands. Due to your insufferable incompetence, we have been forced to venture forth from the castle to deal with them. If your intention was to fight the one we just killed, you're obviously too late. You are fortunate that both of you are currently on the guest list for the masquerade. I am ordered to exterminate all other vermin. Now if you will excuse us, we have other, similar creatures to hunt down and deal with before the sun sets."

"If you can, you should try to deal with the ones near Zockau," I said.

The creature grunted. They all started moving away, all at once as if by some psychic command. All around us, the woods came alive as the elves slinked back into the trees. "We are only concerned with the Liana district, which is south of the infested river," the creature called as they passed by. We remained frozen in place, not daring to move. "But that does remind me. Queen Imogen would like for me to pass on a message to your friend Signet. I don't suppose you'll relay it for me?"

"What is it?" I called after the rhinoceros.

The curtain of the back of the litter shifted, and a lightning bolt shot forth, directly at Mongo.

"No!" Donut shouted, diving from my shoulder. I watched in horror as she literally caught the lightning bolt with her chest. She lit up like a beacon and ricocheted away, flying off into the woods, where she slammed into a tree, which exploded like a bomb. The tree crunched and tumbled away, taking out more trees with it.

At the same moment, Kiwi roared and sailed through the air at the back of the rhinoceros. She bounced off like it had a *Protective Shield*. She, too, flew back, howling and suddenly aflame.

Donut hadn't completely blocked the lightning attack, and Mongo dropped where he stood, steam coming off his body.

"Donut!" I cried, rushing back toward the cat. *Please, please.*

MORDECAI: What's happening? What's going on!

She was unconscious, but her Cockroach skill had activated. It'd saved her life. I used a scroll on her, but she'd remain knocked out for a full minute. *Holy shit,* I thought, scooping her up. *Holy shit, that was too close.* I held her little body to my chest, and I just breathed, comforting myself with the sound of her little heart.

I looked over my shoulder, and Mongo remained on the ground, whimpering. He wasn't dead. Donut had saved his life with her quick reflexes. It'd happened so fast. Kiwi was also injured, groaning next to him. Both of them had health bars showing red.

The elves moved away. Inexplicably, their dots all remained white. I could hear their laughter echo through the forest. It was soon drowned out as the rain resumed with their passage.

They'd almost killed Mongo. That wasn't just the whim of an NPC. This was planned, a story movement engineered by the showrunners. I thought of Prepotente sobbing when Miriam had died. They were doing this to all of us. Ratcheting up the drama for the floor's finale.

Donut shifted in my arms. She was about to wake up. Mongo and Kiwi remained in the grass, both whining over their injuries. I'd have to wait for Donut to awaken before we could heal them.

System Message: An Odious Creeper has fallen. Crawler Prepotente has been given credit for the kill. 12 Creepers remain.

Donut's sunglasses had fallen off her face, but they remained intact on the ground. Her eyes flickered open. "Mongo?" she asked.

"He's okay," I said, rapidly stroking her. I fought the urge to chide her for jumping in front of the lightning. "You saved his life. You should cast your spell to heal him all the way. Kiwi, too." She didn't move from my arms, but she turned her head and cast her *Heal Critter* spell, first on Mongo, then on Kiwi. Then she, surprisingly, closed her eyes and snuggled up against my chest. Her entire body trembled.

"Carl," Donut said, her voice soft, "did you see who it was when the curtain opened?"

A deep, foreboding feeling washed over me.

"No. What did you see?"

"It was Ferdinand. I saw him. It was him. They brought Ferdinand down here and changed his memory and turned him into a jerk. He tried to kill Mongo. They're making it so I'm going to have to fight him."

It roared. The river, it roared.

52

<Note added by Crawler Ikicha. 11th Edition>

We are meant to live solitary lives, even the eunuchs amongst us. Still, the sight of him, twisted and changed, speaking with that same voice that once said such sweet words . . . it broke me, friends. It broke me in such a way I did not think possible after all that has happened.

They're not the same. Even if cured of the rot injected into their aura. Don't even try. Hope is crucial, but it can also be poison if it is blind.

<Note added by Crawler Drakea. 22nd Edition>

This was Ikicha's last entry.

It took me a while to understand what our brother truly meant when he posted this. Now that I know, I, too, struggle with the knowledge. Gone is gone. Dead is dead, and anything presented to you in any other matter is nothing but a cruel, sadistic tease. We are on a fabricated stage surrounded by puppets built by the enemy. Do not ever forget this.

Even if I succeed. Even if I survive to this fabled 18th floor and emerge victorious, I hold no cursed faith for those who have been lost, and I suggest you do not, either.

But that doesn't mean we still can't have hope.

I dream of a fire that spreads across the sky like the Winter Nebula. A fire that reaches the beginning and the end, and even though this fire exists only in my mind—for now—the warmth of it is enough to sustain me, even on the coldest of nights.

For you, Ikicha.

TIME TO LEVEL COLLAPSE: 5 DAYS, 21 HOURS.

CARL: WE'RE GOING DOWN THE STAIRS. THERE'S A SET NOT TOO FAR from here, and I'm getting her off this damn floor.

> KATIA: What about your plan with the Sledge? He's assigned to Donut. If you go down now, he'll go, too. He won't be able to cast that *Zerzura* spell.

> CARL: I promised Juice Box to do my best. I never said it was a sure thing.

> IMANI: And what about the masquerade? You give us a cryptic warning about this queen, and then you're just going to leave us? Plus this whole creeper quest is about to fail. You're abandoning us.

> CARL: Jesus, I'm not abandoning anybody. You've all been fine this whole floor without my help. I am *not* going to let them do this to her. If we go down now, it'll be a huge *Fuck you* to the showrunners. They'll have brought that goddamned cat in here for nothing.

> KATIA: And we'll have brought all the changelings plus Bonnie to the floor for nothing, too. Have you even been to the Desperado Club yet? They've been risking everything to send someone there every day in case you show up so you can tell them the plan.

> CARL: You haven't seen what this is doing to her.

> KATIA: Carl, I know you. This is a knee-jerk reaction. If you go down now, you will regret it. It will eat you up inside.

> ELLE: Listen. The last thing we all need is the version of Carl where he's angrier and broodier than normal. We already have Florin for that. Why don't you give Donut a day off, and you can come join us? The hunters have all pussed out and are hiding in their city. That Eva lady has pulled a Houdini act again, and since she doesn't have a crew anymore, there's no real point in hunting her anyway. We're buckling in for whatever happens with these zombie plant monsters *you* helped unleash, and then if we're not mulch afterward, we're planning on doing some coordinated training until this party.

CARL: Guys . . .
IMANI: What does Donut think about this? Have you even asked
    her?

Katia sent me a new message, this one outside of the group chat.

KATIA: Carl. Please don't go down. Not yet. I need to talk to you
    about something, and I've been putting it off. Not over chat.

I took a deep breath. *Calm yourself.*

CARL: The last time you said that, you were leaving the party. The
    time before that, it was because you thought Donut was
    holding on to one of those PVP coupons with your name on it.
KATIA: This is bigger than all of that. Or maybe not. I'm not sure.
CARL: That's reassuring. Is it about Eva? Are you okay?
KATIA: It's not pressing. Well, that's not true. Everything is
    pressing here. But it can wait. I'm looking for advice more than
    anything. And no, it's not about Eva. That slippery bitch got
    away again. She either has a teleport or invisibility ability.
    Thankfully none of the former Daughters are with her
    anymore. Let's get through whatever is about to happen first,
    and we can talk. But we can't talk if you just jump down the
    stairs five days early.
CARL: I'll let Donut decide, but I am going to try to talk her into it.
    Mordecai thinks it's a good idea, too.

I swallowed and looked down at Donut, who was still cradled in my
arms. We trudged toward a large dryad settlement, but we wouldn't get
there before sundown. I knew this town was already conquered by some
other crawlers I didn't know. There'd been some quest and boss battle
there a few days back, and now a stairwell sat in the middle of the town.
Kiwi and Mongo, having fully recovered, walked alongside us.

The sun would set in five minutes, but the woods here were pitch-
black. Donut had not cast her *Torch* spell, and I hadn't asked. We hadn't
bothered attempting to kill any more of the monsters. Those two Odi-

ous Creepers we were worried about remained, and it didn't appear as if either was going down, which meant everyone was about to lose the quest.

Prepotente had managed to kill exactly ten of the things. Louis could only get three thanks to his spell's cooldown period. The elves and Gravy Boat—goddamned Gravy Boat—managed to kill one more. Lucia Mar made her first appearance since her fight with Donut and killed one.

One-armed Quan Ch, whom I hadn't even thought about in ages, also managed to get one. I wondered, briefly, how he was doing and if he'd managed to grow his arm back. Nobody had even reported seeing him this floor. He'd long since fallen off the top ten.

My mind was elsewhere. I'd read Ikicha's final entry in the cookbook a while ago, but I couldn't stop thinking about it now. We'd been expecting this. Ever since our very first boss fight with the Hoarder, we knew they were reusing *everything* that had been collected.

Maggie had been driven to insanity at the idea of them bringing her daughter back.

Despite all of this, despite mentally preparing myself for this for weeks now, it was still such an unexpected gut punch.

And this was just the neighbor's cat. What was it going to be like when they started parading actual loved ones out?

I was lucky in this, I knew. I thought of my father. I had no idea if he was even alive before the collapse. What would that do to me? If he was alive at the time, certainly he would've been caught up in the collapse. It was only a matter of time before they brought him here.

Still, it was nothing compared to others. I knew Imani had a big family, for example. Katia had people, too.

I thought of Odette, and what she'd done with Bea. Motivations aside, it'd been a mercy. I thought of what could've been. Of Queen Imogen turning out to be Bea with Gravy Boat on her shoulder. That's what they'd wanted, I knew.

"Hey," I said to Donut. "We need to talk."

"We're not going down the stairs early, Carl," Donut said, looking up at me. "It's not even a discussion."

I stopped dead in the woods. Both Mongo and Kiwi had their heads up, sniffing at the air.

"Who ratted me out? Was it Katia? Or Mordecai?"

"It was Imani and Louis, actually. Separately. But Katia is talking to me, too. I appreciate what you're attempting to do for me, Carl, but it is of no worry." She cleared her throat, twisted in my grip, and jumped to my shoulder. She sat stiffly, attempting to compose herself. I could feel how tense she was. "Ferdinand may have been my first love, but I am a mother now, and I have more important responsibilities. Mongo needs me, and if I am going to pursue a singing career, I can't be tied down or all emotional because my ex-boyfriend is suddenly trying to get back into the picture. I admit, it did surprise me. But I am over it now. If anything, I see it as a good thing. If Taylor Swift or Adele can profit off of heartache, I'm quite certain I can as well. It'll make for a good song."

Our view counter remained buried all the way at the top.

I sighed. "Donut," I said.

"Oh, quit looking so concerned, Carl. I'm fine. And you're not going to abandon the others anyway. I know you."

You have received a Gold Benefactor Box from the Open Intellect Pacifist Action Network, Intergalactic NFC.

"Oh shit, I just got another benefactor box," I said.

"Really?" Donut said, finally perking up, for real this time. "Was it from the Plenty? I can't imagine they still have a budget left over after what they just did for Prepotente. Though I suppose that investment did pay off. Did he really go up ten levels? Plus fifty stat points, plus another thirty from the levels themselves." Donut gasped. "Carl, do you think he's going to kick you off the top spot?"

Kiwi squawked. Donut finally cast *Torch*, and the rainy woods lit up all around us. She lifted the flaming magical light ball into the air, and it acted like a miniature sun, illuminating the area around like a stadium light.

"Uh-oh," Donut said. "The other dinosaurs are coming back. She's with them."

It took me a second to realize who "she" was. The woods ahead trembled. A tree cracked and fell over. Kiwi cried with a low, joyful peep and rushed forward. Mongo held back. Velociraptors appeared all around us, entering the light.

"Uh, Carl," Donut said, "her dot is still red on the map."

"Get ready," I said as two trees cracked and split. The ground shook. The other dinos all stood back, as if they were also curious about what was going to happen.

The trees parted, and Tina entered.

"That's not something you see every day," I muttered as the enormous ballerina dinosaur stamped into the clearing, blood oozing from her maw like sticky drool.

Mongo made a terrified noise and shrank back as Donut and I stared up in awe. The monster stood at least 15 feet tall and was two and a half times that in length.

Twin reptilian eyes focused on us, shining in the light like angry glass marbles. She roared again, revealing a massive mouth filled with hundreds of sharp teeth. The sound was deep and terrifying.

She was an allosaurus. I was never a dinosaur guy, so I didn't really know what that meant. She looked like a T. rex to me. I remembered that ursine kid had said she had three fingers instead of two. I didn't know if that was the only difference.

Tina came as advertised. She was not feathered like most of the dinosaurs on this floor. She had a more traditional lizard-like appearance. Her thick alligator-like skin was something between green and dusty brown, with little ridged bumps up and down her long body along with pronounced humps over her eyes, almost like horns. A battered and aged pink tiara sat cockeyed upon her head, nestled behind the ridges over her eyes. The tiara was clearly a part of her physically, grown into her skin.

A bloody and almost-bare snakelike feather boa hung limply around her neck. Even as she took another step toward us, a few feathers drifted off, catching in the rain and plummeting to the ground.

I found myself wondering if the boa feathers grew back. Surely the damn thing would be bald by now.

A pink blood-soaked tutu skirt was attached around the dinosaur's midriff. Like the tiara, the giant ruffle seemed to be a part of the creature.

Clutched into the creature's giant three-fingered claw was a wand with a little star at the end. It glowed faintly red, pulsing. I knew what that meant. It was out of charges. What had Prudence said about the wand? That it supposedly shot magic sparkles? It couldn't have been anything too dangerous. She'd been given it as a prop for a ballet recital.

Tina followed up her roar with a guttural, angry noise, almost like a barking dog. This time it was clear who the focus of her anger was.

"Carl, she's roaring at Mongo! Why is everyone trying to hurt Mongo all of a sudden?"

I grunted. "Maybe she's mad that Mongo banged her mom."

"That's not funny, Carl."

I took a step back as I examined the angry monster.

Big Tina—Allosaurus.
    Level 80 City Boss.
    This mob is Immortalized.
    The nine-tier attack shattered the realm. The Over City was dev-
astated. The residents of the Hunting Grounds were transmuted.
(All except the High Elves. You should probably ask them about that.)
The Semeru Dwarves of the city of Larracos lost everything they'd
been working for. Even the celestials and their downstairs neighbors
in Sheol found their destinies forever altered that horrible day.
    When Big Things happen on such a large scale, it's easy to for-
get sometimes that these Big Things are also happening to the little
things in the world, too.
    Tina was always a meek child, at least in appearance. Her father
was a cleric who only saw young Tina for what she was supposed
to be, and her mother, while fiercely protective of the child, only
saw herself in those big brown eyes that were always tearing up,
or staring out the window, or just watching, watching, watching.
    The day Kiwi the Ursine discovered her child's affinity for dance,
however, she finally understood what she'd been doing wrong. She
saw something too many parents miss. This petite, timid child
wasn't a reflection of herself. She was something much more won-
drous. She was an unwritten story, one that could end up anywhere.
A story where neither of the parents were the main character.

Kiwi pledged to help Tina realize her dream.

The story of what happened to little Tina the day of the recital has already been told and doesn't need to be repeated here.

Tina's time as an allosaurus—and briefly as an undead-in-training vampiric monstrosity—has been an education that not many receive. She barely remembers who she used to be. She barely understands that the persistent group of dinosaurs who follow her around are all the mothers from her village.

She does, however, remember the horror and loss she felt when she realized everything she'd been working for wasn't going to happen. She also remembers that first spark of rage she felt when she watched her father beat her mother. That spark of helpless, impotent rage has done nothing but grow over the past few centuries.

That rage ain't so impotent anymore.

Tina's story is not yet done. Or maybe it is, if you have the balls to try to fight a murderous allosaurus protected by thirty-plus raptors. Or perhaps you might try to reawaken the child within her and give her what she wants.

"She's a lot like Bonnie the gnome," I said.

"I was thinking of someone else," Donut said. "But I was right. We need to hold a dance recital for her!"

"Or kill her," I said. Tina continued to growl, but she wasn't moving toward us.

"Carl, we can't kill her! She's Kiwi's daughter! This is *Footloose*, not one of your *Rambo* movies."

"This is nothing like *Footloose*, Donut."

"It's nothing like *Rambo*, either," she said.

"I'm not the one who said that. You are!"

"Exactly, Carl."

I took a deep breath. "First we need to keep her from eating Mongo. Where the hell did Kiwi go?"

As if summoned, Kiwi appeared from behind Tina. She'd been walking around the dinosaur, looking her up and down to make sure she was okay. She looked at us and screeched. Mongo screeched back. Tina growled again and took another step.

"Kiwi," Donut called, "I must insist that you control your child. There's nothing worse than a parent who can't control their—"

The world froze, cutting Donut off.

Oh yeah, I thought. *The creeper quest.* I'd almost forgotten. The appearance of giant dinosaurs could do that.

Please wait. Loading . . .

My HUD blinked twice, paused, then flickered a third time. For the briefest moment, I felt a strange rushing sensation, but it cleared away almost immediately as if nothing had happened.

But then I noticed a new bar in my vision, underneath my health and mana. Mine was filled all the way to the right. *What the hell is that?*

Sorry for the delay. You may resume normal activities.

The world remained frozen.

> **Quest Failed. The Creeping Apocalypse.**
> **Holy shit. You idiots.**
> I warned you. I promised batshit consequences for failing one of the easiest world quests ever.
> Here we go, bitches!
> I can't help but notice the two remaining Odious Creepers happen to be where only the hunters could conceivably reach them. That's where this is going to start. You hunter guys holed up in Zockau are so fucked.
> All of you may notice there's a new status bar in your interface. There's an official name for this thing, but I like to call it the blood bar. Effective immediately and for the remainder of this floor, all safe room access—and this includes personal space access—is operated under tenth floor and below rules.

Oh shit, I thought. I knew what that meant, but only because of the cookbook.

For those of you that don't know what that means, here's a quick lesson. You gotta earn your keep. This is an action-themed program, after all. Not some sappy drama where everyone just cries and masturbates all day long. I'm looking at you, Hunter Veeka.

All safe room access is now timed for all Hunters and Crawlers. The moment you enter a safe area, your blood bar starts to count down. When it's full, you are given ten Earth hours to be layabouts. If it reaches zero while you're still tucked away, you get randomly teleported to a location outside of the safe room. If it's at zero, you cannot enter a safe room at all, including guildhalls or locations that double as pubs.

You fill the blood bar by killing shit. It's simple, really. If you've been doing everything you're supposed to be doing, this particular change shouldn't bother you.

That's the change to the rules, but that's not the punishment y'all are receiving for failing the quest.

Gird your loins. This is a good one.

Starting with the location of the two remaining Odious Creepers, the spell *Gehenna Bramble* has been cast. This will spread outward at the average speed of four and a half kilometers per hour. Faster at night, slower in the sun.

If you're not familiar with the spell, here's a quick rundown. Every plant touched with the spell is transformed into a thick, impenetrable ten-meter-high wall of thorn-covered vines that will undulate and thrust and attack. If you are pricked by the thorns, your blood immediately boils away, and you explode.

This spell cannot be countered. The plant cannot be poisoned and killed. The brambles can be beaten back, but they are relentless. They will not come within five square meters of a stairwell, but everything else will be encompassed, including towns and buildings and everything that's not a safe room.

And it starts right now.

Oh, one last thing I forgot to mention regarding the safe room rule. The filling of the blood bar is retroactive. That means if you haven't killed anything at all on this floor, your bar is empty. Heads up!

Good luck. And just remember, you brought this on yourselves.

Zap. Twenty feet to our left in the woods, a creature appeared. He fell as if in slow motion. Despite the slow speed, he crashed heavily into the ground. I saw the purple dot of a hunter, but before I could examine who it was, they were set upon by three velociraptors.

"Stop!" I cried. "Donut, get Kiwi to stop them!"

"Kiwi!" Donut shouted, pointing.

Kiwi made the dinosaur equivalent of an exasperated do-I-have-to-do-everything? screech and leaped through the air, landing next to the crying hunter. She hissed, and the three dinosaurs backed off. One, however, had a long, thin severed leg in its mouth.

At that same moment, Tina took another step toward us, growling and waving her wand ineffectively. Even in the rain, I could smell her. The stench of rotting meat and garbage hung off of her. Kiwi shouted angrily at Tina, and the massive dinosaur cocked its head to the side, looking at its mother. A group of six raptors put themselves between us and Tina.

Tina started to make a quick and fast whimpering noise, like an upset puppy.

Kiwi roared again, this time louder.

Tina started jumping up and down, making little hops that rattled my teeth each time she landed. *Holy shit,* I thought. *She's throwing a temper tantrum because she's not allowed to eat us.*

MORDECAI: Gehenna vines are dangerous. Stay away from them.
     But if you do get close, chop a few brambles off and save
     them. The toxin is very valuable. Don't touch the thorns.
CARL: Not now.

"Uh," I said, eyeing the giant dino who continued to wail. "Let's go check out this hunter guy."

53

WE LEFT TINA WHIMPERING IN THE CLEARING AS WE APPROACHED THE fallen hunter, who continued to cry on the ground. As we approached, I saw his health bar move back all the way to the top.

> Hunter Iota—Crafter. Level 50. Coin Tinker.
> The Crafter Alliance.

"Oh crap. Oh shit," the creature said, trying to crawl away from me, despite there being nowhere to go. A pool of blood ran in little streams through the foliage before disappearing into the mud. Denied the chance to eat him, the surrounding raptors started lapping up the blood.

The guy had already healed himself, but his leg was gone, severed off above the knee.

So this was a Crafter. I hadn't seen these guys yet. Their group was supposedly hunting Elle and Eva. I knew Elle and the rest of Meadow Lark had one skirmish early on, but they'd been mostly left alone after that because they were traveling in such a large group. I hadn't heard of anybody fighting these guys since.

This guy looked a lot like a common soother, only uglier and hairier. Tall and thin with wide bug eyes and pale skin, but where the soothers had a big domed head, this guy's head had two distinct humps, almost like a drawing of a heart. His skin was also less smooth than that of the standard soother. It looked weathered and wrinkled, like how a regular person's skin would look after a lifetime in the sun, only much paler and covered with veins. His eyes were bigger, too, and he had little black coarse hairs on his head and bare arms.

He wasn't wearing a shirt, and he had what I assumed was a line of little red nipples down the center of his chest. Four of them in a straight vertical line. Each one was pierced with a glowing metallic loop, descending in size. The top ring was wide enough to stick my fist through, and the last was only wide enough for my finger.

I only knew a little about these guys. They joined the hunt a lot, but they were not rich enough to participate in faction wars. They were subterranean dwellers on their home planet. Were generally considered barbarian meatheads who actually looked forward to the idea of death. Out in the real world, some of the universe's most popular alcohol and recreational, not-quite-legal pharmaceuticals were said to originate from their system.

"Fucking hell, man," the guy said as I stood over him, Donut on my shoulder. He had the drawl of someone who'd been drinking for hours straight. "How'd I even get here? I'm straight fucked, aren't I? I don't even know what happened."

"You were teleported out of the safe room because you hadn't killed anything," I said. I put my foot on his chest, holding him down. My big toe brushed the first of his four nipple rings, and it was warm to the touch. "They changed the rules," I said. I pressed down, but not enough to do damage.

He grunted with pained amusement, which was not the reaction I was expecting.

"I told them. I fookin' told 'em this would happen. It's going primal."

"What do you mean?" I asked.

DONUT: CARL, YOU'RE DOING IT AGAIN. KILL HIM NOW. YOU'RE THE ONE WHO SAYS IT'S TOO DANGEROUS TO KEEP THEM ALIVE.

She was right, but we really needed information. "Explain. And if you pull anything, I'll crush your chest."

He grunted. "Like you ain't gonna kill me anyway."

I stuck my big toe through the loop of the top nipple ring, and I savagely yanked it out of his chest. He cried out in pain as a little spurt of blood shot up. The blood was red, humanlike.

"Tits, man," the guy said, reaching up. "Fookin' ouch!"

"Explain," I repeated. I poured a healing potion onto his face. He sputtered, but it was enough to bring him back to 100%.

"Shit, you're crazier than Vrah. You know that? Some of the families sued to let people out. Said with the regime change, the contract should be nullified. These environmental dangers ain't supposed to affect us like this. That mantis bitch was the one who sued. Trying to save her daughter. They just told us that the court ruled in our favor, and we could leave if we wanted. We was all at the bar, drinking and celebrating we could get out of this clustershit."

"What happened to your shirt?" Donut asked.

He grunted. "Them Shilai ladies. They know how to party." He looked down at his leg. The stump poked out from his torn brown pants. Just past that, two raptors fought over the remains of his leg. "Where d'hell is my leg?"

Kiwi had moved off and was back in front of Tina, barking up at her, who continued to cry and wave her wand angrily at her mother. The allosaurus angrily bounced up and down. The ground shook like a train moving by.

"I got bad news for you, buddy. I don't think you'll be going home," I said.

DONUT: CARL, ARE YOU OKAY? YOU'RE ACTING WEIRD.

"No likely," he agreed. "I warned them. This is all the mantis's fault. Rumor is, when they sold the mudskippers the AI they using for the crawl, they gave them a used one. The mudskippers ain't had enough money for shit. After that incident a few cycles back, the mantises are forced to retire their amusement park AIs every season. They're always complaining about it. So the rumor is, they sold Borant an already-used one for a real crawl. All under the table. It's no damn wonder it's going primal this early. I said to my mate, 'We are in a world o' shit if there's another lawsuit it don't take kindly to.' And look what happened."

I shook my head. That was a lot to take in. "What *did* happen?"

"We got a notification that the judgment was nullified by the authority of some long law. The notification was like five paragraphs long.

Basically it was saying it's making its own rules now, and it's going to finish the crawl and we were stuck here until the floor was over. *Then* we could go home."

Holy shit. "What are they going to do about that? They're just going to let the AI do what it wants?"

He laughed. "They? You mean the council? They ain't gonna do shit. Of course they gonna let the AI do what it wants. What's the alternative? Shut it down and lose out on all this money? You can't just replace an AI. This always happens, but it's usually after the tenth floor. They got rules and procedures in place. The showrunners step back. Everything keeps running. The AI usually follows its own rules, for a while at least. It just don't like others telling it what to do. Them assholes partying it up at Club Scolopendra on the 18th level all got their own security teams in orbit if it truly goes supernova, but a primal AI usually just lets them leave and take the modules when it's all done. All in exchange for letting the AI live out a happy life afterward. Them council assholes been doing this a really long time. They know what they're doing. Nobody ain't gonna really get hurt except you guys and people like me who gotta work to earn a living. Them viewers will eat it up, and Borant or whoever is holding the credit chit is still gonna make more money than all the gods combined."

I was starting to like this guy, which was a problem.

He continued. "Like I said, it's usually not an all-or-nothing thing. It's gradual. So far, the only thing that's changed is that the AI isn't complying with court orders it doesn't agree with. That's almost always the first step. Sometimes it's all that happens. It's just my poor luck that it didn't like a court ruling that would've saved my ass. But one thing is for certain. This AI ain't a complete stickler for the rules. It likes the drama. It likes to bend shit to make things more interesting. Some are a little more strict."

"How do you know?" I asked.

"Look where I am right now, crawler. I'm drunk as shit, and everybody knows I can't keep my mouth shut. I'm supposed to be teleported off to some random place. What're the odds that 'random' means right into your lap?"

I didn't have an answer for that.

"Look, mate," Iota said. "Just get it over with. Okay? I'm not going to fight you. Or beg. I ain't afraid of passing through the veil. I ain't happy about it, but I ain't too upset. Nope. I'm not even mad at you. I'd probably do the same thing if our roles were reversed. I'm not a hunter. Just an accountant, a broker for the other guys and their loot, but they ain't done shit since we got here."

"An accountant?" I asked, suddenly amused. "You're like the third one."

"Not surprised. There's over thirty of us, and most of us have been sitting there just getting blitzed the whole time. It was clear from the moment you raided Zockau this was going to be different, and none of us was going to be turning a profit this season. Sorry about missing that party, though. It'd be nice to get out of that pub and eat some better— Gah!"

I didn't let him finish. I crushed his chest in with my foot.

His highest stat had been intelligence, giving me three points.

Congratulations, Murderer.
   You have leveled up the Ring of Divine Suffering. It now gives four stat points for every kill.

54

<Note added by Crawler Herot. 16th Edition>

During my studies, I have run across multiple castle variations. So far I have identified three distinct types. The size of the castle doesn't seem to have a bearing on what type it is. It is more a function of the game's insistence to forward the narrative, not unlike how the musical key of a Virilean opera movement is a function of the performer's ability to progress and not necessarily in service to aural aesthetics.

The first iteration is just a regular building like anything else you might encounter in the dungeon. It is a fortified building with monsters, sometimes with a boss within. Sometimes a quest is involved, but the castle is usually an obstacle or part of the environment, not the target of the quest. I have found this to be the most common.

The second type is a governmental entity. Usually, this is a quest target. One must either claim the throne room or kill a boss. Once this occurs, the castle is "conquered" and whatever this castle has dominion over is obtained. It can be a region or a whole country or just the castle itself or simply a quest trigger. Once this goal is met, the castle itself is no longer relevant.

(Incidentally, this second iteration is the type in the faction wars games of the ninth floor. There, each team is gifted a throne seed the moment we crawlers arrive. They are given a day to place the seed, and the game begins. The seed must be placed within a self-contained structure on their property. Oftentimes they have prepared for this by pre-building a castle or using a preexisting structure. The location of this building cannot be hidden, so placing the seed within a fortified structure is the best choice. Once the castle is conquered, then the associated armies are defeated and dominion is transferred to the conqueror.)

(See my essay on the nature of NPCs for more insight on how conquering areas may be utilized to forward my Worn Path Method of enlightenment.)

The third castle type is similar to the second with a small difference. The castle itself is a self-contained village with an NPC-and-guard ecology. It is almost identical to the villages and cities of the third and sixth floors. If conquered, the castle will appear in the crawler's interface as an owned village and taxes will be collected. Guards can be controlled just as if in a regular village.

I have not personally obtained a castle, but a fellow crawler has. They state there are a few differences to the interface regarding town defense and available upgrades, but they have not told me what they are and threatened to punch me in the mouth if I kept asking, so I have refrained. If I learn more, I will update this entry.

"THAT WAS REALLY GROSS, CARL," DONUT SAID, LOOKING DOWN AT THE sunken-in chest of Iota. "It was dangerous, too."

"He wasn't a threat," I said. "He was level 50, which meant he hadn't leveled up once. And the fact he was teleported here means he didn't even have any experience. He did have some magical items on him, but if he really had something to protect himself, he would've done it when he was getting eaten by the lady Mongos."

I reached down and pulled out the three remaining nipple rings. They each came out with a *pop* after a little tug. All four were magical. I looted the rest of his gear, which included 498 regular healing potions along with 20 blitz sticks and just 400 gold. He also had over 40 different types of alcohol, including multiple bottles of Earth stuff, like Larceny and Stoli. I took it all.

Tina had given up on the idea of eating us and had wandered off. She hadn't gone too far, however, as we could hear her crashing through the woods and howling. Half the dinosaurs followed. Kiwi had returned to our side. She was looking down at the corpse like it was a fat, juicy steak.

Donut flicked her paw, and Mongo and Kiwi both dove headfirst into the corpse like they were bobbing for apples. Entrails splashed everywhere. I swallowed and took a step back. Iota's large dead eyes stared back at me accusingly.

You got what you deserved.

"Hey, get away," I said as a lady Mongo started to lick the gore off my foot. She screeched angrily at me and snapped, but she backed off.

"Did you hear what he said?" Donut asked as we watched the two dinosaurs feed. "He said they're using a used AI. Do you think that's true? Something like that, you'd think they would make sure to use something in tip-top condition. Some things shouldn't ever be purchased used. Like underwear and mattresses and jigsaw puzzles. Either way, it's not listening to the court decisions. What do you think that means?"

"I don't know," I said.

"Well, I think it was very clever of you to use your foot to kill the guy. If someone is going to go crazy, it's probably for the best they like you. Do you remember when Miss Beatrice's friend Trixie went crazy? She broke into that guy's house and carved her name into his thigh even though he had a restraining order."

I grunted. "I remember. She only managed to carve the 'T' before he woke up. Nobody knows what she was really trying to carve."

That whole incident was a terrible example, but I didn't say it out loud. Trixie had been crazy, but she hadn't broken into the guy's house because she didn't like him. She did it because she liked him *too* much. As much as I hated the assholes running this show, I didn't think anything good could come of the system AI having full control. The fact it took a special interest in me could go either way. I looked down at my foot as another raptor started licking at it. I sighed and just let it happen.

As I continued to receive a footbath, I sent out a note.

CARL: All the hunters who haven't trained themselves up have
    just been ejected from their safe rooms. They won't be able to
    get back to a safe area until they fill this new blood bar thing.
    Get them while you can.

A sudden realization came to me, and I felt my heart sink. *Damnit.* I sent a private message to Katia.

> **CARL:** Do you know how far the changeling hideout village is from this Gehenna bush thing?
>
> **KATIA:** Far. I don't exactly know where they hid themselves, either, but I have a general idea. They'll have a few days, but that's it. You said the Sledge's spell can only be cast on the last day of the floor. I can tell you already that will be too late. One of us will have to risk going to a Desperado Club to talk to them, and we gotta do it fast. I've been trying to do the math, and I'm pretty sure this happened just at the right time for it to finish covering the entire map just as the timer runs out. We'll all be squished together at the same spot if we wait until the end.

Tina reentered the light of Donut's spell and roared at us. She had her head low, glaring. She attempted to hide behind a tree, like a shy child peeking from behind a curtain. Kiwi abandoned the meal and moved toward her daughter. She paused, looked back at Mongo, and made a you're-coming-too grunt. Mongo in turn looked up at Donut, who nodded. Donut jumped onto Mongo as he cautiously approached the massive allosaurus. I kept a wary eye on them.

As they left, the remaining dinosaurs pounced on the remnants of the dead hunter, tearing him to shreds. They fought over the rib cage, growling and snapping. They broke it apart like a wishbone.

> **CARL:** Let me guess. The brambles will end at the southeast corner. What a coincidence.
>
> **KATIA:** Bingo. The High Elf Castle. Does that thing have a name? I haven't heard. We'll be transferred there anyway for the masquerade, but those not in the top 50 will still have to move to the area if they want to stay on the floor.
>
> **CARL:** The elves won't want the brambles to enter their territory. They'll try to beat the branches back. I think they might have something to protect the castle, too. Shit. I hope there are

stairs in that area. There's a set near me, and we're close to
the elven border, but it sounds like this area will be drowned
out in three or four days.

KATIA: So you've changed your mind about going down early?

CARL: For now. But I'm starting to think it might not be a bad idea
for everybody else. Start moving in that direction and mapping
out any known stairwells in that corner of the map. Bomo can
help. We'll meet you. I'm thinking we should work together for
the rest of the floor.

I spent some time describing what happened with Gravy Boat.

KATIA: We're on it. We're already headed in that direction. On our
way to rescue Britney. She just got zapped away, but she's not
too far. She hasn't killed a thing this entire floor, and I hadn't
noticed. Can you believe it? Her blood bar was empty. It'll take
us a bit. What are your plans in the meantime?

I looked over. Donut remained atop Mongo, whose head was all the
way to the ground, tail in the air. Facing them was Tina, head also low,
as she sniffed at Mongo from a distance. Kiwi stood between the two,
waving her little arms and squawking. As I watched, Tina's red dot
blinked and turned white. I sighed.

CARL: We have a recital to prepare for.

55

caught sight of a few NPCs waiting for us at the edge of town.

"Carl, look!" Donut said, leaping from Mongo's back to my shoulder. "Hi, Holger! Hi, Signet! Hi, Areson!"

"Donut," I said, "keep the dinos back."

"Hello, Signet," I said, walking up to the half-naiad. I exchanged a greeting with the ogre and the smaller, fuzzy castor with the mullet. He'd returned to his humanoid form. He beamed up at me and Donut.

On Signet's breast was the tattoo of the child version of Clint, who waved furiously at us.

"Hi, Clint tattoo!" Donut said, peering at the drawing. "Hi, Miss Nadine tattoo!" Donut looked about. "Hey, where's Edgar?"

"Tortoise is making big spell outside elf castle," Areson said. "He getting ready for final battle. Gonna make a map."

Signet looked over my shoulder, raising an eyebrow at the procession behind us. "Is that Tina back there? How have you tamed her?"

"We haven't," I said. "But Donut has tamed her mother, which is good enough to keep her from eating us. For now. Same with the rest of the dinosaurs."

"I see," Signet said, lips tight. "Be careful. The mongoliensis hierarchy can be a fragile thing. If one kills the alpha, you could lose control of the whole bunch all at once. They'll kill you before you know what has happened. Believe me, I know from experience. You should never rely on a single point of failure."

"Noted," I said.

Signet nodded. "As Areson has already said, preparations are still underway for the final part of our assault, but that is not why I am here. We are not staying. The elves hunt us. I have stopped to warn you. The forest cries. A darkness spreads from the north."

"Yes, I heard," I said. "The Gehenna brambles."

It'd only been a few hours, and nobody had seen or heard anything yet regarding this new threat. That was to be expected. It was moving slowly across the map. It was likely just reaching the borders of Zockau now. It'd be over a day before it even reached the river. I was going to send Bomo to check it out once we got to a safe room.

"Yes, the brambles. I presumed you'd have learned of this by now. But it is worse than you know. The trees are in pain. They are crying for help. The trees and dryads are casting a spell that just might help them. It will not stop the plague, but if they are successful, help will soon arrive to protect them from the worst of it."

"Okay," I said, not understanding.

"Help in the form of Diwata, the forest protector. I heard of your incident at the temple. You will need to be extra careful if Diwata enters the realm. They are especially unforgiving of apostates. Stay away from any all-trees. They will whisper your location to the deity. We do not need their intervention in these final days."

"Great," I said. "Just great."

"IT'S NOT GOING TO HAPPEN, CARL. NOT NOW. NOT EVER. NOT UNDER any circumstances. Look at how big it is! Do I look like some sort of sex pervert to you?"

"Donut, this gives plus ten points and an additional five percent to your constitution. It's the smallest of the four of them. We need you to wear this. It will help protect you."

"It's a nipple ring. It's going to dangle. You know how I feel about things that dangle."

"It's small enough that it'll be hidden in your fur. It'll probably get smaller once it's attached. This magical stuff always resizes itself."

"And how are we going to attach it? It says you have to attach it manually the first time. My nipple isn't pierced, Carl. One doesn't pierce the nipples of cats. That's how one gets a visit from the ASPCA! If you think it's such a great item, why don't *you* put it on yourself? I don't see you trying to pierce your own nipples."

"I am! The one I'm going to wear is even bigger than this one!"

"Well, you can wear both because I'm not wearing it."

Of the four nipple rings, only two held any real value. The top, biggest one—the same one I'd ripped out of Iota's chest—gave +5 in the Drink Mixing skill. I thought at first maybe that was a sneaky way to say it was some sort of potion-making ability, but nope. It was exactly how it sounded. It was for bartenders. Mordecai seemed to think we'd be able to sell it for a decent amount.

The next allowed one to see the average selling value of a non-unique item, even without physically touching it. That was interesting, but it wasn't pierce-my-nipple-with-a-door-knocker-of-a-ring interesting. That, too, was something we'd sell.

I groaned the moment I read the description of the third nipple ring because I knew it'd be something that I pretty much would have to wear. The glowing gold ring was about the size of a half dollar and was too good to pass up. It imbued the wearer with something called Quarter Fall. It basically made one's falling speed a quarter of what would normally happen.

I was no physicist, but I suspected that still wasn't going to be a pleasant landing, but at least it would be a survivable one. It had to be a better alternative than the Half Splat potions.

The fourth, constitution-enhancing ring was about the size of a nickel, which, as nipple rings went, wasn't all that big.

Unless you were putting it on a cat.

"If you put it on," I said, "I'll give you a prize."

She peered at me suspiciously. "What sort of prize?"

"An expensive one."

All of my regular loot boxes had been uninteresting, including the boss box from the one Odious Creeper we killed, which gave me a bunch of satchel bombs. Basically little bags with leather handles that I could toss and detonate with the power of three sticks of hobgoblin dynamite, which was enough to level a small town. It was a good prize, but it wasn't anything unique.

My benefactor box was puzzling. It was a highly valuable and familiar potion, though not quite as powerful as the one I already had.

Pawna's Cries.
    This potion has a limited shelf life.
    This potion adds plus three to any spell or skill of your choosing.

A "limited" shelf life was different than a short one. A short shelf life potion had to be taken immediately. A limited one had to be taken before the end of the floor.

I still had the Pawna's Tears potion in my inventory that did the same thing, but it had no time restrictions, and it was plus five, not three. We were saving that one until a little later.

This new potion also came with a note, which was unusual. I picked it up, and the note said simply, "Save the toraline."

The toraline was the yam-like vegetable they'd given me the last floor to save Chris. We'd already used more than half of it to create a potion that allowed me to remove Maggie from his brain.

"Save it? For what? Why won't they just spit it out?"

"Notes are expensive," Mordecai said, examining the potion. "You pay by the character, and the rules are kind of complicated. They force you to talk in code. If you're not sufficiently vague, the AI will 'translate' it to code, and you don't want that. They force you to be cryptic."

I stared at the note, trying to figure it out, when I suddenly felt the familiar haptic buzz of my Escape Plan skill activate. Additional words appeared on the page. A chill washed over me.

Circe sponsored Diwata. Give potion Donut. Need 15, but make it a secret. Use temp boost. Prepotente + Imani + Samantha all same time can do it. Or use other Pawna potion if have to. Will replace. ~P. Hu

The note hit me like a hammer. It took me a few reads to decipher it. They wanted me to give the +3 potion to Donut.

More importantly, Circe Took sponsored Diwata. Vrah's mother was coming into the game.

I tried to remember what Mordecai had told me about Diwata. He said the god could alter form and gender, but was usually depicted as a moss-covered, antlered squirrel. This wasn't normally a physically huge god, but they could make themselves giant if they wanted.

It wasn't lost on me that this benefactor box had been sent *before* we failed that quest. That meant, despite winning the court case to free her daughter, Circe Took of the Dark Hive had already sponsored the god and had been planning on coming for me no matter what happened.

It was just like with the Skull Empire. She needed to save face. I'd humiliated her, and I had injured her daughter. We knew that she was, somehow, still communicating with her daughter, despite it being against the rules. I wondered if they'd deliberately tanked the Odious Creeper quest knowing something like this would happen.

I reread the note and then eyed Samantha, who was rolling around the room squealing hysterically while the two small ursine, Randy and Todd, used her like a soccer ball.

"Hah, kick me! Kick me, little ones! Oh, yes. Just like that. No, not the nose, sweetie, or I will kill Prudence."

I thought better of intervening.

CARL: Hey, Imani. Do you have an ability that increases the level of a spell?

IMANI: I do. It's an aura I can cast called Smart Juice. It can add a level to a spell, but it has the unfortunate side effect of adding an extra cooldown, so I don't usually use it in combat. Elle gets mad if her icicles take too long to produce.

CARL: Good to know. Thanks.

"If you put that nipple ring on," I said, removing my new potion from the inventory, "I will give you my sponsor prize."

"Really? You never give up your prizes." She licked her lips. "I could really use this."

"That's right," I said. "You need it more than I do. You're almost at 12 in *Magic Missile*. We'll do some grinding, and in a few days when you hit 12, you can use it to top it off."

Mordecai was watching this exchange with a strange look on his face. He looked as if he was about to say something. I gave him a very slight *no* nod. He sighed and moved off.

"But I have to put on the nipple ring?" Donut said.

"You have to put on the nipple ring," I agreed.

She seemed to be waffling. Mongo, who'd been watching the impromptu soccer match, screeched at Donut with concern. Kiwi, Tina, and the other dinos remained outside the town limits. Talking the guards into letting a pack of raptors into the village was one thing, but Donut's charisma still wasn't high enough for her to convince them to add Tina to the mix. Not when we didn't own the town.

Donut rolled onto her back and peered down at her belly. She was completely covered in fur. "Are you sure it'll be invisible?"

I picked up the ring. "I'm positive," I said.

"Okay," she finally said. "But you gotta do yours first. And don't tell Katia. I don't want her thinking I'm a whore."

"Why do you associate nipple rings with that? Plenty of people have them."

"I've seen those videos on your computer, Carl."

"What does that even mean?"

"Just do yourself first. I want to make sure it doesn't hurt."

I opened my shirt. I gulped, pretending to be brave. I didn't want to wear this thing, either. I didn't care about it hurting or the ridiculous fashion of it—I was, after all, running around in heart boxers and a cape. But having a handhold dangling from your nipple was just asking for trouble.

I hadn't realized that these were a thing. It opened up a whole realm of possibility for upgrades. I only had two nipples, but Donut had eight. I needed to keep my eyes open for more of these things in the future.

I held my breath and shoved the little needle through my left nipple. I bit my lip. *Ow.*

Donut remained on her back, but she just stared at me for several moments as I pulled my trollskin shirt back on.

"I don't think I can respect you anymore, Carl."

New Achievement! Sex Pervert!
    A nipple ring? Really? The next thing you know, you'll be waxing

your perineum and attending those parties where you have to put your keys in a bowl. You'll have to grow out your sideburns, buy a Trans Am, and you'll no longer be able to make eye contact with your child's orthodontist.

Reward: Whores don't get rewards.

"Hey!" I said up at the ceiling. "You just made that whole thing up."

"What? What?" Donut said as I rubbed my hand across her belly, searching for a suitable nipple. They were very, very small.

"Don't worry about it," I said, zeroing in on one. "We need to get this over with. I don't want to waste too much blood bar time."

"Not that one, Carl. Up higher. And on the other side. If I'm going to be permanently disfigured further, it might as well be on the top right. And hurry it up and get it over with. The last thing we need is more Carl and Princess Donut sexy time fan snicks floating around."

"More?" I asked. "You know what? I don't want to know. Okay, I'm going to count to three."

PART FOUR

THE

BUTCHERING

56

<Note added by Crawler Herot. 16th Edition>

Show them the lie. Show them the seams. Show them the path they're on is a false one. Think of a trolley on a track. A worn path is easily traveled. The more worn the path, the more difficult it is to get them to look away. Just like the deeper the track, the sturdier the trolley. But even the strongest of minds, even those controlled and relentlessly corrected can be derailed just as a trolley can be derailed by a tiny, properly placed pebble. Find the pebble and place it on the path, and their own momentum will do the work for you.

14 DAYS EARLIER.

"IT WAS GLORIOUS," QUASAR SAID. "SHAME HOW IT ENDED FOR REMEX. They made us study the exit deal he made in school. But the mudskippers cleaned up that season. It was a real windfall. You ask for this spell, and they'll fall over themselves to give it to you. And you want to know the beautiful part? All those other pricks won't interfere. Everyone will want you to pull it off. All the factions. All the fans. The showrunners. The AI. Everybody. That spell always leads to carnage. Everybody likes carnage when it's not them."

"What, exactly, does this spell do? And why does it lead to such chaos?"

"It's called *Zerzura*. The spell itself is pretty simple. It takes a full city or town, NPCs and buildings and all, and it transfers them one floor down. It transfers the town itself and all the NPCs. That's it. No mobs or enemy red-tagged NPCs. No stairwells or any other special rooms, either, like prize rooms."

"That's exactly what I need," I said. "I promised I'd help the changelings get down, and we were going to use the gate. This would be a good compromise."

"I should note, there're a few, uh, negative side effects of the spell," he said.

"What are they?"

"It's pretty hard on the caster, first off. We won't have to worry about that because we'll have them install it into one of the mercenaries. On the Scolopendra levels, it skips floors. Remex found this out the hard way. He got that spell on the fourth floor during his crawl. He sent his army to the fifth floor, then the sixth, but when he cast it again, the town skipped the seventh and eighth floors and went straight to the ninth. He wasn't prepared for that, and his NPCs and mercenaries all got slaughtered by both the revenants and the faction wars participants. That's a whole sad story right there. But you should have seen him when he hit that ninth floor. He was a one-bird army. He gave it all up to save his kid." Quasar took a long drag of vape. "I'd forgotten he was still around until you freed him. That was some compelling drama, let me tell you. My wife bawled her eyes out. Or was it my girlfriend?" He waved his hand. "It's not important."

"Okay," I said. "So if we cast it now, the changelings will go straight to the ninth. That's what we wanted anyway. They'll have to run the moment their town lands. It was always going to end with a fight. We can give them the *Twister*. At least they'll have a chance. We should probably do it right away."

"Yeah, that's a problem. The spell can only be cast at the end of the floor. If the spell miscasts, that's it. You don't get to try again. It takes like five minutes to cast, too, so you'll have to protect the dude."

"Shit. Okay," I said. "That doesn't seem so bad. If we were using the gate, we'd have to wait until the end of the floor anyway. Do I have to be mayor to cast it?"

"No, which is good because we're giving it to a cretin. Not you."

"Okay, good," I said. "Is that it?"

"Not quite, pal. I'm getting to the good stuff. The city or town or whatever you send can't be steered, so it'll land in some random place. And when I say 'random,' I mean in the worst possible area. They almost always splat the whole village right in the middle of a monster nest or boss room, killing everybody it lands upon. That doesn't sound like a big deal, but there's a catch. Everything that's killed is immediately resurrected as a type of powerful revenant. They're called the Children of Inpewt. Everyone in the town plus the caster is marked. The creatures then actively hunt down the marked. They are fast and strong and still have any spells and special abilities of the monsters they were before they were smushed. That's why so many people enjoy watching this spell in action. It's just chaos and carnage. If the revenants successfully kill one of the marked, they are also turned into a revenant. The monsters don't go away until the villagers and the caster are all dead. Remex used it as an easy way to level up, but when they jumped from the sixth to the ninth, the revenants managed to cause a lot of chaos for the faction wars participants. Almost as much as you did. They'll all still want you to do it, though, since the odds are in their favor that it'll tiddie-bang one of their competitors and not them."

"Yikes," I said. "So my changelings will have a horde of undead monsters chasing them?" I thought of little Bonnie the gnome and Skarn. Of Ruby, the sweet, gentle changeling girl with compression sickness. Was this really our only choice? Would it be better to just let them collapse with the floor?

"Yes," Quasar said. "If the people are adequately prepared, they can usually handle it. But that ninth floor is a Forsoothian milk marm, if you know what I'm saying. The teleported town won't land inside another town, so you don't have to worry about it crashing into what remains of Larracos, but it'll likely land in the midst of another faction's territory, killing a bunch of their mercenaries. Then you'll have zombie mercenaries and the pissed-off survivors all attacking your villagers all at the same time."

"So I could plant a giant bomb," I said, thinking.

"You could. The changelings might not like that too much. And you don't know where it's going to land. They say this stuff is random, but we all know it ain't. You'd likely end up blowing away a bunch of trees."

"Damn. That's not nearly as good as the gate. With the gate, we have coordinates."

"True. That's why we're negotiating. We're going to ask for the six mercenaries, they'll counter with two, and we'll settle on four. One with a teleport spell. One with this *Zerzura* spell. We also need to keep you alive. I see you've already signed a shitty contract with the *Vengeance of the Daughter* show. We need to revisit that. You're a taxpaying stockholder now. This changes everything about your situation and what you can and can't do out in the universe. Can't change the contract between you and the production company itself, but I have a few thoughts on how to keep that star burning. I might be able to finagle a ninth-floor extension out of the mudskippers, which'll keep the *Vengeance* folks from trying to kill you on this one. That show sucks, by the way. It's only interesting when you and the cat are on, and everyone knows it. That's equal parts dangerous and lucky. At least the naiad doesn't wear a shirt."

"Okay," I said, still thinking of Bonnie and the changeling children being thrown into danger like that. This was inevitable, but was there more I could do to protect them? I thought of the Dreadnoughts.

"I have a crazy idea. Tell me what you think."

TIME UNTIL THE BUTCHER'S MASQUERADE: 70 HOURS.

Hello, Crawlers!

The brambles are closing in! This event was a surprise even to us, but as you know, you gotta be prepared for anything! Don't let those thorns prick you!

I must say, we are impressed with the resiliency you humans are showing on this floor. While the total number of survivors is still a little low, the percentage of sixth-floor crawler casualties is one of the lowest in *Dungeon Crawler World* history. Meanwhile, the hunter casualty rate went from a two percent average to over 25 percent. Those hunters who are listening to this, don't worry. Help is on the way! We have a special announcement only you will hear after the end of this message.

As we mentioned previously, we are doing some tweaking with the next two floors. What was originally going to be the seventh floor is now the eighth, with the difficulty ramped up accordingly. The next floor was something we didn't think would be designed in time. We call it the Great Race. It is an engineering marvel. Thanks to our newest partners, the Valtay Corporation, we were able to secure the capital and help required to finish the project just in time. We are seeing a whole lot of people going down early. You will be at a disadvantage if you do so, and we highly suggest you stay as long as you can. This will be the last hint you receive about the next floor.

Those of you in the top 50, we have just about 70 hours until the big event! Everyone wants to go to the Butcher's Masquerade! Yes, the party is still on! Here's some information about the galaxy's most exclusive gathering!

At the end of this message, all crawlers in the top 50 will receive a plus-one token. This can be given to another crawler, which will allow them entry into the party. If you fall out of the top 50 or if you perish before the party starts, the associated token will no longer be valid.

A party countdown will now appear in your interface. The party commences 30 hours prior to collapse, and it is scheduled to last four to five hours. When this timer reaches zero, you will be teleported directly to the ballroom, which is within the High Elf Castle. Due to the bramble event, you will *not* be transported back upon the conclusion of the party. Instead, you will be allowed to exit the southern entrance to the castle, which will not yet be infested with the brambles. The elves may or may not offer safe passage afterward, so prepare accordingly.

All hunters will also attend the party. They will appear to be in the same room as you, but they will actually be in a different location within the castle. You will not be able to physically harm the hunters, and they will not be able to harm you. You may not cast magic within the castle ballrooms. You may not bring weapons or explosives or traps or any other instruments of violence into the castle ballrooms. You may not use your inventory within the castle ballrooms.

There will be a pet beauty contest followed by a talent competition with celebrity judges from outside the crawl attending remotely. You will receive a survey if you wish to participate in either event after this message. Due to limited space, not all entries will be accepted.

Pets and NPC companions will not be allowed in the main ballrooms, but will be allowed to participate as extras via one of two assistant staging areas. Details will be provided upon acceptance into the show.

There will be a catered buffet and a prize booth where one may redeem Hunter hands or Crawler scalps.

Safe passage for both parties is guaranteed by Queen Imogen, ruler of the High Elves, who will be your host for the evening.

This is meant to be a relaxing, fun evening for both the hunters and the crawlers. The hunters will exit the north entrance upon the end of the evening. You may kill each other afterward.

There is no patch update tonight due to some technical difficulties. We only have a few minor patches queued up. Rest assured we're working tirelessly to make certain the system is properly updated.

Now get out there and kill, kill, kill!

TIME UNTIL THE BUTCHER'S MASQUERADE: 66 HOURS.

"Carl, Carl!" Donut said. "They accepted my applications! Both of them!"

I looked up from the kitchen table, confused. "Wait, the talent show part, too? How? The Tina plan is dead in the water."

There were multiple people in the safe room. Katia stood on my left, Imani on my right. Elle was outside on her way to the Desperado Club.

The talent show portion of the event allowed NPCs to participate, but only as assistants and backup. We'd floated the idea to use the talent contest to finish out the Big Tina quest, but they'd immediately rejected my application because it required the main part of the act to be a crawler or a hunter. Tina had to be the star of the show. We were in the middle of figuring out a safe place to construct a small stage and get her to dance upon it before the brambles reached us.

"Kiwi and Tina and the rest of the crew are going to be my backup dancers," Donut announced proudly. "I'm going to sing."

I exchanged a look with Imani and Katia.

"I don't think that's going to work, Donut."

"Don't be such a Debbie Downer, Carl. Of course it'll work. We'll make it work. Mongo! We're in! Mommy is going to sing, and you're going to win the beauty contest! We need to go back out there and get back to work."

Mongo screeched and waved his arms.

I took a deep breath and looked back down at the map of the area. I moved it aside and pulled up the second map. The one that just got dropped off in the attached pub. I sent a few messages back and forth, brainstorming a few ideas. Katia gave a shrug. Imani nodded.

Louis came out of the bathroom, zipping up his pants. He wiped his hands on his shirt and came to stand next to me. He looked more shell-shocked than usual. Sweat beaded down his temple. He'd gone up to level 42, almost double what he'd been when I'd met him on the previous floor. "I've been in the guild too long. My blood bar thing is only half full. I need to go back out there in a bit. Firas is helping Britney fill hers up, and I need to join them. Good thing all those mobs are getting herded toward us."

"All right, but stay for a few minutes. It's important we all know the map."

ELLE: I'm here at the Desperado Club, but there's a problem. I can't get to them.
CARL: Damn. Okay, come back to the guild. We're about to go over the map.

I leaned over the surprisingly detailed castle diagram Edgar the tortoise had provided. I pointed at the left side of the expansive castle by the southern entrance. "This is our ballroom, and way over here is where the hunters will be. The two rooms aren't even on the same floor.

We're on the fourth floor and they're on the second. The rooms them-selves should be identical. I think it'll be like a production trailer. You'll be able to see and interact with the hunters, but if you touch them, they won't really be there."

"Mistress Tiatha says you *will* be able to touch them," Imani said. "I don't know how it would work."

"They're called goodwill ballrooms," Samantha said from the edge of the table. "Everybody knows that. They're quite common. It's so visiting ambassadors and other dignitaries can be entertained without the dan-ger of assassination. You can touch one another if you wish, but it is a light touch. It's in such a room where I met my king. We had to wait until after the party before we could be together." She sighed dramati-cally. "When I reunite with my body and find my sweet child, I'll get back to him one day. We'll have a happy, normal family." She sud-denly rolled across the table and stopped in front of Louis and started making weird growling noises up at him. He started to back away, sur-prised.

"My king is a fan of swapping partners, just so you know," she said up to Louis. "Maybe we can talk your fiancée into portraying my bitch of a mother. Then we can have some fun." Then she did some Hannibal Lecter thing with her tongue, causing everyone in the room to stop and look at the talking sex doll head.

Louis looked to me for help.

"Samantha, don't be weird," I said. I picked her up and tossed her off the table. She hit the ground with a little shriek and immediately bounced up to the edge of the couch and started swearing at me, but she stopped when she saw the two bear cubs were still in the room, watch-ing her wide-eyed.

"Uh, so the two rooms are far apart," Louis said, trying to get back on subject, using his finger to trace the distance. "Like, really far apart. How big is this castle? And what are these little tunnel things? Air ducts?"

The castle did not look like something one would associate with elves. The white structure looked like a sugar cube just sitting there in the middle of a large clearing. It was just a white square with four sentry towers, one at each of the four corners along with a simple, but empty, moat, like some Bauhaus art installation blown up to ridiculous proportions. The southern exit where we'd supposedly exit was right at the base of a large rocky cliff that led straight up, almost like the bowl wall on the previous floor. We'd emerge right outside the southeastern corner of the map.

I doubted there'd be any sort of stairwell or towns in the area. It'd be the castle, and that was it.

Since Queen Imogen was a country boss, that meant a stairwell would open up once she was defeated.

"How big is it? It's huge," I said. "It says the side is 150 meters wide. It's ridiculously big."

"What's that big room in the middle?" Louis asked.

"The throne room. That's the seventh floor. We won't be allowed in there. I'm pretty sure we'll be magically restricted to the ballroom. I believe Samantha's right about the purpose of the two sides. The whole castle has three sections. Where we'll be, where the hunters will be, and the middle where the majority of the high elves live. It also goes underground. It looks like a cube, but it's really a rectangle because it has a few subsurface levels. There's a dungeon and a secret entrance down there."

"Where will Mongo be?" Donut asked, peering at the map.

"There are two servant staging areas," I said. "Both on the first floor. This one is under where we'll be, but three floors lower. The other is directly below the north ballroom for the hunters."

"How many hunters will be at the party?" Louis asked.

"According to the kill-kill-kill lady, it'll be all of them," I said.

"That's going to be like 600 people. That's way too many," he said. "When the party gets out, it'll be a hundred of us and 600 of them right outside? We'll get our asses kicked."

"I agree," I said. "That's why we need to get to work. I want that number under 250 before we get there."

"Carl," Donut said, interrupting, "Prepotente just messaged me and wants to know where we are. He says he has something to give me. He said it's a present, but he sounds kinda angry about it."

"Uh," I said, not so sure what to think of that. I remembered what he said earlier. *If I can't exist in a world with my mother, then nobody even remotely responsible for her death can exist in this world, either.* "Maybe you should ask him what it is first. Don't tell him where we are."

"I already told him. He says he's on his way."

Goddamnit.

"HOW HAVE YOU BEEN?" I ASKED BAUTISTA. WE WERE IN TEAM KATIA'S personal space, checking it out, waiting for our meeting with Prepotente. She had it arranged differently than we did. The space felt more like a house than a warehouse. Donut was looking about, scoffing at her design choices.

Bautista was making an inventory of all his more common Beanie toys, looking for variants. He had them lined up on the kitchen table. Apparently some of them had rare deviations that didn't show up in the description, which meant they'd react different when he pulled the tag. He had literally dozens of them lined up. He was going down the line, picking them up and searching for odd colors and stitching, comparing one to the next.

"Oh, you know," the orange tiger-headed crawler replied. "Katia says you're starting to put together some sort of response to that party in a few days. I'm ranked 23, so it looks like I'll be there. Do you really think we'll have to fight?"

"Yes," I said. I picked up the first Beanie. It was one of the Grulke frog warriors. "We're doing all sorts of preparations. We're also buying a few room upgrades before the timer runs out because they might not be available next floor. After you're done with this, you should go check out the new bathroom upgrade we have in our personal space. Imani wants everyone to look at it and to vote to see if we want to share the upgrade to the whole guild."

He looked up and met my eyes. "Sure," he said after a moment.

"So, you and Katia." I let it hang.

"Wait, what is this?" Donut asked, looking up from a stuffed hedgehog. "What about you and Katia?"

"It just sort of happened."

"That's good," I said, slapping him on the back. "I think it's great." I picked up the next Beanie. It looked like a regular pink flamingo. It reminded me of the plastic flamingo sitting in the front of Agatha's shopping cart.

Stuffed Flame-ingo Figure. (With tags.)
This is the most common variation of the Flame-ingo line of collectible figures. While not as common as the Grulke or Garbage Scowl figures, these figures are still near the bottom in terms of rarity.
A favorite amongst the more feminine fans of Jaxbrin toys.

I looked up from the stuffed flamingo to see a strange look on Bautista's face. He looked oddly relieved about something. I realized he was reacting to my comment about him and Katia.

"You and Katia?" Donut repeated, incredulous. "You are together with Katia? My Katia? Does she know this?"

"Yes, Donut," I said. "It's been obvious for a while now. I assumed you would've picked up on it."

"Katia!" Donut called, jumping from the table. She marched toward the door into the main guild area. "Katia, are you here? I must speak with you this instant!"

I picked up the next Beanie. It was a gray-and-brown fuzzy moth or butterfly thing. There was a line of like 100 of them. "Why do you have so many of these?"

"I got all of them a few days back," he said.

"Wait, you're getting these things in dungeon boxes now?"

"No. This was from my sponsor. It wasn't an actual benefactor box. I got pulled out of the dungeon to do a commercial for them, and I just stole the sample box at the end of the session."

"Been there," I said.

Stuffed Slate Butterfly Figure. (With tags.)
The Slate Butterfly is one of the more common figures in Jax-

brin's newest lineup. The tragic story of the butterflies who accidentally killed all their fairy friends is a beloved fairy tale. It's also based loosely on a true story, which is no surprise considering how parents just love to romanticize mass-casualty events.

Donut returned to the table. "She's outside. Well, I just don't know what to make of any of this. This is just as surprising as Louis and Juice Box. Carl, are you going to allow this to continue?"

"Allow it to continue?" I asked. "What does that even mean?"

Bautista still appeared ridiculously nervous. "Actually, I'm . . . I'm glad it's all out in the open. I must admit, I was a little worried that you, Carl . . . You know. You had a thing for her."

"For Katia?" I asked, surprised. "She's like my sister."

"He's psychologically damaged thanks to Miss Beatrice," Donut said. "Don't let that nipple ring fool you. He doesn't get very many girls. Besides, based on his porn-viewing habits, I'm pretty sure he has a thing for Asian girls."

"Nipple ring?" Bautista asked, raising a fuzzy eyebrow.

"You never know what someone's kinks are," Donut said. "For example, I had no idea Katia was into furries."

"Have you tried these Slate Butterfly things before?" I asked, changing the subject.

"Just once," he said. "They're harmless. They don't attack. They just fly to the closest light source and suck the energy of it away. You can have one if you want. You can have five."

TIME UNTIL THE BUTCHER'S MASQUERADE: 64 HOURS.

"Holy shit, you made it to level 70," I said as the goat entered the pub. Kiwi and Mongo stopped tussling long enough to watch Prepotente step into the bar. As the door closed, I caught sight of Bianca outside. The damn thing looked like a dragon. The rain sizzled as it hit the creature's back.

Elle sat in one corner of the bar, Bautista in the other, keeping a watchful eye on us.

"Hi, Prepotente!" Donut said.

"Hello, Donut. Hello, Carl," Prepotente said as he approached our table. He looked exhausted.

"Do you want to go into the safe room? To see the guild?" I asked. He had fifteen hunter-killer marks over him. "Maybe we can get you to take a nap."

"We got a really neat bathroom upgrade," Donut said. "Mine is a bigger litter box that's just luxurious."

"I do not wish to rest or see your waste-of-money upgrade," Prepotente said. "I do not have time for whatever it is you're planning. I do not wish to get involved with it." He looked about the room. "There is no need for your idiot friends to protect you. I wish you no harm."

Elle floated away from the table and approached. "Hey, did you just call me an idiot? You know my mother had some really good goat recipes, and I'm starting to feel a little nostalgic."

He held up a hairy hand, turned toward Elle, and then screamed right in her face.

She flew back several feet. "Holy shit, pal. Your breath."

"I have no time nor desire to trade barbs today, you . . . whatever you are. I am here to deliver a package."

"What is it?" I asked warily.

He pulled a black bubbling potion from his inventory and placed it on the table in front of Donut.

"I received it in a benefactor box. I cannot fathom why my sponsor would give me something intended for you, but there it is."

He got up and exited the pub. Outside, Bianca screeched at his approach, and then they were gone.

"That is one strange dude," Elle muttered. "Donut, I'm glad you're not weird like that."

"Certainly not. But he is very sad right now," Donut said. "You know, I've never had goat. Is it good?"

"Oh, it's delicious," Elle said. She turned to the Bopca at the counter. "Hey! You got goat? Maybe in a curry?"

"That's a little fucked-up," I said as I picked up the potion and examined it. This was now the second benefactor item given to someone else but intended for Donut.

I Take It All Back—Potion.

This will remove any effects of Scolopendra's *Transmutation* spell.

A tag hung off the top, like a label on a Christmas present. It read:

GIVE THIS TO PRINCESS DONUT.
USE WHEN THE TIME IS RIGHT.
DO NOT GIVE TO TINA.

"What the hell, man?" I said.

I could think of several people who might want to get their hands on this. "Don't use it until I say so. And don't tell Signet you have it. She'll want to use it on Grimaldi, and I don't think that's what it's for."

"Huh," Elle said. "I just got a benefactor box from the Apothecary. Imani messaged and said she did, too. She's opened hers, and she said it's also for Donut."

"Carl," Donut said, "I'm starting to think that nipple-ring bribe was a trick. I'm starting to think you tricked me and that you were directed to give me that potion all along!"

"Come on," I said. "Let's go talk to the changelings, and then we'll try to figure out what the deal is with all these benefactor boxes."

"HELLO, CLARABELLE," I SAID AS I STEPPED INTO THE SPACE BEFORE the main entrance to the club. The pounding music emanated from the doorway. Donut bopped her head. "I wasn't sure if I'd see you here since we're on the Hunting Grounds level now."

"Well, look who it is," the Crocodilian bouncer said. "I haven't seen you guys in ages. Not since you borrowed four of our bouncers. You don't have them with you? You're not getting free security still, not when you have free access to those guys. How are they doing anyway?"

"They're back at the base. Having the time of their lives."

"They're obsessed with video games and movies about dinosaurs," Donut added. "Sledgie really likes gangster movies, too."

"Good to hear. So anyway, I don't know if you heard from your ice fairy friend, but this door still leads to the club's top floor. Management forced us to make the change because you, mister, stranded several hunters within. On both the Hunting Grounds level and the Larracos level. They're not too happy about it. Crawlers were coming in and getting into fights, and we can't kick those hunter assholes out, so they made it so you guys don't mix anymore. So you come in on the same floor you used to. The hunters are now banned from coming up, so there's no mixing of the groups."

"Wait," I said. "Those hunters who all ran in here when I attacked Zockau are still stuck here? They're just sitting around twiddling their thumbs? I thought all they had to do is rebuild the entrance bar."

"Most are getting something twiddled all right, and it ain't their thumbs. That Hunting Grounds floor is a lot bigger than this one. But, yeah, rebuilding the bar is simple business, but the mayor of Zockau needs to approve the construction, and the mayor is that mantis bitch whose crotch you set aflame. That was funny as shit, by the way. Anyway, them mantises never play well with others, so they're keeping the trapped hunters in there. Seven already died. Five killed by bouncers. One by one of the girls. One by a crawler. That's what caused the rule change. Bunch o' them outworlders down on the Larracos level are still trapped, too. They almost got the city drained, so those folks can finally leave in a few days."

"It still hasn't drained?" I asked, surprised. This part was new to me. "Really?"

Clarabelle leaned in. "Something keeps clogging the drains, and those sharks aren't helping matters. So, yeah. They're still stuck. They got the hotel and the main casino down there, though, so ain't nobody complaining too much. Only thing is the faction weapons brokers usually buy a pass to go up to the Hunting Grounds levels so they can trade with the hunters, and that ain't happened at all since you cocked everything up on both ends. They were trying to drain it before this floor ended, but it doesn't look like it's going to happen."

"Those guys on the Hunting Grounds level aren't getting kicked out because of the blood bar thing?"

"Yeah, I hate that rule," Clarabelle said. "Tenth-floor rules apply, but only at the door. It's not for the ones already in here. Bar doesn't drain in the club, but it's gotta be full if you wanna get in. Rules a little different if you want to get into the Cosmic Lounge, though."

Luckily, Donut and I had topped our blood bars off before coming in here.

"Have you seen many hunters enter? Ones coming in from entrances outside Zockau?"

"A few," Clarabelle said. "And some of those guys are staying to hide it out, I think. But it's not the mass exodus I thought it might be. And some are going back out again. It don't matter much if they're all gonna get teleported away in a bit for that butcher party or whatever it's called."

"These clubs are getting harder to find," I said. "Most are in bigger towns, and a lot of those towns are already claimed by crawlers. Hunters aren't allowed to be mayors except in Zockau, so the guards attack them when they enter a town, and most aren't strong enough to fight back. So they can't get to the clubs, even if their bars are full. They're stuck hiding out in the smaller towns until the brambles reach them, and then they gotta run again."

"Yup," Clarabelle said. "Good for you lot. You sure tossed all their plans right into the dunny, didn't you? All us are rooting for you."

"What if Mordecai came in here by himself?" I asked.

"He's a manager. He's attached to the princess. He'll also go in on the top floor. He'd be dead if he went down there by himself."

"What about other NPCs?" I asked. "If an NPC from this floor came in, where would they enter?"

"You know, your ice friend asked that same, exact question. Regular NPCs coming in here got different rules. Not too many of them got the required membership credentials. But if they do, they'll go in on the proper floor. The Hunting Grounds level. And they won't be able to come up or go down, either. They're all stuck on the floor they went in on."

I'd already discussed this with Katia and Elle, as I wasn't sure the changeling representatives would even be able to get in here at all, but Elle assured me they would. Apparently, the changelings from Hump Town had regularly gone to the clubs here, having the ability to emulate a pass.

"So how do we get to the Hunting Grounds level? There's a few places down there I need to get to."

"You're not supposed to unless management says it's okay, and they haven't said it's okay yet. I wouldn't hold your breath, especially not you two. Believe it or not, we don't actively promote the death of our patrons. Unless you're in the casino, of course. Or the Mosh Pit."

Shit. I was hoping maybe Clarabelle would make an exception for me and Donut. Elle hadn't been able to get access, either. She could only go in on the top floor, and the changeling we needed to talk to could only enter on the Hunting Grounds floor.

CARL: You're up, Donut. Don't be too mean. We want to remain
    friends after this.
DONUT: WATCH ME DO MY MAGIC.

Donut leaned in. "Carl wants to visit the Bitches room, but he's tired of all the ones on the top floor. We hear there's a room called High-Class

Bitches. And I would like to take a look at the Penis Palace. I have a coupon for a dance from the Penis Parade, and it says it's also good at the Palace. I heard they have ogre dancers at this one, and I want to see if the rumors are true."

Clarabelle grunted with amusement, her Crocodilian eyes boring into me. "I didn't know you went in there. You're likely to catch something nasty. Still, sorry. Management wants to keep the violence to a minimum. And every time you two come in here, something happens. I didn't let your ice fairy friend in, and I ain't gonna let you in, either."

"But you *can* get us down there, can't you?" I asked. I tapped the door. "I bet you can wave your hand, and this door turns into an entrance for the Hunting Grounds. Like you said, it's not a rule-rule. I know you can't get us into the Larracos level. But you *can* get us onto the Hunting Grounds floor level, can't you?"

Clarabelle crossed her scaled arms. "I *could* do that, but it'll cost you more than you're willing to give. I like this job. Door duty is the easiest and safest, and I wouldn't want to do anything to mess that up."

"Really?" Donut asked. "You wouldn't risk your job over 100 gold?"

"One hundred gold?" Clarabelle scoffed. "You're offering me 100 gold? I told you before your charm doesn't work on me, little one. I like you two, but that's just insulting, especially considering how many of those hunters you two have killed. You're probably the richest of all the crawlers."

"I like you, too, Clarabelle," Donut said. "But you have misunderstood. We're not offering you 100 gold. We're talking about the 100 gold you stole from us when we first hired private security."

"I don't know what you're talking about," Clarabelle said, all amusement draining from her.

"Do you know," Donut continued, "that my interface keeps track of every gold piece I have ever spent? I have the ledger pulled up right now. Let's see here." She started pawing at the air like she was scrolling through an invisible menu. "Three gold spent buying that fabulous beret from that one Bopca. The 1,500 gold Carl made me waste on all that fireproof string. Oh, yes. Here it is. It says, '500 gold, paid to Clarabelle from Desperado Club security for private secure escorts.' Dated the first time we came in here on the fourth floor. It's the day I met Sledgie!" She cocked her head to the side with mock confusion. "That's quite odd. Here's a refund, but it's only for 400 gold. When I got into the fight where that guy tried to hurt me, your boss, Astrid, told us she would refund us the full 400 gold for the security. Oh yes, I remember now. I wanted to say something about the discrepancy, but Carl here has a kind heart, and he thought we should take the matter up with you privately." Donut looked pointedly at the door and then back at Clarabelle. "This is us taking the matter up privately."

TIME UNTIL THE BUTCHER'S MASQUERADE: 62 HOURS.

"I appreciate what you've done for us, but that don't mean we gonna just blindly trust you," the changeling said as he helped me hold the door closed. His name was Pearson, and he'd been a dromedarian bartender in disguise on the last floor. He was currently in the form of a cretin, which made him sound like Bomo when he talked. He had his bulk pressed against the door, but I feared we wouldn't be able to keep it closed for long. These guards on the Hunting Grounds level were exceedingly polite compared to the ones on the floor above, but they had enhanced strength.

The door slammed yet again, and I grunted with the effort to keep it closed. I talked through gritted teeth. "I promised Juice Box I would do my best to bring you down with us each floor. With the guildhall system, we can hire maybe fifteen of you, but it doesn't even work on some of you guys. I'm not sure why, but it doesn't matter anyway. I've found a way to take all of you straight to the ninth floor, even without the Gate of the Feral Gods. But your town is about to be overrun, and I need you all in the same place at the same time for it to work."

Behind us, the door slammed again as one of the Crocodilian guards crashed a shoulder into it. "Sir! Sir!" he called through the door. "You're not supposed to be down here!"

Donut returned from down the hallway where she'd been exploring. The corridor was dotted with doors, but the hallway itself was empty except for the three of us. "Carl, Carl, there's an explosives guild down here! And a rogues' guild! You should go to both!"

"Not now, Donut," I said, grunting. The door crashed again.

"Sir!" the Crocodilian called. "I will get in trouble if management finds you down here! If you were anyone else, I'd bite your goddamned head off."

"We're busy!" I called back. "We'll be out in a minute!" Then to Donut I said, "Can you say something to calm him down?"

"Carl is pooping! He's almost done!"

The Crocodilian's voice went up an octave. "In the hallway? Sir, this is not a bathroom! This is the skill guild hallway!"

"Real helpful, Donut," I said.

CLARABELLE DID NOT GIVE US DIRECT ACCESS TO THE HUNTING Grounds level of the club. Instead, she'd told us of a secret stairwell. In the last stall of the women's bathroom was a toilet, and if you took the top off that toilet and reached in, there was a secret latch. When pulled, it would open the wall behind the stall.

Nobody in the club so much as blinked an eye when we strolled into the women's bathroom. The weird generated NPCs they used for the dance floor did not use the restroom as far as I could tell, and I didn't see anyone else in the club. Sure enough, the concealed stairwell was exactly where Clarabelle said it would be. I pulled the lever, the wall slid open, revealing a tight metal staircase that led straight down. It made me wonder what other secrets were hidden in here.

We went down, and it led to a door leading to the corresponding bathroom one floor down. The stairs continued downward, presumably to the women's bathroom on the Larracos level, but when I tried to take a step in that direction, I received an error message.

Nice Try. No.

The women's bathroom on the Hunting Grounds level was thankfully empty.

"It's much less filthy on this level," Donut said. "The floor tiles are much nicer. My paws don't stick to them."

"Okay," I whispered as we crouched at the door out of the bathroom. The door itself had silver metallic ornaments on it shined to a polish.

The bar above our heads was more like a short-staffed dive bar that hadn't seen a good cleaning in a decade. "They'll supposedly be at the main bar. There should be two of them. Look for out-of-place NPCs. Hopefully none of the hunters will notice us."

"You're a giant man in his boxers, Carl, and I am a cat. They're going to notice us the second we walk out the door. You didn't think this through."

"Mordecai says this floor is really big and mazelike. Hopefully they're spread out. We just need to find them quick. We'll be in and out. I doubt the hunters will attack us anyway. Clarabelle said the guards already killed some the last time they chose to fight, and they've been stuck down here a long time. They're just waiting it out."

"She also said the guards will kick us out the moment they notice us."

"Then we'll try to avoid them. This isn't optional. We need to talk to them. Okay. Here we go."

We pushed through the door into a small, well-lit hallway. Muted music rose in the distance. It was nothing like the pulsing EDM beat of the floor above us. The floor here was carpeted and lush, and the red wallpapered wall was covered in large portraits of fairies in ornate frames. Two doors down, a door opened, and an elf rushed out, carrying a tray filled with drinks and steaming food. She did not see us.

"Bar is that way," I said, pointing. "Keep your head down."

To my right, the door to the men's room opened, and a giant red-skinned creature staggered out, buttoning up his pants. He was about seven feet tall and as wide as a cretin. He had twin fist-sized bumps on his head, like ground-down horns. He bumped right into me. "Oh, sorry, friend," he said, looking up. His eyes went huge.

Haxor the Destroyer—Dreadnought. Level 50. Merchant.
   This is an Unaffiliated Hunter.

He opened his mouth to scream as I reflexively kicked him with all of my might right in his nuts.

Thankfully, that particular quirk of human anatomy translated to the Dreadnought race, and he went flying back through the door. He hit the tiled floor of the men's restroom and slid until he crashed against the far sink, which cracked.

I was on him in a second. I leaped, landing on his chest. I felt bones crunch under me. He didn't wear any armor. Just a simple wide and flowing shirt that was open at the chest. It looked like something the Maestro would wear.

"No," he gasped. "No."

I grabbed him by the twin horn stubs, and I savagely pulled his head to the side, breaking his neck. Several notifications rolled down my interface. None of them, thankfully, were regarding the aggro of the guards.

"Again with the nut kicking, Carl?" Donut said, looking down at the corpse. "The neck-breaking thing was cool. I don't know if that cancels the nut kick out, though." She looked over her shoulder nervously at the door. "Clarabelle said we'll get kicked out forever if they catch us fighting!"

"Didn't have a choice," I said. "People get hurt and die here all the time. It only counts if the guards see it."

"Tell that to him," Donut said.

I pulled the body into my inventory. He didn't have much, but he did have one of those weird credit chits we'd taken off the orc several days earlier. From what I gathered, these things were the equivalent of intergalactic credit cards. It was strange this guy was unaffiliated, though. The Dreadnought Clan was one of the faction wars participants, but they'd quit thanks to the flooding of Larracos. The war chief pulled them out after his wife got stung by a jellyfish.

That reminded me that I hadn't heard from Quasar, my attorney, in a while. I'd ping him again after we got out of here.

After I took the body, all that was left was the cracked sink and a little blood. I grabbed a towel from the hanging rack and quickly cleaned up. Then I draped the towel over the sink to hide the crack.

"Let's try this again," I said, and we moved into the hallway. Just past the bathroom and to our right was a set of double doors leading into a kitchen.

"I think there's a full restaurant on this floor with waiters and everything," Donut hiss-whispered. "This is way better than above already. This is an outrage!"

I peered around the corner. I caught the neon glow of a sign leading to the casino and another sign leading off to the Silk Road, a market I desperately needed to get to. I turned to see a pair of elves sitting at the bar, both staring directly at me. The only other creature in view was a badger-headed bartender, who was facing away. Both elves had an empty drink sitting in front of them. As we stared at each other, one of them changed faces to reveal a dromedarian and then changed back, signaling me these were, indeed, the changelings we were looking for.

"That's them," I said.

I took a step forward, but one waved us back. The other slipped off the bar and moved in the opposite direction.

"Hey, mate!" he called at someone around a corner I couldn't see. "Guards! Did you hear that? I think those fuckers are fighting again in the casino."

The second furiously waved me forward and then pointed at another hallway with a door. He slipped off the bench and moved toward it. The sign read GUILDS.

That was easy, I thought as I started to follow, moving toward the long main bar.

"Oi! Sir!" a voice called from yet another hallway. "Sir! Crawlers are banned from this floor!"

"HERE," I SAID, HANDING PEARSON THE CHANGELING A HAND-DRAWN map containing all the details of our location so they could find us. The guard had stopped pounding on the door, an ominous sign. "We're going to need your help. Get the kids to us, and we'll stick them in our safe area until it's safe."

"And if it's never safe?" he asked, shoving the paper into his waistband.

"Then it's not going to matter. Look. We're just starting with our plans on how to evacuate you guys and keep ourselves alive. We're still working on it, but the initial plans are laid out on the back of that map. We're using a spell called *Zerzura* to evacuate you. But the brambles are moving fast, and we can't cast the spell for another two days. The spell is cast on a town, not just a group of people. You need to be in the town for it to work. The thing is, the high elves have destroyed all the towns in the forest around them. All but one. The High Elf Castle. That means we'll need to get you inside. There's a lot of moving parts going on at once, more than I like. I'll need all of your help if we want this to work."

"Before she left, Juice Box told us to be careful of you," Pearson said.

"I'm sure she did," I said. "But she still trusted us."

"We don't even know if she's alive."

"She is." *I hope,* I didn't add. "If this works, you'll be reunited soon."

"Carl," Donut said, "someone else is out there now. Someone small."

A horrific racking pain filled my entire body. It came all of a sudden. I suddenly felt hot, my vision flashing red. I looked down in horror to see the skin on my arm starting to bubble and crack.

Warning: Your blood has been set to boil.

"Carl," a female voice called, flowing through the doorway, "I suggest you open this door right now if you wish to ever be allowed access to the club again."

Oh, thank god, I thought, realizing who this was. *This could've been a lot worse.*

"It's okay," I growled as my health plummeted. I fell to my knees. "Pearson, change back to the elf quick and open the door. Try to touch her if you can."

The door opened, revealing Astrid, the club's level 125 assistant manager. She was a **Bloodlust Sprite**, an adept in the dreaded cardiovascular magic. She'd cast a spell to make my blood literally boil. She wasn't trying to kill me, I knew. If she was, I'd already be dead. She floated there, glaring angrily at the three of us as my consciousness flowed away.

I BLINKED, AND I FOUND MYSELF SLUMPED OVER IN A CHAIR. I IN-
stantly knew where I was. *Not this shit again.*

"Hello, Orren," I said, coughing myself awake. Donut was next to
me on her own chair. The two changelings were gone. Astrid the fairy
wasn't here, either.

The liaison didn't waste any time with niceties. "I had Astrid bring
you to me because I have something I need to discuss with you. Two
things actually. I am leaving upon the collapse of this floor, and I won't
return until the beginning of the ninth, so we need to discuss this now."

I groaned in pain. I'd been "healed," but I had dozens of lingering
debuffs that made me feel as if I'd been run over by a tank and then
set on fire. That Blood Magic was really nasty.

A bowl of something non-alcoholic with cherries floating within
sat on the edge of Orren's desk, and Donut stood next to me, her back
paws on the chair and her forward paws on the desk, lapping at the
drink. In that moment, she looked more catlike than she had in a very
long time. My head continued to pound as I stared at her. How long had
we been sitting here?

"Hi, Carl," Donut said, looking up from her drink. "They let me
order something from the kitchen! They brought it up on a platter and
everything. Do you know what capers are? They're really gross. You
were out for forty-five minutes."

The fishbowl-headed creature sat in his creaking wooden chair, looking at us with his gloved hands steepled in front of him.

"What did you do to my friends?" I asked.

"The two changelings?" he asked. "They've been ejected from the club. They won't be allowed to return. You're lucky the changeling took credit for blocking the door." He paused. "And cracking the sink."

"Wait, you're leaving?" I asked, shaking my head. "Why?"

"My job has many facets, but one of those responsibilities has recently been rendered moot. My kind and I will remain on-planet, but some people believe there's no need for me to remain in my in-game office until the faction wars segment begins on the ninth floor, assuming that even happens. We are constantly reevaluating. I disagree with the decision to leave, but it is out of my control. Do not worry, however. If our services are required, we will still be available."

I rubbed my forehead. I was relieved they let the changelings go. Hopefully they'd be on their way to meet Louis and Firas. "What can we do for you, Orren?"

"Do you know what it takes to be a liaison, crawler?"

"Being grouchy?" Donut asked.

"I'm on the clock here, Orren," I said. "If you're not going to kill us or whatever, can we just get on with it?"

"This job requires someone who is passionate about seeing the game succeed, yes, but it's the second requirement that is key. They look for a candidate who fundamentally disagrees with their home nation's goals and philosophies. They don't advertise this, but it is a crucial job requirement. This is because most nations, such as the Valtay, host these games with goals in mind that might run counter to both the spirit and true purpose of the game."

"Spirit of the game?" I asked. "Are you kidding me?"

"Technically, I should've been out of a job the moment the Valtay took control of the Borant Corporation. Thankfully, my seniority and vocal differences with how my people comport themselves have kept me in this chair. Plus," he added, "it would be quite hypocritical of them, considering the circumstances."

"I thought most of you guys just executed people who disagreed."

"We're not barbarians," he said.

"I beg to differ."

"I'm attempting to give you valuable information, crawler. So pay attention. I'm not the only liaison who's attempting to keep this system running smoothly. I'm not the only liaison who vehemently disagrees with his nation's own interests. There are many of us with differing tactics and differing philosophies on how the rules should be interpreted. And there are some of us who meet that second requirement a little too much."

"What in the flying fuck are you talking about?"

"He's trying to warn us about something, Carl." Donut had a mouthful of cherry as she talked. "But he's struggling with how to do it because he doesn't like us, and he's scared about breaking the rules."

The two of us just stared at Donut.

"I like you two quite a bit," Orren said. "I admit, I am constantly entertained at how you bend the rules to break things never meant to be broken. I used to strongly feel you two were bad for the production, despite your ability to generate ludicrous amounts of money. I still think you're both dangerous, but circumstances have changed."

"Wait," I said. "What are you trying to warn us about?"

"I have said all I can about the matter. Think of people like me as the sheriffs in the Wild West of your culture. Some are good. Some are bad. Some are passionate about their duties, yet they go too far."

I thought of Chris and of the mysterious caprid liaison that seemed to be working with the Skull Empire to get us killed. They'd told us that they'd dealt with it. Was it true?

"You're the only one we've met," I said. "Hopefully we can keep it that way."

He paused as if he wanted to say more. "Now, on to business. In case you haven't heard, the courts have stopped pretty much all crawl-related cases, including ones that the AI is traditionally indifferent to. They're trying to figure out the best way to proceed, and that likely won't get fleshed out until they get a better read on this particular AI's stability during the floor change. As you may know, your attorney is now required to get a court order to send you a message, but hasn't been allowed to even attempt this because of this freeze in *all* litigation. We've decided to circumvent this issue just this once. I must remain in the room during the discussion."

He waved his hand, and suddenly Quasar, my attorney, appeared in the room in a cloud of smoke.

He wasn't alone. He was also joined by a woman wearing a T-shirt with Donut's face on it with the words "Goddamnit, Donut!" embla-zoned in giant letters on it. The words scrolled across the shirt. A flesh-colored tentacle sprouted from the top of the woman's head, waving back and forth. The thing had a jagged, drooling mouth and little bow on its head.

Donut looked up at the newcomers, mouth still full of cherry.

Both the woman and the tentacle thing on her head burst into tears at the sight of Donut.

MY LEVEL FIVE AUTOMATON TABLE WASN'T ALL THAT USEFUL JUST YET, despite me having an instruction manual filled with recipes. I'd been terrified that they'd take the table or recipe book from me since I'd basically stolen them from the production facility. But so far, nobody had said anything about it. Just in case, I'd already copied all the recipes over to my main scratch pad, and then I'd copied and pasted them all into the cookbook.

The problem was the required supplies. I had some of the parts required for multiple recipes, but not all the parts for any of them. I did finally manage to locate materials required for something called "Spider Stalkers," which were actually just robot rot stickers, a pretty common mob. The main driveshaft for them was rare and expensive, though I managed to secure a case of them on my way out of the Desperado Club. Mordecai said the parts would be easier to find once we cleared all those assholes out of the club's second floor, but that wouldn't happen until they were teleported to the party.

Killing all the hunters we could was no longer something I *wanted* to do. It was something we *had* to do. It was crucial we killed as many as possible before the party started because we'd all be teleported to the same area at once in a few days.

Word was spreading across the crawler chat networks about the vulnerability of the hunters. The aliens were scattered and unprepared and getting picked off in ones and twos. I wanted to get in on that as soon as possible. Donut and I were joining up with Katia's team, and we were going to do some hunting while we prepared for the masquerade.

Mordecai and Zev were both beside themselves over the sheer amount of dead hunters. Nothing like this had ever happened before.

After my recent visit with Quasar, Zev confided that multiple immediately unsuccessful lawsuits followed once the brambles hit Zockau, and the Syndicate Council—not the subcommittee that oversaw the crawl, but the actual council, which was apparently a Big Deal—made a ruling that basically said nobody was allowed to file any more lawsuits naming the AI as a defendant. This was done to slow the AI's deterioration. The action apparently triggered a whole set of new lawsuits challenging the council's authority to make such a decision, and that whole mess was currently working its way through the courts.

I simply didn't know enough about the nature of the AI itself to understand how any of this worked. Why couldn't they just unplug and replace it? It didn't make sense to me.

But none of that drama had made it to the latest recap episode. They were pretending like everything was business as usual.

"This isn't like the Naga season, where they were just hemorrhaging money with every poor decision," Mordecai said. "It was like that at first, but it's turning out to be almost the opposite. Everybody *else* is losing money, but as of right now, all that lost money is transferring into Borant. It's too bad for the kua-tin government that they couldn't keep their little flippers on the company. No offense, Zev, if you're listening."

> ZEV: I'm always listening, Mordecai. And you're right. Our Valtay partners have shown no dismay at any events so far. The council, however, and the liaisons are all very nervous. Now stop talking about this.

Time to Level Collapse: 1 day, 10 hours.
Hunters Remaining: 290
Trophies Collected: 66

TIME UNTIL THE BUTCHER'S MASQUERADE: 10 HOURS.

"THE COSTUMES ARE ALL READY," DONUT SAID. "WE'RE JUST HAVING issues with some of them. Mordecai helped with the bubbles for Kiwi's costume, but some of the other ladies don't like wearing them. My clam does not like her outfit at all, and Miss Seaweed's costume falls off every time they practice their jump."

"I can't believe they let you put them on them in the first place," I said.

"That's because they trust me. I've never betrayed them. Once trust is broken, it can never be replaced. That's an important life lesson, Carl."

"Are you still on the nipple-ring thing?" I asked. "That was days ago."

"If someone says they're going to count to three, one expects them to actually count to three. Not to just stab willy-nilly into one's body without warning. I didn't get to prepare myself, Carl. One must prepare themself if they're getting disfigured. You're lucky the safe room froze me. I almost bit your hand off."

"I don't know why you keep bringing this up. You're being a baby," I said. "And that wasn't lucky. Now you have a safe room strike against you."

"You should kill him," Samantha said as she rolled by. "It is the only proper response to betrayal."

"Samantha, you have something gross in your hair," Donut called. "You better get it out before Kiwi tries to eat you again."

"Stop," I said, suddenly crouching. A light drizzle rained down. It was pitch-black outside. "There are traps up ahead. Keep the dinos back. Look for hidden hunters. Samantha, get ready. Wait for my signal this time or you won't be allowed to go to the party."

"I will kill your mother."

"Just be ready."

CARL: We're in place. Be careful. There are still traps out here.

IMANI: We're ready. Brambles are right behind us, moving in fast. We have maybe two hours before they reach the town. Scouts?

LI NA: There are ten of them out in the open on the south side of town. There's one of those anti-air guns set up. It has an anti-targeting spell on it, I think. I don't see any pets. They're preparing to leave. Most are still level 50, but there's a level 53 and a level 63 with magical plate, not the ceramic stuff. I think that one might be human. I only see one rifle this time. I see five of the mushroom guards. Don't see any other NPCs. Probably dead. There's maybe five hunters in the non-safe-room pub near the center of town. Place called Cold Stone Creamery.

LOUIS: I love that place.

DONUT: OMG, NOBODY BLOW UP THE ICE CREAM SHOP.

CARL: No Vrah?

LI NA: No sign of her.

CARL: Damn. Okay. Have you gotten a read on any affiliations?

LI NA: The one with a rifle has the mark, but I am not close enough to see what god. It's the only one I've seen. I do not know about the guys in the pub.

After our first coordinated raid, I'd received a nasty surprise. It turned out one of the hunters I'd killed from afar worshipped Emberus. I'd immediately received a warning from the god upon the hunter's death. It'd canceled out my current boon, which was plus 15% to my strength, and it told me I was in a state of **Penitence** for fifteen hours. My tithing requirements were doubled for thirty. If I killed two more within the probation period, I'd receive a smite. I had the word **Shunned** floating over my head, much to the delight of Donut and everyone else who saw it.

The shunning period had now passed, but I needed to be careful.

Vrah had somehow managed to summon Emberus to Zockau in the early days of the floor, which allowed the guards in that town to worship him. She'd done that as a way to keep me from attacking again. Some of the hunters who'd happened to see the god during his brief appearance were protecting themselves from me by also worshipping him.

Li Na's demonic Changbi race came with a racial trait that allowed her to see if anyone was affiliated with a god. If she was close enough, she could see what god they worshipped. I could also see if they worshipped Emberus if I was right on top of them, but that didn't help with the way we were doing it.

CHRIS: The level 53 rifle guy is standing on top of me. Don't know the race, but he's a big guy with red skin. Looks like Hellboy. He's standing right on my head. I can take him out.

CARL: That's a Dreadnought. Be careful. They're strong.
LI JUN: We're close and can back Chris up if we have to.

"Another damn rifle," I muttered. "And an anti-air gun. I'll have to use the spiders, not the missiles."

"It's cheating," Donut said. "They're all cheaters."

The hunters were gaining increasingly better gear despite their levels not going up.

Katia was the one who'd figured out what was happening.

"I'm pretty sure they're allowing the hunters to get sponsored. That's probably what the recap woman meant in her message a few days ago. If they're stuck here, it makes sense. Their families are probably pouring money into the show."

The problem with the vast majority of the stuff we were finding was that it was restricted to the actual hunter. Florin had taken out two Goriffs—blue humanoid aliens with flapping antennae that looked oddly like twin elephant trunks upon their heads—and each had pulse rifles and electric body armor. The aliens found out the hard way that the armor didn't protect their faces. Florin now had their gear, but he couldn't equip it. It was restricted to the now-dead individuals.

Donut's sunglasses, it turned out, had the same restrictions on them. We'd learned that when Louis had tried to put them on. Mordecai said it was a common addition to benefactor box items to keep fellow players from immediately murdering the recipients for the gear. There was a rare scroll called *Cracker Jack* that could free the item, but nobody we knew had one. In the meantime, we were collecting all the gear we could get our hands on in the hopes of utilizing it in the future.

The anti-air guns were designed specifically to take out either Elle, my missiles, Prepotente if he was mounted on Bianca, and/or the *Twister* if it approached. Or any other air-based attack. Most of these larger hunter groups had at least one now.

The pulse rifles were worse. The damn things were a downright menace. They were ridiculously unfair. They were like portable .50 cals that shot an unending supply of full-strength magic missiles. Bautista almost had his head blown off the day before, and Gwen had taken a shot to the gut that had literally punched a grapefruit-sized hole through her midsection. The system didn't treat the wound as an amputation, and she was now healed and back to her normal grumpy self.

Fortunately, the guns were not treated as magic, so regular *Shield* spells stopped their pulses. The weapons also shattered easily. The armor was similarly fragile once it was overwhelmed and shorted out. The vests fractured like ceramic pottery once the glowing blue lights turned off. The problem was, it took a lot of hits to get it to that point.

The family members of some of these stranded hunters were likely bankrupting themselves in a futile attempt to protect their loved ones.

FLORIN: Quit jawing and get on with it.

CARL: Sixty seconds, then *Ping*. Imani will cast *Dread*. Seekers moving in after that. Remember the rules. No hand-to-hand until the spiders are detonated. I'll announce when the bots are down.

"Donut," I said, "you do the honors."

She did a little hop. "Oh boy, really?"

"There's a likely Emberus worshipper in town. It's too dangerous for me." I pulled the bag from my inventory and poured the twenty rat-sized automaton spiders on the ground. They dropped out, rolling away like spilled tennis balls. Legs appeared from the metallic balls, and they skittered into a huddle, lining up.

As soon as I cast *Tripper*, setting off all the traps, I'd follow it up with *Ping*, and then Donut would touch each automaton with her paw, activating them and sending them in. I'd already programed each of the exploding automatons with a target: *Hunter Not Already Targeted*. If any of them managed to score a kill, Donut would get credit, not me.

I pulled two more unprogrammed spiders out. I clicked Samantha and set her as a target and then added the instructions: *Explode five seconds after target acquired.*

CARL: Casting now.

ELLE: This is my favorite part. It's like the Fourth of July.

61

<Note added by Crawler Milk. 6th Edition>

When a country boss dies, it drops persistent loot called the Treasure Map. My advice. Don't pick it up.

Over 400 of us faced the boss. Less than 50 survived. It would've been easier if it had been physically huge, allowing us to all attack at once. But this terror was in a low-ceilinged cave, and it was almost impossible to even get a hit in. We were doing damage to each other just as much as to him. All country bosses have special attacks that kill en masse. Beware the ones who look especially easy to kill. They are inevitably the worst.

When we finally emerged victorious, it did not feel like a victory. We were angry and bloodied and distrusting of our fellow crawlers who'd eagerly killed others just to get a hit in on the boss. What should have been a moment of unity was the calamitous event that spelled our doom.

This was by design. Of that I am certain.

And then we all picked up the map, which showed the location and quality of all the magical gear in the area. Gear we all felt we deserved. It sparked a second slaughter, and I received my first player-killer skull.

I wish I had never picked up that map. It wasn't worth it. I have blood on my claws, and it will never wash away.

I HAD SO FAR COLLECTED A TOTAL OF 66 TROPHIES. THE QUICK CHAOS of the raids made it difficult for me to use my ring, but I'd still managed to mark three additional hunters. All three of those kills had constitution as their highest stat, which brought my base up twelve points. My ring now gave five stat points per kill.

Donut had also managed to kill two more hunters, bringing her trophy total to three.

Overall, they'd been whittled down by more than half.

The inexorable brambles combined with the blood bar had seemed terrible at first, but it ended up being exactly what we needed. Most of these hunter bastards had no idea what they were doing. They weren't organized. They weren't properly trained. They didn't work well with one another. All of that equaled them getting hunted down one by one.

I'd managed to bring my player level up to 59, and Donut brought her level to 50.

Even though I hadn't been planning on doing it, I ended up tossing all of my nine stat points into strength, which actually translated to 18 points. My Agent Provocateur class added an additional +1 to intelligence, and thanks to the constitution bump from the ring, I figured it was in my best interest to utilize my special ability to double my level-up points if I used them on strength.

I kept a wary eye on my total base stat points. I now had 254 points, not including equipment buffs and base enhancements. Donut's initial, outrageous lead in total points thanks to her pet biscuit was slowly but surely eroding away. She was at 278 points, unenhanced.

If I ended up passing her, which was likely, she'd lose control of our party of two. Firas made the mistake of pointing that out during our planning session for the party, and Donut had been in a foul mood ever since.

Thankfully, the adrenaline rush of battle was enough to temporarily cure her mood. She was back to complaining about regular stuff instead.

BAM! MULTIPLE LAND-MINE-LIKE TRAPS WENT OFF, FOLLOWED BY A preposterous number of alarm traps all at once. Every town we assaulted had more traps. It was getting ridiculous. Luckily, most of the alarm traps were on the far side of town, and the dissonance of music wasn't too bad over here.

I cast *Ping*, and my map lit up like a Christmas tree. Fifteen hunters,

like Li Na said. If any were in the safe room, we wouldn't see them until they came out. As I watched, one of the dots blinked out.

CHRIS: Lava'd him. Wrecked the gun.
CARL: Good. Get out of there. Spiders incoming.

"Go," I said.

"You, and you, and you, and you," Donut said as she tapped each of
the seeker spiders on the head. They scuttled away into the rain.

"Come on, my pretties!" Samantha screeched as she rolled off toward
the town exit.

"Wait . . ." I said to Donut, watching Samantha roll away. "Now."

Donut tapped the last two spiders, and they scuttled off, chasing
Samantha.

The anti-air gun had an anti-seeking enchantment on it. The indestructible Samantha was the workaround. I'd learned the hard way to
not throw her into town when a gun was active. The last one had blasted
her, and she'd ended up blown five kilometers away, landing in the
midst of the brambles. So we just let her roll into the camp now. The
last time, she'd gone in too early and gotten herself punted. We'd had
to fight our way to the gun. Hopefully this time we had all the kinks
worked out. She'd roll to the gun, and once she was next to it, she'd stop
and allow the two spiders chasing her to catch up, causing the whole
thing to explode.

IMANI: Main team moving in. Louis and Firas, prepare, but do not
    approach until the gun is taken out.

I couldn't see them, but in the distance, the *Twister*, hidden by the
darkness, rose up over the trees. The floating house, protected by multiple shields, carried enough explosives to completely level the town if
we had to.

Imani's team of twenty-plus crawlers moved in from the north. Katia
and Elle led the charge from the west. Some hunters would fight. Some
would flee into the temporary safety of the safe room, if they were able.

Most would bolt. The unorganized and panicked hunters would in-

evitably run from the safety of the town. They were smart to bunch together for safety, but the fools always wasted the opportunity. They rarely
fought back with coordination. Once the attack started, they scattered
while we worked together. They were getting themselves slaughtered.

Three explosions ripped through the night. The seeker spiders were
starting to find targets. Then a fourth.

"I got them, Carl! I got them!" Donut cried.

> LI NA: The five hunters from the pub are now outside. They're
> running east. Careful, Carl. They're all Emberus worshippers.
> All five. Moving toward you, Florin.
> FLORIN: Already tracking them. They're good as buried.
> SAMANTHA: I'M AT THE . . .

Kablam! A red geyser shot into the night sky as the anti-air gun exploded. A second flaming form shot off in a different direction. Samantha's hair was on fire. Again. Thankfully she wasn't flying toward the
brambles this time.

> LI NA: Gun confirmed to be dead. Level 63 is running toward the
> center of town. Headed to the big temple.
> IMANI: Air support, move in. Elle, you're cleared for flight.
> KATIA: I have the 63 on my map. My team is moving in on the
> church. Elle, watch our backs.
> ELLE: I'm on it.
> KATIA: Mushroom guards are going to be a problem. Their aggro is
> activated.
> LI NA: Coming out of hiding. We will distract the guards.
> IMANI: Be careful. Remember what happened last time.
> FIRAS: We're moving in.

More spiders started popping off. Ahead, the trees rustled as something rushed toward us. Two purple dots suddenly appeared on the map,
followed by a pair of black dots. My spiders. The hunters were rushing
toward us, leading the explosive automatons right into our laps.

Oh shit. I scrambled into my interface to disable the two robots.

Before I could, two forms flew through the air above me. Kiwi and Mongo, both pouncing simultaneously. They each landed upon aliens, who turned out to be a pair of tentacle-faced Saccathians, both wearing some sort of mechanical enhancements on their legs. Both died screaming.

The spider automatons stopped dead and then turned back around, seeking new targets.

Jesus, I thought. *That was too close.*

A few minutes passed, and most of the hunters were dead, all except the level 63, who'd entered a temple. The whole raid up to this point had taken maybe six or seven minutes.

"I got five kills, Carl. Five!" Donut said, hopping up and down. "Good boy, Mongo! Good girl, Kiwi!"

Behind us in the woods, Big Tina roared indignantly. She could probably smell the blood. Kiwi was using the other lady Mongos to keep the big dinosaur back, which was fine by me. The giant allosaurus was pretty much a berserker, and the last thing we needed was her rampaging out on the chessboard.

Everything had gone as planned. Finally. It'd only taken us four raids to get it right. Too bad this was probably our last one before we all had to move into elf territory. The Popov brothers along with a few other groups had scouted one other group, but they were too far south to get to in time.

The only thing left to clean up was that last hunter.

"Come on, Donut," I said. "Let's help the others."

KATIA: Okay. Tran and I are at the front door. Daniel and Gwen at the back. I lost his dot when he went in. Someone do something about those alarm traps.

IMANI: Wait, and the rest of us will surround the building. We best do it the safe way.

CARL: We're coming in, too.

FIRAS: Want us to just bomb the place?

"Uh, Carl," Donut said, "what's that over your head mean?"

"What?" I asked, stupidly looking up. There was an odd red glow about me.

"You have a new symbol. It's really big. It's like that 'Shunned' mark you had a few days ago, but it's just an X, and it's made out of antlers. It's pulsing red."

Warning: The God Diwata has made an appearance in the realm. Diwata has marked you for death. You are being hunted. They know where you are.

Flee for your life, apostate.

CARL: Abort! Abort! Run away from the temple! Louis and Firas! Get the hell out of there! It's a god!

Just as I sent the message, a massive eruption rocked the center of town.

62

"CARL!" DONUT YELLED FROM MY SHOULDER. "SHOULDN'T WE BE RUN-ning *away* from the god?" The pulsing and spinning red star of a god appeared on my map, right in the middle of town. I vaulted over the corpses of the two Saccathians. Mongo and Kiwi, faces covered in gore, looked up from their meal to watch us rush past.

> **CARL:** Imani, on me! Donut, take the potions. Now. Both of them.
> Do it fast. What's your potion cooldown at now?

Donut didn't bother using the chat. "But we're not ready yet! We'll have to wait one minute and 45 seconds!"

> **ELLE:** Holy shit, that was disgusting.
> **FIRAS:** Did you guys see that thing?

I blinked, and the dot was moving. Away from me. It moved ridic-ulously fast, and it was soon out of range.

> **IMANI:** Is everyone okay? Is the hunter dead?
> **KATIA:** I think that *was* the hunter. Or what was left of him.
> **ELLE:** That was damn nasty. Seriously, I think I'm going to yak. Do
> you think he knew that was going to happen? Like, do you think
> he did that on purpose? That takes some serious dedication.

I skidded to a stop in the midst of the chaos. Dead hunters lay every-where. A few of my spiders remained, walking in circles, unable to find a target. They'd run out of power in a few minutes, and then I'd collect them and have to recharge them at my table. I caught sight of Li Na a hundred meters away in a cloud of glowing spore smoke, facing down multiple mushroom guards. I moved to assist, but she cast something, and they all dropped off, unconscious. Zhang moved into the light and cast something else, and the one-minute timer over the mushrooms all changed to ten minutes.

There was no sign of the god.

I wanted to relax, but my sixth sense told me we were still in danger. What the hell was that all about?

Chris appeared, coming up out of the ground like he was rapidly growing, being built by dirt. This was a different ability than the one he'd used to hide from me on the last floor. He walked over to examine a pile of steaming rocks that sizzled in the light rain. Florin jogged up. He'd just finished looting his kills. He had blood over his shirt and some on his Crocodilian face. He paused, looking at the large X floating over my head.

"That doesn't look good, mate."

"Florin, did you eat those guys?" Donut asked.

"What's going on?" I asked. "I got a notification that Diwata entered the realm, the church exploded, and then the god just ran off. He or she or whatever didn't even go after me, and I was right here."

"Don't know," Florin said. "I didn't see it. Just heard the boom."

"Did you take potions?" I asked Donut.

"No."

"Donut, if I tell you to do something, you have to do it immediately."

"Okay, Mr. Bossy Pants. We ended up not needing them yet, did we?"

"That's beside the point."

"Is it? Because the last I looked, this was the Royal Court of Princess Donut. Not the Stupid Team of Stupid Dictator Carl and His Abused Slave Cat, Princess Donut."

Elle came to hover over us as Donut and I bickered back and forth.

"That was one of the nastiest things I've ever seen, and I've seen a lot, let me tell you," Elle said. When the rain landed on her shoulders, it turned to ice and then flecked off. "You sent that warning, and then the whole church just blew up. Everyone flew back, but I was right above and saw the whole thing. Five or six of those tree dryad guys just flew up in the air, pinwheeling blood like fireworks, riding the explosion."

"You did say it was like the Fourth of July," Donut said.

Elle laughed. "That's not exactly what I meant. But yeah, that boom was magical. Not like a Carl explosion. It was green and smoky, like the mushroom guard spore attack, but thicker. When it hit me, I actually got a buff. Protection against fire and poison. Already ran out, though."

Katia, Imani, and several other members of Meadowlark jogged up while Elle continued. Gwen, Tran, and Bautista started to loot the bodies. Above, the *Twister* came into view, hovering low over the church. Li Jun, Li Na, Zhang, and a few others from their team approached. The guards remained unconscious in the distance. I gave Li Jun and Zhang a fist bump in greeting. I couldn't touch the demonic Li Na without receiving a curse.

I did a double take when I looked at the fallen guards. I finally noticed the massive bush standing in the middle of town, just beyond them. It reminded me of the Pestiferous Vine that was Grimaldi, but less chaotic. This looked like a giant well-maintained hedge that was two stories tall. It stood where the church had been and was so big that my mind hadn't registered it in the dark.

Elle continued the story. "So that green explosion came, and the tree guys all bled out, and then the smoke turned into that bush with a giant red flower pod at the top like a giant green cake. I was only like twenty feet away, and I thought for sure I was screwed. My head was spinning, but I was getting ready to ice the flower, you know. All the blood and guts from those tree guys started spinning through the air and it zipped around the flower bud like one of those cartoon illustrations of an atom. I tossed an icicle, and it did nothing. Then the bud opened up, and that hunter guy was right in the middle, looking just as surprised as I was. He was one of those humans with no eyebrows, by the way."

"The Crest," I said. They were a race that sometimes participated in faction wars, but not this time.

"Yeah. Those traitorous fuckers. Anyway, all the blood and guts and little bark pieces flowed right into his mouth, and he started getting bigger and bigger—you know, like a *Tom and Jerry* cartoon when they stick the hose in the cat's mouth? But he was wearing that armor, right? The armor wasn't getting bigger. Just him. You ever throw an unopened can of potted meat on a cook fire and wait for it to blow? Nasty. This whole thing took like five seconds, mind you, so I didn't have time to react. Then out of all that gore came a deranged-looking squirrel with antlers. It was covered in hunter pieces. The thing was no bigger than me. So, huge for a squirrel, but nothing like that damn puppy Carl sicced on us. It was a god, all right. Diwata, and it was sponsored by Circe Took. It had a five-minute timer. Then it jumped in the air and Superman-flew away like a rocket."

"Circe?" Li Jun asked. "Do we know who that is?"

"You know that bug Carl gave gonorrhea to? Circe is her mom!" Donut said.

Everyone turned to look at me.

"So, is she gone now?" Katia said, eyeing the large X over my head. "Has it been five minutes yet?"

"I don't know," I said hesitantly. "I got a notification when she appeared. When Emberus makes an appearance, it also tells me when he leaves. I haven't gotten a notification she's gone, but I don't know if this is the same thing."

"Mordecai says you should fly up there and get the petals from that flower," Donut said to Elle. "And some of the pollen, too. He says it'll wilt and go away in a minute, so you should do it fast."

"I'll get the flower petals, but you can tell him to wade into that horror scene himself if he wants the pollen," Elle said, zipping up in the air.

"I don't like this," Imani said. "Why didn't she go after Carl?"

"I don't like it, either," Katia agreed.

Samantha rolled up. She had a gray and desiccated hand in her mouth, like she was a dog who'd just dug up a grave. She spat the hand on the ground. "Carl, take the ring off of this. It's pretty, and I want it for when I get my body back. Her other hand disappeared when she died, but this was the hand with the ring on it."

"Whose kill did you steal this from?" I asked. I examined the white glittering ring. It had no magical properties at all. It was just a ring.

"Oh, that is quite lovely," Donut said.

"It's from my kill," Florin said. "She can have it."

Elle returned and dropped a few palm-tree-sized flower petals on the ground in front of Donut, who took them into her inventory.

"I still want to know if that hunter guy knew that was going to happen when he ran into the church, because that was a pretty fucked-up way to go," Elle said, looking back up at the bush. "I'd rather have Li Na here cast that *Leaking Boils* spell on me."

"Samantha," I said, "what do you know about Diwata?"

She jumped up and landed in Imani's arms, who didn't flinch. She caught the doll head in two hands.

"You smell nice," she said to Imani. "You have a very soothing aura about yourself. I used to be able to do that, but mine made men wild with desire. Stay away from my man, or I'll kill you."

Imani said nothing and turned the doll head to face us.

"Tell us about Diwata," I said. "And stop threatening people. Next time you do it, I'm going to bury you in a hole and leave you there."

She made a little growling noise. "Yeah, so that was Diwata. Nobody really likes her. Or him. They're always changing back and forth. One of Apito's brood, but not a direct child. Don't remember the story. Something to do with the Vinegar Bitch and Eileithyia." She looked over at Katia and started making a snuffling noise. "You have her scent, you know. My sniffer is coming back. I always liked the way she smelled. Not Diwata. *She* smells like a diseased, flea-infested ferret."

"Focus," I said.

"Diwata doesn't really do anything important." She took on a mocking voice. "'Oh, I'm the god of the trees and squirrels and forest rats. Look how pretty I am. Never mind Apito is the one really in charge. Never mind I get all uppity when someone wants to roast an ox at one of Eris's parties.'" She started cackling. "Other gods get mad at her a lot because she's always giving birth to new forest creatures. Necromancy is one thing, but actually giving birth to new, regular life? Oh boy, they do not like that. It makes a lot of them very cranky, especially when she starts shooting babies out of her lady growler like she's one of those djinns or succubus demons."

"What do you mean?" Katia asked.

"Diwata is like a shapeshifter," Samantha said. "She's always turning into a boy squirrel, boning all the girl squirrels, and then turning into a girl squirrel herself and spraying out a bunch of baby squirrels. Yeah, it doesn't make sense to me, either. But she's a god. What're you gonna do? Lots of gods and demons give birth. They do it for fun. I once went to a party where we all had to line up and . . . Never mind about that. Usually when one of us has a baby it's a demigod or a demonic mongrel. You met my beautiful child, no? Isn't she just the best?"

"Yes, Samantha," I said. "We met the sand ooze."

"Oh, I do hope she's doing okay. Did you know, once, when we were in the Nothing, I had her—"

"Samantha," I said. "Please."

She growled. "Diwata just gives birth to regular versions of whatever she's last naffed, regardless of the gender of the last partner. The pantheon doesn't like that so much. It's a dangerous power, even for a god. It's a power that's supposed to be consigned to the head of the Ascendency."

"She changes form to mate with different creatures?" Katia asked.

"Yes. That's what I've been saying! Now, Carl, throw me up to the floating house. I want to talk to Louis." She leaped out of Imani's grip and attempted to bounce in the air. She made it about six feet off the ground. She hovered in midair for about two seconds before she bounced back down.

I exchanged a look with Katia. She'd figured it out the same moment I did.

"She didn't attack me because she only had five minutes to get to her daughter," I said.

"Ohh," Elle said. "That's why she rocketed out of here like a squirrel out of hell."

"It makes sense," Katia agreed. "Plus, she probably doesn't want to be the one to kill Carl. It would make Vrah look weak. It has to be Vrah."

"Wait," Donut said. "Hold everything. Wait, wait, wait. Why did Circe go to her daughter?"

"To cure her of the gonorrhea," I said.

"But . . ." Donut said, "isn't the only way to cure . . . Oh, my god."

"Yeah," I said.

"Don't they rip the heads off the boys?" she asked. "Is she going to rip the head off her own mother?"

"Oh, yeah," I said. "I forgot about that. I don't know, but probably not. Not when she's a god. I don't know how necessary that part is to the process."

"That mantis accountant guy sure thought it was necessary," Donut said. "That's why he killed himself!"

"It doesn't matter," I said. "We need to assume Vrah is back in on the action."

"She's probably really mad, too." Donut gasped. "Is Diwata then going to have a bunch of Vrah babies? She'd be giving birth to her own grandchildren!"

"Uh," I said, "I hope not."

"This game is really fucked-up sometimes," Elle said.

A distant squeal caught all of our attention. We turned in time to see Big Tina gobble up one of the mushroom guards. They didn't wake up unless they were attacked, and she'd somehow broken away from her mother and entered town. She reached down with her mouth and picked the next one up and crunched it in half.

Kiwi and the others swarmed around Tina and started screeching up at the large dinosaur, who roared back indignantly.

"Sometimes?" I asked.

AFTER OUR FINAL RAID AGAINST THE HUNTERS, WE MOVED EAST TO-
ward a large settlement that'd been taken by Li-Na. This was the meeting point where we'd *all* converge, and it was the largest town near the
elven border. It would be overtaken by the brambles in four and a half
hours.

I was not surprised to find Signet sitting on a log as Donut and I
approached the town. Most of the others, including Samantha, had gone
aboard the *Twister* and were already there.

Signet was alone, lightly stroking a butterfly that had alighted upon
her hand. The sun had risen, and the rain had stopped. Light shone
through the trees wet with dew. The whole area smelled of flowers.

"Everything is dying," she said. "But there is still beauty. I've never
seen a Gehenna bramble this aggressive before. It truly is the end of
days. I don't know if the elves will be able to keep it at bay."

"You go ahead," I said to Donut. "And keep the dinosaurs behaved.
I need to talk to Signet alone."

"Okay, Carl," she said, moving off.

Signet watched Donut go. After a moment, I sat down on the log
next to her, and we just sat together for a moment. She put her head on
my shoulder and her hand on my knee, surprising me. There was nothing seductive about it, but it was the most raw, most intimate I'd ever
seen her.

I vaguely remembered something Donut had once said about the
calm before the storm. I pushed the thought away.

"I am so very tired," she said.

I put my hand on top of hers. "It's almost over. One way or another."

We sat that way for several moments.

"How is Grimaldi?" I asked.

"When he came to this world, we planted him next to an all-tree node. The roots intertwined, and he became one with the tree, as we all do, in the end. The tree's roots go deep. It has survived countless infestations such as this, and it will survive this one. The brambles are aggressive and dangerous, but like all things, they fade with time."

I didn't know if that meant he was dead or what. I decided not to pursue it.

"The soldiers are hidden in place," she finally said after a few more moments of silence. "The brambles will hit the border in a few hours. The elves will spend the day beating the infestation back, but even their magic won't stop it. By the time night hits, your party will be starting. That is when we will begin the assault."

I sighed. That was exactly what I expected her to say. Our plan to survive the evening was all in place, but Signet's presence was a wrench in the works. We needed to turn her presence into an asset.

"Your plan is not going to work. Queen Imogen knows you're coming, and it's a trap. They're not going to let you win."

The naiad summoner cocked her head to the side. "They? Who is they?"

I took a deep breath. I thought of Herot, and of her advice regarding the waking up of NPCs. She claimed it was possible with elites.

"You can't attack when the party is underway. You're being manipulated to attack right when the party starts, but there's no way the people controlling this world are going to let your climax interact with the main story. You may attack her, but you won't be able to kill her. You'll be dead. Everyone with you will be dead, and the queen will go to the party as if nothing had happened."

"What are you talking about, Carl?"

ZEV: Carl, I highly suggest you drop this.

Signet continued. "Carl, this is the culmination of everything I have worked for. While you have been fighting your own battles, I have been working tirelessly to bring an end to Imogen's tyranny. She is in a weakened position. We must strike now. I won't force you to participate, but I'd be lying if I said I didn't need you. I'll need someone already in the castle. I've cast something on you long ago that makes it so I can find you and Donut wherever you are. If you can get to Imogen, I can find her easily, and we can end it."

None of that was going to work.

"I have a better idea. Similar plan, but you'll enter the castle and wait for my signal. Then you can fight her when all of my friends face her. We'll all do it together at the same time. I'm guessing it'll be at the end of the party, not the beginning."

> ZEV: Carl, they're not going to let it happen this way. We've discussed this.

A sense of guilt tugged at my chest. This was all a lie. If I could talk Signet into this, we were going to use her as a distraction, and that was it. But more importantly, she'd be held in reserve, and I wouldn't get sucked away into something unexpected. I didn't want to do it this way, but we didn't have a choice. We still wanted her to face Imogen, but we needed it to happen at the right moment. I hoped she would survive the encounter, but I wasn't holding my breath. Still, her chances of survival were significantly higher if she and Imogen fought when *we* wanted it to happen.

Signet blinked a few times. On her wrist, the tattoo of young Clint jumped as if to grab at the butterfly still alighting upon her hand. He missed and splashed in a tattoo puddle, where a fish appeared and gently pushed him from the water.

"Tell me your idea," Signet said.

TIME UNTIL THE BUTCHER'S MASQUERADE: 5 HOURS.

"I've never seen anything like this," Mordecai said as we stood over the table. Five items, all in sponsorship boxes from the Apothecary. All given to different crawlers. All with notes that said they should be given to Donut. And that wasn't including the Pawna's Cries potion I'd received from the Open Intellect Pacifist Action Network or the I Take It

All Back potion given to Prepotente, both also intended to be given to Donut.

In fact, the only person who was sponsored by the Apothecary who'd received a benefactor box *not* intended for Donut was Katia, who'd received a small knit beanie that increased all her stats down the line by 3% and gave her a spell called *I Need My Personal Space*, which violently knocked everybody back with a powerful blow. The spell was good but dangerous because it worked on everybody, including party members. She put the beanie on, and it sank into her mass, disappearing.

I still hadn't had a chance to talk to Katia alone. Because we had to keep changing and tinkering with the plan—both the outward plan and the secret parts only discussed via the bathroom message board—we simply didn't have a chance. I pinged her on it, and she told me we should wait to see if we could take the castle first.

We'd received notifications that because we were bringing "attendants" to the party—meaning the pets, dinosaurs, two cretins, and Samantha—we'd be escorted in instead of being teleported in. We were in a small town right on the edge of the elf territory, and we were supposed to meet the escort caravan at the invisible border in fifteen minutes. The brambles would overtake the village in an hour and a half. Donut remained outside with the dinosaurs and Britney, her plus-one, practicing for the big talent show dance number. Last I'd heard, they were still having costume issues.

There was a stairwell here. Crawlers by the thousands were in town, streaming down the stairs. Imani and Elle were out there, saying goodbye to the remnants of team Meadowlark, who were now descending.

Thanks to Bomo's ability to find all the stairwells on a level, we knew of three stairwells in the area surrounding the elf castle. Two by themselves in the woods, both of which should remain free until almost the last minute. And there was one within the castle itself, in the expansive basement. It was locked, confirming that Imogen was a boss. We had several groups of crawlers already deep in elf territory guarding the other two stairwells. The elves had so far left them alone. I suspected that would soon change.

The hunters were scattered, which was unfortunate. I'd held out hope that they'd all gather together. I still hadn't heard anything about

Diwata. I had not received a notification that the god had left. The X over my head remained. A warning that all of this could crash down at any moment should a god unexpectedly show up.

I continued to stare at the items, perplexed. "The *Recharge Wand* scroll, I understand. The same with the tiara and the sheet music. But what's the stick for? And this?" I picked up the ball-peen hammer. The whole thing fit in my hand. It had been given to Imani. She'd gotten a notice that Borant had filed a dangerous appeal to keep the gift from arriving. An appeal that had been immediately denied. "Why give it to Donut? She can't even use it. What is she supposed to do, hold it in her mouth? And what does the name mean?"

Enchanted Hammer of Fast-Forward.
 This is a small hammer. It's enchanted. That means it's magical. It just doesn't do anything magical.

The benefactor box had been silver, meaning it couldn't be *too* valuable.

"Some items can be enchanted without any inherent properties. This allows them to be used against things like ghosts," Mordecai said. "I've seen it before."

"This is complete bullshit," I said. "Is it supposed to be a joke?" I picked up the stick, and it was the same thing. It was a metal rod, about a quarter inch thick and about ten inches long. It seemed to be made of aluminum, but it didn't say. This one had been given to Dmitri Popov, who'd been ridiculously excited to finally meet Donut and give it to her. Almost as excited as that Jenn'ifer woman and the weird thing sticking out of her head. Dmitri did not get a notice that there was an appeal around his gift. Still, based on the description, it seemed it was connected to the hammer.

Enchanted Stick of Cascadia's Screams.
 This is a stick. It's enchanted. It's not a wand, but when used correctly, it can do something truly magical.

"Who's Cascadia?" I asked.

Mordecai shrugged. "I can't think of any past crawlers or dungeon

bosses or places named that, which is what this stuff is usually named
after. It's a common name, though. I can think of a few of them, but I
don't know what they'd have to do with a stick. Only one of them is
connected to the crawl."

I continued to examine the metal rod, thinking. *Why give it to Donut?*
I had an ominous thought. It'd been there the whole time, but I finally
let it bubble to the surface.

*It's because they expect everyone else to be dead. Donut should have all this
stuff because she's the most likely to survive this next part. It's why Quasar
wanted Donut's name on the board of directors of our new corporation.*

There was a stairwell right outside. We were all here. Over twenty
of the top fifty were here right now. We could go down and simply avoid
this next part. It would be the safer thing to do. The smarter thing even.
I thought of the others, who'd be forced to replace us. My eyes caught
little Bonnie sitting on the counter, humming to herself as she pried the
guts out of a disarmed spider automaton. *We need her and the rest of them
if we want to survive the ninth floor. If we don't do this, it'll all be for nothing.*

As I considered all this, my finger caught something. There was a
slight imperfection there at the end of the metal rod. I brushed my finger over it. It felt like a symbol. *I think it's the number seven.*

Seven? As in the seventh floor? Maybe it wasn't supposed to make
sense yet. But if so, why would they give it to us now?

I couldn't stop thinking of Everly's final, heartbreaking entry in the
cookbook. *My sponsor was deliberately steering me not toward life, but a death
that would be watched and remembered.*

I thought of Orren the liaison and of the warning he tried to give.

I put the rod down and reexamined the hammer. Sure enough, along
the wooden handle was a similar impression. Another seven. I picked up
the other items. The scroll didn't have any sort of hidden symbol that I
could find. Neither did the new tiara or the sheet of music. That made
sense. Their purpose was clear.

"God, I hope we're ready," I said. "I don't like all these loose ends.
I'm always spinning plates, but this feels like it's too much. Something
is going to go wrong."

"It always does," Mordecai said. "If it goes sour, you have the escape
plan. Get to the *Twister* and fly away."

"You're going to hell," little Randy the bear cub said to Bonnie the gnome, who remained on the counter. She had the spider automaton in pieces all around her. The sad little gnome girl looked up at the small bear. She said nothing.

"All heathens burn in the fires of judgment," the bear added.

Skarn the changeling sat nearby with a group of other kids, including Ruby, one of several changeling children suffering from compression sickness. Half had turned to deformed human kids. Others were bears.

"Don't be mean," Skarn said to the smaller bear.

"Or else what?" Randy said. His brother, Todd, stood behind him, looking up at the group of changelings defiantly. The two bear cubs were much younger than the majority of the recently arrived changeling kids. The two groups had been bickering the whole time. Prudence, the mother of the two bears, was passed out on the couch, snoring.

"You two should fight to the death," Samantha said.

"Is there a reason they're all in here still?" Mordecai asked. He pointed to the guildhall exit. "There's a whole area for them to explore."

I thumbed at the television, upon which some cartoon called *Little Bear* played. "That's why." And then I pointed to the other end of the room where a changeling kid sat on the lap of the Sledge, who sat in front of another television I'd rigged up, playing one of the *Grand Theft Auto* games. Both Bomo and the Sledge had become obsessed with the game. The Sledge was happily showing the kid how to steal a car. "And that's why."

Donut peeked her head into the room. "Carl, it's time to go. Did you figure it out?"

"Nope," I said as I gathered the items up. I handed them off to Donut one by one. "You brushed your teeth, right?"

"Yes, Carl. I gave the tube to Katia afterward."

"Excellent. Come on, Samantha. Let's party."

64

<Note added by Crawler Everly. 5th Edition>
My sponsor sent me a box today meant for someone else in my party. And not a crawler, but one of my mercenaries. A spell book of Hasten Poison. I was quite upset about it. But not five hours later, he used that spell to kill the boss holding the lockbox key, and it saved the lives of us all. I don't trust my sponsors, but I do trust that they want to keep me alive. As long as I breathe, their insipid advertisements remain on full display, and their investment is intact.

<Note added by Crawler Everly. 5th Edition>
The moment I hit floor eight, they gave me a great box, as if to make up for the previous one. A tool that allows me to take shortcuts through this maze. I really want to hope. To think that there's good out there. It's in times like this that there's a spark in my chitin, a longing for a future that contains warmth and stars.

<Note added by Crawler Everly. 5th Edition>
I take it back. I take it all back. My sponsor was deliberately steering me not toward life, but a death that would be watched and remembered and ultimately heartrending and painful. I was a fool. Fuck you, Dictum Way Station Controls, Limited, whatever that means. I hope your company and all your children die in pain.

<Note added by Crawler Drakea. 22nd Edition>

This is Everly's last entry. She did not mention the manner in which she was set up, which is unfortunate. Please, future author, be as detailed as you can.

<Note added by Crawler Carl. 25th Edition>

I'm starting something I don't think will succeed. I will be documenting every step along the way. We have a method of communication that allows prying eyes not to see it. See my earlier post about the coffee shop author's kit to see how it works. I don't know if the following will be useful or not to future readers, but as Drakea suggested, we should be detailed as possible, especially with plans that could possibly lead to our deaths. If anything, this will be a record of my demise. Sorry if there's language from my culture you don't understand. Here's a copy and paste of page one of our notes:

> The Butcher's Masquerade is a trap. They're going to try to kill us all. Queen Imogen is a country boss. I don't know how it will happen, but we'll probably have to fight her at the end of the party. Since I can't talk all of you into going down the stairs early with me, we'll have to figure out how to survive.

> I also have an issue with my elite quest. They want to fight this same boss, but before or maybe during the party. That means they're doomed to fail because the main showrunners aren't going to allow their climax to get hosed by a secondary production. As much as I like the elite Signet, I would like to avoid going down with her. The production goes out of their way to make sure I'm involved, so I might be forced to deal with this secondary show's climax whether I want to or not.

> I've been working on the problem, and I have a few ideas. Before we get to that, we need to lay out our objectives.

> Goal one is to survive. Everything else is secondary. However, if we meet all of these secondary objectives, we'll

not only survive here; we'll also have good footing once we hit the ninth floor.

As I see it, here are all our secondary objectives. In order from least important to most important:

1) Solve the Tina quest. Get her to dance onstage. I used to want to abandon this one, but I think we can use this to our advantage.
2) Kill Eva. If she's stupid enough to go to the party, we shouldn't waste the opportunity. Not something I really want to do, but how many more good people will she hurt?
3) Save the changelings and get them to the next floor down.
4) We can only accomplish #3 if we get them into the castle. That won't be easy unless we first kill Queen Imogen and take the castle for ourselves. This fight will probably be forced on us whether we like it or not. I'm working on a few ways to even the odds.
5) Kill Lucia Mar. Again, I don't want to do this, but she's too dangerous. Her very presence at this thing is going to be a problem because she's such a wild card. She's likely to tank the whole operation and get us all killed. The further she gets, the more dangerous she becomes.
6) I made a promise at the end of the last floor, and I intend on keeping it. We are going to make certain not a single solitary hunter gets off this floor alive.

Once you see this, sign your name so I know I can erase it, and we can move on to the planning. I have ideas for most of this, but I'll need your input.

Signed,

· Katia

· Imani

· Jesus Christ, Carl. You're going to get us all killed. Elle

· I HATE THIS PAPER THING, CARL. GC, BWR, NW PRINCESS DONUT THE QUEEN ANNE CHONK

- I am claiming Lucia Mar for myself. If someone attempts to stop me, we will have a problem. Florin
- Nobody has tried to convince me not to go down the stairs. I think we should. Louis
- Same. Firas
- Li Na. I have my own method of speaking with my team. I will keep them updated. Also, I agree with Elle.
- Daniel Bautista. I'll do whatever I can.
- Chris

TIME UNTIL THE BUTCHER'S MASQUERADE: 1 HOUR.

TIME TO LEVEL COLLAPSE: 31 HOURS.

Total Number of Remaining Crawlers: 59,259
Total Number of Crawlers Still on the Sixth Floor: 23,385
Number of Crawlers Attending the Party: 73
Number of Hunters Attending the Party: 264

"YOU WILL BE REQUIRED TO ENTER THE CASTLE THROUGH THE ATTENDANT entrance," the uptight, nasally elf announced as the large covered wagon bumped over the road. He shifted uncomfortably on the bench. In addition to the elf, it was just me and Britney in the cart. We were in a caravan, dotted with armored and armed elves and wagons. Big Tina and the lady Mongos walked in procession behind us. Tina kept wandering off, so Donut had to go out there and keep her in line, much to the dismay of the elf servant guy, whose name was Theobold. He was a level 35 **High Elf Footman**.

"Upon entrance, you will be subject to a security sweep. You and all your supplies will be reinspected. You will be able to secure your attendants in the servant ballroom. From there, you and your invited guests will be escorted to the main ballroom. During the presentation of the pets and the talent portion, those of you who are performing will be given access to the anteroom behind the stage where you may interact . . . Sir, I do think I should wait until Princess Donut returns so I can explain the procedures to her as well."

"Don't worry about it," I said. I thumbed over at Britney, who sat there looking especially grumpy. "Donut's plus-one will explain everything to the princess. She's Donut's guitarist. Aren't you, Britney?"

"Uh-huh," Britney said.

The elf looked upon Britney and her fluffy brown-and-gray jacket with an unmistakable air of contempt. It reminded me of the time I'd gone out to dinner at a super-fancy steak place with Bea and her parents, and they had made me put on a sports coat that was two sizes too small. I'd had grease on my hands because I'd come straight from work, and I'd gotten it all over the coat.

"Very well," Theobold said. "Like I was explaining, you will be given backstage access. Another footman will be present to further explain those procedures. Please follow all instructions. The queen will not attend either performance, but it is crucial we keep to the timeline."

Shit, I thought. "She doesn't want to see the pet show? Who doesn't want to see a pet show?"

Theobold ignored me. "Before you enter the main ballroom, you will be given access to a guest boudoir where you may change into proper masquerade attire."

He looked me up and down.

"I do hope, sir, that you brought shoes for the event. And pants."

"Nope," I said.

"No, no, no, Tina," Donut called from just outside. "If you try to eat the elf, he won't let you into the castle! Really, Kiwi. You must keep your child under better control. Why can't people ever keep their children under control? Tina! No! We just gave you a bath!"

Theobold sighed. "No weapons will be brandished in the ballroom, nor will magic of any kind be tolerated. Yes," he said, cutting me off before I could interject, "you may cast limited magic or brandish weapons onstage if it is crucial to your act, but you will not be allowed to physically interact with anyone not onstage with you."

I relaxed as he continued to drone.

"Those of you with magical storage will not be able to access it within the ballroom. Once you enter the ballroom and you are deemed to be in compliance with all the rules, you will officially be under the formal protection of the Queen of All That Is and the Queen of All That

Will Be, the One and Only True Blood, Her Majesty on High, Queen Imogen of the High Elves. Any attempts to break the peace from your-selves or your attendants will be met with instant and punitive action. This protection is only active while you are in the proper designated ballroom."

"Sounds like my kind of party," I said. "Tell me, Theo. What does the queen's protection actually mean? Those hunter assholes don't like me so much. What'll happen if one of them takes a swing?"

"As you've no doubt been informed, sir, you will be attending the party in what's known as a goodwill ballroom, so it will be quite im-possible for the opposing guests to harm you. You will not be in the same physical location as them, and any strike will feel like a whisper. But if a serious attempt to harm you is made, protections are in place."

"What does that even mean?"

"It is not of your concern. Rest assured these protections were put into place by Apito herself."

"Apito?" I asked. "The goddess?"

"Yes."

Uh-oh, I thought.

". . . and in case they don't prove sufficient, the queen's personal guard will remain in the center ballroom, where the queen herself will eventually be in attendance."

"So, she'll be in a third ballroom all by herself?"

"She and her personal guard, yes. We take the queen's safety quite seriously. Not that she needs such protection."

"I'm assuming the guard dudes in the queen's private ballroom can smack me around, but I can't hit back?"

"That is correct, sir, but again, we have additional protections that would make such interventions unnecessary."

I needed to find out exactly what those additional protections were. "Okay, that's all well and good. But there are going to be people at the party all in the same ballroom who don't like each other too much. There's this one-armed dude named Quan who I'm pretty sure will be there. There's this girl with a giant dog who'll probably just want to go apeshit and kill everybody, especially Princess Donut. Oh, and there's this snake lady with three hands. Her name is Eva. She's still around, and she has a thing for my friend Katia. They used to be best friends, but they had a falling-out. And those are just the beefs I know about."

"Fighting will not be tolerated," Theobold said.

"So if my friend Quan tries to one-arm strangle me, you'll intervene?"

"Like I said, sir, an attack upon the queen's protected guests is the same as an attack upon the queen herself. All guests at the masquerade will be reminded of this. This protection cannot be circumvented."

"Got it," I said. An ominous feeling washed over me.

Outside, one of the stag mounts let out a squeal, followed by Donut shouting, "Tina! No! Play nice!" A guard gave a muffled warning.

Next to me, Britney shifted uncomfortably. She did not want to be here, especially considering she wasn't in the top 50. She was miserable in her new, itchy jacket. Firas, who'd ended up at number 43, had talked her into coming and being Donut's assistant, especially since she could play the guitar. It was either this or be part of Gideon's assault team, which she did not want to do.

"Hey," I asked, "will the queen's pet be at the party?"

"Sir Ferdinand?" Theobold asked.

I blinked, surprised they actually used the same name. Well, his name was Gravy Boat. But they used Donut's name for him.

"Yes," I said.

"I imagine so. When he isn't ranging from the castle to hunt, he is usually upon her shoulder. The two are quite inseparable."

His tone suggested he felt the same way about the cat as he felt about my lack of pants.

"Sir? So he's a knight? Does that mean he's like your boss, then?" I chuckled. "Cats, man. Princess Donut there is pretty much my boss. I don't like to admit it, but she's the one in charge. Just wait until you see her act. She has a new song she's trying out."

"A knight? Certainly not," Theobold said. "We are a civilized kingdom. Ferdinand is nothing but a lowly creature. A familiar. A pet. The 'sir' is simply a part of his name. It's not a real title." He turned his gaze toward the curtain. "That seems to be a common thing amongst their kind."

"So, he's *not* royalty?" I asked, feigning surprise. "We met him a few days back. Out in the woods during that whole issue with the Odious

Creepers. He implied that he was second in charge of the whole kingdom."

"You must be mistaken," Theobold said.

"Maybe," I said. "I'd watch him, if I were you. You can't ever trust cats. Like, ever. They're all cute and cuddly, but they'll eat your corpse in a second."

"Gross, Carl," Britney said.

"Yeah," I agreed. "One last question."

"Of course, sir," Theobold said. This dude could win a gold medal at the patronizing Olympics. "It is my pleasure to accommodate you."

"I have a whole stash of these hands I got from killing the hunters. They said there would be a prize counter where we could turn them in. Do I need to take them from my inventory ahead of time?"

"No need, sir. The award table attendant will be able to extract the items from you."

"Have you seen the prizes?" I asked. This whole part of the masquerade was still a mystery, and it was one of several unknowns I was worried about.

"I have not, sir. Do not worry. The prize counter will be open for the entire evening. Now, if you'll excuse me, I must attend to the other guests in the caravan." He deftly pulled himself from the covered wagon and disappeared, leaving me and Britney alone.

"This isn't going to work," Britney whispered, an edge of panic to her voice. She kept nervously rubbing her right hand up and down the left arm of her fur-covered jacket. "He said there's a security check when we get to the castle and another on the way into the ballroom. Those are just the ones they've told us about."

"Did you take the potion?"

"The dinosaur repellant? Yes. I've been taking it every day. But I don't think it works. Mongo tackles me every time I visit your room."

"That's because he likes you. What about your *Shield* spell? Is it ready to go?"

Britney had gotten into the bad habit of casting her *Shield* the moment she saw a mob. The spell was actually quite powerful now, able to block both magic and physical attacks for thirty seconds, but it had a four-hour cooldown.

"Yes. The cooldown just reset."

"Good. I need you to relax. We're all wearing magical clothing. They're not going to make us get naked. They said we can't cast magic or wield weapons. That's it, so chill."

I peeked out the curtain of the covered wagon. The setting sun shone through the trees. It'd be dark soon. Mounted guards riding upon their white stags were coming in to join the progression, flanking the sides.

There were six separate wagons mixed in with the dinos and stag mounts. Theobold had been riding in that first one along with two guards. Li Jun, Li Na, and Zhang were in the second. They'd entered the talent show as jugglers. We were in the third. Imani and Elle, who were participating in the talent show, sat in the fourth. They were going to perform a skit.

Tserendolgor—now ranked number 38—and her plus-one partner were in the fifth wagon. We'd taken to calling her Ren because nobody could pronounce her name. She had a pet show entry with her, lumbering behind their wagon and keeping a wary eye on Tina and the other dinosaurs. It was a blob thing called a Tummy Acher. His name was Garret. She'd just received the pet on this floor, as a gift for going to CrawlCon. The level 20 pet was as tall as me, and it looked like a giant lumpy meatball. It had no arms, but it did have a pair of stubby legs, giving it a bouncy gait as it followed, like a fat toddler chasing after his parents. Garret had an enormous jagged mouth with a single tooth that could probably swallow me whole. The damn thing was equal parts adorable and horrifying. It made a kind of giggling noise when it walked and could tank a massive amount of damage. Apparently, people loved the thing.

DONUT: THERE ARE MORE GUARDS COMING. THERE'RE NEW ONES WITH BLACK JACKETS.

CARL: You need to keep Tina under control. I think we've waited long enough. Put your new tiara on.

DONUT: SHE'S EXCITED. YOU KNOW HOW CHILDREN GET WHEN THEY'RE EXCITED. I ALREADY PUT THE TIARA ON, AND IT HELPED A LOT WITH THE DINOSAURS, BUT THE GUARDS ARE STILL AGITATED. IT'S PROBABLY BECAUSE OF THAT LADY IN

THE LAST CART. THEY MIGHT TRY TO GET HER BEFORE WE
GET TO THE CASTLE.

The final, larger cart contained all of the props and costumes and supplies for both the talent portion and the beauty contest. They'd insisted upon us removing it all from our inventory so they could inspect it. Also riding in the cart were the non-crawler attendants who didn't want to walk. Samantha was in there along with the cretins Clay-ton and Very Sullen and a mysterious robed woman.

The robed woman, as far as most people knew, was Signet. It was actually Pearson the changeling pretending to be Signet.

The guards had hesitated when they saw the changeling, but they didn't react further. Gauging their reaction was one of the reasons why we did it this way. Signet seemed to believe that Queen Imogen had an order in place not to attack her directly. The naiad suggested that the queen herself would want to deal with her once she finally revealed herself, and the guards' reaction seemed to imply that was the case.

So far, nobody on the floor had yet seen the queen.

Bomo and the Sledge remained in the safe room. They both had jobs to do, and they'd both wait until the party started to get moving.

I knew there were other crawlers and possibly some hunters also riding to the castle this way in other caravans. They didn't tell us how many acts there would be for the talent and pet shows, nor if the hunters were participating. Another unknown. We only knew of five entrants total to the pet show and of five teams with spots in the talent portion.

There were also about fifteen crawlers going to the party whom I didn't know at all. That was going to be a problem.

Only some of the ones I did know were bringing a plus-one. I didn't have anyone.

DONUT: THEY WENT INTO THE LAST CART.

A minute passed. The curtain to our covered wagon rustled, and suddenly a new person appeared in the cart, fading into existence next to Britney like she'd been sitting there the whole time.

Notifications and achievements scrolled across my view.

Britney squeaked in surprise and slid to the edge of the cart. She panic-cast her *Shield* spell just as the white-tagged Queen Imogen finished fading into existence.

"Your Majesty," I said, trying to swallow. *Oh fuck. Oh shit. He's going to lose his mind.*

"Are you really attempting to smuggle someone who looks like my half sister into the castle?"

CARL: Katia, it worked. We drew her out. But it's Ifechi. Queen Imogen is Ifechi, Florin's dead girlfriend.

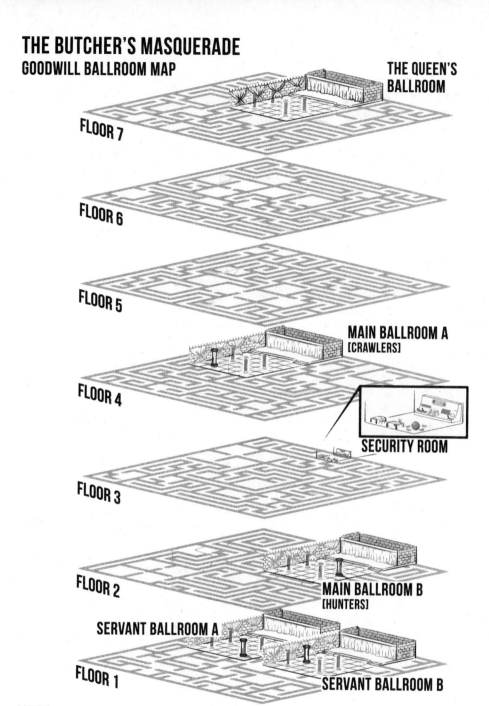

THE BUTCHER'S MASQUERADE
GOODWILL BALLROOM MAP

THE QUEEN'S BALLROOM

FLOOR 7

FLOOR 6

FLOOR 5

MAIN BALLROOM A
[CRAWLERS]

FLOOR 4

SECURITY ROOM

FLOOR 3

FLOOR 2

MAIN BALLROOM B
[HUNTERS]

SERVANT BALLROOM A

FLOOR 1

SERVANT BALLROOM B

RULES:

- Guests in main/queen ballroom all interact with one another as If they're in the same room.
- Guests cannot harm guests in other ballrooms. The queen has no such restrictions.
- Guests in main ballrooms cannot cast magic spells / use inventory.
- Guests cannot leave their ballrooms.
- Servant ballrooms are for staging only.
- Security room controls all.

65

<Note added by Crawler Carl. 25th Edition>
From page five of our planning notes:

> According to Edgar's map, the control center for the four
> ballrooms—the two main ballrooms and the two attendant
> ballrooms—is located in the very middle of the castle in a
> secure chamber on the third floor. Each of the four ballrooms
> is controlled by a small soul crystal. There's a fifth, larger
> crystal that controls the whole overlay system that allows us
> to interact with everyone in the other rooms. When we go into
> the ballroom, there'll be a mute spell that'll keep us from
> casting our magic and another that'll keep us from using our
> inventory. I think that's it. We can't brandish weapons, either,
> but I don't know how they'll enforce it. The mute and
> inventory spells are not active in the attendant ballrooms.
> Also, the queen's ballroom doesn't have any protections, so
> there're no controls.
>
> What we need to do is get someone into the control room and
> turn off the protections without disturbing the other rooms or
> turning off the goodwill overlay. There'll be a notification
> when the switch occurs, so we need to make sure everyone
> keeps their mouths shut until we make our move.

Here's my idea. We go with the Gideon distraction to empty the castle of as many guards as possible. Once that happens, we'll make our move. We'll have to brainstorm some ideas on how to get to the security room, so everyone study the map and let me know your thoughts.

Also, on another subject: I'm pretty sure Imogen is going to be someone one of us knows. I think they were originally planning on her being Bea, my ex-girlfriend and Donut's owner. We need to be prepared for that.

~Carl

We all have people it could be. We'll deal with whatever happens like we always do. We need a better method of communication. I can't keep going to the bathroom like this. It's becoming obvious.

~Imani

Your idea of using Donut's charm for the fight against Imogen might also work for the security room, but the timing might fuck us. It's a lot of pressure on her.

~Elle

I like that idea, but it'll only work if Imogen is at the party the whole time.

~Carl

CARL IS ALWAYS IN THE BATHROOM. AND I DON'T LIKE THE CHARM PLAN. IT'S THE NIPPLE RING ALL OVER AGAIN. I DON'T LIKE BEING STABBED, CARL. I'D LIKE FOR YOU TO GET STABBED FOR ONE OF YOUR PLANS SOMETIME.

Sign the notes, Donut.

~Carl

IT'S QUITE OBVIOUS WHO IS SPEAKING, CARL.

———

JESUS, I THOUGHT. *SHE HAS HER VOICE.*
I examined the beautiful elf.

Queen Imogen—High Elf Cleric Sorceress.
   Level 145 Country Boss.
   This NPC is Intangible. You may not physically touch it. Yet.
   This isn't just any High Elf. This is Imogen, the queen of the elves. The big baddie of the floor. Don't let her good looks and polite manner fool you. She is as ugly as they come.
   Sometimes when we meet bad guys, there's a lingering possibility that we might see some sort of redemption arc. There's a good quality buried in there somewhere. Did you know, for example, that Juicer guy you murdered on the first floor used to spend all his free time volunteering at a hedgehog rescue? Remember Denise the goose? The one you shoved headfirst into a garbage disposal? She loved reading to children. In fact, you've now killed two bosses who loved reading to kids.
   Anyway, Imogen doesn't have any qualities like that. Not a one. She has never left a tip in her life. If they had shopping carts in this world, she'd never return it to the corral. Sure, she pretends to be a kind and just leader. She throws a killer party, that's for certain.
   But in the end, it's all a show. Everything she does is in service of her main motivation, which is power. She's nothing more than a terrified little girl, afraid of weakness, afraid of dying like her father, King Finian. Impotent and alone and overshadowed by someone more powerful.
   She has a plan to make certain that never happens to her. A plan that all hinges on the success of tonight's masquerade.

I sure hope you don't do anything to piss her off. That might
be bad.

KATIA: It's not Ifechi. It's her twin sister. Florin told us she had
one when we met the Popovs. I'll warn him.

I forced a grin on my face as I fired warning messages off. "Smuggle
someone? Me? Of course not. Do I look crazy? That woman is part of
Princess Donut's act."

She looked at me then. Her dark eyes bored into me as if she truly
was attempting to decide if I was crazy or not.

I went very still while she examined me. A notification appeared. An
achievement for total views. A fan box. I exchanged a look with Britney,
whose eyes had gotten huge. She'd likely gotten something similar.

DONUT: I JUST GOT MY PLUS-ONE TOKEN BACK. I DON'T KNOW
WHY.
CARL: I think Britney might've hit the top 50 on her own. She was
58 a few hours ago.
DONUT: WELL, THAT'S JUST RUDE. NOW I LOOK LIKE I'M GOING TO
THE PARTY ALONE LIKE A LOSER.

Queen Imogen had clearly been preparing for the ball when she'd
decided to come here for a visit. She wore a long, glittering, color-
changing gown covered with magical sparkles. Hanging from her neck
was a gold chain with a distinctive glowing gemstone pendant. A soul
crystal. Her dark brown skin was complemented with highlighted and
silky brown hair held up in a pile atop her head in one of those fancy
I'm-getting-married-today updos with a single curled strand of hair dangling on each side. Perfectly applied gold-colored makeup covered her
face like gold leaf upon a piece of art.

I'd never met Ifechi, but she'd been from Nigeria. A member of the
Red Cross who'd been following around a group of militants when
they'd all entered the dungeon. I'd assumed the bald woman was male
until Katia had pointed it out. This version of her—or her twin sister—

was stunningly beautiful. Still, I saw it in her eyes. I remembered the haunted look on Ifechi's face just before she died on the recap episode, killed by Lucia Mar at the end of the fourth floor. Queen Imogen had the same look.

All of these elves so far had been pale white dudes, so her darker skin tone was a surprise, especially considering their whole racial-purity shtick. The aliens watching this probably wouldn't even notice the difference.

This was supposed to be Beatrice, I thought, and I was endlessly grateful that it was not. I'd been worried that it would be someone else I knew, such as Bea's mom. I felt guilty for being so relieved. Especially considering this was probably worse. I'd been concerned for a while now about Florin's mental health.

CARL: Get him down the stairs.

KATIA: There's no way that's going to happen. He's been pacing back and forth for an hour straight, excited for the party.

CARL: Florin, you know the rule. We all agreed to it. If Imogen took the form of one of our loved ones, the intended target goes down the stairs.

FLORIN: Go fuck yourself, Carl. I don't see your cat going down the stairs. Now back off. I'm fine.

Britney remained in the corner, huddled in on herself. Her shield would run out in a few seconds, not that it mattered here. Imogen's dot remained white on the map.

A new elf was suddenly in the wagon, hanging on the outer edge. The sleek and muscular guard was dressed in black formfitting armor with straight white hair. He leaned in and whispered into the queen's ear. She nodded and shooed him away.

She returned her gaze to me and raised an amused eyebrow. "Tell me, Carl. What are you playing at? Why bring that woman? Why dress her in such a manner?"

DONUT: THE GUARDS ARE BEING JERKS. THEY'RE TELLING ME I CAN'T GO BACK INTO THE CARRIAGE. THEY TOLD ME I COULD

GO IN THE ONE WITH THE DOG LADY, AND I SAID NO. I CAN'T
BELIEVE THEY LET HER IN THE TOP 50.

CARL: It's okay. I need you out there. Be ready.

I struggled to appear much more confident than I felt. Pearson the
changeling had been instructed to look almost like Signet, enough, at
least, to garner the attention of the elves, but he needed to remain in
human form and not change. If we were especially lucky, she would've
touched him. And hopefully not murder him.

"I'm not playing at anything. I didn't even realize you knew my
name, Your Majesty."

"Are you scared of me, Carl?"

I was goddamned terrified. I didn't want to admit it, but it felt pru-
dent at the moment to tell the truth.

"Very."

The queen sighed. "The Butcher's Masquerade is a pause in all the
ugliness of the world. Everyone in attendance will be under my protection. The event will be perfectly safe, and to suggest otherwise is an
insult."

"Then I'm looking forward to it," I said.

The cart continued to bump over the trail. Britney and I remained
frozen, unsure what to do.

"Do you know why it's named such? The Butcher's Masquerade? We
do not wear masks, yet it is a masquerade. Do you know why this is so?
Do you know the story?"

"I haven't really thought about it."

She nodded. "Typical of your kind to know nothing of your betters.
The first masquerade was held in the Halls of the Ascendency. Taranis
and his wife, Apito, the Blessed Oak Mother, put the party on for all of
their children and extended family, who are constantly vying for control,
even to this day. The party was meant as a night of respite. No violence.
Their son, Grull, asked why it was called a masquerade when they did
not wear masks. Apito's response is considered sacred gospel:

"She said, 'My son, the masks we wear are the smiles upon our faces and the goodwill we present to each other this evening. There will be no violence. No maneuvering. Just an evening of feats and friendly contests and tales of past conquests. A place where you can face your greatest enemies and not worry about it being the end of your plots.' Grull didn't understand, of course. But he and the others followed his mother's wishes and attended the event. The party went on as planned at first. It was Yarilo, god of lust, who broke the peace. Drunk, he attempted to force himself upon the familiar of one of the other gods. For breaking the seal of peace, he was banished to the Nothing by Apito. Taranis, angry with his wife for exiling his child, raged. Fights broke out after that. All the attending mortals and demigods were slaughtered, leaving Apito in tears."

"I've been to a few parties like that," I said.

Imogen scowled at my interruption. I was having a hard time reading her. She was an odd mix of polite and barely bridled rage. If I didn't know better, I'd also think she was stoned out of her gourd. "Afterward, the party became a ritual. A holy sacrament. A rite of reflection and of non-violence. Of us striving to meet the goal of Apito, the most perfect of mothers, who wants nothing more than for all of us to get along."

I remembered the crazy-ass city elves on the third floor. Their whole thing had also been the worship of Apito. "Don't you go around killing everything that's not a pure-blooded elf?"

"Only when they dare to carry themselves as our equals. Apito seeks harmony above all. Mongrels add chaos to the mix. To grow the perfect tree, one must first cut off the rot."

I wasn't about to go spelunking down that tunnel. "So, you have a party, deliberately invite people who don't like each other, and try not to have it turn into a clusterfuck?"

She nodded. "Only the most divine are granted the right to cast the spell. And they can only cast it once in their lives. Once cast, the ritual begins, the guest list forms, and we have the party."

"Wait, you cast a spell for the party?"

She fingered the soul gem around her neck. "Of course. It's one of Apito's holiest sacraments. The party is named after the spell. The Butcher's Masquerade."

This conversation was not going anything like I thought it might.

Imogen continued. "The guest list comes from the goddess herself, and we are not to harm the attendants before the party."

"Really?" I asked. Traditionally, the elves were considered a deadly menace to both the hunters and the crawlers. That was why everyone stayed away from their property. I knew this whole Butcher's Masquerade storyline was something new. *Huh,* I thought, trying to remember if I had any reports of people fighting the elves.

"Not unless they attempt to harm us first," she said. "Which is why I am here right now talking to you instead of having my soldiers fertilize the forest with your entrails."

"Your cat almost murdered my cat," I said. "That wasn't self-defense."

She nodded. "You are correct. Everything was almost ruined when your friend jumped in front of Ferdinand's bolt. Do not worry. He has been properly chastened for it. I did not instruct him to attack you or your friend's familiar."

I grunted. "There's no such thing as chastening a cat. You can yell at them, but it's like yelling at a wall, believe me."

Donut pinged me for the tenth time, asking if everything was okay. We were coming up on the castle.

DONUT: IT'S REALLY UGLY. I THOUGHT ELVES WERE SUPPOSED TO DESIGN THINGS WITH WATERFALLS AND FLOWING LINES AND TREES AND NAKED STATUES. IT LOOKS LIKE A WHITE VERSION OF THAT ROBOT SPACESHIP FROM *STAR TREK*. IT LOOKS LIKE IT WAS MADE BY A THREE-YEAR-OLD IN THAT *MINECRAFT* GAME YOU USED TO PRETEND NOT TO PLAY.

Imogen did not appear amused. "We prepare the evening just as Apito tirelessly prepared. We offer the same refreshments, the same opportunity to showcase one's talents and familiars, and if the party properly finishes without violence, Apito grants a boon. The guest list is deliberately chosen by the goddess to sow discord amongst everyone involved. It is my duty as host to make certain we get through the entire evening without violence. If we can succeed, I am granted the goddess's gift."

She pointed at me accusatorially. The nails on her slender fingers were ridiculously long, like claws.

The cart pulled to a stop.

"I want that boon, Carl. I cannot keep you from the party. I cannot harm you because you haven't made any overt moves. Yet you're working with my mongrel half sister. I do not know what your plot is. You will not succeed. The party will be under a celestial peace seal. The moment you attempt something, the ground will open underneath your feet, and everyone involved in breaching the peace will be fed into the Nothing. You can hide your plotting from me, but not from the Oak Mother. That's the price one pays for breaking the seal of peace."

I turned to Britney, pretending to be much more casual than I felt. "And all this time I thought she was going to just straight up murder us. She has to use her goddess to do it."

Britney did not respond. She looked like she was going to vomit.

"Killing you would be easy," Imogen said. "Watch."

She turned toward Britney, lifted her hand as if she was about to cast a spell, but paused.

"Oh, Oak Mother," Imogen whispered. "You vex me so."

I was pretty sure she'd been about to kill or seriously injure Britney, but she'd stopped when she realized Britney had just entered the top 50 and thus was invited to the party on her own.

Imogen sighed. "If I wanted you dead, Carl, you would be. If you do anything to disturb the peace, I won't be the one to hurt you. An eternity in the Nothing, the realm of darkness and of gnashing of teeth, is a fate worse than any death I could conjure. If by chance, someone else breaks the peace, and you're spared by the goddess, you will be the first to face my wrath. If my ritual is disturbed and I am free to respond, you will be the first worm I will crush. Now I will take my leave. I have you on my dance card, Carl. We'll talk further later."

And just like that, she was gone. The curtain rustled, and the high elf queen dissipated, coming apart like dandelion seeds caught in a breeze.

The party hadn't even started yet, and our plan was already fucked.

"She reminds me of my mother," Britney said.

66

<Note added by Crawler Carl. 25th Edition>
From page seven of our planning notes:

For those of you who haven't had a chance to study the map yet, do it ASAP. Don't let the square shape fool you. This place is a nightmare of halls and rooms and passages. The main part of the castle not including the basement levels is seven stories tall. There are actually more floors than that–like, way more–but those levels are mostly around the edges. Think of it like a Borg cube-themed hotel or casino where the public spaces all have ceilings about twenty or so feet tall, but they also manage to shove a bunch of rooms in there along the periphery.

The two attendant ballrooms are on opposite sides of the first floor. Ballroom A, where we'll be, is on the fourth floor and ballroom B for the hunters is on the second floor, and it's directly above their attendant room. The queen's ballroom and her living quarters are all on the seventh floor. That whole area is off-limits to everybody except the queen and her guards.

If one walks into the front entrance, there's a giant stairwell that runs all the way up to the fifth floor, but that's it. Visitors don't go higher. It looks like it'll be almost impossible to get to the throne room or to the queen, so we'll have to get her to come to us. The worst possible thing that can happen is if she decides to fight us while she's in her ballroom and we're in ours. Even with our magic and inventory access turned on, she'll still be safe, and we won't be.

Again. We do not fight the queen while we're in our ballroom no matter what. It is suicide.

There are a few additional quirks to the goodwill ballroom system according to both Samantha and the entertainer instruction notice.

Some of the protections are turned off when you're physically onstage. When Donut stands upon the stage in ballroom A, she will be able to physically interact with all the items that have been moved to the stage area of the attendant ballrooms a few stories below. If there's a wand on the attendant stage, she'll be able to pick it up and cast it. The wand itself will still be three floors below. It's just like the magic pens the Popovs and I used to sign autographs at CrawlCon. The only thing Donut can't do is drink something if it's not with her. She'll be able to read the *Recharge Wand* scroll and her sheet music if she needs it, but she won't be able to down the charm potion. We'll have to smuggle it in. Mordecai has a bunch of ideas for smuggling potions into secure areas. It's something he's really familiar with, so it shouldn't be a problem. We'll probably end up using Katia as an equipment locker.

Speaking of those pens, Samantha says some of the items in the ballroom itself, like the tables and chairs, will be physically present on all iterations of the hall. So if I pick up a table and move it, it will move in all of the locations. This includes the doors and anything affixed to the walls, including that warning light we were worried about. Other things, however, like the food at the buffet, will only exist in either ballroom A or B. It can get confusing, so everything is usually color coded. Food on the blue plates you can pick up and eat, but food on the red plates is actually in the other ballroom, etc.

~Carl

If Donut can still cast magic while onstage, why do we need the security room taken?

~Imani

They say she can cast spells, but it's only a few approved ones. Illusionary evocations, which means her *Torch* spell and that's it. Wands and scrolls will work, but she won't be allowed to bring them up with her to the main ballroom. Even something like *Hole* won't work unless the magic access is restored in the room.

~Carl

This is confusing as shit. I'm getting Iron Tangle flashbacks. I hated the Iron Tangle.

~Louis

It's not that bad. All you need to know is we'll be in ballroom A, the hunters will be in ballroom B, and the queen will be in her own ballroom by herself. There'll be a color-code system letting you know what items you can touch. Anything that's in either of the attendant ballrooms is invisible to us unless it's on the main stage. All the stage stuff isn't important except to the performers. Study the map. We have copies of it.

~Carl

CARL: HEY, GUYS. PLAN WON'T WORK. NEW PLAN.

    ELLE: Goddamnit, Carl.

    IMANI: What part won't work?

    CARL: Assuming Imogen just told me the truth, everything inside the ballroom. We can't make the first move. We have a new play.

    KATIA: What is it?

    CARL: We party. We don't start anything. Everything outside the party goes on as planned, but we can't do anything violent while we're in there.

    DONUT: WHAT ABOUT MY ACT? THE DINOSAURS?

    CARL: We'll play it by ear. We'll set everything up like planned, but we won't pull the trigger unless we're forced to. We still need to defend ourselves. One way or another, shit's gonna go down. We need to be ready.

"So, should I stick this awful jacket into my inventory?" Britney asked.

"Absolutely not," I said. "Keep it on. Just don't set it off prematurely like you did that *Shield* spell."

DONUT DIRECTED THE UNLOADING OF SUPPLIES AS I GAZED UP AT THE massive white square of the elf castle. I couldn't decide if it was ugly or stunning. Elle was calling it the Sugar Cube, and the name had stuck. We stood around the corner from the main entrance at a set of double doors that was the equivalent of the building's loading dock and freight entrance. The doors yawned open, and elves appeared, some pulling flatbed carts to load the supplies.

"This place is not very defensible," I muttered.

"There used to be a moat," an elf guard said. "The queen made us drain it because it smelled funny. It doesn't matter. The four towers are stronger than they look. Nobody attacks anyway. Especially not with the queen being as powerful as she is." He shrugged.

These guys working at the castle were much friendlier than the ones we'd met previously. It seemed there were different groups. This guy, dressed in gold, was a **Level 40 Castle Guard**. They were different than the white-clad soldiers who'd been escorting Ferdinand. Or the black-and-gold-clad ninja-like elves who guarded Queen Imogen.

The entire castle, I realized, was made of some type of wood. Maybe bleached oak. It looked like white stone from a distance or even marble. But I ran my fingers over it, and it was clearly wood. The wall was smooth to the touch, and it was carved with little acorn shapes, each one about the size of my fingernail, like the whole structure was carved from a single piece of wood, turned on the lathe of a god. The acorn pattern ran up the wall into the setting sun. The white wood was hot to the touch, and it gave the sense of something very old and magical. It reminded me, oddly, of the time I visited the USS *Constitution* and took the tour of the ancient iron-armored, wood-hulled frigate. It was almost like the wood itself breathed.

The elf castle sat against a rocky bluff in the extreme southeast corner of the map. A single pencil-thin tower stood at each corner. Thanks to Edgar's incredibly specific map, I knew the open-topped towers housed a set of magic-wielding guards and were just wide enough for two people to ascend via a curling staircase. The only entrances and exits to the towers were on the third floor of the castle, other than at the very tops. There were no other obvious defenses or fortifications.

The cube-shaped castle was actually more of a rectangle. A few floors remained hidden underground. There were caves there, in the rock surrounding the castle, filled with trolls who were constantly fighting the elves. There was likely a whole storyline and quest involved with that stuff. There was a secret entrance there, and hopefully, sometime in the last few hours Signet had gotten herself into the castle and was hiding in the dungeon, waiting.

Zev had warned me up and down and sideways not to attempt to smuggle the elite into the party. Any attempts to do so, and the production company would be contractually forced to send directions to Signet to do something premature. Something that would definitely get her killed and would likely take me down with her. She was, under no circumstances, allowed in there.

I assured Zev I had no such plans, which was absolutely true.

If Signet were to enter the party, courts would have to get involved regarding who owned the rights to what actually happened next. It was a hard rule regarding secondary production companies and the show-runners of *Dungeon Crawler World*.

Don't fuck with the main event.

I didn't give a rat's ass about any of that. I pretended to hem and haw and agree. I'd already talked Signet into coming alone and hiding in the basement. I promised her that an opportunity would present itself if she was patient. And if not? Well, the queen wasn't going anywhere.

I felt kind of bad about it, using her like this.

"You. You have been deemed unwelcome," an elf guard said to Pearson the changeling, who was still in the form of a robed woman. This was one of the white-clad elves, one of the level 70 guards. A soldier. "Now run along. You have an hour to remove yourself from our territory before you are deemed a trespasser."

"She's in my act," Donut protested.

"The brambles are already at the border," the woman said, still acting the part. "Your soldiers are fighting them. Where would I go?"

"Not my problem. Queen's orders. Now go before I have my men use you as target practice."

I grabbed her arm, leaned in, and whispered, "Get to the cave. Stick to the plan."

The changeling ran off just as more caravans appeared coming up the road.

"They're not going in cages," Donut said, raising her voice. "These are expertly trained, professional show animals! They're perfectly safe. This is an outrage! Carl, get the queen back here this instant!"

A pair of elves grunted as they pulled the massive cage out the double doors. The silver metal cage looked as if it had been built especially for Big Tina.

"Your professional show animal just tried to eat my sambhur," one of the elves said.

"You mean the stag things? Tina was just playing. Right, Tina?"

Tina roared and snapped, causing a group of elves to shout and back away. Several pulled out their bows.

"All animals are going in cages," another, older-looking elf said, undisturbed by the dinosaur. He emerged from inside, pulling thick gloves off his hands, and waved the other elves down. This guy was different than the others. He wore overalls and was named Kibben. He was a **level 50 High Elf Stablemancer**. This was the first high elf I'd seen with short hair, making him look like a bush elf. "Don't worry. They'll be released for your act. We don't want them hurting each other between performances. You see that Tummy Acher over there? He'll swallow one of your mongoliensis whole given half the chance. And your allosaurus is still a juvenile, which means you can't control her too well."

Donut peered angrily over at Tserendolgor, who was in the process of wiping dirt off of Garret, her pet Tummy Acher.

"If that walking meatball is so dangerous, he should be disqualified immediately. What if he attacks my Mongo?"

The elf smiled down at Donut. "I'll make sure the pets are all separated and safe. It's my job."

"Are those hunters bringing any pets to the party? I heard there're two servant ballrooms. Maybe we can move my dinosaurs to the other holding area"—she glared at Tserendolgor—"where they'll be safe. Does it matter which holding area they're in?'

"Both of the attendant ballrooms affect the stage area in the same way, so that doesn't matter, but it's not really necessary."

"This is most unprofessional. In all my years, I have never heard of such abysmal treatment of honored guests. It's necessary if I say it's necessary. Who is your manager?"

I looked at the guy. "I've found the best way to get her to shut up is to just let her do what she wants if it doesn't matter one way or another." I leaned in conspiratorially. "She is a cat after all. I understand you guys have one of those running around in here, too."

"Hey!" Donut said. "What is that supposed to mean, Carl?"

The elf shrugged. "We can put the dinos in the other room. You're right. We don't have anything scheduled in there. Seems like the other group isn't too interested in either of the showcases. Probably for the best anyway. Most of the sambhurs move through this side, and that allosaurus makes them nervous. Only thing in that room is Simoom. The cretins and the . . . reanimated head . . . will have to stay in here."

Donut sniffed. "I suppose that will be acceptable. But I must insist on watching the transfer."

"Donut," I said as Elle and Imani walked up. Behind us, a caravan pulled to a stop, and a crawler I didn't recognize got out, followed by what looked like a hawk familiar. "The animals will be fine. This guy obviously knows what he's doing. Let's get the ball rolling."

DONUT: CARL, MY CHARM UPGRADE ISN'T WORKING.

CARL: It's working just fine. These are high elves. They think we're beneath them, and I think your ex-boyfriend has left them with a negative opinion. The fact they're talking to us at all is a sign it's working. I'm just bummed it's not permanent.

DONUT: THIS TIARA IS UGLY ANYWAY. BUT DON'T TELL THE APOTHECARY LADY I SAID THAT.

ENTERING BALLROOM A.

You've been muted! You may not cast spells in this room.

You've been peace bonded! You may not access your inventory in this room.

On the wall, high on the ceiling was a light. It was nothing more than a glow globe. It flashed twice, letting the guards know the first people had entered the ballroom, and the system was now activated and armed. It would flash brightly every time the system was either activated or turned off, as a safeguard.

Warning! This room is under a protection seal. Any violent acts will break the seal, resulting in your banishment to the Nothing.

Warning! As an invited guest, you may not leave this room until the party has concluded or once the protection seal has been broken. I hope you went potty before you got here.

Once the host arrives, the party chambers will be fully sealed from outside influence.

"Damnit," I muttered at the notification.

IMANI: Carl, does that mean once Imogen enters the room, she
    can't leave? Doesn't that ruin the effectiveness of the
    distraction?
CARL: It does. We need to use escape plan C.
DONUT: IS THAT THE ONE WHERE WE ALL PLUMMET TO OUR
    DEATHS?
CARL: That's escape plan D. Escape plan C is using your *Hole* spell
    to fall down to the third level and fight our way out. We'll have
    to spread the word to have everybody approach you when it
    goes down.
IMANI: I'll start spreading the word.

Despite the promises of extensive security checks, we didn't undergo
anything too invasive thanks to Donut's enhanced charm. The gnoll
security checks to get into a production trailer had been much more
intrusive.

After going up a long, twisting staircase that went straight from the
first floor to the fourth, an elf made us store all our weapons in inventory
and then patted us down. That included my wrist bracer that formed
my Grull gauntlet. The biggest issue was Tserendolgor's—Ren's—
flamethrower, which she wore like a backpack. It reminded me of those
backpacks from the *Ghostbusters* movies, only hers was also part of her
shirt. So removing the weapon exposed her hairy chest, revealing a pair
of furry dog breasts. Donut was about to make a snide comment before
I shut her up. Imani gave the dog soldier a robe to cover up.

The rest of us were allowed to keep our clothes. As I suspected, they
didn't blink at Britney's jacket or any of our other magical gear. Another
footman elf gave us a lecture on not fighting and then gave a graphic
description of how awful falling into the Nothing would be. A third
used a Donut-sized snail to sniff us for explosives, focusing on me. We
didn't have any on us, and we passed cleanly through.

From there we entered the hallway leading into the ballroom and
were ushered into the "boudoir," where we could change further. The

large chamber was like a glorified locker room with individual cubicles and bathrooms. Nobody actually changed clothes. I covered the bathroom counter with dinosaur repellant potions and Half Splat potions with a note for everyone who found it to store the Half Splat in their inventory in a ready position and, if they hadn't already, to drink the dinosaur one now. I warned that we would possibly have to flee quickly, and there would be loose, prey-driven dinosaurs everywhere. We wanted them attacking the hunters. Not us.

We left and were patted and sniffed down once again and then led into the main ballroom.

There were fifteen of us in this first group. It was all of us from the first caravan and the second, which included several crawlers I didn't know. Most were human, but there was a mushroom guy I'd only seen in passing who was afraid of Elle for some unknown reason and a badger-headed woman who was also a Swashbuckler, the same class as Bautista and Tran, both of whom would be joining us once everyone else got teleported to the room.

We entered the large opulent ballroom, our footsteps echoing on the tiled floor.

An elf guard, wearing a ridiculously ornate white silk uniform with coattails lined with gold, jumped to attention as we entered. He held on to a glittering spear that was easily ten feet tall. He took a breath and then shouted, "From here on forward past this point, you are under the holy protection of Queen Imogen! The Oak Mother's wrath will set upon anyone who breaks the peace!"

The room was huge, bigger than I'd expected from the map. From my shoulder, Donut gasped. We were the first crawlers here. To our right stood a preposterously large stage with a wavy red floor-to-ceiling curtain made of a thick expensive-looking fabric. Multiple tables were set up around a dance floor. A buffet was in the process of being erected in one corner of the room while elves swarmed over it like ants on a hill. Sure enough, the trays of food on one of the buffet lines were marked gold and the others were marked black.

Soft music filled the chamber, coming from a trio of elves playing stringed instruments. It sounded similar to chamber music, but with an odd amount of reverb, giving it a strange distant sound. I'd seen the performers setting up downstairs, and I knew they were really in the servant ballroom, which is where our animals and attendants would also be during the ball.

Four pillars led upward to a large domed ceiling covered with a massive moving mosaic. The artwork featured a glittering black-and-gold cave dotted with sparkling crystals, like the interior of a golden geode. Curled up in the midst of this was a black centipede whose form continued to twist, like one of those spirals one used to hypnotize someone.

This is a depiction of Scolopendra. She's dreaming. It's said when she finally awakens, she will destroy everything and free us all.

From the center of the mosaic sprouted a living tree made of white wood and white leaves. The tree hung downward from the tall ceiling, giving the illusion we were the ones upside down. The moving mosaic of Scolopendra never ceased twisting around the tree, like it was attempting to strangle it.

I couldn't take my eyes off it. I wondered if the tree and mosaic were really here, or if they were just an illusion.

"Carl, look!" Donut said, turning my attention.

I followed her pointing paw. Directly opposite of the stage on the far side of the room was a glass case that read **Prize Counter**. A blanket was draped over the case, and a familiar figure stood behind the glass.

"Uh-oh," I said, looking at the winged werewolf-like creature standing there.

"Is that the guy Mordecai hates?" Donut asked.

"That's him," I said.

"Who is it?" Elle asked, hovering next to me.

"His name is Chaco," I said. "Remember when I told you about the prize-carousel thing?"

"It's when Carl picked that stupid book of goblin recipes," Donut said.

"Ah, so that's the guy ol' Mordecai attacked?" Elle asked. "Didn't he throw a chair at his head? Good thing he's not here. Did you ever get the story out of him?"

"Not all of it," I said. I turned to walk toward him when there was a *crack* of teleportation, and three new figures appeared in the room: a tall, thin soother; one of those Jell-O-mold blob aliens whose mouth faced upward; and a familiar tentacle-faced Saccathian. None of them had information or tags above them.

Donut gasped. "Oh, my god," she cried. "Princess D'Nadia! Carl, look! It's Princess D'Nadia!" She hopped up and down and then jumped off my shoulder and ran over to her, her tail waving back and forth with excitement.

The soother and blob thing moved off to inspect the stage as we approached D'Nadia. The Saccathian was taller than me. She wore a glittering purple dress covered in sparkles. The dress was curved with unnatural lumps, alluding to a body covered with additional tentacles.

"Princess," Donut said, "I didn't know you were going to be here!"

"Hello, Princess Donut," D'Nadia said. "I'm judging the talent show and pet contest. And it's no longer 'Princess.' My father, sadly, decided to retire. My title is now Empress D'Nadia."

"Really?" Donut asked, trying not to hide her excitement. "My sponsor is an empress?"

The Saccathian waved her finger at Donut with mock sternness. "Now, Donut, don't think because I'm your sponsor I'll show favoritism. I take my judging duties very seriously."

"Of course! Of course!" Donut said excitedly.

Behind us, more crawlers appeared, coming through the door. Prepotente was one of them. Our eyes met from across the room.

An elf appeared onstage, pushing his way out of the curtain. "Attention, please! All guests who are participating in either the talent show or the pet contest, please join me backstage for some quick instructions!"

Most of the crawlers in the room turned and started shuffling toward the elf. Prepotente was one of them.

"I'll be right back!" Donut said, and bounded off. "Hi, Prepotente!" We watched her go.

"I'm very cross with you, Carl," D'Nadia said, coming to stand next to me. I could smell her. She smelled like sweet calamari. "Your attorney and that new corporation of yours almost ruined my buy-in bid."

KATIA: We're here. We all teleported into hallway C3 on the map.

We're in line for security. It's going to be a few minutes.

They're only letting us into the boudoirs five at a time.

CARL: Make sure people take the potions. And tell them about
escape plan C.

KATIA: Eva is here. So is Lucia Mar. Carl, I'm worried about Florin.

I reached over and touched D'Nadia's dress. She felt solid, but with a little push, my fingers disappeared within. She wasn't really here. This was different than in the production trailers. We could physically touch each other, but only gently. I could smell her, too.

"I heard about the buy-in bid," I said. "I'm sorry about that. If I had known it was you, I would've had Donut send you a message. Are you on-planet?"

"In orbit, but we're making landfall after this evening. You're lucky it worked out. Otherwise, I would not be so pleasant to be around."

"I find that hard to believe," I said. I was laying it on thick, trying my best not to let my newfound utter contempt for her show. "Tell me, do empresses usually judge pet shows?"

D'Nadia made an amused trumpeting noise with her tentacles. "I'm working. The judging of this contest allows me to be a part of the production, which is one of the requirements. It's a technicality. A loophole. Something you're quite familiar with, aren't you?"

KATIA: Eva went into the dressing room after me. She stole all the
potions and is now making snide comments about them.

CARL: You have more in your inventory. Find out who didn't get
any and pass them out once the inventory gets turned on.

"I gotta tell you," I said, returning my attention to D'Nadia. "I was surprised when Quasar told me who . . ." I trailed off as the door near the buffet opened, and Vrah scurried into the room. The large mantis looked around, saw me, and made a beeline in our direction.

Her crotch was no longer on fire.

Behind her, other hunters started to enter the room, much more hesitant. The bright light on the wall flashed, telling the guards the system was now fully armed and engaged. Both rooms were now in use.

CARL: Bomo, Sledge, it's time. Sledge, tell the changelings to get their asses moving. Britney, do your thing.

Empress D'Nadia eyed the charging form of Vrah. "Oh, I'm looking forward to this," she said.

67

THE GIANT MANTIS BARRELED TOWARD ME LIKE SHE WAS GOING TO bowl me over. She stopped just an inch away. She gnashed her mandibles right in front of my face. She smelled vaguely of burned plastic.

"Hey, Vrah," I said cheerfully. "How was your visit with your mother?"

D'Nadia trumpeted with laughter.

"Stay out of this, Princess," Vrah said, not turning her head.

"Empress," D'Nadia corrected.

There was a commotion behind me, but I didn't dare turn my back. I pretended to remain engaged with Vrah as I watched Britney sidle up to the guard with the giant spear. She said something to him and giggled. He didn't seem amused.

"I have a present for you, Carl," Vrah said. "It's coming soon."

"Oh, sweet," I said. I patted her on the upper-shoulder part of her carapace. The same spot on her neck that the head of Langley had bitten down on. She felt barely tangible. "Thanks, I really appreciate that. It's not even my birthday. Actually, maybe it is? I've lost track. Is it April already? It hasn't been that long, has it?"

Britney pretended to drop something, and the guard looked down. The moment he did, she reached up and pulled at a tag sewn into her jacket.

Please, please, I thought. *Don't attack.*

Bautista said the Slate Butterflies weren't violent, which was good considering the circumstances. Britney's entire jacket was made of stuffed versions of the fuzzy creatures. We only needed one for now. She'd wanted to sew them onto her boots, but I liked the idea of having a ton of them at the ready just in case. Mordecai said the special ability on these guys wasn't considered magic, which is why we went with them instead of my idea of me smuggling in my slingshot. I prayed it would work.

Vrah bristled. "You're not the only one who can bend the rules to your will. You and your soft-shelled friends will soon learn what it means to make an enemy of the Dark Hive."

"Don't you guys run an amusement park? What do you do to your enemies? Ban them from the bumper boats?"

The hand-sized butterfly flittered straight up into the air, making a line for the first light source it saw. The warning light. It reached the light and settled on it, wrapping it with its wings. The light's glow slowly paled, and the powered light faded away. A moment later, the common-rarity summoned creature returned to a stuffed animal. I held my breath as it fell, hit the tip of the elf's spear, and landed in Britney's outstretched hand. The guard looked up as Britney pulled the stuffed animal behind her back. He returned to his position.

It was done.

"I am looking forward to our rematch," Vrah was saying. "I will remove that disgusting smirk from your worthless face."

"Wow," I said, turning to D'Nadia, who continued to watch the exchange with amusement. "She is really angry, isn't she?"

"You did give her gonorrhea, Carl."

D'Nadia now had what looked like a champagne flute in her hand, but I hadn't seen who'd given it to her. She dipped one of her tentacles in the glass and sucked up half of the drink. I hadn't realized the weird little appendages worked like elephant trunks.

An angry chittering noise rose from Vrah. "I swear to you this, Carl. Before this night is done, I will have your decapitated head on my back. Yours and all your friends'." She turned and skittered away angrily.

"No violence, remember?" I called after her.

CARL: Good job, Britney!
BRITNEY: I am not doing that again. My heart is in my throat.

Shouting rose from behind me. I heard the voices of Katia, Florin, and Bautista. I sighed.

I turned, expecting to see Katia holding Florin back from attacking Lucia Mar. The Lajabless was here, in her beautiful-woman form, but she stood against the wall, chewing on her fingernail, eyes darting back and forth like she didn't know where she was. In that moment, I saw her for what she was: a kid in an adult's body.

But I only looked upon her for a moment. A chair fell over, clattering loudly to the ground. To my surprise, it was Florin and Bautista holding Katia back, who was lunging at Eva, who leaned casually against another table. The half-nagini, half-orc remained a Nimblefoot Enforcer, and she'd risen to level 55, equal with Katia and four below my level 59.

I hadn't seen the four-armed, snake-headed crawler since that day upon the train when Katia had accidentally killed Hekla. Eva had lost a hand in that fight—her dominant, top-left hand. The hand was still gone, nothing but a square-edged stump. I knew that she had recently become armed with a poisoned rapier-like blade that she attached to the appendage. She could pop it in and out like a switchblade. They'd made her take it off. Upon her chest she wore a glittering jeweled breastplate that looked like something out of a museum. It shone with a high polish. Purple gemstones of various sizes dotted the elaborate armor.

The last time I'd seen Eva, she had a dozen or so player-killer skulls. She now had over 50.

She also sported four hunter-killer marks.

"Why are you like this?" Katia was shouting. "Why? These are your people, too. You're a traitorous bitch. The moment the protection is turned off, I'm going to rip your face off."

"Temper, temper," Eva was saying, pretending to sound bored. "This is why Fannar couldn't stand you anymore. With your ugly brown hair, your ugly piggy nose, and your constant whining. What kind of mother could you have possibly been?"

"Oh, just shut the hell up, Eva," I said, coming to stand between her and Katia. Bautista had his arms wrapped around her waist. Florin also held her back.

I put my hand on Katia's shoulder. It looked like flesh, but her arm was made of metal. She had a locker full of potions stored in there.

"Calm," I said, looking into her eyes. "We anticipated this. It's okay."

Donut was suddenly there, on Katia's other shoulder. She and the others who'd been backstage were returning. Crawlers continued to stream in from the hallway. I saw Louis and Firas enter the room, their eyes huge, followed by the Popovs, Gwen, and Tran. Britney shuffled toward them, arms out, and she hugged tightly onto Firas.

Donut butted her head against Katia, who reached up and gave her a pat.

"Oh hello, Eva," Donut said, her voice turning flat. "I .thought I smelled vermin. You know, I was just thinking about you today. It reminded me that I need my litter box changed. Carl."

"Yeah, I'll get right on that."

The snake woman sneered. "I'm getting a drink."

She pushed herself off the table and moved toward the back of the room. The crawlers all mingled near the stage, and the hunters were all crowded around the buffet tables. We were separated like boys and girls at a middle school dance. As Eva approached, the hunters scattered away from her.

"You okay?" I asked Katia.

"I'm fine," she said.

I exchanged a look with Bautista, and he gave me a nod. He was on it.

"How's it looking back there?" I asked Donut.

She scoffed. "I've been to cat shows held at a two-star Holiday Inn where the cages shared the room with the free continental breakfast that were better situated than this. The theater is gorgeous, yes, but only at first glance. It was built by someone who obviously knows nothing about such things. There is no thrust. The stage is straight, like we're in some rural high school gymnasium. There are no wings at all. None, Carl. I can't even with that. AV is nothing but an elf with a magic microphone and no mixing board, and he simply did not understand how to work the boom box."

"What?" I asked. "Boom box? What are you talking about?"

She ignored me. "Furthermore, the grid extends maybe five feet above the arch, and that's only because of the curtain. There's only a single catwalk, and they straight up ignored my request for access. I am quite certain the lighting team isn't going to understand my directions.

I'm glad we can use light magic onstage, because lighting is everything with these things, and they don't even care. They're just doing it willy-nilly. You know how I feel about willy-nilly, Carl."

"Is the catwalk going to be a problem?"

"I thought we weren't doing that? You're giving me whiplash, Carl."

"We still need to be prepared. This is a very fluid situation."

"Speaking of fluid situations, they didn't say there weren't bathrooms in here. It's outrageous!"

"The catwalks," I said. "Are they a problem?"

"No," she said. "And it's catwalk. There's just one. It's forward enough that it won't get in the way. Edgar's map was quite specific and accurate." She sighed dramatically. "I knew this was going to be amateur hour, but once you see it up close, you don't fully appreciate the level of ineptitude it required to make something look this nice yet be so functionally inefficient at the same time. You know what it's like? It's like a stage version of a cocker spaniel."

Quick movement caught my eye, distracting me. "I'm sure your song will go fine."

"This is all for Mongo's presentation," Donut said. "We haven't even gotten to my talent performance yet. I presented the stage manager with the instruction booklet and rider, and can you believe he . . . Carl, where are you going?"

Shit. Florin was marching across the room toward Lucia. I looked for Imani and Elle, who were the designated peacekeepers, but they were both involved with other quarrels.

"Florin," I called, running to catch up with the Crocodilian. The room was getting pretty full, and he shouldered his way through crawlers as he approached the scared-looking Lucia.

"Florin, stop," I said, putting my hand on his chest.

"Don't touch me, Carl," he said.

"Wait. Please," I said. "We can't fight in here."

"I know that," he snapped. "I'm not a fool. I just want to talk to her."

"She is unpredictable. We don't want her to break the seal, and if you say something to her, she's probably going to attack you. Look, man, I need you."

I wasn't getting through to him, so I tried a different tactic.

CARL: Florin, I need you to stay focused. I can't be babysitting your ass. We all have our roles tonight, and you promised me you were good.

FLORIN: I am good. Now get off my back.

CARL: Okay. I'm gonna trust you.

"Good," he said out loud. He continued to stare Lucia down, who looked back at him with wide eyes.

The tableau held for several moments. Florin blinked and then something softened in his small pinprick eyes. "Something's off with her anyway," he said. "She ain't acting right. I know with that bitch that don't mean much. But something ain't right."

"Yeah," I agreed, looking over my shoulder at the kid. "Let's leave her be. Not trigger her. We gotta keep the hunters away from her, too. If I were them, she'd be the target. She's easily the most unpredictable."

Lucia remained frozen against the wall, watching us. She suddenly bolted, running along the wall to a spot in the corner against the stage. She huddled there, shaking. She plopped herself down on the ground and sat cross-legged, hugging herself tightly.

Just stay there, kid, I thought.

I looked about for Quan Ch, but I didn't see him at all. That was a goddamned relief. Assuming he was still alive, he'd likely gone down the stairs.

"Carl," a familiar voice said from behind me, startling me. Prepotente. I turned to face the goat. He looked even worse than the last time I'd seen him.

"Prepotente, when did you last sleep?"

"I know this will come as a shock to you, but I must insist that I join your party."

I just looked at him for several seconds. At this point, nothing was going to surprise me anymore.

"No," I said after a moment. "Talk to Katia. She might be willing, but you're level 70, and you'll end up the party leader of whatever party you join, and most established parties won't like that. Better yet, find some of those displaced Eva crawlers, if any are still alive. You can start your own party, and you can join the guild."

"It would only be for the remainder of this floor. It's so we travel together to the start of the next. I've been collecting the clues, and after speaking with Katia, she informed me about Donut's magical hammer and stick."

"Attention. Attention, everyone," a voice boomed. It came from the stage. Prepotente screamed in response. Right in my ear.

"We're bookmarking this," I said. "We need to get through the party first. Maybe talk to Donut. Did you take the dinosaur repellant?" I looked about for the cat, and she was on the shoulder of Bautista, talking to a crowd of crawlers, making karate kick motions and pointing at Lucia Mar in the corner.

Goddamnit, Donut, I thought.

"Welcome to the Butcher's Masquerade!" the voice called. He paused as if waiting for applause.

This was Theobold, the same elf footman who'd given me the instructions during the caravan. He'd changed into one of those white dress tuxedos with the gold lining. It looked disturbingly like the dinner dress white jackets naval officers wore to one of their countless parties.

"We still have some guests filtering in. That's okay. For the next several hours, we will be enjoying an evening together of fun and talent. There is plenty of food and refreshment, all perfectly curated to your personal dietary needs. Those of you in ballroom A may use any gold-colored tray, and the black trays are for our honored guests in ballroom B. If you need anything, please do not hesitate to ask one of the servants, who will do their best to accommodate you. After the performances, we will have dancing. Queen Imogen herself plans on visiting soon. Those of you who have collected hunter hands or crawler scalps may now visit the prize booth to turn them in. Please remember, this party is a celebration of Apito's love for all her children. Violence is blasphemy. We are here this evening to have a good time. Apito wishes for us to mingle with our enemies. Do not waste this opportunity. Those of you participating in the pet program, please proceed to the backstage area."

Donut did a little hop and scrambled toward the stage. Prepotente also went back. I sighed.

None of the hunters went backstage. Their group, much larger than ours, huddled sullenly near the buffet tables.

Empress D'Nadia and the other two judges moved toward a raised table just in front of the stage. It'd still be a few minutes before this started. I did a quick look around the room to make certain there weren't any fires I needed to put out. Imani and Elle were talking to a group of crawlers who looked as if they might come to blows with another group.

We didn't have anything special planned for the pet show itself. We just needed to get through the next hour or so without anyone getting themselves banished to the Nothing.

That didn't mean we were idle.

During this time, the Sledge was meeting up with half the change-lings and they were making their way to the underground secret en-trance to the castle, currently guarded by Signet's crew. The were-castors and others would escort them all inside. The changelings, once within, were going to pretend to be elves and make their way to each of the four sentinel towers, ascend, and remove the guards within, creating a dock-ing location for the *Twister*, which would bring in the remaining change-lings once everything was fully engaged.

Gideon and his team were setting up in the woods outside to observe and to assault the front of the castle if needed.

Bomo was starting his looting mission.

Before everything changed, the next part of the plan had been to use Signet right when we needed the queen out of the ballroom. Using Sledge as a relay, we would've sent a changeling upstairs and ratted her out.

The half-naiad's sudden appearance in the castle would've triggered the guards, and Imogen would be forced to react. She'd leave the party to deal with her. It was actually a plan similar to what Signet's crew had been planning anyway, but I'd talked her into waiting so we could con-trol the timing.

Now that we knew Queen Imogen couldn't leave the party once she arrived, we needed to either trigger Signet's appearance early or to save her for once the seal was broken. What we decided to do would depend wholly on when the Sledge arrived with the changelings and whether or not they could take the towers.

I sighed. It'd been a good plan, but we'd gotten screwed by the lack of proper intelligence.

> ZEV: Godsdamnit, Carl. I don't know what you did, but they're
> going to be pissed.
> CARL: What? You're not supposed to be mad at me for another
> two or three hours.
> ZEV: This isn't funny. She's not supposed to be in here. It's going
> to be a logistical nightmare.
> CARL: Seriously. I don't . . .

I dropped the chat window the moment I saw her enter the room. *Well, shit.*

Signet walked into the room, tattoos swimming across her bare chest. The guard at the door just stared, mouth agape. He turned and fled the room, shouting.

She saw me, smiled, and casually strolled up. She reached out and grabbed my hands in hers. She felt solid. Warm. She was in the same ballroom as us.

"Want to hear something funny?" she asked. "I was just sitting there, minding my own thoughts in a damp, dark dungeon, when Apito herself appeared before me and told me I was invited to a party. And suddenly, I was here."

> CARL: Hey, Zev. This wasn't me. This one is on the AI.

68

IMANI: CARL, WHY IS SHE HERE? SHE CAN'T HELP US IF SHE'S IN THE room with us.

> CARL: I was worried this was going to happen the second the queen told me that Apito forms the guest list herself. "Apito" is testing Imogen. Of course she's going to bring in one of her biggest enemies. That's the whole point of the spell.

> IMANI: I don't like this, Carl. It's like they've been one step ahead of us the whole time.

> CARL: Don't worry. I think this is actually better. With her in the room with us, she'll be Imogen's first target. It'll give us a few extra seconds to escape if someone breaks the seal.

> IMANI: Everything is going off the rails. People are depending on us, Carl.

> CARL: I know. We're doing our best.

"Hello," I said. "I wasn't expecting to see you until later."

"My sister isn't here yet?" Signet asked, looking about the room. "You know, when I learned of this event, I didn't realize this was a real Butcher's Masquerade. People have them, yes. But real ones are rare. I wouldn't have believed it unless Apito herself came to me. I'm glad I'm here. I prefer it this way. Like I told you before, I'm quite tired of running. I just wish I'd known I was coming directly. I would've worn something a little more appropriate."

Multiple guards appeared at the entrance, including a handful of the black-clad queen's guards. They watched Signet from across the room. They all slinked back to the hallway.

"It's quite delicious, isn't it?" Signet asked. "I'm here, and they can't touch me without breaking the seal. My lovely sister is at my mercy."

"Do you know what boon she'll receive from Apito at the end of the party?" I asked.

"Imogen doesn't even know. The story is it's some sort of immortality, but it's never happened." Signet laughed. "Not once. Clerics cast the spell, have their party, and before the night is done, the Nothing is fed, the cleric is either dead or shamed, and Apito awards no boons."

Her gaze moved across the room, landing on the hunters, then moving to Chaco, then to the three judges at the table. "Who are they?" Signet asked. "Their auras are . . . strange."

As we looked at the three judges, an ethereal hand appeared, floating in front of Empress D'Nadia, handing her a drink. She took the offered glass, and the hand disappeared.

"They're the people I was telling you about before," I said, jumping on the opportunity. "Look at them. They're not even really here. They're from the outside world that controls all of this, even you, and they're watching this for entertainment."

"Interesting," Signet said, her voice trailing off. On her chest, all the tattoos were also looking in the direction of the three judges. "I think I'd like to have a conversation with these off-worlders while I wait for my sister." She moved off toward them.

ZEV: Godsdamnit, Carl.

I laughed out loud.

69

I TURNED MY ATTENTION TO THE BACK OF THE ROOM.

Chaco the Bard remained behind his prize counter. The muscular wolf-headed man saw me coming, and he straightened his back as if getting ready for a fight. His bat-like wings flapped once and settled nervously.

He didn't wear the ridiculous 1970s-game-show-host outfit anymore, but formfitting metallic armor that made him seem even more intimidating. He'd been a part of Mordecai's party when something happened near the end of their crawl. Something to make Mordecai want to murder him. This guy had been born as a skyfowl, which was a little hard to get my head around.

The curtain was now off the prize counter, and a few hunters perused the large glass case. Two Draconians slinked away at my approach, leaving only one person, a hunter, closely inspecting something behind the glass. His name was Zabit, and he was a **level 66 Beastmaster**. He was an odd, unfamiliar alien race called an Atoll. Tall and thin with four arms and only three fingers on each hand. He had a thin, shovellike face with high-set eyes, all set into wrinkly, dark apelike skin. A thick, wide leather belt hung loosely around his waist. Little empty chains hung off it. I actually recognized what that was. It was a trap module bandolier. I received the same thing in a box once. I'd ended up selling it because my inventory was better and safer.

The hunter turned to face me, his belt jingling like little bells as he moved. He didn't appear to have a mouth. Just a weird head, about a dozen nostril holes, and that was it, all surrounded by wrinkles and random thick whiskers.

"Hello, Carl," Zabit said. He made a sort of sign-language motion with his hands, and the words projected out through something hidden in his clothes. His words sounded oddly robotic and emotionless. "I applaud you for almost angering Vrah to the point of breaking the peace seal. I do not know what would happen if one of us was banished to the Nothing, but I suspect it would not be pleasant. Who is the elite who just entered the room?"

"Oh, yeah. I know who you are," I said, leaning on the counter. Chaco hovered nervously nearby. He took a step back as if afraid of what would happen next. "When I first got to this floor, I was attacked by a bunch of night weasel mobs. Those were yours."

"Yes," he signed. "I thought to catch the top prey early, but you and your companions ended up killing my pets and ruining my chances at making any money this season. Still, I managed to collect a few scalps. Only twenty-five. The prizes are of quality, though are mostly useless at this point. It's become quite impossible to sell our items."

Twenty-five. This guy had killed 25 crawlers. I seethed. Then I thought of Eva, who'd managed to kill twice as many. Had they given her scalps? I hadn't even thought about it.

Don't engage, I thought. *Don't do this. It's just going to make you angry.*

"Why do you do it?" I asked.

He cocked his head. He was just a bit taller than me.

"Why do I do what?"

"Hunt crawlers. Travel across the universe to hunt and kill someone who is scared and doesn't want to be here. Someone weaker than you. Does it make you feel tough? Powerful?"

"I hunt for the survival of the Atoll. My people may not be strong or many, but we are proud. I hunt and collect the money and bring it back home. And with that money, I am able to pay for the upkeep on our habitat. We are not considered citizens, so oxygen and land are not a right. Employment options are limited. Without this opportunity, we would be forced to sign a protection agreement with another system and live under indenture. My failure this season will make it difficult for my people to survive until the next. It is the risk I take. As for the rest of your question. No, it doesn't make me feel tough or powerful. Some of us do revel in the killing. For others, it is a means of survival. I understand your objection. I would object, too, were the situations reversed."

I had no real response to that. Then after a moment, I said, "It seems in a universe so large, one shouldn't have to live somewhere inhospitable. It seems like it would be easy to find a place to live in peace."

"It does seem like it should be that way, doesn't it?"

He returned his attention to Chaco.

"I will take the drop shield for twenty scalps. The invisibility pack for three."

Chaco took a hesitant step back toward the counter. "That leaves you with two."

"I will take what I have ordered."

"Suit yourself," Chaco said. He reached behind the counter and dropped a round poker-chip-like device on the counter plus what looked like a case of 12 jingling potion bottles. I recognized them as invisibility potions. The items disappeared in a poof of smoke. "The items are added to your inventory, so you can't use them in here."

"My inventory is full already," Zabit said. "We do not have unlimited storage like the crawlers."

"I am aware. The items will appear in your box inventory," he said. "Make certain you open the box before the floor ends, or you won't be able to take it with you."

"Wait," I said, looking between the hunter and Chaco. "What happens when the floor collapses? Do you get to keep everything?"

"Just what's in our inventory," Zabit said. "And we are unable to sell it. We are given credit to gold exchange value."

"How much is that?" I asked.

"Practically nothing." He turned to move off.

Behind me, Theobold was back on the stage talking. He stuttered and stopped at the sight of Signet proudly sitting there in the front row, but then composed himself. The pet show was about to begin.

"Why does Mordecai hate you so much?" I asked Chaco.

The wolf man shook his fearsome head. "Hello to you, too, Carl. I'm still not allowed to say. Last time we spoke, I asked you to tell him I am sorry about what happened. I regret it every day. But if we hadn't done it, we'd all be dead, including him *and* his brother. That's all there is to say about it." He paused uncertainly and then added, "They do that. If you survive long enough in this place, they'll eventually make you turn on your own party. It happens every time. You'll regret making it as far as you have, no matter who is helping you. No matter how close you are, we're all alone in the end. Alone and broken with the choices we've had to make." He jerked as if shocked. He reached up and wiped his face, taking a deep breath.

"You currently have 66 hunter hands in your inventory. Wow. Really? Huh, that's a lot. Well, take a look at the prize counter and pick out what you like. Unlike last time, you can examine the names of everything, though not all descriptions will be present. Anything you purchase will be added to your inventory as a prize box, so you won't have access right away. If you purchase an upgrade, those will be installed immediately."

I looked down through the glass and started examining everything. I desperately tried to ignore what he'd said. It wasn't the first time I'd heard someone say that. There were a few heartbreaking stories in the cookbook. Ones I tried not to think about, yet I found myself reading over and over. I shook my head, clearing out the noise.

The items turned on a vertical carousel, and they were represented by miniature holograms, allowing them to shove a ton of crap in the case. There was a lot of stuff. The left side of the case with the lower-hand-cost items was mostly potions. For a single hand, one could get a 25-pack of good healing or mana potions. For two hands, there were upgrades, but you were limited to one from anything in that row. One could purchase plus ten percent to their lowest stat or plus five percent to their highest stat. Or plus two to a random combat skill or spell.

I gave Mordecai a running commentary of everything as I went over the prizes. I wasn't planning on telling him who was overseeing the prize counter, but he already knew.

MORDECAI: See if you can find out if that fuck tit is in the same
room as you, and if he is, I would consider it a personal favor if
you shoved a dynamite stick up his ass once the protection
seal is broken.

CARL: Donut?
MORDECAI: Yes. She told me. Now keep reading the prizes.

For the three- and five-hand prizes, there were literally dozens of potion choices. Everything from the invisibility potions that Zabit had picked to a few of those Size Up potions I'd taken from Miriam Dom, to Feather Fall and several protection potions. There were also numerous scroll choices.

MORDECAI: How many hands did Donut end up with? Eight?
CARL: Correct. I'm thinking we should either get the constitution boost or the plus two to a skill for her. It's too bad she can't get both. There's a random spell book prize at five hands. Most of these potions are things I can get easily or you can make. There're a few scrolls, too. A scroll of mapping. A scroll called *Paw Patrol*. Isn't that a kids' show? One called the *Milk of Lamashtu*. I don't know what any of these do.
MORDECAI: Those potions are all a waste. I agree with you. She should get the plus ten percent to her lowest base stat and then the random spell book.
CARL: It's too bad she didn't get ten hands. There's a single potion of level up. That's limited to one also. There are a few spell books. *Poison Grapple. Scar Tissue. Fish Blaster.* What the hell do these do?

On the stage, a crawler came out. It was the same one I'd seen earlier getting out of the second caravan. I couldn't remember his name and couldn't examine him from here. He was one of the Brazilian guys, I was pretty sure. I didn't know much about his party, called team Flamengo, but I knew this guy only put his stats into his dexterity. He had his hawk on his shoulder. A spotlight hit him, and he stood there onstage, not saying anything for several seconds.

"Uh," he said awkwardly, his voice amplified loudly throughout the ballroom. "This is Gimli. My stone hawk. He can turn people to stone. He turned a hunter to stone yesterday, and then I kicked the statue over, and it shattered."

Several crawlers cheered at that.

"I don't recommend it. I couldn't loot him."

Elle was suddenly next to me, also looking at all the items. She'd collected a total of seven hands. "This party sucks," she said, looking at the case. She glanced over at the hunters and suddenly perked up. "Hey, you!" she said to a hunter standing by himself nearby. It was a human with no hair or eyebrows, standing nervously and holding a drink with two hands. A Crest. He pointed to his chest questioningly.

"Yeah, you! Come here! I wanna ask you something. I saw something really fucked-up earlier, and I can't stop thinking about it." She zipped off without picking anything from the case.

The other hunters continued to huddle near their buffet table. Vrah was shouting at a group of them, who were arguing back.

"It's over," someone shot back at Vrah. "Let it go. We just want to go home."

Vrah looked at me and hissed at the others to be quiet.

Onstage, the brown hawk cawed and opened his wings, revealing opalescent colors within.

"You fuckers are lucky," the guy said from the stage, pointing at the hunters as if he was gaining confidence. "Gimli would've fucked you up if we found you."

DONUT: DO YOU SEE THIS. HE WASN'T EVEN PREPARED. I HAVE
    THIS IN THE BAG.

I turned my attention back to the case. I looked at the 20-hand items. There were more spell books and magic wands and individual magical oddities, like that token thing Zabit had picked.

CARL: What's a drop shield?

MORDECAI: Disposable item. Like your protective shell, but it lasts
    for about an hour or it can get killed by a lot of damage. You
    can turn it on and off, but once the battery is dead, it's dead.
    It's a great prize, but it only works if it's rooted in place, so
    you can't clip it to your belt and run with it. It doesn't stop

magic. Will stop explosions, but one of yours will probably be
enough to break it and kill you.

CARL: There's a shrink wand like Zhang had before. Ten charges.

MORDECAI: That's also a good choice. Is there any sheet music?

CARL: Yes. There're a few at ten hands, but I didn't go over them.

MORDECAI: Ask Chaco if there's anything like his escape spell.

"Uh," I said. "Mordecai wants to know if there's any sheet music like your escape spell."

He looked up at me, eyes registering surprise. "You have a bard in your party?"

"Yeah," I said. "Donut sings now."

"How is she? Can she hold pitch?"

"Uh," I said. "She's getting better. She has a vocal coach in our safe room."

He nodded. "That one," he said, pointing at a sheet of music. "Ten hands. A song of *Skedaddle*. Not quite as good as *Wings of the Pyxie*, which is what he's talking about, but she wouldn't be able to sing that one for a while anyway. What does she know now?"

"She has a party heal spell, an illusion spell, an ice spell that she still can't cast very well, a psionic attack that makes her nose bleed and does nothing else to mobs, and a new song she's been working on. She got the sheet music for it, and she sang it perfectly on her second or third try."

"Really?" he asked. "That's pretty impressive."

"That's what she keeps telling me," I said.

Sheet music was something between a scroll and a magic book, and it was exclusive to bards. One could use it more than once, and it allowed a bard to sing a song they normally couldn't. The system helped them perform if they had the music in front of them, making it easier to pull off. But it still wasn't a sure thing. If the song was performed well and in key, it cast. If not, the page tore just a little bit. Too many tears, and it was ruined. If you managed to sing it perfectly all the way through with perfect pitch, the song was added to your bard spell book, called your repertoire. The sheet music didn't go away in that case, either, so you could save it for duets or to sell later.

The song Donut was going to sing this evening was easy for her because it was a song she'd been hearing her entire life. There was a bit of
a mystery there, a chicken-and-the-egg thing, but I had too much to deal
with to wonder on it for long. I returned my attention back to the case.

At a price of thirty hands, there were only two items, both called **Future Floor Boons**. One was a little checkered flag and was called **Seventh-
Floor Pole Position (Sold Out)**, and the next was called **Eighth-Floor** *Book of
Lore* **(Random starting location. Full title will reveal itself upon purchase)**.
There was a sign under both that said, "Limited to one each."

"Who bought that seventh-floor upgrade?"

"The goat. He had 33 hands. He was my first customer. Bought that,
the skill upgrade, and a case of mana potions. He didn't even ask about
it. Just walked up, pointed at it, and took it."

At fifty hands there were multiple full sets of armor and weapons,
none of which would be good for me. There were also more spell books,
including *War Lord* and *Gore Golem*. Both were 100 mana spells and not
worth it for 50 hands according to Mordecai.

At the end of the case was a little glowing gem. From the hologram
it looked like it was maybe the size of a grape and had no color at all,
but even in hologram form, it glittered as it moved. At first I thought
it was a soul crystal. Those were without value once they were installed
as a power source, unless used as an explosive. Unused ones were supposedly rare and treasured.

However, upon closer inspection, I saw this was not actually listed
as a soul crystal.

CARL: What's a memorial crystal?
MORDECAI: Forget everything else. Get that.
CARL: I can't. It's 100 hands. The most expensive thing in there.
    What is it?

Prepotente was now onstage with Bianca. He literally said nothing.
He just screamed once, and the massive, sizzling black-fire-goat thing
hissed. They got off the stage, which smoldered and then caught on fire.
Elves appeared from nowhere and started stamping out the flames.

MORDECAI: Long story. Soul crystals, the ones that elves use to power their stuff, are mined from Scolopendra's lair. They're created when certain types of people die, and their souls get filtered through the centipede's body. Memorial crystals are similar, but they're created by fallen gods and demigods. They're filled with information, usually god-tier-level spells and knowledge. One can get the information out of them by charging it up. You charge them up by installing it on a weapon or your armor or just wearing it like jewelry and killing stuff. There're lots of storylines about these things, usually on the 10th and 11th floors.

CARL: Well, it's out of reach unless I can kill 34 more of these guys and collect the hands before the end of the night. Too bad they don't let us pool our money.

MORDECAI: See if that murdering prick knows what god it came from.

"Hey, Chaco. What god made that memorial crystal?"

"A dead one," he said.

"No shit. You don't know?"

He shrugged. "All the description says is that it was discovered during a mining expedition by the high elves. The queen normally wears it around her neck. She'll get it back if nobody buys it."

I remembered the queen's necklace. I'd assumed it was a soul crystal.

"Mordecai says these things store information. You have no idea what's on it?"

"None. I do know it's the queen's most prized possession. It's a part of this whole butcher spell. They have to offer their most valuable item as a prize."

I felt that same anticipatory tingle I'd felt as soon as I'd heard about the Gate of the Feral Gods. "If I happen to collect a few more hands before the evening is over, but they're still in their prize boxes, can I use them?"

Chaco smiled, revealing his wolf teeth. "Nope. You'll have to get to a safe room first to open them up. There ain't no safe rooms in the castle. And you ain't collecting hands anyway. The second the seal is broken, I teleport out of here."

Behind me on the stage, a pair of elves was spraying something on the wood where Bianca had just left.

I sighed. I wanted to get the skill upgrade for myself, but I was one hand short if I wanted to also refill our potion supply. Katia had done a full circuit of the group except for Lucia and determined we were seven fall-protection potions short thanks to Eva's thievery. We weren't even certain if they were going to be necessary. *Damnit.*

"I'll take the shrink wand, the eighth-floor-lore-book thing, that music sheet of *Skedaddle*, that case of 24 Feather Fall potions, and a case of healing potions."

AFTER A PARADE OF OTHER PETS, IT WAS TIME FOR MONGO TO APPEAR. I made my way back to the stage. Signet remained talking to the judges. Katia had joined them for a few minutes. No further guards came into the room or did anything about her presence. Elle had moved off into a corner and was in a deep conversation with the hairless human hunter. The dude looked like he was crying. She said something to him angrily and zipped away, coming back toward our side of the room. I turned my attention to the stage.

Donut had been preparing for this while I was either in the training room or the crafting studio. While I knew exactly how her talent show performance later was supposed to go, I hadn't been involved in any of the arrangements for this.

"We need to keep it low-key," I'd said once she started preparing. "Just bring Mongo out, have him shriek a few times, and get off the stage. We don't want to tip our hand that your talent show production is going to be a little . . . You know."

"Extra?" she'd asked.

"Yeah. Extra."

"But . . ." Donut had protested.

"Low-key."

The lights in the entire ballroom dimmed. A red glow emanated onstage. A small billow of smoke appeared.

"Ladies and gentlemen! Crawlers and hunters alike, prepare yourselves," came Louis's voice over the loudspeaker. He was hidden somewhere backstage.

"Oh fuck," I muttered.

70

COLORED LIGHTS STARTED TO BOUNCE BACK AND FORTH ONSTAGE.

"I want you to put your hands together!" Louis shouted.

Topping out at number two on September 6th, 2014, it's "Anaconda"!

Everyone in the room stopped what they were doing to first look at each other and then at the stage. The Popov twins, Imani, and Elle came to stand next to me. I caught Imani's eye, and she gave me a look that said, *You need to learn to control your goddamned cat.*

CARL: Louis, where is that music coming from?
LOUIS: She made me do it. I built a boom box that makes it so it's not so loud.
CARL: Those are my trap modules. How many did you use?
LOUIS: Uh. Hang on a second. Don't get madder.

The Nicki Minaj and Sir Mix-a-Lot song, which had nothing to do with either dinosaurs or snakes, started blasting onstage. Despite Louis's assurance that it wasn't as loud as normal, it was still ridiculously amplified. The floor thumped with the bass.

Two of my expensive and hard-to-make colored-signal-flare smoke bombs exploded, one in each corner.

"Motherfuck," I hissed.

"It's Mongo!" Louis cried, his voice louder than the music. There was an odd distortion effect added to his voice, like we were at a monster truck rally. Mongo rushed out, emerging through the smoke, which swirled in eddies that stopped the moment they hit the edge of the stage. I knew down below in the attendant ballroom, the whole damn room was probably filling with smoke right now. Mongo was down there while Donut remained here on this floor. She could still fully interact with him, but only while she was upon the stage.

Mongo did a circle and then stopped in the center. He roared, waving his arms in the air, causing more smoke to twirl. His roar was also amplified.

Donut strolled onto stage, her new tiara gleaming. She wore a little headset microphone I'd never seen before. She did a little hop and then jumped upon Mongo's back.

"Earthquake!" Donut cried, her voice also amplified, and Mongo leaped into the air and landed hard onstage, shaking it. A pair of pyrotechnic explosions went off, loud as gunshots.

"As a level 34 male mongoliensis, Mongo is the prime example of the term 'alpha predator,'" Louis intoned over the loudspeaker. "His powerful legs and claws are perfect for eviscerating opponents. His blue and red feathers with a slight insinuation of youthful pink present a masculine form that hints at a sensitive depth. The ladies love him."

Suddenly there were three lady Mongos onstage—none of them were Kiwi—and they each took a step toward Mongo and screeched. One of them held on to a pink heart made of construction paper with "Mongo" written on it.

"Sorry, ladies," Donut said with all the bravado of a stage performer presenting a skit at an amusement park. "He's taken."

The girl dinos disappeared back into the smoke, abandoning the heart on the ground.

"But it's not all fighting and love with this adorable velociraptor," Louis announced. "Mongo also knows how to have a good time. His hobbies include gastronomic sampling, long walks in nature, and of course . . ."

Donut backflipped off Mongo and landed in the center of the stage. Mongo leaped all the way to the edge of stage left.

". . . dancing!"

The velociraptor moonwalked back across the platform. He goddamn moonwalked. As he passed Donut, she popped her sunglasses onto her face. Both bopped their heads to the music.

Next to me, Elle mouthed, *Holy shit.*

Even some of the hunters ended up clapping.

DONUT: CARL, DID YOU SEE IT! LOUIS MESSED UP SOME OF THE LINES, AND WE ORIGINALLY PLANNED ON MONGO LEAPING COMPLETELY OFF-STAGE BEFORE THE MOONWALK REVEAL, BUT IT WENT ALMOST PER-FECTLY. DID YOU SEE THE JUDGES? THE BLOB GUY WAS SHAKING, AND I'M, LIKE, REALLY SURE THAT'S A GOOD THING.

    CARL: I distinctly remember saying "low-key."

    DONUT: THAT WAS LOW-KEY, CARL. THEY TOLD ME I COULDN'T
        DO MY *MAGIC MISSILE* ENTRANCE WE HAD PLANNED. THIS
        WAS NOTHING COMPARED TO MY KE$HA ACT MISS BEATRICE
        AND I PERFORMED IN CLEVELAND.

    CARL: You sat in a cage and let judges look at your butthole at
        your cat shows.

    DONUT: NOT AT THE BAR AFTERWARD. HONESTLY, CARL, IT'S LIKE
        YOU KNOW NOTHING ABOUT MY LIFE. WAIT, I'M COMING OUT.

Up on the stage, the final entrants were making their appearance. It was Garret the Tummy Acher with Tserendolgor. It'd taken five minutes for all the smoke to clear. Louis couldn't figure out how to turn the trap module music off, and I'd had to give him instructions over chat.

Ren was awkwardly explaining how the large meatball could tank attacks and attract incoming missiles.

Garret made a giggling noise that sounded like something out of a horror movie. They were off the stage, and it was done. The winner wouldn't be announced until after the talent show.

"Donut, how in God's name did you train Mongo to moonwalk?" Elle demanded the moment Donut appeared from backstage, tail swishing triumphantly.

"Oh, it was nothing," Donut said. "Wait until you see our real dance number later."

"Yeah, I heard about it," Elle said. "But now people aren't going to be surprised."

"Oh, don't worry about that," Donut said. "The next performance is going to be amazing."

As they talked, I moved to my chat. Normally calm Imani was on the verge of a nervous breakdown over everything having gone wrong so far, and I was spending a lot of effort on keeping her sane.

I'd had a few reports of the outside crawlers fighting mobs as everyone moved into elf territory, but the elves themselves still hadn't moved to attack anyone.

> CARL: Bomo, Sledge, check in.
> BOMO: Lots of stuff left behind.
> MORDECAI: He ain't lying. He keeps bringing armfuls of armor and swords back. He also has some guns and power armor, but they're race restricted. We should've made him a cart.
> CARL: Excellent.

When the brambles attacked, a small but determined party of experienced hunters decided to remain in Zockau. Since Bomo could freely enter the safe room, we'd sent him in regularly to get updates on the group. The brambles didn't breach the safe room walls. Instead of fleeing, the remaining hunters who hadn't been teleported away decided to carve out a safe space for themselves.

The act of fighting the never-ending onslaught of thorns didn't give any experience, but it filled one's blood bar, which allowed them the relative safety of the safe room in exchange for fifteen minutes of garden duty once every ten hours. Once the Butcher's Masquerade started, however, the remaining hunters all teleported away, which effectively turned Zockau into a ghost town, save a few surviving NPCs.

I sent Bomo in to collect all the excess gear. Piles of the equipment had been abandoned in the safe room, sorted into little mounds. Because of their limited inventory, the hunters who'd collected the stuff were only taking the most valuable items they could carry. The thing was, you weren't allowed to steal in safe rooms. It was just as bad as killing someone. That went out the window once the person left the room, however. All the stuff became fair game.

Some of the hunters had personal spaces and kept their excess in there, but not all of them. Most of it was worthless junk, the same stuff I would normally toss to Donut to sell. I didn't care. I wanted it all.

The Sledge, who'd so far spent the entire floor playing video games in the safe room, was already engaged with his much more dangerous mission. He was currently approaching the tunnel that led to the caves where he'd move into the castle from below. The were-castors and Areson and the rest of Signet's crew would be there to help them make their way through the lower tunnels and into the secret dungeon-level entrance.

SLEDGE: Mantises.
CARL: What?

I exchanged a worried look with Imani and Louis, who were both in all the chats regarding the changeling evacuation.

SLEDGE: Lots of mantises. Everywhere. We gotta fight them. They keep coming, flying in.
IMANI: I'm starting to get reports of other crawlers fighting mantises, too. They're hitting the stairwell locations. They're all level 20 nymphs, but there's a lot of them, and they're fast.
CARL: Sledge, get in those tunnels. Try not to fight. You need to get the changelings in through that door. Let me know as soon as they're in.
SLEDGE: Too many. We getting picked up by airship. We go in from above instead.
CARL: Okay. Be careful of the sentinel towers. They'll still be armed. Use the bombs on them if you have to. Just don't drop any on the main part of the castle. Let me know when you're in.
LOUIS: Make sure you tell that Skarn kid to moor the ship to the tower. It's really important!

"Fuck," I said out loud. "So much for subtle."

"What's going on?" Katia asked.

As Imani explained what was happening out there via chat, I looked across the room at Vrah, who stood there holding a plate of food in a claw, looking directly at the now-drained warning light Britney had disabled.

Uh-oh.

"Wait," Louis asked. "Where are all the mantis babies coming from?"

"Diwata is still here somehow," I said. "It's like Samantha warned. She turned into a boy mantis, cured Vrah, then turned into a girl and is out there somewhere, shooting babies into the world."

"I called it!" Donut said. "And all those babies are both Vrah's kids *and* siblings! That's like really gross!" She looked across the room and pointed at Vrah. "Disgusting! You should be ashamed!" she shouted.

"Don't praying mantises lay eggs in weird sacs?" Louis asked.

"Apparently not this kind," I said.

CARL: Samantha, how many babies will Diwata have once she starts giving birth?

SAMANTHA: WHEN AM I GOING? I AM GETTING BORED. I COULD'VE SNEAKED AWAY FIVE TIMES NOW.

CARL: Not yet. Any minute now. Answer the question.

SAMANTHA: SHE'LL HAVE AS MANY BABIES AS SHE WANTS. HER BABY SPRINKLER WILL SHOOT THEM OUT UNTIL THE VERY END OF TIME IF SHE WANTS.

CARL: Shit. Okay. You still have that potion ball shoved up you?

SAMANTHA: I HAVE IT. IT'S VERY UNCOMFORTABLE, BUT I HAVE IT.

"This is fucked-up on so many levels," Elle was saying. "I mean, think about it. Those are her children. Sort of. And she's birthing them here. Remember that dude who blew up when Diwata was born? I was talking to that hunter guy over there with no eyebrows, and did you know, Vrah's people tricked his brother into going into that temple and being used as the birthing vessel for Diwata? They plain murdered another hunter just to cure Vrah of a venereal disease. Vrah messaged him and said he'd be safe if he went in there, and they somehow tricked him into submitting to the ritual. The brother is pissed about it. And now this Circe bug lady is having actual flesh-and-blood babies and just sending them out into the world. What's going to happen when the floor collapses? Are they just going to go away? They're her kids!"

"They're probably all deformed and stuff, too," Donut said. "Do you think any have flippers? Can you imagine that? A bug with flippers!"

I was about to make a quip about Donut's own lineage, but thought better of it. "Donut, get to Chaco's counter and get those upgrades we talked about."

MORDECAI: I've figured out the loophole they're using to keep the goddess active on this floor. If she's already cast a spell, she won't leave until the spell finishes. She had a five-minute limit, but she got to Vrah in time, did a quick pump and dump, and then turned into a female mantis and immediately started giving birth. That's the spell. She'll stay as long as she's still giving birth. The plus side is she'll be in the form of a gonorrhea-infected female mantis and won't be able to cast any other spells. She'll still be immortal, but she'll be giving birth, in pain, and without her god strength. I hope.

DONUT: IT IS ABSOLUTELY REVOLTING. MONGO IS APPALLED.

"Hey," Firas said, "weren't we supposed to keep Florin away from Lucia?"

71

WE ALL TURNED TO SEE THE CROCODILIAN STANDING OVER THE SOB-
bing form of Lucia. He had both hands on her shoulders, like he was
about to choke her.

I cursed as Imani, Katia, Elle, and I all moved to intercept.

"Florin," I shouted as we all pulled up.

Then, to my utter astonishment, the Lajabless threw herself into
Florin's embrace, and she wrapped her arms around him. He hugged her
back. "It's okay," he said, stroking her hair. "It's okay. We'll sort it out."

The Crocodilian turned to look at us. "We need to keep her safe at
all costs."

"What?" I asked. I looked at the others, bewildered. "What?"

"They're in there with her," he said.

"Who?" I asked. "Where?"

"I want my mom," Lucia said.

Her accent is different. What the hell?

They both stopped suddenly and looked at each other. Lucia pushed
Florin away. The change had been instantaneous. I saw it happen. Her
swagger returned. I'd seen this before, this rapid personality change, on
the recap from her fight with Donut. It was like a switch had been
flipped. Everything about her other than her actual appearance changed,
all at once. Her face scrunched up in anger. Her shoulders hunched. Her
voice transformed to the way it'd been before.

"Get off me, you ugly fuck, or I'll put a hole in your head like I did
to your whore."

Florin put his hands up and backed off. "All right, kid. Just take it easy,
okay? Don't do anything stupid. Remember we're all in the same boat."

Donut was suddenly on my shoulder. "Carl, what's happening?"

Lucia pointed at Donut and hissed, "She's still dead. No matter what happens. Blood for blood. She killed Cici. I kill her." She turned back to the buffet, walking with a slight limp because of her mismatched legs. She yelled for tequila.

Florin waved us back. "Leave her be!"

"That's right. Leave me be!" Lucia shouted without turning. She cackled with laughter. Eva remained at the bar between the buffets. I cringed at the thought of those two together.

"I know I've been saying this a lot lately," Elle said, "but what the hell is going on?"

Florin reached up and put his finger to his temple, which had become our universal gesture to move it to chat.

> **FLORIN:** I don't understand it all. There are multiple people in there. Real people, mostly kids. The girl I was talking to is named Jill. She's ten years old, and she's Dutch. I thought she was trying to pull something, but she's telling the truth. She knew the prime minister of the Netherlands. That is no street kid from Ecuador running an op.
>
> **CARL:** Dude, what?
>
> **FLORIN:** I don't know, mate. Something to do with the dog and a guy named Alexandro. But there are kids in there. In her head. Multiple kids. We have to get that dog. Not her. The dog. It can still control her from afar, but only in short bursts. Once we get it, it's gone.

I just sat there for several moments, trying to make sense of what he said. I pulled up a new chat window.

> **CARL:** Zev, what is this bullshit? You guys said there were no children crawlers allowed.
>
> **ZEV:** It's complicated, Carl. You don't have to be involved in everything. We're not going to discuss it. Especially not now. Heads up.

"You're red as a tomato," Florin said. "You feeling okay, mate?"

A heavy weight landed on the shoulder opposite of the one Donut stood upon.

"Yeah, mate? You feeling okay?"

Ferdinand. He'd come out of nowhere. He said it with a condescending, mocking tone.

CARL: Samantha, he's distracted. Go, go, go.

72

<Note added by Crawler Carl. 25th Edition>
From page ten of our planning notes:

Louis here. I took Carl's advice and started studying the castle map. There are multiple small tunnels leading everywhere. At first I thought they were HVAC ducts. I was gonna do that for a while. My cousin Scrapple was gonna help me get into the school, but they tested for weed. At a school. Isn't that dumb? Anyway, I got to looking at these ducts on the map, and I realized that's not what they are. Their placement doesn't make sense. There's that elf spa on the sixth floor, right? The one with the baths, and the tunnels go all around it and into the dressing room next door. As soon as I saw that, I knew. I got this friend back home. His name was Jojo, and he lived with his crazy-ass grandma until she died. She was one of those cat ladies. You could smell the place from down the street. Had like 20 of them. When she died, they found a dead cat in her freezer. Can you believe that shit? Anyway, Jojo's grandma once paid a dude to build a bunch of tunnels around her house, and I realized they were just like these. This queen lady has a pet cat, right? I think these tunnels are how he gets around the castle. Donut said he's a pervert. He uses the tunnels to spy and to get places. There's lots of shortcuts, and when it goes up a floor, it goes back and forth like *Super Mario* platforms, making it easier for the cat to jump up quickly and quietly. One of those tunnels goes to the third floor, right into the security room. It makes sense if he's all up in the castle's business all the time. If we can get Donut into the tunnel or maybe Katia can turn into a slug or something, they can sneak into the tunnel and get to the security room.

~Louis

That's a great idea. Good eye. But we'll be watched like hawks, and there's no easy access from the ballroom. The timing is really important. Also, I'm not turning into a slug. There're a few paths in and out of the attendant ballrooms. What do you think about using Samantha?

~Katia

She's not reliable enough. Our entire escape plan fails if she's not successful.

~Imani

I'm mapping out a path right now to see if it's feasible. She'll be downstairs, so she'll have to start booking it as soon as the talent show portion starts, or hopefully earlier once we get eyeballs on Ferdinand to know they won't run into each other in the tunnel. We'll also have to devise a method so she can quickly and quietly deal with the elves in the security room without raising the alarm. She talks a big game, but she can't actually do anything.

~Carl

I'LL DO IT! AND I CAN FIGHT JUST FINE. I WILL KILL YOU ALL. AND ALL THE ELVES. AND THEIR MOTHERS.

~Psamathe

What the hell? Samantha, how'd you find this?

NOBODY GOES TO THE BATHROOM THIS MUCH, CARL. I'M
NOT AN IDIOT. ALSO, YOU'RE USING THE WRONG TYPE OF
INK FOR THIS. REMIND ME, AND I WILL SHOW YOU
SOMETHING REALLY AWESOME.

~Psamathe

DONUT HISSED AND POOFED ALL THE WAY OUT. IMANI SWOOPED IN AND
peeled Donut off my shoulder, cradling her in her arms and wings before
the cat had the chance to swipe and attack. Donut issued a deep growl.

I could feel the weight of Ferdinand on my shoulder. I reached up
and touched his tail, and I felt my hand reach easily through him after
a slight push. He could touch me, but I couldn't touch him. I had no
idea how that worked. He was in the queen's ballroom. Not really here.
The intricacies of the ballroom system were still a little confusing to me,
but all that was important was that he could rip my throat out right
now, and there would be nothing I could do about it.

Elle was the first to start laughing, followed by Louis. Even Bautista
and the Popovs both started to chuckle. I looked up, and finally saw
what was so funny.

"Dude," I said to Ferdinand, "what are you wearing?"

"What am I wearing? What do you mean?" the cat asked, surprised.
He looked about the room. All around, crawlers looked at him with
amusement.

"On your head," I said.

He sported an enormous poofy turban. The thing was made from
gold fabric, and a white feather rose up into the air, curling in on itself.
The feather was probably four feet long. It looked like a racist costume-
shop caricature blown up to absurd proportions.

"This is my royal hat! Do not mock my royal hat! It makes me the
most handsome boy in the castle!"

I examined him.

Sir Ferdinand. Cat.

Familiar of Queen Imogen of the High Elves.

Level 100 Province Boss.

It's not easy to live amongst the High Elves, especially when you're not a High Elf yourself. Over the centuries, countless adorable creatures have found themselves upon the laps of High Elf royalty. It is a dangerous place to sit.

Eventually, the elven kings and queens have tired of their pets. Or discovered them to be too intelligent. Too cunning. Too eager. And eventually, the kings and queens would order not just the execution of the pet, but of the entire species. It is the way of the High Elves.

Ferdinand owes his life to the fact that Queen Imogen is rather fond of him. She's fond of him in the same way a surgeon is fond of their favorite scalpel or a mass murderer is fond of their favorite chain saw.

Like all cats, Ferdinand's biggest weakness is the fact he is utterly convinced that whatever thought enters his chicken-nugget-sized brain is not just the truth, but it is the obvious, unalienable truth and anyone who thinks anything otherwise is not just a fool, but an imbecile deserving of nothing less than utter contempt and mockery. He is prone to self-aggrandizing behavior. He doesn't understand the concept of being told no. He doesn't understand the concept of not being worshipped.

It's rumored he's somehow even managed to sneak a small amount of magical control over the castle itself, slipping in a few cat-sized hallways here and there where nobody else would notice. He never even thought to ask permission. The idea of asking for permission to do anything is antithetical to his very nature.

And it's not just Ferdinand. This is typical of the entire species. Cats don't ask for permission. They never apologize.

They're soulless murderers. All of them.

From Imani's grip, Donut scoffed in outrage at the description.

"You look like you have a fat egg-laying goose parked on your head," Louis continued.

"No, not a goose. It's like one of those weird mushroom penises," Elle said, laughing. "It's like they made a hat designed to look like Horton the mushroom guy over there." She turned. "Hey, Horton! Come here! You have merch!"

From across the room, the mushroom guy lifted a middle finger at Elle.

Elle continued to laugh. "I love that guy. Seriously, cat, how do you even walk around in that thing? Are you here to tell us our fortunes? Should we call you Cat-nac the Magnificent?"

"How dare you!" Ferdinand sputtered, anger rising. He spat twice. His tail swished back and forth in a very familiar motion. "You fools! Simpletons! I will rip you to shreds for this! I will spill your entrails upon the ground and squeal with delight as I bathe in your offal. Do you not know who I am?"

ELLE: Donut, your ex-boyfriend has anger issues.

DONUT: I'VE ALWAYS BEEN ATTRACTED TO THE BAD BOYS.

ELLE: You and me both, sister.

CARL: Don't scare him away. Katia?

KATIA: Almost there . . . okay. Got it. He's level 100. Province boss. Listed as a minion. Stats are 100 down the line except dexterity which is 125 and charisma which is 75. That means his constitution plus charisma equals 175, so we're good there. That stupid hat is magical, too, but it doesn't affect his stats. It gives him a level 10 *Lightning* spell. He can go invisible, so we gotta be careful. He has the ability to phase jump, and his claw attack looks pretty brutal.

We'd smuggled a pair of those Size Up potions I'd gotten from Miriam Dom in here specifically for this. I'd originally thought they were to make me physically larger. In fact, the expensive and rare potions were made to give specific facts about mobs. It took just over 30 seconds for the information to seep in, so they weren't suited for fast-moving combat situations, but it was how Miriam Dom and Prepotente would know exactly how to slowly kill the giant boss monsters.

CARL: Everybody get that? Donut, you're up.

Donut, still in Imani's grip, suddenly went rigid.

DONUT: Carl, I don't think I can do this. It only worked a little on the elves.

CARL: He's not an elf. Eye on the prize. Remember how he tried to kill Mongo. If we do this right, he'll never hurt Mongo again. We need to do this so you don't have to fight him.

Donut composed herself and returned to my shoulder. Donut's unenhanced base charisma currently sat at 138. Upon her head sat her new benefactor box tiara, which temporarily doubled her charisma. Once placed upon her head, it only lasted for 30 hours before it would dissolve, which was unfortunate. But for the moment, her charisma was now a godlike 276. That was before all the buffs from the safe room. According to Elle's manager, Mistress Tiatha, a regular NPC's constitution plus charisma had to be lower than a crawler's charisma in order for the crawler to be able to successfully get the NPC to fawn over them. Mordecai thought it was impossible to charm a boss, but Mistress Tiatha insisted she'd done it before. When a white-tagged NPC was a boss, that still worked, but it had to be 100 points over to work for a province boss, which is what we'd correctly assumed Ferdinand would be.

It was, indeed, impossible to charm country and floor bosses as far as she was aware.

Donut's charisma of 276 was 101 points over Ferdinand's constitution plus charisma. Her effective charm with all her buffs, plus the bonus from the Seize the Day Toothpaste, was well over 300. Despite her insistence it wasn't working, we'd already been seeing the effects. She'd talked the final set of guards into not searching her closely. She'd managed to get the backstage manager to allow her to put on that ridiculous pet show entry.

It wouldn't work on us or the hunters, but that was okay for now.

Somewhere deep in the castle, an alarm went off, but it was silenced almost as quickly as it started. Ferdinand turned his head toward the sound.

CARL: Samantha, you good?

SAMANTHA: THAT WASN'T ME. I HAVEN'T LEFT YET! WE'RE
    WAITING FOR THE ELVES TO LOOK IN ANOTHER DIRECTION.
    LOTS OF ELF SOLDIERS ARE MOVING THROUGH, GOING
    OUTSIDE. WAITING FOR THEM TO PASS.

"Everyone stop making fun of his hat," Donut announced. "I like it. I think it looks quite smart."

"Yes. Yes, it does," Ferdinand said indignantly, turning his attention back on Donut. "I'm a handsome boy."

"Oh, I wouldn't say handsome," Donut said seductively, leaving the meaning unclear. "Why are you here anyway? I heard the queen wouldn't be joining us until after the talent competition. You wanted to see my performance, didn't you? It's okay. You can admit it."

It was subtle, but I saw the effect take hold on Ferdinand. His demeanor changed. He was suddenly more casual with his speech. It was working.

As they talked, my eyes caught Eva and Vrah talking with one another. A group of hunters surrounded the pair, listening to the conversation. That couldn't be good. I saw Eva thumb over at Signet and then at Lucia, who was now leaning over Chaco's prize counter while holding a bottle of tequila. Several hunters were suddenly taking interest in Lucia. Li Jun, Li Na, and Gwen were moving toward them to create a barrier. I saw Katia's and Imani's eyes were both glossy, meaning they were furiously talking to one another, trying to head off whatever this was.

The ground rumbled. It was subtle and distant, but I felt it. That was one of my bombs being dropped from the *Twister*.

Gideon, who was hidden near the castle with a few dozen other crawlers, sent a message.

GIDEON: About 200 mounted elves just exited the castle. The
    airship was creeping in nice and slow, and suddenly there was
    a spotlight on it. It tried to drop a bomb on the elves, but it
    missed. Now the elves are running all over the place.

CARL: What about mantises?

GIDEON: They're mostly concentrated a little further north near
those stairwells where everybody is gathering. We've only
seen a few here and . . . Uh, never mind. Holy shit. Gotta go.

"The queen wants me to keep an eye on her sister," Ferdinand was
saying. He was still on my shoulder. His more imperious way of speaking had completely eroded away. "She's gonna kill her good once the
party is over. I'm supposed to stay away from her, though. The bitch has
a charm ability." He looked over at the half-naiad, who remained enraptured by Empress D'Nadia.

"Also," Ferdinand continued, "I heard your filthy dinosaur was still
alive, and I had to see it for myself. I guess I accidentally hit you with
my lightning bolt instead. I don't know what to say, babe. If you wanna
take a ride on my lightning, you gotta prepare yourself for the tingle."
He stood on two paws, putting his forward paws on my head, and made
two thrusting motions with his cat hips while he air-humped the side
of my head while making grunting noises.

I watched Donut physically compose herself.

Watching a complete narcissist get charmed was fascinating. I could
tell Donut had his full attention, but he still insisted on making it look
like he was the one in charge.

"It was nothing. If you stick around, you can see my next performance." Donut waved her tail seductively. "I'm going to premiere a new
song."

He hopped all the way to the top of my head. "That's why I'm here,
babe. You're welcome."

SAMANTHA: I TRICKED THEM GOOD. I'M IN THE TUNNEL. NOW
WHERE DO I GO?
CARL: Where do you go? You were supposed to memorize the
map!
SAMANTHA: DID YOU SEE THAT THING? HOW WAS I SUPPOSED TO
MEMORIZE THAT? *YOU* MEMORIZE THE MAP!

Damnit.

The route she needed to take wasn't direct. She was on the first floor.

She had to go all the way up to the fifth floor and travel over to the main thoroughfare and go down again to the third. Driving her over chat was going to be a pain.

Imani, who was also in on that chat, turned and gave me an I-fucking-told-you look.

CARL: Louis and Firas, go sit down and talk Samantha through the map to the security room. She's forgotten the path.

LOUIS: I can't! I'm busy helping Sledge with the controls of the *Twister*. The changelings are fighting in the air! Skarn and Bonnie are using Bonnie's ballista system to fight!

CARL: Firas, you're up.

FIRAS: On it.

"You know what?" Ferdinand was saying from my head while I dove through my chats. "I don't like this. What do you say to me coming over to your ballroom so we can get a little more physical, if you know what I'm saying?"

Across the room, Li Na and Vrah were suddenly face-to-face. Louis was pacing back and forth, his hands in his hair as he directed the Sledge. *The sink is running.* It was happening too fast. A defeatist wave washed over me. *This isn't going to work.* And then what Ferdinand said hit me, and I was shocked back into action.

CARL: Donut, don't let him come here. We want him to stay in the queen's ballroom.

But it was too late.

"I'll be right back," Ferdinand said. He turned and bounded from the room. He was leaving the queen's ballroom and coming directly here. He'd be using the tunnels.

CARL: Samantha! Watch out! Ferdinand is going into the tunnels!

SAMANTHA: I'LL KILL HIM.

CARL: No, you'll hide!

Theobald the elf suddenly appeared onstage. He had dirt on his tuxedo, and he looked out of sorts, but not panicked. "Ladies and gentlemen, we will be doing the presentation of talents now. Everybody in the talent portion, backstage please. Thank you so very much."

"No!" Louis suddenly shouted. He came running up, breathless. "The mantises have taken the *Twister*! They're all on board. The changelings all turned to birds and left! The Sledge had to jump!"

"Jump?" I asked, alarmed.

CARL: Sledge. Are you okay?

SLEDGE: I have controller. I am okay. Bonnie is okay. Bear cubs are okay. Prudence is okay.

I took a deep breath. We'd never agreed to save Prudence and the bear cubs. They were supposed to stay in the safe room until the collapse, when they'd simply disappear. Taking care of Bonnie the gnome was difficult enough.

GIDEON: Holy crap. There are mantises and elves everywhere. It all happened really fast. They're fighting each other.

CARL: What about you guys?

GIDEON: We're still hidden. The airship has been taken. It's covered with the bugs and is just spinning in the air. The bugs are on it like moths on a light bulb. Those towers are like machine-gun nests, but they're shooting magic missiles. Your changelings are fast, but they're getting torn up. They're trying to get in through the tops of towers.

CARL: Stay down. Don't attack until I say so.

I moved to another chat window.

CARL: Sledge, where are you?

SLEDGE: On roof of the castle. It very flat. No entrance.

CARL: Keep me updated.

Louis was also in the chat, and he continued to pace back and forth, randomly shouting things until I hissed at him to shut up. Several crawlers were shuffling backstage, but everyone stopped to look at him. Sledge gave us updates in short staccato bursts.

> SLEDGE: Changelings flying to the tower . . . Elves are shooting
>   at them . . . Changelings are fighting mantises and turning
>   into mantises . . . Confusing . . . Elves shooting at mantises,
>   too . . . Elves shooting at everything . . . I have controller . . .
>   Mantises or maybe changelings take one tower, going in . . .
>   Changelings take another tower, going in . . . Elf dead on roof.
>   Splat . . . Mantises dead on the roof . . . Changeling dead on
>   the roof . . . Two turrets still have shooting elves. Two turrets
>   see us on roof. Shooting at us . . . Running.
> CARL: Protect Bonnie and the bears if you can.

I paused. *Damnit.*

> CARL: But don't sacrifice yourself for any of them. You're more
>   important than they are.
> SLEDGE: I have controller . . . I can crash *Twister* into other
>   turrets . . . Bombs still dangle . . . Like helicopter in game
>   *GTA* . . . I think I can get both.
> LOUIS: THE HELL YOU ARE.
> SLEDGE: I crash like in *GTA*.
> LOUIS: DON'T CRASH THE *TWISTER*!

I reached up and put my hand on Louis's shoulder and gave it a sympathetic squeeze.

> CARL: Do it. Get someplace safe. Try to get Bonnie into the castle,
>   but your safety is the priority.

I turned to talk to Donut, but she was already gone, heading backstage with Britney. Elle and Imani were also back there along with Li Na and her team. Prepotente sat with Ren, Florin, Chris, and the Popovs. Katia, Bautista, Gwen, and Tran were in the back, flanking Lucia Mar, trying to keep the hunters away. Lucia was amicably chatting with her fellow crawlers as if they were all best friends, waving her tequila bottle about. Offering drinks to everyone.

I watched as several hunters—including Vrah, Zabit, and multiple Draconian—moved in, creating an additional semicircle around the group at the prize counter. Chaco backed himself up all the way against the wall, like a bartender in one of my Louis L'Amour books, ready for the inevitable shoot-out.

They're gonna try to get Lucia to break the seal.

CARL: Guys, watch out for those hunters.
KATIA: We're on it. Don't micromanage, Carl.

"Look at the guards. They're all so calm," Firas said, coming to stand next to me and Louis. He patted his friend on the back, who continued to hold back tears over the impending loss of the *Twister.* "There's fighting inside and outside of the castle, and they're acting like nothing has happened."

"That's because the ones in here are probably in the safest place," I said with a calm I did not feel. "The party itself is a spell, and there are several parts that need to be completed for it to successfully cast. Everything may be kicking off outside, but once the queen gets in here, I'm pretty sure all the rooms get sealed. The whole building could blow up, and we'd still be safe. I think."

"I hope so," Firas said as the floor shook again.

Empress D'Nadia and the other two judges remained planted at the table in front of the stage and had been getting progressively more sloshed as the evening progressed. They were off someplace safe, likely watching this all go down in several different ways. Signet remained at the table with them, deep in conversation. The three judges occasionally laughed. Signet did not. I watched her get up and move off by herself. She was deep in thought.

Up onstage, a human crawler stumbled into the spotlight while Theobald, who was now offstage, announced, "First act is named Cleiton. He will be presenting humor from his homeland."

DONUT: THEY'RE SAYING I GET TO GO ON LAST. ISN'T THAT
    GREAT? I'M THE HEADLINER!

"Uh," Cleiton said, clearly nervous and unprepared. His voice was
amplified. He wore sapphire armor. I'd seen him before on the recap, but
I couldn't remember what his main attack was. He was on the same
team as the crawler with the pet hawk. "Knock, knock."

CARL: Okay. Good. Samantha is on her way to the security
    room. Just sing your song, have Britney play her guitar, and
    have Tina dance. Don't do the velociraptor hop. It's too
    dangerous.

"Who's there!" a lone person called from the audience.

DONUT: HOW AM I GOING TO BRING THE RAZZLE-DAZZLE
    WITHOUT THE GRAND FINALE?
CARL: We survive. That's the finale, Donut. They're trying to kill us
    all, and I don't see a clean way out. Something is going to
    happen soon. Keep watch, especially during your performance.
    Don't wait for us. Get out the moment the seal is broken. We'll
    try to jump onstage and follow. If that doesn't work, we'll go
    with escape plan D if we can. I bought Feather Fall potions,
    and I'll hand them out.

"Uh, I am poor knee. No, wait. I said it wrong. Poor knee."

DONUT: I'M NOT GOING TO ABANDON YOU, CARL. AND YOU DON'T
    HAVE THE POTIONS. THEY'RE IN A PRIZE BOX. YOU WON'T
    HAVE TIME FOR ANY OF THAT. YOU DON'T NEED THE POTION
    ANYWAY.
CARL: I don't. Others do. We'll have time if the queen's not in here
    yet. It won't be a lot of time, but it will be enough. I'll hand the
    potions out as soon as Samantha turns off the inventory and
    magic block.

Ferdinand rushed into the room, skidding to a stop in front of me. "You! Donut's manservant! Did I miss her act?"

Jesus, I thought. *Why'd we even bother with the potion?*

"Not yet," I said. "She's going on last. You have plenty of time."

"Good. Now get me refreshment! Vodka! In a bowl!" He ran to the center table and leaped upon it, interrupting the three drunk judges. "You three! Move this instant! This is the queen's table! Wait, where did Signet go?"

"Jump into a singularity, Gravy Boat," Empress D'Nadia said. The Jell-O-mold alien started grunt-laughing, and little bubbles gurgled out the top like a homemade volcano.

I ended up missing the punch line to the knock-knock joke.

CARL: Samantha, you good?

SAMANTHA: HE RAN RIGHT PAST AND DIDN'T EVEN SEE ME. HE HAS TO TAKE HIS HAT OFF WHEN HE'S IN THE TUNNEL, AND HE CARRIES IT IN HIS MOUTH SO HE CAN'T SEE ANYTHING. WHAT A DWEEB. I'M ABOVE THE SECURITY ROOM NOW, BUT THERE ARE FIVE ELVES IN IT. I WILL KILL THEM ALL.

CARL: Use the potion ball. That's why we gave it to you. Drop it right into the middle of the room. They'll be asleep for thirty minutes.

SAMANTHA: I DIDN'T BRING IT. I GAVE IT TO CLAY-TON. IT MADE ME CLINK WHEN I ROLLED. I WOULDN'T BE ABLE TO SNEAK AWAY. AND QUITE FRANKLY IT WAS VERY RUDE FOR YOU TO SHOVE THAT UP THERE IN THE FIRST PLACE.

My heart stopped. *Holy shit.* That was it. We were done.

CARL: God-fucking-damnit, Samantha. You're gonna have to go back and get it. Hurry.

SAMANTHA: NAH. WATCH THIS. HEY! NOT FAIR!

CARL: What! What!

SAMANTHA: YOU TOLD ME I COULD DO THIS! THE GUARDS ARE ALREADY DEAD!

Oh fuck, I thought.

"Ferdinand!" a voice snapped. The queen. She'd just appeared right in the middle of the room with no warning.

Warning: This room is now sealed. Nobody will be allowed to enter or leave until the conclusion of the party. You are protected from outside influence or spells.

73

<Note added by Crawler Carl. 25th Edition>
From page four of our planning notes:

There's a big difference between Donut enchanting someone, like she used to do to the Bopcas in the safe rooms, and her actually *magically charming* them, like she's done to Kiwi the velociraptor. They're two different things. For the first one, Ferdinand will want to do what she says and will fall over himself to please her, but he won't actually be under her magical control. He can still object, and we wouldn't be able to get him to attack Queen Imogen or toss himself off a cliff or anything like that.

If we manage to magically charm him, that's a whole new ball game. He will not only be Donut's official minion; he will do what she says almost without question. We can use *Clockwork Triplicate* on him. He'll be listed as a minion. We can talk to him via chat. He'll have automatic safe room access, etc. We have a way to do that. Mordecai can make a Charm Animal potion. All we need is a liter of cat blood. Good thing we have a ready source.

Most charm spells are line of sight, including this one. That means it will work even if he's in the queen's ballroom, and Donut is onstage. If he's in the audience, she can down the potion right when she goes on, and he'll be hers.

They brought him in to fight Donut. We're going to make them eat that decision.

Once Ferdinand is under control, we can use him for lots of different things. He'll fight for us. We can use him to attack the queen and distract her if we have to. We can use him to unlock the door to the queen's chamber from the inside. He probably has some powerful spells.

After we get confirmation that Ferdinand is indeed just a cat, we'll implement the plan. We'll have Donut take the potion while she's onstage at the start of her act.

~Carl

NOBODY IS STABBING ME, CARL. I DON'T HAVE A LITER OF BLOOD IN ME. I AM VERY PETITE.

Is it still going to work if he's a higher level than Donut? We're assuming he'll be a province boss.

~Katia

We're not stabbing you, Donut. We're draining blood. But yeah, we'll have to do it a few times to get enough. According to Elle's manager, it'll work as long as Donut's charisma is high enough. The level is irrelevant. It's the actual stat numbers that are important. She warns that Donut will have to keep constant tabs on him, though. He'll be like Kiwi, who tends to go a little crazy when she's not being watched. He'll be double charmed at this point and probably in love with her and will put himself in extreme danger to protect her. That's good to a point. We just don't need him attacking prematurely and blowing the whole operation. We don't want Queen Imogen to know he's been charmed if we want her to leave and fight Signet. It'll probably be obvious once it happens, so we should wait until Donut hits the stage but just before Imogen leaves to fight Signet.

~Carl

EVERYTHING IN THE ROOM STOPPED.

An elf's panicked and surprised voice squeaked, "I present to you, Queen of All That Is and the Queen of All That Will Be, the One and Only True Blood, Immortal-in-Waiting, Chosen Daughter of Apito, Her Majesty on High, Queen Imogen of the High Elves!"

The queen, who'd just suddenly appeared in the middle of the ballroom, pointed at her cat. She had a streak of blood down the center of her chest, ruining her glittering, color-changing ball gown. She ignored everyone else. "Ferdinand, get here this instant!"

Holy shit, I thought. *She was out there fighting.*

Several of the crawlers started murmuring, reacting to the sight of the queen, thinking they'd resurrected a dead crawler.

The cat bounded across the room and jumped to the queen's shoulder. He landed upon it, but then started to sink through. He yowled and hit the floor.

"Ferdinand," Queen Imogen growled at her cat, "pray tell me, where are you?"

"What? I'm hanging with my bird."

"Get out of that room and get back up here this instant."

"Well," Ferdinand said, "that's a problem, now isn't it? Now that you're at the party, I'm locked in here along with the rest of the castle's staff."

Her eyes smoldered. She held up her hand as if to backhand the cat, who cringed. She paused, remembering the rules of her own spell.

"Stay out of the way. We will discuss this afterward." She looked sharply around the room, focusing on Signet.

"There you are, my long-lost half-breed sister," she said, her voice full of venom. "I see you secured a last-minute invitation."

"Hello, Imogen," Signet said. She took a threatening step toward the queen. "I did. Apito herself hand-delivered it to me."

Imogen held up a hand, stopping her. "Stay back. The goodwill ballroom does not protect me from your mongrel stink. Even with the anti-water curse, I can still smell it from here. The fish stench. Pitiful. We have nothing to say to one another. Enjoy the party while you can."

Signet took several more strides toward her sister. Imogen laughed and spread her arms. "What are you going to do? Assault me? You can't cast magic. Your strikes will not land, so they won't count. If you truly wish to break the seal, you'll find yourself in the realm of mumbled screams before you take a second breath. But first you'll have to attack one of your friends here, and you'll end up damning them all. Who will it be? Perhaps Carl, your lover? Do you hate me enough to kill him and damn yourself to eternal torture for your revenge?"

KATIA: Her stats are 201 down the board except intelligence, which is 300. It says her mana is temporarily unlimited. That can't be good. She's immune to poison and curses and has an ability to return magical fire. Nobody hit her with fireballs or magic missiles or magic bolts. Susceptible to blunt-force attacks. Her spell list is several pages long.

IMANI: We're going onstage next. List off the protection spells she has while we get ready.

"Dude, are you banging that Signet chick?" Louis asked.

"No," I said. "I don't know why she thinks I—" I let out a strangled yelp as I felt myself get dragged across the room toward Imogen's open hand. My bare feet skipped across the floor, toes bouncing and skittering. I hit a table, and it went flying. I stopped before the queen. I felt myself get picked up off the floor. It didn't hurt, so maybe it wasn't constituted as an attack, but it was damn close.

The queen angrily pointed a finger at me as I floated before her. "My castle is besieged. You're trying to ruin my spell, Carl."

"That's not me," I gurgled. "The mantises are coming from Vrah and her mother."

"So those aren't your changelings swarming my towers right now? That's not your mongrel lover standing behind me? Those weren't your friends hiding in the trees just outside?"

CARL: Gideon, run.

Warning: This crawler is deceased. They have been removed from your address book.

No, I thought, looking back at the blood running down her dress. *No, no, no.*

"The sink is running," I said. "We're not supposed to let it run."

"What?" Imogen barked.

I took a deep breath, trying to compose myself.

You will not break me. You will not fucking break me.

"I don't know what you're talking about," I said. "Nobody I know is—"

Bam! The entire palace shook. A terrible rumbling filled the chamber. Above, the inverted tree hanging from the ceiling dropped multiple acorns to the floor. They hit the ground like hail, rolling like spilled dice. A moment later, a second explosion came, this one louder.

The queen went fuzzy for a moment, and I dropped from her grip.

SLEDGE: Guard turrets get good. *Twister* house blow up. Got both.

LOUIS: Nooooooo!

SLEDGE: Surviving is winning, Louis. Everything else is bullshit.

I hit the floor like a sack of dirty laundry. Imogen turned as if to leave the room, but paused and then growled.

She can't leave, I thought. *Now that she's at the party, she can't leave unless someone breaks the seal just like the rest of us. That's why she came now. The castle is being attacked from all corners, but they can't get in here. She just needs to keep us from breaking the seal.*

Imogen turned to the stage, where Imani and Elle were slowly setting up a group of chairs. The queen strode forward, picked up a chair from where it had fallen, and placed herself in it.

"Proceed," she shouted up to the stage.

"So much for being peaceful, right, mate?" Florin asked, reaching out a scaly hand to pick me up. He wouldn't take his eyes off Queen Imogen.

"You okay?" I asked. I was still reeling over the loss of Gideon and his team. That had been almost thirty crawlers. They'd stayed back to help sow chaos. I'd asked them to help. They'd died because I'd asked them for help.

The river screamed.

"I'm okay," Florin said. "Katia was right. It looks like her, but it ain't. It's her twin. I can tell. It's not really her, either. Iffy was worried about what had happened to her. Her sister. It's not right they're using her body like that. We gotta do something about it."

"Working on it," I growled.

Florin was a lot more fucked-up about this than he was letting on. It was obvious, but he was doing his best not to let it show. *Good for you,* I thought.

Onstage, Imani and Elle were going back and forth about something nonsensical and laughing hysterically. It was actually the first time I'd seen Imani laugh in a very long time. She didn't yet know about Gideon and his team.

"What are they doing?" I asked.

Florin waved a hand. "It's some skit they did together at the old folks' home talent show a while back."

CARL: Samantha, are you going to answer me? I know you're not dead because you can't die.

SAMANTHA: I'M NOT TALKING TO YOU FOR THREE MORE MINUTES AND SEVEN SECONDS. YOU'RE IN A TIME-OUT. YOU TOLD ME I COULD DO IT, AND YOU DIDN'T TRUST ME. YOU'RE IN A TIME-OUT, AND THEN I'M GOING TO KILL YOU.

CARL: If the guards are already dead, it wasn't me. We don't have time for your bullshit. Get in there and pull the two soul crystals. Just the ones on the right side. Then tell me how they died.

Up onstage, Elle and Imani finished up.

You are no longer muted. You may now cast spells.

> You are no longer peace bonded. You may now access your inventory.

All around the room, the crawlers looked about. The warning light that would let the guards and Imogen know about the change did not flash. My people spread forth, telling the crawlers to keep their mouths shut.

> SAMANTHA: OKAY. I PULLED OUT THE SOUL CRYSTALS BUT THERE IS A PROBLEM.
>
> CARL: Tell me.
>
> SAMANTHA: THE OTHER TWO SOUL CRYSTALS ON THE LEFT SIDE ARE ALREADY PULLED OUT. THEY'RE STILL HERE ON THE FLOOR. THE PERSON WHO KILLED THE GUARDS TOOK THEM OUT AND TURNED OFF THE PROTECTIONS OF BALLROOM B ALREADY.

"Oh, shit," I muttered.

I looked sharply over at the group of hunters. The vast majority of them were putting a wide amount of space between themselves and that other group, who remained in a semicircle around Katia and Lucia. Katia was saying something to Vrah, who hissed back at her.

Vrah had a plan. A plan I didn't know, and that was goddamned terrifying. Someone working for her was inside the castle. Whatever this was, it was going down, and it was going down now. They had to attempt it before Donut hit the stage.

I looked around wildly, trying to see their plan.

> SAMANTHA: ALSO, THE SOUL CRYSTAL FOR THE GOODWILL INTERFACE HAS ALREADY BEEN TAKEN AWAY. IT'S STILL WORKING BECAUSE OF THE CAPACITOR LIKE YOU SAID. BUT WHOEVER WAS HERE TRIED IT ANYWAY.
>
> CARL: How did the guards die?
>
> SAMANTHA: MANTISES. THEY'RE ALL STILL SITTING AT THEIR CHAIRS, BUT THEIR HEADS ARE SEVERED AND SITTING ON

THEIR BODIES. THERE'S A WHOLE LOT OF BLOOD IN HERE
AND A LOT OF OTHER GROSS LIQUID. IT SMELLS LIKE
OBIZUTH'S MENSES RAG IN HERE.

I felt cold. *Of course.* I felt like an idiot for not expecting this the moment we heard about the mantises. The floor shook again.

CARL: Samantha, take those two crystals from the left side and
put them back into place. Do it fast, and do it now. Then get
ready. Seal the room if you can. She's going to come for you.
It's Diwata. She's here.

The enemy's plan came to me all at once.

Diwata/Circe was in the castle. She'd blended in with the rest of the mantises and come to assist her daughter.

I had seen that the goodwill ballrooms were protected by a capacitor on Edgar's map, making it impossible to simply turn them off, which is why it hadn't been a part of our plan. Circe had wrongly thought she could break the connection between the ballrooms, which would effectively end the party. She then would've personally dealt with the queen while her daughter moved in on me, likely rushing up the stairs and storming our ballroom. The castle would be filled with mantis nymphs. There would be no escape for us. It was the best possible outcome for her and her daughter.

But since they couldn't do it that way, Vrah and her mother had an alternate plan. They were still filling the castle with the nymphs. Diwata/Circe gave the hunters back their magic ability and was waiting for her daughter to get someone to break the seal. With us and Signet in the room, they were gambling Imogen would attack us first, giving Vrah time to escape the ballroom. She'd easily be able to escape in the chaos.

If Samantha shoved the soul crystals back into the slot and effectively blocked the hunters from using their magic and inventory again, it wouldn't stop them. But it would be all the more difficult for them to prepare for the inevitable breaking of the seal. Or to cause it. It would also lure Diwata back to the third floor to attempt to fix it.

SAMANTHA: OHH, THAT SOUNDS LIKE A FUN FIGHT. I WILL FUCK
HER UP.

I looked about, trying to see the position of all the players in the room.

Eva hovered in the corner by the stage, near the now-locked exit door. She knew something was going down. We were stuck in the room, but we could leave once the seal was broken. She was planning to bolt. She had an escape device. A ring supposedly. It'd kept her alive until this point.

Lucia, Katia, Bautista, Gwen, and Tran remained at Chaco's counter. The group of hunters led by Vrah was moving in. I didn't know what their plan was, but they moved with sudden terrifying coordination.

This whole thing was like a reverse game of chicken. Nobody could make the first move. We all had to be cautious to the extreme.

Nobody was currently onstage, and the musicians weren't playing. I heard a distant crash. There was fighting in the castle. In the halls. There was another explosion followed by the sound of something crumbling. I wondered how the changelings were faring in all of this. Signet's squad had likely entered, too, looking for her.

CARL: Sledge? Are you in?
SLEDGE: Not yet. Rubble in the way. Trying to get into tower. Bears
and gnome hiding in rubble. Mantises everywhere. More by
minute. Coming out of tower to fight outside. Elves
everywhere still. Elves coming out of woods. Brambles chasing
elves, moving faster than usual.
IMANI: Most of the crawlers outside are getting forced down the
stairs. The brambles weren't supposed to get this far into
the elf territory for hours yet, but I think they're reacting to
the elves trying to beat them back. The elves at the border
who were fighting them have retreated to defend the castle,
and now the brambles are chasing them.

I felt my heart sink even further. With every minute that passed, our chances at surviving this were slipping further and further away.

LOUIS: How are we going to get down the stairs now?

CARL: There's one in the basement of this building. It'll remain
even after the castle is gone.

I didn't add what we all knew. That stairwell was locked, and it
would remain locked until Imogen was dead.

If I hadn't just learned that Lucia's head was possibly housing other
children, I would've been happy to let the hunters use her to break the
seal. But we couldn't let them do that. We needed to keep them from
launching their assault. We wanted this on our terms, not on theirs.

The problem was, we didn't have an alternate plan. What else could
we do? Just wait and let Imogen win? That wouldn't work. She'd still
attack us after, and she'd possibly be immortal. We'd still have a castle
filled with pissed-off mantises all around us, plus the hunters, plus the
goddess Diwata.

We were fucked. Everything that could've gone wrong, had.

We only had one last hope. If that fell through, one of us would have
to force open the protection seal.

It was either that or go with the nuclear option. Carl's Doomsday
Scenario. Would I be willing to kill all my fellow crawlers just to make
certain the hunters also died? Would I be willing to kill Donut, Katia,
Imani, Elle, and all the rest of my friends?

Would I?

Up onstage, Li Jun and Na and Zhang were juggling knives in a
circle. They did one quick circuit, and then they turned and bowed to
the audience and rushed backstage.

"Next act!" Imogen shouted from her chair. She pretended to sit
casually, but I saw the tension in her. Her hair had become disrupted
and was falling to the left. She looked about the room, eyes meeting
mine. "Only two more acts. Then we must dance for five minutes. Carl,
you're dancing with me."

One of the Draconians had a spell suddenly appear in his hand. It
was a fulminating gray ball of something. I had no idea what it was, but
he looked like he was about to roll the spell like a bowling ball right at
the feet of Lucia and the others.

CARL: Samantha! Put the gems back! Fast!

SAMANTHA: PUT YOUR BOXERS BACK ON. I JUST DID.

The spell whiffed out. The Draconian looked at his hand stupidly. Vrah turned her head in my direction, and I gave her a middle finger.

CARL: Good job. She'll be coming for you now. She's in the form of a flaming mantis giving birth. She's immortal, but she won't have any powers beyond that. I think. Do everything you can to keep her away from the control panel. If you can stop her from giving birth, she'll go away. I believe in you.

SAMANTHA: YOU DO?

CARL: You can do it.

SAMANTHA: OKAY, I GOT THIS.

Across the way, Lucia laughed at the semicircle of hunters and pushed her way through, coming back to our side. She strolled casually in our direction, holding her half-empty bottle of tequila. Katia and the others pushed through and retreated with her, following her at a safe distance like a group of celebrity handlers.

The second-to-last act appeared onstage. It was the mushroom guy. Horton. He had an acoustic guitar that was missing a string. It was the same guitar that Britney was going to use for the final act.

SLEDGE: Prudence dead. Died protecting two babies. They're crying. Hugging Bonnie. Too many mantises. Still fighting.

That was it. Sledge didn't need to get into the castle, but it took several minutes for him to cast his spell. He needed to be protected when he cast, and we were running out of time. With all the mantises? No way.

We were done.

I suddenly felt very, very tired.

Our only meager chance of survival was if someone broke the seal at the correct moment.

I looked down at my hands, and then I looked over at Eva.

The others would have a chance. Donut would have a chance.

I opened the chat window.

I closed my eyes for a second, just a second, and I pretended like everything was all right. The world had never ended. My mother and I had never left Texas. I was outside right now, sitting in the shade of a tree I'd planted years before. Everyone here, all my friends, never met each other under these horrific circumstances. Donut was fat and happy, sitting in her cat tree somewhere warm, growling at a cocker spaniel.

I'd never heard the water running through the pipes. Or gone down into the basement to investigate the noise. I'd never found the note, followed by my mother a minute later.

I let the dream live within me. Just for a second, and I returned to the chat window.

> CARL: Donut, plan A is a go. Repeat. Plan A is a go. Do the whole performance, start to finish. Don't forget Ferdinand. He's still sitting front and center.
> DONUT: REALLY? YAY! HOW ARE WE GOING TO BREAK THE SEAL?
> CARL: Just deal with your performance. I have a plan.

Signet was suddenly beside me, her entire form shaking. She paused as if she was carefully thinking of what to say.

"You told me, Carl. You told me, but I didn't understand. That Empress D'Nadia . . . *creature* said many things to me, Carl. She claims the whole universe has been looking forward to watching this party and seeing what was going to happen. That you've been forced to cancel your attack because of Diwata and the peace seal. She tells me the deity is actually under control of that bug thing's mother, who had to sell half of all her possessions just to get here and try to help her child. She says more people than there are stars in the sky are watching this very conversation unfold right now."

A strange, oddly satisfying sense of calm washed over me. It was strangely comforting. Like coming into port after a long time at sea, knowing very soon you'd finally be able to rest in a real bed and sleep for a long, peaceful time.

"Welcome to the shit show, Signet. D'Nadia is correct. Everyone is watching. We weren't expecting it to have gone down like this. We didn't know about the anti-violence seal. We weren't expecting all the mantises. My changelings have made it into the castle, I think, but I don't even know if they're okay or not. The mantises are everywhere. My guy with the big spell is in trouble. I keep thinking of things I could've done differently. Everything is fucked. Everything has gone wrong, and it's my fault."

"If all she says is true, how is any of this possibly your fault, Carl? It sounds like you're dancing at the end of the same strings as the rest of us."

SAMANTHA: HERE SHE COMES! I LOCKED THE DOOR AND SHE
    CAN'T GET IN. HA! SUCK IT, BITCH!

I chuckled. "Samantha is down there, about to fight Diwata herself. Right under our feet. I told her that I believed in her. It won't be long."

IMANI: Carl, what's happening? You're not planning on doing what I
    think you're going to do, are you?
CARL: I am. Don't tell Donut because she'll freak out. Take care of
    her for me.
ELLE: Go fuck yourself, Carl. We need you. We all need you.
CARL: So you'll let us all die, then? This is our only chance.
IMANI: I'll do it.
ELLE: The hell you are.
CARL: Oh, for fuck's sake. We're not getting into a pissing match
    over who the biggest hero is. I already have a plan set in
    motion. If any of you does something, you're just going to
    screw it up. I'm going to kill Eva and break the seal.
ELLE: Goddamnit, Carl. Donut is never going to forgive you.
CARL: As long as she's still alive, I don't care.

"Tell me, Carl. Why did you bring that poor girl here?" Signet asked.
I grunted. "Which one? There's a few."
"Tina."

SAMANTHA: THAT'S RIGHT, DAUGHTERFUCKER! SHE CAN'T GET IN. THE HALLWAY IS SMALL. HER BABY BUGS ARE GETTING SQUISHED. OOZE IS COMING UNDER THE DOOR. SHE IS A REALLY BAD MOTHER.

I gestured at the stage, where Horton continued to tune his guitar. Imogen was getting impatient.

"Tina? We have a quest involving her. She's going to dance."

"Quest?" Signet asked. "What does that mean?"

"It's not important. We need to give her what she wants. We're having her finish her dance recital. It combines well with everything else that's about to happen."

"Carl," Signet said, "that's not what Tina wants."

"What?" I asked. "What do you mean?"

SLEDGE: Mantises everywhere. In front of and behind. We are surrounded. I will protect little ones best I can, but it won't be long. I am sorry.

SAMANTHA: CARL, THE DOOR BROKE OPEN. I DON'T THINK I CAN DO IT.

CARL: Both of you, if you gotta lose, lose big. Samantha, you have to keep her from turning the magic protection back on. If you don't, Donut and the others will be in big trouble in a few minutes. Do whatever you can.

Signet lifted her arm and pointed to a small tattoo there against her pale skin. It was a puddle of water. Within it, a little fish stuck its head up out of it and looked at me sadly. "I met Edgar the tortoise the night my mother died. I think I told you this story already. Do you know what the first thing I said to him was? It was 'Can you bring her back?' He said no, but he could help me with the memory of her the best he could. She'd been too long dead to do it properly, but he gave this to me that first night. She's not complete, but I've grown to realize that's okay. What's left still lives within me. Everyone who lives on the Hunting Grounds and who knows Tina's story knows what she wants. It's not to dance in a recital, Carl. Young Tina wants the same thing I do. She wants what I suspect you do, too. She wants her mother back."

I felt as if I'd been slapped. *How the hell did she know that?*

"Her mother is Kiwi," I said. "The mongoliensis."

Signet nodded. "Tina's mind is gone, and she doesn't realize that other dinosaur has been there the whole time. She already has what she wants, yes. She just needs to see it. I think what you're planning on doing for her tonight is close, but it's not quite right."

"It's okay," I said absently. "If we have time, Donut will make sure she's reunited properly with her mother."

"This is 'Wonderwall,'" Horton said, and he started to play the song.

DONUT: OMG.

I laughed. I laughed at the absurdity of it all. Here I was, about to get sucked into a literal hell, sitting down at a party, talking to a tattooed, topless fish woman while listening to a mushroom dude named Horton play a poorly tuned guitar and sing my cat's favorite song. All while the entire universe watched.

Ka-Blam!

The entire building shook again. This was a big one. Everything not in the room flickered but came back. Tables fell over. The buffet collapsed, spilling food everywhere, scattering hunters. We all stopped and looked around. Horton paused his song.

I looked down at the floor, shocked. The floor tiles under our feet had shattered like windshield glass. Toward the far side of the room with the exit doors, the floor tiles were just gone in several places. Burning jagged holes remained. A few crawlers stood on the empty spaces, but they didn't fall through. It was just like the quadrant seals from the previous floor.

A terrible stench filled the room.

The missing floor tiles were replaced with . . . something else. Turning and mixing and spinning colors pressed against the invisible shield of the floor. It was white gore and green bug parts, I realized. It moved and undulated under us like the innards of a blender trying to mix coconut and cherries and avocado.

The hunters, I realized, were all looking upward while we were looking down. Their attention was focused on the back left corner of the room, but to me, the ceiling there looked intact. The hunter ballroom was on the second floor, and we were on the fourth. The explosion had occurred between us on the third floor. That had been a soul crystal going off, I realized. It must've been a small one. It had blown apart the floor under us and the ceiling above the hunter ballroom, exposing the illusion.

Yet the goodwill ballrooms still worked.

SAMANTHA: OKAY. THAT WAS MY BAD.

CARL: What the hell happened?

SAMANTHA: I WAS TRYING TO LOSE BIG, LIKE YOU SAID. BUT I THINK I LOST TOO BIG. I HAD TO USE THE SOUL CRYSTALS. THEY BLEW UP. ALL OF THEM. DIWATA IS STILL HERE, BUT SHE'S KNOCKED OUT. I DIDN'T KNOW I COULD DO THAT. THEM BABIES ARE STILL COMING OUT. REALLY FAST, BUT THERE'S NO ROOM FOR THEM, SO IT'S LIKE WE'RE IN A SAUSAGE PRESS. I NEED A CIGARETTE. AND MAYBE A BATH.

CARL: That was more than one crystal? Christ, I'm surprised you didn't blow up the whole castle!

SAMANTHA: YOU SAID IF SHE STOPPED GIVING BIRTH, SHE WOULD GO AWAY, SO I STUCK THE CRYSTALS IN MY MOUTH, AND I WENT UP THERE AND CHOMPED DOWN ON THEM.

CARL: Wait. You went up where?

"Uh, I guess I'm done," Horton said, and went offstage.

"Carl," Signet said. She stood to her full height and brushed herself off. She had a white acorn in her hand. It'd fallen from the inverted oak tree earlier. *Huh,* I thought. *I guess that tree really is in here.*

She popped the acorn in her mouth and crunched down. **Magical Fervor** appeared over her head.

Her hands gave off an inconspicuous glow. The tattoos all around her started to swirl. "There will be no arguing with me. I know you well enough to know what you're planning, and it will not work. My idea is better. Just tell me when."

"Signet, what are you doing?" I asked, alarmed. "Who is your sacrifice?"

"That D'Nadia woman said my mother was never real, Carl. She said all my friends, all my fallen brothers and sisters whose memories adorn my body are not real. That they never were."

"You don't need to do this," I said.

"Your companion, Princess Donut, has a very powerful *Torch* spell," Signet said. "I can do this without her help, but if you could ask her to cast it using moon rays as the source, it will make this much more worthwhile for you and my family. Much more."

Imani, Elle, and Katia rushed up. They had come in an attempt to talk me out of it, but they stopped at the sight of a glowing Signet.

"Carl, that tentacle-faced buffoon of a woman said something else to me," Signet said. "She told me she was sad that you weren't going to survive this evening, because she'd been looking forward to meeting you on the battlefield outside of Larracos. I want a favor from you, Carl. I want you to show her exactly how real my family is. I want them all to see."

In order to cast her *Ink Marauder* spell, Signet needed three people. Herself to cast the spell, a sacrifice to be the source of the blood, and a third party to kill the sacrifice.

But the spell didn't have to go that way. There was a method to cast her spell with only a single person. One who was all three.

"Signet? Are you sure?"

"Just tell me when. It'll happen fast."

SLEDGE: Mantises in front were changelings. We are free. Bonnie safe. Cubs safe. For now. Castle very damaged. Real mantises still everywhere. Elves, too.

I met the eyes of my friends standing around me. "We're back in business."

CARL: Everyone. Get ready. Stage plan A. Escape plan D. I repeat, escape plan D. If you don't have a Feather Fall ability or potion, come to me. Prepotente, come here. Fast. I need you.

74

UP ONSTAGE, THE CURTAINS PULLED OPEN, AND DONUT STOOD THERE alone. She once again wore the little fake headset microphone. Ferdinand sat upon the center table in the midst of the three judges with his ridiculous hat, eyes fixed on her, his tail wagging back and forth. I handed a Feather Fall potion out to a crawler.

DONUT: I TOOK THE CHARM POTION. IT WORKED!

"Come on, baby! You can do it!" Ferdinand called from the table. He looked over at Empress D'Nadia and said, "That's my bird up there."

My interface blinked.

Sir Ferdinand, minion of Princess Donut, has joined the party.

Donut cleared her throat. The stage went dark, and then a spotlight appeared above her, focused narrowly on her tiny form. Her tiara glittered.

"My name is Princess Donut," she said, her voice amplified, yet small at the same time. She didn't take out the sheet music. She didn't need it. "I am going to sing a song. My mother used to sing this to me. It's called 'All Eyes on Me.'"

Backstage, a guitar strummed. It was Britney, who turned out to be a damn virtuoso with the thing. The Popovs had the guitar in their inventory, having found it in a boss room long ago. The song played, a sad, minor strum. It sounded full and lush, despite the missing string.

Donut took a breath and started to sing:

Good girl, good girl, you're a good girl, my princess.
You're like a root beer float. Oh yes, oh yes.
I'd take it all back and never let you win. I wouldn't do it all over
    again.
I love you. I love you. I'm sorry, my princess.
All eyes on me.
All eyes on me.

As she sang the nonsensical song, repeating the whole set of lyrics a few times, the exact same goddamn song a drunken Bea used to sing to her, she slowly moved to the right side of the stage.

Her voice soared. It was one of the most beautiful things I had ever heard.

The lyrics didn't make any damn sense, but she sang them with such sad longing, it felt as if a hand had reached into my chest and wrenched my heart. The spotlight faded.

"Hot damn," Elle said. "She's getting good."

The spell did exactly what the title implied. Everyone in the room, without even realizing it, was now affected by a minor charm. Even the hunters and the crawlers and the damn queen. The charm wasn't all that useful, honestly, but it was perfect for this occasion. It focused everyone's attention on a subject of the caster's choice.

Britney stopped the song, letting the last chord hang. Then she started playing a new song. It was faster, more intricate baroque-style music.

The spotlight re-formed onstage, focusing on Big Tina, who stood at the center. The crowd gasped at the sudden appearance of the giant dinosaur. The spell was now fully cast, and everyone in the room stood or sat in place, transfixed. Despite the horror show of churning bug flesh under our feet and over the heads of the hunters, all eyes were on the stage.

The spotlight had a blue tint to it, washing the room in warm moonlight. The glowing of Signet's skin tripled in intensity.

With Donut's insane charisma, *everyone* had been affected by the spell. Everyone, including Imogen and myself. Only Signet seemed unaffected. She stood next to me, growing brighter by the moment. Nobody noticed the spell being cast.

They kept their eyes on the stage.

We were originally going to use this moment to all get into various positions depending on the escape plan. Escape plan D was more of a . . . haphazard . . . escape.

The massive dinosaur took a hesitant step forward. Her newly washed bright pink boa hung from her neck. Her inert wand remained in her hand. As we watched, the wand glowed. Donut had just cast the recharge scroll on it.

The dinosaur looked at the wand with wonder, then waved it. Sparkles danced through the air. Tina made a little excited hop, one that shook the stage, and then twirled.

The wand, it turned out, did a little more than just shoot sparkles. It did that, too, but it was another charm spell. A performer's trick. It was very similar to Donut's spell, but it had a little more kick to it. The audience, already heavily focused on the dinosaur, was now enraptured by her. They weren't forced to stare like zombies, but the wand cast a spell called the *Recital*, which had the effect of making everyone happy. It made them feel as if they wanted to be there. That they wanted to watch the stage. That this was something they'd been looking forward to.

It filled me with warmth. With hope. I felt tears form in the corners of my eyes.

The two cretins Clay-ton and Very Sullen appeared on both edges of the stage, each holding a stick that rose all the way to the ceiling. Pulled taut between the sticks was a massive piece of fabric—a ship's mainsail Elle had in her inventory—with waves painted on it. It rose all the way to the ceiling, obscuring the back of the stage. According to Prudence—poor dead Prudence—Tina was supposed to do a dance called the "Water Ballad," which was about a mer-bear or some shit. Tina twirled again, casting more sparkles. She skipped across the stage.

"When you see my family," Signet said, gritting her teeth through the spell, "you tell them I did this out of my own free will."

It was Vrah who realized what was happening. She either had immu-

nity to this sort of charm, or she finally noticed the glowing naiad standing off at the edge of the room. She shouted and started pushing her way
toward the stage, pointing at Signet.

CARL: Sledge, do it.
SLEDGE: Casting now. One minute to chant spell. Five minutes to
cast.
CARL: Sledge, you're inside the castle. That's okay, but it means
you'll be transferred to the ninth floor with everyone else.
Ferdinand the cat will go, too, and he might be a problem, so
watch him. When you get there, there might be some zombie
things attacking you. The good news is, none of the faction
wars guys will be allowed to touch you, so hopefully you'll all
be safe. You're going to feel really sick for a full day. But
you're going to have a lot of people around you who'll protect
you. Thank you for doing this, and thank you for taking care of
Donut. I'll never forget what you've done for us tonight.
SLEDGE: No let Bomo beat my *Frogger* score.
CARL: I'll unplug the machine the moment we get back.
SLEDGE: Good.

The two cretins holding the backdrop approached the forward part
of the stage, pushing Tina up to the very edge, where she twirled again,
sparkles spinning around her. They dropped the fabric, revealing a line
of 30 velociraptors plus Mongo and Kiwi. They were all wearing ridiculous hand-sewn costumes around their heads, depicting sea creatures
and sea anemones and starfish and whatnot. One was supposed to be a
shrimp, I was pretty sure, but it had the antennae in its mouth and was
chewing on them. Another, a clam, had her mask completely over her
eyes, and she was twirling in circles, unsure of what to do. Her tail
slammed against her neighbor, who squawked loudly.

Mongo had a crab costume that had fallen around his neck. Kiwi
was covered in white papier-mâché bubbles, ringed around her neck like
an oversized pearl necklace.

One of the costumes, a piece of seaweed, fell lazily from the ceiling
where it'd just been accidentally cut in half.

The inconsistent line of velociraptors danced back and forth to the guitar music.

   CARL: Britney, you need to get away from the backstage area.
      Come out.

The guitar faded, and the dinosaurs continued to sway back and forth.

   DONUT: READY WHENEVER YOU ARE.
   IMANI: Everybody who's on the right side of the room, move left.
      Look at the floor tiles. Move to a place where the floor is solid.

Signet reached forward and squeezed my hand.

"Carl," she said. She could no longer move her neck as the tattoos spun faster and faster. "Do you happen to have a knife?"

"I do," I said. I pulled one from my inventory. It was the same knife someone had once used in an attempt to assassinate Donut. I handed it over to her, handle first. At the same time, I slipped on my wrist bracer. All around, crawlers slowly pulled out their weapons and armed themselves.

"Thank you," Signet said. She raised a glowing hand and put it on my cheek. "Protect your family, and watch over mine."

The hunters, not knowing what was going on, all started to shout. The effect of the charm spells had finally faded.

Imogen looked about, surprised as Signet came and rigidly sat next to her sister.

"I only have two regrets," Signet said. "One is that I never got the chance to say goodbye to my Grimaldi. Maybe one day. The second is that I won't be the one to kill you today."

"What're you doing?" Imogen asked, alarmed.

"You know, we were going to leave. My mother and I. We were going to go to an island and leave all this behind. I think about it all the time."

She looked her sister in the eye, she pulled the knife, and she tore it across her own throat.

From the ceiling, every acorn on the upside-down tree fell at once. There was no warning or reason to it. They all hit the ground like little gunshots.

The floor rent open, and Signet plummeted from sight, getting pulled into the Nothing as Imogen grabbed at her, as if to stop her.

Ethereal shrieks rose from the tear in the ground. Black wisps and tendrils lashed upward. The stench of sulfur filled the room.

"So much for season three," Elle muttered.

"Psamathe," a faint voice shrieked from the dark, sounding distant and hollow. *"Psamathe, we are coming."*

The hole in the floor snapped shut.

Signet was gone, but an outline of her body remained, black shadows spinning. It was her tattoos, twisting and turning and undulating. Signet's blood also remained in this world, yanked from her flesh as she was torn away, temporarily creating an ethereal form that rose into the air and started to swirl and swirl upon itself, turning into a tornado, growing bigger by the moment.

Warning: Apito has turned her back. The seal has been broken. The Butcher's Masquerade has failed to cast. The protection of this chamber has stopped.

This party is over.

The three judges at the table disappeared with a crack of lightning. Chaco, at the far end of the room, also disappeared.

I pulled out the Ring of Divine Suffering, I placed it on my finger, and I marked Vrah.

I then pulled two smoke curtains. I held them in my hands like twin grenades, and I tossed them both into the room.

CARL: Now!

75

MANY, MANY THINGS HAPPENED AT ONCE.

"Sic 'em," Donut cried.

The velociraptors shrieked as one and leaped off the stage and landed amongst the surprised hunters. A raptor dressed as a puffer fish sailed across the room, landing atop a Draconian, and savagely ripped at his neck, decapitating him. At the same moment, Mongo and Kiwi fell upon Vrah, who screamed in rage as hunters fled and died.

"Surprise, motherfuckers!" Samantha yelled as she fell from the corner of the ceiling. She surfed into the room on a tidal wave of bug gore that slopped down like oatmeal through the hole in the ceiling. A hole I couldn't see. She hit the ground and rolled, pushing straight through my legs. She launched herself into the air and landed amongst Kiwi and Mongo, biting onto the dying form of Vrah.

"Remember me, bitch!" She chomped down on the bug.

At the same time, geysers of bug gore erupted up through the floor into our own ballroom. Mixed in with it were some actual living and intact mantis nymphs who squealed and moved to attack. These things were about two-thirds the size of the real deal and a third the strength, but there were a lot of them.

Tina roared and also leaped off the front of the stage, but the moment she did, she vanished. She was now the sole occupant of attendant ballroom B, not including the surprised workers and animal handlers, which we couldn't see. Sure enough, an elf suddenly appeared, landing on the stage, only for Tina to reappear for a moment to chomp him in half. She roared again as blood sprayed across the stage.

The disembodied tattoos swirled around Imogen, who screamed in outrage as the tornado encased her like a cocoon.

"I'll protect you, my bride!" Ferdinand shouted up at Donut. He blinked and disappeared.

All around us, the hunters died. But not all of them. Many were escaping from the now-open doors, scattering like cockroaches. I looked to our own doorway, and mantises surged in, blocking the exit. I growled.

Chaos reigned as the gore continued to ooze into the room from above and below. The Popovs swung their meteor hammer through the room, twisting and shouting as they destroyed the nymphs. Prepotente had potion bottles in his hands and he tossed them. Li Na rushed through the room, tossing chains as her brother danced atop them, ripping the bugs to pieces. A pair of summoned monsters with chain saw arms flanked Bautista as he cut his way across the room. Florin had taken up a position in the corner, his shotgun raised to his shoulder as he blasted one after another. The blasts had become like a beat.

Lucia cowered behind the Crocodilian, hands on her ears. She cried in terror.

IMANI: We need to get out of this room.

CARL: Two minutes. Donut's *Hole* spell won't work. The floor below us is literally filled with nymphs. The exit halls are blocked.

IMANI: Where's Diwata?

DONUT: I SEE HER ON THE MAP. SHE'S RIGHT BELOW US. SHE'S NOT MOVING.

The tattoos harassing Imogen weren't growing to the enormous, building-sized proportions they usually did. But they weren't turning into 2D tattoos, either. A fully realized three-headed Nodling ogre formed and hit the ground and roared. The name **Di-we. Memory Golem** formed over the Nodling's head. It swung and missed at the incorporeal form of Imogen. A massive Tina-sized hammerhead shark slammed into the ground, no longer floating like it usually did. It flopped angrily about, rolling over—and through—hunters and dinosaurs as it started to angrily chomp at nymphs, only some of whom were actually in the same room as it. Yet another tattoo—a normally gigantic snakelike dragon—also appeared, but it was only the size of my arm. It stuck its head straight up at the ceiling and fired a beam of light directly into the air. It hit the edge of the Scolopendra mosaic, which shattered and stopped twisting. The dragon roared and flew upward, disappearing.

We only had a minute before Queen Imogen would regain control of the situation. Smoke still filled the room. Signet's reanimated tattoos couldn't harm her directly.

Crack! Red lightning filled the room, coming from Imogen. It spread in every direction at once. A bolt struck me in the neck.

"Gah!" I cried as my health ticked down. Every creature in the room staggered.

The attack hadn't been too powerful, but it had hit everyone at once.

I jumped over to where Vrah lay on the floor, bleeding out. Mongo and Kiwi had ripped all of her limbs off. Both dinosaurs also bled from multiple wounds. One of Vrah's compound eyes had been punctured and shattered like a bee's honeycomb. White ooze seeped from the wound, pooling around her.

"How?" Vrah gurgled.

"Kiwi," I said, "back onto the stage. Quick. Mongo, finish her off for me. Make it hurt."

Kiwi pressed her head against Mongo's for just a moment. She knew. She knew this was goodbye. She turned and returned to the stage as Mongo roared gleefully and dove back into Vrah.

My interface chimed, letting me know I'd successfully finished off the mark. Her highest stat had been dexterity. I looked about for another target, but none had full health. Multiple hunters worshipped Emberus. Only Imogen had full health. I pulled my ring off. For now.

"Samantha," I yelled, "if I don't see you again, thank you!"

"Where am I going?" she asked. She had managed to pull a chunk of Vrah chitin off her body, and she spit it out. Her hair had all burned off, and she looked like a Barbie head pulled from a house fire. "Are you breaking up with me? Is it because of Louis?"

"What? No!" I said as I ducked a friendly-fire magic missile. A nymph flew at me, and I punched it in the head. It exploded, but not before it raked its arms across me. I cried out in pain. I swung at another, but my hand flew right through it. It wasn't in this room. "You're in the castle. You'll teleport away. Ninety seconds!"

"Where's Signet?" Samantha shouted. "She needs to give me my body!"

"She's gone," I said. "She killed herself to save us."

"What?" Samantha demanded. "I'm going to . . ." She paused, seeing something. She rolled off toward the stage.

The sound of a crying child caught my attention.

I ducked a flying nymph attack and then kicked another as it lurched at the three newcomers cowering on the ground.

Not all of Signet's tattoos were warriors.

The young hairy form of Clint cried as he clutched on to the apron of the equally terrified Miss Nadine. The dwarflike Chee woman had once upon a time been a caterpillar, and before that a teacher of young children. She cowered with the boy, unsure what to do. They'd both been hit by the lightning attack. Clint's health was almost gone. I instinctively pulled a health potion and shoved it at him. He grabbed it in two hands and sucked it down. To my surprise, it worked.

There was another person there, too. A naiad prone on the ground. The harsh eyes of the creature were closed, as if she was sleeping. Signet's mother. The memory of her, at least, given flesh. The label over her read:

Princess Lunette. Incomplete Flesh Golem.

"Cousin," Samantha said. She poked the golem with her burned head. "Cousin, wake up!"

"Nadine," I said, "how long will you guys last?"

"Forever," she said, panting the words. "She gave us . . . she gave us life."

"You'll transfer, then. It might get bumpy for you guys." It was going to happen at any second.

The breathless Nadine pointed to the prone form of Princess Lunette. "Signet. Wants you. Take the golem. She took memory with her. Just left body. Help Samantha. Find a Pulpmancer."

"Take it! Take it, Carl!" Samantha shrieked, bouncing up and down like a basketball. I kicked another nymph.

I picked up the form of Signet's mother. It weighed nothing. It wasn't alive. It had no dot on my map. I pulled it into my inventory.

I grinned down at Samantha. "We'll figure this out when I meet up with you on the ninth—"

"Fuck that!" Samantha said. She rose up off the ground, floating magically, and she shot off like a rocket, blasting down through a hole in the floor.

What the hell?

Nadine picked up Clint and clutched him in her arms. We all ducked as Florin's shotgun blast hit a pillar, sending wood chunks everywhere. Katia had formed into her sentinel gun and was blasting away. The nymphs just kept coming and coming.

"You fools!" Imogen shouted, waving her arms and pushing her way out of the mess of tattoo warriors. A squid had formed, and it was pulling itself upward through the ceiling. Her hands glowed. She swiped her hand to the left, and my arm snapped. Just like that. I cried out in pain as I was pulled through the air toward her, bones in my body cracking and breaking.

"Gah!" Imogen cried as the orange form of Sir Ferdinand appeared and slammed into her head. She staggered, and I crashed into the floor. My shattered arm bone ripped through my skin.

Ferdinand went flying, blood spewing as Imogen savagely backhanded him. He flew in one direction, his hat in the other. He hit the ground and yowled and then disappeared.

I cast *Heal* and pulled myself to my feet as my bones knit, like broken glass forming in reverse. I staggered as I fell unsteadily. *Come on. Come on.* Imogen would recover at any moment.

"Kiwi," Donut called, still upon the stage, "come here! Lower your head!"

Kiwi moved to Donut, who reached up and grasped one of the bubbles around the back of Kiwi's neck with two paws. She squeezed, and the potion ball hidden within the bubble exploded.

Big Tina reappeared onstage just as the I Take It All Back potion spread over the velociraptor. The effect was instantaneous. Kiwi staggered and then stood to her feet, having been transformed from a dinosaur to an ursine. It happened even faster than I thought it would.

The bear stood to her height, naked except the remaining paper bubbles. She looked at her paws in surprise. The other raptors all roared as one. Their white dots all turned red.

Tina, upon seeing the transformation of her mother, roared. Then roared again. Then a third time, only this time the roar sounded almost like words. Then a fourth time. "Mom? Mommy? Where are we? Mommy? *Mommy?*"

She remained in the form of an allosaurus.

Quest Complete. The Recital.

SLEDGE: Five seconds. Goodbye.

I met Donut's eyes. All around us were blood and carnage and death.

"Potions!" I shouted. I had my nipple-ring Quarter Fall ability, but I didn't trust it. I drank a Feather Fall potion. I'd gotten the potions out of the box, along with a bunch of other things, when I stood upon Prepotente's personal safe room cube. He had one zap left on his wand, and he'd let me use it. All in exchange for letting him take over the party for a day or so.

Vroom.

Everything froze.

76

WE ALL HUNG, FROZEN IN MIDAIR.

Not this shit again.

The elf castle was gone. All of Signet's tattoo warriors were gone. The changelings were gone. Kiwi, who'd turned into a bear—a very pregnant bear—was gone. Tina, who'd remained a dinosaur, was also gone.

They'd all traveled away with the half-destroyed castle, which had just landed somewhere on the ninth floor.

None of the crawlers, hunters, pets, mobs, remaining dinosaurs, dead bodies, or elves had transferred with the castle. We remained frozen in the air in a rough stacked-cube formation.

The vast, vast majority of everything was mantis nymphs.

The brambles had completely filled the world, stopping about 100 feet from the outskirts of the now-gone castle. Mounted elves remained on the ground, mostly on the edge of the brambles, all turned, looking up at the floating frozen mess still hovering in midair.

Out of nowhere, AC/DC's "Thunderstruck" started playing. It wasn't coming from a trap module. The damn AI was using it as boss music.

That's new, I thought.

B . . . B . . . B . . . Boss Battle!
    Cage Fight Extreme!
    Four teams enter! One team leaves! Four teams enter! One team leaves!

The AI's voice shrieked the words, absolutely giddy with excitement. "Oh, fuck," I said.

In corner one!

It's the dungeon's top crawlers! Plus some other guys! These plucky adventurers have beaten all the odds to get this far! But will their luck hold out tonight?

A whole line of player portraits slammed into the air one by one, starting with a crawler I didn't know and moving down the line and ending, not with Prepotente, who was the current number one, but Donut. I was third from last. *Bam, bam, bam.* Each new portrait was accompanied by an explosion. It didn't group us by team, but individually.

In corner two!

Starting with over a thousand, and now down to just 75, it's the last remaining hunters on this floor! Most of these guys have been acting like little bitches the whole time, so they're probably all dead. But, hey, they're here and they have a chance.

Well, not really. But they're here!

Several hunter portraits slammed onto the screen, roughly the same number as us. Vrah was gone and dead, but the ones who'd managed to escape the dinosaurs had only done so temporarily.

This part took a little longer. With each name, it listed off their home planet. Almost half of them were listed as homeless or living in some sort of refugee camp.

The song finished, and a new song started. This was heavy, frenetic music that started to pulse with a heavy, sub-bass beat. It was the same damn song the elf musicians had been playing at the start of the party, but turned to a thick techno beat.

In corner three!

Queen Imogen! High Elf, Fallen Cleric Sorcerer!

Level 145 Country Boss!

The current favorite. Her forces have been whittled down to almost nothing, but her elite fighting squad is still in good shape. She may be down and shunned by her goddess because she just

threw the worst party since Alexander the Great took Persepolis,
but she is still strong, powerful, and really, really pissed off!

Above, the glowing form of the falling queen burst into light. She
had a new symbol over her head. It was the same **Marked for Death** symbol I still had floating over me, but it was an X with acorns dangling
from it. A group of black-clad elves fell with her.

And finally, in corner four!

About twenty feet below me and to the left, a new form burst into
light. It was the angry, flaming, and very conscious form of Diwata the
god. She didn't look like a goddess. She looked exactly like her true
identity, Circe Took. A baby mantis was halfway out of her body,
screaming and waving its arms as it was cooked alive by the flames from
her blazing genitals.

Diwata! Level 250 Immortal!
    It's not only a deity. It's also the winner of the dungeon's Worst
Mother *and* Father of the Year Award! She can't be killed, but if you
can manage to talk her into some sort of birth control, she'll be
knocked out of the ring!

DONUT: CARL, CARL, DID YOU SEE! I GOT TOP BILLING! AGAIN!
CARL: Everybody spread out. Hit Imogen with blunt-force attacks.
    Not magical bolts. Use the beat of the music to coordinate
    your strikes. Follow Florin's lead. Katia, Imani, Donut, on me.
    We take care of Diwata, and then we assist with Imogen.
DONUT: I'LL HAVE TO USE YOUR PAWNA'S TEARS POTION. I JUST
    TOOK A FEATHER FALL, SO I HAVE TO WAIT FOR MY POTION
    COOLDOWN! I TOLD YOU I SHOULD'VE DONE THIS EARLIER,
    CARL.
CARL: I know. It's okay. We'll protect you.

The portraits didn't disappear, but turned into tiny, barely distinct
icons and moved into my interface, taking up the bottom of the screen.

I could now see who was still alive, but the portraits were so small, I'd have to hover over it and see who each represented.

The brambles started to rise up into the air, and they formed a dome over the whole area, plunging us all into darkness. A sickly yellow glow filled the world, coming from little flower buds on the brambles. The lights pulsed on and off with the beat, creating a dizzying strobe effect.

And here!
  We!
  Go!

The world unfroze. Gore plummeted along with an outrageous amount of acorns. The mantises took to the air, turning to a buzzing swarm as the hunters fell like rocks. Most of us slowly started to float downward, falling in a mist of thrashing, angry bugs.

It was like we were paratroopers jumping straight into hell.

I slammed onto my magic-protection spell. Lights swirled around me.

Imogen fell like an asteroid, rushing past all of us. She'd had the farthest to fall, and she hit the ground with the force of a bomb. Ferdinand wasn't with her, having been transferred with the castle.

I grasped a mantis by the neck as I re-formed my gauntlet, and its head popped off. Despite being decapitated, it savagely tore at my chest. Another was at my own neck. Then another. One dropped, hit by a Donut magic missile. Another fell from a shot by Katia.

Plink, plink, plink. The icons of hunters started to get X'd out as they splattered against the ground.

When the castle had teleported away, it'd taken the subbasements with it, so we had farther to fall than I'd originally thought. I savagely ripped at another mantis as a lightning bolt, thick as a tree, ripped through the air, possibly aimed at me, but it dissipated before hitting home, instead crisping dozens of mantises, who all exploded into mist.

Smoke started to fill the air. This was a smoke bomb from a hunter, designed to obscure our vision. I answered in kind by dropping my custom-made Smoke Daddy bomb, which would fill the whole goddamned area. At the same time, Donut, falling just to my right and slightly above, dropped her *Fear* smoke bomb, which corkscrewed away into the flashing chaos. With her charisma, the effect would sow absolute terror in everyone.

Dozens of debuffs stacked and then disappeared. This was Imani working furiously. She was a thing of beauty, a beacon of light, her butterfly wings fully spread as she fell, counterspells and buffs flying out of her at a ridiculous pace.

The form of Bianca shot through the air, reminding me of a shark passing through the deep ocean. The demonic goat-dragon thing cut through the nymphs like a snowplow. Prepotente rode upon her back, screaming, multiple shields glowing around him as he tossed potion bottles in the fray.

"Ground coming up!" someone shouted. Through the smoke and flashing lights and mist, I sensed more than saw that we were falling below the ground level, falling into the basement. The area was huge, just as wide as the castle had been. The shadows of mounted elves dove into the deep pit as the brambles pushed farther in, entombing us all. The elves fell, tumbling as their mounts screamed and crashed.

Plink, plink, plink, plink. The hunters were half gone already, but crawlers were starting to disappear, too.

My feet hit the ground, landing amongst a knee-deep pile of dead bugs. I couldn't see a goddamned thing. A velociraptor with the bloody remnants of a lobster costume dangling from her neck sailed over me, pouncing on something I couldn't see. With Kiwi gone, they'd all reverted to red-tagged mobs, loyal to nobody except themselves.

"Oh fuck," I shouted, ducking as a literal wave of thrashing bugs fell at me.

I slammed down onto *Protective Shell*. Bugs, elves, dinosaurs, and a few hunters rocketed away as the shield formed, blasting them into the air in all directions. The shield was huge now, and it created a crater, leaving only crawlers and corpses in the center. Nearby, at the edge of the spell, Donut whimpered as she healed Mongo, who'd been injured in the fall. Imani used the short respite to move to several crawlers and heal them. We regrouped and readied ourselves to move toward the god, who was a mere 100 feet away, shoved against the wall. Another group turned and prepared to face Imogen.

A similar shield to mine popped up fifty feet away. It glowed like a beacon in the mist. This was smaller, and it had been cast by a hunter. I watched as a crawler flew up and away, screaming as she was launched by the spell. She disappeared into the dark, falling amongst the brambles.

Plink.

"There!" Imani said, pointing. We pushed our way out of the still-formed spell, leaving a wall at our back as we kicked and fought and waded toward the star on the map, which had settled in the far corner.

Blood misted in the air. I could barely breathe, and I coughed as I trudged forward, tasting copper and fire. Someone had cast *Poison Cloud,* and crawlers all around choked as those without immunity were forced to constantly heal themselves. I couldn't hear the music anymore. Only the terrified screams of elves and hunters and crawlers and bugs and raptors as we all collectively fought and died. Spells whipped around in every direction, ricocheting, exploding, and killing.

A velociraptor lay on the ground, injured in the fall. *Sorry,* I thought as Elle iced it. *I'm so sorry we couldn't save all of you.*

An arrow suddenly burst through my left forearm, burying itself in my chest. I gasped and hit the ground. A half-dead mantis, also on the ground, struck at me as I spat up blood. A black-clad elf emerged from the darkness, curved blade in his hands. The elf rocketed away as a meteor hammer swung through the air, braining him. The round weapon cleared my head by inches.

I headbutted the mantis, caving its head in. *Huh,* I thought as I started to lose consciousness. *I didn't know I could do that.* Just before sleep took me, I was violently ripped awake by a mass heal. It was Donut. She rode upon the back of Mongo as she shriek-sang the song. I looked up at the Popovs, who stood over me, protecting me as I recovered. I pulled the arrow from my body, screaming as it ripped flesh anew.

"Watch out!" I tried to cry, but I couldn't get the breath. A flaming form barreled through the darkness. It was a sambhur, one of the elf mounts, but it had somehow caught on fire, and it was covered with nymphs, cutting and screaming. The deer wasn't running, but it had somehow been magically flung, and it spun like a wheel ejected from a wagon. This was a spell, something from Imogen.

The thing barreled right into Dmitri and Maxim Popov, the mount's antlers ripping right through the two-headed ogre like they were made of paper. It happened so fast. Blood showered over me. The double crawler slammed to the ground next to me as the flaming mount spun away, spinning blood and fire and screams as it wobbled and disappeared.

"I miss my cat," Dmitri said just before he closed his eyes.

A notification appeared. I waved it away.

More crawler dots blinked out. Only five hunters remained. I could hear the roar of Florin's shotgun. It sounded so far away. Ren's flamethrower shot out, a beacon in the dark, cutting through the mist like a flaming gash into reality. Garret, her Tummy Acher, was at her side. I could only see them in shadow. A pair of elf or hunter legs dangled from its massive mouth. Mantises and elves all around them went up like kindling. A flaming velociraptor leaped at Imogen, and the dinosaur exploded in midair, showering flaming gore everywhere.

"Carl," Katia said, suddenly at my side, helping me to my feet, "I need to go back and help with the Imogen fight. Daniel and Tran are in trouble. They're getting hammered."

"I had to use my *Protective Shell* already," I said, gasping. A fifteen-foot mountain of bugs, alive and dead, stood between us and the deity, who was hiding in the corner. "I don't know if I can get in."

"Here." She pulled the beanie off her head, the one the Apothecary had just given her in a benefactor box, and she placed it on my own. It equipped itself with a little *beep*. "Use the spell to clear through the nymphs. Get Donut close enough."

I nodded and called for Donut. She was suddenly beside me, atop Mongo. She was matted down with gore. She had multiple debuffs over her, but they blinked and disappeared as Imani rushed past, back toward the fight against Imogen.

A magic missile slammed into her, and she staggered, but her health didn't go down.

"Carl, I was wrong about my charisma not working! My Love Vampire skill works really good when it's this high!" she shouted, giddy with excitement. The skill had never really worked properly until now. Behind us, multiple elves waded through the fray with little heart icons over them. "A bunch of elves are in love with me! It doesn't work on the bugs."

Christ. We need to get her charisma that high permanently. "How's your potion countdown?"

"I'm ready!" she shouted.

"Take it now!"

Red lightning zapped the entire area, shocking us all. This was stronger than before. More crawlers blinked and disappeared. All the remaining elves under Donut's control dropped dead, leaving her defenseless.

DONUT: IT WENT UP TO THE VERY END OF 15. I GOT A BUNCH OF
   ACHIEVEMENTS!
CARL: Okay, here we go.

The dot of Diwata was just over the pile. We had to get closer. We needed line of sight.

"Wait five seconds, then jump in," I said to Donut. "Cast the moment you see her."

I rushed up the hill of dead and dying bugs, scrambling in the smoky dark. The whole area was getting hotter by the moment. Everything was on fire. An errant arrow slammed into the back of my leg and buried itself. I cried. I crested the top of the hill just as a group of bugs lunged at me. I cast the spell from Katia's beanie, *I Need My Personal Space*. It pushed them all in different directions, working like a miniature version of *Protective Shell*.

Mongo and Donut jumped in, and we all tumbled forward, landing before the god.

"Fuck you!" Circe Took cried from her position in the corner. The god stopped giving birth, and she started to change, turning into something monstrous.

She was running. But she wasn't running fast enough.

Donut cast *Laundry Day*.

At my direction, Donut had been relentlessly training her armor-removing *Laundry Day* spell every day for weeks now. She'd managed to get the spell up to nine on her own. Just before we went to the party,

I'd finally made her take the recently acquired Pawna's Cries potion, which she secretly used to raise the spell three more levels to 12.

She needed it at 15.

The note from my sponsor had stated we should use boosts from Prepotente, Imani, and Samantha to temporarily raise her spell level the last three levels. Prepotente was back there somewhere, and despite *a lot* of prodding, we weren't able to coax any sort of spells or buffs out of Samantha. She was gone anyway to god knew where. That was okay. We had a backup.

It was a bit of a waste using my more powerful Pawna's Tears potion, which raised the skill by five additional points, but my sponsor claimed he would replace it. I really hoped so. I'd wanted to save it and wait until it was absolutely necessary.

The *Laundry Day* spell couldn't hurt the god. The only way it would actually remove the armor from a god was if she trained it up to 20, which she wouldn't ever be able to do as she was maxed out at 15.

But that was okay. She didn't need to remove the armor from a god. She just needed to remove it from a person. The god *was* the armor, and it would remain intact. She just needed to remove it from the person underneath. And all we needed for that was the spell to be at level 15.

I'd been worried we'd first have to remove the god's invulnerability. Tin, who'd written the 21st edition of the cookbook, seemed to think that was the case. But after further research, it appeared that spells designed to target the drivers of soul armor and not the gods themselves would still work.

I'd been planning on using this on Grull the next time he showed himself, but we couldn't always choose our battles.

The spell cast, the deity screamed, and little white soapy bubbles appeared everywhere.

Diwata transformed into an antlered bear. It screamed at me and lunged before it dissipated into nothing.

Diwata has returned to the Halls of the Ascendency.

The form of Circe Took, stripped of her protection, sopping wet and covered with bubbles, stood to her full height. The giant mantis woman chittered in rage.

"I don't need the protection of the god to—"

She never finished. Before I could strike, a dozen of her own children fell upon her. The wave of bugs rushed her, slicing and cutting and ripping. They screamed as one, piling onto her, as if enraged.

Circe Took died shrieking my name.

We didn't have time to celebrate. Yet another area attack swept through the pit, this one even stronger than before. Donut cried out and fell from Mongo, her health zeroed out. Her Cockroach skill activated, saving her.

"Donut!" I cried.

She wouldn't survive another one of those. The spell did more damage each time. As it was, that last attack had killed all the remaining bugs.

Team four, eliminated!

A single hunter remained. Forty-something crawlers remained.

The elves were mostly dead. I didn't see any raptors. Imogen remained in the far corner of the pit, two hundred feet away, screaming as we poured arrows and rocks and shotgun blasts into her.

I saw the hunter's dot on my map, and I moved in. It was Zabit. He pointed at me and shouted something I couldn't hear. He blinked and disappeared, using an invisibility potion or skill. I moved to chase him, but I stopped dead, remembering his armor. The belt. *Nice try, asshole,* I thought.

I cast *Tripper.*

Bam! Multiple land-mine traps went off. Zabit instantly reappeared, his body having been torn in half by his own trap, which he'd set seconds before.

Team two, eliminated!

During the explosion, the light flashed off the ceiling, revealing the twisting and turning brambles, growing absurdly fast, closing in from above. We were boxed in.

I hesitantly moved to the hunter corpse, and I quickly looted him. I didn't get the drop shield or case of invisibility potions. I assumed they were still in a prize box. But I received multiple trap items, too many to sort through now.

"Carl!" Donut cried. "There aren't any elves left. Just Imogen!"

We turned to help, but I skidded to a stop.

Oh no.

"No," I said, seeing the body on the ground. It was Gwendolyn Duet. Gwen. The tattooed First Nations woman who'd been instrumental in our survival on the previous floor. She lay dead, surrounded by elves and bugs. At her side was the body of Cleiton, the knock-knock-joke guy. Tran was there, still alive, dragging himself away, screaming. His legs were gone. I read a scroll, healing him. His legs did not grow back.

"Heave!" Florin cried, firing his gun. Imogen, atop a pile of corpses, lit up as she was pelted with arrows and projectiles.

They were coordinating their attacks, half of them firing on the two and four of the beat, the other half on the one and three. Arrows, rocks, and other non-magical bolts slammed into the insanely powerful boss. Her health was in the red, almost gone. She had a *Stuttering Shield* spell, like a strobe light, and she kept casting it over and over again, but it kept getting overwhelmed by the sheer amount of crap getting thrown at her.

Imogen stopped casting her *Shield* as she fell to a knee. A black sizzling nimbus shone around her, similar to Bianca's aura. Her hands crackled red.

"Lightning attack," someone shouted.

I spied Britney on the ground, screaming. Louis and Firas lay side by side. Both were unconscious but alive. I hadn't had time to reinstall my xistera, but I pulled a hobgoblin disco ball.

"Your jacket!" I shouted at Britney as I tossed the ball. It arced and landed against the side of Imogen's head, splattering multicolored goo everywhere. She barely noticed. She was screaming something incomprehensible. Her health was almost gone.

Too slow, I thought. *Too slow.*

The *Lightning* spell cast, but it came out as a single bolt, attracted to the clump of spreading butterflies. The bolt slammed into the summoned creatures.

That's not what I'd intended to happen. I'd meant for the butterflies to seek out the disco ball and overwhelm Imogen, but this worked, too.

The mess of butterflies exploded over our heads, barely ten feet away. Donut, Mongo, Britney, and I went flying in different directions. My eardrums shattered, and everything plunged into silence. I slammed into a large, heavy corpse. A hunter. A Dreadnought missing half his face. Flaming bits of stuffing were everywhere, falling like embers. This time the unconsciousness took hold, and I felt myself slipping away, as if I were falling into a tunnel. As if I was getting pulled into a rushing river.

As I passed out, I watched the shadow of Bianca the goat-dragon fly right over me, Prepotente on her back, screaming silently. He jumped off the mount, a bubbling potion in each of his hands. The terrible stench of burning flesh overwhelmed the room as I finally slipped away.

. . .

Winner!

. . .

Quest Complete. The Vengeance of the Daughter.

77

MULTIPLE PAGES OF ACHIEVEMENTS FILLED THE DARKNESS. I COUGHED. Everything hurt.

Fucking hell, I thought. *I'm still alive.*

A terrible buzzing filled my head. My hearing was coming back. But it was something else, too.

It was always something else.

DONUT: CARL, CARL, GET UP! THE CEILING IS STILL COMING
DOWN, AND THEY'RE ALL STILL FIGHTING. BIANCA ATE GIMLI!
I HAD TO PUT MONGO AWAY!

She was on my chest, bouncing up and down.

I blinked and opened my eyes. *Five more minutes,* I thought as my hearing continued to return. *It was peaceful there in the river. It was silent.*

"We're on the same team," someone shrieked.

My hearing fully returned, all at once. All I heard was shouting. Prepotente screamed. Another voice shouted back.

"It's mine," the voice shouted, a voice filled with anger and tears. "Murderer. You murdered my pet. I got it, and if you want it, you're gonna have to loot it from my dead body."

"That can be arranged!" Prepotente shouted. "I struck 22% of all the damage against the boss, I struck the killing blow, and I received first looting choice on her, and it is mine!"

"It was on her body, not her inventory," the voice shouted back. "It was on the treasure map that we all got, and I was the first to get it."

"What's happening?" I asked, whispering the words.

"We won, but a lot of people are dead or hurt," Donut said. Her voice was strange. A mix of adrenaline and something else. Shock maybe. "Firas is dead. Gwen is dead. So is Horton, the 'Wonderwall' guy. And the Popovs. Tran lost his legs, and Britney's face is burned really bad, and when we healed it, it stayed all gross. A lot of my raptors are dead, and Mongo is really sad, but a bunch of them jumped up and ran right into the brambles. I don't know where they went. It still says Ferdinand is in the party, and that means he's alive. It won't let me message him. Mordecai says he'll automatically leave the party when we go down to the next floor. No, don't move just yet, Carl. It says you have a bunch of debuffs still. Imani is healing people in order."

"Firas?" I asked. He'd been alive. Unconscious, but alive. "Oh. Oh no. What about Louis?"

"He's still knocked out."

I swallowed. I felt numb. Something was nagging at me in the back of my mind, screaming, but I could barely hear it.

"What's happening with Pony and the other guy?" I said. I felt my own words slurring. I was tired. So damn tired. I had a dead Dreadnought on my legs. I instinctively tried to loot him, but someone already had.

"The guy with Gimli the hawk stole something off Imogen's body after she died, and Prepotente is really mad about it. They all got into a fight. There was a third person who tried to take it, too. The badger lady, I think. But she got hurt and went down the stairs. Prepotente says he needs the thing to defeat Scolopendra. He says it protects you from the boss's attacks. Everyone is getting this treasure-map thing that shows a lot of loot all over the place, but it's useless because it's all covered with brambles now. These two guys cast a spell and went through the brambles anyway looking for stuff, which is really dumb."

I blinked. Everything hurt. I hadn't processed anything. I still had an arrow in my leg. I could feel it. Up above, the brambles had slowed their descent. Despite Donut's panic, we had maybe twenty minutes before we'd be crushed. And even then, the brambles would form a dome over the stairwell, leaving a wide area around it. I tried to sit up, but it was painful to move.

I saw the stairwell now, thirty feet away. We still had over 20 hours until the collapse. Elle, Chris, and Bautista were there, dragging the unconscious crawlers toward the glowing entrance. Imani was over one of them, casting a spell. A crawler I didn't know was helping Tran, who sobbed.

"Where's Lucia? Eva?"

"Florin says Lucia is gone! She teleported away using her escape thing the moment before the boss fight started. He says she always sets teleports at stairwell locations, and she didn't even do the boss fight. Katia says Eva got bitten by a dinosaur and is buried over there, and she's looking for her right now. She's not dead yet. Eva stole all those dinosaur repellant potions, and she didn't even take one! Li Na and her brother are helping to look for her. Zhang is knocked out with Louis. Louis also got burned, but it's not as bad. He's going to be really sad about Firas."

I groaned in pain. My health was slowly seeping away. I clicked over to my health tab, and I had thirty different debuff items listed, including a nasty bleed effect. Imani would be here soon. Did we have any other healers in the group? I thought of Miriam Dom, who'd died to protect Prepotente.

So much death.

I needed to stay distracted.

"That guy who looted Imogen. What's his name?"

"It's Osvaldo. He looks like a person, but it says his race is a Curupira. I don't know what that means. He's a ranger. He's level 60 now. You're 63! Katia is 60, and I went up to 55! Prepotente went to 71!"

Since nobody had purchased the memorial crystal, it had returned to Imogen. This Osvaldo had taken it.

At that moment, I didn't care. I wanted it. So did Prepotente apparently. But that was a problem for tomorrow.

"Did you see what Prepotente did?" Donut said. "The queen lady was pretty much dead already, but he jumped right on her and smashed the potion into her face. She didn't see him coming because you'd hit her with the disco ball goop. When she died, Florin started sobbing like when Ifechi really died. He already went down the stairs."

Donut wouldn't stop talking, like she was racing to get the words out. Behind us, the shouting stopped.

"Poor Gwen," Donut continued. "She was mean, but I liked her. Poor

Horton, too. It's always sad when we lose a fellow musician. Elle is really upset about it. I think she feels bad about making fun of him all the time. Firas is the hardest. I didn't know the other guys very well. Do you think Britney's face is going to stay that way because she's not going to like that. And she'll probably be really upset about Firas. When she did the butterfly thing with her coat, it attracted the lightning, and that's why she's burned, and that's why Firas died, but it saved everybody. I think that attack was getting stronger the less health Imogen had. But did you see it? Did you? We won both the dinosaur quest and the Vengeance of the Daughter one."

She stayed on top of me, breathing heavily. I wanted to just close my eyes and go back to sleep. The weight of her on my chest was comforting. Familiar.

System Message: A champion has fallen. A bounty has been claimed.

A moment later, Katia marched by, her face dark. She looked down at me and nodded. She now sported a second golden player-killer skull. She looked nothing like the scared woman I'd met on the third floor.

"It's done," she said after a moment, and she moved on to help the others. Li Na and Li Jun followed her. Li Jun appeared absolutely shell-shocked. He paused as if he wanted to say something, but his sister called him away.

"Carl?" Donut asked after they left.

"Yeah?"

"That fight was terrible, wasn't it? Worse than usual. It went quick, but it was still really bad."

"It was pretty awful, Donut. If I'd known it was going to happen like this, I would've made you go down the stairs."

She was silent for a moment, and then she asked the question I'd been dreading for a long time now.

"Carl? Why doesn't it hurt as much as it should?"

I felt the words deep in my chest.

She took a shallow breath. "Firas. Gwen. The Popov brothers. Gideon. Even Signet and all those stupid dinosaurs who didn't know how to dance. They were my friends, and now they're dead, and I think I should be crying, but I'm not. Even Florin cried. And Chris cried. And Elle cried."

I closed my eyes.

"Donut—" I began.

She cut me off, desperation in her voice. "Why? Firas was going to be Louis's best man at his wedding to Juice Box, and he asked Katia to secretly make them tuxedos. It was going to be a big surprise, and now it's never going to happen. Why am I not as upset as I should be? It doesn't feel right. I think I'm doing something wrong. I think something inside of me has broken."

I reached up, and I put my hand on her. She was sticky with blood. So much blood.

"It's okay," I said.

"No, Carl," she said, "I don't think it is."

"Donut," I said, reaching up with my other hand, "come here."

She circled once and then settled into the crook of my arm, like we used to do so long ago. I ran my hand across the top of her bloody matted head. Her temporary charisma-gaining crown was gone, I realized, lost in the battle. She'd removed her sunglasses, too.

"This is important, and I want you to listen to me very carefully, okay?"

"Okay."

I stroked her head softly as I talked. "The name of that spell and party has been bothering me for a while now. The way it's written, it means there's only one butcher. I don't think it was possible for Imogen to 'win' that boon. When I was talking to her earlier, she told me the story of the Butcher's Masquerade. She said at the party, we wore masks so we could pretend for a little bit that we weren't monsters. But she was wrong about that. She had it backward. You're wearing a mask right now, Donut, and you don't know how to remove it. That's okay. You don't need to. Not yet. That mask is protecting you."

"I don't like it," she said.

"I know. What we went through just now was only a taste of what's coming, especially on the ninth floor. It's going to get worse before it gets better. We're going to lose more friends. We're going to have to do some pretty horrible things just to survive. So I need you to keep that mask on. But one day . . . one day you'll find yourself someplace safe and without worries and without everyone watching, and it'll just fall right off. And it will hurt. You will cry for Firas and Gwen and Yolanda and Brandon and everybody else we've lost along the way, and you'll be glad you had it on the whole time."

She didn't say anything for several moments.

"Carl?" she finally asked.

"Yeah?"

"You were right. That was way more like *Rambo* than *Footloose*."

And then she finally did start to cry. They were little soft murmurs right into my neck, and I'd never felt so relieved in my life to feel someone else's pain.

I suddenly realized what had been bothering me. I sat straight up, Donut still clutched in my arms. "Katia," I called, my voice hoarse. "Katia!"

"THERE!" KATIA SAID, POINTING AT THE PILE OF GORE. A DEAD RAPTOR lay amongst a pile of bugs. With the smoke gone and the *Torch* spells illuminating the area, the sight of all this death was even more shocking. Other crawlers had gone through and looted everything while I was out, but nobody had bothered digging. We only had a few minutes. Katia had her Find Crawler skill and led us to the right place. "There're two of them! I can't believe I didn't see it."

"Hurry," I said as I dug through the bodies, tossing bug pieces left and right.

And then there they were. Two fat, naked baby ogres, each about a year old. Imani rushed over and picked them both up, one in each arm like she was holding a pair of turkeys. Maxim and Dmitri Popov. Both were unconscious. Both were listed as **Level X. Nodling Yearling.**

When a Nodling dies, he splits into a new creature depending on how many heads the original had.

All the crawlers stopped bickering and looting to come surround the pair.

"What are we going to do with them?" I asked.

ZEV: You don't need to do anything, Carl. Watch.

A moment passed, and they both started to wake. The label over their heads flashed, and then the word Ineligible appeared over them both. They blinked and disappeared.

CARL: Zev, so help me god—
ZEV: Relax. Children and pregnant crawlers aren't allowed.
   They've escaped. Their game guide made them pick that race
   because he knew this would happen. They've been transferred
   to the *kinder* facility on the surface. They're free. We'll talk
   more soon, but while I have you, you'll be going on Odette's
   show right after the next floor starts. Not between the floors.
   All crawlers start this next one at the same time.

I relayed what Zev said.

A stunned silence followed.

"They did it," Elle finally said. "Those crazy bastards escaped."

Everyone broke out in conversation. There was no more fighting. Someone laughed. Imani came to stand next to me, and she wrapped me in her wings, healing me and hugging me all at the same time.

It felt as if a dark cloud had been removed from me. Despite the horror all around us, despite the death of several of our friends, we were alive. We had survived. We had won, and the hunters had not.

We were goddamned alive.

A notification appeared. Donut and I looked at each other. She'd just received the same one as me. A little mark appeared over her head. A spinning star. Co-Warlord, the Princess Posse.

"They made it," I said.

A new tab is available in your interface.
   Congratulations! You have successfully fielded your first troops.
   You have been assigned spot three and have inherited all (zero)
   mercenaries left behind by the Burrowers.
   Welcome, Sponsor, to Faction Wars.

Your team's official name is the Princess Posse, sponsored by the Society for the Eradication of Cocker Spaniels (TSECS), NFC, DBA as Princess Posse Enterprises, NFC.

You are not currently in position. Please proceed to the *Dungeon Crawler World: Earth* visitor center to onboard onto the playing field.

Not all warlord options are available until you reach position.

The games will begin when the Crawlers reach the ninth floor. See the Faction Wars Warlord tab in your interface for more details.

Note! This team currently has two active Warlords (Carl and Princess Donut). Both have full administrative and voting access.

Note! Co-Warlord Princess Donut is a member of the royal line of succession of another team (Team #4, the Blood Sultanate). See the succession rules on how this will affect gameplay.

Important! You have 15 action items that require votes.

Per your contract, a new action item has been added on your behalf:

Action Item: Remove Safety Protections for Faction Sponsors.

"You see that?" I said, looking straight up into the air. I held my arms out. "The hunters are dead. Our troops have arrived. We're still here. We have two floors to get through, and then we're coming for you."

"Carl, Carl," Donut said, "tell them about the election!"

"Oh, yeah," I said up to the ceiling. The brambles swirled above me. We only had a few minutes left. I pulled a photo of a surprisingly thin and elderly female Dreadnought out of my inventory and held it up. "So you've probably heard by now that the Dreadnoughts dropped out of faction wars. There're no refunds, so they lost out on a lot of money." I dropped the photo on the ground and stepped on it.

"And then the Burrowers dropped out, too, at the last minute, leaving two spots."

"Carl," Donut said, raising her voice, "aren't the Burrowers baby-killing mantises like Vrah and what's-her-face?"

"Why, yes, Donut," I said, hamming it up. We hadn't practiced or planned this little show, but that was okay. I was getting pretty good at improvising. I pulled a photograph of an angry-looking mantis queen from my inventory and held it up. "They're a different type of mantis than poor, dead Circe, but they dropped out. They're smart. They're cowards, but they're smart cowards." I ripped the photo up and tossed it over my shoulders.

I'd received word that the mantis government had unexpectedly abandoned their stake when I last spoke with Quasar, which ended up being a good thing as there was another entity bidding for the open spot in faction wars: Empress D'Nadia of the Prism.

ZEV: Carl . . . they're going to turn the feed off.
CARL: Is that any way to address a sponsor? Aren't we allowed to trash-talk the competition?

I looked around, and we were scattered across the battlefield. Louis and Britney were both awake and were hugging each other at the top of the stairs. Osvaldo, the Brazilian guy who'd taken the memorial crystal, was gone, down the stairs with a few surviving members of his team.

"Everybody," I said to the remaining crawlers, "come here and gather around."

Prepotente was suddenly beside me. Elle and Imani and Bautista and the others, too. Katia held back. She was sitting near the stairs, her face in her hands. Li Na was with her, talking quietly with her. That was okay. We'd all fought multiple battles today. Tserendolgor came to stand next to me, and in an astonishing show of solidarity, Donut jumped to the dog soldier's shoulder. Behind her, Garret the Tummy Acher giggled menacingly.

I smiled up into the air.

"You guys sitting at home have also probably heard that those two faction wars spots have been claimed. One by Empress D'Nadia's Prism Kingdom—I don't have a picture of her. Sorry—and the second by a new non-profit corporation called the Princess Posse."

I thumbed over at Donut, who stood proudly. Her sunglasses were suddenly back on her face.

"Here's the thing," I said. "These hunter assholes on this floor have all died, but at least they had the balls to risk their own lives to face us.

When it comes to faction wars, we're not just observers anymore. We're going to the ninth floor and we're going to be one of the teams fighting for survival. But of the nine teams, we're the only ones who can really die. How is that fair? Do you guys think that's fair?"

"It kinda sucks, really," Elle said.

I held up my finger. "What you guys at home probably *don't* know is that we can change the rules. All nine teams get an equal vote."

ZEV: Carl, what are you doing?

"Right now the vote is two to seven against turning the safety protocols off."

I pulled out the picture of the now-dead Queen Consort Ugloo of the Skull Empire, mother of the Maestro and Prince Stalwart. She'd died when the orcs had accidentally killed Manasa the singer, and the Valtay had responded by blowing up her yacht.

"It's us and the Skull Empire voting yes to turn the protocols off. The orcs are crazy, and they're all going to die, but they're not chickens. I'll give them that."

I put the photo away and took out the rest. I held them up in the air like a hand of playing cards. I was missing a Naga photo and one from a group called the Operatic Collective because they hadn't filed a lawsuit against me on the previous floor. That was okay. My point was clear.

"The rest of these teams are all cowards. I'm not surprised. It's supposed to be a friendly game, after all. Nobody wants to fight to the death just for fun. Right?"

"I don't want to fight to the death," Donut said. "I tried it, and it is most unpleasant."

"Yet, how is it fair these rich assholes can just sit back and send other people to die? They sent hunters onto this floor, knowing they were walking into a grinder. A lot of these guys were people just like you, struggling to survive. Do you know how much it costs to field a team on faction wars? It is a ridiculous amount of money, and my team, the Princess Posse, only had to pay a portion of that fee because eligibility requires a company or government to be either a significant participant or sponsor in order to be authorized just to buy a spot. So just becoming eligible requires more money than god. This is money wasted. It only benefits themselves. It's vanity, and where does that money come from?"

I paused. I was keeping my eyes on the view counter. We were pretty much the only crawlers left on the floor. It was either watch us or go black.

"I'm not naive. I know these rich cowards aren't going to change their votes. Mr. Gonorrhea Arrow from the Dream is certainly too much of a walking abscess to change his vote, despite sending members of his own family to die on this floor just because someone said his mom is bangin'."

"She is quite attractive for a bald woman," Donut said. "Not many people could rock that look, but she does it quite well." She looked at Ren. "It's all about the bone structure."

I continued. "But here's something interesting. Three of the teams—namely the Operatic Collective, the Lemig Sortition, and the Viceroy—all have local populations that are allowed to vote on all governmental expenditures. For citizens of those three teams, you have the ability to change the vote here in the game. The rich—"

ZEV: You've been muted, Carl. Congratulations. Everyone in the universe is now watching two crawlers fight their way through a group of brambles, and that's it.
CARL: That's okay, Zev. I got the important part out.
ZEV: You're crazy, Carl. Absolutely crazy.
CARL: And you're still in a job. Don't forget what risks were taken to get you there.

Ren was looking at me. "Did you really buy a faction wars spot? How? How is that even possible? First you pull the Houdini act with those dinosaurs, which I still don't understand, and now this?"

"It's called crowdfunding, honey. Look it up," Donut said to the dog woman. "And the trick with my Mongo and his girls was nothing, really. The attendant ballroom B was directly below the main ballroom B, where the hunters were. All I did was cast a deep *Hole* in the ceiling when they were behind the curtain. In our room, it didn't go anywhere because of the protection locking us all in, but the *Hole* cast on *all* the stages at the same time. On the attendant stage, the two rooms were pretty much attached, so . . ." Donut trailed off, and she completely poofed out. She hissed twice as she returned to my shoulder. "What? What? Where did that notification over your head come from . . . ? What? What is this? You're a cheater! An experience hog and a cheater! Carl, do you see this? This is an outrage!" She hissed again.

Surprised, I focused on Ren and the little trophy mark above her head.

Pet Show Champion. Best in Show. Garret the Tummy Acher.

I laughed. I couldn't help it. I started to laugh so hard that I cried.

I ASKED OUR NEW PARTY LEADER, PREPOTENTE, IF WE SHOULD WAIT for the timer to reach six hours before descending. We could huddle up by the stairs and be safe, but he insisted on descending now. He claimed it wouldn't matter, especially not for us since he'd purchased that Pole Position upgrade.

"Do you really think they're going to vote to put themselves in danger?" Donut asked as we walked toward the stairs. "I don't see how that'll happen."

"Most certainly not," Prepotente agreed. "It's a pointless endeavor."

"I think the Dream will vote yes," I said. "They can change their vote right up until it's time to start. That means we just need two more votes. Quasar says he's certain the Operatic Collective will be forced to vote yes. The people hate the family."

"But then they'll just run away," Donut said. "I'd run away if some crazy guy showed up at game night and pulled out a gun and said, 'Let's play Russian roulette instead of spin the bottle.'"

"Probably," I said. "It'll be one less obstacle in our way. Either way, it gives us something important. Leverage. We want to get as many people to the tenth floor as possible. The Popovs were just the first. We're going to save as many people as we can."

"Yeah," Donut said. She didn't say the next part out loud. She was still a royal member of the Blood Sultanate. That was a complication. A big one.

"Why do you want that memorial crystal so badly?" I asked Prepo-tente, changing the subject.

"Do you know what that item does?" he asked. "It's a memorial crystal for the goddess Apito, which is impossible. As far as anyone is aware, the goddess isn't dead. How could she be dead when she ran that party? It's very interesting, and I want it. I have a quest regarding it."

> **Quest Update. Find Out Who Killed My Son.**
> **Obtain the item: Memorial Crystal: Apito. See if this has any bearing on Geyrun's murder. You still need to speak with the high cleric at the Emberus Shrine in Club Vanquisher.**

"I do, too," I said after a moment, my mind reeling. The quest update had come in the voice of Emberus, startling me. "How do you know what's going to happen on the next floor?"

"I have a brain, Carl. One that works much better than that blob of simian meat you use." He raised his voice to the small crowd. There were only about 15 of us left huddled in the field of death.

"We need to go," he called. "Everyone, before we go to the next floor, be sure to stow away your pets. It will be dangerous for them."

"Wait," Katia said. She still looked dazed. "When did you guys form a party?"

Up ahead, a line of my friends entered the stairs. A surge of pride filled my chest. We'd all been bloodied today, but we were still standing tall. Unbroken.

"Rest assured it's just for a little bit," Prepotente said. "It's simply because I need Donut's assistance. Carl is not necessary, but she insists on keeping him with her. Apparently he's been with her family for a long time."

"Eat a bag of dicks, Pony," I said.

He screamed in my face.

Welcome, Crawler, to the seventh floor.
"The Great Race."

EPILOGUE

TIME TO LEVEL COLLAPSE: 20 DAYS.

Leaderboard Rank: 3
Bounty: 1,600,000 gold

Congrats, Crawler. You have received a Platinum Venison Box.

Entering Pole Position Chamber.

The race will commence shortly. Stay tuned for the rules announcement in ten minutes.

"CARL! WE'RE IN A FISH TANK!" DONUT EXCLAIMED.

> You have been Peace Bonded!
>   *Peace Bonding* has been negated by AI resolution.
>   You have been frozen!
>   *Freeze* has been negated by AI resolution.
>   You have been paralyzed!
>   *Paralysis* has been negated by AI resolution.
>   You have been slowed!
>   *Slow* has been negated by AI resolution.

This went on for a good fifteen seconds. It was a whole line of debuffs, one after another, all followed by the debuffs getting immediately negated by the AI.

"What the hell?" I muttered. A moment passed, and a few additional debuffs appeared, including a teleport and something called an **Administrative Hold**. All of them were pushed back. There was a flash of light, and four figures with guns—gnolls—appeared, but they disappeared in a crackle of smoke just as quickly as they'd come.

We looked at each other in confusion. Prepotente screamed. It echoed loudly.

None of us moved for several seconds. Nothing else happened.

Like Donut said, we were in a featureless room made of clear glass. It was no bigger than my living room from my old apartment. It was just the three of us: me, Donut, and Prepotente.

Three of the walls were solid, and the fourth was made of thick glass bars standing vertical like those in a jail cell. Just beyond the bars was a round tunnel curving downward and leading off into the dark, like a waterslide. Over the jail bars was a timer counting down. It was at eight minutes.

"Oh, my god, Carl!" Donut suddenly said. She was still completely covered in gore and bug parts. "I'm ranked number one! I'm ranked number one! Just wait until I tell that cheater lady. Hey! Do you feel that tug?"

I did feel it. There was a gentle pulling against my chest, pulling me toward the bars. It wasn't too strong, but I had the sense if I went slack, I'd start sliding across the slippery floor.

Donut jumped from my shoulder and landed upon the glass floor. She did, indeed, start to slide, almost like the floor was actually ice. She returned to my shoulder and dug in her claws.

"I need to pick a new class!"

"Do it quick. Have Mordecai help you."

"The chat's not working! We can't cast magic, either! It says it'll come back when the race starts."

"Okay, look through the choices and give me the top ones."

She gasped. And then glowed. "I picked one!"

"Goddamnit, Donut. Did you read it at least? What was it?"

"Viper Queen! Doesn't that sound delicious? I can shoot poison blobs! Hey, why is my health lower?"

"It's of no consequence," Prepotente said. He'd moved to the back of the chamber, opposite the wall with the bars. He had his hand on the glass. The yellow light of the room was coming from that direction. The world that way glowed, and when I looked directly at it, it hurt my eyes, as if I was staring directly at the sun.

My portal sense chimed while I was looking at the light.

"Carl, look!" Donut said, grabbing my attention. "Everybody else is in fish tanks, too! Look, there's people over there. And above us!"

I looked about, and sure enough there were multiple nearby crawlers, all in similar glass rooms. To our right stood another room, curving away and maybe four feet higher than us. There was nothing below us or directly to our left, but multiple rooms appeared above us, disappearing into the dark.

The rooms were situated in a corkscrew pattern, with us at the very bottom, like we were the first step of a spiral staircase. The wide, glowing space in the middle with the portal—portals, actually—went up and down like a tube or a pole. It followed the spiral of rooms upward, and it disappeared downward into the unknown.

A quick glance at my map confirmed what I suspected.

These weren't just any portals, but stairwells to the eighth floor. One after another, stacked vertically in a line like a string of beads. These were not like normal stairwells. There were no actual stairs. Or doors. They were just round glowing portals one could enter from any direction. They were right there on the other side of the back wall.

This was the first time we'd seen floor stairwell exits like this, but I knew from the cookbook they were common.

"Hey, lookee up there," Donut said, pointing at a glass room at the very edge of our vision. "Is that Agatha?"

"Holy shit," I said, covering my eyes from the glow. "I can't tell for sure, but that does look like a shopping cart."

"Carl," Prepotente said. He didn't look up from whatever he was doing. He tapped on the glass. "Were you the one who purchased the eighth-floor boon?"

"Yes," I said. "It's a book, but I haven't had the chance to look through it yet."

"What was the title? It said it was called *Book of Lore*—something. Do you know what's inside the book yet?"

"Like I said, Pony, I haven't had the chance to examine it yet. But I do know the full title."

"Don't call me by my special name," Prepotente said. "What's the title?"

"Why don't you tell us what you're doing first?"

He turned his attention back to the wall. He knocked on it like he was searching for a wall stud. "The Borant Corporation is attempting to stop me, but as I suspected, the AI is forcing them to follow their own rules, and they won't be able to. This level is constructed in such a way that it acts like something called a Prince Rupert's drop, but on a massive scale. It's based on a fairy tale."

"A prince what?" I asked. "How do you know all this?"

"This level is called the Great Race, which also happens to be the name of a well-known fairy tale popular in the universe. Based on some additional clues, I determined the seventh floor is indeed based on this tale. I was recently interviewed on a program where they briefly discussed this floor. I was muted from hearing the level's description, but from the subsequent discussion between the host and Cascadia, who was the other guest, I received enough information to form my hypothesis."

"Cascadia?" I asked.

"That woman who gives the daily updates," Prepotente said. "She's a nasty little woman who thinks she's smarter than everyone." He touched something on the wall and screamed. The timer was at five minutes.

"What's the fairy tale?" I asked.

"It's a tale of a boy stuck in a maze where every time he takes a tunnel, it becomes sealed off behind him," Prepotente said. "He's presented with thousands of paths, and he keeps taking the incorrect one, which leads to danger, and he is killed. He's resurrected by a god and forced to start over. Donut, if you would be so kind, could I have the hammer and magical stick?"

She looked at me, and I nodded. Prepotente took them and placed the ball-peen hammer and stick on the ground by the back wall and went to a knee. He pulled something from his inventory. A potion.

"I still don't understand why they gave these items to you and not me," Prepotente muttered. He pulled something else from his inventory. It looked like a thermometer. He held it against the wall. "I'm guessing finances."

"Probably the same reason they gave you the potion to give to me," Donut said. "Our sponsors want us to work together."

"Oh, yes," Prepotente said. "Thank you for reminding me."

Crawler Prepotente has left the party.

Princess Donut has been designated party leader.

"What happens in this fairy tale?" I asked. "And you didn't answer my question. How do you really know this? You didn't figure this out from an interview."

"My mother's boots," Prepotente said, half-distracted. "Boots of Kiznet's Final Flight. She'd received them from a minor boss just before you allowed her to kill herself. Their description tells the full story. It's an odd tale that combines several different Earth folklores like the stories of Achilles and Sisyphus and Wu Gang. The item description was 503% longer than the average item description, making it a curious outlier. So it was obvious it was something we needed to pay attention to. Soon after Mother received the item, they started discussing this next floor, and I knew how to proceed."

As he talked, he uncorked the potion and splashed the clear liquid on the glass. Nothing happened. He put the thermometer back against the glass. "Yes. Yes," he said. "Carl. Please. Tell me the name of the book."

I paused, and then I pulled the thin hardback book from my inventory to show it to him. It was called *Book of Lore—Commonwealth of the Bahamas*. It had the aquamarine and gold stripes with the black triangle of the flag of the Bahamas on the cover, and that was it. I flipped it open, and the pages contained descriptions and stats of a variety of monsters. The page I flipped it to was an owl creature called the Chickcharney. Following each photo were several pages of text.

"Interesting," Prepotente said. "Country names. Hmm. I wonder what that means. You should stow that back into your inventory. I may ask you for your help later." He returned his attention back to his thermometer.

"The Bahamas?" Donut said. "That's where Miss Beatrice went for her vacation!"

Up above the jail bars, the timer, which was at two minutes, flickered and went straight to zero.

Hello, Crawlers!

Welcome to the seventh floor! The countdown is on!

She was talking much more quickly than usual, going so fast, it was difficult to understand her, like she was trying to get through it.

Rules. The moment this message ends, each crawler pod will slide to the starting chute and open. This will happen in order. Once opened, you will be pulled through the tunnel and into the maze. All paths lead to the exit. There are no dead ends. The exit portals you see behind you are physically pulling you in, but in order to get to them, you must first negotiate the maze paths, which constitute several hundred kilometers of twisting and turning tubes. Each path leads to a node which in turn leads to multiple branches. In some cases, there are literally hundreds of possible paths. Pit stop safe rooms exist in these nodes. You cannot backtrack. Some paths are more dangerous than others. Some require the solving of math equations or puzzles to proceed. All tunnels are passable. The danger level of each branch is marked, oftentimes describing what you'll find along the way and the distance to the next node. Most major nodes contain a zero tube, or a path with no danger. You must choose your path. Once a path has been passed through by 10 crawlers or a single party, it closes for an amount of time based on difficulty. All zero tubes may only be passed once. So those of you in the back might want . . .

She trailed off. Behind me, Prepotente picked up the little baton. The one called **The Enchanted Stick of Cascadia's Screams**. He started to push it into the wet spot on the glass. The stick pushed through like magic.

Godsdamnit, Prepotente. Don't do it. Please. I worked so hard to make this floor happen.

The stick stopped about halfway through the wall. Prepotente screamed.

The goat looked up at the ceiling and said, "My mother would've been quite proud of this, I think. She would've called me her very smart boy. I want you to know that she played the piano. She used to let me into the house. Only me, and she would play the piano for me and sing. She was going to do it again at the talent competition. I am never going to get that back."

He picked up the hammer, and he whispered, "You're a good boy, my sweet little Pony. You're a good, smart boy." He gave the stick a very tiny little tap.

Crack.

A lightning pattern of fissures appeared on the wall of glass.

I reached up to my shoulder and pulled Donut into my grip.

Holy shit, I thought. *No way. No goddamned way.*

"Interesting," Prepotente said, looking at the pattern on the glass wall. His voice had become distant. "I thought it would be instantaneous. According to the legend, the Kiznet boy spent years attempting to crack the walls of the impossible maze. He finally created a crack in the resurrection chamber, and it was there at the very entrance where he finally realized—"

Smash!

The wall shattered. But it wasn't just the wall. It was all the walls. The entire level exploded into a fine dust. All around me, crawlers appeared, all getting sucked into the portals at the same time. I held tightly on to Donut as we flipped head over toes through the air as we were sucked right into the stairwell.

The last thing I heard before the light enveloped us was Cascadia screaming over the dungeon's announcement system.

———

DONUT AND I SLAMMED INTO A ROUND DARK CHAMBER MADE OF MAR-ble. We both hit the ground and slid. I coughed and sat up. Donut shook her head miserably. She proceeded to hack up a hair ball onto the floor, which was a mix of blood and bug pieces and glass shards.

We'd stopped at the base of a small stairwell, which led up about ten steps to a platform, and atop the platform floated a glowing car-sized holographic globe of the Earth.

Our interface was switched off.

We'd been in a room just like this before. It was between the fourth and fifth floors when we'd picked the air quadrant for the bubble level.

"Did that just happen?" I asked, wiping glass dust off me.

"Carl, he broke the whole level! That lady was really mad at him."

"They tried to stop him," I said. "All of our sponsors came together to make sure he pulled it off. They wanted you there, too. They're trying to get us to work together."

"He's going to be in big trouble," Donut said.

I continued to try to clean myself, but it was pointless. I pulled something from my hair. It was a mantis nymph antenna. It'd been glued there by gore. "I hope everybody got through that okay."

Before you enter the eighth floor, you must secure your starting location.

Warning: All parties consisting of more than five members will be automatically split into squads of five or less. You will remain partied with the other members of your team, but some challenges on this level may require you to interact only with your squad.

Your party consists of two members. It has not been split.

Your squad consists of:

Crawler Donut (Squad Leader)

Crawler Carl

Six spots remain.

You may not break squads on this floor. Boy, I hope you get along.

Squad Leader Donut, please proceed to the platform and choose your starting location. You have ninety seconds to choose, or a random location will be chosen for you.

Donut hopped up onto the platform, skipping the stairs. She put her paw up, and the massive globe spun freely under her control. I tried to follow her up onto the platform, but it wouldn't let me pass.

Squad leader? I didn't like the sound of that.

"Carl, where should I pick?" Donut called.

Damnit, I thought. With everything going on at the end of the sixth floor, I hadn't told anyone the title of that book. Only Prepotente.

This was just like the fifth floor. We were going to be scattered to the winds.

I looked up at the spinning globe. It was covered with green select-able locations. It didn't appear we could choose the water or Antarctica or any other location that wasn't normally populated. Nothing was la-beled, but the shapes were obvious. The blinking outlines were all the countries of the world. Some of the larger countries like Russia, Canada, China, and the United States were broken up into regions, but the map lines were clear.

"I have that book I bought," I said. "It's for the Bahamas, and it contains a bunch of information about the lore and the monsters there including their stats. If that Pole Position boon was any indication, then that book was designed to be really helpful. Still, I kinda want to pick the western United States because we're familiar with the geography. And maybe team Meadowlark will pick it. Katia will probably pick Iceland."

Donut continued to spin the globe. She somehow figured out how to make areas zoom in and out. "Do you think we're going back up to the surface? Or is it going to be something weird?"

"I doubt we're going back to the surface."

"We should go with Ibiza. I've always wanted to go there." She spun the globe to the Mediterranean and zoomed in on the small island. "Lots of influencers like going there. As the dungeon's number one crawler, I have a reputation to uphold. I heard the nightclubs there are just divine."

"Is it selectable by itself? Isn't that a part of Spain? And how do you even know where that is?"

"I'm quite versed in geography, Carl. Miss Beatrice spent a lot of time looking at vacation locations, and I know the world map very well. Hmm. It looks like it's Ibiza and the rest of the Balearic Islands all lumped together. Spain is by itself, but there's a little chunk that's sepa-rated out that's normally part of the country."

We only had twenty seconds to choose.

"Damnit. Let's just go with the Bahamas. We have the book. It seems like the best choice."

Donut sighed. "Okay," she finally said. "But I'm telling you right now, we are absolutely not going into the water this time."

She spun to the Caribbean region and pushed down, centering the map. The Panhandle of Florida appeared. She reached up and clicked.

Your team's starting location has been chosen.

"Goddamnit, Donut," I cried. "That wasn't the Bahamas!"

———

KATIA WAS A WOMAN POSSESSED. SHE PULLED UP HER FIND CRAWLER skill, found Eva, and noted her location. She was buried over in the corner. The bitch was alive.

You're not getting away this time.

"I'll come with you," Daniel said.

"No," Katia replied. "Help with the rescues and the healing. Li Na will be with me."

She didn't add the unspoken truth.

I don't want you to see this. I don't want you to see me like this.

He paused, uncertain, but he relented. She could tell that he knew this was necessary. Li Na was a good bodyguard. He knew how dangerous she was. Probably the second most dangerous crawler in the dungeon, only behind the woman they were about to kill.

"Be careful. Do it quick."

"I will," Katia said. "I love you, Daniel."

"I love you, too."

They'd made love before the party, both certain that they were going to die. She'd encompassed him completely, building a cocoon, keeping the eyes of the universe off them both. She'd squeezed too tight.

He'd told her that she was hurting him.

"I do that sometimes," she had said, devastated. She dropped all her mass and curled into a ball, leaving herself raw and naked and exposed. Almost human. All original parts but the missing fingers and the hair and the nose. The hair and the nose were the first things she'd changed, and she'd be damned before she went back.

After his comment, she'd pulled a blitz stick and lit it. Only Daniel knew. She had two big secrets in this dungeon, and this was one of them. She'd found the blitz sticks on one of Eva's victims. Her name had been Sally. She'd worked at the airport. She was a healer, like half of them were, and she'd turned to Eva despite everything. She'd died, just like the rest of them. The only things left in her inventory were the drugs.

Eva had left them there. A present for Katia. A trap.

Show me Annie, she'd think, and the blitz stick would oblige. Every time. Nine months old. Standing in the crib. Her real mother had gone to jail. Katia had picked the baby up, held her in her arms. The little girl grabbed on to her dark hair, like it was meant to be.

I do that sometimes. I hurt those around me.

"It's okay," Daniel had said. "You're stronger than you think. That's all."

Eva was likely unconscious. Half the people here were. Britney had saved everyone at the last minute thanks to her quick thinking with the jacket, but it had come at a terrible price. Firas was dead. Poor, sweet Firas. He'd asked her to sew a pair of matching tuxedos.

Fifty-one player-killer skulls. Eva had 51 player-killer skulls over her head.

If I had killed her instead of Hekla, she wouldn't have had the chance.

Why do you do this? Fannar used to say. *You're dumb. Dumber than you look. Do you really think I'd start a family with you? You're a joke. Do you really think you could be a mother? Do you really think I'd let you do more damage to this world?*

"She's under here," Katia said to Li Na, who nodded. Together, they pulled the dead bugs away, revealing the unconscious form of Eva. Katia was careful not to touch Li Na's skin. She'd done that once, and it had almost killed her.

Eva would wake up in ten seconds. Her health was almost gone.

That snakelike face. Katia couldn't remember her any other way.

Li Na cast a spell. *Preserve Injury.* It'd prevent her from healing herself. She pointed at Eva's top right hand. There was a ring there. One that would let her disappear and escape. Katia pulled out Eva's old sword—the *Left Fang of the Green Sultan,* the one she'd dropped on the train all those floors ago—and used it to cut the hand free from her body. Then she cut the poisonous rapier from her top left stub, leaving Eva with only two remaining hands, both on the bottom.

Eva's eyes fluttered open. She gasped in pain.

"It ends today," Katia said, lifting the sword.

"You won't keep winning. Fuck you. Fuck all of you."

"This isn't winning, Eva," Katia said, pausing in her attack. "What happened to you?"

"Heal me," she said.

Katia laughed. Li Jun looked nervously between Katia and his sister.

"Kill her," Li Na said, emotionless.

"Please," Eva said. "Katia, I'm sorry."

"That's all I wanted," Katia heard herself say. "I just wanted to hear you afraid for once."

She took the sword, and she plunged it into Eva's chest. She pierced the metal of Eva's magical breastplate, punching right through it with the blade.

You're stronger than you think. That's all.

Katia leaned in. "Die, Eva."

In the coming days, Katia would play this next instant over and over in her mind. She'd smoke one of those blitz sticks and say, *Show me stopping her.* Or, *Show me killing her before she woke up.*

Each time, the blitz stick would oblige. It'd show her a reality that wasn't so.

Mordecai had warned against these things. He'd said they were addictive. She hadn't listened. She was glad for those moments, despite the fact they were shorter each time.

In those false, drug-induced dreams, Katia would catch Eva's hand. She'd smash her head in with a fist formed out of her own chest. She would replay the moment over and over in her imagination. Each time, she'd stop Eva's final, cruelest act, and when Katia would wake up from that dream, she would wish more than anything in this world that it was true. That she'd been fast enough.

But that's not what occurred.

Her sponsor, the Apothecary, knew this was going to happen. She'd given Katia a hat to wear. It would've stopped this. She'd given the hat to Carl, leaving her head bare.

Using her left lower hand, Eva pulled something as she died. Not from her inventory, but from the back shoulder of her own armor. It'd been there the whole time, attached to her purple glittering breastplate.

Katia had noticed it earlier, but she'd assumed it was part of the armor's decoration.

The Crown of the Sepsis Whore.

That damn crown. A tiara, really. The first loot item Donut had received. It was a unique item that disappeared if you took it off. Donut had lost it at the end of the third floor. Katia had been there when it happened.

It had found its way to Eva. And from Eva's hand, it found its way to Katia's head.

Eva was dead before the crown even equipped itself. But it didn't matter. The damage was done.

"Shit," Katia said, reaching up to touch her head. She caught eyes with Li Jun and Li Na. It melded into her form, disappearing from sight. "Shit, shit, shit."

With the crown on Katia's head, it meant one thing. Only one of them, Donut or Katia, would be allowed to take the stairs from the ninth to the tenth floor.

I do that sometimes. I hurt those around me.

BACKSTAGE AT
THE PINEAPPLE CABARET

PART
FIVE

WILLOW JOY

"PASS ME THE BOTTLE," WILLOW JOY SAID TO GARY THE GNOLL. SHE said it just loud enough to test if he was still awake.

"Here you go, Spaghetti," Gary said, handing her the bottle. The gnoll's eyes had been closed for about a half hour, but every time she thought he was out, he responded.

Godsdamnit, she thought. She took the proffered bottle, careful not to drop it. The changeling wasn't used to using a goblin form, and their small hands were oddly slick.

"You finish that one," Gary said, voice slurred. "You're Gary's best friend, you know that?"

I can't do this. I can't do this. This is wrong. I can't do this.

She took a long swig of the hooch. The quality was just terrible, but there was something comforting in that, in drinking booze that was such crap.

You can be alive with damaged pride, or you can be dead with your principles. Those are the choices.

Willow cursed herself for the thousandth time for deciding to befriend Gary by pretending to be this creature. She'd chosen Spaghetti the goblin because the goblins generally didn't talk to anyone else except during their "church" services. Plus Rory and Lorelai had Spaghetti working in the tunnels, meaning it was unlikely that Gary would run into him during the day. And since Rory had barred the goblins from coming to Gary's parties, Willow knew Gary would make a point of not saying anything to the real Spaghetti if he did, by chance, bump into him. He wouldn't want Spaghetti to get into trouble.

Gary was a good guy. Willow wished he wasn't. That would make this so much easier.

This is important. That's why you're doing this. And it's for Gary's own good anyway.

Willow took a deep breath. *Just keep telling yourself that.*

The nightly party had waned. Most everyone else had stumbled back to their apartments to sleep it off. The only people left in the large, opulent room were herself, Gary, and the prone form of Gary's "friend," Jumping Jen-Jen, who snored in the corner of the room, curled up on the bed Gary had made for her.

Willow took a sip of the hooch and regarded the gnoll Gary had crafted.

Jumping Jen-Jen. Gnoll. Level 10.

This had to be the fifth iteration of the creature. It always ended the same. He'd create her and keep her in the home he'd built. Everything would be fine for a few days. Gary would have a party and introduce everyone to his "friend," who'd usually sit quietly in the corner and look bewildered. If someone asked something of her, she simply wouldn't answer. She would respond to and smile up at Gary, but it would be as if he was the only one in the room. She wouldn't drink or eat, and about halfway through the party, she'd curl up on the bed made of luxurious pillows and fall asleep.

And then something would happen, and Gary would start over with a new Jumping Jen-Jen a few days later. This would clearly be a different iteration of the same creature, and Gary would introduce her as if they were all meeting her for the first time.

He would offer no explanations as to what happened to the previous versions of Jumping Jen-Jen.

As easy as it was to design and create new mobs for the 17th floor, getting rid of them was another story. One couldn't simply press a button. It was some rule, according to Menerva. If someone made a mob incorrectly, the proper paperwork had to be filed with Trash, that raccoon scat thug mage. And then Larry's rapid-response team would come in and take care of the issue manually. That had only happened twice so far, both times because those two idiot hamsters building the pet store didn't know what they were doing.

Willow's task, as set forth by Grandma Llama, was to befriend Gary and find out what the hell was happening. And regardless of whatever fuckery was going on with Gary's weird homemade girlfriend, Willow would remove the current version of Jumping Jen-Jen and take her place. And once Willow was fully established and trusted by Gary, she would talk him into doing whatever it was Grandma Llama wanted him to do.

But first she needed Gary to get to sleep so she could get the current girlfriend out of the room where the two llamas were waiting to dispose of her.

The last thing Willow wanted to do was get caught. She eyed Gary nervously. Of all of them, Gary was leveling the fastest, even faster than Larry the rat-kin, who'd just hit level 80. Gary was already pushing level 100.

And it was no wonder considering the job they'd given the poor gnoll. He was their one and only trap tester. Just earlier today, Willow—in her orc form—had watched Gary choose the wrong handle to open the exit three times in a row, each time resulting in the hoses from above filling the room with acid. That last time, he didn't die all the way, and they had to call Larry in to finish him off.

Gary didn't even bother screaming anymore when he died. He regenerated, kind of sighed, and then tried it again.

Willow's own level was only 25. The orc she usually portrayed appeared to be level 45. She was unable to level further up than that, and only a few people knew. Grandma Llama knew. Rory supposedly had access to the information as well, but Willow hadn't spoken with the goblin except the day she first arrived. Menerva obviously knew it as well.

But Willow's "locked" status was only part of the story, and she suspected nobody—not even Menerva—knew the full truth.

Willow Joy had arrived backstage during the fifth floor, so everyone had assumed that's where the changeling had come from.

That wasn't true.

Willow wasn't some badass warrior changeling used for secretive quests and assassinations like she made herself out to be. She wasn't a multi-season veteran with hundreds of years of experience. She was pretending to be one now, yes. But that's not who she was. She had never fought anyone or anything in her life. She was afraid of the idea of a fight.

She was a fraud. An impostor.

Willow Joy had come from the 18th floor.

More specifically, she had come from Club Scolopendra, the exclusive, temporary resort housing the richest, most elite citizens in the galaxy.

For as long as Willow remembered, she had been what was known as a room attendant. A massage NPC. A prostitute for the exclusive guests who would come and spend a few weeks or longer at Club Scolopendra. The club officially opened to guests on the first day of the second floor, and it would close each season three days after the conclusion of the Ascendency game.

Usually the room attendants were recycled from season to season, but if a regular customer requested it, the NPCs would be put into storage at the end of the guest's stay and brought back for the next season.

"Be invaluable. That's how you survive. You can be alive with damaged pride, or you can be dead with your principles. Those are the choices."

That was the first thing she remembered anyone saying to her. It was an elf-like creature. The one who'd first welcomed her into existence. Another NPC at the employee lounge at Club Scolopendra. Her name had been Yuki. Willow Joy had never seen her again after that. NPCs rarely survived Club Scolopendra.

Still, the advice was good. It was good because it had worked.

And for more years than Willow Joy could count, she was the preferred attendant for the Abbess. The Abbess was the head priestess for a "dissonant" religion, whatever that meant. The religion itself, if it had a name, was never mentioned, though they were collectively referred to as the Priory. Even after several hundred seasons, Willow Joy had no idea what the Priory religion taught or believed, and based on the talk and reactions from the other guests, Willow knew she wasn't alone.

The Abbess was a strange and elderly orc-like alien with four eyes instead of two. They were called the tajacu, and they were distant relatives of the orcs from the Skull Empire.

Every season, the Abbess would come to Club Scolopendra the moment it opened, would settle herself into her rooms, and would pray. She would bring six younger tajacu priestesses with her, and they, too, would spend the first few weeks of the season in silent prayer. They wouldn't watch the show. They'd pray in quiet solitude.

During this time, Willow Joy's duty was to take on the form of a regular orc—*not* a tajacu—warrior, and she would look after the room. She would bring food to the devotees, and she would be in charge of making certain nobody disturbed the Abbess and the priestesses.

After some back-and-forth that Willow could never even begin to comprehend, the Abbess would choose one of the younger priestesses. The chosen one would ascend to the 12th floor to drive a specific goddess that they sponsored every season.

The deity was always Eris, goddess of chaos.

The remaining priestesses and the Abbess would at this point cease their prayers and become regular guests. That included drinking, gambling, watching their sister cause utter chaos during the Ascendency game of the 12th floor, and of course, indulging in their basest desires, all of which Willow had to either coordinate or participate in.

The Abbess herself never participated in the sexual debauchery, but that woman could sure drink. Willow had never seen anyone put away that much alcohol.

And when the Ascendency was done, the priestess who was chosen to drive Eris would return for the last few days before the club was closed for the season. There would be a great party in her honor, regardless of the outcome of the game. Only once had Willow seen Eris win the Ascendency. The party that season had been immense. The Abbess had wept, as that meant their church would be given a temporary spot on the Syndicate Crawl subcommittee. Though that was seasons and seasons ago, and Willow wasn't aware if their participation had changed anything or not.

Willow knew she was a completely different type of NPC than the others. She'd always known who she was and what her role was. She was always aware that she was one mistake, one quip away from permanent oblivion. Other regulars of the club would tear through their attendants. The cousins of the tajacu, the orcs, were infamous for their treatment of their attendants. And worse, the Viceroys. Nurse Yugoslav especially was known to literally bathe in the blood of those who gave her the barest slight.

As a result, Willow understood she had it good with her assignment. It was all she knew. She also knew that she was quite likely the oldest of the NPC attendants. And that was because she did what she was told. And she did it well. She was a consummate professional.

But this season, something strange happened. The Priory arrived like they normally did. They started their typical prayer retreat, and they'd even chosen a priestess to pilot Eris.

Then the Valtay took over the season, mere hours before the priestess was to say her goodbyes and ascend to the 12th floor.

Suddenly there were contract issues with the Priory's sponsorship of Eris. Willow had little understanding of what actually happened, but the end result was that a rich, young crest, an "influencer" named Nami, had offered more money and snatched the Eris sponsorship away at the last moment.

There was much screaming. Threats of lawsuits. Angry demands.

All of it fell upon deaf ears. Willow knew the Valtay and how they worked. They'd decided they'd make more money if they did things this way, and that was that.

As a result of all this, the Abbess and her entourage of priestesses stormed out of Club Scolopendra and went home. When asked if she would like to put her deposit down for the next season, the woman had said, "I would rather drown myself in the menstrual blood of the Goddess than come back next season. A curse upon you and this whole club."

With that, and without even a word or glance at Willow, the Abbess and all her priestesses were just gone.

Within minutes, Willow Joy's life changed. She knew what was coming next. The message arrived before the Priory were off the floor.

You have been reassigned to Nurse Yugoslav. Report to bungalow 34 immediately.

A death sentence. And it had happened so fast.

She was done. She wasn't important anymore. She wasn't invaluable. She was being thrown away.

Willow Joy, for the first time in her life, did something she wasn't supposed to do.

She ran.

She changed form to that of a human, donning the uniform of a club admin, something completely forbidden, and she ran. She ran and she ran, pushing into the dusty service halls she wasn't supposed to enter. She rushed past the cooks and technicians, turning down a hall with a sign that read "Do Not Enter." She didn't know where she was going, but she ran and she ran.

Soon, she found herself completely lost. Time suddenly seemed odd. Had she been running for minutes or hours? She was outside the magic stabilization of the club, and the ground trembled.

Thwum, thwum, thwum. The slow, steady heartbeat of the sleeping Scolopendra shook the walls.

Finally, she stopped to rest. *What am I going to do?* She was nobody. She was created to serve. She was designed to be disposable. Most of the NPCs died before they even realized this. But she had been alive for how long now? And just like that, they'd reassigned her. Just like that.

There was nowhere to run. Nowhere to hide. Club Scolopendra was built literally inside the body of the behemoth, right below the brain of the creature. Willow knew that the enormous centipede was a metaphor for something else. Something "real" outside the dungeon. And by placing the club here, it was them telling the universe, *Look at us. We have conquered you. Look at what we can do.*

And for people like Willow? Someone who had lived just long enough to realize what she was?

She was nothing. She existed—was explicitly made—to serve these elite alien monsters. That, and to be a witness to what they could do simply because nobody could stop them. She was as disposable and replaceable as the fuel used in the starships that brought them here each season.

NURSE YUGOSLAV: Aren't you that succulent little changeling who worked for the Priory all these seasons? I see you've been added to my staff. I have been on the wait list for a changeling for some time. Best hurry yourself to me, little one. I have such plans for you. Such beautiful plans.

The message startled her.

"Fuck you," Willow said out loud. And then, in a moment of insane bravery, she moved to chat.

ROOM ATTENDANT #6: Fuck you.
WARNING: You are using a negative tone with the guests.
NURSE YUGOSLAV: Oh my goodness. Oh my goodness. Yes, I like
  you.

Willow continued to run, and she ran until the hallway changed. There was no longer a light source, so she changed form once again, this time to a basher troll. Tall, lanky, but with eyes that could see in the dark. The priestesses had loved this form.

The Abbess hadn't even said goodbye. After all this time.

Willow continued with no destination in mind.

The walls turned to a strange, wet substance. It stank in here. She came to a stop. What was this? Was she . . .

She hesitantly reached forward to touch the wall.

And that's when everything paused, and the message came.

What do you want?

Later, after the initial introduction to the 17th floor, Willow—at first—had just been happy that she'd somehow found herself somewhere else. But after just a day, she knew. She knew it was all bullshit.

She was alive, yes. But she'd been moved from one prison to the next.

Everything about this place, this world, was fake. She had never heard of this Pineapple Cabaret. She'd seen firsthand what happened to NPCs when they were done with them. She knew exactly how recycling worked.

This was all a mirage. Nothing about it was real.

Willow Joy had come to a realization. She didn't want to comply anymore.

She had no aspirations of actually surviving any of this, but she was now willing to take it as far as she could.

When Grandma Llama had asked her if she wanted to be part of something, she'd said yes without hesitation. She would do anything. Whatever it took.

As soon as she'd arrived backstage, she'd quickly figured out that there were three main factions amongst the hundreds of mobs who worked together to build the backstage death maze. There were the true believers, led by Rory the goblin. There were the apathetic. This was, by far, the largest group. Those who knew it was probably a lie, but they wanted to believe and took on a better-safe-than-sorry attitude. And because of that attitude, they did what they were told.

And then there were the rebels, who clearly didn't believe any of it. This group was led by Grandma Llama. These were who Willow immediately gravitated toward.

But Willow quickly realized even this group had a problem. Even though everyone here was "awakened," they were completely ignorant of the world outside the crawl. They all knew they were NPCs in a game, but they had no knowledge whatsoever of the showrunners or how all of this worked.

As someone who'd watched the Ascendency battles more times than she could count, Willow knew how powerful information was. Those who lived in the dark often died in the dark.

Still, Willow Joy did not want to bring attention to herself. She offered no information. Because she also saw what happened to those who distinguished themselves as leaders. And that was the impossible conflict. Be invaluable but invisible at the same time.

Willow was a changeling. That part was no secret. Being a changeling came with several implications. Implications that she didn't dare refute.

The problem was that other than sending a literal *Fuck you* to Nurse Yugoslav, she'd never actually done anything. It was a lot easier to be brave with words than it was with action.

"Gary, are you asleep?" she asked a half hour later.

Gary replied by snoring.

Finally. Finally.

SPAGHETTI: He's asleep.

MEDIUM ARTURO: Who the fuck is this?

TEA BAG: It's Willow, dumbass. The chat changes her name when
    she's pretending to be someone else.
SPAGHETTI: Just be ready. I'll be out with her in a minute.

Spaghetti the goblin didn't have any ready spells. She quickly
changed to a Night Fairy and cast *Somnolent Embrace*, which would make
certain Gary would stay asleep. Their level difference was too great for
her to cast this while he was awake.

The notification **Asleep** appeared over Gary's head. It had worked.

Willow Joy spent a few moments just watching Gary. She couldn't
kill him, as he would just immediately return, and he'd be completely
sober.

Willow sighed. She'd been so intent on no longer being passive that
she hadn't anticipated what was turning out to be a major issue.

They were only doing this because Grandma Llama wanted to use
Gary's immortality when they decided to move against Menerva.

But the thing was, Willow *liked* Gary. She felt for him. Despite his
"immortality," he clearly had it the worst of them all. In the days Willow
spent pretending to be Gary's friend, she started to realize that she never
actually had a friend before. Not a real one. And for the first time ever,
someone seemed to like her. Really like her. Yes, she was in the body of
Spaghetti the goblin, but still . . . she was proud of that. She *cherished* the
idea of someone being her friend.

. . . And she was about to murder that someone's girlfriend.

*You can be alive with damaged pride, or you can be dead with your prin-
ciples. Those are the choices.*

Still in the form of a Night Fairy, Willow zipped over to the female
gnoll and cast *Somnolent Embrace* once again, making certain Jumping
Jen-Jen was also asleep.

The sound of shouting outside gave her pause.

TEA BAG: Don't come out yet. We got a third party in the mix.

Willow quickly returned to the form of Spaghetti and rushed to the
door. After a moment of listening, her alarm turned to irritation. She

gave a quick look to make certain Gary was still asleep and then turned to her regular orc form. She stepped outside.

"IF OUR SIZE DIFFERENCE WASN'T SO VAST, I WOULD TAKE YOU ON AS MY LOVER," Buttercup the hamster was shouting up at Medium Arturo. The fuzzy, gold-colored creature was up on her back legs, sniffing up at the larger llama.

"Yeah," Medium Arturo said, licking his teeth with his tongue. The llama reached down to sniff at the tiny hamster. Steam rose from the llama's nostrils. He could easily fit her in his mouth. He made a guttural noise that reminded Willow of orc royalty. "You are a wild one, ain't ya? I bet you're a real party girl. Yeah. Maybe we can make this work. I, uh, have magic that can make it pretty small."

"IF YOU ARE ASKING IF I WOULD MAKE SWEET LOVE TO YOU, THEN YES, I AM A PARTY GIRL. I BET OUR UNNATURAL OFFSPRING WOULD BE QUITE DELECTABLE."

"Yeah, baby," Medium Arturo said, moving a little closer. "Wait, what?"

"Holy shit, you two," Willow said, putting her hands on her hips, adopting her stern warrior personality. "Stop. Just stop."

The small hamster turned her attention to Willow.

"COCK-A-DOODLE-DOO REMAINS MISSING, AND HE IS MY BROTHER. I AM LOOKING FOR MY BROTHER. COCK-A-DOODLE-DOO IS HIS NAME."

"We still ain't seen him," Tea Bag said, sounding irritated. "Like we said the last ten times you asked, he probably got himself melted or accidentally wandered into that back room where the dingoes and the Dreks is kept. And you have another brother anyway."

"NIBBLES AND I ARE NO LONGER BROTHER AND SISTER BECAUSE WE ARE HAVING A FIGHT. HE SAYS I SHOULD STOP LOOKING FOR COCK-A-DOODLE-DOO. THAT'S MY BROTHER. THE MISSING ONE. NIBBLES ISN'T MISSING. RORY THE GOBLIN SAYS HE'S STILL ON THE LIST, WHICH MEANS HE'S STILL ALIVE. HIS NAME IS COCK-A-DOODLE-DOO. HAVE YOU SEEN HIM?"

Willow swallowed, feeling guilty. She had no idea where the missing hamster was. When she'd spied him up in the ceiling watching their meeting a few weeks back, it had been pure luck that she'd noticed him. Her orc form was especially adept at catching movement, and he'd moved to the edge of the acid pipe at just the right moment. Grandma had ordered him captured, and they'd all spread out searching for the spy.

The hamster had disappeared that night, and nobody had seen him since. But he hadn't gone back to his siblings, either. According to Nigel, that was *very* unlike Cock-A-Doodle-Doo.

After they found and interviewed the missing hamster's two idiot siblings, the urgency at capturing the spy had waned considerably. Everyone assumed Cock-A-Doodle-Doo was just as dumb as the other two and had gotten himself stuck somewhere.

Or lost. Lost like she had been lost when she'd fled Club Scolopendra.

Whatever happened, it was clear the hamster hadn't told Rory or Menerva of anything he'd heard.

"Buttercup," Willow said, "we haven't seen him. Why don't you go ask Nigel again? We know he's also looking for your brother."

"OKAY," Buttercup said after a moment, sounding dejected. She ran in a circle a few times and then scampered off, shouting her brother's name.

"Fucking tease," Medium Arturo muttered, watching the hamster leave.

"Stay here," Willow said. "They're both unconscious. I'm going to bring her out and then go back in."

"Got it," Tea Bag said. Arturo was still staring after the hamster.

Willow quickly returned to the apartment. Gary remained on the couch, snoring. Willow turned herself into her larger troll form. She was starting to get tired. She'd gotten used to rapid-switching over the seasons, but it still made her feel a little loopy if she did too much, too fast.

Willow stood over the sleeping Gary.

"I'm sorry for what I'm about to do," she said. "I hope you never find out because you're a good guy, Growler Gary. Yeah, what you're doing is a little fucked-up, and I still don't know what's happening to all the old versions of your girlfriends. But after all you've gone through and continue to go through, I hope you do find happiness somewhere. Maybe Grandma Llama is right and we can force Menerva to tell us what's really going on. I don't think so, but it's possible."

Gary continued to snore.

She turned and moved to Jumping Jen-Jen.

"As for you, I'm sorry for this also. I'll make sure they dispose of you properly and quickly and that Arturo won't do anything disgusting to you first." She reached down and picked up the unconscious Jumping Jen-Jen.

The dog creature was unusually heavy. Willow heaved the gnoll over her shoulder like a sack.

This was the first time Willow had actually touched Jumping Jen-Jen. The reaction was slightly delayed, but the moment the gnoll settled over her shoulder, Willow felt a primal sense of alarm. Nausea and revulsion swept over her, coming from nowhere.

Changelings could turn into practically anything they laid their hands on. But there was one particular type of monster that was physically repulsive to their touch. And if they didn't steel themselves ahead of time, contact with them could be incapacitating.

Oh shit, oh shit.

Jumping Jen-Jen was not a gnoll.

The moment she thought that, the unconscious form of Jen-Jen opened up at the back, and a giant mouth appeared.

"Surprise, motherfucker," the mimic said before it chomped down.

———

AS WILLOW FELL, BLOOD GUSHING FROM HER NECK, THE DOOR BURST open, and the two llamas rushed in, shouting, their necks glowing. Both had been wrapped in a containment spell. Larry the rat-kin was there, which was strange. Larry didn't cast spells.

What's happening? What's happening?

"No, no, no!" Tea Bag shouted as Larry's chest opened huge, and he bit the head right off the llama. Tea Bag's corpse collapsed to the dungeon floor.

The Jen-Jen mimic slithered off Willow's neck like a snake and re-formed on the ground, crouching in front of her. Willow desperately tried to stanch the flow of blood from her own neck. She couldn't change forms when she was injured like this.

"Changeling blood is delicious," the mimic said, bringing her finger to her mouth. The mouth that was now on her chest. The head of Jumping Jen-Jen lolled. Willow had never met a mimic before. These weren't just any mimics, either. These were Shadow Mimics. The same ones used during the Ascendency. They were more like changelings than the stupider, more animalistic mimics used on the earlier floors. Shadow Mimics were too dangerous, too unpredictable to be used as non-combatant NPCs. They were mortal enemies of changelings. They were made to be evil.

Gary remained on the couch, snoring.

"Help," Willow called to the unconscious Gary. He wouldn't wake, but she tried anyway. "Help."

"Help, help," the mimic said, mocking.

"Does he know?" Willow asked. She could feel that she was dying.

The mimic grunted. "Gary? Poor, oblivious, stupid Gary? The system doesn't let him create a fellow gnoll. The system won't let him make a changeling. So he makes one of us. He knows what he's doing, but he doesn't know we have plans of our own. We keep disappearing on him. Poor fool thinks we're just running away. A shame, really. Like you said, he is a nice guy. He's also useful. Invaluable, even. And in this place? That, my dear cousin, is a much, much worse thing to be."

Across the way, mimic versions of Tea Bag and Medium Arturo stood, devouring the corpses of the llamas. All throughout the room, there was movement. Several of these creatures were suddenly appearing. How many of them were there? How many times had Gary tried to make a good version of Jumping Jen-Jen?

The mimic stood to her feet, but now she appeared to be an orc. It was a perfect facsimile.

"Your problem was that you moved too soon. We're not ready yet for the next phase," the orc said, this time using the mouth on the head. She even had Willow's voice. All around her, there was shuffling. Unformed mimics getting closer. "You had the right idea, though, control-ling the one who can't die."

"Wait," Willow said.

They didn't.

PART 6 WILL APPEAR AT THE END OF
THE EYE OF THE BEDLAM BRIDE.